"*How Firm a Foundation* pre seen
in real life: conscientious peo|)ath
God wants them to take. Onc< :wn
with confusion and indecisio. .t is
found to be not a straight roac ..u .uau, for it leads through
Calvary. Marcus Grodi's characters illustrate what is played out daily
all around us—and in us. Anyone who takes the Christian faith at all
seriously will see himself in these characters because he knows that he
too is on the path."

—Karl Keating, author
Nothing But the Truth

"In the midst of the myopic miasma of most modern fiction, Marcus
Grodi's novel shines forth with the clarity of crystalline grace. Whereas
many modern novelists sneer contemptuously at the perennial problems of life, much as an adolescent might sneer at the wisdom of his
elders, Grodi steers beyond the sneers to a calm and considered reflection upon the problem itself. A problem, in his eyes, is not something
to be sneered at or complained about; it is something to be solved. I
cannot praise this novel enough. It follows in the noble tradition of
Newman's *Loss and Gain* but brings the Newmanesque ruminations
upon the meaning of life from the detached decorum of nineteenth
century Oxford to the desolate desecration of contemporary America.
Any discerning reader who has grown weary of the juvenile posturing
of post-modernity, would do well to pick this book up and begin
reading. It is fiction for grown-ups, the sort of book that might literally change the direction of one's life. Perhaps, indeed, it should come
with a warning: Read but Beware. You might never be the same again!"

—Joseph Pearce, author
Christian Imagination and *Wisdom and Innocence*

"For the second night in a row, Gloria and I were both up well-past
midnight reading *How Firm a Foundation*. But, I can assure you this:
it won't happen again, because we both finished it last night. It is
really a tremendous book. It will no doubt be used of the Lord to
bring many to the fullness of the truth."

—Bruce Sullivan
former Church of Christ minister

"On-going conversion—deepening faith to which we are all called—is a delicate dance of grace, insight, wonder, struggle, suffering, and joy. How does someone think, pray, and work through the process? Marcus Grodi offers a masterful presentation—practically the inside scoop—of the layers of challenge: interpersonal, pastoral, emotional, and, of course, spiritual. The difficulties are real; the truths are compelling."

—Kimberly Hahn, author
Life-Giving Love

"This novel is unique among stories of conversion. It is a fictional composite of the true life experiences of many converts whom Mr. Grodi has worked with as President/Executive Director of the *Coming Home Network International*. Throughout this compelling narrative, as in all divisions among Christians, the basic issue is: by what means can we know the full truth of the Gospel? In the unfolding of this story we see Stephen and others forced to contend with the problem of authority and then by providence led to the final answer—Christ's answer—surrender to Him and His Church."

—Rev. Ray Ryland
Chaplain, *Coming Home Network*

"*How Firm a Foundation* is a remarkable achievement. For the first time ever, Marcus Grodi has given readers a realistic and compelling view into two worlds—the inner dynamics of a Christian denomination, and the struggles of a dedicated and honest man of God who slowly witnesses the underpinnings of his faith crumble, only to be replaced by solid bedrock. I'm confident you'll enjoy this book. Thanks, Marcus; you've done a superb job of storytelling."

—Bud Macfarlane Jr., author
Pierced by a Sword

HOW FIRM A FOUNDATION

ALSO BY MARCUS GRODI

Journeys Home

MARCUS GRODI

HOW FIRM A FOUNDATION

C H *Resources*

PO Box 8290
Zanesville, OH 43702-8290
877-455-3208

Coming Home Resources
PO Box 8290
Zanesville, OH 43702

Coming Home Resources is a registered trademark
of the Coming Home Network International, Inc.

Library of Congress Cataloging-in-Publication Data

Grodi, Marcus C. (March 2, 1952)
How Firm a Foundation / Marcus C. Grodi

ISBN 0-9702621-2-4
1. Fiction
2. Religious fiction

Scripture texts normally used in this work are taken from
the Revised Standard Version of the Bible,
copyright 1966 by the Division of Christian Education of the
National Council of Churches of Christ in the United States,
and are used by permission. Other Scripture quotations are from
the Authorized (King James) Version of the Bible, 1611.

Cover design by Devin Schadt, Saint Louis Creative
Layout and design using Pagemaker 7.0 by author
Photo of Marcus milking taken by son Jon Marc

To my father,
Daniel Edgar Grodi
1927-2002

Did you ever know that you're my hero,
And everything I would like to be?
I can fly higher than an eagle,
For you are the wind beneath my wings.

Wind Beneath My Wings
Jeff Silbar, Larry Henley

[Charles] had now come, in the course of a year, to one or two conclusions, not very novel, but very important: first, that there are a great many opinions in the world on the most momentous subjects; secondly, that all are not equally true; thirdly, that it is a duty to hold true opinions; and, fourthly, that it is uncommonly difficult to get hold of them.

from *Loss and Gain*
A novel by
John Henry Cardinal Newman

CONTENTS

Part I

The Lord is My Shepherd,
I Shall Not Want

1

Snow blanketed the new england countryside as a congregation welcomed their new assistant pastor with the gift of his favorite hymn.

"How firm a foundation, ye saints of the Lord,
    Is laid for your faith in his excellent word!
What more can he say than to you he hath said,
    To you that for refuge to Jesus have fled?"

One would like to call it singing, but agnostic neighbors as well as one bellowing hound might take issue. To the newly ordained Reverend Stephen William LaPointe, the out-of-tune, bagpipe-sounding voices were music to anxious ears. He bit the inside of his cheeks as his emotions waffled between ecstasy and tears.

"Fear not, I am with thee; O be not dismayed!
    For I am thy God, and will still give thee aid;
I'll strengthen thee, help thee, and cause thee to stand,
    Upheld by my righteous, omnipotent hand."

The congregation of two hundred thirty studied Stephen's silhouette against the whitewashed plaster wall. His six-foot frame and average build dwarfed the shorter, stouter senior pastor, Bradford T. Malone, who had long prayed for an assistant. But Stephen's sandy, shoulder-length hair and winsome smile, coupled with his evangelical enthusiasm, were already making the balding and paunchy senior pastor remember that "one must be careful what one prays for."

For Stephen, no words more clearly expressed his understanding of his calling than this glorious early American hymn. It declared his own conviction that the truth of his faith, the truth of his preaching and ministry was built upon the firm foundation of the Bible—"His excellent Word!" For the Reverend Malone, this was but an echo of convictions gone by.

"When through the deep waters I call thee to go,
   The rivers of woe shall not thee overflow;
For I will be with thee, thy troubles to bless,
   And sanctify to thee thy deepest distress."

Stephen's seven-month-pregnant bride, Sara, sat in the front pew straining to hide her terror. Her smile was an inaccurate measure of what lay beneath. The words to this third refrain of her beloved's favorite hymn taunted her as she contemplated the role she must now accept— a role she had neither desired nor pursued, nor for which she felt worthy. As she sang with feigned enthusiasm, she prayed that these strangers might be blind to the true meaning of her tears: the painful, reluctant abandonment of the wonderful things that piety would never buy.

And her prayers were answered, for the congregation saw only a beautiful, supportive wife and mother-to-be, whom they presumed they had hired along with her husband.

"When through fiery trials thy pathway shall lie,
   My grace, all sufficient, shall be thy supply;
the flame shall not hurt thee; I only design
   Thy dross to consume, and thy gold to refine.

"The soul that on Jesus hath leaned for repose,
   I will not, I will not desert to its foes;
that soul, though all hell shall endeavor to shake,
   I'll never, no, never, no, never forsake."

The hymn concluded with a loud and long "Amen". The elderly organist raised her aching, arthritic fingers and allowed the music to fade into expectant silence. The congregation resumed their seats, and all eyes focused on the new assistant, all ears awaiting his first sermon.

Stephen, dressed in a black academic robe accented with a red liturgical stole, stood up on weak knees and climbed into the elevated central pulpit. When the founding fathers built this white, wooden Congregational church in the mid-1700s, there were no amplifiers, high-fidelity speakers, or microphones. Preaching was a full-voiced art, projected to those seated in the back pews—and it was the only entertainment in town.

From this elevated precipice, Stephen towered above the congregation. Both the authority and grave responsibility of this pulpit drew him upward. The words of Jesus passed through his mind like words on a marquee: *Whoever causes one of these little ones who believe in me to sin, it would be better for him if a great millstone were hung round his neck and he were thrown into the sea.* Jesus will hear every word he preached, so he'd better be correct. At that moment, however, Stephen had no way of knowing that one day this verse would become a haunting and debilitating burden too heavy to shoulder.

He studied his new church family, and was reassured by their welcoming yet reserved New England smiles. Standing in this historic pulpit, Stephen was confident that this was the moment, the very purpose for which he had left everything behind for seminary.

Raised a Lutheran, he had progressed with the usual complaints through the customary rites of passage—baptism, Sunday school, confirmation, Sunday worship, Luther League, summer camps, and Bible schools. And though this cumulative religious data had flowed into the appropriate folds and nodes of his brain, it clotted spiritually somewhere before it had reached his heart. When he left his family and friends for college, Stephen left his Lutheran faith behind.

After three years of raucous campus life, the persistent witness of a church-going fraternity brother and now life-long friend, Jim Sarver, finally softened Stephen's self-centered heart. The power of this conversion so dramatically altered every sinew of his life that Stephen's one goal ever since had been to help others experience this same powerful, life-changing love of God.

Now nine years later, the Reverend Stephen W. LaPointe opened the Bible to read the text he had carefully chosen for this, his first sermon at Sleepy Meadow Congregational Church. From Proverbs chapter three, he began reading:

"Trust in the Lord with all your heart,
    And lean not unto your own insight.
In all your ways acknowledge him,
    And he will make straight your paths."

This had been his favorite scripture ever since Jim taught it to him in college. For too long Stephen had leaned on his own insight and found himself lost. Then, through Jim's testimony and the preaching of a local Congregationalist minister, Stephen rediscovered his Christian faith and the need to trust fully in Jesus. In seeking to acknowledge the Lord in everything, Stephen discovered this scripture to be limitlessly true: God had straightened out his path, had brought him into the pastoral ministry, and now to this pulpit and to these people.

And also to his beautiful wife, Sara, sitting there below him, who in two months would deliver their first child.

"Before I begin, please join me in a moment of prayer," he said with less confidence than he showed.

The congregation bowed their heads in unison. Stephen glanced down at Sara, her brown hair tied back the way he liked it. She winked and smiled, revealing the dimples that always made him melt. Then bowing his own head, Stephen prayed for God's guidance. Yes, God was the primary recipient, but *how* he prayed and *what* he prayed conveyed an important message to this new flock.

The communal "Amen" reverberating, Stephen raised his eyes to a sea of new faces and new needs—some with hardened hearts in need of compassion and renewal; others with hearts ready for a challenging inspiration. Before a word left his lips, he loved them and hoped with anticipatory joy for long years as their assistant shepherd.

2

"Excuse me, but does this gash need stitches?" the woman asked, pushing a grubby child forward. "You see, I was chopping carrots and little Howie was only trying to help…"

"I'm sorry, ma'am, but I'm not a doctor. I only look like one."

The elevator door opened and Stephen, dressed in his new three-piece, "hospital-go-a-visiting" navy-blue suit, pointed the mother and her wounded son toward Emergency.

Stephen entered and pressed *Seven* and smiled as he considered the irony of this mother's honest mistake. Years ago, he had wanted to become a doctor, inspired by the television superstar, *Marcus Welby, M.D.,* but God's long-range planner rarely syncs with our own.

At *Five* the door opened, and a disheveled orderly entered backwards, pulling a gurney. A wailing woman in her mid-40s clung to the patient's limp, bandaged hand.

"Scuse me, Doc," the orderly said.

Stephen crowded into a back corner as IV bottles rattled.

"Oh, I'm not a doctor."

"This is the staff elevator, mister," the orderly responded, still shifting for more space.

"I'm sorry, I didn't…"

"Says it next to the door. The visitor elevators are around in the main lobby."

"Sorry. I'll remember next time." Stephen knew this, of course, but Reverend Malone had encouraged him otherwise, saying the staff elevators were quicker and more readily available. Plus, Stephen would more likely avoid queries from visitors and staff. So far this hadn't worked.

The woman continued to weep, kissing the hand of who Stephen guessed to be her unconscious son. His head, completely swathed in bandages, appeared grotesquely swollen above his pale, lifeless face.

Stephen watched awkwardly. He felt that he ought to say something comforting, but words failed him. Instead, he stared straight ahead at a plastic-covered certificate posted on the stainless-steel elevator wall. Richard Schnittker, the state elevator inspector, had signed it and thereby guaranteed that this elevator could hold 1,200 pounds. A quick calculation of the mother and the orderly, both overweight, the patient and his gurney, plus himself at 180, told him that they were safe for the time being. Two more of any of their girths, however, and they were in trouble. He reached into the inner pocket of his suit coat and removed his appointment book to appear purposely distracted.

These first two weeks at Sleepy Meadow certainly qualified for the proverbial frying pan into the fire. Reverend Malone had reviewed everything that both he and Stephen needed to do every day, week, and month. He had pointed out all the necessary stops—St. Luke's and Memorial Hospitals, Sleepy Meadow Nursing Home, and Fishbaine's Funeral Parlor—and then yesterday after morning worship, Reverend Malone and his wife, Myrtle, escaped for three weeks to Aruba.

At *Seven* the orderly pushed his patient out into the hall with hardly a glance of caution in either direction. The distraught mother stood paralyzed against the elevator wall.

"May I help you?" Stephen asked as he reached to steady her.

"Are you a doctor?"

"No, ma'am. I'm a minister."

Stephen still felt self-conscious saying this.

"Is he your son?" he asked, helping her catch the speeding gurney.

"Yes," she said between sobs. "He wrecked his cycle. We told him this would happen, but he wouldn't listen."

What to say? Stephen might be an ordained minister with three years of seminary and six years of previous work in the "real world," but he was still at least ten years younger than this distraught mother. Who was he to presume his wise words of comfort upon her? His courses in counseling were to have prepared him, but still, he seemed to be play-acting.

"His father and I warned him to wear a helmet, but..."

Her words were lost as the orderly pushed through the traffic of nurses, doctors, and visitors, and entered room 714 on the left. Stephen followed the mother past another patient in the first bed.

"Hey, keep it down!" the roommate bellowed.

"Now just be patient, Mr. Bernstein," the orderly said. "This will only take a minute."

"I *am* a patient, and this is my room, dammit!"

"You know this is a double room, and that this young man is your fourth roommate."

"Well, just keep it down, or I'll call my lawyer."

"Yes, Mr. Bernstein," the orderly replied as he pulled the curtains separating the beds. A nurse entered dressed in a blinding white gown, and together she and the orderly transferred the unconscious young man to the permanent bed.

"Mrs. Carlsted?" the nurse asked.

"Yes."

"I'm Nurse Hartshorn, and you need to sign some papers."

"Will he be all right?"

"We'll need to wait for the doctor. Your son has suffered a massive skull fracture and has lost a lot of blood. Only time will tell."

As the mother signed, Stephen studied the scene. He reviewed mentally the four people before him for whom Christ died. Under the touch of his presumably comforting hands was a mother in terror of losing a son. *Was she a believer? Was she praying inwardly or just lost in despair?*

To her right under hospital sheets, intravenous sustention, and residual anesthesia was a young motorcycle rebel on death's door. *Had he ever made a commitment to Christ, possibly as a teenager at some summer camp? Or was he a prodigal soul reaping his just reward?*

On the other side of the curtain was crotchety old Mr. Bernstein, absorbed in an afternoon soap. His few words were enough to indicate his contempt for the human race. *Did anyone, family or friends, ever pay him a visit? Did faith have any place in this man's heart?*

And then there was Nurse Hartshorn. *Did she see her work as a channel of God's love, or had years of putting up with patients like Mr. Bernstein hardened her heart? Did she see Christ in every patient, or were they only "gomers," as described in that cynical novel about the medical industry?*

"The doctor will be with you in a moment." Nurse Hartshorn smiled perfunctorily, turned, and left.

"Here, ma'am, sit here close to your son," Stephen said as he guided the mother to the chair nearest the bed.

She extended a trembling hand up to her son, but on feeling his cold limpness, she recoiled and again was lost in weeping.

Though actually uninvited, Stephen assumed that he was welcome. His seminary notes contained copious outlines for hospital visits just like this, and his readings had fleshed these out. But it was Reverend Malone's single whirlwind tour that had kick-started his academics into action. This, though, was his first solo visit, and he felt like the rookie he truly was. *What should and shouldn't I do?*

Stephen cradled the woman's shoulders with one arm and touched her clenched hands with his other hand.

Again at a loss for words, he chose the only course of action that made sense. "Would you like me to offer a prayer for your son?"

Without looking up, she nodded yes.

Now, what to pray? He recalled when he was seven years old and his family's Lutheran pastor had visited his father, who was dying in the hospital. The prayer, which Stephen only vaguely remembered, had been resplendent with high-sounding theological platitudes leading smoothly into a communal recitation of the Lord's Prayer. Still repulsed by his nominal Christian upbringing, Stephen was intent on being more helpful, more sincere, and more Christ-like.

"Heavenly Father," he began. He prayed for healing and mercy for the son and comfort for the mother and family. He asked for God's will to be done and then quoted a psalm that spoke of trust in God's providence. Finally, like the minister of his youth, he too ended with the Lord's Prayer, giving his words a stamp of authenticity.

After his "Amen," she followed suit, but then to his surprise she blessed herself with the sign of the cross.

She's certainly no member my church!

"Father?" she began to ask.

"I'm not a priest."

She hesitated, and then, looking up into his face for the first time, asked, "Reverend, do you think Billy is going to heaven?"

What do I say now? Stephen thought in a panic. *This family must be Catholic or Episcopalian, I don't know. How am I to know whether this boy knows Jesus? Does this mother even know Jesus if she's Catholic? Where should I begin? There's hardly time, nor is it even appropriate to try leading her through the "Four Spiritual Laws." But does this woman need to know* facts *right now, or merely words of consolation?*

"Ma'am, the Bible teaches us that whosoever believes in Him…"

"Who are you?" a male voice interrupted from the door.

Stephen jerked up and saw the hulk of a man dressed in greasy coveralls whose profile blocked the light from the outer hallway. As the man came toward them, Stephen stood up quickly, pulling back from the woman.

"My name is Reverend Stephen LaPointe, and I was…"

"Stealing sheep, I suppose. Thank you, you may leave now. Our priest will be here soon." The man stood with his back to the window, gesturing Stephen out.

"I'm sorry, I didn't mean to…"

"That's okay, I appreciate it," the mother said. "Thank you."

Stephen nodded and slipped uncomfortably between the man and the bed and out into the hall.

"Oh, John!" he heard from the room, and looking back he saw the man and his wife lost in an embrace. Stephen turned toward the elevators, wondering where he had gone wrong. He checked his appointment book again for the name and room number of the person he had originally come to visit.

"Good Lord," he grimaced. *Mr. Bernstein, Room 714. No way I'm going back in there!* "Maybe tomorrow," he said as he continued toward the elevator.

The clock on the wall in the nurse's station read 4:35, so Stephen decided to get a coffee before the chilly ride home.

Reverend Malone had encouraged him to linger for at least fifteen minutes in hospital cafeterias: "You never know whom God might bring into your nets," he had said. "Every person there is either a member of our church, a fallen-away member, or a potential member, and five minutes of your time might make all the difference."

Feeling gun-shy from his most recent fiasco, Stephen took his coffee to a table furthest from the few people present. As before, he studied the scene, trying to see through the eyes of Christ. At a table near the food counter were a young father and five children. The children, all under ten, were joking, laughing, and being rowdy, while the father, embarrassed and angry, struggled to keep them at bay. *Was their mother here for surgery, or was she giving birth to yet another screaming "papist"?* This was St. Luke's, the only Catholic hospital in this southern Vermont county. Members of Sleepy Meadow Congregational usually went to Memorial Hospital, but old Mr. Bernstein's condition had required equipment that only this hospital was able to provide, so here he was.

Maybe that was why they mistook me for a doctor rather than a minister, he thought. But then again, he got the same treatment wherever he went in his three-piece suit.

At another table, a covey of doctors and nurses sat discussing something in hushed tones, maybe some in-house controversy. Several tables away, a couple held hands, exchanging soft words and pregnant smiles.

Across the room at the table farthest from him, a man sat by himself, staring out through the large picture window. He wore a leather jacket, and his black hair was slicked back all the way to his collar.

Stephen watched, but the man remained motionless.

OK, Stephen, he prodded himself, *are you going over to him, or wait for some priest to swoop in?* Sufficiently scorned, he rose with his coffee, and walked toward the man.

"Afternoon," Stephen asked gently when he reached the table.

The man sat back with a start and focused on Stephen. "What do you want?"

He looked to be about Stephen's own age, with a pleasant though unattractive face that at present was twisted by a scowl. His most distinguishing feature was his thick, wire-rimmed glasses perched high on a straight Roman nose. Blessed with perfect eyesight, Stephen couldn't imagine being constrained to seeing the world through the distorted tunnel of those lenses.

"Sorry to bother you. I noticed you were sitting alone, and wondered if there was anything I could do. My name is Reverend Stephen LaPointe," he said, extending his hand.

Reluctantly, the man accepted Stephen's handshake and said, "Sorry to bite your head off. I'm Walter Horscht. Please, have a seat." The scowl relaxed, replaced by an expression of concern. "My wife Helen is here…we're having…she's having a baby."

"Congratulations. Is everything going all right?"

"I think so. I got tired of waiting in the lounge, so I thought I'd come down for a coffee and a smoke. They said they'll page me if anything happened."

"Do you live here in Sleepy Meadow?"

"No, we live up in Red Creek, but the company health plan sent us here." Walter studied Stephen more closely. "I take it you're not a Catholic priest?"

"No, I'm the new assistant at Sleepy Meadow Congregational. Are you a Catholic?"

"Hell, no," Walter answered with a laugh. "As I said, I wouldn't be here if the company hadn't forced us. As soon as the baby's born, we're gone."

"Are you a member of a church in Red Creek?"

"No, not exactly. I grew up with religion, but gave it up in the service. Couldn't stomach all the do's and don'ts."

There was a moment of awkward silence as Stephen calculated his response, but Walter continued, his attention diverted to his coffee. "However, with the baby coming, and with Helen hounding me about it, I've been kinda reconsidering, you know, for the baby's sake."

"Well, Walter, that's as good a reason as any to come back to Jesus."

"Now don't get me wrong. I'm not saying *I'm* ready for all that Jesus crap. I just think it would be good for the baby and Helen."

"Sure, Walter, I understand. But tell me, if you don't mind, what do you have against all this Jesus *stuff?*"

Walter turned his face to look straight into Stephen's.

"Reverend, I'll tell you. My parents were the strictest type of Baptist fundamentalists. They scrutinized and judged my every word and deed by their damned puritanical rules. My father rarely spared the switch. When I escaped their clutches for Vietnam, I mooned their life and faith goodbye, and was glad to leave their hellhole for the next."

A Vietnam vet, Stephen noted to himself. *Thank God for college deferments.*

He studied the man before him, who had again turned toward the window. Walter's rough exterior looked like so many others who had chosen to check out of mainstream American culture. Stephen wondered how much brutality and bloodshed this man had witnessed—or inflicted. *Lord Jesus, forgive and bless this brother.*

"I'm sorry that your experience of Christianity was a bad one," Stephen said, "but in reality our Lord is very loving and merciful. He doesn't dwell on our sins. He forgives them, and then helps us forget them and move on."

"That's well and good for you Brooks Brothers types," Walter said with a snap of his face. He then looked down and rose to leave. "But as I said, I was considering this for the sake of Helen and the baby."

"Here, Walter," Stephen said, rising, extending the first of his newly printed cards. "I'd like to be of help to you and your family if I can. Would you like me to pay a visit to Helen and the baby?"

Walter took the card and stuffed it into the back pocket of his black jeans. "Sure, thanks." He zipped the front of his jacket and started toward the exit. After a few steps, he stopped and called back without turning. "Helen's in room 265B. If you see her, tell her I love her. I need to get to work."

"Gladly, Walter."

Stephen watched him exit into the cold, run to a rusty blue pickup, jump in, and speed off.

But as the pickup receded into the encroaching darkness, Stephen felt the chill of an intangible foreboding.

3

THE FLICKERING LIGHT FROM THE CANDLE made the rafters appear to dance and sway. Sara didn't expect Stephen home for several hours, because the hospital had called him back in. Apparently, a woman whose husband he had met yesterday was in danger of losing her baby. With the New England boiled dinner simmering on low in the crock-pot, Sara slipped upstairs for her long-awaited attic rendezvous.

Since the Malones owned their own home, this hundred-year-old manse had been conveniently available for the new assistant and his pregnant wife. It was drafty and needed more than a mere can of paint, but Sara refused to complain—it was a house and not another apartment.

She struggled up the last few steps, out of breath, as was to be expected of any woman eight months pregnant. Scattered around the attic with no particular organization were the discarded memorabilia of thirteen previous clergy families. Sara thought the mostly trash intertwined with decades of spider webs would be fascinating to sift through, but this was not her immediate concern.

She moved cautiously with her candle stub to a more recent addition of boxes, trunks, and file cabinets in the far corner near the stone chimney. Here were the treasures that represented Stephen's and her individual lives before they had become one.

Progressing from box to box, she held the candle close to read the descriptions, which she had hurriedly scribbled months before with a black magic marker.

"Wouldn't you know it," she said aloud, finishing the complaint silently. *The box I want is on the bottom.*

Tilting the candle slightly over a loose brick projecting from the chimney, she formed a puddle of wax to hold the candle secure. This freed her hands for the search. After setting aside boxes marked *STEPHEN'S CLASS NOTES, CHECKS: 74 THRU 81, TAXES: 74 THRU 81,* she reached her target. She dragged the box marked *PERSONAL: SARA* out over the dusty floorboards and then pushed it closer beneath the light of the candle.

A shiver went up her spine as she peeled away the duct tape. She had not counted on the intense cold of the unheated attic. In the box were bundled and loose photographs, newspaper clippings, letters, diaries, plus other paraphernalia that together summarized Sara's twenty-five years of New England life.

The expanse of her world to date had ranged as far southwest as Norwich, Connecticut, where, as a young girl, her father, Joseph Bondforth, had commuted to New York City. Then it extended northeast to Freeport, Maine, where during her teenage years, her father opened his own accounting firm in his ancestral town. Next her world expanded in a triangle to Campion College in South Boston, for both her undergraduate and graduate studies in American history. Finally now to the northwest, to Vermont, where she was trying to fill the daunting shoes of a pastor's wife.

She scoffed at the embarrassing photos of her as a high school cheerleader but even more at the irony cast by brash photos of her as a rebellious, bra-burning college feminist. One particular photo of Mary, Louisa, and Tess made Sara laugh with shame. These three ex-friends from her sophomore year were making irreverent gestures on a statue of Father Eleazer X. MacKraken, the founder of Campion. She had certainly drifted far afield.

As she was growing up, her family had been regular members of various Congregational and Unitarian churches. Other than mealtime prayers, however, they rarely discussed their faith. Christianity was more a social thing than a conviction. Attending a Catholic college had hardly been Sara's goal in life, but Campion offered her a scholarship too good to refuse. Given the College's progressive liberal environment, her nominal faith posed no complications, and she easily ignored what she considered the archaic remnants of Catholicism's Dark Age superstitions. Occasionally she attended a small stone Congregational church a few blocks from campus, but, for the most part, she just slipped through her undergraduate years as if her nominally Christian heart was Teflon-coated.

A series of horrendous choices then had followed, which she hoped would forever remain buried.

Leafing through more photos, she found one of her first with Stephen. He had been working as a seminary intern at Second Congregational in downtown Boston, while she was beginning her master's program. On a major rebound in her faith, she was searching for some thread of meaning. Then, one Saturday, a friend invited her to a meeting of Christian singles at Second Congregational. Sara went along hoping to find answers, and what she found was the man she would one day marry.

In the photo, they were standing together beside the pond in the Boston Public Garden. Sara thought she could read on her face the terror that was growing in her heart as she realized what marriage to this evangelical seminarian would mean.

This wasn't the time, however, for such reminiscences. There were two specific items she must find and immediately destroy.

Ever since their first night in this old manse, this had become her obsession. Stephen was lying with his head on her stomach, listening to the faint, pitter-patter heartbeat of their seven-month-old baby. It kicked Stephen right in the face, and they both laughed. Then it kicked again, but this time in a different way. A soft pain went down her solar plexus, a pain so vaguely familiar that it brought it all back. It was then that she knew she must make this trip to the attic.

She continued sifting impatiently through bundle after bundle, straining under the diminishing glow of the candle, until she found the first envelope of her search. She ripped it open and began sorting through more photos. Yes, there it was: a wedding picture of herself in jeans and a garland of daisies in her hair, and beside her, in jeans and no shirt, stood her then beloved, Frank.

*   *   *

"THANK YOU FOR COMING, Reverend LaPointe," Helen Horscht said with words slurred from exhaustion after twenty-four hours of on-and-off labor.

Upon entering the room, Stephen was once again taken aback by the unique beauty of Helen's face. The curves and balance of every feature seemed somehow perfect, as if God had modeled her after a sculpture by Michelangelo. Even with her auburn hair damp from the stresses of labor, she was still beautiful, and when placed mentally alongside her husband, the picture posed an enigmatic and troubling contradiction.

"You're more than welcome. How are you feeling?" he asked.

"Much better now. The pain has been awfully intense."

"Have they located your husband, Walter?" Stephen glanced around, but saw no signs that anyone had been there since his second visit that morning.

"No, they haven't," she said. "It was his day off, but normally he tells me where he's going."

"Well, you just relax. I'm sure he'll call or stop by soon. Is there anything I can do for you?"

"No, thank you," and with that she turned to the wall and wept.

Stephen patted her shoulder lightly and then left. He asked the nurse at the station across the hall, "Is everything going fine?"

"Yes, the doctor will be here soon, and then we'll induce."

"Do I have time to get a coffee?"

"Yes, of course."

"Thanks."

Stephen glanced at his watch and then headed for the elevators. He wished he were home with Sara. Every night since Malone had left, he had been out on some call or supervising some lay committee. He wondered how Sara was holding up. It was bad enough that he had to learn how to be a pastor by trial and error, but there were no manuals at all for becoming a pastor's wife. And given her past, there was no guarantee that she would succeed.

*   *   *

MY DEAR BROTHERS AND SISTERS, do you hear His voice? Do you hear Him calling you? He is, you know. He knows you better than you know yourself. He knows your past and your present. He knows your needs and He knows your heart. And He is speaking directly to you."

With this, the evangelist paused to point up and out and around from his podium on the fifty yard line to the thousands of listeners in the stands under the dome of Eisenhower Memorial Stadium.

"He is beckoning to you, 'Come to me, all ye who are weak and heavy laden, and I will give you rest.' Will you not come to Jesus, Who loves you so much that He gave Himself for you, shedding His blood on the cross for the forgiveness of your sins? Will you not come? Will you not come?"

Men and women began descending from every direction down the aisles and onto the playing field.

"Will you not come? What is it that holds you back? Are you afraid? Are you proud?"

The pleasant-toned, two-hundred-voice choir began singing a familiar hymn of invitation:

"Just as I am, without one plea,
    but that Thy blood was shed for me."

Walter strained to hold back the tears. His friend Raeph Timmons had dragged him along, but Walter swore that it would make no difference. He also refused to tell Helen that he was going because he didn't want her to get her hopes up. He would have nothing of this Jesus crap.

Yet now he wanted to go forward. He wanted to be forgiven. He wanted to start over. He wanted to believe. But he couldn't let Raeph see this, even though this was exactly what Raeph and his wife, Patty, had probably been *praying* for, *damn them!*

Then Raeph stood up and began to go forward. He was a deceptively slight man. Underneath his loose-fitting clothing, Raeph was the strongest man Walter had ever known. But what had drawn Walter to him, back when they were recuperating as roommates in a Veteran's hospital, was Raeph's fathomless heart. He never got riled. He always loved. His Christianity was not a put-on; it was real.

"Where are you going?" Walter asked incredulously. "You don't need to go forward."

"We all need forgiveness, Walter. I've already given my life to Jesus, but I want to give it to Him again. Do you want to come with me?"

Walter looked out at his friend through teary eyes and fogged-up glasses. Fighting back a smile he said faintly, "Yes." With that, the tough, explosive veteran dressed in black stood up and stepped out into the aisle, shaking with sobs.

"Just as I am, and waiting not
    to rid my soul of one dark blot."

Walter was sure he looked stupid, grasping shoulders to steady himself as he descended the steps on wobbly legs, but he didn't care.

Something had changed; something was different inside. He didn't know what it was, but it felt great.

"To Thee, whose blood can cleanse each spot
     O Lamb of God, I come, I come!"

"Yes, Lord, I'm a'comin'," Walter said with a smile as he reached the turf.

Raeph stopped to direct Walter forward to the rows of folding chairs surrounding the podium. There a male counselor welcomed him.

"What's your name," the counselor said, extending his hand.

"Walter...Walter Horscht."

"Have you come to accept Jesus as your Lord and Savior?"

"You're damn right, but will He accept me?"

The counselor sat down beside him and they talked.

Raeph stood back, giving his friend space to receive grace. This had certainly been a long time coming. Ever since they became friends in that VA hospital, Raeph had tried to break through Walter's tough defenses with the Gospel. Now here he sat meek as a lamb, reciting the sinner's prayer.

"Just as I am, Thy love unknown
     hath broken every barrier down;
Now, to be Thine, yes Thine alone,
     O Lamb of God, I come, I come!"

Suddenly Walter stood up with raised arms and shouted above the refrains of the choir and the mumbled prayers of hundreds of repentant sinners, "Thank you, Lord! Praise you, Jesus! I love you, Lord!"

Raeph smiled with joy. Grace had gotten through. Jesus had cracked his friend's shell. But as he watched Walter prance around in ecstasy, kicking his legs like a Russian dancer, Raeph's smile dimmed. There was another side to Walter's character. A dark side, like another personality that might lash out suddenly in unreserved bitterness. Raeph had witnessed this many times over the past few years, but it was Helen who had suffered the most.

As Walter joined hands with a woman in a tight red dress on his left and a businessman in a pinstriped suit on his right, Raeph wondered whether grace had penetrated deeply enough to touch this other side.

*   *   *   **

STUDYING THE GLINT in Frank's eyes, Sara realized what she should have known all along.

After having finished her undergraduate degree, she had accepted a teaching position at a local public high school. It was there that she had met Frank, the science teacher. He was at best a nominal Catholic whose moral life made him a man of drastic contradictions. Sara was ignorant of Catholic moral practice, so she had guessed that Frank's occasional trips to the confessional allowed him the freedom to live as he pleased. Their dating got hot and heavy fast, and to her consternation, she became pregnant.

Her teaching career had just started, so she was vulnerable to the many voices in her life—including those of her parents as well as the father of the child in her womb—that encouraged her to end the pregnancy. But she was too afraid to do this alone. So, Frank said he loved her, and they got married. A radical campus priest, a close friend of Frank's, arranged for a quick private marriage—one that asked few questions and made fewer demands. A real '70s write-your-own-vows marriage.

They moved in together, and for a few weeks they actually *felt* like husband and wife. She even started to *feel* that she might grow to love this man.

Then during spring break, she went by herself to the clinic.

Sara now held the photograph at an angle over the flame of her candle. The photo began to burn and then crinkle into ashes. She set it down on the brick beside the candle and watched it disintegrate.

"Burn, Frank," Sara said with an edge of finality. "Burn."

She returned her attention to the contents of the box. More letters, photos, a half-finished diary, an outdated teacher's certificate, and then the bottom of the box.

"It isn't here," she said with panic. She glanced around at the other boxes. "No, it's got to be in this one."

She started over, looking more carefully through each packet of photos, letters, and documents, until she found it. She held the receipt close to the flame and, with horrific agony, remembered...

SHE PARKED HER CAR a block away, pausing to hear whether anything inside her would argue against what she was about to do, but she heard nothing. Never in any of her religious training had she heard a convincing argument against a woman's right to an abortion. At Campion, she had encountered what she considered *self-righteous fanatics* preaching the Catholic party line, but they had been easy to ignore, given her Congregationalist convictions of freedom of conscience. Instead, the pro-choice arguments at feminist rallies turned her heart—arguments saying that, in many circumstances, abortion was the most loving and civilized choice.

Wearing inconspicuous clothing and hiding behind dark glasses, Sara left the sanctuary of her car. When she turned the corner around a large, boarded-up building, she found herself face-to-face with a crowd of pro-life picketers. Dozens of people were marching in a circle, brandishing what she considered hideous posters with pictures of aborted fetuses, offensive pro-life slogans, and religious symbols. People were kneeling, praying with beads. Others were singing folk hymns. People were passing out pamphlets. As she took this all in, she realized that several women had guessed why she was there and were coming toward her.

The urge to turn and run gripped her, not because she had changed her mind, but because she hated confrontation. She didn't want to talk to anyone; she just wanted it to be over.

They were about to greet her when she lowered her head and walked straight through them, past the picketers, past the bead-speakers, around the pamphleteers, and on into the clinic. She refused to hear a word.

A year later, after she had been seeing Stephen for several weeks, she told him about Frank and their quick divorce. At first she thought this had driven Stephen away, since he began breaking dates for ridiculous reasons. Then one evening Stephen showed up at her apartment unannounced with a bouquet of roses and a bottle of wine.

SARA AGAIN PICKED UP THEIR PHOTO from Boston Garden and tried to recall every detail of that wonderful evening that had sealed their relationship.

"YOU SEE, SARA," Stephen began awkwardly after popping the cork, "when I heard about your divorce, I began questioning whether I should even date you. It sounds judgmental…"

"I should say," Sara said with feigned annoyance, for she knew his concerns were probably right.

"Now just listen," he said, clinking glasses and kissing her. "I just needed to be sure, that's all. I believe that the Bible is the sole authority for our faith—for everything I believe and teach. Jesus spoke clearly against divorce and remarriage, so I was unsure what to do. I wanted to ignore it all, as do so many other modern Christians, but if I can't follow Jesus' word, what can I follow? I was stumped.

"Then this morning Reverend Gaston, my senior pastor, took me aside. He knew I was struggling with this. He said that sometimes when one is stuck in the quagmire between seemingly contradictory Scriptures, the only way out is to prayerfully make the most logical choice. He confirmed what Jesus had said about divorce and remarriage, and then asked, 'Stephen, do you remember the passages where Jesus forgave the woman at the well who had five husbands, or where he forgave the woman caught in adultery?' I said, 'Yes, of course.' 'Do you believe that Jesus has forgiven Sara?' And I responded, 'Yes, I'm sure He has.' Then he said, tapping my chest with his forefinger, 'Then why can't you?' I had no response except to say that, of course, I too forgive you, and therefore I have no reason to hold back my love."

Stephen apparently now had no reservations, but Sara did. The thought of being a preacher's wife was paralyzing, and given her past, the combination was an embarrassing oxymoron.

Then she let most of it out—all but about the abortion. She enumerated her failures and shortcomings, her doubts and apprehensions about filling the shoes of a pastor's wife.

And somehow, God gave Stephen the grace to sit patiently and listen. After hearing every conceivable reason why their relationship could never work, he reached out and cradled both her hands. He then said, "Sara, there's an old saying that expresses it best: 'There, but for the grace of God go I.' If I am even the least bit worthy of being a minister, it is only because of what Jesus has done in my life—not because of anything I have done or refused to do. I, too, have made many mistakes—many in and after college that I prefer to forget. But God in His loving mercy has changed me, and I know that He loves you even more than I do."

Stephen looked into her green eyes and gently caressed her hands with his lips. "I know that He will do for you what He has done for me and for millions of others," Stephen continued. "He wipes away the stains of our past with His forgiveness. He recreates our hearts with His love, making us into new creatures. He helps us become what we were supposed to be if we had never sinned. I'm not asking you to marry me because you are perfect or because I expect you to become perfect—though I expect both of us to try," he said, adding levity as was his custom.

"And I'm not asking you to marry me because I believe that God has called us together—which I do believe. And I'm not asking you because somehow underneath all that diminishing feminist exterior I see hidden the makings of an ideal pastor's wife—which I also do see. No, I'm asking you for one reason: because I truly love you."

Sara held the receipt from the South Boston Family Clinic, the last piece of evidence of that shameful blot on her past, up to the flame and watched it burn. She had told Stephen about Frank, but never about this—*He would not understand.*

A door slammed downstairs.

"Sara, I'm home."

Sara jumped and lost her balance, falling backwards onto the pile of boxes, knocking them over with a crash. The flaming document flew from her hands onto a bundle of old newspapers.

"Sara, what's happening?" Stephen cried out, bounding up the stairs three at a time. In the corner he saw a stack of papers on fire, a burning candle on the chimney, and two feet emerging from a pile of boxes.

"Sara!" Quickly he used his sport coat to smother the flames, and then turned to Sara, who was struggling to extract herself.

"Sara, what happened? Are you all right?"

"Yes, yes, I'm fine. Is the fire out?"

"I think so, but what happened?" he said, helping her to her feet.

"Oh, I was sorting through some old correspondence, and, well, I guess I fell. Can we go down now?"

"Sure, here, let me help you."

Stephen walked her to the stairs, and then preceded her down, assisting her until she was safely in a living room chair.

"I better go back up and make sure the fire's out completely," he said.

"But…"

"Don't worry, I'll be right back."

Stephen rushed back up the stairs. He first checked the smoldering papers. Deciding to take no chances, he picked them up by the twine that bound them. He then broke the candle free from its wax mooring and turned to leave. Under the flicker of the flame, he noticed a partially consumed scrap of paper. Holding the candle closer, he read what was left of a letterhead: *STON FAMILY CLI.* He tried to read farther.

"Stephen, please come here."

"Yes, dear," he said, turning from the fragment and proceeding quickly down the stairs. "Boy, there's a lot of discarded trash up here."

"Yes, I know," Sara said with uncertain relief.

4

Two years later…

A SUDDEN BRILLIANT FLASH OF LIGHTNING preceded by ten seconds the resultant deafening crack. This then echoed into diminishing rumblings among the hills surrounding Red Creek Congregational Church.

"Two miles yet and comin' closer."

Around the perimeter of four folding tables in the musty church basement sat a group of eight men and women. Each reverberating luminescence elongated their silhouettes against the bookshelves on the far wall.

"That puts the storm directly over your farm," said the Reverend Brian Smith. He sat alone at the head table, his black clerical shirt open at the collar, his white tab dangling from one side. His full head of black hair graying at the temples was well groomed as usual, but his normally pleasant, jovial expression was tainted by some distant distraction.

"I remember once back in '37," began Miss Irene Drewer, but another flash and an even quicker peal of thunder cut her words short. She and her twin sister, Elsie, sat at the table to the left of Reverend Smith. They were in their eighties, never married, and attended every church activity. This was their life. Irene generally did the talking, though, since Elsie was embarrassingly plagued with an incurable stutter. Elsie rarely was able to utter a complete sentence, except when she sang. In the choir, she was a doe set free, for mysteriously her voice was flawless and perfect in song. With each crack of thunder, Irene sat stone still as if unaffected, while Elsie cringed, looking around furtively into every dark corner as if searching for some nemesis.

"Hopefully, Clem 'n the boys'l finish'er up while thar's still pow'r." Mr. and Mrs. Fred Spivens sat along the table facing Reverend Smith. For these third-generation dairy farmers whose sons now ran the business, this weekly gathering was a thoroughly enjoyable extravagance that was an unjustifiable luxury back when their lives were hamstrung by two hundred Jerseys.

"Now thar's a generator, Fred, so don't you fret," Mrs. Annabel Spivens countered.

"Eh'up."

Along the table to the pastor's right sat three men who were the proverbial three musketeers of the church—always together, always up front, and generally a welcome mixture of seriousness spiked with whimsy—Ben Ware, the plumber, Raeph Timmons, the heating and cooling specialist, and Walter Horscht, the production manager at the injection molding plant in nearby Piscataway.

Ever since Walter's conversion at the crusade two years ago, he had been a radically different man. He gave up smoking and drinking, he began wearing his hair conservatively short, clean, and brushed neatly back, and he replaced his black anti-social attire with the Brooks Brothers wardrobe he had previously berated but secretly admired. Now his normal attire was a blue button-down Oxford cloth shirt, khaki pants, and penny loafers. With his thick wire-rimmed glasses he almost looked scholarly. Practically overnight he had become a Bible-toting, gospel-preaching, clean-talking disciple of Jesus, much to the mixed reviews of his family and friends.

Yet, they were generally ecstatic over his reversal. When he had showed up the next morning to greet his wife and their new daughter,

Stacy, Helen couldn't believe that he was the same hot-headed, hardened war veteran she had married. He was completely remorseful. On his knees, he begged not only for her forgiveness but for her help in starting over. From that moment on, his previously unpredictable and seemingly uncontrollable energies had become rechanneled into an unreserved defense of Jesus and His Word. In the end, Walter became even more conservative than the parents who had once driven him from the faith. He resolved, however, to prevent this from happening to his own sweet pea, Stacy, and especially to prevent anyone the likes of what he used to be from ever touching her.

Another lightning flash was followed immediately by thunder and the heavy onslaught of rain.

"She's here now," said Ben with a knowing smile, as if his being a plumber made him an expert in anything involving water.

"Guess we'll see whether your repair of the church drains and sump'll work," said Raeph.

"It'll work," Ben replied, his smile diminishing as he shot a quick glance toward the utility closet.

"What a great night to continue our study of the End Times," Reverend Smith began. "Jesus said in His Olivet discourse, 'For as the lightning cometh out of the east, and shineth even unto the west, so shall also the coming of the Son of man be.'"

Elsie glanced quickly around, cowering deeper into her chair.

"Now Elsie, Jesus didn't mean specifically *this* lightning."

They all laughed, including Elsie, who sat up a mite straighter.

"Walter, could you read from Matthew 24, verse 9 through 14."

"Sure, pastor."

Walter opened his leather bound King James Bible, which he had received as a child and now carried everywhere. It looked as though it had been through the wash. Under the echo of rumbling thunder he began reading with the same suspenseful intensity one might read a tale by Poe:

> "Then shall they deliver you up to be afflicted, and shall kill you: and ye shall be hated of all nations for my name's sake. And then shall many be offended, and shall betray one another, and shall hate one another. And many false prophets shall rise, and shall deceive many. And because

iniquity shall abound, the love of many shall wax cold.
But he that shall endure unto the end, the same shall be
saved. And this gospel of the kingdom shall be preached
in all the world for a witness unto all nations; and then
shall the end come."

They sat quietly listening to the rain. Ben kept his eyes glued to
the bottom of the utility door.

"Sounds a bit like this day and age."

"Sure does, pastor," Walter said.

"Of course, this could also be said about many other times in
history, but never more so than today," said Reverend Smith. "And
with Israel having become a nation, fulfilling the necessary Old
Testament prophecy, and the gospel having been preached to the far
corners of the globe, the time is truly ripe. Are we not living in a
time of great hatred and wickedness? A time filled with cold, self-
centered hearts and overflowing with falsehood and false teachers?"

"Pastor, I've got to tell you about a book I just read," said Raeph.
"It's called *The Late Great Planet Earth*, and it has changed my life.
I've always believed in the Second Coming of Jesus, but never
imagined that it could be this close. The author says that all the
signs point to an imminent rapture of the faithful."

"What's that?" asked Fred.

"Look a little farther down in Matthew and you can read about
it," said Reverend Smith. "Raeph, how about reading verse 40 and
on."

"All right." Raeph turned the page and began reading:

"Then shall two be in the field; the one shall be taken,
and the other left. Two women shall be grinding at the
mill; the one shall be taken, and the other left. Watch
therefore: for ye know not what hour your Lord doth
come."

"Boy, I hope the boys get the milking done," Fred said with a
smirk. "I'd hate to see Clem left behind to finish up all by his
lonesome."

They all laughed except for Elsie, who was staring at her pastor
for clarification, and Walter, who was reading on in the text.

"The idea is that before the Great Tribulation, the church—those who are true believers in Jesus Christ—will be raptured or translated into heaven, leaving unbelievers behind," Reverend Smith explained. "But up until the Rapture, the faithful will still undergo persecution, hatred, and the undermining of their faith by false teachers."

"Pastor," Walter asked.

"Yes, Walter."

"Who are the false teach…"

Lightning flashed and cracked, and the lights in the church went out. Elsie screamed. The illumination from additional lightning flashes made their dark silhouettes into an eerie rendition of the Last Supper, and the reflection from Walter's two lenses made Elsie think of an Oriental spy in an old black-and-white murder mystery.

"Now take it easy," Reverend Smith said calmly. "There's a candle in the cupboard behind me." He reached back to extract an altar candle and held it up to the flame on Fred's butane lighter, which Fred had conveniently flicked.

"I s'pose we ought to get home to make sure the generator's kicked on," Fred said to Annabel.

"Us, too," said Irene. "Our cat Fidget is probably affright."

"Maybe the good Lord is telling us we've talked enough for one night," Ben quipped anxiously.

"Hardly," said Walter. "I'm sure the lights will come back on in a moment. I'm willing to keep going if anyone else is."

"I'm in no hurry," said Reverend Smith. "Anyone who wants to stay can, and the rest can follow Fred's flame out to the parking lot."

"Thanks, Pastor, see ya Sunday."

Fred and Mrs. Spivens, Irene and Elsie filed out behind the flame hand-on-shoulders, like prisoners in a chain gang. Left behind around the tables were Reverend Smith and his three musketeers.

"Please, Pastor, who specifically are the false teachers that Jesus mentions?" Walter continued. "How can we know?"

The four men, hunched close to the flickering candle, had the appearance of a clandestine meeting contemplating some dire conspiracy. And any passers-by wondering this wouldn't be far wrong.

*　　　*　　　*

"PLEASE, STEPHEN, come right in."

"Thank you, Reverend Malone. You wanted to see me?"

Stephen sat down in a leather-upholstered chair and sank in until his face barely rose above the senior pastor's large oak desk. Reverend Malone sat comfortably in a swivel executive's chair, the back of which extended at least a foot above his rounded shoulders. He was wearing what to Stephen looked like a traditional smoking jacket, which fit appropriately with Malone's ornate pipe from which emerged the pleasant scent of cherry mixed with rum.

The past two years had been extremely full and rewarding for Stephen. He had shared in every aspect of the pastoral ministry, from baptisms, confirmations, marriages, and funerals to counseling, home visitations, preaching, and teaching—all under Malone's constant supervision. At first Stephen worried that Malone was going to delegate everything to him and then lay back, but this had hardly been the case. Malone was a busy and effective pastor, and Stephen appreciated him for this. This didn't mean, however, that they had always agreed. Over the past six months in particular they had battled head to head over many issues, and the popularity of Stephen's Wednesday night Bible studies and monthly stint in the pulpit hadn't helped.

But Stephen was grateful for his senior pastor's model and his fatherly attention. Stephen was beginning to feel that when the time came, he would be ready to take on the role of pastor—but he didn't believe yet that he was ready.

"Yes, thank you for coming over on this stormy night," the senior pastor began. "I'll be out of the office the next few days, so I wanted to get this off my chest. Mrs. Pearson called."

"Oh, what now?"

"I know, she seems to get bent over the least things, but in this case I think she's right. You and I have had our friendly disagreements over the issues of salvation and justification, and up until now I've put up with what I consider an exorbitantly narrow viewpoint, especially in your sermons. Nevertheless, Mrs. Pearson and others have complained that you're making them feel insecure about their relationship with God, while at the same time ramming eternal security down their throats."

"My sermons must be hitting a bit too close to home, I take it?"

"Stephen, you know as well as I do that the viewpoint you teach is only one of many. Your emphasis on the 'Four Spiritual Laws,' on responding to an altar call, on 'accepting Jesus as your Lord and Savior,' all of this is but the narrow-minded concoction of twentieth-century Evangelicals. It's all well-meaning, grant you, but in the end it cheapens the faith. It makes conversion comparable to a fast-food restaurant—come forward, say a prayer, voila, you're guaranteed heaven."

"But that's an unfair caricature of what I preach. I always emphasize the necessity of a converted heart and a sincere change of lifestyle. The assurance of salvation doesn't mean that a person can now sit back and relax in sin."

"But that is the way it too often is interpreted and sadly practiced. Listen, Stephen, lifelong members like Mrs. Pearson may not have had the same 'born-again experience' that you had and that you believe everyone should have, but believe me, she is a good Christian."

"But what is a 'good Christian,' Reverend Malone? It seems to me that members like Mrs. Pearson presume they are *saved* because their ancestors built this church, because they have always had a family member on the board or on some church committee, or because they happen to be one of the church's largest donors."

"In all those things, Stephen, you only see attempts to earn salvation because her life of faith doesn't fit into your mold. Instead, I see these as the selfless giving of time, talents, and money for the work of the church."

"Oh, come on, Reverend Malone. Mrs. Pearson? You've complained yourself about her using her wealth and family's position as a fulcrum to manipulate the church."

Malone rose from his chair to gaze out his office window. From there he had a clear view of the front of the white church building accentuated by the illumination from two ground-mounted spotlights. The rain falling heavily at an angle gave the impression of a church under siege.

From Stephen's perspective, Malone's silhouette with his pipe clenched in his teeth and smoke rising around him portrayed either the profile of Sherlock Holmes or Alfred Hitchcock.

"Stephen, some day you'll understand. An old pastor once cautioned me to think always like a good general who must choose his battles carefully. On the whole, I agree with you. Mrs. Pearson's faith does need a good kick in the pants, but as the pastor of this church I also need to be sensitive to her feelings and trust in the timing and influence of the Holy Spirit. I need to be sensitive to the needs of the long haul, not only the moment."

"But what if Mrs. Pearson was frightened by tonight's lightning display and died? Would her longstanding membership, her influential family, and her money get her into heaven?"

"Stephen, again I agree with your sentiments, but only God knows the sincerity of her heart."

From the depths of his cushy chair, Stephen stared up in frustration at his senior pastor. To Stephen this *was* a battle worth every ounce of his effort—where would he be if his friend Jim had not confronted him about his own need for conversion? To downplay this was the slippery slope to modern liberalism, to the social gospel. But beyond that, Stephen was dumbfounded that Malone was trying to justify folding under the pressures of money and power.

In the end, Stephen's only response was a blank-faced "Yes, sir."

"Listen, Stephen," Malone said as he turned back from the window, "in reality this is probably all a moot point. I know you don't agree with my politics, but you will, once you find yourself in my position, which may be sooner than you think."

"What's that?" Stephen said, sitting up.

"Red Creek Congregational is losing their pastor. I spoke with Reverend Smith yesterday, and he is interested in having you apply as his successor. I concurred with him."

"When is this happening?"

"Within the month. Smith is moving to a church in St. Johnsbury to be near his ailing mother. If you are interested, and if they are, you could be their pastor in, say, three months. What do you think?"

"This is awfully sudden. I'm not sure I'm ready."

"Stephen, cut the false humility. You've been ready and antsy to hold the reins of leadership for a long time."

"I'll need to talk this over with Sara."

"Can you let me know when I get back on Wednesday?" Malone said, extending his hand and moving toward the door.

"Yes, I think so," Stephen said, accepting the handshake, struggling up out of his chair. "And thank you, thank you for your confidence."

"You've earned it, Stephen. But until then, how about saving your hell-and-brimstone fervor for Red Creek?"

"No problem, sir. The soul of Mrs. Pearson and her money are in your tender care."

"Thanks."

*   *   *

STEPHEN'S RIDE HOME was a bit precarious, not only because of the torrential rain and occasional fallen branches, but because his mind was awash with a tsunami of afterthoughts. When he had left for his meeting with Malone that evening, he hadn't the slightest notion that his drive home would be consumed with the ramifications of moving on to a new congregation.

What will Sara think? he wondered with a hint of trepidation. *She's just become comfortable here, and only barely accustomed to her role as a pastor's wife. Is she ready to face the more demanding pressures of a solo pastor's wife?*

Yet, Stephen's mind kept returning to his disagreement with Malone. He abhorred Malone's modernist, truncated compromising of the gospel. *In the few short minutes that we argued over how to coddle to the whims and financial blackmail of members like Mrs. Pearson, hundreds of people died apart from Jesus. We are not to pamper to their weaknesses, but exhort them to change, to surrender to Christ.*

Something deeper, however, was eating at Stephen. Every time that he and Malone had disagreed over some issue, Malone had been able to fortify his opinion effectively from Scripture.

Three years of study and debates at seminary had solidified Stephen's uncompromising belief in the inerrant, sufficiency of the Bible. Like most evangelical Christians following the lead of Martin Luther and the other sixteenth century Reformers, Stephen accepted *sola scriptura* without question—that the Bible was the Christian's sole trustworthy source for truth.

During those seminary debates, often in the cafeteria late at night, he had argued his Congregationalist-Evangelical-Calvinist beliefs against seminarians who held Methodist, Pentecostal, Baptist, Episcopal, Lutheran, Presbyterian, Assembly of God, Church of Christ, or other doctrinal positions. At the time he was consumed in defending what he *knew* was true, and denouncing what he *knew* were misinterpretations of Scripture. He didn't see it a problem that these sincere, believing Christian brothers—and sisters—also believed in *sola scriptura*. He merely assumed that their presumptions were blinding them to the Bible's true meaning.

These two years under Malone, however, had made him painfully frustrated. He felt stymied in all of their scriptural debates because they always ended in a stalemate between his collection of Scripture passages and Malone's. If he pointed to verses arguing salvation by faith alone, for example, Malone countered with verses emphasizing the necessity of love or baptism or good deeds. If Stephen built a scriptural case for eternal security, Malone turned to dozens of verses that confirmed the possibility of apostasy. And Malone wasn't necessarily defending the position he believed; he was only arguing that no single position was true. He was arguing for individual freedom of conscience.

Up until this evening, until this moment as he pulled into the driveway of their manse and contemplated dashing through the rain to the front porch, Stephen had written all of this off as but the process by which sinful human beings argue their way closer to the truth, almost as if it was some kind of game. But he might soon become a solo pastor to whom a congregation looked for the reliable discernment of biblical truth. This was no longer a game. The eternal destiny of souls might depend upon whether what he was preaching and teaching was true. Was he ready to take this responsibility onto his shoulders?

Stephen's immediate decision, however, was whether to sit patiently until the rain died down or run like a banshee to the front door. It struck him as funny that this was analogous to his quandary over whether to remain comfortably as an assistant at Sleepy Meadow or brave the onslaught of responsibilities at Red Creek.

A face peered from the kitchen window, and Stephen knew what his decision must be. He held a newspaper over his head against the driving rain and ran like a banshee.

*　　　*　　　*

"IT'S DIFFICULT TO IDENTIFY precisely whom Jesus and the writers of the New Testament were referring to as false teachers," Reverend Smith said as he looked across at Walter through the flickering glow of the candle. "Like snakes in the grass, they can be sly and deceptive. The

Bible tells us, though, to 'test the spirits,' and using the criteria of Scripture we can at least identify some of them."

Reverend Smith turned slowly through his Bible. "Here, listen to what the Apostle Paul wrote in his second letter to Timothy:

> ...in the last days perilous times shall come. For men shall be lovers of their own selves, covetous, boasters, proud, blasphemers, disobedient to parents, unthankful, unholy, without natural affection, trucebreakers, false accusers, incontinent, fierce, despisers of those that are good, traitors, heady, highminded, lovers of pleasures more than lovers of God; having a form of godliness, but denying the power thereof: from such turn away.

"Now does that sound like today or what?"

"Couldn't be a better description of the world I see," Ben said.

"Especially those 'without natural affection,' Paul's politically correct way of identifying homosexuals," said Raeph. "Makes me sick."

"Yes, the world is truly going to hell in a hand basket, and that's a sign," said Reverend Smith with intense seriousness. "The last days are upon us, and I wouldn't be surprised if these lovers of self and money and perversity wake up some morning soon and find us all gone, raptured to the right hand of Jesus. In the meantime, false teachers working as pawns of the devil will attempt to corrupt the church. They will teach a false gospel that enslaves people rather than frees them. Here, listen."

He turned back a few pages, and then with a glance at each of the men around him, continued reading.

> "Now the Spirit speaketh expressly, that in the latter times some shall depart from the faith, giving heed to seducing spirits, and doctrines of devils; speaking lies in hypocrisy; having their conscience seared with a hot iron; forbidding to marry, [and commanding] to abstain from meats, which God hath created to be received with thanksgiving of them which believe and know the truth.

"OK, my friends, which religion forbids the marriage of its

clergy and nuns, forces its members to abstain from meat on Fridays, and gives heed to 'seducing spirits, and doctrines of devils' by praying to the dead?"

"I knew it!" Walter exclaimed through gritted teeth.

"Yes, Walter, the Roman Catholic Church. Our forefathers left Europe for this continent to escape the clutches of the Pope—the antichrist—and his horde of demonic teachers, but they followed us here and have infected every community, every institution with their heresies."

Lightning flashed, making them all jump.

"Reverend Smith," said Raeph with excitement. "I read another book recently by an ex-priest who became a Baptist minister. His name is Gary Harmond and he heads a ministry called Former Catholics to Catholics, FC2C, which tries to rescue Catholics from the clutches of the Pope."

Reverend Smith smiled. "I know Gary. I've heard him speak. We have some of his tracts in the church foyer that clearly reveal the Catholic Church for what it is."

"His story is convincing," Raeph continued, "and reveals the false teachings that were ramrodded down his throat in seminary. One particular argument he uses clearly proves the lie of the papacy. The Catholic Church points to Matthew chapter sixteen to prove that Jesus chose Simon Peter to be the first pope and the rock of the Church. But in the original Greek, Jesus' new name for Simon means 'little stone or pebble.' On the other hand, it was Simon's confession of faith that became the 'rock' or 'large boulder' upon which the church was built. The whole development of the papacy was built on a twisting of Scripture."

"The sixteenth-century Reformers all pointed to the pope as the antichrist and the Catholic Church as the 'whore of Babylon,'" Reverend Smith added, "but in the centuries since, the Catholic Church has infiltrated our country, our government, our culture, even our own churches with its lies, periling millions to hell."

"What do you mean, infiltrating our churches?" Walter asked.

"Ever since the Reformation, Catholic priests and laymen have secretly come amongst the faithful, posing as sincere believers, polluting and watering down the true gospel, sometimes with legalistic rules that enslave people's hearts, other times with liberal ideas that lead to complacency and sloth. Here, listen."

Reverend Smith rose to retrieve a book from a nearby shelf.

"This book by a Presbyterian theologian named Boettner, called *Roman Catholicism,* is, in my mind, the best presentation of the truth about the Catholic Church and its twisted plans to overpower the world. After enumerating this in great detail, the author declares:

> The time has come to put aside false tolerance and to let the world know the facts about Romanism. The public has been duped too long...Protestants must be made to see the great danger that threatens them. The hierarchy'— and by this he means the pope, cardinals, and bishops— 'makes no secret of the fact that it is out to "Make America Catholic."...The hierarchy seeks to gain control, and to a remarkable degree is gaining control, by placing its agents in key positions in the government, the press, radio, television, movies, education, and labor movements, all over the nation. And for the most part, Protestants are fast asleep!"

"But how can we determine whether someone is an infiltrator?" Walter asked with rising concern.

"It's not easy," replied Reverend Smith, "but mark my words, they're everywhere."

The pastor turned his focus to the candle's flame, and then with a serious, troubled expression said, "I need to tell you guys something. You're the closest to me of all the members. I found out just two weeks ago that I'm being pressured to move. Apparently some members here don't like what I'm preaching and have complained to the head office. They're pressuring me. I've decided to accept the call to a quiet, small church in St. Johnsbury, way off the beaten path, supposedly to be near my dying mother, but between you and me, she's just fine."

Walter stood up, kicking his chair back from the table. "They can't do that! Your dismissal requires a congregational vote."

"Yes, *they* can, Walter, because they can make it rough for me. I've come to the conclusion that it may be for the best."

"Are infiltrators behind this?"

"Walter, I can't say. I only know that someone with influence doesn't like my version of the gospel."

Suddenly the lights came back on, as well as other electric

appliances around the church, filling the stillness with a host of competing noises.

"Listen, brothers, I need to get back to the family. How about a final prayer, and then let's call it a night."

"All right, Pastor," Raeph said, "but know that you are in our prayers."

"Thanks. Let's pray."

As Reverend Smith led them in prayer, Walter's mind raced with questions driven by anger. *How can we let this happen to Reverend Smith? How can I protect my family in these last days from the lies of these Roman infiltrators?* He racked his brain for what God might be calling him to do.

Ever since the night of his conversion, Walter had been certain that God was calling him to accept some special assignment and that his entire life up until that moment had been its preparation. As a Marine assigned to the special assignments division, he had been called to perform many tasks which he was sworn to conceal— tasks he prefered to forget. An order would be given in code, and without any questions he was expected to obey.

Now as a Christian, he looked to the faithful centurion of the Gospels as his model of obedience. *Are you calling me, Lord, to do something specific to put an end to the influence of these infiltrators?*

Reverend Smith concluded their prayer and then led his faithful three musketeers up to the front entrance. Passing through the foyer, Walter noticed the tracts Reverend Smith had mentioned and grabbed one for the road.

"Good night," Reverend Smith said with a sorrowful smile.

"See you later, Pastor," Raeph said as the spokesman. "You'll be in our prayers."

They ran out through the rain to their cars.

As the interior of Walter's new gray Caprice station wagon began warming up, he sat examining the tract entitled "Are Roman Catholics Christian?" Though it was in the form of a miniature comic book, Walter was deeply moved by how the artist effectively portrayed the pagan, idolatrous sources of Catholic teaching, particularly those concerning the sacraments. He was shocked to read how Catholics become citizens of two countries, enslaved under the political rule of the Pope in Rome, and how Catholic priests control them through the incriminating information collected in the confessional. Each picture and its captions turned his stomach and strengthened his resolve to do everything within his power to rescue Catholics from the grasp of the evil one.

The tract ended with a prayer, which he prayed with conviction: "Dear heavenly Father, thank you for revealing the truth about the Catholic Church. I reject this false church of Satan, and accept Christ's sacrifice on the cross as perfectly complete. In His precious name, please forgive me my sins. I accept Jesus as my Lord and Savior and trust Him alone for my salvation."

As he put his station wagon into gear, he made a vow to never be duped by any wolf in sheep's clothing.

5

"CREATE IN ME A CLEAN HEART, O God," Stephen sang softly as he paced the second-floor hallway. William was nearly asleep in his arms. Stephen had tried many strategies to encourage his ever-energetic two-year-old to sleep alone in his own room, but to date, the only successful maneuver had been to soothe him off with song, lay him down, and then sneak out quietly.

> "Restore unto me the joy of Thy salvation,
>   and uphold me with Thy free spirit;
> Create in me a clean heart, O God,
>   and renew a right spirit within me."

Stephen paused to listen. Steady, solid breathing; no movement; the feel of a limp bag of grass seed. *He's asleep.* Carefully Stephen laid William down in the crib, covered him with a blanket, and then backed out. Halfway down the stairs, he again paused and listened. *Nothing! Great.*

Passing first through the kitchen, Stephen poured two glasses of white wine. Though some Congregationalists were still puritanical, most were less concerned than other Protestants over the drinking of spirits. Since Sleepy Meadow was a melting pot of converts from other denominations and a wide array of scruples, he and Sara guarded their consumption. When alone, however, and intent on a quiet evening of marital intimacy, a glass of wine helped set the mood.

As he entered the compact yet cozy living room and handed Sara her wine, the familiar theme song from *St. Elsewhere* was introducing the evening's escape into exaggerated hospital chaos.

"Why, thank you, my dear," Sara said with a knowing smile.

She had apparently anticipated his motives, for she was already dressed in a peach-colored negligee modestly covered by a white terrycloth robe. And her message did not fall on blind eyes. Ever since William's birth, they had been trying unsuccessfully to give him a sibling. They were intent on succeeding, however, and the time was ripe.

"Did William succumb to your crooning? Um, this tastes good."

"So far, yes."

"Good. Come, sit by me."

Stephen cuddled up beside her and greeted her with a kiss.

"The new wallpaper in the bathroom looks fine, dear," Stephen said tactfully.

"Mrs. Heibert helped me. She measured and cut while I pasted. Wait until you see what she has in store for the kitchen: a light green and red motif with baskets and apples. She also has some creative ideas for this living room."

"Remember, please: two men also live in this house."

"Yes, don't worry. I promise we'll keep the feminine frills to a minimum."

Stephen couldn't put it off any longer. He had avoided it during their late dinner and then postponed it until after William was asleep.

"Sara, I need to talk with you about something Reverend Malone told me tonight." He pressed the mute button on the television remote.

"What is it, another complaint about doing too good of a job?"

"Hardly, but then again, his main reason for calling me in was to warn me to back off on how I preach the gospel. Seems I've been offending Mrs. Pearson and a few other large donors."

"So what are you going to do?"

Sara admired Stephen's preaching, but even she was still learning to appreciate his intensity.

"Actually, he's taken the matter into his own hands. He has recommended that I leave Sleepy Meadow and move on to my own pastorate—that I apply for the vacant pulpit at Red Creek Congregational Church."

"You mean he wants you…he wants *us* to leave?" Sara pulled away slightly. "We just got here. I'm just starting to feel at home in this broken-down shack of a manse. I'm making friends, I'm being accepted as more than a stranger in this congregation, and I'm even getting used to be referred to as 'the minister's wife.' He can't make us move now."

After a pensive sip of wine, Stephen answered carefully. "He's not making us move. Rather, he is encouraging me to consider this great opportunity. He believes that I am ready, and I think so, too."

"But Stephen, I just wallpapered the bathroom! William has lots of great playmates in the neighborhood, and we're within walking distance of everything we need. Why would we want to move?"

"Sara, way back when we were dating we talked about all this. I told you that a minister's family must remain unattached to any location, to any church, or to any people. Like the Apostles, we must always be willing and ready to follow the Lord whenever and wherever He calls."

"Oh, Stephen, get off your high horse. That all sounds fine on paper or when you're pontificating from your pulpit, but how can I stop from making friends or trying to make where we're living feel like a home? Are William or any future children never to have any lasting friendships?" With this, she pulled farther away.

This isn't going well, Stephen thought with panic.

It hadn't taken many weeks for this idealistic minister to discover that marriage brought a wider range of challenges than he had ever imagined. He had yearned for an intimate partner, a friend, a soulmate who, with a matching abandonment to God, would walk beside him open to any leading of the Spirit. But within weeks, he recognized with nervous apprehension that marriage was exactly what his counseling classes had taught him to teach others: "Marriage is two unrelated streams from sometimes drastically different sources coming together into one, with the convolution an often prolonged and dangerous series of rapids and waterfalls." Marriage was at best tough.

It wasn't so much that all of his priorities, habits, and interests were now under scrutiny; he had expected this. Rather, Sara began complaining whenever some aspect of the ministry took his attention away from the home, from William, and from her. He couldn't leave the house in the evening without some cutting comment, and invariably if he had to stay up late on a Saturday night finishing a sermon he received a cold shoulder when he came to bed. He sometimes felt unfairly trapped between two competing claimants on his loyalties: he had heard and responded to God's call, dedicating his life to serving Christ with his whole heart, yet Sara was demanding that his primary call was to her and his family. Progressively, every aspect of his life was evolving into a struggle between competing vows. He knew that other clergy were able to survive this and continue to minister successfully; he only prayed that he could.

"Sara, please. I wouldn't be considering this if I didn't think that this is what God is calling us to do."

"What God is calling *us* to do? How can you know? How can you be absolutely sure that this is what God wants for our family at this moment, at this time in our lives? Why couldn't this merely be Reverend Malone's will for getting you out of his hair?"

This wasn't the first time they had gone around and around about how to discern the will of God. Stephen, the good Calvinist, believed that nothing happened apart from God's plan. Not a sparrow falls without His knowing it—without, in fact, God, in His infinite wisdom, planning it, predestining it. Therefore, when things "happened," when opportunities arose, good or bad, Stephen always saw in them the providential hand of God.

Sara, on the other hand, was less theological and more earthy. Things happen, and people manipulate and connive for their own selfish purposes. In every decision, she looked for a self-centered lining. How God's plan fit into this she hadn't the foggiest. Instead, given her past, she fought for self-preservation, and now for the preservation of her family. She didn't distrust Stephen. She only wondered sometimes whether he was able to balance his priorities fairly.

Stephen stood up and began pacing. He knew of no easy way to win this argument. He spoke nervously. "How do I know for sure that God is calling us to move? On the one hand, I don't know. He doesn't drop these kinds of orders down from heaven in the form of stone tablets. But on the other hand, I am absolutely certain from experience that He does lead, that He does have a plan for our lives."

"Sara, please understand, I was not pursuing this move. It wasn't my idea. I was content to stay here as long as it seemed God wanted us here. But I knew for certain, down here," he struck his chest, "as Malone was speaking, that this was of God; that it was time for me to move on, to accept this opportunity as a gift from God. And I can think of no adequate reason to doubt this."

"But doesn't it matter what I feel in here?" Sara screamed, striking her chest in a mock gesture.

"Mommy," came a cry from upstairs. "Mommy."

"There, you woke the baby," Sara complained.

"I woke the baby?"

Sara marched upstairs without further comment, handing Stephen her glass half full.

He watched her disappear, leaving their decision in a lurch. He downed the remainder of both glasses and sat down, bewildered, in the threadbare recliner that had come with the manse.

"Dear Jesus, what am I going to do?"

Resigned to the dismantling of the evening's agenda, he unmuted the television. After a few minutes of *St. Elsewhere*, he discovered that he was witnessing the parallel dismantling of a medical intern's marriage because of the parallel demands of his "caring" profession.

Stephen switched the television off and threw the remote onto the couch. *It would be much easier if there was someone with authority over me, planning and guiding my career; someone at least with spiritual wisdom with whom I can share my concerns. But as it is, it's up to me to discern God's Call—and then convince Sara that it's the right move for our family as well as my career.*

"Why must it always be so complicated just to do my job?" he said softly. And he remembered Paul's words of warning: *I want you to be free from anxieties. The unmarried man is anxious about the affairs of the Lord, how to please the Lord; but the married man is anxious about worldly affairs, how to please his wife, and his interests are divided.*

"OK, Paul," Stephen said as he went to the kitchen for another glass of wine, "what's your advice for a married pastor?"

Part II

Green Pastures, Still Waters

1

A BRISK DECEMBER WIND swirled about the vacant streets, resurrecting wispy snow spirits that vanished mysteriously into the night. In thousands of cities around the world, Saturday midnight was the climax of every week with glaring lights and marquees, dancing and drinking, and lonely hearts anticipating at least temporary companionship. But in the tiny Vermont hamlet of Red Creek, all was dark, and most were snug in their beds.

All was dark, that is, except the magnesium street light guarding the town square, like an ancient town crier proclaiming "Midnight and all's well," and one other solitary light. It leaked from between the curtains of the pastor's office at Red Creek Congregational Church.

Earlier in the week, moving vans had arrived and unloaded, and Stephen, Sara, and two-year old William had arranged themselves and their few possessions into their new home. Now after three busy days of fending off charitable as well as inquisitive neighbors and scoping out the few convenient shopping spots, Sara and William were contentedly asleep. Stephen, however, was still awake, putting the final touches on his inaugural sermon, to be delivered first thing in the morning.

It wasn't some nuance of the text that was keeping Stephen up, though. On the contrary, he was eager to present himself and his family, his goals, dreams, and priorities to this his first solo congregation. Rather, it was the sweet and sour mixture of joy and terror that pressed in upon him as he considered the responsibilities he was about to shoulder.

Stephen listened anxiously as the phone rang on the other end of the line.

Three years ago, the elders of Second Congregational, Boston, had ordained him by the laying on of hands. He had accepted this as God's mandate to go forth and preach the word, without compromise, without error. He also knew that one day he would stand face-to-face with Jesus to answer for how he had led or misled His—*God's*—people.

Now, as a solo pastor, he would face a barrage of ministerial decisions, which he would make either alone or in agreement with a committee. In Congregationalism, every decision falls under the authoritative scrutiny of the local congregation, so Stephen's challenge would be to persuade the sometimes defiant flock to follow his lead while at the same time convincing them that every decision had been their own. Thus, Stephen would allow lay committees to decide the basic order of worship, the styles and amount of music, the Sunday school schedule, the distribution of the budget, the celebration of religious holidays, as well as mundane choices like the color of the sanctuary curtains. By watching Reverend Malone, Stephen had learned the necessity of dodging these potentially volatile issues.

The line rang again. *He's probably asleep. I should hang up,* Stephen thought. *But then again, he might be halfway to the phone.*

So he waited.

Some decisions, though, he dared not delegate, because how he handled these would be the measure of his pastorate. Congregationalism being what it was—the ultimate democratic society—one false word, action, or insinuation on Sunday could mean unemployment on Monday. When he faced these crucial administrative decisions, he planned to consult with other clergy as well as his growing library of books on pastoral ministry. He also planned to confer selectively with Sara, recognizing that the pressures and bias of her position as the pastor's wife might skew her objectivity.

But now as he prepared for his first morning in the pulpit, one unanticipated decision held him hostage. It was admittedly insignificant, even petty given his Congregationalist freedoms and the multitude of legitimate decisions that could quickly disengage his pastorate. Consequently, he had been too embarrassed to poll the local clergy, and especially Sara. Yet now he was unable to move forward.

"Hello?" a tired male voice answered at the other end.

"Jim. Hey, it's Stephen. Sorry to call you so late."

The mere sound of Jim Sarver's familiar voice brought Stephen welcome relief. After being separated for several years after college, he and Jim had found themselves together again at seminary—a seminary Stephen had chosen specifically because that was where his old friend was going. Jim had already married Cindi and was living in the married dorms, while Stephen lived with the single seminarians. Although Jim's responsibilities as a husband, student, breadwinner, and eventually father allowed him little time outside of class, their friendship remained strong. Jim had gained a reputation, unpopular in some camps, as a staunch defender of the literal interpretation of Scripture. It was this unwavering conviction that eventually led Jim to transfer his ordination from the Congregational Church to the more conservative Presbyterian Church of the East.

"Again so soon?" Jim said. "We go months without a peep and now twice in a week. Are you ready to tell your new flock 'what for'? Shape up or ship out?"

"Very funny. From what I gather, this church is already terribly wounded and divided from the last pastor's fanaticism. He had half of the church staying up nights awaiting the Rapture, while the other half schemed to tar-and-feather him for implying that they might be left behind."

"There's a bit of that here, too, though Presbyterians tend to be stuffed shirts when it comes to anything apocalyptic. If it ain't clearly stated in some part of the *Book of Confessions,* they won't buy it."

"*Book of Confessions*—you're lucky. All Red Creek Congregational has is a short creed they wrote themselves fifty years ago that essentially states that they will live by the Golden Rule. Everything else is up for grabs."

"Leaves you lots of leeway."

"Yeah, lots of room for confusion, compromise, and complaints."

"Now don't say I didn't warn you," Jim said. "Remember that this was the reason I switched over to Presbyterianism. Having a *Book of Confessions* and a *Book of Order* built on the collective wisdom of the church from its inception is a great check on craziness."

"Well, don't get a hernia patting yourself on the back. Where in those books of wisdom did your General Assembly find the authority to declare that a woman has a right to kill her unborn child?"

"I know, and there are many of us who are actively trying to reverse that decision. The pro-abortion platform only won by a small majority. But this is your nickel. What's up?"

"I'm up against the wire, and I need your advice. I'm stumped by a decision that on the surface sounds ridiculous, but the longer I wrestle with it, the more significant it grows. Are you ready?"

"Shoot."

"Should I or should I not wear a clerical shirt and collar?"

"Boy, that is a big one," Jim said laughing. "Wait until you have to choose between black, blue, gray, red, or lavender; short sleeve or long; full collar or tab!"

"I knew in you I'd find a sympathetic ear, but seriously, may I unload on you for a while?"

"Why not, everybody else does."

"As you know, in Congregationalism there are no guidelines or restrictions on clerical dress. Each pastor can decide for himself so, ultimately, this decision is completely up to me—it should be no big deal.

"But over the past three years, a thought has been eating away at me. You and I are on the same page when it comes to recognizing that we live in a relativistic culture. An increasing majority of people, even Christians, assume that truth is dependent solely upon individual preference, situation, or gut feeling."

"That's right," Jim said. "Look anywhere, listen everywhere, everyone has a different opinion on what is *true*—and don't you dare impose your view on anyone else."

"As evangelical Christians, we assume the basic gospel message that Jesus is the only true way to God. He cleared this up when He boldly proclaimed that 'no one comes to the Father except through me.' But Jim, doesn't it bother you that beyond this basic truth, everything else seems up for grabs?"

"What do you mean?"

"Choose any area, like what a person must do to be saved. At first, I found it comical, all the different and conflicting opinions between Christian traditions. While Catholics still believe that salvation must be earned through works, we Protestants teach salvation by faith alone. But what Lutherans understand this to mean is different from what Baptists, Episcopalians, Methodists, Pentecostals, you Presbyterians, and we Congregationalists believe. Taking this a step further, Southern Baptists don't agree with

American, Conservative, Free Will, or Primitive Baptists; United Presbyterians don't agree with Evangelical, Reformed, or Orthodox Presbyterians; and we Congregationalists have almost as many views as we have churches."

"That's what happens when you throw out the historic creeds and base *truth* on a congregational vote," Jim said.

"Excuse me, but wasn't your General Assembly's decision to become pro-choice a bit of democratic theology?"

Jim was silent long enough to strike Stephen as significant.

"Well?" Stephen said.

"OK, all the Christian denominations that I know of have some democracy in their theology," Jim finally conceded. "The leaders do the best they can to discern the truth of Scripture in relation to modern issues."

"So what happened? Did your Presbyterian leaders mishear God, misinterpret Scripture, or just fail to do their *best*?"

"Probably a little of all three."

"Then you and I agree that your denomination screwed up when it voted pro-choice?"

"Yes, of course."

"Jim, it sounds like you and I think that we are better interpreters of Scripture and more intimate *hearers* of God than the leaders of our denominations," Stephen offered.

"Well, I have noticed too often that those who don't fare well in the pulpit or parish end up in high levels of denominational leadership."

"But Jim, doesn't it bother you that what you and I believe and teach is radically different from that of so many good, faithful Christians of other traditions? Up until recently none of this bothered me—it never raised a red flag—until this stupid issue brought it all to the surface.

"Jim, I've read every reference in my library on clerical dress, and made a mental comparison of all the ministers I know, and all I come up with is confusion. When I was a kid, my Lutheran pastor always wore a white clerical tab in a black collar. Then that first Congregationalist minister you introduced me to years ago refused to wear a clerical collar. His congregation was hard-pressed to get him to put on a tie.

"Then at seminary, we rubbed elbows with students from over

forty different denominations, each of which had its own guidelines for clerical dress. At Second Congregational, Boston, the clerical staff wore those Puritanical collars, with two long white tabs representing the two testaments of the Bible falling down upon their black academic gowns. Later, at Sleepy Meadow, I followed Reverend Malone's lead. His clerical habit was a white shirt and colorful tie. During the week we wore suits, while in the pulpit we dressed in black academic gowns, accented with red stoles.

"And now I'm on my own," Stephen continued. "I'm head pastor with complete freedom on how to communicate my pastoral authority to the members of Red Creek Congregational and the community. Of the other clergy in town, some wear business suits, while others choir or academic gowns over a shirt and tie. Still others go the whole nine yards with clerical collars, robes, and seasonal stoles. On the other extreme, the Assembly of God minister wears a lavender leisure suit."

"So you've decided to follow his lead."

"*Her* lead, and so far it's the only model I've ruled out," Stephen answered. "The history here at Red Creek Congregational has been sporadic, different with each minister, almost as if each purposely chose to break any previous pattern. Tell me, what do you and the staff do at First Presbyterian?"

"We wear clerical collars, robes, and seasonal stoles; the whole nine-yards."

"Why?" Stephen challenged.

"For me, the question was 'Why not?' The long-standing practice of the pastors here has been to wear full clericals on Sundays and suits the rest of the week. Sure, some argue that clericals inappropriately elevate clergy above the laity, but others counter that clericals add dignity and help establish authority. Honestly, Stephen, since I had no reason to buck the tradition, I just went with the flow. If the ministers here had always preached in golf shirts, I probably would have done the same."

"Well, I see pluses and minuses in both wearing and avoiding clericals," Stephen said.

"So wha'cha gonna do?"

"Jim, I can't shake this off, because it all points to a much bigger issue. Isn't it wrong that, like the relativism in our modern culture, everything in the pastoral ministry is up to personal preference—as if Jesus gave no instructions for how His followers were to establish, practice, and preserve the ministerial office? Every clergyman I know has a different and often conflicting opinion about everything. Is everything that we do and teach—from insignificant things like this to eternally important things like who Jesus was— merely up to individual opinion? Is it truly insignificant whether I wear a collar, or whether my congregation celebrates the Lord's Supper, or whether these members were even baptized, or whether they are Trinitarian, or whether mothers carry their children to term or abort them for whatever reason? How can I be sure that what I am teaching and preaching and doing is true?"

That growing, subliminal voice had finally blurted out what actually was keeping Stephen up nights. In the morning, he will step into the pulpit of Red Creek Congregational as the resident authority on what was true. But to what extent does he have the authority to declare that what he preaches, in contrast to the other ministers in town, is true?

"Stephen, you're blowing this all out of proportion. Remember that quote from Augustine we learned back in seminary: 'In essentials, unity; in nonessentials, diversity; in all things, charity'? Clerical dress falls under nonessentials, so there can be great diversity. The Trinity and divinity of Christ are essentials, and the diversity we find in these issues is the result of doubt, ignorance, rebellion, or just plain pride. The main problem is the lack of charity. Come on, my friend, lighten up. You have arrived! Enjoy the fact that you are about to pastor your own church."

"Jim, you're right," Stephen said, looking at his name emblazoned across a sheet of the church's new letterhead. "These people probably won't even give a rip what I'm wearing as long as my sermon doesn't infringe on their plans for the afternoon."

"That's right. So tell me, what are you going to wear?"

The wooden schoolroom clock on the wall opposite Stephen's desk struck 1 a.m. He needed to get beyond this issue and go home.

"I guess I'll wear what I wore at Sleepy Meadow. I'll wear a black robe and my Celtic preaching cross and avoid the clerical collar, since it's a holdover from Roman Catholicism anyway."

"Sounds OK by me, but don't get too hung up about Roman Catholic holdovers. If you do, you'll have to avoid almost everything we believe and practice. Let's face it, Stephen, our understanding of the Trinity as one God in three persons—which you and I both fight to defend in our New England Unitarian culture—is only indirectly based on Scripture. It came from the decision of a handful of Catholic bishops back in the fourth century."

Stephen knew this from seminary, but he hadn't thought of it in relation to his present mental gymnastics—and he didn't want to go there. *Hadn't Jim just referred to the doctrine of the Trinity as one of those essentials which demand unity?*

"Jim, thanks for hearing me out. And sorry to keep you up. Are you ready for tomorrow?"

"I suppose. I'll be preaching on Jesus' miraculous feeding of the five thousand to a room full of skeptics who believe that this was a miracle of 'sharing.'"

After warm farewells, Stephen hung up. He turned his attention to a clothes rack across the room. Tomorrow morning he will don the robe, but leave the black clerical shirt behind. As he stared, the shirt taunted him for his indecisiveness, in this issue as well as the myriad others that he had always taken for granted.

2

BEFORE THE LAST VERSE of "God Be With Us Till We Meet Again," Walter slipped from the oak pew without a word to Helen or Stacy. He exited the sanctuary through the rear entrance, and descended the wooden steps three at a time. Most of the congregation would leave through the side door directly into Singleton Hall, which connected the 200-year-old church to the 20-year-old office annex. Walter was trying, however, to beat the rush to the front of the greeting line, because he was ecstatic over who was now their new pastor.

He cut sharply around the southeast corner, his unbuttoned overcoat billowing behind him. Cautious to avoid any ice patches, he careened by an overgrown juniper bush, and then hurdled skillfully several unanticipated canine deposits.

Over the past few weeks, he had heard the new pastor's name mentioned as rumors leaked from the search committee, but it hadn't clicked. Then when Reverend LaPointe stood in the pulpit, in his black robe and silver cross suspended on a chain around his neck, Walter was elated. Here was the very pastor who had taken the risk of talking to him "while he was yet a sinner."

Just like Jesus! Walter thought with excitement. *The pastor who was there for Helen when I wasn't; who comforted her after she delivered my sweet pea.*

He had always intended to thank him, because it was LaPointe's encouragement that had convinced him to go with Raeph that night to hear the evangelist. But he always put it off and then forgot.

But now LaPointe was here, his new pastor. Walter was ecstatic. They had feared that the loss of Pastor Smith would be the downfall of this congregation, but now there was hope.

He turned right around the southwest corner at full throttle and attempted another right turn up the steps into Singleton Hall. On a blind patch of ice, however, his feet slipped, sending him at full speed into a snow-covered hydrangea. Extracting himself quickly, he then had to locate his thick glasses, which he had lost in flight. Groping, he found them in a drift and placed them back on his nose.

Resuming his quest, he rushed into the hall only to find, through lenses blocked by residual snow and condensation, the line already two dozen deep. His strategy had failed, but at least he was ahead of the remaining 130.

He entered the line in front of Mrs. Willamette Guilford, smiling, but her glare said that she wasn't amused.

"Walter, where'd you go?" Helen asked as she and Stacy came forward to join him. "And why are you covered with snow?"

"Don't ask," he said, brushing his coat. "I tried to beat the rush, but obviously a few others had the same idea. Can you believe who this is?"

"Not in our new hall, Mr. Horscht," scolded Mrs. Guilford.

"Yes, sorry," he said walking back outside. Once clean, he returned into line next to Helen, under Mrs. Guilford's glare.

"You know," Helen whispered, "I wondered the first time I heard his name, but didn't get my hopes up. He was so kind to us."

"Stacy, please stay in line," Walter snapped.

Everyone said that two-year-old Stacy was the spitting image of Shirley Temple—the same curly blond hair, dimples, cheerful smile, and, sometimes to Walter's dismay, the same energy. Since Stacy begun walking, he and Helen rarely had a moment's rest. At present, the start and stop of the reception line was a challenge for Stacy and her vigilant parents.

Hearty laughter rose from the front of the line. Apparently someone had shared a private joke with Reverend LaPointe and his family.

Charles Singleton! I should have known, Walter complained silently. *Trying to win favor before the rest of us even get to greet him.*

Walter presumed that it had been Singleton and his clique of liberal, social gospelites that had orchestrated Pastor Smith's departure.

They never miss an opportunity to belittle conservative Christians as old-fashioned, out-of-touch fundies, and especially to ridicule any talk of the coming Rapture—almost as if they were organized to do so.

Walter saw them as seeds of Satan planted in their midst, tares among the wheat sent to strangle and starve the faithful. He noted Reverend LaPointe's welcoming smile, but assumed it was merely conventional courtesy and not a signal between scheming compatriots.

The line moved forward another step. Irene and Elsie Drewer were now greeting the LaPointes. As usual, Elsie hung back in embarrassment. The prayer group had once prayed over Elsie, demanding, "in the name of Jesus," that whatever demon was behind her uncontrollable stuttering to "come out and leave her!" But nothing happened. In the end they all felt sheepish, as much for themselves as for Elsie.

"Fine sermon, Pastor LaPointe," said a man Walter only vaguely knew. "Great to have you on board."

"Thank you," LaPointe answered, "We're glad to be here."

The woman beside LaPointe, who Walter presumed was Mrs. LaPointe, smiled her response. Between them was a blond-haired boy about Stacy's age, whom the Mrs. constantly needed to corral. The facial resemblance to his father was striking.

"Now you're not going to ram that Rapture malarkey down our throats like our last pastor, are you?" the next man asked LaPointe.

I can't believe ol' Wimple actually asked this, Walter laughed to himself, *but I guess it shouldn't surprise me. He's one of Singleton's cronies.*

"Well, sir," LaPointe answered, shaking Mr. Wimple's hand, "I don't intend to cram anything down anyone's throat, except maybe the gospel." Those within hearing laughed, breaking the awkwardness of the moment, leaving Mr. Wimple to exit with a "Humph!"

Several more greeters exchanged pleasantries, until it was time for the local dairy farmers, Fred and Beatrice Spivens, to move forward.

Now how'd they get up there? Walter complained with a smile.

"Welcome to Red Creek, Pastor LaPointe," Fred said.

"Thank you."

"That thar's an in'tresting cross your wearing."

"My mother gave it to me."

"It's nice, but ol' Pastor Smith wore a collar. Are you ordained?"

"Oh hush, Fred," his wife scolded. "Don't mind him, he's just a tease. Welcome to our church."

"Thank you, ma'am."

Fred and Beatrice left smiling.

Several more greeters passed through, until Walter and Helen were only one away. But this was Sue Humphries, the Sunday school superintendent, whom Walter feared might take as long as the previous two dozen.

"Oh, Reverend LaPointe, it is so good to have you here, praise God. And Mrs. LaPointe, what a blessing to..."

Walter tuned out but watched closely. LaPointe and his wife were smiling, nodding their heads, listening. Then LaPointe gave a furtive glance toward his wife that in Walter's mind communicated, "How are we going to get by this one?" When Sue reached over to greet Mrs. LaPointe, Walter moved in.

"Hello, Reverend LaPointe. Remember me?" Walter said, extending his hand.

"I don't seem to recall..." LaPointe responded with a look of puzzlement.

"Well, what about my wife, Helen?"

With this, LaPointe's face lit up with recognition.

"Why yes, of course, now I remember. Helen and Walter Horse..."

"Horscht."

"Yes, and this must be little Stacy," Stephen said, bending down to shake her hand. "Let me introduce you to my son, William. He's your age. And this is my wife, Sara," he said, straightening back up to adult level.

They greeted each other and as Helen and Stacy passed on to Sara and William, Walter held back.

"Walter, I'm sorry I didn't recognize you," Stephen said. "You're dressed differently than..."

"I know, that's to be expected. My conversion on the night of Stacy's birth made some radical changes in my life. I've wanted to thank you for talking to me in the hospital, encouraging me when I was hard set against anything to do with Jesus.

"I guess that 'Jesus stuff' finally broke through?"

"It made a different man of me." Feeling the impatient glare of Willamette Guilford, he cut to the chase. "Tell me, Pastor LaPointe, are you planning to continue the Sunday evening Bible studies?"

"As soon as possible. How about next week?"

"Great. Thank you," Walter said, shaking LaPointe's hand furiously.

"You're welcome, Walter, and I presume you'll be a regular?"

"Wouldn't miss it."

"Good, see you then," LaPointe said, tactfully moving Walter forward.

"Helen, please let's get together," Walter heard Sara LaPointe say as they pulled away from the line. "I'm sure the kids will enjoy each other."

"I'll call you tomorrow," Helen answered.

"Please do."

Walter led his family through Singleton Hall downstairs for coffee, juice, and doughnuts. He couldn't hide his broad smile. *Thank You, Jesus,* he prayed inwardly. *I was afraid You had abandoned us, but surely You have sent us this man. May he lead fearlessly in the footsteps of Your servant, Pastor Smith. I pray he is just as informed about the coming events, and courageous enough to speak out.*

Seeing his closest friends already marshalling the doughnut table, he yelled, "Raeph, Ben, you won't believe who this pastor is."

3

"Goodbye, sara. Please, let's keep in touch," Tess Darby said as the two hugged and then parted in front of Campion Student Union.

This had been exactly what Sara needed. Wiping the tears from her eyes, she began strolling for one final look around campus before starting home.

The first few weeks at Red Creek had taken their toll. Stephen's workload was greater than that of his assistantship at Sleepy Meadow, and the number of people who stopped by day and night to welcome them and share their views on what he ought to be doing was distressing. She was appalled by their self-righteous meddling. Daily, her doubts about whether she had the mettle to be a pastor's wife increased, regardless of Stephen's constant encouragement. Combined with William displaying all the lingering symptoms of the terrible twos, Sara began to panic.

While still at Sleepy Meadow, a flier had arrived announcing a series of sesquicentennial lectures at her alma mater. Her favorite professor, now semi-retired, was to speak during Christmas break on "The Private Lives of the Founders of the Republic." She instantly wanted to go, but given the craziness of everything, she hesitated to ask. After picking the flier up and putting it down over a dozen times, however, she finally got the nerve.

"Of course, Sara. It will be a great escape for you," he had said. He even arranged for his mother to come from Hartford to watch William for the weekend, which more than sealed her decision to get away.

The long drive alone across New England from Vermont to South Boston in the whiteness of January was panacea enough. She stayed at a hotel within walking distance of campus and spent hours exploring her old haunts. The lectures were invigorating and reawakened her desire to continue her graduate studies, but given life as it was, she knew this was impossible.

As she paced slowly across the quad, surrounded by the century-old brownstone buildings that represented a mostly wonderful period of her life, she was disturbed by her divided heart. Certainly, she would return home to her husband and two-year-old son, both of whom she loved dearly. But a lingering, tempting, uncomfortable voice taunted her about how much she had given up when she consented to become a minister's wife.

And it hadn't helped that *he* had been here.

She hadn't even considered this possibility. Why should she? His interests had been science, not history. Yet there he was, yesterday afternoon, in the last lecture of the day, sitting several rows ahead.

AT FIRST, from the back, she wasn't certain that it was he. But then he began peering around, searching, and their eyes met. He smiled, but she turned her attention back to her old professor who was discussing the rivalry between Hamilton and Burr.

She could not ignore, though, how good he looked. The same warm, friendly eyes and beckoning smile. Six years had brought some recession to his hairline, but this only added a welcome sign of maturity. She fought to keep her eyes forward, especially whenever she noticed through her peripheral vision that he was staring back at her. At the close of the lecture she hurried from her seat, to escape through the farthest door, but he found her.

"Sara, please," he called above a crowd of students anxious to begin their Saturday night revelry.

She stopped just short of leaving the building, fighting against her conscience warning her to run. She felt his hand touch her arm and then, turning, she found herself facing the man she had once called husband.

"Hello, Frank."

"Sara, you look great. How are you?"

He spoke as if he was oblivious that this was the first time they had seen each other since he had abandoned her, since he had walked out that summer after her *procedure*. Lawyers eventually had finalized the divorce in their absence.

The longer Sara looked at his insensitive smile, the more she wanted to hit him. Instead, she broke from his grip and made for the door.

"Sara, please. I'm sorry, terribly sorry."

She again stopped. He gently turned her around and, crouching to look up into her down turned eyes, he repeated, "Sara, I am truly sorry."

"But you left, without a word, without a note. You just took your stuff, and then the only thing I ever saw of you again was your signature on a divorce petition."

"Sara, can we talk?" Frank said pointing toward a room off the main hallway, full of vending machines, snack tables, and chairs. "How about a coffee? It will give me time to list all the reasons I was a self-centered jackass."

His smile was contagious, and against every inclination, her frown relaxed as she walked with him into the same room where other young men had once wooed her. He bought coffees and brought them to her at a table by the window.

"Actually, Sara, I probably don't need to go through all the details. I was terribly wrong, from beginning to end. My whole reason for our marriage in the first place was dishonest. I wasn't ready to settle down, but didn't know what else to do when I got you pregnant. The underlying problem was that, though at first you were just another object of my immoral lust, I began to love you. I married you because I didn't want to hurt you. When the pregnancy was no longer an issue, I panicked, because by then I truly loved you. But I wasn't ready. I had learned from our living together how terrified I was about failing as a husband, a responsible provider, and a father. So I bolted."

Sara listened, noncommittal, safely behind her Styrofoam cup.

"I'm ashamed of what I did, but it's good to get it out. I drove nonstop to California. I bummed around for a while and stayed mostly lost in drugs and booze. When the lawyers tracked me down, I was stone drunk in my apartment. I signed the papers as if I were giving a student a hall pass. I was cold and heartless, and terribly lonely."

He sipped his coffee, waiting for some response. Getting none, he stood to pace.

"After several months of this, I came back to earth—actually, I came up from the gutter. I got sober, started teaching in a public high school in Santa Monica, and even began attending church again. But this time not a Catholic church. A large independent church. My life changed. I got religion, as some might say."

Sara was speechless. She had wished a different future on Frank.

"In 1986, I came back looking for you. I wasn't sure why, except to at least apologize and help you in whatever way I could. That's when I discovered that you had remarried, to a minister of all things, serving some church in Vermont. God certainly has a strange sense of humor," he said with a sad smile. "Sara, I only want you to know how sorry I am, and hope you can forgive me."

Awkwardly, Sara reached across and touched his hand. "But why are you here this weekend?"

"When I came back I rediscovered how much I missed New England, so after completing my term, I took a teaching position up in Essex. Now I live in a small cottage overlooking a beach near Rockport. When I saw the flier on this series of talks, I had a hunch you might be here. So assuming the worst that might happen was sitting through a few boring lectures, I took a chance. It is good to see you."

"You, too, Frank," Sara said. "Our mistakes were mine, also. Maybe they helped force us to grow up."

"They certainly led to my own conversion of heart. Please, tell me about yourself. What's it like being a pastor's wife?"

"Ain't that a hoot. The last thing anyone could have imagined," she said, "but I'm basically happy. Stephen has just started his first solo pastorate at a country church in mid-state Vermont. We have a two-year-old son named William."

"So thankfully," Frank said awkwardly, "there were no lingering complications?"

"No, thankfully," she lied a little. "The pressures of the new church were getting my goat, so I decided to take a break for my first revisit to Campion."

"Has it been a good visit?"

"Yes and no," she said, looking toward the door.

Frank saw this as a hint, but wasn't ready for their reunion to end.

"Sara, how about for old time's sake joining me for dinner? No complications or expectations. It would just be good to keep talking."

Voices from every direction bombarded her brain and tore at her heart. She looked across at this man she had once loved, whom she truly had tried to envision as a lifetime partner. He was just as handsome as the first time she had met him, even more so, for his conversion had somehow softened his features. She wanted to lean forward and kiss the lips that once had captured her heart, but the instant she sensed this urge, she knew what she must say.

"No, Frank, but thank you." She rose to go, extending her hand. "I'm glad we ran into each other—thank you for taking the chance, but we've both moved on, and cannot go back. In my position, I feel guilty even talking with you."

"Seriously, Sarie, just dinner, that's all."

His use of her pet name almost won the day.

"No, I can't."

SHE HAD KISSED HIM ON THE CHEEK, and then, trying to appear calm and collected, had exited into the night. Thankfully, she had run into Tess Darby, once her closest classmate, who distracted her thoughts for the rest of the weekend.

Now she stood at the far end of the quad. Turning a full circle she surveyed the panorama of her past, matching the nostalgia with the teeming uncertainties of the present.

Did I make the right choices? she pondered sadly as she made her way toward her hotel.

But she halted in front of the one campus building she had never entered, St. Edmund Campion Chapel. As a student, she had walked this path hundreds of times without the slightest notice. After her divorce, she had even less interest in Catholics and their religious hypocrisy, let alone in entering this Roman sanctuary. Yet, she was a different person now, a person of faith, and the sight of this monument to Catholic spirituality piqued her interest. It was somehow beckoning her, and she decided to stop.

Excited but nervous, she found the large wooden doors unlocked. Cautiously she pulled one open, hoping she was not interrupting some Catholic gathering, but the sanctuary appeared empty.

She advanced slowly inside, and was taken aback by the beauty of the light pouring in through the large stained-glass windows. She was unable, however, to proceed any further than the back pew.

Sitting motionless, she moved only her eyes as she studied everything around her—the rough-cut granite walls and columns, the arched windows, the life-sized statues, the rows of flickering candles, the ornate wooden front altar, and the intricately carved crucifix peering down from the front wall. She stared with amazement, surprised that what she always assumed would be offensive and gaudy was instead beautiful and comforting.

But this was the first time she had been in a church with a statue. Many of the Congregational churches she attended refused to display even a cross. Now as she studied the face of a statue that she guessed was Mary, she strangely perceived that it—that *she*—was smiling at her. Mary's stone arms were extended before her with rays of stone light pouring forth, symbolizing, she supposed, Mary's love flowing onto Catholics.

Uncomfortable, she pivoted to examine the other side of the sanctuary, and her foot hit against something. A padded kneeler. She had never been in a church with kneelers—she had never knelt in a church before—and though she had read about Catholics kneeling in idolatrous worship before statues just like those now staring down upon her, she nonetheless was drawn to kneel in prayer.

Reaching down, she carefully lowered the kneeler to prevent it from banging on the marble floor. She dropped her knees to the pads, folded her hands on the back of the pew before her, closed her eyes, and became lost in tears.

Words of sorrow poured forth, leaving behind a contrite space in her heart. A dozen times she declared, "I'm sorry," begging God to forgive her and to help her forgive herself. For ten minutes, she knelt and prayed, listening yet wondering whether she should expect anything in return. Under Stephen's tutelage she had grown to believe in prayer, but intellectual pride usually squelched her hope.

Opening her eyes, she quietly sat back on the pew. She gazed cynically around at the Catholic art that was so foreign to her New England Protestant tastes: a statue of a monk in a robe holding a skull, a picture of Jesus with red and white rays exuding from his heart, and a statue of a small blond-haired child clothed in flowing royal robes, holding a golden orb. Repulsed, she wanted to run.

Suddenly the sound of someone walking in the front of the chapel startled her. A hunched, dark-robed woman was crossing before the altar, carrying a long, brass candle snuffer. She bowed slightly as she passed the crucifix, and then proceeded to light some candles.

Sara bolted from her pew, tripping over and banging the kneeler. Without looking back, she charged into the large wooden door, propelling it against the outside wall, and dashed away from the church, down the walk toward her hotel.

Desire driven by guilt overcame her. She ran to get home to Stephen, to William, to their new home and church family, even to the congregation's demanding and demeaning expectations of her as a pastor's wife; to get away from this past she should never have opened, and especially away from the man who was now only hours away in Rockport.

*   *   *

STEPHEN FELT A MITE CLAMMY as he sat in the church basement. He considered mentioning this to Ben Ware, sitting across the table, but changed his mind. He knew that the church plumbing wasn't the cause of his present discomfort, and besides, diverting the subject that tangentially would be too obvious.

Next to preaching, there was nothing Stephen enjoyed more

than teaching the Bible—nothing, of course, except intimacy with Sara. Stephen believed that examining and exegeting, comparing and contrasting biblical texts was the closest that modern man could get to hearing the voice of God. He would always remember that exhilarating moment in seminary when Dr. Nicholas, his favorite theology professor, drew their attention to the eternal significance of that text in Paul's second letter to Timothy: "All scripture is inspired by God and profitable for teaching, for reproof, for correction, and for training in righteousness, that the man of God may be complete, equipped for every good work."

"And since the most accurate translation of the Greek word for *profitable* is *sufficient,*" Dr. Nicholas had argued, "all Scripture is inspired and *sufficient,* and thus the bedrock for *sola scriptura*. The entire Reformation initiated by Martin Luther and then fine-tuned by the lawyer-scholar John Calvin and the other Reformers turns on this important assumption."

Ever since his first year in seminary, Stephen had been teaching Bible studies at some church or youth group, but he had been anticipating this first study in his own church with nearly uncontrollable excitement. He had planned to start immediately on his second Sunday in town, but everything had escalated so quickly— which was precisely why Sara had gone away for the weekend.

I hope the break has been good for her. She should be getting home about now, he thought, glancing surreptitiously over the heads of his companions to the clock across the room.

At 7:15, he had arrived to arrange the tables in a formation that would most effectively promote free sharing. In time an inquisitive nine had straggled in: Fred and Beatrice Spivens; Irene and Elsie Drewer; Robert Gorman, the chairman of the church board; Wanda Fritz, the director of Christian education; Raeph Timmons; Ben Ware; and, Stephen's greatest on-site promoter, Walter Horscht.

As was his custom, Stephen had opened the study with prayer, and then made the mistake of asking where Reverend Smith had left off. Apparently Smith had been leading them through a three-month examination of the End Times and the coming Rapture—one of Stephen's least favorite subjects. Of all the things the seminarians argued over, this had been the most volatile and least reconcilable.

After a half hour discussion, Stephen concluded that Smith had taught them that the Rapture was imminent. And by this group's enthusiasm, it was obvious that most of them heartily accepted every word of Smith's panic-ridden scenario. Robert Gorman and Wanda Fritz, the only apparent dissenting voices, were disturbingly reticent. This, therefore, put Stephen and the former minister on opposing sides. Certainly Stephen believed in the Second Coming of Christ. At least once every year he preached a sermon guaranteeing that Jesus was coming again in our lifetime—if not in the clouds as predicted, at least for each person at the moment of death. But the publication of a raft of sensationalist books warning of the Rapture's imminence kept the topic ripe in too many minds.

It again had been Dr. Nicholas who had convinced him that the Rapture was at best a modern heresy of major proportions. He had documented clearly that no Christian theologian of any repute had taught this idea before it was proposed by a controversial English preacher named Darby in the nineteenth-century. Then, after this idea was heralded as uncontravertable truth in the footnotes of the Scofield Study Bible, fundamentalists everywhere began accepting it as gospel.

But Dr. Nicholas had proven to Stephen's satisfaction that the Bible nowhere teaches a rapture of the Church in which God would rescue the faithful from the coming tribulation long before Christ's Second Coming. Nicholas' simple proof consisted of demonstrating that in every instance, any scriptural reference to a rapture of believers coincided with Christ's Second Coming. Christians will have to suffer through any coming tribulation just like everyone else. All the present books built around the assumption of a coming Rapture, no matter how enthusiastically convincing, were, therefore, spurious and led believers into groundless presumption.

Stephen recognized that many of the people to whom he was now to minister had ignorantly accepted this theory, hook, line, and lobster cage. But he no more wanted to discuss the End Times than he wanted to put his tongue to a frozen swing set.

Tonight, however, he had been blindsided, and now they were waiting for *his* interpretation of Matthew 24.

He looked with glazed eyes at the passage and once again considered inviting Ben to take a look at the sump pump. *Should I beat around the bush to avoid alienating the regulars in my first month here? Thanks a lot, Jesus!*

"First," he began, "it is important to recognize that there are many conflicting opinions about the meaning and application of this passage..."

As he said this, that nagging thought hounded him. *Why are there so many conflicting opinions on this? I thought Jesus promised that the Holy Spirit would lead us into all truth? What's wrong with this picture?*

"...and I don't just mean opinions held by misinformed troublemakers, but legitimate, faithful, Bible-believing scholars and pastors. This is one of those sticky-wickets where faithful people can agree to disagree. There is one verse in this chapter, however, that all agree is of supreme importance: 'But of that day and hour no one knows, not even the angels of heaven, nor the Son, but the Father only.' Jesus warns that we are to 'Watch therefore, for you do not know on what day your Lord is coming.'"

"But Reverend LaPointe," Raeph asked respectfully, "didn't Jesus castigate the Pharisees for ignoring the signs of the times?"

Walter chimed in, remembering Reverend Smith's argument, "And given what Jesus and the apostle Paul said about the signs—wars, rumors of wars, famines, earthquakes, rampant immorality, false prophets, etc., etc.—wouldn't you agree that this points to today?"

"Yes, all these signs are more than evident today," Stephen said, "but they have been evident to some extent in every age. During the Dark Ages, especially during the infestation of the plague, many predicted the imminent coming of Christ, but they were wrong. I believe that these signs have been repeated throughout the ages because in every age Christians are called to be ready to meet their Savior."

That phrase "I believe" echoed in his subconscious: *So what if this is what you believe. Why is your opinion more accurate than Reverend Smith's or the authors of those best-selling books? When did you ever write a book?*

"But what did Jesus mean about two men out plowing in a field," Raeph asked, "one being taken, the other left? Or two women grinding, one taken, the other left?"

Stephen waited to see whether anyone else would venture an explanation, but all were looking to him. Even the two whom Stephen presumed might be on his side were waiting for his "authoritative" explanation.

"This is referring to the Second Coming of Christ," Stephen

said. "Some will rise to spend eternity with God; others will spend eternity in Hell apart from Him."

THIS MADE WALTER UNCOMFORTABLE—not the point about Heaven or Hell, but LaPointe's apparent disbelief in the Rapture. Here was his champion, the one he had hoped would carry on the campaign started by Pastor Smith; the one he had bragged up to all of his friends. *But what had I based this hope on?* Walter wondered. *A bold visit in the hospital or some kind words said to Helen when I wasn't there?* This thought ate away at him, for he had often suspected that others were trying to steal Helen's affection.

"But, Reverend LaPointe," Walter demanded, "what do you say to this?" He searched through his Bible for those verses Reverend Smith had shown them. "Here in Paul's first letter to Timothy: 'Now the Spirit speaketh expressly that in the latter times some shall depart from the faith, giving heed to seducing spirits, and doctrines of devils; speaking lies in hypocrisy; having their conscience seared with a hot iron; forbidding to marry, and commanding to abstain from meats, which God hath created to be received with thanksgiving of them which believe and know the truth.' To whom does this refer?"

"WELL, WALTER," Stephen answered, "when Paul wrote this he was referring to heretical pagan and Jewish sects that had infiltrated the growing Christian communities, polluting the gospel with falsehood."

"But today?"

"We probably can't identify this with any one specific group. Throughout history there have always been false teachers spreading false teachings among the faithful."

How can you be sure that what you are teaching is true? Stephen asked himself.

"But wouldn't you say that this most clearly describes the Catholic..." Walter started to answer.

"Rev...rev...rever...end La...La...Pointe?"

Only the hum of the sump pump broke the silence as everyone glared with surprise at Elsie. No one could remember ever hearing her ask a question.

"Yes, Elsie."

"Ver...verse thir-teen," she asked with determination. "Wuw...what does it mum...mean?"

Her beckoning look said more than her simple request. It cut through all of their subsequent jostling of opinions.

"Well, yes, Elsie. Let's see what that verse says." Stephen turned his attention back to Matthew 24:13 and began reading to the group: "'But he who endures to the end will be saved.'"

Stephen had read through this portion of Scripture many times, always focusing on what Jesus was saying about His Second Coming, but he had missed the significance of this short verse.

He who endures to the end will be saved, he read again silently.

OK, Stephen, the voice taunted, *how you gonna jive this with your belief in once saved, always saved?*

Every answer his mind posed had a counter. The inner voice rang with the same demeaning, cynical tones that Reverend Malone had used to ridicule his belief in eternal security.

"Elsie, Jesus is reminding us that there will always be attacks on our faith," Stephen said. "He said that if the world hated Him, it would also hate us; but also remember that He promised that He would never leave us or forsake us, or as it states in Romans chapter eight, 'We know that in everything God works for good with those who love him, who are called according to his purpose.' Elsie, there is nothing to worry about, no matter how scary the times get, because if by His grace we are in Christ, then by His grace we will endure to the end."

She smiled, nodding her head several times in appreciation. She then sat back, looking meekly around.

Stephen glanced at his watch. "Looks like we've used up our allotted time," Stephen said. "I've certainly appreciated our discussion, but we haven't had a chance to talk about what book we will study. I was hoping we might consider shifting to Paul's letter to the Romans..."

*　　　*　　　*

"WALTER!"

"Yeah."

Raeph was hurrying to catch Walter, who had barged from the basement as soon as the session had ended. Walter was unlocking his Caprice wagon.

"What'd you think?"

"I don't know, Raeph. He likes to skirt the issues."

"Well, it was his first time, new church, new people. I think he sounds balanced."

"Yeah, I'm sure he's fine. Listen, I need to get home. I'll call you later in the week."

Walter started the engine and pulled his door closed. Raeph stepped back and watched his friend's car spray stones as it left the parking lot.

STRAIGHTENING THE CAR after a hurried turn, Walter brought his mind back to the thought that had driven him from the church basement: *What if Reverend LaPointe isn't what I thought him to be?*

4

Seven months later...

THE PASSING OF TIME is a mystery we all share. Pulling into the driveway late again for dinner, Stephen felt that it had been eons since they had moved to Red Creek. Yet, at the same time, it seemed like only yesterday they had crammed their bags into his Fairmont sedan to follow the moving van here. Actually, it had been only eight months and torrents of pastoral, marital, and parental responsibilities—successes and failures—had passed over the ministerial dam.

Turning off the ignition, and grabbing his briefcase bulging with sermon materials, he knew he once again had failed.

The postage-stamp lawn in front of the manse was identical in size and sparse layout to the homes on either side, except that his was two weeks beyond needing a trim. William was a hyper-energetic two-and-a-half year old, far too young for the task, so Stephen had no one to blame but himself.

Passing the front picture window, he noticed the oily haze as the orange reflection of the setting sun reprimanded him for ignoring Sara's constant plea to clean the windows. On the front stoop, he paused: *Am I ready for this?*

One week ago this very night, they had celebrated the joyous discovery that Sara was three months pregnant. Since William's birth, she had suffered two miscarriages, so this news was fraught with prayerful caution. For Stephen this was a sign that all was well—the previous pregnancies being outside of God's perfect timing. For Sara, well, Stephen couldn't tell. She appeared joyful, but there was a fleeting sadness. Or was it fear? Stephen couldn't tell. What she needed was more help around the house, and some relief from their ever demanding "Steamboat Willie." But his schedule of appointments, committee meetings, and counseling sessions, teamed with his need for more time to plan, prepare, and pray, and frustrated by unpredictable interruptions like funerals and congregational crises—all of this and more prevented him from giving this relief.

He checked the mailbox and pulled out a fistfull of bills. New England Light, Bernie's Trash Removal, Bowerston Loan—*Never enough money,* he complained—bill after bill, until he came across a personal letter to Sara. From someone unnamed in Rockport.

Must be an old classmate she met at the conference.

He bundled the letters back up, and as he grasped the handle of the aluminum screen door, it came off in his hand. He prayed: *Lord Jesus, please, have mercy on us this evening!*

"Honey, I'm home. Sorry I'm late again."

"Can you play with William for a minute?" she called from the kitchen. "I'll get dinner back out on the table."

Her tone sounded surprisingly calm.

"Daddy!" William said as he ran out from under his mother's skirt.

"Hello, William," he said, kneeling to return his hug. *Why does this feel like I'm coming back from a long trip?*

The two of them turned their attention to whatever imaginary war William had been fighting with a menagerie of plastic soldiers, cowboys, Indians, dinosaurs, kid's-meal critters, cartoon characters, and stuffed animals strewn around the living room.

"Dinner's ready," Sara called.

"Come on, William, time to eat," Stephen said.

"No, we just started."

"Maybe we can play after dinner," he said, knowing this was a ruse.

"Hello, dear," he said, kissing Sara and helping William into his high chair.

"Have a good day?" she asked. The genuineness of her smile was indecipherable.

"Oh, the usual. How about yours?"

"Well, let's pray first."

They bowed their heads, while William reached for the fried chicken.

"Now please, William, we have to pray first. Fold your hands..." Stephen repeated the daily routine, assuming that one day William would get with the program.

After saying the prayer, filling his plate, and taking a few bites, Stephen asked, "So now, tell me, how was your day?"

"Not bad, actually. The morning was the usual battle. William demanded constant attention, while I tried to catch up on laundry and cleaning the bathroom. By noon I needed a break, so we took a picnic lunch to Rogers Park. Helen and Stacy were there. While the children played, Helen and I gabbed about everything under the sun."

"How are they doing?"

A nasty rumor had captivated the gossip channels of tiny Red Creek. Apparently Helen had checked into St. Luke's emergency room with a badly bruised eye and a broken arm, supposedly from tripping down the back stairs of their home. She claimed she hit her eye on a box of rubbish and broke her arm when it became entangled in the railing. The rumor mill spread a different story, however, and wherever Walter went the locals gawked.

"William, please," she said, righting his sipper cup. "Now, eat your chicken leg. Mommy made it specially for you."

"I want applesauce," William countered.

"You've had more than enough sugar today," she said, as much for Stephen's ears as for her overly energetic son's. After redirecting William's attention, she returned hers to her husband. "Everything Helen tells me confirms her story. If she's hiding physical abuse, she's hiding it well. I've seen no reason to doubt their love for one another. Have you talked with Walter yet?"

"I called him at work, but had to leave a message. Maybe I'll hear something tonight."

"Tonight? What do you mean tonight? Do you expect him to call you at home?"

Stephen studied her as he sheepishly chewed his chicken.

"I'm sure I told you. There's an emergency board meeting tonight at eight to settle a squabble about a new Sunday school curriculum."

"You didn't tell me." She slammed her napkin hard on the table, and kicked back her chair to rise.

"Sara, I told you. I..."

"Well, I don't care. In eight months we haven't had eight evenings alone."

She dumped her half eaten dinner into the garbage and added her plate to the already overflowing stack of dirty dishes.

Resisting the urge to shoot back a defensive rebuke, Stephen paused to study his wife. Watching her attack the dishes, he was touched by what a caring, loving, faithful, diligent, and responsible mother and wife she had become. Her turned back reminded him shamefully of how he had almost rejected her because her past was so far from the preferred lily-white credentials. Once they were married, Sara had been reticent, even cynical about joining him in daily prayer or Scripture study. Then, as life will have it, her escalating openness coincided with his overwhelming busyness. In time she had established her own daily devotional routine while he struggled to even make time for grace before meals. More frequently now, Sara was adding Spirit-led spice into church, family, and neighborhood discussions, a sure sign of her spiritual growth. *What more could I want?* But that wasn't the right question. *What more does she want and deserve?*

He rose from his chair and walked up behind her, placing his hands on her sides. Initially she tensed from the rage brewing within, but feeling his firm and persistent grasp as he enveloped her in his arms, she relaxed and accepted him. They nuzzled cheek to cheek.

"Honey, I'm sorry," he said softly. "I'm sorry our life has become so crowded with distractions. You know that I'm never gone for selfish reasons. Listen, I promise that tonight I will tell the board that since you're pregnant, whenever I'm out for an evening on church business, I'm going to spend at least an extra hour at home the next morning giving you a hand. How does that sound?"

"Oh, Stephen, they won't agree to that."

"They'll just have to."

He turned her around and kissed her affectionately. Behind them was a sink full of dishes that will wait until tomorrow. In the small dining area was a partially consumed dinner that will morph into leftovers. And in his high chair sat William, who watched with toddler jealousy as his mommy cuddled the other man in her life.

*   *   *

WALTER SAT GUARDEDLY in the front pew at Grace Open Bible Church. Knowing the popularity of this best-selling author and speaker, he had arrived an hour early to claim a few prime seats. Glancing around repeatedly for familiar faces, he nevertheless found himself a stranger in a large, modern, nearly full sanctuary. In three minutes the speech was scheduled to begin.

Positioned directly in front and above him on the raised, red-carpeted platform, beneath ceiling-mounted spotlights, was a clear Plexiglas podium. At its base partially blocking his view, was an enormous arrangement of white roses, ferns, and baby's breath. Walter considered moving but there were now no other options.

"Here you are," came Raeph's familiar voice as he claimed the seat to Walter's right. "You must have surged through when the janitor opened up. Seen him yet?"

"Nope," Walter said. "Not yet, but he should be starting any second."

The sanctuary lights dimmed slightly as a gray-bearded man in a tight-fitting maroon suit crossed the platform. After tapping the microphone and signaling someone offstage to start the tape, he began.

"Our speaker this evening needs no introduction, for I am sure most of you are familiar with his books, tapes, and tracts. For the unfamiliar, Reverend Gary Harmond was born, baptized, and catechized a Roman Catholic. After seminary he was ordained a Catholic priest, and served as such for over ten years until by God's grace he found the Gospel and Jesus Christ. After resigning from the priesthood, he earned a master's degree in theology from Durham Theological Seminary and was ordained as a Southern Baptist. Of course, we won't hold that against him."

This brought the expected laughter from the non-denominational, evangelical crowd.

"He pastored for six years, but recognizing a dire need, he founded Former Catholics to Catholics—better known as FC2C—to reach out to Roman Catholics with the gospel of Jesus Christ."

Walter shot a smile towards Raeph. For months they had been counting the days until Harmond's rare appearance so close to home.

"Put on your seat belts!" Raeph whispered.

The emcee continued. "He's with us this evening to retell his story and then answer your questions, so please join me in a hearty welcome, the Reverend Gary F. Harmond."

A thundering applause of more than two thousand hands shattered the anticipatory stillness. The crowd rose, united in one boisterous standing ovation.

Walter clapped his hands enthusiastically above his head. He turned around smiling at the crowd as if he were somehow responsible for the evening's speaker.

From red curtains framing the left side of the platform, a tall, stout figure emerged. His prematurely white hair was combed back and high above his red, stern face. His black preaching robe trimmed in gold braid billowed behind him as he stormed center stage. Grasping the podium he shouted with exaggerated theatrics, "Rome is out to get you if you don't watch out! I know..." and then in a subdued voice, glaring around with a smirk at his highly receptive audience, "...because I was there!"

He stepped back from the podium as if driven back by the escalating applause. Raising his right hand, pointing heavenward, he transformed their horizontal ejaculations of praise to the vertical. Allowing them an extended period of extemporaneous worship, he then raised his left hand, and with two slowly descending palms, like a maestro in control of a large orchestra, he led the crowd in a decrescendo into silence.

"All sovereign and eternal Father," he began in prayer.

As Reverend Harmond's words filled the hall, Walter barely contained his excitement. Glancing around, he saw heads from wall to wall bowed in pious petition. His eyes filled with tears of joy, for this was the most spirit-filled gathering he had attended since that crusade where his soul was rescued, redeemed, and reborn. He looked up at their highly honored guest, whose face was pinched in an expression of earnest appeal. Harmond's imposing figure with arms extended made Walter think of Moses parting the Red Sea or Abraham begging God to spare Sodom.

Suddenly, while still praying, Harmond opened his eyes and . glared down directly at Walter. For what seemed an eternity their eyes remained locked together. Harmond's intensity was unsettling.

"Lord, give us the wisdom," Harmond continued, his attention focused on Walter, "to recognize false teachers in our world, in our community, even in our midst, and the courage and fortitude to stand against them."

Why is he glaring at me? Walter asked himself. He was unsure whether to turn his eyes away or respond with a timid smile. Then Harmond's glare changed slowly into an accepting grin. Walter smiled back and knew in that instant that the Lord was about to catapult his faith into a new dimension.

*   *   *

"I'M SORRY, MEL, but I don't want my children's faith encumbered by myths like Heaven and Hell, the Devil and demons, sin and damnation." Ms. Ruth Singleton was beside herself with frustration, almost to the point of tears. "Jesus freed us from sin and commanded His followers to love one another; to forgive and care for one another. *This* is what our Sunday school curriculum should focus on."

"And Ruth," Mel Tiebold said, "I am not about to submit my daughter's religious education to the minimalist reductionalism of your liberal feminism."

Stephen was caught in a hornet's nest. He had heard rumblings of this apparently ongoing debate, but this was the first time he had encountered its intensity. Robert Gorman, the chairman of the board who was responsible for keeping the meeting under control, was sitting back from the table, looking to Stephen for guidance. The volunteer Sunday school staff had been pressing for a decision because they were beyond the due-date for ordering the fall curriculum, so some resolution was necessary.

"Just because Jesus freed us from sin," Mel continued, "doesn't mean we can now ignore it. And just because liberals like you don't *believe* in Heaven or Hell, or the Devil and demons, doesn't mean they don't exist. Jesus spoke as much about the reality of these things as he did about love. You can't have one without the other."

"I can, and so can my children," Ruth shot back. "Modern scholarship has shown that the true gospel of love can clearly be freed from its ancient, ignorant, superstitious, and, if I may say, chauvinistic elements. It must be demythologized."

As he listened patiently to these two highly educated board members fight it out—Ruth, a social studies teacher at Red Creek

High, and Mel, the science teacher at Mount Hope Christian Academy—Stephen understood more clearly the forces that led to Reverend Smith's demise. These two strong, unwavering voices were but the spokespersons for the two factions that divided this otherwise peaceful country church. Stephen, like the pastor before him, sided with the second, more conservative and traditional faction. This was certainly obvious in his teaching and preaching. He was even a bit puzzled now by how warm and receptive the liberal faction had been to his hiring.

There was a complication, however. The Singletons and the Tiebolds represented two of the oldest families in the church as well as the community—pillar families whose great-great-great-grandfathers had built this church. Often these families with their ancient credentials were a bother, especially to new pastors. They presumed, at least in an unspoken way, that their long ancestral membership gave them certain privileges—maybe even special wisdom into how the parish and its pastor should run the church. Usually, however, this "wisdom" boiled down to something like: "Just leave everything the way it's always been. If it ain't broke…"

Some pastors sardonically referred to such families as card-carrying members of the *Thorn in the Flesh Society.* Rumor had it that this clandestine society assigned at least one *thorn* to every church. Secretly they attended national, regional, and state conventions of the *TFS* to stay current on the latest schemes to make their pastor's work particularly difficult. As a result, these "pillar" families, whose firsthand knowledge of their church's past could theoretically be of great assistance to a new pastor, were too often barriers to needed change.

Ruth's husband, Charles, who had greeted Stephen so warmly on his first Sunday, turned out to be the local circuit judge and chairman of the town's board of regents. The new office annex had been financed through the benevolence of their extended family, in honor of Reverend Isaac Singleton, one of the church's nineteenth-century clergymen.

Stephen would have preferred, however, to side with Mel Tiebold, for he would want his son William to hear the *whole* gospel, not a modernist truncation. But the Singletons and their cronies, who numbered fewer than a third of the congregation, nonetheless represented more than two-thirds of the giving.

The memory of Reverend Malone's prophetic words awakened Stephen into action.

"Ruth and Mel, please sit down."

The two descended reluctantly, glaring at each other.

Knowing that the two had been born and raised together in this backwoods Vermont town, before Ruth went to an Ivy League women's college on the east coast and Mel to an evangelical college in the Midwest, Stephen wondered if there was more to this debate than conflicting theologies. *Had they been childhood sweethearts until one spurned the other?* The thought of these two hitched as husband and wife almost made him laugh out loud, but instead it led him to ask himself, *How in God's name am I ever going to resolve this?*

Stephen stood up to claim control of the meeting.

"All of you understand better than I do how this issue, as well as many others, divides this congregation right down the middle." *Or at least into one-third, two-thirds.*

"You also know that the wrong decision here could fragment this church, because neither side seems willing to compromise. What is sad is that both sides affirm that Jesus commanded us to love one another, but neither side seems willing to do this."

"But every time this issue comes up..." Mel began.

"Please, Mel, let me talk. There is no hiding the fact that I lean towards the more conservative evangelical curriculum..."

With this, Ruth sat back hard in protest.

"...but I promise that this week I will carefully review both proposed curricula from cover to cover, as well as another program that might be more acceptable to both sides. Then next week, same night, same time, I will give you my recommendation. Will this do?"

"That doesn't give us a lot of time," Ruth answered. "We're already late for the publisher's deadline."

"Ruth, what would you have me do?" Stephen asked her. "Force a decision on us that might exacerbate an already divided, bitter church? What kind of model is this for our children?"

No one responded, so Stephen moved on. "So we'll decide this next Wednesday evening," *Lord willing.* "Is there any more business we need to cover tonight?"

He remembered the promise he had made to Sara, but one look at the dozen faces around him—expressions quite different from those in da Vinci's rendition of the Last Supper—convinced him that this was hardly a receptive moment.

*　　　　*　　　　*

"ANY QUESTIONS?"

Reverend Harmond had just completed a condensed, yet inspiring rendition of his conversion from Roman Catholicism to Jesus Christ. With accusatory details, he had reviewed how the nuns of his youth had forced him to accept superstitious and idolatrous myths. They had introduced him, he declared, to a religion of works-righteousness instead of challenging him to accept Jesus as his Lord and Savior. All through seminary he had made every effort to fulfill each ritual meticulously, reciting the Daily Office and the liturgy of the Mass, but he never read the Bible freely on his own. He became ordained and served ten years as a priest, but like Martin Luther he always felt like a failure, unloved by God.

Until, one day, he met an ex-priest who helped him break free from Roman Catholic "enslavement." This ex-priest, he said, patiently walked him through the Scriptures, showing him the many ways that Catholicism was both unbiblical and unchristian. Harmond explained how "by grace the scales fell from his eyes," and he experienced "a powerful conversion to Jesus." Within a year he resigned from the priesthood, and the rest was history.

With tears, he also told how God had honored his willingness to surrender. A year after resigning, rejected by family and friends, he became reacquainted with an old girlfriend from high school. Devastated that he had chosen the priesthood over their love, she had concluded that God was calling her to become a nun. When they met again, she was going through her own crisis of faith as a result of the massive changes imposed by the Second Vatican Council. Harmond told her about his conversion, and within a year she had left her habit behind and become his wife. God had restored their lifelong love.

Now, as the applause was dying down and people were returning to their seats, Reverend Harmond opened the floor for questions.

A middle-aged man squeezed past others in his row and rushed to a microphone in the center aisle.

"Pastor Harmond, what was the key issue that finally convinced you to leave Catholicism?"

"There, of course, were many, many things, but the pivotal eye opener was when I discovered that the verse used by the Catholic Church to establish the authority of the pope does not teach this," Harmond said. "They claim that in Matthew 16:18, Jesus declared Simon Peter the rock upon which He would build His Church. But that isn't what it says."

With this Harmond drew their attention to the text and outlined in detail the argument that the Greek term used by Jesus refers to Simon as merely a "little stone." Instead, it was the faith expressed in Simon's bold proclamation that would be the "large boulder" upon which Jesus would build His Church.

"Once I saw that the supposed authority of the pope was nothing more than a later creation of a corrupt church, two things happened: first, I saw through all the strange theologies that had crept in under the influence of corrupt, power-hungry popes, and, two, I discovered the trustworthiness of the Bible. I discovered *sola scriptura* and used every spare moment to read it. Now my life and faith in Jesus are inspired, guided, and constrained by Scripture alone.

"Any other questions?"

Walter had one, but he hesitated. Three people were already standing in line. Besides, he was worried that the crowd might laugh at his conspiratorial suspicions.

A woman asked whether Catholics truly worship Mary, and Harmond said they most certainly did, offering many details.

A young man asked why Catholics believe in Purgatory, and Harmond said Catholics see this as a second chance after death to earn their entrance into Heaven.

An elderly woman, who admitted to being an ex-Catholic, asked about the rosary and other devotional practices from her childhood, like the scapular. Harmond, again offering evidence, called them pagan, superstitious infestations from the time when Catholicism became the official religion of Rome under Emperor Constantine.

The line to the microphone was now empty, so Walter, with a burst of courage, shot out of his front-row seat. Another man, however, beat him to it, so Walter reluctantly waited behind him. The man was medium height, with dark hair and a mustache, and he stood before the microphone with a large, open leather Bible.

"Reverend Harmond," the man began, "thank you for your candid testimony, but can you straighten something out for me, please?"

"If I can," Harmond said.

"The Bible teaches in Second Timothy that 'all Scripture is inspired by God.' To which Bible does this verse refer?"

"Well, of course, this verse doesn't refer to any particular English translation, but to the original in the Greek and Hebrew. My preference is the King James Version, but there are other acceptable translations."

"I wasn't asking which English translation, but which Bible? Specifically, which collection or canon of books? Any honest historian knows that up until the Council of Rome in 382 A.D., there was no official collection of books, but multiple, conflicting lists. So, to which collection of scriptural books was Paul referring?"

Walter, more consumed with nervousness about how he would pose his question without embarrassing himself, was oblivious to the man's dialogue with Harmond.

"Sir, I appreciate your question," Harmond said confidently, "for it gives me an opportunity to clear up some confusion. When Paul wrote this he was, obviously, referring only to the Old Testament, for as of yet none of what would soon be considered the New Testament was understood as Scripture. They were just letters or gospel accounts written by apostles or their disciples. We now know, however, that the Holy Spirit who inspired Paul's words was speaking through him in reference to the entire canon of Scripture."

"Please forgive my persistence, but you haven't answered my question. To which collection of Scriptural books was Paul referring? Which specific Bible is inspired and sufficient?" he said, holding up his leather Bible for emphasis. "The canon established by the Council of Rome as inspired and trustworthy had seven more books than your King James Bible does. In fact, those seven books were included in the same Greek translation of the Old Testament that Paul used and to which he was here referring. How can you be certain that your incomplete collection of books qualifies for Paul's reference?"

"Excuse me," Harmond said, "but may I ask which translation you are holding up so brashly?"

The man hesitated, lowering his Bible, and then answered, "Why, the New American Version."

"As I thought—the modern Catholic Bible—and you're here to confuse these good people."

A low murmur rose from the audience as they considered the traitor in their midst. The man, however, looked straight ahead at Harmond.

"No, I'm not here to confuse, but to clarify."

"Sir, I do not agree. I am always willing to debate you and other so-called Catholic apologists, but this is not the time or the place. So if you would, please be so kind as to step aside for the gentleman behind you."

"But you have avoided my question..."

"Would you gentlemen in the back please assist this man out? Apparently he is intent on being disruptive."

Harmond's confrontation woke Walter from his self-indulgence and aroused his ire. In obedience—though Harmond had not asked specifically for his help—Walter grabbed the man.

"Reverend Harmond has asked you to leave, so move it," he said.

Walter turned him around and led him forcibly towards the exit. In so doing, Walter relinquished his place in line, but he had his answer already. *Was there truly clandestine Catholic infiltration into the Protestant Church?* The man in his grasp, who so slyly had tried to trip Harmond up, was the only answer he needed.

*   *   *

AFTER EXTRACTING HIMSELF from the meeting, Stephen decided to detour downtown instead of going straight home, to Burt's Ice Cream Bowl for a hot fudge sundae. Snack in hand, he crossed the road to consume it peaceably in Rogers Park.

The first thing he encountered was a gaggle of children enjoying a late-evening romp on the merry-go-round. The speed of their rotation was certain to fling one or more onto the concrete. His inclination was to barge in and take control as the only responsible, sensible adult within screaming distance. *Where are their parents? But why squelch their fun and be mean old Reverend Spoilsport?* He turned away, and walked indifferently to a bench behind an overgrown azalea bush. *Now I know why ol' Mr. Grumley prefers this bench.*

He gazed up at the brilliant full moon, savoring a mouthful of ice cream. *How am I going to tell Sara that I wimped out on my promise?* But his mind turned quickly to other things.

How am I ever going to reach the Singletons with the truth of the gospel?

In the four years since seminary, he had encountered many Christians like the Singletons—more committed to their Congregationalist heritage than to the faith upon which it was built; more committed to Plymouth Rock than Jesus the Rock; more interested in peace and love than faith, repentance, and conversion.

How can I break through their shells of self-sufficiency, to see that to love and establish peace, they first must have converted hearts—that apart from Jesus they can do nothing?

On the other end of the spectrum, he thought of Mel Tiebold and how fanatics like him could be just as bothersome. Mel's literal fundamentalism was an embarrassment. Certainly Stephen believed that the Bible was inerrant and that the Genesis accounts of Creation were historical. Nevertheless, he allowed some leeway in interpretation. *Seven days, seven eras, or seven bazillion years—the fact that the sun and the moon weren't even created until day four necessitates some latitude in interpretation other than 24-hour literal days.*

But for Mel, this was the touchstone for orthodoxy: to hedge here was a slippery slope to declaring that the entire Bible was a collection of myths. Mel was a two-fisted science teacher with a science textbook in one hand and the Bible in the other. If they ever disagreed, the Bible always won—and the parents who sent their children to Mount Hope Christian Academy wanted it this way. For this and other reasons, Stephen questioned whether he would want William, and their new child in the womb, to attend this bastion of hyper-fundamentalism.

An adult yelling interrupted Stephen's thoughts. He peaked around the azaleas in time to see Mel Tiebold ordering the children to get off the merry-go-round and go home.

Which way will Mel leave? Dang, he's coming straight at me!

Stephen rose quickly from the bench and stalked around the azaleas, keeping them between Mel and himself. Once Mel was on his way, Stephen realized that the bench was no longer a safe haven.

Might as well go home.

He walked through the now empty park. The bright August moon projected his shadow across the merry-go-round, still spinning from a child's last defiant shove. In his mind's eye he saw a vision, which struck him as somehow prophetic. There were four groups of people. The first was the six children gaily spinning at breakneck speed, oblivious to any potential danger. They'd done this hundreds of times—what was there to fear? Then there were the children's parents sitting at home glued to television screens, eating popcorn, assuming that nothing could happen in sleepy Red Creek. Third, there was himself, an ordained caregiver in the community keenly aware of the potential danger and the children's ignorance, but rather than bear their ridicule, he walked silently past. Finally there was Mel, who recognized the danger, warned the children, and sent them home. He did this out of love, even though the children complained and reviled him.

Stephen stopped in front of his church, now dark, and recalled the Singleton-Tiebold feud. Stephen knew on which side of the fence he stood—on which side he had always stood—but the thought of Ruth gave him pause. She was no mental slouch, having graduated near the top of her class in both her undergraduate and master's programs. And though Mel caricatured her as an uncaring, man-hating feminist, she was often more loving and Christ-like than was Mel, whose fanatical defense of orthodoxy—take-no-prisoners— reeked of modern Pharisaism. Both were sincere in their convictions, but sincerely contradictory. *They cannot both be sincerely right— unless there is no right answer to their debate. So one of them has to be sincerely wrong, or at least misled.*

He recalled his previous arguments with Reverend Malone over salvation and justification, and then his more recent dilemma over clerical dress. On all of these issues, he took stands against equally adept people who held significantly different positions. *In the end, how do I determine which side is true? I believe that where I stand is true—but how can I be certain?*

The vision came alive again in his mind, as bright as the moon, and he perceived a deeper meaning. The children represented his congregation, living their Christian lives and presuming all was well, because their "divinely appointed" caregivers generally let them "live and let live." Whenever the caregivers challenged their presumptions, however, the congregation's claws came out.

Stephen knew it was his responsibility before God to make sure that his people were spiritually safe and secure, that they were headed without any doubt towards eternal bliss. He also knew that there were many with lives bordering on heresy or moral bankruptcy. Sometimes he responded to their waywardness as he had done with the children, walking silently by without a word of warning. Other times he was like Mel, exhorting them to straighten up or burn, which always brought hate calls or mail.

To what extent, however, am I like the children's parents? To what extent am I blindly misleading my congregation—telling them they are fine when they are not?

Then he perceived a fifth group in his vision: children who had remained home, because their parents believed that children should not be roaming around after dark. These parents represented in Stephen's mind the other ministers in town—Methodist, Presbyterian, Lutheran, Baptist, Nazarene, Catholic, and Episcopalian—who taught their people differently than he did, sometimes drastically so. Remembering Christ's warning, he wondered: *Is it possible that I am a blind guide?*

In the specific issue being debated by Ruth and Mel, Stephen was certain that Mel was correct, but he had been equally certain in his arguments with Reverend Malone. In the end, "orthodoxy" was determined by whoever can muster the longest and strongest platform of verses. *Upon what should I base my deciding vote between Ruth's "modernism" and Mel's "traditionalism"? There are Scriptures to back both sides, and I know ministers who believe as Ruth does. The existence of entire Sunday school curricula promoting her view at least confirms that there are influential, educated Christians who believe this stuff.*

But that doesn't make it true, Stephen protested, *yet how will I prove to Ruth and Mel, to the board, and to myself that my interpretation is the clearest expression of Scripture?*

Up until this moment, he had never questioned what he *knew* by the witness of the Spirit to be true, but now this nagging sense of uncertainty wouldn't leave him alone.

He turned around to gaze at Faith United Methodist, his nearest "competitor." He remembered with deep regret a long-forgotten cafeteria debate with a seminarian named Carl. They had begun seminary together and with racquetball as a mutual interest had become close friends. Carl was a staunch Methodist, carrying on a three-generation tradition of Methodist ministers. One evening over a casual ice cream sundae—the connection to his more recent snack gave him pause—they discussed predestination versus free will. For an hour they sat nose to nose, Bibles in hand, parrying and countering chapter and verse, until the irreconcilable clash of Stephen's Calvinism with Carl's Wesleyanism sent them to their rooms. They didn't speak for the remainder of the school year. When Stephen returned in the fall, Carl had transferred. They had never spoken again. The last he heard, Carl was pastoring a Methodist church in Saskatchewan.

Stephen glanced up at the moon following him, and remembered Paul's warning in Ephesians: *Never let the sun go down on your anger.*

"Lord Jesus," he asked several steps from his front porch, "were my Calvinist convictions that eternally crucial that they justified rejecting this good Christian brother? Carl was just as committed to Scripture as I was. How can I be certain that my evangelical-Calvinist interpretation is *the* one true interpretation?"

The bulb in the porch light was burned out, so he thankfully couldn't see the unmown grass or the dirty windows. But when the screen door handle came off again in his hand, he wondered how many other ways he was blinded by the darkness.

5

Six months later...

W INTER AND SPRING were playing an obdurate tug of war, like stubborn opponents of contradictory opinions. Whenever a thaw seemed imminent, another Canadian front blasted across Lake Champlain, giving the lingering snow new life.

For the LaPointes, seamless days of gray skies stifled whatever joys remained from William's first truly cognizant Christmas. The birth of their second son, Daniel, was an ecstatic blessing, but the painful news that Sara could no longer bare children dampened their joy. Apparently there were complications from some previous procedure, of which Sara claimed ignorance. The whole family, therefore, was quite ready for the uplift of Easter.

Amidst the clutter of his desk, Stephen set aside his outlines for the remaining Lenten sermons, and laughed cynically at the church's plans for Easter. In the late 1700s, when the non-conformist settlers established this church in the backwoods of Vermont, no New

England Congregationalist celebrated any of the now universally accepted Christian holy days. "Roman idolatry," they had decried, and for the same reason, no religious artwork was allowed in the church. Consequently, a weathervane was mounted on the fifty-foot steeple instead of a cross.

Over time, however, the stress of transforming culture had surrendered to the flow of American Protestantism and the spirit of progress. Now they celebrated all Christian holidays and had a large wooden cross up front in the sanctuary. And to top it off, every Christmas they proudly erected the county's largest nativity scene. Stephen sniggered at the thought of the church's founding fathers spinning in their graves at the abhorrent sight of graven images of Mary, Joseph, and Jesus polluting the church lawn.

Possibly to offset the appearance of buckling under to Rome, the populace also had accepted alternative traditions. Now Santa Claus, Halloween, and the Easter Bunny overshadowed and sometimes even replaced St. Nicholas, All Hallows' Eve, and the resurrected Jesus. The more religiously committed members warned against the pagan origins of these aberrations and called for a return to the "pure celebration of these holidays"—the same celebrations their forefathers had considered papist and pagan.

Even more so, however, Stephen considered how aghast the forefathers would be over what he was about to do. Out of his briefcase, he retrieved the final draft of the eulogy he was about to give for a young man named Ronnie.

After worship on Sunday, Marty and Phyllis Gibson had pulled him aside. Their nephew, Ronnie, who had been living in Chicago, died recently. His family wanted to hold Ronnie's memorial service close to home for family and friends and to place him in the family plot in Red Creek Union Cemetery. For some undisclosed reason, however, the new pastor at the family's United Methodist Church north of town was unable to officiate at the funeral, so they wondered whether Stephen would.

Although members of the church's more liberal faction, Stephen liked the Gibsons. They were regular, front-pew attendees, met every challenge with an optimistic smile, and were generous in every pledge appeal. When they asked, therefore, he accepted immediately. Now, however, he wished he had some legitimate way out.

From the scant information he gathered from the Gibsons and

a brief meeting with the grieving family, he learned that Ronnie had been born and raised on the outskirts of Red Creek. He had been baptized and catechized at what was then First Evangelical United Brethren Church. He graduated from Red Creek High and then went to college in Chicago. A quiet student, he got good grades, stayed out of trouble with the law, and after completing his undergraduate studies, accepted a job in sales. Within two years, however, he became deathly sick, and now two years later he was dead. During this time, he remained with friends near Chicago, so his death came as a shock to his parents.

Uneasy with the shallowness of his evolving eulogy, Stephen had called a phone number that Ronnie's father had surreptitiously slipped him. By the time Stephen had hung up, he was in a devastating quandary.

The voice on the other end of the line had been the Chicago friend who had taken care of Ronnie to the end. He had declared matter-of-factly that Ronnie had been an outspoken, practicing homosexual and continually had spurned his parents' pleas to reject his lifestyle and return home. When diagnosed with HIV, Ronnie became angry and lashed out at everyone, but showed no signs of remorse. He blamed society for his death sentence by AIDS, never his own lifestyle. "To the end," his friend had said, with a tone that to Stephen sounded a bit too flippant, "Ronnie cursed God and his family. He wanted to be cremated, but the family refused."

With this information, Stephen then understood several things: why the family had been so guarded, why the family's pastor had been conveniently unavailable, and why Marty and Phyllis Gibson, ignorant of their nephew's lifestyle or cause of death, had asked so innocently for his help.

Stephen had no reservations about where Scripture and God stood on the issue of homosexuality, and where practicing, unrepentant homosexuals probably spent eternity. Even though modern Christians were becoming more open and less uptight about this lifestyle, he believed that this was merely a conformation to modern immorality.

His quandary now stemmed from what he would say with clear conscience to the mourning and mostly oblivious family and friends.

Three times he had composed and discarded sweet sounding eulogies before he arrived at the present version. It, too, was fitting to the title—"good words"—but it avoided any comments about

Ronnie's spiritual destiny. In the end, he decided to focus on what can be learned from such a young man's death: None of us knows when God might call us home. Are we ready?

With his Bible and eulogy in hand and his parka collar up around his face, he made his way from the office annex out into the cold. When the Fairmont's engine refused to start, he wondered with nervous humor whether the ghosts of the founding fathers were intervening to prevent him from giving the church's blessing to a young man so uninterested in God's mercy.

*   *   *

"Mom, hello. What a pleasant surprise," Sara said, catching her breath, trying to sound genuine. She had just nursed Daniel to sleep in his second-floor bedroom and distracted William with toys in the basement when the phone rang on the main floor.

"Well, don't act like I've been distant," Marjorie Bondforth said. "It's only been three weeks since I was there helping you after Daniel's birth."

"I know, I didn't mean it that way. I just wasn't expecting your call. How are you? Are you calling for any specific reason?"

This last sentiment clearly expressed Sara's qualms about this rare call from her normally distant and detached mother. Sara owed her feminist and agnostic past to the dominance of her mother who, since being widowed, had become quite a socialite. When Marjorie heard about Sara's "infatuation" for a seminary student, she had belittled her. Then when she discovered that Sara intended to marry him and become a pastor's wife, Marjorie essentially disowned her. To avoid the wedding, she had feigned a bronchitis attack and stayed incommunicado for nearly a year. Eventually, after William's birth, Marjorie began making inroads for reconciliation, and now with the birth of their second son, her mother almost sounded interested in acting like a grandmother. But from experience, Sara presumed there must be some urgency that necessitated her mother's call.

"No, no, dear, nothing specific. I was just wondering how you and the baby and, of course, William and Stephen were doing. Must there be some specific reason for me to call?"

"No, but face it, Mother, you rarely call just to say 'Hi.'"

"Well, that's behind us now, dear. So how's Danny?"

"*Daniel*, Mother. We want to avoid the nicknames. He's doing quite well."

"Keeping you up nights?"

"Yes, all night, I'm afraid to say."

"Is Stephen helping more this time?"

"Mother, Stephen has always been helpful."

"But I thought you said…"

"I only meant that when William was born, Stephen was extremely busy getting accustomed to his first pastoral position. He helped every night as much as he could, as he is doing now."

To some extent, Sara had to cover up for Stephen. Yes, he was getting up whenever it was necessary to walk Daniel back to sleep, but he wasn't liking it. Now after a month of sleepless nights, she and her husband were hardly acting like best friends—but she wasn't about to give her mother grounds for an "I told you so."

"Well, you know I could move up there and help if you wanted," Marjorie said.

This nearly knocked Sara to the floor. *Mother offering to abandon her fast-paced New York social calendar to…help? Beyond conception.*

"Mother, are you serious?"

"Of course, dear. You know that there's really nothing left here for me. I could be there in a couple days if you wanted."

"Well, I don't know. The thought never…I'd have to ask Stephen, of course."

"Listen, honey, I'm offering to come up and help you, not your husband. He doesn't need my help."

"But, Mother, I presume that if you're serious about this, you will stay here with us. Stephen obviously has to be in complete agreement." Sara knew this would never happen, and wasn't quite sure she wanted it to. Nevertheless, her mother was actually offering. *This must be some kind of act of God.*

"But, mother, I promise that I will make every effort to convince him. It would be good to have you here—to help with the boys and spend some time together." Her voice broke off.

"Sara, is everything all right?"

"Yes, of course."

"Now, honey, I realize we could have been closer as a mother and daughter, but I want to be there for you now."

Sara wished she could spew it all out to this woman for whose acceptance and love she had yearned from childhood. She wanted to tell her about the countless lonely nights when Stephen was out on church business; about the unfair, stifling expectations from self-righteous people who couldn't themselves live up to their own demands; and about the eroding, uncomfortable, even dishonest contradictions between her stagnant, doubt-ridden inner life and the prissy, "grace-filled, and Spirit-led" facade she had to don grudgingly before these people as well as her husband.

"Didn't I warn you about the puritanical frustrations that awaited you if you married this fundamentalist?" her mother said.

But it was because of her mother's own form of self-righteous bigotry that Sara refused to open up.

"Mother, you were wrong. I have a great life, a loving and generous husband, and two beautiful boys. God just never promised that all marriages would be as flawless and joyful as yours."

Halfway through saying it, Sara regretted this cheap shot, but completed it anyway. From early on Sara had known of her father's philandering and her parents' contractual marriage. She presumed that her mother had long relished the freedom that awaited her after her father's passing.

"That was unnecessary," her mother said.

Sara felt the familiar coldness descend between them like a scrim in a theatrical portrayal of dreams.

"Mother, I didn't intend to hurt, only to remind you that one should take the log out of one's own eye..."

"Don't preach at me," she said with such vicious rage that Sara pulled the phone from her ear as if to avoid contamination.

"Mother, I..."

"Here I call to offer help, to set my whole world aside, and what do you do? Spit at me. Stab me in the back."

"Mother, I hear Daniel crying upstairs."

"Yeah, sure. Whenever things don't go the way..."

"Please, I have to go. Goodbye."

Sara hung up. Once certain that the line was dead, she picked up the receiver and set it aside. Her mother would be calling back immediately, seething with rage.

Daniel wasn't crying. The upstairs was silent. She stuck her head into the basement stairwell, and heard William talking contently as he narrated the fierce onslaught of an army of plastic soldiers and critters against his wooden block fortress.

Determined to enjoy this respite, she quickly refilled her coffee cup and retired to the living room. For a moment she watched Ethel and Lucy stuff their faces with chocolates on a rerun of "I Love Lucy," but she wasn't in the mood for slapstick. She switched off the television and retired to a glider facing the front window.

Her view extended out across their snow-covered lawn, across partially cleared Main Street, and over the town square where farmers used to corral livestock during trips to town. Through the blowing snow, she strained to make out the shapes of Adam's Dry Goods, the Good Morning Cafe, First Security Bank, and Angel's Macramé and Boutique. Around to the right, out of sight, was the church.

This was her world, her life. She sat still and silent for a long moment, until she could no longer retrain a voice from within.

She was right, you know. Is this the life you wanted for yourself?

Sara reached over to the end table for the family Bible and turned to her favorite book—Philippians. Despite all the doubts with which she continued to wrestle, she yet had grown to cherish the calming and reassuring words of Scripture. Lately in the midst of her loneliness—with no friends or family nearby, the children in their infantile worlds, and Stephen always gone—the Word had become her one solace. She began rereading some of Paul's advice on how to manage loneliness and discouragement:

> Do all things without grumbling or questioning, that you may be blameless and innocent…forgetting what lies behind and straining forward to what lies ahead, I press on toward the goal for the prize of the upward call of God in Christ Jesus…Have no anxiety about anything…Not that I complain of want; for I have learned, in whatever state I am, to be content…And my God will supply every need of yours according to his riches in glory in Christ Jesus.

"Lord Jesus," she prayed aloud through tears, "please, help me survive this hell…and please, don't let Stephen find out."

*   *   *

SCRIVENER'S WAS THE ONLY FUNERAL HOME IN TOWN, and the crowd paying respects was surprisingly large. Stephen hung back against a wall of the parlor, observing the intriguing mixture of mourners. Most were familiar townsfolk, a few from his church. Others were strangers, and to Stephen and a few other gawking locals, their dress, radical hair-styles, and demeanor shouted that they were Ronnie's friends from out of town.

Stephen watched as the mourners proceeded in line for their brief moment with the deceased. They processed lock-step, as if someone had choreographed their movements. Standing in line, most with hands clasped before them, they inched forward silently. Their faces bore expressions of solemn dignity, and they spoke only in hushed, guarded tones. Any giggles or antics from children were quickly squelched. Upon reaching the bereaved parents, they shook hands and delivered soliloquies of condolence, fitting to their relationship with the deceased. Next, they waited nervously for the mourners standing before the coffin to pay their respects and move on. Finally, once the way was clear, they delicately walked forward, gazed down upon the dead, and paused for an appropriate passage of time. What followed was a wide assortment of facial responses ranging from startled awe, stony silence, quivering sadness, and smiling consolation. Stephen assumed that if these mourners were like himself, their thoughts were mixed with genuine memories, prayers, and petitions as well as calculations as to whether their period of respect sufficiently conveyed true reverence and compassion. Once this time had been met, though, they moved on quietly until, after signing the guest book, they either left for work or home, or buddied up with friends to carry on with previous conversations.

Seeing that the line had dwindled down to nothing, Stephen moved forward.

"Hello, Mr. and Mrs. Gibson."

"Hello, Pastor LaPointe."

They shook hands. Mrs. Gibson wiped away a tear. Mr. Gibson appeared detached.

"Very nice expression of affection and support from your friends and family," Stephen said.

"Yes," Mrs. Gibson replied, "Ronnie would have been touched. Have you been to see him yet?"

"No, I wanted to wait to go forward with you."

"Thank you."

She took his arm and, with her husband trailing behind, led him to the coffin.

Ronnie was wearing a navy blue suit, which Stephen assumed was not his normal attire. His black hair was neatly trimmed and combed flawlessly to one side, which Stephen also assumed was by order of his father. His face was gaunt and more flesh-colored than his pale hands, probably due to makeup. But what captured Stephen's attention was Ronnie's angry sneer. Apparently the mortician had done his best to create an impression of peacefulness, but there was no question about it: Ronnie's eyes and lips were set in a defiant snarl. It reminded him of Jimmy Cagney in *Angels with Dirty Faces* on his way to the electric chair, or in that film where Cagney died on top of a burning oil refinery: "Top of the world, Ma!" Ronnie's expression betrayed no sign of remorse.

Stephen struggled for something consoling to say, but was speechless. Ronnie's mother finally broke the silence, speaking softly and more openly than she did in their previous meeting.

"Pastor, he really was a good boy. I don't know why he did what he did. We tried to keep close to him, but he wanted nothing to do with us or our faith. Many times I sent him religious materials to open his heart, but, well, several months ago he sent them all back in a box. He wrote that he had refused to read or listen to the material, that he never would, that he wanted me to stop, and..." she broke off to wipe her eyes, "...that we should just go to hell. Pastor, I'm telling you this because I know you've got a big task before you. Please know that whatever you say, I will understand."

She looked up at Stephen, and continued.

"I wish my son had been a model Christian man, but that wasn't to be. I know that God loved him, and we did all we could to convince him of this love in Christ." Turning back toward the corpse, she whispered, "But Ronnie chose his own destiny." Touching Ronnie's cold hands, she spoke solemnly. "As it says in the Book of Hebrews, '...it is impossible for those who were once enlightened, and have tasted of the heavenly gift...if they shall fall away, to renew them again unto repentance, seeing they crucify to themselves the Son of God afresh.' All we can do now is pray for God's mercy."

This mother's stark recitation stunned Stephen, for this was one of those few Scripture verses for which he had no definitive response—a verse that from any angle appeared to contradict his evangelical convictions of "once saved, always saved." The best explanation he had heard for this awkward text was that the apostate person had only *appeared* to be enlightened, remaining unconverted and unsaved.

Stephen was preparing to counter her statement—to claim that *if* Ronnie had at one time in his life accepted Jesus as his Savior and Lord, and *if* he had surrendered his heart to God's grace, then Ronnie was still, even though defiant and rebellious, covered by the righteous blood of the Lamb—but Stephen caught himself. He remembered that this family and probably most of this crowd were Methodists. They didn't believe in eternal security but in freedom of the will, freedom to turn away from grace and away from salvation.

He remained silent before the coffin. Ronnie sneered up at him.

But for that matter, Stephen's mind raced, *my evangelical views clash even with pure Calvinism. A true Calvinist presumes that Ronnie's destiny was solely dependent upon God's election: long before Ronnie was even born, he was either predestined to Heaven or hell. One can guess another person's eternal destiny by examining his 'fruit,' as Jesus had said, and so by all reports, Ronnie probably didn't have a chance in ...*

"Oh, Emily," Mrs. Gibson said as she turned away to greet a woman waiting patiently in line.

For a second Mr. Gibson locked glances with Stephen, but then he turned away to follow his wife.

Mercifully, Stephen had been granted a stay of embarrassment. He took one last pensive look at Ronnie and then left to sign the guest book. Turning away, he saw a familiar face glaring at him in shock.

"Why hello, Walter," Stephen said with his right hand extended. "I didn't realize you were friends with the Gibsons."

"What are you doing here?" Walter said in a hushed, gruff tone.

"What do you mean?"

"Are you actually conducting this charade? Ronnie no more deserves a Christian funeral than does Charles Manson."

"Relax, Walter. Funerals are more for the living than the dead," Stephen said. "Why, may I ask, are you here?"

"John Gibson works with me at the plant. He's a good friend, and his son was a terrible trial. John just wants this whole thing over with and his son buried and gone. But why are you performing this service? They're Methodists. It sounds to me like their minister had more sense than you about avoiding this one. What hopeful thing can you possibly say about this ungrateful kid who basically spat on his family and faith and flaunted his immorality?"

"Excuse me," said a woman who had touched Stephen's sleeve. "May I speak with you a moment?"

"Yes, of course. Excuse me, Walter."

Stephen followed the woman away from Walter's suspicious stare. She looked to be about his own age, moderately attractive, dressed sharply yet conservatively in a black dress. She led him to a quiet corner away from the crowd.

"I realize, Reverend LaPointe, that it is nearly time to begin, but I need to ask a question."

Stephen thought he saw in her face some resemblance to Mrs. Gibson, so he assumed she was one of Ronnie's aunts.

"All of us here know about Ronnie's lifestyle, and why he died. This is no mystery," she said. "The question is, where is he now? From your perspective, is he going to Heaven?"

Stephen couldn't believe his ears. Just when he was hoping to skirt the issue, it snuck around and bit him. He studied the woman's expression but couldn't discern whether she was a conservative who believed that Ronnie was frying in hell, or a liberal who figured "I'm OK, you're OK, we're all OK, so what the hey?"

"Ma'am, you know I can't claim to know that. No one can," he said. "That is up to the mercy of God, who knew Ronnie's heart better than anyone does, even Ronnie himself. I believe, as Scripture claims, that anyone in Christ is a new creation, the old is gone, the new has come. If sometime in his life Ronnie had accepted Jesus as his Lord and Savior, even if Ronnie continued to fall back into sin, than he will be saved by grace through faith, not by his own righteousness but by the righteousness of Christ. If Ronnie is standing even at this moment before Jesus and is being asked why he should be allowed into heaven, the issue is, what is Ronnie's plea? If he accepted Christ in this life, then he can point to Jesus and His righteousness, and God will blind his eyes to Ronnie's sins. The question is, Mrs...?"

"Mrs. Rita Brownstein. I'm Ronnie's older sister."

Good Lord, Stephen thought. *How many toes have I already stepped on?*

"I didn't know he had any siblings," Stephen said sheepishly.

"Let's just say that my parents aren't too happy with me right now."

"Well, Mrs. Brownstein, the question is whether your brother ever made this commitment and surrendered his life before he died. Do you know whether this was the case?"

"As a matter of fact, he did make that commitment," she said. "He went forward when he was fifteen with a bunch of friends at a summer Bible camp and gave his life to Jesus. He returned home excited about his faith, but this only lasted a few weeks.

"But there is something I want you to explain," she continued, with pointed intensity. "Sure, I'm terribly sorry for Ronnie's death. At one time we were close, but then he became belligerent about his lifestyle. He flaunted it, especially knowing how we felt about it. Once he even brought home one of his lovers and humiliated our parents. But Reverend LaPointe, how can you possibly believe that some adolescent altar call, no matter how sincere, can wipe away any responsibility or guilt for the way he chose to live the rest of his life?"

Lord Jesus, I don't need this! Stephen complained inwardly.

"Well, if his life remained unchanged, it's possible that his conversion was insincere," he replied. "Maybe he only went forward out of peer pressure. The Bible says that one must confess with one's lips and believe in one's heart. He may have confessed outwardly, but maybe he didn't believe inwardly."

"How convenient," Rita said. "I've heard this rationalization many times from you Evangelicals. You tell everyone who comes forward to your altar calls that no matter what they now are saved, yet if they fall back into sin, you merely claim that their conversions weren't genuine. Wouldn't it be more correct to say that only those who endure in holiness until the end can be saved?"

There is that verse again to haunt me, asked so innocently by Elsie: 'He who endures to the end will be saved.' Who is this woman?

But Stephen had a set response for this. "Actually, you've made the distinction yourself. No one can be certain about anyone else but himself or herself, since we cannot see into anyone else's heart. Eternal security is a matter between us and Jesus. Even if we look at another person's lack of fruit, we can't judge, for they may be truly repentant and converted inside."

"So what are you going to say to this crowd of mourners that knows my brother's 'lack of fruit'?"

"Actually, you've helped me work this through. I hope to say much of what we've just discussed, but as tactfully as possible. So if you will excuse me, it's time to begin." He began to walk away, but she stopped him.

"Then just remember something when you're up there, and maybe it's best that I fully introduce myself. My name is *Reverend* Rita Brownstein, my family's Methodist minister, and I'm glad this is your funeral and not mine, even though my parents resent me for refusing to do it. I believe that your description of eternal security is neither eternal nor secure, for you basically have an out clause for every contradiction. If some believer falls away, you merely say that he was never truly converted. Well, my friend, that is hogwash and precisely why I am a Methodist. I teach that every person has freedom of the will and the responsibility to choose God and grow in holiness. If they don't, like my rebellious brother Ronnie, they can fall away and lose their salvation. I pray that God has mercy on his soul, but I'm hedging any bets."

"But then you end up defending that a person can earn salvation through works, through sinless living?"

"No, you are confusing the issue with extremes," she said. "We are saved totally by grace, and our sanctification is the result of our responding to and growing in grace. Conversion is never a one time event that guarantees heaven. Conversion is the beginning of a process that must be fleshed out and completed throughout the rest of our lives as we seek to fulfill Christ's command to become perfect as our heavenly Father is perfect."

"But," Stephen countered, "as Luther and Calvin convincingly argued, our wills are completely depraved from the fall. We no longer have the ability to do anything worthy of God's approval and forgiveness. There is nothing we can do to earn our salvation and, likewise, nothing we can do to lose it; yes, salvation is a free gift of grace, but as such it can not be earned or lost."

"Actually, it is God's freely given grace that empowers us to respond in obedience," Reverend Brownstein answered, giving no ground. "Jesus said, 'Whoever believes....' Believing requires an act of the will, and in the mystery of God's sovereignty, human beings have the complete freedom to choose God or turn away."

"But…"

"Excuse me, Reverend." A man dressed in a black suit, obviously one of the funeral home attendants, was trying to interrupt tactfully. "It's time to begin."

Being guided forward, Stephen looked back at Reverend Rita, who was sending him forth with a sardonic smile that said, "Good luck!"

Stephen stopped short of the center aisle between rows of folding chairs full of guests waiting to hear what words of encouragement he might muster for this seemingly hopeless occasion. To his right by a door was a wastebasket. He opened his Bible, removed his eulogy notes, and cast them away. He then walked down the aisle, up to the coffin now thankfully closed. He turned around, laid his Bible on the wooden lectern, and began, "We are gathered here today…"

But inside, he was begging: *Lord Jesus, please, give me the words, and then get me out of here.*

*   *   *

THE CARS WERE LINED UP with the familiar black flags, their engines running, spewing clouds of exhaust into the frigid air. The hearse nudged forward, and the caravan for Ronnie's last earthly journey began.

Walter watched from the parking lot feeling terribly depressed for John, the father.

Once the last car was out of sight, he reentered his Caprice wagon and began his own procession back to the plant. His mind, however, was a maelstrom of angry, contemptuous, suspicious inner voices that all focused on Reverend LaPointe.

"What a bunch of meaningless, noncommittal, beat-around-the-bush, namby-pamby bull crap," he said to no one in particular. "He seems faithful enough, he makes the rounds of the hospitals and homes, his sermons are generally good, his Bible studies are interesting, but there's that other side—that elusive layer that he keeps hidden."

As he drove speaking out loud, he accentuated his comments with hand gestures.

"Sometimes I see him holding back. He's about to explain a

point of faith, but then he hesitates, as if he's unsure whether it's true; or maybe he's calculating the most middle-of-the-road, least offensive way to say it."

He stopped at a light and noticed that the driver next to him was glaring. Smiling back and giving a facial-hand gesture that said, "Oh, it's just crazy old me," Walter turned back toward the light, and sped off quickly when it turned green.

"There's always something that he's hedging about. First it was about the End Times, and now it was about sin and salvation. He's just not good old Pastor Smith."

And doesn't he seem to play it both ways with the Singletons, the Gibsons, and the other liberals in our church?

"Whenever he has to take sides between those modernistic liberals and us faithful Christians, he weasels his way through with some compromise."

And what about his involvement in the Clergy Association?

"That's right. Pastor Smith refused to have anything to do with that gaggle of liberals and heretics, and a papist to boot!"

Isn't this all what a papist infiltrator might do? Always trying to look good to all sides, keeping all sides happy while slowly lulling everyone into heresy? Giving the impression of being faithful, yet congenially fraternizing with the enemy, if the enemy IS his enemy?

Walter sat up straight. This thought had never crossed his mind. Sure, he believed, as did others, that the Catholic Church had infiltrated Protestant churches, but to consider LaPointe a candidate?

"He can't be."

Yet, as he began reviewing all of his concerns about Reverend LaPointe in the light of how he perceived an infiltrator might act, in every case LaPointe fit the bill.

"But this is too strange…"

And then he remembered.

"At the end of the memorial service, after he delivered his watered-down eulogy, after he invited us to stand for the Lord's Prayer, after he sent us forth with the usual benediction, he gave us a blessing, in the name of the Father, and the Son, and the Holy Spirit."

Walter knew that other Protestant ministers also did this, sometimes raising their arms out and over the congregation in the form of a blessing.

"But I swear that I saw him, just before he raised both arms…I saw him start to raise only his right hand first, just like a priest might do. Then he pulled back slightly, and raised both arms together."

Walter couldn't believe what he was thinking—what he might have discovered.

Who can I tell? Who can I ask? Raeph? Ben? Should I call Pastor Smith? No, I need to keep this to myself, for now, but I will keep my eyes and ears open.

Walter put his foot hard to the pedal with an exhilarating sense of excitement. Being convinced that there were worldwide conspiracies attempting to gain control of our country, our church, and our world is one thing. But to have uncovered this conspiracy in one's own back yard is a great work of God's grace! *Thank you, Lord. Please, guide me as I seek to do Thy will!*

Part III

Paths of Righteousness

1

Six years later...

How can i know god's will for my life?

In the eleven years since Reverend Stephen LaPointe was ordained, he had heard this question dozens of times, mostly from young adults on fire for their faith, trying to discern *exactly* what God wanted them to do. Rarely was the problem a matter of knowing what to do, but of accepting the seemingly mundane task to which God already had called them. Although most of the world appeared oblivious to this, sincere seekers of all ages asked this question, and for Stephen there *was* no greater question.

In the mirror before him, Stephen saw a slightly graying man on the verge of turning forty. Thankfully, the black robe hid his expanding waistline. He affectionately grasped the pewter Celtic preaching cross that had hung from his shoulders for over four hundred sermons. From the sanctuary down the hall, he could hear the organist lead the congregation in the opening refrain of *We Gather Together* as they awaited his entrance.

Eye to eye, he examined himself, and recalled how, fourteen years ago, convinced that God was calling him into the ministry, he had set aside his secular career to enter seminary. When he had read what Jesus had told the rich young ruler—"Go, sell what you have, and give to the poor, and you will have treasure in heaven; and come, follow me"—Stephen knew that Jesus was also talking to him. Now years later, his pastoral calling had been confirmed many times over by pastors, seminary professors, family, and friends, as well as his experiences as a seminary intern, an assistant, and finally the last eight years as a solo pastor.

His years at Red Creek had consisted of hundreds of sermons,

Bible studies, and committee meetings, and a nearly seamless flow of hospital, nursing home, and home visits, spiced with dozens of baptisms, marriages, counseling sessions, and funerals. These demands certainly had made home life at times testy, and Sara had none too often let him know it. Yet, to his satisfaction, Sara had grown into the role she had been expected to play. William was almost ten years old, and had established himself as one of the upcoming stars in basketball and baseball. But at six-and-a-half, Daniel was proving to be their more challenging son.

All in all, though, the years had been good to them, yet Stephen knew that "God's plan for his life" at that moment was to move on. Not because there were any controversies that necessitated his exit, but because he was anxious to start fresh somewhere else, to build on his successes and learn from his mistakes.

In January he had surreptitiously submitted his resume to a list of Congregational churches looking for pastors. In May a letter had arrived from Respite Congregational Church. This slightly larger congregation in upstate New Hampshire had recently lost their pastor and was actively seeking a "young, enthusiastic minister, committed to the Gospel and the Great Commission." Stephen knew of no better self-description, so he applied, interviewed, and preached a candidating sermon. By July he had been hired. He was to begin next Sunday.

Now he only had to go out into the sanctuary and say good-bye.

*   *   *

THE PEOPLE OF RED CREEK had turned out in surprising numbers to bid farewell to their pastor. Most hated to see him leave, because his preaching, teaching, and pastoral leadership had helped the church grow in numbers and enthusiasm. Some were offended that he had turned his back "so soon" on their needs, "just because Red Creek is small and insignificant."

Stephen had just finished preaching his farewell sermon, and the congregation plus visitors were gathered in Singleton Hall to say their good-byes. Adults milled around in groups, some with Stephen and Sara, sipping punch, munching cookies, and reviewing the memories of the past eight years. The teens were clustered off in one corner away from the younger children in the nursery. But two nine-year-olds were off by themselves, cookies and punch in hand.

"What's it like where you're going?" Stacy Horscht said, holding back tears.

"Oh, I don't know," William LaPointe responded. "I've only been to the new church once. It has a large playground with a ballfield and some hoops, and the town has a park with a pool. Our new house is right next to the church."

William had come to know many kids through the church and at school, but none closer than Stacy. When they were younger, their mothers often brought them to Rogers Park to play together. William had grown to feel like a brother to her. He had defended her as her knight in shining armor in their make-believe games, and in real life when Brad, the local bully, tried to push her around. Sports had threatened to come between them, but still through it all, they remained the best of friends. Of all the people saying good-bye, there were no two so sad.

"Sounds great," Stacy said unconvincingly. "Did you meet any of the kids yet?"

"Some at the church. I think there's a few in the neighborhood."

"What's the school like?"

"I don't know. I guess I'll find out tomorrow morning."

"Stacy?" A gruff voice was heard above the din of the crowd.

"I've got to go, William. I'm going to miss you," Stacy said holding out her hand.

"Me, too." He took her hand shyly.

"There you are," Walter Horscht said as he grabbed Stacy and pulled her away. "Come on, we've gotta go."

"'Bye, William. You won't forget me, will you?"

"Of course not."

Walter pulled Stacy through the crowd toward the front exit.

"Helen, please," he said.

Helen was standing with Sara LaPointe, saying their good-byes. Hearing Walter, she leaned forward and embraced Sara. They held hands and, after a few final private words through tears of friendship, they parted.

"But, Daddy, why do we have to go so soon?" Stacy said, struggling to keep up with her father's pace.

"No whining, we've said our good-byes. Now let's go home."

Helen glared silently at Walter as she opened the car door.

"Now don't you start. You know how I feel about Reverend LaPointe. This is the best thing that ever happened to Red Creek. He may be a good preacher, but as I've told you, I don't trust him."

"Walter, whom do you trust?"

He glared at her with a look that said, "How dare you confront me in front of Stacy!"

Helen lowered her glance and entered the car. Stacy got into the back seat, and in silence the family rode home.

2

Respite congregational church was founded in 1796 by the same cluster of nonconformist families who established the town of Respite. Having become exasperated by the Federalist politics of post-Revolutionary Boston, they made their second escape from "tyranny." The first escape had been three generations earlier when their ancestors sailed from England to the Colonies. Later, the great-grand children, finding their lives, livelihood, and faith compromised by the chicanery of power-hungry politicians jostling for position in the new United States of America, sought another "new Jerusalem" in the wilderness of extreme northern New Hampshire—a "respite" from the "times that try men's souls."

The first church building had been a log cabin that could barely hold the five original families. A continuous influx of discontented settlers had forced first an addition and then an entirely new structure by the mid-eighteen hundreds. In 1896, a suspicious fire destroyed this edifice one day before its centennial celebration. Now ninety-nine years later, some families still hold grudges against others whose ancestors had been the suspected arsonists. By 1901, a new larger sanctuary was completed, and except for new paint and a few minor repairs, this was the same structure in which two hundred thirty people sat awaiting the first sermon of their new pastor.

"Heart of my own heart, whatever befall,
Still be my Vision, O Ruler of all.

"Amen," the congregation sang out with gusto as they completed their new pastor's second favorite hymn, *Be Thou My Vision*.

"Good morning," Stephen said to a sea of new faces.

"Good morning, pastor," the congregation responded in various shades of unison.

"Let me say first that my family, seated before me," he said pointing down to Sara, William, and a fidgety Daniel in the first pew, "and I are thrilled to be here with you this morning." He looked at Sara for confirmation, and was glad to receive a loving nod. She had resisted their first move from Sleepy Meadow to Red Creek, but this time she was more than ready—for new faces, a new neighborhood, and perhaps a less demanding, more understanding body of believers.

"For my text, I have chosen what I consider my life's verse. This Scripture was recited at my ordination, and it stood as my text for my first sermons at both Sleepy Meadow and Red Creek. As I joyfully contemplate accepting the responsibilities as your pastor, I can think of no passage that more clearly describes our being called together. Please follow along as I read Proverbs chapter three, verses five and six."

Having read these verses hundreds of times since his conversion more than fifteen years before, Stephen lifted his gaze out to his new flock, and recited from memory, "'Trust in the Lord with all your heart, and lean not unto your own insight. In all your ways acknowledge him, and he will make straight your paths.' Before I begin, please join me in prayer."

He watched his new congregation bow their heads exactly as his previous two congregations had done, as if they had all attended the same school of Sunday piety. As he led them in beseeching God for guidance and inspiration, for open minds and hearts, he also prayed that this new pastorate would have as many blessings as the last.

Red Creek had had its unique trials, especially with the small band of rabble-rousers led by Horscht who increasingly questioned his sincerity. In general, however, the congregation had responded well to his leadership, teaching, and preaching. All in all, he looked back with contentment. Standing in this old yet new pulpit, he prayed that this new family of believers would indeed be a *respite* where his own family could grow in faith and love.

As he prayed, he noticed a small brass plaque fastened to the top of the pulpit facing him directly. It stated simply, WE WOULD SEE JESUS.

"And may our attention this morning be not so much on the speaker," Stephen said in closing, "but upon Jesus, for it is He who we have come to see. In His Name we pray, Amen."

Seated in a pew close to the front were Adrian and Ginny McBride. In their early thirties, these two had become, through their recent adult conversions, like reborn children. They had liked Reverend Wilkins, whose preaching and personal attention had turned their hearts toward Jesus. With bewilderment, they had watched the battles within the church destroy his leadership and confidence, and now they were anxious to hear whether this new pastor would continue to feed their spiritual hunger.

"My sermon this morning will consist of three short sections. In the second section, I will summarize the goals I have for our first year together, and then follow this with a brief reflection on this great text from proverbs. But first, I want to state right up front the top two priorities of my life."

For weeks Stephen had pondered how he should begin this new pastorate differently than he had his last. The conundrum over clerical dress that had so paralyzed him at the outset of Red Creek was now but a humorous memory—he was still embarrassed that he had been so bewildered by such an insignificant issue. For a much longer period, however, he remained perplexed by the conflict of opinions that exists between otherwise sincere Bible-believing Christians. In time, though, this too had passed, for the endless flood of pastoral demands pushed this well back out of consciousness. Now he was determined to make two issues clear from the start.

"First, I want you to understand this about your new pastor. My number one commitment and priority is to Jesus Christ, my Lord and Savior. There are no compromises here. I believe as the Scriptures teach, which I accept," he said, holding up his leather bound Bible, "as the inerrant Word of God, the one firm foundation for our lives. I believe that Jesus is the Son of the Living God; that

He was conceived by the Holy Spirit in the womb of Mary, a humble Jewish girl; that He was born in a manger in Bethlehem; that He was baptized in the River Jordan by John the Baptist; that He preached the good news of the kingdom of God; that He healed the sick, exorcised demons, and performed miracles to demonstrate His glory as the Son of God; that He was betrayed by one of His own Apostles; that He was tried, condemned, scourged, crucified, died, and buried for our sins; and that He rose again for our salvation. I believe that you and I are saved by grace through faith in Jesus, that our sins are forgiven, and if we accept Him as our Lord and Savior, we will one day stand before God whiter than snow, washed clean by the blood of the Lamb, by the righteousness of Christ. I don't want you to have any questions about where I stand on the Gospel."

Other than an occasional cough, the rustling of a few hymnals, and two boys in the back battling with spit wads, he heard and saw nothing that indicated major dissent, so he continued. "Do you know what is posted here on this ancient pulpit? Some time in the past, a brass plaque was attached to tell me exactly what you want from me. The plaque states simply, 'We would see Jesus.' Well, I promise you that by God's grace Jesus is what you'll get.

"Hearing no complaints," he paused to look around quizzically, but only drew laughs of support, "I must also state a second commitment and priority. I presume that there will be no complaints about this, either, but it is important that I make this perfectly clear from the start. My second commitment, of course, is to my wife Sara and to my sons, William and Daniel. I believe that just as God called me into the ministry, that He called Sara and me together as husband and wife. The covenant we made to each other in our wedding vows was just as Jesus stated, 'The two shall become one.' The pastorate involves many demands, as I'm sure you are aware, but I must never allow these demands to compromise my family. If I fail as a father and a husband, than I have surely failed you as your pastor. The Apostle Paul commanded his congregations to 'Imitate me as I imitate Christ,' and this is the same expectation that I accept: I am to give you a model to imitate. So, I am asking you to help me remember that, next to Jesus, my first priority is to Sara and my family."

Stephen studied his new congregation. He was mostly greeted

with confirming smiles, and an occasional elbow from one spouse to the other. Sporadically, however, he saw blank expressions that he tallied as possible votes of dissent. This he would find out soon enough.

"With this clearly established, let me now review a few of the goals I have for our first year together."

*　　　*　　　*

THE PARISH HALL of this 90-year-old church was in the basement, actually the first floor. To enter the second-floor sanctuary, worshipers ascended a wide and long course of wooden front steps. This arrangement gave the sensation of ascending into the presence of God, as well as portraying to the non-church-going neighbors what the holy were doing on Sunday.

To enter the parish hall, one either descended a front interior staircase or went around and in through a side door. It was from the latter that a bevy of children had escaped from the mostly adult reception, and with them had come Sara.

She had excused herself to keep an eye on the boys, but actually she needed fresh air. The September heat wave had only increased the mustiness of the crowded hall. The thought of inhaling the incubated residue of nearly a hundred years of church socials, receptions, Bible studies, and committee meetings had driven her from her third new-church reception.

She was happy for Stephen, and felt he deserved this new opportunity to use his gifts. Through the closing door she could see him surrounded by members of his new flock—*their* new flock— laughing as he struck a strange pose, probably the punch line of some joke. Smiling, she said to herself, *This was the right choice, for both of us.*

Outside it was a beautiful day. The white clapboard church sat on a hillside surrounded by a mixture of oak, maple, beech, and fir trees, whose emerging autumn colors glowed amidst the pervasive green. Sara glanced upward at the tall steeple that seemed less like a pointed spire than an infinitely long pathway that receded into eternity. She closed her eyes as the clear morning air quickened her spirit. Silently she prayed, *Lord, please, may this third try be a charm. May this be the place and the people where I finally can grow to accept—to love—my role as Stephen's wife. And please, may our marriage...*

"Excuse me, Mrs. LaPointe?"

Sara broke from her meditative pose. "Yes?"

Standing cautiously before her was a young couple dressed conservatively, he in a dark navy-blue suit and she in a yellow ankle-length print dress. Their picture-book beauty startled Sara.

"We're Adrian and Ginny McBride, and we just wanted to welcome you to Respite," Adrian said as the three shook hands. "That's our eight-year-old son Sammy on the swing."

"That's our two boys on either side of him," Sara said.

In awkward silence, they watched the children play, until Adrian spoke again.

"Ginny and I have been members of Respite Church all our lives. We came up through all the church programs and were confirmed together. After being high school sweethearts, we were married in the sanctuary."

A glint in Ginny's eyes shouted the continuing intimacy of their love.

"But it wasn't until a couple of years ago that our faith really came alive," Ginny added.

"That's very nice," Sara said.

"We just wanted you to know that, well, with all the divisions in our church, we want to do all we can to help you and Pastor LaPointe feel at home."

"Divisions?" Sara asked with guarded surprise.

"Nothing different, I'm sure, from what happens in every church. We just have a number of groups that can't see eye to eye on certain issues of theology. Ginny and I love the Lord, and try to stay detached from all this. Anyway, we just want you and the pastor to know that we are here to help in any way we can to bring healing to our church."

"Why, thank you, Adrian and Ginny," Sara said, letting Adrian shake her hand again, "I'm sure Stephen will appreciate your help and benefit from your experience here."

"Please don't hesitate to call us," Adrian said, as they excused themselves.

Stephen didn't tell me we were coming into a divided church, she thought with disappointment as she watched this couple retrieve their son and head to their car. Returning her gaze to the spire pointing upwards to the abode of God, she asked, *Lord, what have you brought us into this time?*

3

Seven years later...

STEPHEN THREW ASIDE the pale green curtains and cracked the sole window in his church study. Though the late winter cold front was adding another layer of powder to the already foot-deep drifts, he preferred a cold draft to the room's mildewed ambiance. Of his three pastor's studies, this was by far the worst. From the moment he first entered this antiquated room some seven years ago, he vowed to have it remodeled, but like so many other urgent tasks, it had been lost in committee.

Crossing to his desk, he grimaced for the hundredth time at the enormous painting on the wall behind his chair—a black velvet, fluorescent portrait of Jesus that some well-respected, deceased member had bequeathed to the pastor's study. In the eyes of the church, therefore, it was untouchable, but Stephen was determined to find some way to have it tactfully removed. So far, his only strategy was to sneak it out and then claim that someone must have broken in and stolen it. He knew, however, that no one would believe this, because it was the last thing that anyone would steal from this church.

Turning his back to the glowing Jesus, he sat to tackle the growing pile of letters, memos, and emails, but decided to retrieve his phone messages first. One from his dentist, another from the board chairman, another from a lightning rod salesman, all of which he noted quickly and deleted.

Then there was another message more in line with his "calling."

"Hello, Reverent LaPointe. This is Adrian McBride. Could we set up a time to meet? Ginny and I...well, I just need to talk to you about what's happening to Ginny. It's tearing us apart. Please call me at work if you can. Thanks."

I was wondering how long it would take before he called, Stephen thought. Rumors had been circulating in this close-knit community. There were no specifics, but plenty of speculation. Ever since their spiritual awakening two years before Stephen had arrived, the McBrides had become obsessively active in the church, Adrian serving as a deacon on several committees, while Ginny taught adult Sunday school classes. But then last fall, Ginny began excusing herself from all responsibilities. To the gossips, her most noticeable quirk was her uncharacteristic aloofness. She had always been the life of every party, but now she only stood back and watched, as if she were "too good for the likes of us."

To his overflowing to-do list, Stephen added, *Call Adrian McBride,* but his conscience nagged him to make the call now.

"I've got to start my sermon prep," he replied out loud to no one in particular.

From a pile of unfinished business, he extracted the sermon folder that read Matthew 16:13-20. Inside were his notes from the sermon that he had preached on this text nearly eight years before at Red Creek entitled, "Who Do *YOU* Say that I am?" Then it had been as a part of a year-long preaching series through the first Gospel, but now he had chosen this specifically to address the crisis that had been dividing Respite Church. With coffee in one hand and the old sermon in the other, Stephen retired to a cracked-leather lounge chair by the window.

Assuming that his previous exegetical work and conclusions were correct, he forsaw no obstacles to making this old sermon fit the present. Nevertheless, he would first reread the biblical text, and then give the Holy Spirit room for any new inspiration:

> Now when Jesus came into the district of Caesarea Philippi, he began asking his disciples, saying, "Who do people say that the Son of Man is?"
>
> And they said, "Some say John the Baptist; some, Elijah; and others, Jeremiah, or one of the prophets."
>
> He said to them, "But who do you say that I am?"
>
> And Simon Peter answered and said, "Thou art the Christ, the Son of the Living God."
>
> And Jesus answered and said to him, "Blessed are you, Simon Barjona, because flesh and blood did not

reveal this to you, but my Father who is in heaven. And I also say to you that you are Peter, and upon this rock I will build My church, and the gates of Hades shall not overpower it. I will give you the keys of the kingdom of heaven; and whatever you shall bind on earth shall have been bound in heaven, and whatever you shall loose on earth shall have been loosed in heaven.

Then he warned the disciples that they should tell no one that he was the Christ.

When Stephen interviewed for this position seven years ago, he had learned of the squabble that had driven Reverend Wilkins to an early retirement. In the late eighties, several couples attended a charismatic renewal conference and had come back bent on revitalizing the church. Their enthusiasm was contagious, and within a few weeks more than fifty people were attending the weekly Prayer and Praise meetings. At first Wilkins had welcomed their fervor. They were accomplishing overnight what he had failed to instill in fifteen years of preaching and chastening. But slowly troubles began to surface. Around one spirit-filled layman emerged an organization of lay leaders under which other church members were to be grouped into cells. Criteria for membership were established and strictly enforced. In time new theologies began to crop up that questioned the salvation of anyone who didn't exhibit some extraordinary spiritual gift.

When Wilkins contested their ideas, the leaders turned against him and challenged his authority. After months of bickering and backbiting, the congregation split in two: one half forming a new home church under the leadership of the unordained charismatic leader, while the other half remained under Wilkins. In time the scenario grew even crazier when the leader of the home church left his wife of twelve years to marry the wife of another man in the fellowship, and yet continued in leadership—claiming that this was "God's perfect Will" for the two families affected and for the community. Some of the separated branch became disenchanted and returned to Respite church, but others remained to this day enraptured by the bold wisdom of their inspired prophet.

In time, Wilkins realized that he was incapable of restoring order, so he resigned, bought a fishing boat, and retired to tend lobster pots off the north coast of Maine. Six months later, Stephen became the new pastor.

Now after seven years of patient, cautious, charitable pastoral care, Stephen finally felt that he had won enough trust from the congregation to take bold steps towards rebuilding their unity in Christ. He had hoped to accomplish this long before now, but every attempt had been like trying to tame an abused dog. Just when he thought he had made progress, some disgruntled member would snap at him with a bitter complaint at a committee meeting or behind his back.

Finally, though, even the most wounded of the members seemed ready for renewal, so to begin, he had chosen this text. From the culture, through the media, and especially from the novel accusations of the self-acclaimed prophet down the street, the faithful remnant of Respite Congregational had become confused about many aspects of their faith. With this text, Stephen wanted them to hear afresh Simon Peter's startling, unreserved, bold proclamation of what the Father had revealed in his heart: that Jesus was the Messiah, the Son of the living God.

He sipped his coffee. At first he saw nothing in his notes that needed adjustment. The sermon followed his usual structure: an introduction with a hook to capture the congregation's attention, followed by an analysis of the text, which flowed into three specific points for the congregation to "take home" for their spiritual edification.

Out of the side of his eye, he noticed the fluorescent Jesus glaring at him. The smirk in His smile reminded Stephen of the Mona Lisa.

I wonder whether old Mr. Weatherby willed this as a sincere gift or a sick joke? Stephen thought.

He returned to his notes, and sat up with a start.

Why did I devote so much of my sermon on the anti-Catholic disclaimers? he wondered. *Had there been a particular reason?*

In one long section, which probably had taken five minutes of pulpit time, he had expounded in detail the Greek discrepancies between Simon's newly-given name and the "boulder" of Simon's faith upon which Jesus would build His Church. Stephen then had downplayed Simon Peter's reception of the "keys of the kingdom" and the authority to "bind and loose" by drawing the congregation's attention to where Jesus later gave this same authority to the other Apostles.

As were his present intentions, Stephen's three points had examined the many contradictory opinions about Jesus in the world around them, the bold truth of Peter's confession as revealed by the Father, and finally the question: who do they themselves believe Jesus to be?

With relief, Stephen concluded that his old sermon was workable. *But what about the anti-Catholic disclaimers?* He had probably included these in his Red Creek sermon with little reflection—this was what he had learned in seminary and subsequently never questioned. *Red Creek did have lots of ex-Catholic members, but is this a major issue here at Respite?*

His coffee was cold, so he went down the hall to the church kitchen for a fresh cup. On his return, he paused by a shelf that contained his New Testament commentaries. Ever since seminary, the size of his personal library had grown in proportion to the increases in his pastoral salary—actually out of proportion because his salary had risen only slightly. Through the steam exuding from his coffee, he scanned his collection, and noticed a commentary he had never read. It had come as a part of a large collection he had purchased at a clergy widow's auction. He didn't recognize the author, but nonetheless decided to examine what this new voice might say about his text.

Comfortably back in his lounge chair, he turned directly to chapter sixteen and began reading. The author began by defending from Scripture how Simon Peter was the first in authority among the Apostles. Given this context, the author then began remarking on the significance of Simon's new name, Peter. He first pointed out that in the Bible, a person was given a new name by God to indicate a new status, like Abram to Abraham, or Jacob to Israel. He then emphasized that in the Old Testament the name "rock" was only used as a name for God, and never for a human being.

Stephen paused to challenge this, but couldn't think of any exceptions. Knowing that Jesus wasn't one to make meaningless gestures, he wondered, *OK, why would Jesus give Simon a new name used previously only in reference to God?*

After listing numerous reasons that the phrase "this rock" could only have referred to Simon and not to Jesus, or merely Simon's faith, the author directly addressed the argument from Greek grammar that Stephen had always used to attack Catholic claims. The author wrote:

> The first thing to note is that even though the New Testament was mostly written in Greek, Christ certainly would have spoken Aramaic, the common language of Palestine at the time. In that language the word for rock is *kepha*. We find evidence of this several times in Scripture when Simon Peter is referred to as "Cephas." What Jesus most likely said, then, was thus: "Thou art *kepha*, and upon this *kepha* I will build my Church." Consequently there was no distinction whatsoever between the two references to "rock."

That Jesus had not spoken in Greek was, of course, no surprise to Stephen, but until that moment, it had slipped his mind in connection to this verse. His mind raced. He stared at the paragraph, scanning the words, his attention darting from phrase to phrase.

"But why then was this Aramaic word translated differently into Greek?" he said aloud. He continued reading:

> In Aramaic the word *kepha* has the same ending whether it refers to a rock or is used as a man's name. In Greek, though, the word for rock, *petra*, is feminine in gender. The translator could use it for the second appearance of *kepha* in the sentence, but not for the first, because it would be inappropriate to give a man a feminine name. So the translator put a masculine ending on it, and there was *Petros*, which happened to be a preexisting word meaning a small stone. Therefore, any significance concocted from the difference of these two Greek spellings is meaningless.

Stephen sat motionless. A cold draft billowed the green curtains. He rose to close the window, and stood gazing out at the snow-covered cemetery. The weathered headstones of eight generations of church members were only half visible. To the majority of humanity, these paragraphs were inconsequential. Only a minute percentage of the world's population were even interested in reading this biblical scholar. For Stephen, however, it was as if the simple truth of this scholar's few words had opened before him a horrific chasm of doubt.

Two things became immediately and plainly clear: the argument that Stephen had learned in seminary and proclaimed ever since— to hundreds of people who trusted him—was utterly groundless. Even more significantly, however, was his realization that here was a perfectly valid interpretation of Scripture that was contrary to what he, his friends, and his seminary professors insisted was the sole interpretation of the infallible Bible.

There it was again.

For several years, he had been able to squelch that nagging voice, to force it back out of consciousness and ignore its charges. Over and over he had scourged himself with the verse, "No one who puts his hand to the plow and looks back is fit for the kingdom of God," until he could re-focus without concern on his pastoral work.

But the voice was back. *How can the Bible alone be a trustworthy foundation of truth if so many sincere believers come up with such defensible yet contradictory opinions FROM THE SAME TEXT?*

Stephen looked down at the commentary in his hand, and read the author's name: *Fr. Eloisious Barns, S.J.*

"A Catholic priest! No wonder."

But so what? Is his argument valid? That's the point.

Stephen opened the book to reread the paragraphs and then farther into the contextual sections. Setting the book aside, he began to pace.

Yes, it was valid, he concluded. *I may not agree with the implications he draws about Petrine supremacy, but the point is, his interpretation of the text is at least as valid as mine. Therefore, I can never stand in front of any congregation and declare my old argument without impunity.*

He grabbed his sermon notes.

What am I to do with this? I can't merely repeat it, and it's too late to change—the text and title are written in stone in the bulletin. The only solution is to focus on the substance of Simon's confession, and avoid the anti-Catholic disclaimers.

The telephone rang. Reaching to retrieve it, the inner voice taunted him: *But how can you be certain that anything you preach from this text is true, untainted by your prejudice, your ignorance, or your laziness?*

"Hello?" Stephen answered with a shake of his head.

"Hello, honey. How you doing?" came Sara's welcome voice.

"Oh, just fine," Stephen lied.

"Lunch is ready."

"Great. I'll be right home. 'Bye. Love you."

He hung up and reached for his overcoat. Again the eyes of the fluorescent Jesus caught his attention, but this time the smirk seemed to be gone. Instead, Jesus was peering deeply into him as if calling him accountable for every thought, every conviction.

Stephen turned off the lights, closed the door behind him, and escaped.

*   *   *

THE FACTORY BREAK ROOM appeared to be rolling as if adrift at sea. This was but an illusion caused by the violent swaying of a ceiling lamp, not from some act of nature but an accident of Walter's exuberance.

For a moment, this silenced his argument, while his audience of two scrutinized him through the gray cigarette haze. Ignoring them, Walter grabbed for the light, missing it once, and then resumed his attack.

"But it does make a difference. The Bible says that in the End Times false prophets will deceive the faithful. Wolves in sheep's clothing will infiltrate our churches, corrupting the Gospel."

"Mr. Horscht, listen," said the young technician, Walter's primary target. "Sure, the Bible does say that, but there's no proof that we're living in *the* End Times."

Walter glared at this newest employee. The thought of recapping all the evidence was debilitating.

"Jon," Walter replied with constraint, "the question is not whether it is *the* End Times. Jesus warned us to be ready at all times. The point is that false teachers are everywhere. They pollute our lives over the radio and television, they control the newspapers and the politicians; they even preach liberal trash from our church pulpits."

"Jeez, Walter, calm down," said the other co-worker, Walter's elder both in age and seniority. "You see a conspiracy behind every rock."

"There is a conspiracy," Walter shouted, standing up. "A conspiracy to capture our souls for Hell, and behind it all is the anti-Christ and his horde: the Pope and the Roman Catholic Church."

"That does it." A vicious snarl rose from a third co-worker who up until then had been sitting with his back to the others, across the room by the vending machines. He shot from his seat and charged. Walter raised his hands in defense, but not quickly enough. The man, a full six inches taller and larger in every dimension, caught Walter on the jaw with a solid right, sending him back, toppling over his chair and overturning the water cooler.

Shaking it off, Walter jumped up to retaliate. He blocked another right, and then buried his own into his opponent's stomach. As the man buckled, Walter lifted him off his feet with an upper left.

"You damned papist," Walter yelled as the door behind him opened.

The plant manager surveyed the scene and said, "That's it, Walter. You're fired. Clean out your locker and get out."

"But he hit me first...."

"I don't care. This is the third time you've caused a fight with your fanaticism. You're through. Get out."

With that, the manager stepped back and pointed to the exit.

Walter turned to his co-workers for support, but they looked away. The man he had sent into the vending machines only managed a faint smile.

"You'll all be sorry for this," Walter retorted, turning directly into his boss.

"Oh, you gonna fight me now?" he said pushing Walter with his chest.

"No, of course not, sir," Walter said backing down. He turned and walked silently down the dark corridor very much alone.

The locker room was empty and drab in its institutional gray. Seeing no one, Walter cried out in anguish, "Lord God, how could you let this happen to me?"

He turned the combination, and opened what for over eight years had been his private sanctuary amidst a world lost in sin. Whatever hassle he might face in the plant or at home, one visit to this haven of grace was enough to rekindle his spiritual resolve.

Carefully, prayerfully, he removed to a New England Patriots sportbag a wrinkled print of Jesus, blue-eyes, long brown hair, full beard, and smiling. This had formed the focal point of his shrine. He then removed three photos of Christian men he sought to emulate: the crusade evangelist who had converted him in 1988; the ex-priest Reverend Harmon, who stood as his anti-Catholic knight in spiritual armor; and a photo of himself with old Pastor Smith. He placed these with reverence beside Jesus. From the top shelf, he then transferred a box containing his arsenal of tracts, books, and tapes. As the title of a tract about the coming judgment of fire caught his attention, he resumed his lament.

"Was I not speaking Your truth? Was I not following Your lead? What am I to tell Helen? How will I provide for them?"

He thought of the Old Testament prophets, ridiculed when their messages were demeaning to God's chosen people. He thought of Stephen, the first Christian martyr. And he thought of Jesus: *"Blessed are you when men revile you and persecute you and utter all kinds of evil against you falsely on my account. Rejoice and be glad, for your reward is great in heaven, for so men persecuted the prophets who were before you."*

Walter stood chastised in his self-pity by the words of this Beatitude. From inside the new sanctuary of his sportbag, the eyes of Jesus watched him. He remembered another word of warning: *"When they persecute you in one town, flee to the next; for truly, I say to you, you will not have gone through all the towns of Israel, before the Son of man comes."*

"Are You saying, Jesus, that You are calling me to move on? To another job? To another place?" He searched the eyes of his Savior for an answer. "Or could You possibly be calling me into full-time ministry?"

Walter stood up as if a light from above had flooded the room in brilliant clarity.

"Whatever You want, Jesus," he said.

But what about Helen and Stacy? came an inner warning. *What about your mortgage? Your bills? And you have no training?*

"Whatever You want, Jesus."

He closed his bag and his locker, and left, "kicking the dust from his shoes," a soldier with new orders.

4

Aᴠᴛᴇʀ ᴀ ʀᴇǫᴜᴇsᴛ, a command, and a threat, William and Daniel finally acquiesced to clearing away the evening dishes. With the hope of catching a few minutes of peaceful conversation, Stephen led his beloved wife with their coffees into the living room. He made straight for his comfortable lounger to the right of the fireplace leaving Sara their new couch to the left. It was obvious, however, by her placement and posture, that she had expected him to sit beside her, but all day he had yearned for this rare moment in his favorite chair.

Without the boys, the tension from dinner was more acute, making it difficult for either to begin. Finally, through the clamor of rattling dishes, Stephen broke the ice.

"Listen, honey, I'm sorry about tonight's meeting."

"It's just that you'll be gone all day tomorrow," Sara said. "You're always off to some board meeting, counseling session, or hospital call, while I'm left home minding the boys."

Stephen sat looking into his cup, wondering how to diffuse this too frequent scenario before it escalated out of control. *If only for once we could simply discuss this. When will she accept that this is a part of my job, and though my trip involves helping members from our last church, it's still a part of my calling?* Stephen knew, however, from fifteen years of marriage, that whenever he scheduled a trip away, Sara invariable sent him forth with a blow-up. *If I could, for once, respond with compassion. Lord, please, please help me.*

"Hey, that doesn't go in there!" shouted William from the kitchen.

"It does too! That's where it was before dinner!"

"Boys," snapped Stephen, "Cut it out and keep it down!"

He studied Sara. The atmosphere was such that no matter what he said, he knew they would argue. He slowly rose and sat down next to her, encircling her shoulders with his left arm. With his other hand, he gently cradled her clenched fists. At first, she pulled back, but then she melted. She began to cry, and Stephen pulled her over into his lap. He held her tightly as her body wrenched with sobs. Stephen had anticipated that Sara would soften under his initiative, but not to this degree.

"Honey, what…what is it? What's wrong?" He held her tighter wondering whether in his cursed busyness there was something else he had missed.

"Oh, Stephen," she said through her tears, "no, nothing out of the ordinary. I suppose it's just the wrong time of the month on top of it all. I just get frustrated with you're always gone in the evenings, and then whenever you're planning to leave town I panic." She held him tighter while another surge of tears and sobbing passed. "Please, please, don't mind me. I'll be all right. I know you need to go. Please give Irene and Elsie a big hug for me. I miss them."

"Sara, I wish I could cancel tonight's board meeting, but you know I can't. I…sometimes it seems that there just isn't enough time to catch a breath." He paused and then continued. "You know this minister's job is not all it's cracked up to be. It's almost impossible to be a good father, a good husband, and a good minister. Sometimes I think if I could do anything else I would, but…well, you know I've been called to this."

"I know, and I don't want you to change. Please, I'm sorry, let's have a good night together."

"Tell you what, honey. I'll get home as soon as I can, and then we can have the rest of the evening to ourselves."

"And while you're fighting the battles with the board," she said, smiling, "I'll send the boys upstairs to read while I cozy-up in front of the TV. My favorite movie is on at nine, *An Affair to Remember* with Cary Grant and Deborah Kerr."

"Hey, I'll do what I can to get the meeting over early so I can watch it with you. Keep the wine chilled!" With this they embraced.

"Come on, you two. Go upstairs if you're going to get all gushy," William said in mock reproach.

"All right, all right. Is everything picked up in the kitchen?" Stephen said.

The routine was back to normal. Sara went to the kitchen to supervise while Stephen retrieved his briefcase from the study. After a farewell kiss, he left for his brief walk across the snow-covered churchyard.

That was some kind of breakthrough tonight, he told himself. *If only all our disagreements could end so well.*

But as he hurdled a drift, the words of a Harry Chapin song from the seventies haunted him:

> *My son turned ten just the other day.*
> *He said "Thanks for the ball, Dad, come on let's play.*
> *Can you teach me to throw?" I said, "Not today,*
> *I've got a lot to do." He said, "That's OK."*
> *And his smile never dimmed and he said as he turned away,*
> *"I'm gonna be like him, yeah,*
> *You know I'm gonna be like him."*
> *And the cat's in the cradle and the silver spoon;*
> *Little boy blue and the man in the moon.*
> *"When you coming home, Dad?" "I don't know when,*
> *But we'll get together then, son,*
> *You know we'll have a good time then."*

*　　　　*　　　　*

"REVEREND LAPOINTE, it looks like all are in attendance except Adrian McBride, so if you would open with prayer, we can get this meeting started," George Patnode, the board president, said, striking the gavel and rising from his chair, initiating the rising of the rest of the board. While most were dressed conservatively in shirt and tie, a dressy sweater, or a sport coat, George wore a pair of gray sweats.

"Let us pray. Father, grant us Your wisdom..." Stephen began as he mentally reviewed the various projects and programs slated for the evening. Most were perfunctory and posed no problems. The only line item that gave him any apprehension was the pending vote to participate in this year's ecumenical Good Friday service. Thankfully, this was the last item on the agenda.

Adrian's absence also distracted him. *I guess I should have called him.*

"Thank you, pastor, and sorry about the sweats. The church basketball team had a semi-final game against Good Hope Methodist. We won in overtime, so I didn't have time to change."

"Or to shower," quipped Larry Howe, the self-appointed board jester whose comic relief and occasionally poignant questions added levity and stimulation to otherwise boring meetings.

"Yes, that's true," George replied, "but maybe it'll help us get done on time. Phil could you read the minutes from the last meeting?"

*   *   *

EAGERLY, Sara prepared for her quiet, intimate evening alone with her husband. As soon as he had left, she shot upstairs for a quick shower and then slipped into a comfortable yet not unflattering nightgown. Covering this with a blue terrycloth robe, she threatened the boys once again to get upstairs and read.

She then scurried around picking up miscellaneous items scattered everywhere by everyone in the house. Her emotions began rising over the family's insensitivity to her constant need to clean up after them, but then she exclaimed, "No! I will not ruin our evening." She forced herself to "suck it up," as William's coach might say, and resumed cleaning without complaint.

Sara was reaching into the utility closet for the vacuum when the doorbell rang. Unlike at Red Creek, their nearest neighbors here had remained quite standoffish, so they received few evening visitors. She glanced at the clock. Seven thirty. It was dark outside, and though she knew this was irrational, she nevertheless always felt apprehensive when she and the boys were alone in the evening.

Quietly, she closed the utility room door. The doorbell rang again—this time twice, with a tempo of impatience. As she moved slowly through the kitchen, she pocketed a small paring knife that was lying on the counter. At the front door cautiously, she peered out through the magnified viewer. It was an unidentifiable man facing away toward the road. Sara waited anxiously for him to turn, and when he did, she recognized his distorted profile as Adrian McBride. With curious relief, she opened the door.

"Hello, Adrian, what a surprise."

Seeing Sara in her robe, Adrian backed off. "Oh, Mrs. LaPointe. I'm terribly sorry. It must be later than I thought."

"No, I just put this on to relax," Sara said,

"Mrs. LaPointe, I'm sorry to bother you and the pastor in the evening, but I heard he was going out of town and I've been trying to see him. I know how busy he is, but there's something I need to discuss with him."

"I'm sorry, Adrian, but he's not home. He's at the board meeting."

"Oh, Lord, I can't believe I forgot," he said with a hard hand to the forehead. "I guess this whole thing has got me so riled up…"

Sara could list the many reasons it was inappropriate to invite Adrian in. Since their first conversation at the initial church reception, Sara had had few substantive conversations with either Adrian or Ginny. Their paths had crossed many times at Sunday worship and other church functions, but she figured it was their overt enthusiasm that compelled her to keep her distance—their assumption that they and she were on the same page spiritually brought out her base feelings of inadequacy.

Nonetheless, like most in the community, she was intrigued by the rumors.

"Please, Adrian, why don't you at least step in for a moment out of the cold."

Adrian hesitated as his pastor's wife, clad in her house coat, held the door open for him, but then he accepted her invitation.

Closing the door behind him, she asked, "Is there anything perhaps I can do?"

"I'm not sure, Mrs. LaPointe," Adrian said awkwardly.

"Here let me take your coat, and please call me Sara. Make yourself comfortable in the living room while I run up stairs for a minute." Seeing his discomfort, she added, "The boys are upstairs doing their homework. Would you like a cup of coffee?"

"That would be fine," he said relinquishing his coat.

Sara hung Adrian's "Sunday-go-to-meeting" overcoat on a peg near the door. After fourteen years the custom still held true: first time visitors into the pastor's domain always overdressed—*as if we would otherwise be offended.* Sara wished this custom would end, for she yearned to have normal friends who treated her like a normal person.

Handing him a coffee, she said, "Please, make yourself comfortable, and I'll be right back."

"Thank you…Sara," Adrian answered.

Walking toward the fireplace, Adrian examined the room for clues into the private life of his pastor. Above the couch was a large painting of green, storm driven waves crashing upon a rocky shoreline.

A brass plaque on the bottom corner indicated that it was from a studio in Rockport.

Turning toward the fireplace, he was startled by a large portrait of Jesus hanging above the mantel. It was a reproduction of an ancient picture he had seen on the cover of one of his wife's books. In Jesus' left hand He clasped an ornately decorated book, while His right hand was raised in a strange position, with two fingers pointing upward and the other two folded under his thumb.

Adrian backed away, puzzled to find this in his pastor's home. He chose a chair near the warmth of the fire.

"I've been told that your family is one of the oldest in the congregation?" Sara asked as she reentered the room, clothed in the sweater and slacks she had only recently removed. She sat on the couch across from him.

"Yes, we've always been members here. My great-great-great-grandfather supposedly helped build the original church. I must admit that when family members gather they talk as if this were *their* church and no one else's. It can get embarrassing, especially when they're oblivious to non-family church members dining with them. I suppose you've already been forewarned about us?"

Sitting directly across from him, Sara was distracted by his handsome, strong, and winsome features. It was obvious how the rumormongers might lustfully suspect infidelity. Everything about his deep brown eyes, neatly brushed-back brown hair, charming smile, and soft cleft chin bespoke of someone with reason to be conceited. It was his self-effacing manner, however, that made it all so alluring. She fought to stay focused.

"Actually, Adrian, several concerned members did caution us about the supposed influence your family wields, but Stephen and I have long since concluded that it is often those giving the warnings that we should fear most. Anyway, I'm glad you stopped by," *as long as you're gone by the time Stephen gets home.*

"So, please, is there any way I can help?"

Hesitantly, nervously, he set his coffee down on the long table that separated them, and began. "How should I begin? It may seem like a small thing to you, but it's tearing our marriage apart. I don't know who to turn to, and Ginny…well, Ginny tries to explain it all to me, but I just can't…I can't accept it."

"What do you mean? Please, tell me, *what* can't you accept?"

Adrian began to speak more calmly about the crisis he had never dreamed would touch his marriage—a crisis he could not stop.

*   *   *

"But chad," George said to the youngest of the board members, a representative of the senior high youth group. Much to the consternation of the older board members, Chad had spiked bleached hair and an earring. But since he was the first string varsity quarterback, a star basketball forward, an honors student, and quite handsome to boot, the board put up with his unorthodox appearance.

"We appreciate your thoughts, and know that it would be a great drawing card to bring other youth to your meetings. Nevertheless, I don't think that we could swing the congregation on installing a sand-pit volleyball court, at least right now."

Another board member, recognized as the church's resident jock, gave a thumb's up to Chad, looking around with an encouraging yet comical look.

"And besides," George continued, "the Theresa Noble Sewing Society would have a cow if we installed a volleyball court before we remodeled the parlor, which they've been harping on for years." *En masse* the board laughed in knowing agreement.

"Not to mention the pastor's study," Stephen added with a smirk.

Again the board laughed, shamefaced, and even Chad nodded, conceding that it was a dead issue.

"But seriously, we will leave your suggestion on the books for future consideration," George said. "All right, any other new business?" With all twelve members showing signs of anxious boredom, he concluded, "Hearing none, Pastor, would you share your proposed changes for the new members' class?"

"Sure, George."

Rising he noted that the clock was pushing eight forty-five, and he envisioned Sara waiting impatiently in front of the television.

"We've just completed the fourth new members' class since I arrived, and as with your previous pastors, I accept this as my responsibility. There are lots of benefits to this, but given that

128

remembering new names isn't my best skill, it helps me connect new faces with names, right, Fred?" Stephen said to George.

"That's right, Pastor Flintstone," George answered on cue.

"I would, however, like to propose some changes to the resource materials. Before you is a list of new books I have chosen. Their theological slant is conservative Evangelical, so there are no essential changes, except in the discussions on baptism, the Lord's Supper, Bible study, and prayer."

This got the board's attention, as Stephen anticipated, for they were always reticent about innovation.

"First, with baptism and the Lord's Supper. It has been my experience that new members who join from other Christian traditions find it disconcerting that we Congregationalists differ so greatly from one church to the next. So I'm proposing some materials that explain why we hold to a more symbolic understanding. With Bible study and prayer, I've also assembled some materials to help new Christians as well as old develop a daily devotional practice centered around Scripture reading and extemporaneous prayer. All of these materials are available over on the side table for your examination, and I'll be glad to answer any questions at the next meeting."

Receiving mostly affirming nods, Stephen felt he had at least temporarily dodged a bullet. He started to sit down, but a voice stopped him in mid-position.

"Pastor, may I ask something?" Larry Howe said. "I'm reluctant to do so in front of this peanut gallery, but something's been bugging me ever since we joined this church."

Fighting through guffaws all around, Larry quipped, holding up his arms in the form of a cross, "All right, all right, back off."

The board quieted down anxious to hear what sticky conundrum Larry might pose this time.

"As you know my wife and I used to be Roman Catholics, and thank God we're here now." Larry gave a demonstrative sigh of relief, which he knew everyone would understand. "Ever since our conversion, Sue and I have become avid Bible readers. We're not Bible scholars by any means, so don't get me wrong, but let's just say I've read the Bible more in the last ten years than in the entire first thirty years of my life. Now, one of the main tenets that separates us

Protestants from Catholics is that we believe that the Bible alone is the sole foundation for our faith, correct?"

"Yes," Stephen responded, hoping this would pass quickly. "Most Protestants hold to *sola scriptura*, though there is great diversity as to how this is understood and applied. You also realize that many Congregationalists no longer believe this. Nevertheless, that is at least what we believe here at Respite."

"Fine. So if I get this straight, this inspired book," Larry said, raising the leather King James Bible that always accompanied him to church, "is the sole foundation for *all* that we *must* believe and practice, especially for our salvation?"

"Yes, that's true." Uncertain where this was leading, Stephen nevertheless anticipated nothing he could not answer.

"Then two things that, as I said, have been bothering me. First, if the Bible is the sole foundation for our faith, then where does the Bible say this specifically? I mean, for something this important and foundational, you'd think it would be stated clearly?"

Invariably Stephen had to explain this to every new members' class, so he knew immediately where to turn. "This is most clearly affirmed in Second Timothy 3:16 and 17. Here, pass me your Bible, I forgot mine tonight."

This brought the expected sniggers.

"'All Scripture is inspired by God and profitable for teaching,'" Stephen read, "'for reproof, for correction, and for training in righteousness, that the man of God may be complete, equipped for every good work.' An alternate way to translate the Greek term given here as *profitable* is *sufficient*. All Scripture is therefore inspired and *sufficient* for teaching, et cetera.

"There are other verses that solidify our belief in the Bible's sufficiency, especially where Jesus quotes the Old Testament as authoritative, and where New Testament authors discourage believers from relying on the traditions of men. In Hebrews 4:12, for example. 'For the word of God is living and active, sharper than any two-edged sword,'" Stephen read, gesticulating with the Bible to emphasize that it was *this* book to which the author was referring. "From this and other passages, we conclude that the Bible is God's gift to His people, who under the guidance of the Holy Spirit are led into all truth."

"Then you would say, therefore," Larry responded, "that the Bible is the pillar and bulwark of the truth?"

"Yes, that is a good way to put it," Stephen said, pleased with the clarity of this ardent church member.

"Then, why does the Bible itself claim something different?" Larry asked with a sly smile. "Please explain First Timothy 3:15."

Stephen paged back, curious about Larry's reference. Stephen had read through the entire New Testament many times, so he was anticipating no surprises. Like most evangelical pastors, he had memorized the most significant verses and had a basic mental image of the rest, but this particular text did not ring a bell.

Locating the page in Larry's Bible, he thumbed down to the reference, and found that Larry had underlined this text. A question mark with an exclamation point had been added in the margin. Stephen scanned the verse silently, but it wasn't until he began reading it aloud that the significance of Larry's question struck him.

Stephen's pace slowed as he pronounced each word more cautiously and pensively. Once finished, he sat silently, marveling that he had failed to notice this passage before. In his own Bible, he had underlined the preceding passages about the duties of bishops and deacons, and the subsequent passage containing one of the oldest Christian creeds. But Stephen was dumbfounded.

Why have I never seen this before? And how do I explain it to Larry and the board?

And Larry and the board waited, bewildered by Stephen's awkward silence.

*   *   *

ACROSS THE WHITE UNDULATING CHURCHYARD, Sara, also, sat in silence. Adrian had finished his story. She certainly had heard of such problems cleaving marriages, but never, as they say, from the horse's mouth. Now she understood, though, how and why it could be so devastating, especially for couples so united by their faith in Jesus Christ.

"Adrian, I don't know what to say or advise. You really do need to speak with Stephen. He'll know what you should do. How are your parents taking this?"

"Oh, I haven't spoken a word about this to anyone," Adrian responded, "but they'll probably be even more disturbed than I am."

"I'm sorry that Stephen hasn't been able to fit you in, but I'm sure he will as soon as I tell him what you've told me. That is all right, isn't it?"

"Yes, please do. It will make things easier if I know that he is aware of our problem."

With this, Adrian rose to leave. "Thank you, Sara, for allowing me the time to talk. You've really helped."

"Oh, I don't know what I've done other than listen. Please before you go, can we have a word of prayer?"

It would have been customary in their shared evangelical tradition to hold hands, and though Sara now felt closer to Adrian through the baring of his heart, she, nevertheless, clasped her hands piously before her, and led them in a simple prayer for God's wisdom and mercy. "And may the Holy Spirit break through the confusion that has so distracted and captured Ginny's mind and heart, so that she might return to the faith she has loved so dearly."

Sara brought Adrian his coat, bid him good-bye with an appropriately reserved handshake, and waited on the porch in the evening cold until Adrian had driven out of sight.

She then returned to the living room with a fresh cup of coffee. Stoking the fire, she wondered not only what Adrian should do, but what she would do if anything this bizarre ever happened to her.

*   *   *

STEPHEN GATHERED HIS THOUGHTS.

"The problem with interpreting texts like this, especially when we compare a verse from one New Testament book with that from another, is that it's impossible to understand fully what these first-century writers meant by their terms—especially now nearly two thousand years later. When Paul wrote here that 'the church of the living God' is 'the pillar and bulwark of the truth,' he had no inkling what the word church would come to mean over the centuries. He surely could not have predicted how church leaders would wrestle with one another for control of the expanding church, or how the Roman Emperor Constantine would eventually settle the whole mess by declaring Christianity the official religion of the Roman people and the bishop of Rome the head of the Church. Paul could not have anticipated that this term would one day be used to describe the corrupt hierarchy of popes, bishops, and priests. Or could he have foreseen the Reformation that God initiated to correct this. Finally, Paul with his limited vision of the world could never have imagined the thousands of Christian groups that now call themselves *churches*.

"Paul certainly must have meant what we believe today," Stephen continued, though a voice from within prodded, *But who do you mean by* we? "The *Church* is not physical structures or hierarchies of bishops, or even some collective list of members' names from all the world's churches. No, the Church is the invisible body of believers encircling the globe—past, present and future—in whom the Holy Spirit dwells by grace through faith, and therefore where God's Word and God's truth are rightly interpreted, taught and believed."

Satisfied that he had temporarily dodged this bullet, Stephen scanned the faces of his board for signs of concurrence. He had given them essentially his pat summary of the New Testament authors' understanding of the term church—he only hoped it sat better with the board than it was sitting in his own conscience. The majority nodded with smiles of support, except Larry.

"But pastor," he asked, "how can a world-wide, invisible, and unorganized assortment of believers be a pillar and foundation of truth? I have friends in other churches who love Jesus and His Word, yet believe differently than I do. Which of us is speaking for this invisible church?"

Stephen studied the man's rough face. Larry managed his family-owned logging company, and his complexion and demeanor had been hewn by many long days outside in the New Hampshire winters.

"The things that are essential, we are to agree on; it's the non-essentials that divide us," Stephen replied with force.

"So you're saying that issues like how or when a person is baptized, or whether the Lord's Supper is truly the body and blood of Jesus or just a powerless symbol, or whether abortion is murder, or whether salvation can be lost or is eternally secure, or whether one adheres to the traditional creeds—all of these are non-essentials?"

Stephen felt like one of the Pharisees Jesus had reasoned into a corner, because regardless of whether he said "yes" or "no," he would invite the ire of any number of board members. *Thanks, Larry,* he complained inwardly, *I really needed this tonight.* And besides, this question sounded vaguely familiar.

"What we are called to consider true are those things that have been believed quasi-unanimously by all Christians, at all times and in all places. The unfortunate conflict between Christian believers stems from ignorance, pride, sin, or the denial of how the Spirit has led Christians from the beginning. We are Congregationalists because we believe that we are preserving the freedoms as expressed by Paul and the other New Testament writers."

Larry was poised with a response, but Stephen continued quickly: "Larry, it's getting late, and besides, I don't think I can completely satisfy your question tonight. If you'd like, we can continue this another time."

"Thank you, pastor. That would be helpful," Larry said reluctantly.

Stephen offered him back his Bible, but for what seemed like an eternity they played tug of war as Stephen held on, anxious to read that verse again. Confused, Larry released his grip. Embarrassed, Stephen did the same, and the Bible fell loudly to the floor.

"I'm sorry, Larry," Stephen said, bending meekly to retrieve it. He then gave it freely to its owner. Evading the ensuing awkwardness, Stephen turned his attention back to George, "That's really all I've got for tonight. If you have questions about the resources on the table, please let me know."

Stephen sat down relieved, but that verse continued to disturb him.

Anxious to refocus the board's attention, George stood and announced, "Let's move on to the last sticky wicket of our agenda: are we as a church going to take part in this year's ecumenical Good Friday service scheduled to take place at St. Anne's Catholic Parish?"

As the board debated the ecumenical issue, Stephen remained unengaged. In the end the ecumenists won out, stressing that any relationships established with the members of St. Anne's Parish would only lead to movement towards Respite Congregational, and not the other way around.

*　　　*　　　*

IT WAS PUSHING NINE-THIRTY when Stephen opened the kitchen door.

Not bad when compared with previous promises, he thought.

Driving up he had noticed that the lights upstairs were off, so he presumed the boys were at least trying to get to sleep. The only light in the house came from the bluish flicker of the television in the living room. He assumed that Sara was probably lost in her movie, and possibly oblivious to his late arrival.

"Hello, anybody home?" he quipped softly from the kitchen. He went to the refrigerator and poured himself a glass of cold white wine. Walking into the living room, Stephen broke the ice with a meaningless, "Quiet night?"

They kissed softly as he took his seat beside her on the couch. Sara, already dressed for bed, was snuggled beneath several blankets and a pillow, lost in the classic Grant-Kerr love affair. They kissed again, and setting his wineglass down and kicking off his shoes, he crawled in next to her.

"You won't believe my evening," she said. "Adrian McBride stopped over."

"Adrian stopped by?" Stephen said, surprised. "That's nice. I presume he was here to see me," he said mischievously.

"Of course, you ninny."

"Then why does he so desperately need to see me? Or did you solve his problem for him?"

"Yes he does, no I didn't, and I think you're going to have your hands full when you two get together."

It was the moment in the movie when the two lovers make their pact to meet again in a year on the top of the Empire State Building, so Sara's focus became diverted. "But I'll tell you about it later. How was your meeting?" she said as she watched the television images kiss.

"Oh, nothing out of the ordinary," Stephen lied. He was intent on an undistracted evening with Sara. *So little time, so many distractions. Lord Jesus,* he prayed mentally, *may this evening be an intimate, quiet night to remember.*

5

T HE ROADSIDE CAFÉ was crowded with truckers. The only available booth was an uncleared one in the smoking section, but Stephen took it anyway. He still had another seventy miles to drive, but he could ignore the nagging curiosity no longer.

"What'll you have?" asked an aging, don't-mess-with-me waitress. She cleared the table, wiping it clean with a sopping rag.

He waited for her to finish.

"What do you want?" she demanded again in a voice that invited the stares of several truckers. Stephen noticed immediately that their sympathies were not with him.

He raised his hands in bewilderment.

With a look of incredulity to a burly customer in the next booth, she pointed to a small crumpled menu behind the usual collection of condiments.

After a quick scan of the options, Stephen said, "A black coffee and a number six, eggs over easy."

She turned away towards the kitchen, with no sign of acknowledgement.

But no matter. Stopping for breakfast was only an excuse. Ever since the board meeting, Stephen had been frantic to reexamine the Scriptures and the answers he had given to Larry's questions—which Larry and he both knew were unsatisfactory.

At four a.m. he had awakened and left Sara sleeping on the couch. After a quick shower and then dressing in his usual mid-week suit, he bid Sara goodbye with a light kiss to her one visible cheek, and drove southeast toward the out-of-the-way mountain town of Jamesfield.

"You did say black?" the waitress said as she placed a coffee and a greasy number six before him.

"Yes," but she was already gone.

The overcooked eggs, limp bacon, and cold toast looked only marginally palatable, so after a few token bites, he pushed the plate aside. From his briefcase, he removed his Greek-English New Testament. Even if it took all morning, he was determined to get to the bottom of those verses in First Timothy, for he recognized the underlying significance in Larry's question.

First he pleaded for the Spirit's guidance, and then reread the verses that until last night he had failed to *see:*

> I am writing these things to you, hoping to come to you before long; but in case I am delayed, I write so that you may know how one ought to conduct himself in the household of God, which is *the church of the living God, the pillar and bulwark of the truth.*

Free from the scrutiny of Larry and the board, Stephen noted, first, that Paul had written this letter as a precautionary measure. Paul was planning to visit with Timothy, but in the event that his plans might fall through, he had penned this letter to pass along instructions on how people ought to behave as Christians. In other words, Paul's preferred means of teaching Timothy was face-to-face.

Stephen sipped the black, keep-you-awake-all-night coffee and silently thanked the Holy Spirit for the delay nearly two thousand years ago that had forced Paul to write this letter. Otherwise the world might never have seen these instructions.

Reflecting further, Stephen envisioned the imprisoned Apostle sitting hunched over a wooden table under the dim glow of an oil lamp. He was writing with a sharpened feather quill on a yellow roll of papyrus. This picture then faded into an image of Paul sitting more casually across a table from young Timothy. The two friends were laughing and sharing chalices of wine—for wasn't this Paul's advice near the end of this same letter? As Stephen considered this, he thought, *Wouldn't Paul have said a whole lot more to Timothy face-to-face than he was able to write on that small papyrus? Did Paul summarize everything that was necessary in this short letter, or was this merely a quick introduction to the more detailed list of things he wanted to deliver in person?*

Stephen turned to Paul's Second Letter to Timothy, and reread the verse that he had assumed would answer Larry's challenge.

All Scripture, Stephen thought. *All Scripture? When Timothy* received this letter, what would he have understood Paul to mean by this? Would he have considered Paul's letter itself as "Scripture," or only a casual, yet important letter from his father-in-the-faith? What would he and Paul have considered Scripture?

"Anything else?" the waitress asked, removing his unfinished breakfast and slapping down the bill.

"Some more coffee, please."

"Hey, this ain't a library," she said as she filled his cup to a positive meniscus.

Stephen started to respond, but again, she was gone.

When Paul wrote this, he thought, returning to the text, *the New Testament as we know it had not been collected. In fact, we're not even sure whether the Gospels had been written yet. Therefore, the only thing Paul could have referred to as Scripture was the Old Testament—which of course at the time wouldn't have been called this, but 'the Law and the Prophets.'*

And also, he continued, *we know from the way the New Testament writers quoted the Old Testament, that they used the Greek translation, called the Septuagint. So the term 'Scripture' here must literally mean the Greek Old Testament.*

He glanced down the page to the footnotes. A chain reference pointed to another of Paul's letters. He casually flipped back to Second Thessalonians 2:15. He leaned back to stretch as he began reading, his mind focused on his previous thoughts, until what he read shot him forward in the booth:

> So then, brethren, stand firm and hold to the traditions
> which you were taught, whether by word of mouth or by
> letter from us.

He read this again, and then again. As he did, the two mental pictures of Paul writing and of Paul teaching Timothy face-to-face melded into a composite that represented in his mind how the Christian faith was passed on from Jesus to apostle to local preacher to the people: by word of mouth and by writing.

Stephen mulled this over, thinking about all three verses at once, and envisioned their interrelationship: *the faith of these early Christians was built on the foundation of the Old Testament Scriptures—the Law and the Prophets. But what was written in them needed to be applied to their new situation in Christ—the ancient Prophetic references to the coming Messiah needed to be explained so that they could be understood in reference to Jesus. This was what Jesus had explained to the two disciples on the road to Emmaus, and what then was passed on through the Apostle's teachings, both orally and in writing.*

Stephen paused as he sensed his thoughts reaching a conclusion. *And if Paul asserts that more was communicated in his sermons and public teaching than he was able to record in his few, short New Testament letters, then, therefore, how can it be accurate to conclude that* only *what is in Scripture is essential? Paul said that we should hold to the traditions taught orally as well as written.*

Traditions.

This word, which he as a Congregationalist rarely used, jumped out at him. Paul was telling these early Christians to hold to *traditions* taught not only in his letters but also orally.

With apprehension, Stephen followed another chain reference. First Corinthians 11:2, *"I commend you because you remember me in everything and maintain the traditions even as I delivered them to you."*

"Traditions again," he muttered, "that he 'delivered'." *I've always presumed that this referred to the written records of Jesus' deeds and words. But why?*

Frantically he followed another reference in the same letter, 4:17, *"Therefore I send to you Timothy...to remind you of my ways in Christ, as I teach them everywhere in every church."*

Teach them...everywhere in every church. Again, Stephen thought, *Paul's normal way of communicating Christian truth. And in this instance, he sent Timothy instead of a letter.*

Another reference came to mind, and this time he knew the verse by memory. Second Timothy 2:2, *"What you have heard from me before many witnesses entrust to faithful men who will be able to teach others also."*

From Jesus to Paul to Timothy to faithful men to others. All through oral teaching without any mandate to write it down or to "look it up in the Bible."

Stephen finished his coffee as his mind raced ahead into what for him was uncharted territory. He turned back to the text in Second

Timothy that he had always used to defend *sola scriptura,* and began reading the verses that immediately preceded it: *"But as for you, continue in what you have learned and have firmly believed, knowing from whom you learned it ..."*

For Timothy this, therefore, meant from Paul, or his parents, or others, Stephen thought, *not from some as yet uncollected New Testament letters or gospels.*

"...and how from childhood you have been acquainted with the sacred writings..."

...which had to be the Old Testament Scriptures. But had he actually read these? Probably not. He was acquainted with these primarily through public readings, probably in the local synagogue and church gatherings. In every way, therefore, he was dependent upon oral teaching.

"...which are able to instruct you for salvation through faith in Christ Jesus."

But the Old Testament is NOT that clear about how one is saved through faith in Jesus Christ—one needs the New Testament to fully understand this. So if Timothy and the other early Christians didn't have a written New Testament yet, how could they know how to interpret the Old Testament correctly and adequately to lead them to Jesus?

As Stephen asked himself these questions, he casually flipped back to the initial text in First Timothy: *"...the church of the living God, the pillar and bulwark of the truth."*

"Hey, buddy."

Startled, Stephen broke from his reflection. Hovering over him was a man wearing a soiled apron over a white tee shirt rolled up at the sleeves.

"Take your reading elsewhere. This ain't first period study hall. I've got regular customers waiting to be seated."

"I'm sorry. I was just reading while I finished my coffee."

"Well, finish it in your car."

The man stood aside as Stephen collected his things, threw down a five to cover the bill and tip, and left.

Once by his aging Fairmont, Stephen glanced back through the cafe window in time to see the man laughing with several of the customers, mimicking Stephen's studiousness.

Anger rose within Stephen, but realizing that any retaliation to their ridicule was pointless, he merely turned away and threw his briefcase onto the backseat. As he headed off toward Jamesfield, his mind returned to where his reflections had left off.

The church...the pillar...the bulwark...the truth.

Stephen envisioned Timothy attempting to convince pagan neighbors to believe in Jesus. *If they answered back, "Why should we believe this lunacy," then what could Timothy have said? If he had said "Because the Scriptures say so," he could only have meant the Old Testament, and we know from the experience of the Ethiopian Eunuch in Acts that just reading the Old Testament wasn't enough. Timothy would have had to convince them through the witness of those who had seen Jesus alive after His death on the cross. But where was this to be found?*

The church...the pillar...the bulwark...the truth.

*   *   *

SARA AWOKE IN A COLD SWEAT. In her dreams, she had been desperately clawing her way up the side of a mountain cliff. Upon awaking, she discovered with relief that the sound she had been emulating was Stymie the house cat scratching at the kitchen door.

An empty wine glass on the coffee table reminded her why she had fallen asleep on the couch, and she smiled. Stephen must have left early for his meeting with the Drewer sisters, and probably had kissed her goodbye while she slept. Groggily she stepped into her slippers, donned her robe, and shuffled into the kitchen where, after letting Stymie in, "her highness" started the morning coffee.

While the invigorating black elixir brewed, she popped a pumpernickel bagel in the toaster and turned on the radio for the local news.

"...SAY SKEPTICS AS THEY CONSIDER WHETHER POPE JOHN PAUL'S VISIT TO CUBA LAST YEAR WILL HAVE AN EASING EFFECT ON CASTRO'S POLICIES, EITHER TOWARD THE ROMAN CATHOLIC CHURCH OR FOR A MORE DEMOCRATIC FUTURE FOR THE CUBAN PEOPLE."

"Oh, shoot! I forgot to tell him," she exclaimed, covering her face with her hands. They had become so absorbed in themselves and then fallen asleep, that she forgot to give Stephen the details of her discussion with Adrian.

Well, I guess it can wait, she thought. She spread cream cheese on the bagel.

"AS CATHOLIC CUBANS CONTINUE TO WONDER ABOUT THE IMPACT OF THE POPE'S HISTORIC VISIT, LET US HEAR AGAIN SOME EXCERPTS FROM HIS MESSAGE TO THE YOUTH OF CUBA, TRANSLATED BY OUR OWN JOSE MANUEVOS.

"'WITH HEARTFELT SENTIMENT I ADDRESS YOU, DEAR YOUNG PEOPLE OF CUBA, THE HOPE OF THE CHURCH AND OF YOUR HOMELAND, AND I PRESENT YOU TO CHRIST SO THAT YOU MIGHT KNOW HIM AND FOLLOW HIM WITH TOTAL DETERMINATION. IT IS HE WHO GIVES YOU LIFE, SHOWS YOU THE WAY, BRINGS YOU TO THE TRUTH, MOTIVATING YOU TO WALK TOGETHER IN SOLIDARITY, HAPPINESS AND PEACE AS LIVING MEMBERS OF HIS MYSTICAL BODY, WHICH IS THE CHURCH...'"

Sara was dumbfounded by these quotes from the Pope's speech given on communist soil, yet also strangely moved. She had never given a second thought to the Roman Catholic Church or its pope, except with her silent assent whenever someone ridiculed him or identified him as the anti-Christ. She was unsure whether she actually believed all this, but then again, she never refuted his critics either.

As she listened, she was amazed at how *Christian* the Pope sounded. *I suppose the anti-Christ would be a masterful liar, but would he proclaim the gospel so boldly to a pagan, communist regime? Why would the anti-Christ try to convert communists to Christ? Did the Pope really say 'I present you to Christ so that you might know Him and follow Him with total determination'? This sounded more like something Stephen might preach.*

Troubled by these contradictions, she switched the radio off. Her mind recalled her visit to the chapel at Campion College, the peaceful warmth of the sanctuary, the scent of lingering incense. Her knees trembled as she remembered kneeling, crying out to God, and receiving His forgiveness. Yet, she also remembered the unnerving setting—the peculiar statues and pictures, and the stooped nun lighting candles—that had driven her out and back to the familiar world of her loving husband and family.

But she quickly buried any reflection on her chance meeting with Frank. Though he had sent her several letters, she so far had not responded.

Returning to her couch in the living room, she stared at the portrait above the mantle. She paused to thank Jesus for all the mercies He had showered upon her, for the past she was able to leave behind, and then it struck her. She was praying to a picture of Jesus, just as Adrian had said Ginny was doing in front of statues and icons. Sara studied the eyes and the hand that seemed to be giving her a blessing, and quickly turned away.

But I was not praying to the picture. I was praying to Jesus whom the picture represents. Yet, she shuddered at the thought of praying to it in the same manner that Ginny supposedly did. *Catholics also pray to Mary, St. Peter, and other dead Christians as if they were gods. Surely, this is idolatry.*

She rose, fleeing from the picture that up until then had been a center of comfort in their home.

"Dad gone?" William said, bounding down the stairs two steps in front of Daniel.

"Hey, slow down you two. Yes, your father left hours ago."

As Sara and the boys progressed into their usual pre-school bantering, she was relieved for the freedom to herd her thoughts into more pleasing pastures, which included her plans to make a day-trip to the mall.

Living in this small out-of-the-way town on the northern border of the United States had its advantages: less traffic and noise, beautiful scenery, and cleaner air. But when it came to shopping, it had its drawbacks. Any substantial shopping excursion to the only mall in the region required a roundtrip of one hundred and ten miles, and this was Sara's agenda for the day.

After William and Daniel had been fed, clothed, and deposited safely on the bus, Sara was free to embark on her excursion into civilization.

With the refrains of the Boston Pops flowing from the tape player and the White Mountains peeking above the trees, she felt as though she were in a movie gliding through the snow packed slopes of the lower Alps. In what seemed like mere minutes, she found herself turning off the highway and into the large mega-mall parking lot.

This beautiful new mall, which featured two expansive floors of typical mall franchises, fulfilled its marketing promise as the ultimate in one-stop shopping. After ten minutes of circular searching, she found an empty space nearly five hundred feet from the mall. Bundled against the cold, she scurried for the nearest entrance.

The revolving doors spun in the wake of previous shoppers, and as she passed through, shaking snow from her coat, the interplay of lights, music, fountains, merchandise, and people of every shape and pace made her dizzy. She knew precisely where on the second tier she intended to shop, but she still perused each window along the way. A donut and cookie shop, a lingerie boutique, an over-priced men's clothing store, a faddish young adults' shop with retro clothing from the sixties, a discount shoe store, an outdoors-camping goods outlet, a card and candle shop, another shoe store, a store for smokers, and more of the usual fare found at malls all across America.

Passing store after store, she developed a glazed, detached stare as her eyes surveyed the same merchandise she had seen on previous excursions. Another clothing store, a high-tech gadget shop, a leather goods franchise, but then her pace slowed to a halt as the blur of sameness suddenly sharpened into crystal clarity. She stood mesmerized before a previously unnoticed shop.

It was not the familiar rows of books and Bibles that had captured her attention, or the shelves of religious gifts, games, statues, prints, and other paraphernalia. Rather, it was the large portrait of Jesus displayed on the rear wall—the identical portrait that hung over the mantle in their living room. Their copy had been a gift from a wealthy family in Red Creek who had brought it back from a trip to Eastern Europe. She had never seen it anywhere else, except in the intimacy of their living room. But here it was.

As she gazed at its familiar features, she slowly entered St. Michael's Bookstore. Other artwork, mostly foreign to her New England Congregationalist senses, caught her attention as she began pacing the aisles. Turning the corner of one row, staring at a small replica of Michaelangelo's Pieta, she stumbled headlong over a woman kneeling low to the floor.

"Oh, excuse me," Sara said, catching her balance and realigning some books she had upset. The woman looked up apologetically as she righted herself. Sara was startled to recognize her as Ginny McBride.

"Oh, Mrs. LaPointe. I'm terribly sorry. I didn't mean to be anyone's stumbling block."

The look on Ginny's face betrayed her own shock at being discovered in this Catholic bookstore by, of all people, her pastor's wife. Sara noticed that as Ginny spoke, she had carefully lowered a book to her side, out of view.

"Oh, that's all right, Ginny. No harm done." Sara was inextricably trapped. If she had spotted Ginny earlier, she would have retreated unnoticed from the store. *But what now?* she thought. *Maybe this is providential—an encounter contrived by a scheming God. The question is, did Adrian tell her about our meeting last night?*

"What are you reading?" Sara chose the frontal attack.

"Well," Ginny said, slowly revealing the book at her side. "This is a book on prayer by St. Francis de Sales, a Catholic bishop who lived over four hundred years ago."

She handed the attractive green and black book to Sara.

"This book is a treasure," Ginny said. "May I read you the paragraph I was reading?"

"Yes, of course," Sara said with a cautious smile.

As Ginny retrieved the book and turned the pages, Sara studied the determined intensity of this pretty young woman. She was certainly a fitting partner to the man she had apparently loved all her life.

Holding the book so that Sara could follow along, Ginny read:

> "God has placed you in this world not because he needs you in any way—you are altogether useless to him—but only to exercise his goodness in you by giving you his grace and glory. For this purpose he has given you intellect to know him, memory to be mindful of him, will to love him, imagination to picture to yourself his benefits, eyes to see his wonderful works, tongue to praise him, and so on with the other faculties. Since you have been placed in this world for this purpose, all actions contrary to it must be rejected and avoided and those not serving this end should be despised as empty and useless. Consider the unhappiness of worldly people who never think of all this but live as if they believe themselves created only

to build houses, plant trees, pile up wealth, and do frivolous things."

Initially, the news that the author was a Catholic bishop put Sara off, but as she listened, she heard words that could just as easily have come from any devout Christian preacher—Stephen could have said them. Twice in the same day—in the same morning—she had been startled to hear truly Christian words from Catholics.

"That's very interesting, Ginny." Sara was struggling against three internal voices: one prodding her to interrogate Ginny about what was destroying her marriage, another coaxing her to hear more from this book, and another screaming, *Run! Get out of this place.*

Sara decided to let Ginny decide. "Tell me, Ginny, what brings you to this St. Michael's Bookstore?"

"Actually, I come often. It always lifts my spirit," she said looking around at the pictures and rows of books. Then turning back to Sara, she asked, "Mrs. LaPointe?"

"Please, call me Sara."

"Sara," Ginny said, "have you ever read a book written by a Catholic?"

"Well, certainly," Sara responded defensively, probing her brain for an example. "Wasn't *Brideshead Revisited* written by a Catholic? Or, let's see, the author of the Father Brown mysteries, wasn't he Catholic?'

"Yes, Waugh and Chesterton were excellent Catholic fiction writers, but I mean books about what Catholics believe. As Protestants, we have opinions about what Catholics believe, based mostly on books written by non-Catholics, but few of us have read books about the Catholic Church written by Catholics."

"Maybe not, but what difference does that make?"

Over Ginny's shoulder Sara noticed a portrait of Jesus pointing to a large red heart on his chest that she considered the gaudiest picture she had ever seen. It reminded her of the artwork she had run from years before.

"Well, what if the priest at St. Anne's Parish was teaching a class on what Congregationalists believe? Would you want him to use a book about the Congregational Church written by a Catholic, a Southern Baptist, an atheist, or a Congregationalist?"

"I get your point," Sara conceded, though unsure where Ginny was leading.

"Exactly. A book by the Congregationalist probably would be more accurate and unbiased. The other authors might miss or ignore key points, or even misrepresent them."

The enthusiasm in Ginny's voice had caught the attention of a shopper in the adjacent aisle. She continued.

"I have found that Protestant writers often repeat myths or exaggerations about Catholic history or beliefs that were never true. When I compare what they've written to counter the explanations given by Catholic writers, I find the Catholic side much more believable and uplifting."

The woman in the next aisle locked eyes with Sara briefly and then turned quickly away.

Sara was experiencing for herself the relenting intensity of which Adrian had spoken. She began fishing for words to diplomatically extract herself, but instead said, "For example?"

"Well, let me see," Ginny said, turning her attention back to the shelves. Extracting a blue and white paperback entitled *The Faith of Our Fathers,* she continued. "This book was written over one hundred years ago by a Catholic Cardinal from Baltimore. In his day, he was highly respected by both Protestants and Catholics."

Sara examined the front cover. The artwork, obviously Catholic, pictured Jesus handing a set of keys to a man kneeling before him.

"Is it not correct that as Protestants we believe that the Bible is God's inspired Word?" Ginny asked.

"Yes, of course."

"And we believe that Jesus sent the Holy Spirit to help us interpret Scripture correctly."

"Yes," Sara answered cautiously. Generally, she would pass questions like this off to Stephen, but what was most disconcerting was that these questions were coming from a younger and less educated woman from her own congregation.

"Well, here's a chapter on the Church and the Bible that demonstrates that God never intended the Bible *alone* to be the sole rule of faith, or for us to interpret it independently of the Church. Cardinal Gibbons writes, 'A competent guide, such as our Lord intended for us, must have three characteristics. It must be within the reach of everyone; it must be clear and intelligible; and it must be able to satisfy us on all questions relating to faith and morals.'

"Now, Sara, doesn't this make sense?"

"Well, sure but…" With lots of shopping to do, Sara was hesitant to encourage the ardent Ginny.

"For example, if God intended the Bible alone to be the one source for all Christian truth, and if, as the Bible states, God desires everyone to be saved, then wouldn't God have made the Bible readily available to every person who has ever lived? Moreover, wouldn't God have made the Bible's message perfectly and unmistakably clear?"

Ginny's enthusiasm was rising.

"But for most of human history, entire civilizations have lived and died without having a Bible to read, if the people could even read one. But even more important, we don't need to look far to see that sincere, Spirit-filled Christians come up with vastly different interpretations of what the Bible says."

Sara was visibly impatient.

"Sara, I know you need to go, but can I show you just one more thing? This will illustrate what the Cardinal is trying to say."

Before Sara could respond, Ginny charged on.

"In this section, he describes the problems that belief in *sola Scriptura* and the right of private interpretation have caused."

Again Ginny held the book so that Sara could follow along, but Sara did so only reluctantly. Ginny read:

> "Thus, one body of Christians will prove from the Bible that there is but one Person in God, while the rest will prove from the same source that a Trinity of Persons is a clear article of Divine Revelation. One will prove from the Holy Book that Jesus Christ is not God. Others will appeal to the same text to attest His Divinity. One denomination will assert on the authority of Scripture that infant baptism is not necessary for salvation, while others will hold that it is…"

This immediately recaptured Sara's attention, for in it she heard an echo of her husband's own voice. Over the years, Stephen had occasionally admitted frustration over "the great cacophony of conflicting Christian voices," as he called it—especially over issues like baptism. Now Sara listened more intently as Ginny continued.

"'Some Christians, with Bible in hand, will teach that there are no sacraments...'"

Yes, Sara said to herself, *this is what we Congregationalists believe.*

"'Others will say that there are only two. Some will declare that the inspired Word does not preach the eternity of punishments...'"

This reminded Sara of two ministers who taught contradicting views on this. One was a preacher in Boston that Stephen and she had heard on their honeymoon. He had proclaimed that in the end all people will be saved—it's just that most people don't know it. Our evangelistic responsibility, according to him, was to proclaim that God loves and accepts everyone just as they are.

The other preacher was her husband. The next Sunday, Stephen had proclaimed "Yes, God loves everyone, but unless sinners turn from their sins and repent, they'll spend eternity roasting in Hell."

"'Do not clergymen appear every day in the pulpit,'" Ginny continued to read, "'and point out on the authority of the Book of Revelation, with painful accuracy, the year and the day on which this world is to come to an end? And when their prophesy fails they coolly put off our destruction to another time.'"

Sara remembered the day last fall when she and Stephen were laughing hysterically in their living room. In his files, he had come across a pamphlet entitled *"88 Reasons Jesus is Coming in 88."* Jesus had obviously not come.

Though Ginny had ceased reading, Sara had continued silently.

"Ginny, this is all quite interesting," Sara admitted pulling her eyes from the text, "and I'd love to continue discussing all this, but I do need to get going. I need to find a birthday present for Stephen, some clothes for the boys, and then make the long drive home before school lets out. Maybe when Stephen gets back from his trip, you and Adrian can come over and together we can discuss these things in more detail." *I'm sure that Stephen will know how to respond to all this better than I do,* Sara thought.

"Sara, here, please take this as a gift from me," Ginny said, pushing the book into Sara's hands.

"No, Ginny. I can't take this," Sara said backing away as if the book were contaminated.

"Please, this will help you and Reverend LaPointe understand where I'm coming from, and why it's causing so many problems for Adrian and me."

Seeing that nothing could dissuade her, Sara accepted the gift reluctantly.

"But when Reverend LaPointe gets home, and after you've both had a chance to glance through it, please, may we get together?"

Sara extended her hand, "Sure, Ginny, and thanks. I do appreciate the gift, but I'd better go. We'll be talking soon."

"You're welcome, Sara, and thank you for listening."

Sara smiled and then hurried out of St. Michael's bookstore. Once around the corner and out of sight, she paused to look again at her first truly *Catholic* book. The longer she had stayed in St. Michael's, the more she began experiencing the same mixture of peace and dread she had felt years before in St. Campion's chapel.

She browsed through the pages, skimming the chapter titles, and wondered what she should do with this book. *Should I take it home to read as Ginny suggested? But wasn't it books like this that caused Ginny to question her Protestant faith? That had put her marriage in jeopardy?*

With an elusive sense of panic, she then recalled her husband's frustration with the same issues this Catholic Cardinal was addressing— and refuting. Looking around and seeing no one watching, she dropped *The Faith of Our Fathers* in the trash. She then hurried off, down the corridor, and into the first men's clothing store she could find.

*   *   *

AFTER PAYING FOR SARA'S BOOK as well as several others, Ginny exited St. Michael's and headed towards a coffee and cookie shop. Turning the corner, she spied Sara standing by a waste can. Ginny pulled back out of view, and watched surreptitiously as Sara paged through the book. When Sara began glancing from side to side, Ginny ducked back, but then peeked again only to see Sara drop the book in the trash and hurry off.

Ginny was more hurt than angry, but then she remembered how she would have acted several years ago if someone had given her such a gift—she might have refused it in the first place.

Once Sara was out of sight, Ginny went directly to the trash bin and retrieved the book. *Hey, I paid for it didn't I?* she said to herself, answering any imaginary accusers.

Eventually sipping a Café Mocha and munching a chocolate chip, macadamia nut cookie as big as her fist, Ginny wondered what she should do with the book. Then sitting back with a smile, meditating on the decadence of both the cookie and her plan, she thought, *Maybe Sara and Reverend LaPointe will get this after all.*

6

THE REST AREA WAS VACANT except for blowing snow and a half-smashed six-pack of beer bottles. Stephen pulled his aging Fairmont alongside a pay phone, and after dialing, pulled the phone inside and rolled up the window against the frigid late winter storm.

He should have been home by now, but he was reticent about facing Sara. There was no predicting her mood after his day-long absence, but even more so, he wasn't prepared to tell her about his afternoon—she would not believe him, let alone understand.

He checked his watch as the phone rang on the other end.

"Hello?" came a distance voice.

"Hello, Jim? It's Stephen."

"Stephen who? Oh yes, that old friend whom I haven't heard from in over a year."

"Well, it cuts both ways you know. But life's been hectic as usual."

"You mean you haven't been out fishing and hunting in that great northern wilderness?"

"I wish, but Jim, I need to talk. I'm calling from a highway payphone. Is this a good time?"

"Sure, what's up?"

"Jim, I've just had the most disconcerting experience of my life. In fact, I can't stop shaking."

"What's her phone number?"

"No seriously, Jim; I don't even think I can joke about this, and you're the only one that might understand." Pausing for strength, Stephen continued, "Jim, do you still believe in miracles and the demonic?"

"Well, given the pandemic skepticism of my denomination, it's hard to, but sure. Why?"

"But have you ever witnessed a true miracle in your own work as a pastor, or actually confronted a demon?"

"Well, I don't know. A miracle where someone who was blind could now instantaneously see, or who was deaf and could hear? No, but I believe our lives are overflowing with God's little miracles that most people merely write off as 'coincidences.' As for the demonic, of course I still believe in the reality of the devil. I've never exorcised anyone, certainly not in the vivid way Jesus did, but I've sure counseled a few who were nasty enough to be considered possessed."

"I'm glad I can talk with you, Jim, because I need an understanding friend tonight. I had an experience this afternoon that I can only describe as powerfully demonic as well as miraculous. You know I've always believed, like Martin Luther, that our spiritual battle is with the world, the flesh, and the devil, but I never expected to encounter evil in the way it is described in the Gospels. Well, I did today, in a way that was both terrifying, yet exhilarating.

"Yesterday morning I received an urgent call from an elderly member of my last congregation. She and her sister, Elsie, had moved from Red Creek to Jamesfield, New Hampshire, and as yet had not found a church home. For years, Elsie had been under medication for supposed mental problems. She was a sweet, faithful woman, but she had one strange quirk: she stuttered uncontrollably, except when she sang. She had a wonderful soprano voice, and had always been one of the mainstays of the adult choir. In normal conversation, however, she usually stared down or remained silent.

"When her sister Irene called yesterday, she was in a panic. Elsie had been hysterical, claiming that she was seeing terrifying visions. Irene assumed that Elsie had forgotten to take her medications, but nothing could get Elsie to settle down. Unsure who to call, she begged me to come see what I could do."

Stephen stopped to look around into the darkness surrounding his car. He had the sensation that he was being watched.

"This morning I drove two hours to their new apartment complex in Jamesfield. When I arrived, I found both sisters sitting in the living room as if nothing at all had happened. The three of us sat for a few minutes, Irene and I talking over old times, Elsie listening contently, but no mention of why I had been called. Then Irene motioned me into the kitchen. Once out of Elsie's sight, she started crying softly, and asked me to please help her sister. Without another word, Irene went to her bedroom, and left me alone. I returned to the living room where Elsie was sitting quietly, rocking back and forth in an old bentwood rocker. Her face was expressionless, staring down at her feet.

"I asked how she was doing, but she just shrugged. I asked her a few other things, and getting nothing, I asked if I could pray for her. With that her face shot up, her eyes glared straight into me, but still she said nothing. I took this as some form of 'Yes,' so I closed my eyes, and began praying. I reached over to hold her hand, but when I touched her she jerked away. I looked up and saw a look like hatred itself. I asked what was wrong and she just glared. I began praying again, and when I mentioned the name of Jesus, all hell broke loose. She started yelling at me in a voice that does not come from a frail, elderly woman. She called me vile names, and Jim, I swear, in the stillness of that living room, her hair was blowing as if in a gale. I was paralyzed with shock, because I realized exactly what I was into. I began praying with a vengeance, begging for all the help that Heaven could give while in the background her verbal attacks continued. In the name of Jesus I demanded that whatever was within her be cast out, but the attacks only increased, louder and viler. I kept praying, clutching my Bible.

"But Jim, the most frightening thing was that as she yelled, she accused me of sins, regretful things that I had done years ago, things that Elsie could never have known—things for which I had long since asked God for forgiveness and had put behind me. But apparently the devil didn't want me to forget. Elsie battered me over and over with all the things that remind me of how unworthy I am to be a minister. I felt like giving up with my prayer; I felt like running, but I knew that this encounter was exactly where God wanted me to be.

"I don't know how long it lasted, though it seemed like hours. Eventually Irene came rushing in through the kitchen door with the man from the apartment above. He shouted over Elsie's screaming accusations, 'Stop! What's happening?'

"With that, Elsie went silent. Her head dropped, and I caught her as she fainted towards the floor. The neighbor helped me carry her into her room. She slept for about an hour while Irene and I talked and prayed in the living room. Eventually we heard her call weakly, and then, Jim, this is when the real miracle occurred."

Stephen glanced into the rear view mirror at the lights of another car pulling into the rest stop. It drove past to his right, turned around, and then backed up in front of the restrooms.

"Irene went into the room ahead of me," Stephen continued, "but stopped dead in her tracks, causing me to bump up against her. I glanced around her and saw Elsie's bright shining face, a smile stretching from ear to ear below half-closed eyes. She raised her arms up slightly toward us, and said softly, without the hint of a stutter, 'Please, come here.' Irene and I went to her on either side of the bed and held her hands. She turned to me and said, clear and steady, 'Thank you, Reverend LaPointe. Thank you.' She looked warmly into my eyes, and smiled like an angel.

"Then she turned back to her sister and said, 'Irene, I love you. Always remember that, and thank you.'"

Stephen's eyes began to well up with tears.

"Irene leaned over and embraced her. The two held each other as if they hadn't seen each other in years. Irene wept profusely, but Elsie just beamed, her face aglow with joy. Then, Jim, as I watched this reunion of love, I saw Elsie's hands and arms go limp and fall away from her sister, her eyes closed, but her face still smiling as if she knew an eternal secret. She was at peace, Jim. Elsie died in her sister's arms, free of the evil that had plagued her for so long."

"Good lord, Stephen, what an ordeal! I have never experienced anything like that."

Stephen listened, but the other car was distracting him. Two men had paid trips to the restroom and then returned to sit, smoking in their vehicle.

"But what has shaken me the most about all this," Stephen continued, "is not so much Elsie's death, but the *realness* of it all.

Jim, there were no 360 degree head turns or green vomit as in *The Exorcist*, but I have no doubt that I truly battled either a demon or the devil himself. I feel as if up until today I've been playing games with my pastorate; I've been playing a role. Yes, I've believed in the invisible, spiritual realm, but there has always been a safe, theoretical veneer. I've expounded my views on spirituality freely from the pulpit like Anna in the *King and I* telling the children in Siam about snow; no, actually more like the King of Siam who believed in snow though he'd never seen it. But now, Jim, I've seen 'snow'—I've directly encountered the demonic as well as the power of God's mercy; I believed it was real, but now I *know* that it is."

"Well, Stephen, I guess from time to time we all need a good shot in the arm to wake us up to the reality of what we believe and teach."

"But that's not the point," Stephen said with frustration, while at the same time watching the two men sitting silently in their dark car. "For years now, I've been bothered by the contradictions between otherwise believing Christians. I mean, hey, few of the ministers I know believe anymore in the reality of the devil and demons. They write it all off as myths for the ignorant. Then last night a board member cornered me with a Scripture that I do not remember ever seeing before, and I could not answer him. This morning I examined the text more closely and came away even less sure of myself."

"What text?"

"First Timothy 3:15. But Jim, the point is this: that verse and a few others that I've only 'seen' for the first time call into question everything that I have believed about the authority of Scripture *alone* to define what is true. This morning I saw this in an academic, theoretical way, but now after this experience, all of this has moved to a new level. It is not merely theoretical; it is real and eternally significant."

Jim was silent on the other end, and Stephen was about to ask why, when he noticed something strange about the other car. Its headlights were dark, but it appeared to be moving slowly. He watched, and sure enough, it was creeping toward him.

"Hey, Jim, I think I better go. There's something strange going on here."

"What is it?" Jim asked.

"Two guys in a car are coming toward me. I'll call you later."

"But Stephen…"

Stephen rolled down the window, and while he replaced the receiver, he turned his engine back on. Suddenly the lights of the other car came on as it increased in speed. Stephen jammed his Fairmont into gear and shot forward. He circled to the right around behind the other vehicle and then out the exit onto the highway. He accelerated to and beyond the speed limit. In the rear view mirror, he watched his pursuers' headlights bob back and forth as they tried to catch him, and an otherworldly panic pierced Stephen's heart.

No matter how fast he sped, they continued to gain on him. The blinding headlights were like two eyes boring into his soul.

Up ahead, off to the right, he saw another light. A road sign read STATE HIGHWAY PATROL, NEXT RIGHT.

Thank you, Jesus!

Without slowing or a warning, he veered sharply into the State Patrol driveway. The other vehicle braked and slowed, but then sped off. The passenger window rolled down, and an arm extended exhorting a profane, cursing gesture.

Stephen sat shaking, his heart racing with anger and fear, and a feeling that he had been unjustly violated.

Why?! What did they want with me? What could I possibly have done to arouse their anger?

A startling realization shook him, which, if he had been driving, would have forced him to pull over and calm himself. *Was this some how connected to this afternoon? Was this some kind of retaliation?*

He stared blankly out into the night wondering if he was safe. Should he stop into the State Patrol or just move on? There was a dim light burning in the State Patrol building, but no patrol cars outside. He glanced back towards the highway and saw no lights in either direction.

Slowly he pulled out onto the highway, assuming that his pursuers had abandoned their prey. *Lord, please, watch over me.*

For the next hour he drove cautiously through the darkness more aware than ever how frighteningly true was the Apostle Paul's warning:

> *For we are not contending against flesh and blood, but against the principalities, against the powers, against the world rulers of this present darkness, against the spiritual hosts of wickedness in the heavenly places.*

Part IV

Valley of the Shadow

1

One week later...

Sᴀʀᴀ ᴏᴘᴇɴᴇᴅ ᴛʜᴇ ʙᴀsᴇᴍᴇɴᴛ ᴅᴏᴏʀ, switched on the light, and froze numb with shock. It had been obvious from the clamor that last night's youth meeting was more raucous than usual, but this was ridiculous. Strewn everywhere, on the haphazardly rearranged couches, folding chairs, and card tables, and mashed into the Berber carpet, were potato chips, popcorn, and paper cups.

Sara's temperature rose, and if the boys had been home, her dissatisfaction would have been felt for miles. Surveying the clutter, she consoled herself by recalling that cleaning up after the weekly meetings was a small price to pay for her freedom from having to lead them. Besides, this non-denominational youth club was attracting sometimes fifty teenagers per week—a feat no other church youth group in the area could match. Consequently, she forced herself to recognize that with every piece of trash she bent to retrieve, she was contributing to the salvation of these depraved, rebellious, over-hormoned teenage souls.

Once she had cleared away the larger items, she began vacuuming, all the time warding off the rising tide of bitterness. Then the vacuum's collection bag exploded. Dust and refuse blew everywhere. She wrestled for the switch and let loose a scream of surrender, only to be stopped short by the front doorbell.

She examined herself, covered with dust, and exclaimed with frustration, "Who can that be!"

The bell rang again, so she ascended the stairs carefully to avoid spreading the mess. Peeking through the curtains, she saw a mail delivery van parked in the driveway.

"Excuse me for a second," Sara said as she opened the door and walked past the uniformed delivery woman. Standing on the edge of the porch, she pummeled herself until a small section of the once pristine snowdrift was ashen.

"Vacuum bag explode?" queried the delivery woman.

"How'd you guess?"

"Been there—done that."

"Well, I don't know who put it on last, but the booby trap worked. What'cha got?"

"Package for you, Mrs. LaPointe."

"For me?" Sara took the inch-thick, Priority Mail package. The return address was unfamiliar though local.

"Just sign here."

"Thanks," Sara said as she scribbled her signature. The delivery woman retreated to her truck as Sara stood studying the package. Though eight inches of undulating snow covered the landscape, the morning sun was quite warm and comfortable.

She pulled the paper zipper that unlocked the cardboard jacket and removed the book she had discarded at the mall.

"What!"

Stunned, she read the attached hand-written note: "Found this and was sure you dropped it by accident. Hope you enjoy it, Ginny McBride."

"How dare she force this book on me!"

She crumpled the book in its wrappings to discard it again, but having felt far too much anger already that morning, she paused to re-examine a statement on the book's back cover peering through the wrappings: *"A plain exposition and vindication of the Church founded by our Lord Jesus Christ."*

As always, she thought, *the Catholic Church seeing itself as the one and only true church.*

She kept reading. The book claimed to "delve into the historical background of virtually everything people find hard to understand about our religion." The reference to history hooked her.

More than willing to avoid the wreckage downstairs, she decided to procrastinate for a spell with her first Catholic book. *And also for the sake of Ginny and Adrian,* she reassured herself. *If we're going to be of any assistance, it will help to know what Ginny has gotten herself into.*

After a quick change of clothes, Sara took *The Faith of Our Fathers* and a fresh cup of coffee into the living room for a brief morning's read.

"Good afternoon. Respite Congregational Church."

"Hello. Is this Reverend LaPointe?"

"Yes it is. May I help you?" Stephen leaned back in his chair, away from putting his final touches on Sunday's sermon. It annoyed him that the board belittled his persistent requests for a secretary. It was nigh impossible to focus on anything for any length of time when he had to answer every telephone call or door knock himself.

"This is Adrian McBride, sir. I was hoping that we could arrange a time to get together."

"Yes, Sara told me you stopped by Monday evening, and she filled me in a little about your predicament."

"Mrs. LaPointe was very helpful and kind. I was wondering if Ginny and I could come over some evening soon to talk with both of you. I think that if Ginny could explain herself with the two of you present, we might together be able to help her."

"Well, I don't know when…"

"Mrs. LaPointe was actually the one who made this suggestion."

"In that case, Adrian, let me ask Sara. What night would be good for the two of you?"

"I know this is quick notice, but I was hoping you might be free this evening. Ginny and I are free, and the sooner we quash this, the better."

This was to be his first free evening home in weeks. He had hoped that Sara and he would be able to enjoy a quiet, intimate evening alone. And besides, he was certain that his already overstressed wife would explode at the suggestion of yet another church-related distraction. *But it had been her suggestion.*

"Adrian, let me put you on hold while I call Sara on the other line."

After a few rings, Sara answered, "Hello?"

"Sara, are you all right?"

"Yes, why?"

"You sound perturbed."

"Oh, it's nothing. Just the mess from last night's meeting."

"Sorry I can't be there to help," Stephen said facetiously. "I have a somewhat precarious question to ask about tonight, though. I'm not suggesting this, mind you, but I need to ask. Adrian McBride is on the other line and wants to take you up on your invitation. He was wondering if they could come over tonight to talk with us."

Stephen braced himself, but was stunned when she responded, "Sure, that's fine, if it's all right with you?"

"Well, OK, if you *truly* don't mind. He sounds urgent."

"I'll make arrangements for the boys to spend the night at the Smeltzers'. Please invite them to come, say, around seven for coffee and desert."

"Are you sure?"

"Yes, dear," she said with feigned testiness. "I agree with Adrian that we should confront this as soon as possible."

"OK, thanks, Sara. I love you."

"Love you, too."

Stephen switched back to the other line.

"Well, Adrian, it looks like tonight's a go. Why don't you and Ginny stop by around seven."

After a few words of farewell, they hung up and Stephen attempted a return to his studies. Sara's cooperative spirit distracted him, though. With a smile, he thought: *Maybe we can keep their visit short enough to have that quiet, intimate evening after all.*

*   *   *

THE WHITE LINEN SHADE and its brass floor lamp base crashed to the floor and Stephen's favorite painting of storm-swept waves plummeted from its wall anchor, shattering glass everywhere when it landed on an ornamental stone frog, all of this the result of a direct blow by a flung copy of *The Faith of Our Fathers.*

Sara immediately felt relief, but also shame and embarrassment. She sat quietly, almost weeping, begging Christ for peace of heart. She went to right the fallen lamp, but when she reached for the painting, she found that the bottom right corner of the canvas was badly bent and creased. *What will I tell him? That it had been ruined when I threw a Catholic book across the room?* A second glance reassured her that the painting was not ruined and could be reframed leaving only a fraction of the crease visible. So she went for a broom and dustpan.

As she swept, she faced her guilt, wondering how she could have reacted so violently. In the book's introduction, the author had forewarned why he saw the dire need to write such a book—"because so many false stories and myths had been spread about the Catholic Church." He wanted non-Catholics to learn the truth of the Church. He was making a winsome plea for her heart, but Sara remained stone cold; she remembered how she had felt in the Campion College chapel.

Then when the cardinal wrote, "Remember that nothing is so essential as the salvation of your immortal soul," she reluctantly agreed to read on.

The first few chapters covered less controversial subjects, such as the Trinity, so she skimmed over these, and proceeded directly to a chapter on the "Infallible Authority of the Church." Here the cardinal boldly claimed that "only the Catholic Church has the God-given authority to teach what is true" and that "her teaching is preserved from error by the Holy Spirit."

This enraged Sara's Congregationalist sensibilities but she kept going, and as she read, she found herself vacillating. At times, the cardinal's arguments seemed reasonable, even intriguing, but she began suspecting that somehow she was being duped.

Sipping her coffee, she read a section where the cardinal's face seemed to leer out at her:

> If your church is not infallible it is liable to err, for there is no medium between infallibility and liability to error. If your church and her ministers are fallible in their doctrinal teachings, as they admit, they may be preaching falsehood to you, instead of truth. If so, you are in doubt whether you are listening to truth or falsehood. If you are in doubt you can have no faith, for faith excludes doubt, and in that state you displease God...

With that, the book hit the wall.

Sara cleaned up the glass and hid the broken picture in the utility closet. But why had this statement so enraged her? *Is it because for years I've watched Stephen struggle with this same question? He tries to hide his doubts, but I have seen them in his face contorted with frustration, so I don't need to hear this arrogant, surely misguided cardinal claim that truth can only be known in the Catholic Church.*

She retrieved the book, its binding slightly broken from flight.

She considered returning it to the trash, but instead placed it on the bookshelf to the left of the fireplace.

Perhaps it might help if Stephen glanced through this before tonight's meeting.

Then a chill crossed her heart. Recalling what had divided Adrian and Ginny, she concluded: *Maybe this is exactly what Stephen does* not *need to see. Could he be susceptible to this cardinal's arguments?*

Sara did not think so, but rather than chance it, she moved the book to the privacy of her utility closet and resumed her cleaning.

I only pray that, if this is the kind of tripe that has so lured Ginny away, Stephen will know what to say to bring her back on track— without getting distracted himself.

2

THE DINNER DISHES HAD BEEN CLEARED, rinsed, and crammed into the dishwasher. The living-room hearth was aglow with a freshly stoked fire, and the first-floor rooms were spotless from Sara's afternoon cleaning blitz. The boys were next door at the Smeltzers until morning, and Sara and Stephen sat waiting at the kitchen table.

"You told them seven, didn't you?" Sara asked impatiently.

"Yes, dear," Stephen replied, also a bit on edge. His afternoon had been one interruption after another, so his sermon was far from ready.

They sat silently, waiting. There was an awkwardness between them stemming from concerns of which neither of the other was aware.

Two headlights progressed slowly up the lane, partially masked by blowing snow, and turned into the driveway.

"I'll pour the coffee and you greet, OK?" Sara said, rising.

"If you'd like." He waited as Ginny and Adrian traversed the icy sidewalk and reached the front step, and then, beating them to the buzzer, he opened the door.

"Welcome. Come right in."

"Thank you so much for letting us come over," Adrian said.

"Hello, Adrian, Ginny," Sara said, walking toward them with a tray of coffee and cookies. "Please, let Stephen take your coats, and then come on into the living room."

As they got settled, Stephen and Adrian exchanged general niceties, but the wives remained noticeably aloof.

"I guess your Sammy and our William are on the same basketball team this year?" Stephen asked.

"Yes, that's right," Adrian replied.

A silence descended as the topics of commonality dried up. Eventually, Adrian spoke. "Pastor and Mrs. LaPointe, I asked Ginny to come with me tonight so that she might explain why she is intent on leaving the church."

"Adrian, I haven't left," she said, calmly and tenderly. "I'm sorry for the turmoil my searching has brought to our family and our marriage."

Adrian took her hands affectionately, as they had done ever since they began dating years before in junior high.

"But I can't help it," Ginny said now addressing them all. "Every day, I am more convinced that what I have discovered is true."

Adrian started to pull away, but Ginny stopped him.

"Please, Adrian, please."

Adrian relaxed. It was obvious to all that his desire to be close to the love of his life was stronger than his revulsion for the choices she was making.

"Ginny," Stephen asked, "why don't you tell us how this all started?"

"Well, I have always been a voracious reader," Ginny began. "I suppose this is one of the few areas where Adrian and I are different. His college degree led to a good job; mine in English literature led to a life seeking adventure and inspiration in books. Last summer I began preparing for an adult Sunday school class I was to lead on the book of Acts. In the process, I became amazed at how ignorant I was about the early Christian communities—what they believed, how they worshiped, how their churches were organized.

"I talked with Ock Turner, the local librarian, and he pointed me to an unfamiliar group of writers called the Apostolic Fathers—Christian writers who had been converted and trained by the Apostles themselves. They're certainly not easy reading, but they are fascinating. At first, I began sharing what I was discovering with Adrian, but his new job was so demanding that I mostly kept it to myself. In time, however, I became convinced that I was in trouble as a Congregationalist Christian. Eventually, as September approached, I knew that I could not teach the class without causing controversy, so I withdrew my name, which made more than a few people mad, including Adrian."

She looked over at her husband and, seeing his support, continued.

"I kept reading the writings of other Church Fathers until a few statements from St. Augustine started me thinking about the Catholic Church. As you know, Pastor LaPointe, all the Reformers quoted Augustine to defend their break from the Catholic Church."

She opened her purse and removed a folded sheet of paper.

"I figured this eventually would come up, so I kept a copy of these statements. The first comes from a sermon Augustine gave to the church at Caesarea around 418 A.D. Now, remembering how Luther and Calvin used his writings, listen to what Augustine wrote against those who in his day broke away from the Catholic Church:

> A man cannot have salvation, except in the Catholic Church. Outside the Catholic Church he can have everything except salvation. He can have honor, he can have Sacraments, he can sing alleluia, he can answer amen, he can possess the gospel, he can have and preach faith in the name of the Father and of the Son and of the Holy Spirit; but never except in the Catholic Church will he be able to find salvation."

"Excuse me as I freshen my coffee," Sara said, with a sudden retreat to the kitchen.

Stephen watched quizzically as his wife left in what he recognized as a panic. Returning his attention to Ginny, he saw that she and Adrian were awaiting his response.

"Ginny, I've not read that quote before," Stephen admitted, "but all it says to me is that even someone as theologically astute as Augustine can be blinded by prejudice. Does the Roman Church still teach this? That one has to be a Roman Catholic to be saved?"

"Actually, yes and no," she replied. "When I first read this and other quotes like it from other Church Fathers, I became nervous, not so much because they might be right and I wrong, but because these writers were so persistent in their claims. They pronounced this without apology, without hesitation, as if it were common knowledge in their day. It was this that led me to buy my first Catholic Catechism, which I read from cover to cover.

"In this I learned that, yes, the Catholic Church believes that she is the Church founded by Christ in His Apostles and entrusted through the gift of the Holy Spirit to preserve, protect, and promote Christian truth. She teaches that the Church was created by Christ to be the channel of grace through which all believers are saved."

Stephen could tell by the edge of a saucer protruding from the corner of the kitchen that Sara was standing just inside, listening. He was at a loss, however, as to why.

"Ginny," Stephen said, "there have always been churches as well as individuals who boldly claim to have a corner on what is true, as if they were the only ones to whom God has spoken. But the key is, where is this found in Scripture?" The instant he said this, he felt himself smitten by the same question that had so plagued him all week.

"Pastor, there are many, many verses that teach this," Ginny quickly countered, "but the one that convinced me was 1 Timothy 3:15."

As she read the verse aloud, Stephen screamed within himself: *Good Lord, not again! That verse is relentless.* He looked up from where Ginny was sitting, and noticed that something was wrong. Something was missing. *My painting. It's gone!*

He looked toward the kitchen, but saw no sign of Sara's return.

"In this verse," Ginny continued, "how could Paul have meant that a bunch of disconnected, independent churches were somehow the pillar and bulwark of truth? Doesn't it make more sense that he was talking about *the* Church proclaimed in the ancient Christian creeds as the one, holy, apostolic and catholic Church."

"But Ginny," Sara exclaimed as she bolted back into the room, "so many evil things have been done throughout history in the name of the Catholic Church."

Sara's intensity startled everyone, especially her husband. He could not remember her lashing out so violently against Catholicism.

"Sara," Ginny continued, "like me, you probably grew up thinking all kinds of things about the Catholic Church, but as you and I discussed at St. Michael's, who did we learn these things from? We learned them from our Protestant Sunday school teachers, preachers, neighbors, or friends, or from Protestant books."

Stephen looked at Sara for an explanation, but was ignored.

"But just because they were Protestant doesn't mean that their opinions about the Catholic Church were wrong," Sara demanded.

"I know that and that they did not intend to mislead us. But Sara, have you ever passed along anything you were told about the Catholic Church without first checking to make sure that it was true?"

"I don't need to check, because I know that I can trust the people who told me."

"But isn't it possible that they had done the same thing?" Ginny pressed. "That they had heard or read something from someone they trusted and then passed it along to you without checking?"

"But come on, Ginny. If what we believe about the Catholic Church is false, then who started the lies? Sincere believers in Christ would never justify lying, no matter what the reason, because they know that they will be accountable before God for misleading others."

Ginny paused before she responded, and Stephen knew why. *Yes, sincere believers in Christ should never lie; they should never "bear false witness against their neighbor." But of course, we're "all sinners and have fallen short of the glory of God."*

"That's true," Ginny continued, "and I don't know how any sincere Christian could justify twisting the facts and passing it off as true. I do know, however, that much of what I believed about the Catholic Church is false. I also recognize that the existence of Protestantism depends upon the propagation of these myths, because once the truth about Catholicism is discovered, a Protestant no longer can justify what the name implies: he can not protest. This is what happened to me. I was ignorant of what the Catholic Church truly believes, but now that I know the truth, I cannot stay away from it."

"But, honey, the Catholic Church is against the Bible," Adrian pleaded. "It teaches all kinds of things that are not scriptural."

"Adrian, nothing could be further from the truth," his wife insisted. "This is one of those vicious myths. The only reason we have the Bible is because the Catholic Church protected it, copied it, and translated it long before the Reformation. It was the Catholic Church that decided which books were to be included in the Bible."

"But what about the popes who have forbidden the laity from reading the Bible?" Stephen asked. "If it is God's inspired Word, then why can't Catholics read it?"

"They certainly may and are strongly encouraged to read the Bible. Here, look," Ginny opened her Bible. "This is my Catholic

Bible. It is available in any bookstore, Catholic, Protestant, or secular. Listen to this quote from Pope Paul VI printed in the inside cover:

> The holy task of spreading God's word to the widest possible readership has a special urgency today. Despite all his material achievements, man still struggles with the age-old problems of how to order his life for the glory of God, for the welfare of his fellows and the salvation of his soul. Therefore, we are gratified to find in this new translation of the Scriptures a new opportunity for men to give themselves to frequent reading of, and meditation on, the living Word of God. In its pages we recognize His voice, we hear a message of deep significance for every one of us.

"Now tell me, Reverend LaPointe," Ginny continued, "can you quote me as strong of an encouragement to read and meditate on the Bible from any of our Congregationalist leaders?"

"That's fine, Ginny, and I'm glad the Catholic Church today encourages its people to read the Bible, but that doesn't explain why the popes once forbade its members to do so."

"Part of that is a myth, and part is true," Ginny said. "I'm just summarizing what I've read, but remember that for fourteen hundred years, all Bibles and books were produced by hand, quill and ink, by monks in monasteries. As a result, Bibles were rare and expensive, so few laity ever held a copy of the Bible, let alone own one. But this didn't matter, because few of the millions of laity could read anyway. After the invention of the printing press in 1450, one of the first books printed was the Latin Bible, and within the next hundred years, Bibles were printed in many languages including German, English, and French. Some of these translations were flawed, however, because they were produced by poorly-trained scholars or careless printers. Consequently, many contained errors.

"After the Reformation, the number of printed Bibles increased, and many contained not only misprints but even intentional mistranslations or notes which either attacked Catholic doctrines or promoted Protestant ones. A good example of this was Martin Luther's own German translation. In Romans 3:28 he inserted the word 'only' where the word did not exist in the original Greek.

"The Catholic Church, therefore, forbade its members to read flawed or misleading translations. It would be comparable to you, Reverend LaPointe, discouraging us from reading the Jehovah's Witnesses' *New World Bible* because it contains mistranslations. The main difference is that whereas the Catholic Church has the authority to protect its members, Protestant pastors can only encourage or discourage."

"*Presumed* authority," Sara retorted.

"Actually, Sara, Ginny is right," Stephen said, which won him a sharp glare. "Whether the Catholic priest's authority is legitimate or not, he certainly wields a power over his members that we Protestant ministers can only dream about. But Ginny, if Catholics are encouraged to read their Bibles, then why do they believe so many strange things that are unscriptural, like Mary's Immaculate Conception or supposed bodily assumption into Heaven, or the worship of statues?"

"Well, let me first say that Catholics do not worship statues," Ginny said. "This is idolatry for Catholics just as it is for Protestants. When a Catholic prays before an image, he is praying to the saint to whom that image points, like a painting of Jesus moves us to pray to Him," pointing to the portrait above the mantle.

"Well, there, another example," Sara said, ignoring Ginny's gesture. "The Bible nowhere advocates praying to the dead. Instead, it calls this necromancy."

"Sara and Reverend LaPointe, rather than deal with each of these issues individually, which are all easily answerable, let me address a more foundational issue. Your basic question is how can Catholics believe so many things that are not in the Bible, correct?"

"Right," Stephen said, with facial confirmations from both Sara and Adrian.

"OK, can any of you show me where in the Bible it says that everything we believe *must* be found in the Bible?"

Stephen had backed himself into a déjà vu experience with a twist. This was similar to the question Larry Howe had cornered him with at the board meeting, but from a different angle. For Larry's question, he had a pat response; for Ginny's, he had none.

Hearing no response, Ginny continued, "All of my life, I accepted the assumption that everything we believe must have some basis in Scripture. Hundreds of times I've heard Protestant preachers defend their ideas with the statement, 'The Bible says,' or they attack someone with the demand, 'Where is that in the Bible?' The truth is, however, the Bible nowhere states that *it* is the standard for all truth. This is a non-biblical assumption that was imposed on the Bible, a man-made tradition that millions of Christians have accepted without examination. And to make matters worse, they can't even agree about what it means. Some believe that they can do whatever the Bible doesn't forbid, while others believe they can only do what the Bible permits. For example, Christians who allow abortion are from the first group, while Christians who are against electricity, going to movies, or using musical instruments in worship are of the second group. The point is that the Bible nowhere claims to be what Protestants have made it."

Adrian was looking desperately to Stephen for help, but Stephen had none to give.

"But Ginny," Sara demanded, "what about all the corrupt popes and bishops and priests and the Mafia and drunken and gambling Catholics?"

"Sara, Catholics don't deny for a second that there have been corrupt popes, bishops, cardinals, priests, nuns, monks, laity, and probably more than you or I can imagine. But this shouldn't surprise us one bit. Reverend LaPointe, when did the Church begin having disappointing members who taught or practiced things contrary to Christ's teachings?"

Stephen hesitated. His usual answer to this was going to play right into her argument, but he had no choice. "From the beginning, but ..."

"Exactly. Of the first handpicked twelve, we find a traitor, a betrayer, and mostly cowards. Of the second generation Christians, we find hordes of adulterers, liars, heretics, etc. In fact, the reason behind every New Testament letter was to correct problems in early churches. And isn't this exactly what Jesus promised? He taught that the Church would consist of both wheat and tares, the faithful and the unfaithful, until the end of time. So the presence of unfaithful members does not disqualify the Catholic Church, but qualifies her to be the very Church Jesus established."

"Nor does it disqualify other Christian churches," Stephen said, a bit flummoxed by the informed eloquence of this otherwise soft-spoken laywoman. The familiar slant to his wife's eyes also told him that Sara was feeling intimidated by Ginny's arguments.

"Pastor, let me say two things to this," Ginny said. "First, Jesus did not ask His Father for thousands of independent, dissimilar churches. He prayed that His followers would be united as one, just as He and the Father are one. Right? And second, listen to this other quote from St. Augustine."

Ginny fumbled for her folded paper, which had inadvertently become a placemat for her coffee, and read: "'There is nothing more serious than the sacrilege of schism because there is no just cause for severing the unity of the Church.'"

Turning with tenderness to her husband, Ginny said: "Adrian, I have come to realize that the Reformation was less a God–centered renewal than a divorce, a ruptured family. I believe that I have no choice but to return home to the Church Jesus established."

"But what about my opinion?" Adrian said in frustration, rising from his seat and turning away from Ginny. "What about our marriage covenant? I thought I was to be the spiritual head of our family. Don't I have a say in this?"

Ginny hesitated, but reaching up to grasp his hands, she answered carefully, "Adrian, I love you more than anything, more than anyone else in the world. You know that. The last thing I would ever want to do is hurt you or our marriage."

After a pause, she continued, "But you also know that Jesus said that following Him sometimes causes conflict between parents and children, brothers and sisters, and even husbands and wives. Darling, I know in my heart that to follow Jesus faithfully, I must return to His Church…"

Adrian pulled his hands away, but Ginny persisted: "But I also know that I love you with all of my heart. I am begging you, please, do not force me to choose between you and the Church. I promise that I will do nothing to embarrass you. I won't make a scene about this, but Adrian, I am convinced that this is what God is calling me to do."

Stephen watched as Adrian walked silently over to the fireplace, his back to his wife. If this interchange had happened a year ago, maybe a month ago, Stephen would have offered stock answers to counter Ginny's claims, to call her to return to her evangelical faith and to the spiritual leadership of her husband. He should have been in control of this meeting; he should have been instructing Ginny. But things were different now.

Lifting his eyes, he found Ginny looking directly at him, into him, anticipating his pastoral intervention, which she presumed would fall against her. He glanced away toward Sara, and her puzzled glare almost startled him into action, but he caught himself. Too often over the past ten years he had relied upon the authority of his office to utter the first thing on his lips to break awkward moments, but he wasn't going to do that now.

For what seemed like eternity, his mind remembered similar occasions in his ministry when the pat answers he had learned in seminary didn't work: his confusion over clerical dress, his arguments with Reverend Malone, his eye-opening encounter with Larry at Respite, his confrontation with Rita Brownstein at the funeral, and his frustrating disagreements with Walter Horscht and his friends. Stephen no longer presumed that his evangelical interpretation of Scripture was the most accurate. And even though he was unprepared to accept Ginny's conclusions, her intriguing answers had formed one more crack in the wall of his confidence in the Bible as the one sufficient source of truth.

Upon what sure foundation am I to base whatever advice I give to this suffering yet sincerely believing couple? Who am I to declare that what Ginny has discovered through her search is wrong, when I am no longer certain that my Evangelical-Calvinist-Congregationalist interpretation is trustworthy?

He stood up and crossed the room to a point directly between Ginny and Adrian. Extending a hand toward Ginny, he invited her to stand beside him. With the other hand, he touched Adrian's shoulder and turned him around. Recognizing her husband's strategy, Sara rose and completed the circle of friends.

Their hands clasped, Stephen said, "Ginny and Adrian, I would rather hold my comments for later. I know that you both love the Lord Jesus with all your heart, mind, and soul. For now, this is what is important. Ginny, I don't suspect that you are planning to make this move immediately?"

"No," she said softly.

"Then Ginny and Adrian, the key is to be patient and love each other. Remember James' instructions, 'Be quick to listen, slow to speak, and slow to anger.' If it's all right, I would like us to wait until after Easter to get back together. This will give me time to consider all that you have said. Is that OK?"

"Yes, fine, Pastor," Adrian answered.

"Then let us pray," Stephen said.

With heads bowed, he led them in a prayer for guidance, for patience, for compassion and truth. He asked that the God of all creation and all truth might lead them all without wavering in the clear and narrow path.

The atmosphere following the "Amen" was heavy, but after a brief period of courteous chatter and cleaning up, Stephen retrieved their coats and bid the McBrides goodbye.

*   *   *

"STEPHEN, what was wrong with you?" Sara exclaimed with pent-up frustration the instant the door clicked shut.

"What do you mean?" Stephen said, still facing the closed door, apprehensive about facing her.

"I don't understand. You said nothing to correct Ginny's misguided claims or to help them toward a reconciliation."

"The purpose of tonight's meeting was cathartic," Stephen replied, turning from the door and walking toward the refrigerator. "Ginny was able to spill it all out freely, without too many interruptions. This way we were able to hear it all, and maybe she was able to hear herself more clearly."

"But, Stephen..."

"Honey," he said, removing a bottle of chilled Zinfandel, "trust me. It might seem like all we did was open the proverbial can of worms, but my work with them is not over. It is over, though, for tonight. OK?" He offered her a glass of wine.

She hesitated. It was obvious that for her it was not over, but she reluctantly took the glass and sipped it silently.

"Sara, what is it? Why did you get so agitated about what Ginny was saying?"

She glanced toward the utility closet, and then answered, "You're right, darling. Let's not let this spoil our evening."

With a kiss on the cheek, she led him into the living room.

Or is this the opportune time to tell her? Stephen pondered as he joined her on the couch. *To come clean about all my doubts?*

He placed an arm around her shoulder as she nuzzled up against him. Together they gazed silently at the fire, now reduced to burning embers. He kissed her forehead and they embraced lovingly. He studied her familiar green eyes, which, though everything else in their lives was evolving drastically, always remained reassuringly constant, like a safe, familiar harbor in a tumultuous sea. With one look, punctuated by the tender glimpse of her smile, she told him that he was loved and, therefore, blessed.

Maybe I'll tell her tomorrow.

Yet, as he turned off the Tiffany table lamp, a phrase refused to dim in the marque of his mind: *The church...the pillar...the bulwark...the truth.*

3

BEHIND A CLOSED BEDROOM DOOR, under the concentrated beam of a solitary high-intensity lamp, before the opened hutch of his grandfather's antique roll-top desk, Walter sat hunched over and motionless. His eyes intensely scanned the archaic, yet holy words on the pages of his King James translation. Occasionally he would snap into action, as his hands moved to underline or to copy onto 3x5 cards a particular verse or phrase that had caught his attention. Then he would return to intense stone stillness.

"Walter?" Helen said, snapping the door open. Walter jumped, 3x5 cards scattered. His pen made an arc across the room onto a pile of dirty clothes, the high-intensity lamp careened onto the floor, and with an upward jerk his thick glasses flew over his head and onto the bed.

"Jeez, Helen!" he said, scurrying to right everything.

"Serves you right, Walter. I wish all I had to do was sit around and read the Bible," she said. "Are you going to look for a job today or not?"

"Helen, don't make me go all through that again," he said, realigning his glasses. "I'm not ready to give up on my calling to full-time ministry."

"Walter," she said, on the verge of tears, "what is it going to take to convince you? It's great that you want to serve the Lord; I couldn't be happier for your enthusiasm. But honey, please, no offense, but no one is confirming this call of yours. Reverend Jenkins hasn't encouraged you."

"He hasn't been here long enough to know me."

"But Walter, what about your friends? Are they encouraging you?"

"Raeph hasn't told me to give up," he said, hunched back over his Bible. Things had become only more difficult since his best friend in the faith took a new job in northwestern Massachusetts. Walter felt like a boat adrift in spiritual chaos.

Helen crossed the room. Steadying herself against his strong shoulders, she passed a hand up through his hair. So much had changed since she had fallen in love with this Vietnam veteran "rebel on wheels," and mostly for the better. His neatly combed, graying-in-the-temples hair stood as a symbol to this. Encircling his neck with affection, she embraced the man of her life.

For a moment, he absorbed her love, but then broke free. "Helen, please, I know what I'm doing. Now if you will just leave me alone, I can finish my morning devotions. I'll be down for lunch at noon."

He turned back to his reading.

"Walter?" she pleaded, but he ignored her. She let her hands drop from his shoulders to her side, and quietly left the room.

When the door clicked shut, Walter dropped his head into his hands.

"Lord Jesus," he prayed softly, "what am I doing wrong? Why aren't You leading me? I have to do something, quickly. We've almost depleted our savings. Did You truly tell me to serve You full-time or not?"

The heavens remained silent, as Walter expected. He looked up to the portrait of Jesus that had always been an inspiration, then over to the box containing the other paraphernalia he had emptied from his locker. Struck by an inspiration, he rose as if in slow motion and proceeded to the box. Reaching down into the heap of books, tapes, and literature, he withdrew the tract that for so long had been his guiding light: "Are Roman Catholics Christian?"

Thumbing through the pages illustrated with comics, he wondered: *Could this be what You are calling me to do?*

With renewed energy, he crossed the room to the bedside telephone and called the 800 number printed on the tract.

"Good morning, FC2C. May I help you?" The woman's voice sounded kind but canned.

"Yes, I was wondering if I could speak with Reverend Harmond."

"Is he expecting your call?"

"No, I just wanted to speak with him."

"May I say who is calling?"

"Walter...Walter Horscht. I'm a great admirer of his work. I've read most of his books and tracts. I was hoping I could ask him a question."

"Please hold, I'll see if he's available."

The telephone audio switched to a tape of Reverend Harmond delivering a boisterous critique of the Catholic teaching on purgatory. Though Harmond was halfway through, Walter knew exactly the points of his argument, for he had listened to this tape dozens of times. After nearly three minutes, as the tenor of Harmond's presentation reached a crescendo, the tape was interrupted by a softer, yet strong male voice: "This is Reverend Harmond. May I help you?"

"Reverend Harmond, I'm a longtime admirer of yours," Walter said, standing in excitement. "In fact, I heard you once at Grace Open Bible Church. You probably don't remember, but I was the one who helped remove that Catholic heckler."

"Why, yes. I never had the chance to thank you," Harmond replied. "Is there something specific I can help you with today?"

"I was hoping for your advice. Ever since my conversion to Jesus about seventeen years ago, I have felt that God was calling me to do something special for Him; as if I was converted for a unique and specific purpose. I was a special assignments officer in Vietnam and was trained to do whatever I was ordered, without question, without complaint. And I believe that this is what God is calling me to. Last month, I lost my job because I was too outspoken about my faith and the truth about the Roman Catholic Church. When I was praying afterwards, I swear I heard God's voice calling me into ministry. It's just that no doors have opened. Then I remembered your work with FC2C and how much your materials have helped me understand the vile nature of Catholicism, and I was wondering if maybe there was something I could do to help you with your work?"

"Well, Walter—I think that was what Ms. Roberts said—I appreciate your offer. God knows there's a lot to be done to halt the prolific spread of papism and to rescue Catholics for Christ. But to be honest, we have no openings for new people. We struggle to support our small staff as it is. Do you have any training for ministry?"

"No, not exactly. After the war, I got a degree in industrial engineering on the GI Bill."

"Have you been working as an engineer?'

"Well, no. I was a foreman at a plastics factory up until last month."

Walter heard some undecipherable noises from the other side of the line, and then again Harmond's voice. "Listen, Walter, I can neither confirm nor deny that God is calling you into full-time ministry, but if you don't mind my advice…"

"That's why I called."

"Yes, well, it's been my experience that God gives us each gifts for the tasks to which He has called us. And please don't make the mistake of thinking that full-time Christian ministry is somehow more holy or fulfilling than regular, secular work. It sounds like God gave you the training and experience to work as His full-time disciple, creatively disguised as a foreman or an engineer. You just need to be more tactful and guarded in your witness."

"But, Reverend Harmond, I know in my heart that He has a special assignment for me."

"That might be true, but in the meantime, I presume you have a family to support?"

"Yes, a wife and a daughter."

"The Bible says, 'If any man doth not labor, let him eateth not.' Your first responsibility is to your family, Walter. The Bible also says, 'Ye have been faithful over a little, I will set you over much.' First things first, Walter. Have you tried to find another job?"

"No, I've been, well, waiting on God, as the Bible says," Walter said testily.

"Yes, the Bible does say 'Wait on the Lord,' but God can't steer a docked ship. I suggest you get back in the work force, pay your bills, focus on being a faithful husband and father. And I promise that if this isn't what God wants you to do, He will honor your faithfulness and steer you in the right direction."

"I suppose you're right."

"Sure, but that doesn't mean that on the side you can't be His witness," Harmond said. "Tell me, exactly how have you been actively witnessing to the Lord Jesus, other than getting yourself in trouble at work?"

"During this past month, I've spent a lot of time getting comfortable with the Internet. I'm active in several anti-Catholic discussion groups. In fact, I'm a member of your FC2C chat room."

"Really? Well, Walter, I truly believe that the Internet is the evangelistic medium of the future. More souls will be saved over the Internet, especially from the clutches of the Whore of Babylon, than through any other medium. I strongly encourage you to utilize your new skills for the glory of Christ."

Cables of constricting disillusionment were suddenly cut and cleared from Walter's heart. Everything made sense.

"Reverend Harmond, thank you so much. You are exactly right."

"Of course, Walter. Now I need to rush to another appointment, but please, keep reading and distributing those books and tapes. You know that FC2C exists only through the generosity of friends like you."

"You can always count on my support."

Upon hanging up, Walter felt rejuvenated. He was relieved about looking for another industrial position, because he had loved his work. But even more so, he was exhilarated to realize that somehow the special assignment to which God was calling him might involve the Internet.

He returned to his desk and switched on his computer. After getting on line, he perused a few of his favorite sites, fishing for leads as to how God might be calling him to use this worldwide medium, until he visited a site he considered one of his archenemies—a Catholic ministry that tried to convert Protestant ministers.

"Yes, that's what I should do" Walter said to himself. "Why not e-mail Catholics directly, sending them information that might open their hearts to the truth about their religion."

And then he remembered.

"And maybe even a certain minister whom I believe is, in fact, an impostor."

4

"WHAT WAS GOING THROUGH MY MIND when I picked this verse?" Stephen exclaimed in the Wednesday morning solitude of his sweltering office. He glanced at a thermometer desk ornament that included a replica of the famous Gloucester fisherman sculpture with his trusty ship's wheel. It had been a fortieth-birthday present from Daniel.

"Eighty degrees! That stupid antiquated heating system." He rose and gave the knob on the radiator a spin that would surely call him back in a few hours when the temperature had dropped to below sixty.

Running his hands through his thinning, graying hair, he returned to his seat and the text of his befuddlement. In January, when he mapped out his preaching schedule for the next six months, he had not anticipated that the concerns of the past would resurface with such vengeance.

"How can I possibly stand before these people with confidence when there are so many contradicting interpretations of this passage!"

Since the beginning of February, he had been preaching from texts chosen to focus on spiritual renewal. For the month of March, he had chosen John 6. Stephen had always interpreted this chapter as illustrating the spiritual journey from hearing, seeing, and following Jesus, to believing and finally knowing Him. But with all his present concerns clouding his mind, he saw other aspects he had never before noticed.

"'Truly, truly, I say to you,'" Stephen read out loud for the dozenth time, "'unless you eat the flesh of the son of man and drink his blood, you have no life in you; he who eats my flesh and drinks my blood has eternal life, and I will raise him up at the last day. For my flesh is food indeed, and my blood is drink indeed.' Good Lord," Stephen exclaimed, throwing his Bible back on the desk.

Up until this week, Stephen had never thought twice about this passage, presuming that Jesus was speaking figuratively. But after rereading these verses repeatedly since Monday, exegeting them in the Greek, and following every cross reference, he was less sure of himself than when he had begun. What most troubled him was that it was obvious from the straight reading of the text that Jesus' audience took Him to be speaking literally. *That is the only way to explain why the Jews were so offended and why many of His disciples drew back from Him, complaining that His words were too hard to listen to,* he thought. *And on top of this, when Jesus had the chance to correct any misunderstandings, He didn't. He merely asked the few disciples who remained, "Do you also wish to go away?"*

What bothered Stephen most, however, was how much more easily the clear reading of the text supported the more literal views of the Lutherans, Catholics, and Orthodox than it did his own more symbolic understanding of the Lord's Supper. And the fact that these three groups also disagreed with each other didn't help matters.

He looked across at the thermostat, which had already begun to plummet. Setting his stack of sermon notes on a shelf beside him, he muttered, "Maybe this afternoon I'll be able to think clearer."

All that was left to do that morning was catch up on his overflowing cup of e-mail. He scanned down through the list of messages he had been putting off for days, past dozens of advertisements and promotional spam, past a few messages from his boys he already had answered, and past acquaintances who generally filled his inbox with jokes that had previously made the rounds from coast to coast. Then there was the week-old message from the head office of his Congregational association.

> *Dear Reverend LaPointe,*
>
> *You are cordially invited to attend a meeting for New England Congregational pastors to discuss "Y2K: What is it and should we worry?" Our goal will be to separate fact from fiction and fear so that we can more readily minister to the needs of our churches at the end of this millennium. The gathering will be held on Thursday, March 18th at 1 p.m.*

"Good Lord, that's tomorrow!" Stephen had put off reading this for so long he almost missed the meeting. "But should I go and make even a bigger pain of myself than I already have?"

Actually, he was surprised that they still invited him to these regional gatherings. Generally, he ended up the sole conservative sour note amidst a gaggle of liberals. He always figured their parties began only after he departed.

At least on this issue, some of us might be on the same page, he thought in jest. *Well, if it's all right with Sara, I guess I'll spend tomorrow seeing what kind of nuisance I can make of myself.*

He continued down his list and came across one from an unfamiliar source: *Thevoiceoftruth.*

With the increasing threat of computer viruses, Stephen was cautious about suspicious e-mail. But the subject line of this one was intriguing: "I know who you are."

"Now who could this be?" he said with a laugh as he double-clicked it. A colorful collage of crosses and Bibles filled his monitor's border, encircling a central message that read:

> *Reverend LaPointe:*
> *You don't fool me. You might be able to put up a good evangelical Protestant front, but I can tell by how you water down the truth of the faith and pussy-foot around important issues, like the End Times, that you aren't what you say you are. Know ye that promoting the work of the Whore of Babylon will lead to Hell. You son of perdition, remember what Jesus said: "Whoever causes one of these little ones who believe in me to sin, it would be better for him if a great millstone were hung round his neck and he were thrown into the sea [of brimstone and fire]."*
> *Beware! And be faithful!*
>
> *Thevoiceoftruth*
> *(If you want more information, go to: www.fc2c.com)*

"What is this person talking about?"

He wondered if it might have been sent to the wrong address, *but the sender addressed me directly.*

He started to shoot something with expletives back in reply, and was poised to send it when he hesitated. "Wait a second. What am I getting myself into?"

Instead, he deleted his response and the original, turned off his computer and the lights, and with a sigh of disbelief went home for lunch.

5

STEPHEN'S AGING FAIRMONT sputtered into the paved parking lot of First Congregational Church, Midstream, New Hampshire.

"I've got to get rid of this monstrosity." *But I'll need that long-promised raise first!*

Stephen had arrived nearly half an hour early, but to avoid having to make small talk with clergy with whom he otherwise had nothing in common, he remained in his car, finalizing his thoughts on the implications of the Y2K bug. Since his initial forewarning in a *Newsweek* article, he had become increasingly concerned by both the intensity as well as the diversity of the warnings. The spectrum of these seemingly well-informed opinions ranged from complete denial ("It's a hoax; a money making scheme!") to agnosticism ("All the opinions cancel each other out.") to nominal concern ("My minimal preparation is nothing more than insurance.") to fear and panic ("All aspects of modern, worldwide culture will grind to a halt.") to apocalyptic mania ("This is the final judgment of God upon our worship of technological progress!").

Since January, concerns about Y2K had been surfacing in Bible study discussions, counseling sessions, and board meetings. Recognizing the need to become informed, he had begun studying literature from a wide range of secular and religious sources. Eventually, he and Sara together concluded that, yes, the Y2K threat was real, but it had no inherent religious apocalyptic connection. *Electric grids might go down all over the world on January 1, but this did not mean we should expect to see Jesus coming in the clouds.*

At the board meeting last week, Stephen shared Sara's and his conclusions, receiving the complete spectrum of responses. The more significant backlash of all this, however, was still further confirmation of his personal struggle with truth: "Which of this hodgepodge of contrary opinions from seemingly well-informed sources should I believe and then convince my congregation to believe? Am I being a faithful messenger or a false prophet?"

And his discussion with Sara last night hadn't helped.

Other cars were entering the parking lot, surrounding his like eggs in a carton, but the drivers were unidentifiable through his steamed-up windows.

Last night, did I squander a providential moment…

THE BOYS HAD GONE TO BED to read the latest Brian Jacques adventure, while he and Sara were relishing a quiet moment in their bed watching a rerun of *Andy Griffith*. In response to a sudden offhanded query about today's meeting, he allowed Sara an unanticipated glimpse into his otherwise private struggle.

"Sara, I'm hesitant to bring this up," he said, pausing to sip a late-night instant decaf cappuccino, "but as I contemplate facing those ministers tomorrow, I'm having second thoughts over this issue of Y2K."

"What do you mean?" Sara responded, only half listening. "Why the waffling?"

"It's not so much that I'm waffling—though it probably sounds like it. It's just this: all the ministers I know—faithful believers and mostly well-informed about the potential threat—have come to different conclusions than I have, and on Sunday mornings from their pulpits, their warnings run contrary to mine."

"So? When did you start worrying about what other ministers preach?"

Am I hiding this that well? But should I tell her?

"Let me ask you this," he said instead. "Tell me something that you believe because it is *true* and not because someone else *convinced* you that it was true."

"What?" she asked, pulling her attention reluctantly from Gomer catching Barney in a citizen's arrest. "You're not making sense."

"Let me use a different example," Stephen said. "You and I studied very hard to come to our conclusion about the immorality of abortion."

Sara's sudden jerk to attention surprised Stephen. He continued.

"Together we read and prayed and discussed, and in the end, we agreed on a position that is contrary to many of our friends, family, and colleagues. How can we be positive that we are right?"

She started to answer, but he stopped her with his hand, "I mean, Sara: is our opinion on abortion merely that—just one opinion among many—or is there one position that is in fact *true?* The Bible says nothing about abortion or when life actually begins, or about many other things which we believe deeply. How can we know that our convictions are any more accurate than anyone else's?"

Sara silently turned her focus back to Barney handing Andy his hat, badge, and lone bullet for the hundredth time. With this, Stephen left the warmth of their quilted comforter and walked to the window. He stared out at the church, illuminated only tangentially by a street lamp.

"Or is truth all just relative," he murmured, "like beauty—up to the eye of the beholder?"

"Honey, what's wrong?" Sara asked, rising and crossing the room. "Why is this bothering you so much?"

This is the time. Tell her about the doubts that are destroying my confidence in being a minister.

But he couldn't, not yet.

"Nothing, dear," he said, turning away from the window, taking her into his arms. "I'm just tired."

He kissed her, and with a smile, pulled her back under the comforter, where their attention turned to other things…

Now AS HE SAT behind the fogged windows of his sedan, ensconced among an assortment of mostly newer, more affluent-looking vehicles, he wondered if he was ready for this debacle.

In the attempt to leave his car, he discovered that the driver next to him had left too little room to open his door. He squeezed his slightly overweight frame through the six-inch clearance and against a mental tirade, and then recognized the neighboring car. He was unable to place it, but he knew he had seen this faded gray Caprice wagon many times before.

Must be some minister I know, but who?

Through the familiar corridors of this upper-crust church where the Association held most of its regional gatherings, Stephen proceeded unenthusiastically.

Grab a cup of coffee, find a back seat, and keep my mouth shut!

At the urn was an unexpected, familiar face, dressed in a three-piece brown suit, looking every bit like just another of the clergy.

Of course! That was his wagon.

"Walter, what an unexpected surprise," he said with feigned enthusiasm.

When Walter turned, he nearly dropped his cup of scalding coffee on their shoes.

"Reverend LaPointe, it's, ah, good to see you."

They exchanged a quick, cordial handshake, but Walter pulled away to straighten his glasses.

"I certainly didn't expect to find you at this meeting," Stephen said.

"Our new minister couldn't make it, so he asked if I might bring back a report."

"But how are you able…?"

"Well, I lost my job last month."

"I'm sorry to hear that, Walter. If there's anything I can do…"

"Time to gather, ladies and gentlemen," came an amplified female voice from the fellowship hall.

"Thanks," Walter said, turning toward the voice, "but God will provide."

In the hall, they found six folding tables arranged in a rectangle surrounded by chairs. Stephen figured he had no choice but to take a seat next to Walter, but this did not happen. Walter lingered. When Stephen selected a chair on the west side of the room, Walter hurried to the south corner and chose a chair essentially out of Stephen's direct line of sight.

Most of the faces were familiar, and the unique blend of those who had chosen to attend confirmed Stephen's presumption that the tone of the meeting would be skeptical. The only friend in the mix, sitting directly across the rectangle, was Scott Turner, the pastor of a picturesque church in the southwest forested corner of Maine. Before Scott's adult conversion had turned his heart toward ministry, he had been both a professional football player and a state champion weightlifter. Now his immense presence caught everyone's attention, especially young boys and men who thought religion was only for sissies. No one dared mention this in Scott's presence, though in reality he was no more than a big teddy bear.

Stephen and Scott exchanged facial greetings, and Scott's wink confirmed that Stephen had at least one compatriot among the fold.

"Time to begin, gentlemen," said the Reverend Irene Strongbridge, the only female minister in attendance and the person the head office normally assigned to convene these sessions. "May we begin in prayer," she said, assuming a stance of Mosaic proportions. "Oh God of all creation, of all peoples, and of all creeds…" she began.

Stephen forced himself to follow her invocation with a charitable heart. Even though he was privately an opponent of women's ordination, he nevertheless knew women who demonstrated exceptional spiritual leadership over their congregations. The woman before him, however, was not one of these. Through her carefully chosen and often demeaning posturing, he always sensed a feminist drive to lord it over her "weaker" male counterparts, and it was generally the more conservative male clergy who suffered under her remorseless harangue.

"And may this God," Strongbridge concluded, "who has brought us together to calm the unfounded fears of our people, guide us by Her ever gentle and loving hand. Amen."

Good grief! Stephen complained to himself. He looked around for any signs of similar discontent, but received a lone confirming cringe from Scott. Walter was sitting back out of view, so Stephen could only guess what this hyper-conservative ex-parishioner was thinking.

"To begin our discussion, I have invited Mr. Bud McNearlan, the owner of Bud's Computer System, to explain the origin and true implications of the Y2K bug."

Stephen added his applause to the small crowd's welcome. For nearly forty-five minutes, this slightly overweight, wrinkle-shirted, skinny-black-tied computer programmer-turned-store manager pontificated in terms he presumed would be simple enough for this room full of liberal arts majors. The gist of his presentation was that Y2K posed no threat to the modern computer industry.

"In short," McNearlan concluded, "I can almost guarantee that the world will not come to an end on January 1, and if any minor problems do occur, stores like mine are readily available to get you up and running with little delay."

On his heels followed an engineer from Consumers Network

Power, who for another forty-five minutes explained why the electric grid was safe and secure. "But to avoid the slightest risk of sporadic shortages," he concluded, "we are doubling our coal and natural-gas reserves."

Next in line was the Reverend Oliver Thornton III, the senior minister of the largest and most influential Congregational church in New Hampshire. His father and grandfather had preceded him first at Harvard and then in that pulpit, and generally, whenever Reverend Oliver Thornton III spoke, most lifelong Congregationalists listened.

"It is a great and humbling privilege to address you this morning on a topic that has the unfortunate potential of spreading unfounded panic among our flocks."

Blah, blah, blah, Stephen summarized mentally. He had no doubt where Oliver the Third's politics lie: anything that might adversely affect the collection plate was verboten. *Time to tune out.* With his head in a listening posture and an expression of genuine interest, Stephen's turned his eyes and mind to his unfinished sermon notes.

"Unless you eat the flesh of the Son of Man and drink his blood, you have no life in you," he read mentally. *These are strong words. Where else does Jesus speak so strongly?*

Stephen racked his memory for all the times Jesus had delivered similar instructions to His disciples or warnings to His opponents, but could think of none with more vocative intent than this strange command.

If taken literally, this borders on cannibalism, and thus why so many abandoned him in disgust. But in what way did He mean it symbolically? If Jesus meant that his followers were to "devour" and "drink" His teaching, then why didn't He just say this? Or why not at least correct them before they ran away?

Lending his token attention to the gathering, he casually turned pages to a photocopy of an interpretation from his favorite Evangelical commentator:

> The dispute which ensued among the members of the congregation was hot and stormy: 'they fought,' says John. They knew that Jesus was not speaking literally; they did not suppose that he seriously implied cannibalism. Yet that was the natural sense of his words; it was an offensive way of speaking, they thought, even

if he was speaking figuratively. And if he was speaking figuratively, they could not fathom what the figurative sense of his words might be. Some had one interpretation, some another; and a wordy strife broke out among them. Is it too farfetched to see in this wordy strife an anticipation of the perennial controversies in which Christians have engaged over the meaning of their Lord's words of institution: 'This is my body, which is for you?'

In verse 54 it is the person who eats the flesh of the Son of Man and drinks his blood that will be raised up by him at the last day; in verse 40 the same promise is held out to 'every one who sees the Son and believes in him'. So, those who 'eat his flesh' and 'drink his blood' are those who see him and believe in him: it is they who have eternal life; it is they whom he will raise up at the last day. In his strange words, then, we recognize a powerful and vivid metaphor to denote coming to him, believing in him, appropriating him by faith.

Stephen thought, *'Eating and drinking' merely refer to 'seeing and believing' as I've always taught.*

He then turned to some comments from a Lutheran scholar:

...the new factor of this section of the discourse...opens up a fresh allusion, this time not to an OT text but to the eucharistic words of Jesus: 'Take, eat; this is my body...' The point then is that bread must be eaten, and we now know enough about the bread to understand that it is the Word and Wisdom of God made flesh in the incarnation of Jesus. That is the essential fact which has to be swallowed, digested and assimilated by those who respond to Wisdom's invitation...

Wisdom's invitation is for drink as well as food. The use of eucharistic language makes the introduction of this correlative to eating inevitable. It should be realized that there is no suggestion intended of the horrifying idea involved in a literal interpretation. The choice of phrase is again entirely controlled by the tradition of Jesus' words at the Last Supper, and is again intended to draw attention to the Incarnation and the Passion. The metaphors of eating and drinking are not to be reduced to the vague notion of spiritual acceptance. Flesh and blood denote the real humanity of Jesus. It is the actual, historical Jesus who is to be taken and assimilated by the believer.

OK. 'Eating and drinking' are metaphores that point to the Incarnation and Passion of Jesus; not mere symbols of spiritual acceptance. Next to the words of an Episcopalian commentator:

Faced with this rejection [by his opponents] Jesus repeats his emphasis on life giving and the necessity of eating his sarx (flesh) in order to have life. The eating is related to abiding. This life is from the Father and believers share it in Christ. Thus, the reference to Jesus' sarx here forms part of a progressive deepening of Jesus' self-revelation coupled with a corresponding intensification of the death which tests peoples' hearts in the same way such cryptic sayings function earlier in the Gospel.

Boy, that really helps. I guess I might as well listen to the Catholic. He turned to a world-renowned biblical scholar, respected by Catholics and Protestants alike:

In this section, the eucharistic theme which was only secondary in vss. 35-50 comes to the fore and becomes the exclusive theme. No longer are we told that eternal life is the result of believing in Jesus; it comes from feeding on his flesh and drinking his blood...in 51-58...a new vocabulary runs through them: "eat," "feed," "drink," "flesh," "blood."

This [stress on eating Jesus' flesh and drinking his blood] cannot possibly be a metaphor for accepting his revelation. "To eat someone's flesh" appears in the bible as a metaphor for hostile action (Ps xxvii 2; Zech xi 9). In fact, in the Aramaic tradition transmitted through Syriac, the "eater of flesh" is the title of the devil, the slanderer and adversary par excellence. The drinking of blood was looked on as an horrendous thing forbidden by God's law (Gen ix 4; Lev iii 17; Deut xii 23; Acts xv 20). Its transferred, symbolical meaning was that of brutal slaughter (Jer xlvi 10). In Ezekiel's vision of apocalyptic carnage (xxxix 17), he invites the scavenging birds to come to the feast: "You shall eat flesh and drink blood." Thus, if Jesus' words in 6:53 are to have a favorable meaning, they must refer to the Eucharist. They simply reproduce the words we hear in the Synoptic account of the institution of the Eucharist (Matt xxvi 26-28): "Take, eat; this is my body; …drink…this is my blood."

All right, Stephen thought, *'eating and drinking' can't be metaphors because if they were, Jesus would be claiming to be of the devil! These four commentators all build their arguments on Scripture, and they all know a hell of a lot more about the Bible than I do. So which view do I tell my congregation to believe?*

A gentle elbow to the side jarred him. He looked up to find that Oliver the Third had left the podium and all eyes in the room were now directed at him.

"Yes?" Stephen asked sheepishly.

"Reverend LaPointe," Strongbridge said, "now that I have gained your attention, we have opened the floor for discussion. I was wondering what your thoughts might be. You always have a way of keeping our discussions interesting."

Yes, quite, Mrs. Strongbridge, Stephen thought, *and you always have a way of ensuring that I am earmarked as a darkling among your liberal elite.*

"Well, a couple of things," Stephen began. "First, I find it significant that all three of our experts—a computer, an electrical, and our long-standing Congregational expert—saw the need to include an out-clause in their statements. All three included the phrase, 'just in case,' which merely reiterates the fact that no one knows for sure whether Y2K will be a bust, a worldwide crisis, or something in between."

The looks from the speakers were not confirming.

"Second, just because we aren't comfortable with the apocalyptic connections that some of our overzealous crazies are attaching to Y2K does not warrant efforts to whitewash potential danger. There are no necessary connections between Y2K and Christ's Second Coming, yet I believe Y2K is a God-given opportunity for us to awaken our congregations to their over dependence upon technology and the world."

Stephen was on a roll. "Wouldn't it be better for all of our families to live more simply? Seventy years ago, the country survived the Depression because the majority of people could still survive without electricity, supermarkets, and microwave ovens. What if our country went down for a week? Could our families survive physically as well as spiritually? To me, 'Seek ye first the kingdom of God' is the point of Y2K, and this is what I plan to preach."

"Yes, there is too an apocalyptic connection, and anyone who denies it is a false teacher!" a voice exploded from the back of the room. It was Walter, but only Stephen knew this. To the rest he was an unknown.

"Excuse me," said Strongbridge, "but I didn't get your name."

With a little less resolve, Walter responded, "Walter Horscht, from Red Creek Congregational Church. Our new pastor asked me to come in his place."

"Well, Walter, I appreciate your thoughts. This meeting, however, was intended primarily for clergy..."

Ignoring her, Walter stood. "The Bible states clearly that, 'When people say, "There is peace and security," then sudden destruction will come upon them as travail comes upon a woman with child, and there will be no escape.' First Thessalonians five, verse three. All of you, along with all the other false teachers in the media promoting peace and security, are only misleading God's people. And Jesus said, 'Whoever causes one of these little ones who believe in Me to sin, it would be better for him if a great millstone were hung round his neck and he were thrown into the sea.'"

It was the second time in a week Stephen had had this verse preached at him, but he couldn't recall the first.

"Please, Mr. Horscht, I will have to ask you to leave if you can't control yourself," Strongbridge declared.

"I don't expect any of you to speak out if you understand the true significance of what is happening," Walter pressed on. "Our old faithful minister did, and he was forced into retirement. But the Bible states clearly, 'In those days, two women will be grinding at the mill; one is taken and one is left.' Matthew chapter twenty-four, verse forty-one. Here Jesus is warning us of the coming Rapture of the faithful and its connection with Y2K, for right now women everywhere are preparing for hard times by storing up grain to be ground as needed. They are the faithful ones; you are the false guides."

"I'm sorry, Mr. Horscht," Strongbridge said, standing, "but could a few of you, please, help me direct Mr. Horscht out?"

As she proceeded toward Walter, a half dozen of the men joined her. Two men took Walter by the elbows and carried him to the exit. Stephen, Scott, and the rest sat in disbelief.

"Jesus warned us about you blind guides," Walter said, his voice diminishing with distance, "and one within your midst is even more a son of perdition."

Son of perdition? Stephen sat up. *Where did I hear that recently?*

"All right, gentlemen," Strongbridge said upon the posse's return, "We have a few more minutes before we need to take a break. Are there any other comments?"

Whatever disruption Walter's outburst might have caused, Stephen was at least glad that the group's focus had been deflected away from him. While two ministers from northwestern Massachusetts discussed their plans to use the Y2K scare to organize a countywide food pantry, Stephen phased out. When the break finally came, Scott quickly cornered him at the coffee.

"Boy, it takes all," he said. "I'm only glad he's not at my church."

"Well, guess what. He was at mine."

"You're kidding."

"No, and by the time I left, I had grown accustomed to these kinds of outbursts on any occasion, except during worship. But how are you doing?"

The two broke from the crowd for ten minutes of private catching-up, until Strongbridge recalled the group.

"Scott, I think I'm going to vamoose," Stephen said. "I have to finish a sermon. Let me know, though, if anything of note happens."

Stephen retrieved his papers, and as nonchalantly as possible, slipped from the church. The space next to his car was now empty, so he more easily entered his awaiting steed. He backed out, and throwing the Fairmont into drive, he screeched suddenly to a halt. Blocking his exit, with a clenched fist pointing directly at him through the windshield, was a gray Caprice wagon.

"Walter, I need to go," Stephen said through the half-opened window.

"I know who you are, LaPointe. You can't fool me," Walter yelled.

Again Walter's words rang like a recent echo, but Stephen could not place them.

"You might blend right in with those liberals, but I know your strategy," Walter left his vehicle and was approaching, both fists swaying violently.

"Walter, what has gotten into you?" Stephen said, throwing his car into reverse. He backed into his previous parking space, and before Walter had time to corral him, he pulled out and away, leaving Walter standing alone.

As Stephen pulled onto the two-lane highway, he glanced back and heard the remnants of Walter's screams: "I know who you serve, and it ain't Jesus. It's the whore of Babylon!"

6

LAYERS OF YELLOW, orange, and red receded into the deep, dark blue of eternity over the forest-covered mountain slopes of the eastern skyline. Morning birds greeted the rising sun with pristine cheers of praise and thanksgiving. A sheen rose from the dew that covered the yet leafless branches and the grasses still awakening from their long winter repose. In the midst of this Eden, on a rickety, wooden folding chair, with only a Bible in his lap, Stephen sat motionless, meditating quietly on the surrounding beauty.

This had always been his preferred morning ritual. The long, cold winter having barred him from this pleasure for so long, he was determined this Friday morning, even though the temperature was still a bit nippy, to re-establish his routine. He loved this time of the day, when the birds were waking up and greeting the morning with unadulterated joy, as if there had been no yesterday; only a first day's burst of grace. Bundled against the chill, he sat alone on the north side of the church, away from the roving eyes of any morning travelers. Facing directly east—the way the biblical Jews and the earliest Christians had done—he let the morning sun warm his face, with the desperate hope that the restoration of this ritual might return peace to his otherwise troubled heart.

For Stephen was ready to quit. He loved the Lord Jesus; nothing had changed there. He loved serving Him and preaching His Word so that others might have an intimate, personal relationship with Him. He considered it the greatest privilege of his life to have been called and ordained a minister of the Gospel; for Stephen, nothing beat the rush of standing in the pulpit proclaiming the good news of God's redemptive mercy and love.

But slowly, over the past fifteen years, pastorate by pastorate, encounter by debilitating encounter, the joy of his calling had been sapped. He wanted only to teach the truth, but what in his seminary days had seemed so clear had become disturbingly elusive and sectarian. Sitting now beneath the encroaching shade of a Norwegian spruce, he enumerated the Christian truths that fifteen years ago as a newly ordained minister he would have died for. In each case, however, to his growing displeasure, he could easily provide a counter view held by otherwise Bible-believing Christians. And as if to confirm all of this, the memory of the surreal, confusing encounter with Walter Horscht yesterday morning was like a knife to his side.

"Lord Jesus," he prayed aloud toward the burning crescent of the rising sun, "what am I to do? Did I mishear You somehow all those years ago? I only wanted to serve You, but now everything has become so confusing. I want to one day receive Your reward, to hear Your words, 'Well done, good and faithful servant,' but how can I be certain that I am leading these people according to Your truth and not merely the opinions of men?

"I want to follow Your word," he said, leafing randomly through the Bible in his lap, "but so many verses can be taken in different ways, that all I see now in Your church is utter confusion. Lord Jesus, please help me."

He turned to the Old Testament, to Proverbs, to the verse that for more than twenty years had guided his life. To the background chorus of the birds, he read aloud. He could have recited it from memory, but he wanted to throw this promise back to God directly from His Word.

"'Trust in the Lord with all thine heart'"—*I tried, Jesus, I tried.*

"'And lean not unto thy own understanding;'"—*I thought I was following Your word, but now I wonder whose understanding I was following: Yours, or Calvin's, or Luther's, or my seminary professors', or the commentators' on my shelves, or some preacher who has the charisma to convince anyone that he has the true meaning of Scripture.*

"'In all your ways acknowledge Him,'"—*Lord, You alone know how sinful I truly am, but have I not tried to do everything in my life for You and You alone?*

"'And He will direct your paths.'"

"OK, Lord, I have believed that You have been guiding me all along: from industry into seminary, into the pastorate, and into the churches I have served. But was I wrong? Did I make the wrong decision when I abandoned my secular career to pursue the ministry? Was I running away from 'the world' to something I thought might be an easier, more holy life—which in the end has proved to be neither?"

Closing his Bible, Stephen leaned back, letting the now half-visible sun bask his body with warmth. Through the bright translucence of his eyelids, he continued to beseech God for guidance.

"Lord, should I attempt to pick up again where I left off in industrial sales? Or should I go back to school to get qualified to teach? Lord, please, I need an answer; I need some kind of sign. I have to do something, because this is killing me. I'm afraid that through my own thinking I have gotten off track. Please tell me, what is it You want me to do? Do You want me to continue as ..."

Something soft, warm, and wet struck his face squarely between the eyes.

"Yuck!" he declared as he sprang forward and wiped away a healthy portion of bird manure. He rushed around the church toward the parsonage, feeling his way with only partial vision.

"Very funny, God," he said as he stumbled onto the front porch, "so what *are* you trying to tell me?!"

"What happened to you?" Sara asked as he barged through the door toward the sink. She was preparing English muffins and coffee for his post-devotional, pre-children repast.

"You won't believe this," he said. "I was praying, laying some options before God, begging for His guidance, and some lousy bird pooped on my head."

"I guess whatever you were asking, God was saying, 'None of the above,'" Sara answered with a beguiling laugh.

"Very funny," Stephen said on his way to the bathroom.

Once cleansed, he returned uneasily to the kitchen.

"So tell me, darling," Sara probed, trying to be serious, "what was it that God was pooh-poohing?"

Stephen could now only laugh with her. "I guess I'm not worthy of that 'still, small voice.' Here, come sit with me."

She sat across from him at the dining-room table, and with clasped hands, they silently enjoyed the now fully risen sun.

"Sara," Stephen began cautiously, but convinced that this had to be done, "even though we haven't talked a lot about this, I'm sure you know that I've been feeling discouraged about my work as a minister."

"Yes, I know that, darling. I can't understand why, because everyone appreciates what you do. You are a fine minister, and everyone likes your sermons and your Bible studies."

Almost everyone, Stephen mused with bewilderment.

"Maybe if you hadn't been cooped up for the last fifteen years in these small churches with their small-town attitude," she continued, "with their lack of vision and expectation, and their ridiculously tight budgets and no supportive staff, you might feel more fulfilled in your work."

Pulling up from his coffee, he looked at his wife in wonderment. "Honey, I think you just might be right. Maybe the answer is that I need to break free from this inward-focused mentality and take on a more responsible position—in a larger church, with a larger budget, a skilled staff, and a mindset that includes an openness to outreach and missions."

Sara looked into her beloved's eyes. "Darling, I think God has answered your prayers. I've known for a long time that you have a lot more to give than these small churches expect or can even receive. If you want to move on, I'm ready. With the boys gone during the day, I think I'm ready to be somewhere where I also can get more involved."

Stephen rose with extended arms, and she responded, rising into his caress. Under the invigorating warmth of the east window, they grasped each other tightly, as they had not done in months. With misty eyes of joy, Stephen whispered into her ear, "Thank you, honey. You are God's greatest gift to me."

7

One year later...

Marge nicholson, the senior secretary of First Congregational Church, Witzel's Notch, was a heavy-set divorcee in her mid-fifties, whose control over the church office ran contrary to the lack of control in the rest of her life. Since the break up of her second marriage and the entrance of her last daughter into college, Marge's whole world revolved around the church. For some, this posed an awkward conflict of interests—between her intense involvement on various church committees and circles and her daily responsibilities as the pastor's gatekeeper. Some members jealously wondered if she ran the church.

As the primary daytime voice for First Congregational, Marge did her best to follow the scriptural mandate to "speak the truth in love." But trying to screen callers and protect the pastor's ever-crowded schedule sometimes got her goat.

"And then next week he's away for a few days on a retreat for Congregational ministers. When he gets back on Thursday, he'll need every available minute to prepare for Sunday worship. So I'm sorry, it looks like the best we can do is ... a week from Tuesday."

The caller on the other end of the line was doing all she could to break through the guard of this gatekeeper.

"I understand," Marge interrupted, "and would like to fit you in sooner, but Reverend LaPointe's schedule these past five months has been unbelievably hectic. He's had to become acclimated to the usual pastoral duties here—which are twice as demanding as those at his last church—and on top of that, there has been an unusually large number of funerals this month. These throw a wrench into whatever schedule he tries to keep..."

The caller was relentless. To Marge, the person's seemingly desperate request for an immediate meeting with the pastor sounded like so many others. *Everyone's problems are always more urgent than everyone else's,* she complained to herself. Marge tried to be sympathetic and tried to listen with discerning ears, but she had heard these pleas for immediate attention too many times before.

As the caller's list of reasons continued, Marge reached into the bottom right drawer of her desk where she kept her supply of bite-size Snickers bars for just such occasions.

"Yes, I know how you must feel." Marge popped another Snickers into her mouth, pitching the wrapper successfully into the waste can across the room while trying to speak without the sound of chewing. "Tell you what, maybe the pastor knows of a window in his schedule that I don't, so if something comes up sooner, I'll call you...OK...sure...I know, but...OK...God bless." With that, Marge hung up. After a quick sip of cooling coffee, Marge returned to what she had been doing before the interruption.

Being a church secretary in the new millennium was different from when she began twenty-five years before. Back then, it was electric typewriters and mimeographs with everything filed hardcopy. Now a computer network interlinked the nine-member staff and then on to the Internet. No more scraps of paper floating around alerting people to missed telephone calls or appointments. E-mail had won the day, and though the hard filing had never ceased, most church documents, databases, and membership information were stored on hard drives.

At first, Marge had fought this move to high-tech. She insisted she could do everything more efficiently the old way. But the young pastor at her last church was both a computer wizard and a patient teacher. For a while, Marge worried that she would fail, but she quickly became not only adept, but a computer advocate. In the final tally, it had been her computer skills that had won her the executive secretary's position at this affluent church.

Marge turned back to her computer and sighed as she read the marquee of large purple letters scrolling across her monitor, *WWJD?* She had created this screensaver to tweak her conscience whenever she received calls like the last one.

One of the more common new tasks she had acquired with all of this computerization was the responsibility of screening the pastor's e-mail. On any given day, Reverend LaPointe might receive over twenty-five electronic messages.

On this particular morning, the pastor's inbox contained thirteen messages. The first two were spam selling some new technological breakthroughs, which she quickly deleted. Three were from personal friends of the pastor. These she passed along without reading. Two others were Christian news summaries, which she read and forwarded. Another was a joke from his son William, which she passed on with a chuckle. Three were from church members wanting information about upcoming committee meetings, reasons for the proposed changes in the Sunday school schedule, and counseling to prevent an impending divorce. She handled the first two and passed the third along.

Then there was an interesting message from the head office that sent Marge diving for another Snickers. Reverend LaPointe was invited to attend a meeting of New England Congregational pastors to discuss whether they should take a united stand on the growing concern over euthanasia. The underlying tone of the message was that they should not. Their gathering was, therefore, to discuss the best means of preaching freedom of conscience vs. the growing pressure of voices haranguing against the inalienable right of every citizen to decide his or her own destiny.

Marge knew that this had to be a general e-mail sent in bulk to every Congregationalist minister in New England, because the head office certainly knew where Reverend LaPointe stood on this issue. Anyone who heard at least three of his sermons in a row knew that he and his family were strictly and unashamedly pro-life. Marge herself was more in line with the views of those at the head office—*Boy, I'd like to introduce my Aunt Tilly to that doctor in Michigan!*

She passed this along without comment, knowing that Reverend LaPointe would accept the invitation.

The final e-mail, which she had postponed until last, came from one relentlessly harassing e-mailer who apparently had followed the Reverend here. Eight times during the past five months, this mysterious source had scolded the pastor with jargon that Marge only partially understood. Each time, after a quick read, Marge would pass these along—she only wished she could eavesdrop on the pastor's answers, if he gave any.

Grabbing a Snickers, she began reading silently: *To one who is blinded by the darkness...*

The pastor's door opened, and Stephen's face appeared. "Marge, could you please come in, and bring those committee reports for the upcoming board meeting."

"Yes, yes, of course, pastor." She jumped back, rolling her chair away from the monitor. "I'll be right there."

Shoot, she said under her breath, and with a click of her mouse, she forwarded the unread message. Collecting the committee files and her coffee, she switched on the answering machine and entered the pastor's inner sanctum.

*   *   *

"THE USUAL STUFF floating in the on the information highway?" Stephen asked, his back toward her as she entered.

He had returned to his cushy leather executive chair and was gazing into the computer monitor on the credenza behind his desk. Apparently, a local carpenter had used the same locally cut maple lumber to build both this credenza-desk combination and the lavish bookshelves that filled all four walls of this remodeled office.

At this new church, with the staff he had only previously dreamed about, Stephen was determined to keep the day-to-day atmosphere light. He took his work seriously, seeing every moment as an opportunity for the Kingdom, but he also recognized the danger of taking oneself too seriously. He often quipped that if God had enough sense of humor to create platypuses and flounders, to make males and females operate emotionally on contradictory timetables, and to choose men like himself to preach the gospel, then he too ought to make levity a regular part of his work. "Be perfect as your heavenly Father is perfect," Jesus had said. This at least meant one must develop a good sense of humor.

"Yes, Pastor, nothing out of the ordinary, except the message from the head office and the one from your anonymous friend."

Stephen turned in his chair to examine Marge's expression, still trying to read from which part of the Congregational spectrum his closest assistant was coming. "Yeah, neither of those were intended to make my day. I suppose I'll need to go to that meeting, voice my opinion, and make more enemies among my 'freedom of conscience' brothers and sisters. It baffles me how these leaders of souls can be sold on the idea that Christ sent forth His disciples to proclaim basically one idea: that anyone can believe anything they want as long as they do it with love. I don't think this is what our Congregationalist forefathers intended us to preach."

Marge got comfortable in the leather chair facing the pastor's desk, saying nothing in reply—only smiling mildly. She generally played her religious cards close to the vest. So far, Stephen had concluded that Marge would do whatever hedging was necessary to keep her boss happy and ignorant of her personal views, because ever since her second marriage had fallen apart, she needed this job.

Stephen reached for a printout of his daily *To-Do* list.

"I need you to help me with a few things before I leave on next week's pastoral retreat," Stephen said. "First, for the up-coming board meeting…"

For the next fifteen minutes, the two reviewed an assortment of pastoral and congregational issues, which at his three previous, smaller churches had barely raised an eyebrow. The music program, for example, had always been one area where he felt comfortable leaving well enough alone. None of his previous three church choirs would have won any awards, but at least they were always compliant about working within his worship plans. Here at Witzel's Notch, however, he inherited three choirs—adult, youth, and children's; plus a men's quartet and two bell choirs—women's and youth. To complicate things, these were all directed by the full-time music director, who played the organ at both services, and, worst of all, was known across the country for several of her published chorales. Like the church's previous pastor, Stephen often wondered who was in charge of worship. Her constant pressure to feature at least two choirs in each service made it a weekly battle to reserve enough time for what he considered the more necessary part of Sunday worship: the sermon!

"And when you've finished the rough draft, please let me see this Sunday's bulletin," he told Marge. "I need to recalculate the time for each element to determine whether something needs to be cut. What do you think, Marge? If I have to choose, which should go: the extra anthem by the women's bell choir, the promotion for the spring bazaar, or my sermon?"

"Oh, I'll leave that to you, Pastor, but you know, the bazaar brings in a lot of money each year, and what would worship be here at Witzel's Notch without a bell choir?" She collected her papers and left with a smile.

Stephen returned to perusing his e-mail, hoping to make a dent in his inbox. Although Marge was surprisingly efficient at screening his messages, he was still unable to keep up. Over 120 messages needed to be read or reread, and then answered, saved, or discarded. As he scrolled through the long list, he skimmed past inquiries from troubled members that required more carefully thought out answers than he was willing to give at that moment. He answered affirmative to the request from the head office, and then there was that letter from "Thevoiceoftruth."

"When is this guy going to get off it?" he asked aloud.

> *To one who is blinded by the darkness:*
> *Why won't you respond to my charges? Is it because they are too close to the truth? You can't escape from my inquiry, for as I've said before, I know who and what you are. And so does the One who has the power to cast you into Hell!*
> *I'm writing for your own good!*
> *Thevoiceoftruth*

Stephen had made the mistake of answering the second of these harassing e-mails. "Thevoiceoftruth" responded with an eight-page, virulent accusation that Stephen was actually a Catholic priest posing as an evangelical Protestant minister to proselytize for the "Whore of Babylon." Nothing Stephen wrote could still the absurd suspicions—*And calling the source a "crazy fool" had not helped.*

Do I answer this time? Stephen thought with bewilderment. *Where does he get this tripe? What have I ever done or said to earn his wrath? Who is he?!*

Without comment, Stephen deleted "Thevoiceoftruth," and moved on to lighter stuff, to messages from friends and a joke from William. At that moment behind closed doors, with a sermon to finish and an afternoon of counseling appointments, he was more than willing to procrastinate.

Stephen presumed that he was sufficiently gifted at erecting an impenetrable front before his congregation, his clergy friends, his board members, his staff, and even before his wife and family. He was positive that his façade portrayed a man firmly committed to Christ and unswerving in his convictions and service.

Nevertheless, within the sanctuary of this new maple-paneled pastor's study, as in the privacy of his heart of hearts, he knew that his move to this church—five times larger in every respect than his last—had not been the answer to his struggles. His move had only made things five times more complicated.

Now every Sunday he preached to an audience twice the size with an interlocking matrix of new problems, so the critical significance of his struggle with truth had only intensified. Each week as he gazed out upon this sea of new, beckoning faces, he remonstrated with himself: *They are expecting me to tell them how to use Scripture to make sense out of their lives, yet no matter what I say, they can find some contradicting voice in some other pulpit of the county. Lord Jesus, please, give me strength!*

Stephen set his short-term sights on working through a dozen of these messages and then returning his efforts to Sunday's sermon but, admittedly, he knew that what he was running away from was his sermon.

Once again, he had been blindsided. In September, when he had mapped out his preaching schedule for his first six months, he had merely followed the same schedule he had used when he began at Respite and Red Creek. The text had been published in last week's bulletin as well as in the Witzel's Notch *Intelligencer,* so he couldn't change it. But each morning, as he studied the text from John 8 and his previous sermon notes, he increasingly wondered whether he himself had truly experienced what Jesus had promised:

> *If you continue in My word,*
> *you are truly My disciples,*
> *and you will know the truth,*
> *and the truth will make you free.*

8

"TAKE YOUR BOOTS OFF downstairs! You know better than that! Do you think I've got nothing better to do than clean up your mess?"

Sara immediately regretted the tone of her words—as she always did after losing her temper. *But these boys should know better.*

Her heart softened as she realized that their excitement might have hampered their judgment. Their father had promised to get home early to take them bowling.

"Come on now, you know better than that," she repeated with more restraint. "When you're cleaned off, come up for a cup of hot cocoa and then back to your books."

Sara was finally starting to feel settled in their new home, though the speed of the change had been exhilarating. Within a week of Stephen's throwing his hat into the ring of available ministers, Witzel's Notch had contacted him, and it had taken only one face-to-face meeting to convince Stephen to accept the opportunity to serve this larger congregation with a larger staff and a larger budget. They had hoped this new start with all of its challenges would help him refocus his vision for ministry, and so far, it seemed to have worked.

She liked this new church, even apart from the good things it offered Stephen. The volunteer opportunities were more sophisticated and diverse. Immediately she had signed up to help as a substitute Sunday school teacher—for Daniel's class—and to help with the crisis hot line. She even considered updating her certification so she could be a substitute history teacher at Witzel's Notch High School.

"Mom, is Dad home yet?" Daniel yelled as he and his brother discarded their muddy boots and winter wear and trudged up the steps. "He said he'd take us bowling if he could break free."

Returning to the present, Sara said, "No, he's still at the church."

Since they had arrived in September, there had only been one Saturday evening when Stephen was home free. Every other Saturday had been consumed by committee meetings, weddings, or unexpected funerals. She chuckled to herself as she recalled that Stephen had actually quipped at a recent board meeting that he might need to start requiring a two-week notice for all funerals.

But admittedly, this was already starting to wear on Sara's patience—especially whenever she went through her monthly hormonal swing. *No, it hadn't taken long for reality to set in,* she said to herself.

This new, larger church meant longer hours, more committee meetings, and higher stress for Stephen—and more time alone for her and the boys. Sara tried to convince herself that she could deal with it emotionally because this wasn't Stephen's choice.

If he could be free, he would, she responded to that inner voice that from the beginning has tempted her with the suspicion that Stephen's visits with women were far from innocent. She was certain to the contrary, but the voice was always there.

"But there's still time. He's only half an hour late," she said to her sons, knowing that he probably would not make it. "Here, drink some cocoa and finish your reading assignment, and you'll be ready to go when he arrives."

"But, Mom, it's Saturday," Daniel complained.

Sara was pleased by how well Daniel was doing in his new eighth-grade class, although he had started three weeks into the semester. He was not the student his brother was, though. William had somehow developed the self-discipline of finishing his homework immediately after school without prodding or complaint.

If only William had remained as cooperative and obedient in other things, she mused. During the past year, William had become continually more rebellious, hanging around with less desirable friends. He had even begun talking back to his father in public—which in any pastor's family was a major no-no. She and Stephen were becoming quite concerned, but they found little time to confront him.

"Oh, come on, Mom," Daniel whined. "Duke and North Carolina are playing on the tube."

Sara had heard this pleading routine thousands of times. Her temper started to rise, but she caught herself, wondering if she should check the calendar to see whether something else might be feeding her emotions.

"Listen, Daniel, you knew the game would be on. If you had finished your work like your brother, you'd be able to watch. And besides," she said on a calmer note, "you've only got one chapter of Dickens to read, so get to it. When you get done, you may watch the game until your father gets home."

Daniel grumbled, but took his drink to his room to force himself through another chapter about Miss Havisham and Pip. William exited to the television, his cocoa elevated toward Daniel in a gloating gesture.

Sara poured herself another cup of cocoa and paused to gaze out the kitchen window, at the now-familiar scenery in their new back yard: a gray wooden swing set left by the last owners, the old sailboat Stephen had always intended to restore, and her grandmother's antique wooden glider—even more in need of repair.

The only consolation to this mess was that it was disguised by six inches of snow. Off in the distance, over the crests of the woods that surrounded their country home, she could see the distant snowy peaks of the White Mountains. There somewhere in the middle was Mt. Lafayette, which Stephen, the boys, and she had climbed on their only free weekend since they had arrived.

As she stared at the beautiful New Hampshire countryside, she uttered a soft prayer of thanks to God for all He had done in their lives—in her life. He had brought her so far, and given her so much. *And to think that I had almost settled for so much less. Now if only I can become the kind of wife and mother You want me to be.*

As she continued gazing at the winter landscape, her eye caught the glare of an approaching car. It was Stephen. He was coming up the main road and would be there in about four minutes. She gulped the remainder of her chocolate, placed the cup in the dishwasher, and started picking up miscellaneous items scattered around the kitchen. Preparing to meet her husband, she wiped away a tear from her eyes, a tear of both sorrow and joy.

9

"If YOU CONTINUE IN MY WORD, you are truly My disciples, and you will know the truth, and the truth will make you free."

With a strong but warm voice of conviction from the pulpit of First Congregational Church, Witzel's Notch, Stephen proclaimed the text that had troubled him all week.

On Tuesday, when he began reviewing his old sermon notes, he knew that he would need to start over from scratch. He was glad this was the first Sunday of the month, because this meant they would be celebrating the Lord's Supper so his sermon could be conveniently shorter. But he still could not avoid the text's uncomfortable implications.

"Please bow your heads for a moment, and join with me in prayer as we prepare our hearts and minds to reflect on God's Word."

Stephen would have to be guarded with his conclusions about this passage; his congregation would not understand. *Besides, I can't*

*let personal concerns color my interpretation of the Bible. I'm called to
preach the Word to this people, unpolluted by private matters, prejudices,
or doubts.*

"Heavenly Father, we thank You for the power of Your Word
which always challenges, inspires, corrects, and conveys Your merciful
love for us. As we listen this morning to Your written Word, please
open our minds to hear Your voice, and our hearts to respond fully
and freely. And may our focus be not so much on the speaker, but
upon Your Son, Jesus Christ our Lord, for it is He whom we have
come to see. Amen."

The congregation took their seats and settled down to hear what
good news their pastor might have for them on this cold and snowy
first Sunday in February.

Stephen paused to gather his thoughts, peering down from his
ornate perch at a few of the now familiar faces that regularly greeted
him as he began each week's message. But on this particular morning,
their encouraging attention did not dissuade his reticence to begin.

On Wednesday afternoon, the true significance of this text had
struck him dramatically. John 8:31-32 was one of those texts that
many Christians memorized, but then regurgitated without
considering fully its implications—without facing what it required
of them. As he revisited this text every morning, he wondered with
growing concern whether he was worthy to teach this people its
most intimate meaning.

"I regret to tell you that I must speak only briefly this morning
on a text that truly deserves a longer, detailed exposition. I suspect,
however, that at least a few of you, given today's NFL playoff, are a
bit more than just relieved."

Stephen received the anticipated laughter, which, as calculated,
helped gain their sympathetic ear. Above the more controlled laughter
came an inordinately boisterous guffaw that Stephen quickly identified
as that of Bill Walker, the president of the church board. Bill was
obviously giving everyone a subtle reminder that it was he who had
convinced them to hire this *great* preacher.

"I believe this concise statement by our Lord was one of those
that was meant to separate the wheat from the chaff," Stephen said.
"Many people followed Jesus for wrong reasons, or at least they
failed to understand fully what following Jesus required. And isn't

this still true? I wonder if there isn't some wheat and chaff that needs separating here this morning?"

Stephen paused to peruse his new congregation from side to side, not with the sneer of a hell-and-brimstone preacher, but with a more winsome grin—one he hoped would communicate that he was preaching not only to them, but also to himself.

"In this section of his gospel, the Apostle John tells us that Jesus was addressing 'the Jews who had believed in Him.' Now John could not have meant, this early in the narrative, that these Jews had believed in Jesus as their Messiah. More likely, John meant that they were impressed by what Jesus was preaching and doing and, consequently, accepted Him as a teacher worth following. Some might have become comfortable with people referring to them as 'the disciples of Jesus.'"

Stephen leaned on his forearms, gaining strength from the firm foundation of this pulpit from which many wiser preachers had cast their nets.

"We also know from the context that Jesus had just made a bold allusion to who He truly was—that He had been sent from the Father above and spoke not on His own authority but on that of the Father. Jesus warned them prophetically that when 'they had lifted up the Son of man, then they would know that I am he.' This apparently sounded blasphemous to many of them, for soon some wanted to stone Him. But yet," Stephen continued, pausing for effect, "Scripture says that 'as he spoke thus, many believed in Him.' Many were undeterred by His strong claims, and continued to be unashamed of being seen in His presence."

Stephen glanced at the clock positioned on the back wall of the church. Long ago one of the wealthier "pillar families" had bequeathed this clock to the congregation. Originally, the well-meaning church board had positioned it on the wall to the right of the pulpit where the congregation, with but a mere shift of their eyes, could determine how close the sermon and the service was to completion. After many hard-fought congregational debates, the previous pastor had finally convinced the board to move it to the back.

"Jesus then directly addressed these believing Jews—and I believe He is also directly addressing you and me, who live and work in the midst of so many who have rejected Christ; who consider the Christian religion a myth or a psychological crutch, and yet still have the audacity, even the pride, to call themselves His followers."

As he uttered this challenge, Stephen's glare landed on Bill Walker. Bill and Mattie were not even sitting in their usual spot. A group of visitors had beaten them to it, so the Walkers were forced to sit on the left rather than the right side of the sanctuary. He only caught Bill's eyes for an instant, but it seemed like eternity. Stephen prayed that Bill would not read anything into this, for his choice of victims had been completely at random. Bill could be overly sensitive, especially if anyone insinuated that his Christian commitment was anything but sincere. He was already the board president when Stephen arrived, and one of Stephen's more vocal confidants had insinuated that Bill had been selected more for his esteem in the community than his Christian convictions.

Stephen quickly turned his gaze, purposely focusing on a few other faces to dilute his possibly misunderstood glance, and then continued with his message.

"On the surface, as we listen nearly two thousand years later, His words sound innocent enough: 'If we continue in His word'—if we live faithfully and radically in line with His teachings—*then and only then* can we consider ourselves truly His disciples—truly Christians.

"And *if* this is true, then He gives us two promises: one, that we will 'know the truth'—we will be convinced in our hearts and minds of the truth about who Jesus is and what this means for our lives and eternal future—and, two, that this truth 'will make us *free.*'

"But what is this freedom? Freedom from what? Oppression? Poverty? Sickness? Anxiety? Ignorance?"

Something began to bother Stephen. He could not identify it, but he sensed a rising uneasiness. Sweat was collecting on his forehead and the back of his neck. Ignoring this, he got back to business.

"Jesus was saying something specifically intended to get a rise out of his audience. The Jews had a certain ancestral pride. No matter what calamity had befallen their nation, no matter what enemy had subjected them to captivity—Egypt, Babylon, Greece, or at that time Rome—no matter how bad things had become, they always considered themselves free. They were God's chosen people. In fact, listen to their immediate response: 'We are descendants of Abraham, and have never been in bondage to anyone. How is it that you say, 'You will be made free?'"

This time Stephen's focus rested on the right side of the sanctuary, passing from the far right of the fifth row inward toward where the Walkers normally sat. His glance was stopped by a strikingly attractive teenage girl with shoulder-length blond hair, a red sweater, and a facial expression that shouted boredom. To her left sat a woman who was surely her mother. She had the same blond hair, though tied up in a bun, accented with the subtle glistening of petite diamond ear studs, and the same striking facial features, though matured and therefore more perfected. She was what the girl would become. Her pleasant, winsome expression was familiar and drew Stephen's attention until they locked eye-to-eye. Stephen self-consciously glanced away to the other side of the sanctuary.

"These first-century Jews had not followed Jesus looking for freedom," he continued, "for as descendants of Abraham, they assumed they already were free. Some might have come to this gifted rabbi to better understand truth, and, therefore, were not put off when Jesus challenged them to follow His teachings. Many roving rabbis probably made the same claims.

"But *freedom*? They didn't worry about this, unless Jesus meant freedom from Rome, but how could following His teachings free them from their cruel oppressors?"

The familiarity of that woman's face pursued him, so as he spoke, he glanced back. But before his eyes found her, they landed on the man next to her. His dark, graying hair was neatly parted on the left and stylishly combed back, but his most distinguishing characteristic was his small, thick, round glasses, giving him the look of a scholar. He wore a bright white shirt, a blue-and-gold striped tie, and a navy blue blazer.

As Stephen stared at this spectacled face, he sensed that the man's intense stare was more than focused attention. The slant of his brow and the set of his jaw gave the impression of bottled fury ready to explode. There was no mistaking it.

Good God in Heaven, Stephen thought in panic. *What is Walter Horscht doing here?*

Stephen labored to refocus on his sermon.

"Uh," Stephen said, struggling. He reached into his robe for a handkerchief, and as he wiped his brow, he again noticed Bill Walker, smiling with arms akimbo, oblivious to the stress Stephen was attempting to hide.

"In the…ah…paragraph that follows, Jesus tried to help them hear, and understand, and hopefully accept the freedom that only He could give. He said, 'Truly, truly, I say to you, every one who commits sin is a slave to sin. The slave does not continue in the house forever; the son continues forever. So if the Son makes you free, you will be free indeed.'

"We know from the rest of this chapter, however, that these particular believing Jews didn't hear what Jesus was trying to say— their pride was too great. In fact, the more that He said and they said, and then back and forth, the worse things got, until in verse 59 we read, 'So they took up stones to throw at Him…'"

What God-forsaken reason has caused Walter to bring his family all the way here from Vermont?

Returning his focus to the written text in the pulpit Bible, Stephen thought: *I wonder what he is going to read into my sermon this morning?*

Stephen steeled his gaze, turning to the left side of the church, to finish his message.

"Jesus had truly struck a sour note. Even after He clearly explained that He was talking about freedom from sin and its effects, it made no difference. They didn't *hear* Him.

"But are you and I any better at hearing, accepting, and taking seriously this freedom from sin that Jesus offers?" His voice cracked faintly as he forced himself through the distractions.

"There is one basic issue I want us to consider in the time remaining. No matter what special connections we think we have with God—whether through family, or church membership, or church rites like baptism, or even through high reputations built on faithful service in church activities, committees, or boards—no matter what privileged relationship we think we have with God, sin breaks it, severing us from our heavenly Father.

"Romans 3:23 reminds us clearly that 'all have sinned and fall short of the glory of God.' Therefore, in some way every one of us has sinned, becoming, as Jesus said, 'slaves to sin.' Consequently, none of us have 'continued in the house,' as Jesus said, or in other words: we have ceased to remain in fellowship with Him."

Stephen had now reached the textual implications that had haunted him all week, and he froze in reflection, as if someone had pressed a pause button. And, in his mind's eye, that someone was, of all people, the Reverend Rita Brownstein—the Methodist minister who had cornered him nearly fourteen years before at her own brother's funeral. Her forceful, mental image glared up at him from the sacred page, but it wasn't exactly her face: her professional, painted smile had been replaced by the defiant, immortal sneer of her deceased brother.

All week this text made Stephen squirm under a theological conundrum from which he naively thought his move to Witzel's Notch could allow him to ignore—a theological contradiction that cut deep into everything he believed, taught, and preached, yet seemed to raise its ugly head at every turn. The idea that a follower of Jesus must "continue" or "remain" in His Word implied that it was possible for a believer *not* to do so.

Stephen was on trial, on the defense of his staunch Calvinist conviction that by grace alone believers can not lose their salvation. Against him stood Rita Brownstein, Reverend Malone, his ex-seminary friend Carl, and thousands maybe millions of other good, faithful Christians who believed otherwise.

Stephen's seminary training had convinced him that only the dogma of the perseverance of the saints made sense out of man's loss of free will from Adam's fall, God's perfect justice and sovereignty, and God's freely given grace. This is what he had tried to tell Rita: *Since there is nothing anyone can do to earn salvation, there is likewise nothing anyone can do to lose it. Yes, salvation is a free gift of grace, but as such it can not be earned or lost.*

But her response had been equally true, for after sixteen years of ministry, he was disturbingly aware of many verses that contradicted his view—verses that challenged people to *choose* to believe, to *will* to obey God, to *follow*, to *continue*, to *quit* sinning, to *remain* true to all the traditions they had learned—to do everything possible to keep from falling away and to avoid those who had.

And nothing had so confirmed this than what Stephen discovered on Thursday morning. He was reading in the book of Revelation where the resurrected Jesus tells John to write messages of warning to seven churches. Jesus was speaking to *believers* when over and over he warned them that it was only those who *remained* faithful, who *kept* his works until the end and therefore *conquered* who would not be "hurt by the second death" or blotted from the book of life. The obvious implication was that some born-again believers might *not* conquer and instead be lost.

He looked down at Sara and then out over to the congregation. *Are any of these people—am I—continuing and 'conquering?'*

Turning his attention back to the written Word of God, another paralyzing thought filled his mind: *Within a fifteen-mile radius of this church are at least twenty faithful, Bible-believing ministers—Methodists, Lutherans, Episcopalians, Pentecostals, Baptists, Nazarenes. If by chance they are preaching on this identical text, they likely are interpreting it differently than I am. Which of us, dear Lord, is preaching "the truth?"*

He jolted back into action, delivering the words of his defense to his unsuspecting congregation.

"From the truth of God's Word expressed in 2 Corinthians 5:17—the truth which Jesus promised we would 'know' and which would make us 'free' from sin—we know that anyone who 'is in Christ…is a new creation; the old has passed away, behold, the new has come.' And the Apostle Paul clarified this in verse 18 by emphasizing that 'All this is from God, who through Christ reconciled us to Himself….'"

A glare of light from the right side of the sanctuary lured Stephen's attention. Turning, he saw that it was a reflection from, of all things, Walter's glasses. *WHY IS HE HERE?* Stephen shouted to himself as he fought to stay on the message at hand. The stress was so intense that he was losing track of where he was in his mental outline. As Stephen stared at this unwanted guest, Walter glanced away and hunkered down behind the high puffy hairdo of a woman seated in front of him.

Stephen turned back, determined to finish.

"The good news that Jesus wanted these believing Jews to hear, and wants us to hear, is that there is nothing that can guarantee freedom from sin and acceptance by God, except our own personal relationship with Him, which is a work of God's grace. Hear what the Apostle Paul wrote in Ephesians chapter two:

But God, who is rich in mercy, out of the great love with which He loved us, even when we were dead through our trespasses—our sins—made us alive together with Christ (by grace you have been saved), and raised us up with Him, and made us sit with Him in the heavenly places in Christ Jesus, that in the coming ages He might show the immeasurable riches of His grace in kindness toward us in Christ Jesus.

"And what he wrote next is directly to the point:

For by grace you have been saved through faith; and this is not your own doing, it is the gift of God—not because of works, lest any man should boast.

"Any of us here this morning who are in Christ—who by the leading of God's grace have accepted Christ as Lord and Savior and, by His grace, are continuing in His Word—are, therefore, set free from the damaging effects of sin. We might *feel* otherwise..."

Which is why I did not want to do this text!

"...but this is something we must believe, something we must trust and know, and therefore live out faithfully in our lives."

Lord Jesus, help me! I must preach Your Word without bias.

"There is one particular word in this important statement by Jesus that we must consider carefully—a word that Jesus used often. This word makes all the difference whether you or I can experience fully the joy of our Christian faith, and that word is the word 'continue.'

"By His grace and by our faithfulness we must continue, we must keep, we must abide in Christ; we must continue in every aspect of our lives—our words and our actions—to follow Christ faithfully. As Jesus will say later in the Gospel of John, on the same night He asked His Apostles to remember Him in the breaking of the bread—which we are about to celebrate—'If you abide in Me, and My words abide in you, ask whatever you will, and it shall be done for you...These things I have spoken to you, that My joy may be in you, and that your joy may be full.'"

Closing the pulpit Bible, Stephen concluded: "As we prepare

our hearts to celebrate the Supper of the Lord, let us each consider how faithfully we have continued in His Word. Let us pray."

As he waited for the congregation to bow their heads and settle down into stillness, he glanced back to Walter, who still was hiding behind the hairdo. Softly Stephen led the congregation in prayer.

The "Amen" was the cue for the organist to begin the introducion for their communion hymn, "Beneath the Cross of Jesus," and the servers to start forward with the silver trays carrying cubes of sliced bread and small plastic vials of grape juice. Stephen sat down briefly, waiting as the servers prepared the communion table—waiting for the moment when he would rise and read Jesus' words of institution. He was also waiting impatiently for the time in about an hour when he could kick off his shoes and relax aimlessly in front of the television, out of the glare of his people.

First, however, he must find out why Walter was here.

*   *   *

THE SERVICE WAS OVER, and the sanctuary was almost empty. Stephen, Sara, William, and Daniel stood at the front of the greeting line along the outside hallway. This led from the west sanctuary doors either out to the parking lot or down to the fellowship hall for coffee and doughnuts.

"Fine sermon, Pastor."

The line always moved swiftly, allowing insufficient time for more than the perfunctory praises, good-mornings, and thank-yous.

"Another good one, pastor," said an older member as he painstakingly passed with a cane and went out to his car. Stephen generally said little in response to such courteous compliments. He just smiled, nodded, and said, "Thank you, come again," or "Appreciate that, have a great week," or, if he knew the person, he might throw in something more personal.

"You hit me that time, Stephen," said a middle-aged man Stephen had been counseling. His wife had left him months before the LaPointes had arrived. "Continuing is always the hardest part, isn't it? Please pray for me."

"And you for me, my friend," said Stephen as the two shook hands affectionately.

As the river of parishioners flowed past, Stephen glanced occasionally over their heads down the line to see whether Walter and his family were getting close, but they were not there. *They must have taken the other exit.*

"Good," Stephen exclaimed with relief.

"What was that, dear?" Sara asked, never dropping her smile as she greeted an elderly woman enveloped in furs smelling of mothballs: "Yes, Mrs. Tourquesny, the quince tarts were heavenly."

"Oh, nothing, dear," Stephen answered, nodding a kind greeting to the creator of the pastries that had driven him and the boys to the bathroom sink. *But why then had Walter come, if not to confront me?*

After the last greeter had passed, Daniel turned to his father. "Dad, every time we do this, my cheeks ache from smiling at a bunch of people I don't even know."

"That's just part of the job, Danny. Imagine how my cheeks feel after three Christmas Eve services. Listen, you all go down for doughnuts. I'll be there in a bit."

The boys needed no coaxing and quickly raced downstairs. Before leaving, Sara raised herself up on her toes and kissed her husband on the cheek. "Is that better? Are you all right?"

"What do you mean?"

"You seemed distracted this morning. Your message was fine, as usual," she said, affectionately squeezing his arm, "but, I don't know…is there anything I can do?"

"No, I'm OK. Just tired from staying up late fine-tuning the sermon. Please, I'll meet you downstairs in a moment, and then let's make a quick getaway. I'm looking forward to kicking back this afternoon."

"Remember, you promised Danny you'd fulfill your raincheck on yesterday's bowling?"

"Egad, that's right," Stephen replied. "OK, but please run interference for me, at least long enough to catch my breath."

"Yes, dear," and with another peck on the cheek, Sara went downstairs.

Stephen retraced his steps up to the pulpit to retrieve his Bible and paused for a moment to gaze out at the empty sanctuary. He recalled the words of the prophet Isaiah that implied that when the Word of God is preached, it never returns empty. *But what will this morning's sermon reap?*

He turned to face the front of the sanctuary where on the blank white wall hung a large, hand-hewn wooden cross. He studied its rough surface, and thought of the splinters that must have chaffed the bare back of his dying Savior. It reminded him of the cross he was expected to bear as a man called to preach the Word, without error "in season and out of season."

And Stephen knew now that he faced but one option.

*　　　　*　　　　*

IN THE FRONT PARKING LOT, Walter, Helen, and their sixteen-year-old daughter Stacy were getting into their gray Caprice wagon. Walter paused briefly before getting in to study the beauty of this ancient New England Congregational church. He removed his glasses and wiped them with his handkerchief. Helen and he had assumed with great expectation that his new position as night supervisor at Levonshire's injection molding plant here in Witzel's Notch would be a chance for his family to start over. They had assumed that First Church would be their new church family. It had never crossed his mind, though, that this would be where LaPointe had also moved.

The outrage that had filled Walter's heart the moment he recognized LaPointe in the pulpit continued unabated—directed both at LaPointe and at the God who was playing such a sour joke on him and his family.

Lord Jesus, why are You doing this?

The image of his last confrontation with LaPointe in that parking lot taunted him, and LaPointe's refusal to respond to his e-mails added infuriation.

But as this ate at his mind, the serenity of the house of worship standing before him made him pause: *Perhaps God has another reason for this apparent coincidence?*

Walter replaced his glasses and looked up at First Church's high steeple, bedecked with a typical New England weathervane—*and not a papist crucifix*, he mused. He sensed a rising surge of spiritual momentum. *Has God specifically called me to this place?*

Speaking aloud to no one in particular, he said with excitement, "Why else did I so unfairly lose my job, and then so miraculously find this better one?"

He looked once more at the church, and then got into his car with a whole new sense of purpose.

Part V

Thy Rod and Thy Staff

1

Long before daybreak Monday morning, Stephen awoke, showered, dressed, stuffed three days' worth of casual clothes into a duffel bag, and stacked the back seat of his new green Wagoneer with devotional books, sermon materials, and his laptop. Quietly, he crept back into the house to kiss Sara and the boys goodbye without waking them. Returning to the garage, he drove for places north, and a three-day escape.

The annual pastors' retreat was in the mountains at The Widow's Mite, an old renovated hunting lodge. It was run by Tom and Suzette Cousineau, an elderly couple who had inherited it from Suzette's grandfather. The enormous two-story log and stone structure consisted of a U-shaped upstairs divided into 12 bedrooms, each facing a wood-railed balcony which overlooked the spacious downstairs living room. At the open end of the "U" was an enormous fieldstone fireplace surrounded by large picture windows that gave a panoramic view of the White Mountains and the large spring-fed pond for which the family's great-grandfather had chosen this location.

Stephen and his fellow clergymen had been meeting here annually for twelve years ever since the retreats had been initiated by Ronald Stang, a conservative Congregationalist pastor from Gloucester. Ron had been concerned about the growing liberalism in the Association and perceived the need for a "by-invitation-only" retreat for evangelical pastors actively "fighting the good fight." This would give them some needed time away for R&R, prayer, and the encouraging fellowship of like-minded brothers.

Ron had chosen The Widow's Mite for many reasons. Isolated in the shadow of the White Mountains, it was centrally located for most New England pastors, it supplied all their needs, and because the Cousineaus were themselves deeply religious, it offered a quiet, devotional atmosphere.

Stephen was more than anxious to reach the serenity of The Widow's Mite. He yearned for the relaxing warmth of the central fireplace where he would gather with friends, some of whom he had not talked to since last year's retreat. Focusing on what awaited him, he began purging himself of the concerns of his congregation and family.

Through the morning twilight, he saw the entrance ramp to the Interstate, and realized that both he and his car were thirsty. So before committing himself to the long haul north, he turned into a convenience mart for gas, a large coffee, and some donuts. The pump lanes were empty, but as he got out, he noticed a gray Caprice wagon pulling in beside a second row of pumps. The driver was blocked from view by a large sign advertising a free car wash with each fill-up. After the Wagoneer had consumed its fill of medium test fuel, Stephen walked inside to pay his bill.

He extended his credit card to a tired yet pleasant young woman dressed in a bright yellow uniform. He studied her artificially highlighted auburn hair, her green eye shadow, her bright red fingernails, and, not least of all, her partially unbuttoned blouse. Instantly his mind was captive to a wide range of inappropriate thoughts, until the woman said sarcastically, "Anything else?"

Raising his eyes, he saw that she had obviously caught the drift of his thoughts. "No, thank you," he said, fumbling as he gathered his morning snacks. He turned away, hoping to bring his mind back to a more appropriate universe, and found himself in a sudden staring match with the last person he expected or wanted to see, Walter Horscht.

Through the fog on his glasses, Walter gave no indication that he had recognized Stephen. Stephen's first inclination was to escape unnoticed, but his pastoral heart thought otherwise. Breaking through the awkwardness, he extended his hand. "Good morning, Walter. I thought I saw you in the congregation yesterday morning. What brings you and your family to Witzel's Notch?"

Walter stepped back, startled, wiping his glasses with his fingers. Stephen could tell that Walter was castigating himself for choosing this of all gas stations.

Reaching around Stephen to pay his bill, Walter responded

nervously, "I'm the new night supervisor over at Levonshire's. Helen, Stacy, and I moved in last week. We had intended to make First Church our spiritual home, but we didn't know..."

There was so much Stephen wanted to ask this mysterious antagonist, but this wasn't the time or the place. "Well, I hope you will. We apparently have a few things to clear up, though. Why don't you stop by my office sometime where we can talk?"

Walter grabbed his change and headed for the door. "Yes, well, I might just do that. Have a nice day."

Stephen watched through the open door as Walter entered his vehicle and drove quickly away.

"What a strange way to start the day, Lord," Stephen said to the cold misty morning. "I just pray that this isn't a portent of things to come."

He re-entered his Wagoneer and headed onto the Interstate. This year he was in charge of the retreat discussions, and he was determined to arrive in plenty of time to set up the chapel before the nearly thirty regulars arrived. Over the weeks of preparation, he had given in to the urge to use this private gathering of friends to go public with his concerns. There was no one at home he could talk to, especially not Sara.

But yet, will any of these seemingly content pastors appreciate my dilemma?

With the glow of the morning sun breaking above the mountain skyline and the distant, invisible ocean coast, Stephen prepared his heart for renewal. Specifically, he prayed that through his prayers and the advice of his friends, he would find clear direction for his future.

*　　　*　　　*

ONCE THE CONVENIENCE MART was out of sight, Walter pulled his wagon to the side of the road. He held the steering wheel tightly with both hands as he calmed himself down.

"Dear God!" he exclaimed, out of breath. "What was that about?"

For several minutes, he stared out into the emerging morning world, shaking his head slightly back and forth as he reviewed all that had happened so recently to him and his family—the serendipitous offer of the night foreman's job, the miraculous sale of their home in Red Creek, and the discovery of their new home which had so pleased Helen. He had taken its nearness to the church as a sign from God, but now he wasn't so sure.

The shock of discovering that LaPointe was their new pastor still rang through his mind like a fit of demonic laughter. Beneath this surged the mental replay of ripping Stacy away from her lifelong friends at Red Creek. She had never spoken so belligerently and with such defiance. Now he regretted even more how violently he had responded. *But she deserved it! She may be a teenager, but that doesn't mean I can't turn her over my knee when she defies me!*

He looked out toward the eastern sky where a hint of red was beginning to appear, and prayed silently: *Lord Jesus, what did You want me to do over there? Did You plan that rendezvous as some kind of encounter? I'm sorry if I failed You, but it just didn't seem like the right time. Lord, what is it that You want me to do?*

He waited, but no answer came—only the aging purr of the engine amidst his now calm breathing. Putting his car back into gear and returning to the road, Walter knew that when the time was right, God would give him a sign.

2

"STEPHEN! Hey, long time no see," said a tall black man with graying, close-cropped curly hair. Seasonally dressed in a wool sweater and insulated corduroy pants, he remained close to the fire blazing in the inn's stone hearth.

"Cliff, it's great to see you. I didn't expect you this year," Stephen said, dropping his bags to give a brotherly embrace to Cliff Wilson, a seminary alumnus and fellow Congregational pastor from Connecticut. "I see you still aren't acclimated to this northern chill."

"Boy, ain't that the truth," Cliff said, turning his backside to the fire. "It's been twenty years since I came north from South Carolina, but I still need all this stuff to keep from freezing."

"You're the only pastor I know who wears long johns as a regular part of his clerical attire."

Stephen was more than pleased to see this old friend. Their

closeness, honed by tough years together in seminary, had never slackened and now returned instantaneously as they shared their first jabs of friendly humor. "How many years has it been?"

"The last retreat I attended was four years ago," Cliff said.

"That long? Well, where have you been? Every year we miss you and wonder why you're staying away." Stephen clasped Cliff's shoulder. "*I've* missed you."

"Well, as you can imagine, being a black pastor in this snow-white, New England, once-puritanical church isn't exactly a piece of cake."

"Hey, it isn't easy for us white dudes either," Stephen quipped, and they both laughed. "Did you move?"

"Yes, I settled in a bit farther south at an inner-city church on the Connecticut shore. It has all the usual preferences for the social gospel. We have our uncomfortable class divisions between the older gray-haired, long-term white members, who now mostly live in the suburbs, and the newer, poorer, inner-city black and Puerto Rican members, but everything has gone miraculously well."

"Where does that leave gray-haired black dudes?"

"At least we're getting old together," Cliff said, pointing to Stephen's own graying pate.

"How's the family?" Stephen asked cautiously, stoking the fire.

Cliff turned to look into the flames. A shadow passed across his face. "I guess that's the real reason I've stayed away. Cecilia moved back to Carolina with the kids. The boys spend a month or two with me each year, and you know about our daughter."

Stephen remembered that there had been a question about the paternity of their youngest child, which had set their marriage on edge.

"I wanted to work it out, but Cecilia was fed-up with being a black pastor's wife in a white world. Two months after the divorce, she married Stephanie's true father."

"Cliff, I'm sorry to hear this," Stephen said. "I remember you two in seminary—we all saw you as the ideal pastoral team. I'm sorry I haven't kept in touch."

"Well, friendship's a two-way street, Stephen. I didn't call or e-mail either. I was just too ashamed."

"Please, let's get together more often. We can meet halfway for lunch."

"I'd like that, Stephen. I've been pretty discouraged lately. This pastoral life hasn't turned out to be what I thought it would."

"Boy, you can say that again." This time Stephen studied the flames.

"How are things with you?" Cliff asked.

"Well, Cliff, on the one hand—on the surface—everything couldn't be better. I've been at my fourth church for five months, and I don't think I could find a better fit. Their conservative evangelicalism matches comfortably with my 'right-wing fundamentalist redneck' theology."

This brought the expected laugh. Stephen was repeating something Cliff once had hurled at him in anger. While seniors in seminary, a disagreement over what was the core mandate of the gospel had tested their friendship. Stephen had emphasized "proclaim the gospel to the lost," and Cliff, "love the downtrodden, feed the poor, and liberate the captives." In the end, the tension had strengthened their friendship and brought balance to each other's convictions.

Stephen hesitated over whether it was the time to tell all. Finally he said, "On the other hand, let's just say that I love Jesus with all my heart, and that I'm eternally grateful for His love and acceptance. Beyond that, well, I'm not certain what I believe anymore."

"Stephen, what's happening?"

"Oh, later, Cliff, there's plenty of time for that," Stephen said, shifting moods. "Hey, it's great to see you, though. Listen, I need to drop off my bags and finish my prep before the rest of the gang starts piling in."

"Sure. If there's anything I can do to help, don't hesitate to ask—I can break away from the fire for at *least* a minute."

Smiling, Stephen gathered his bags and proceeded upstairs to select a bedroom. Ascending, he half wished that no one else would come. He would enjoy spending an uninterrupted afternoon alone with Cliff, for there were few with whom he'd rather reveal his doubts—especially since he had helped Cliff wrestle through his own period of uncertainty during their second year in seminary.

Fifteen minutes later, Stephen descended with his devotional materials. He had changed into clothes that were more relaxing: a plaid lumberjack shirt, a pair of corduroys, and leather chukka boots. Cliff rose to help.

"Tell me, Stephen, who's coming this year?"

"The usual suspects," he said. "Actually, I don't know since I wasn't in the registration loop, but no one has mentioned that any of the regulars aren't coming."

"What about Jim Sarver?" Cliff queried with a tone that implied inside information.

"What about him? I haven't heard one way or the other." With feigned detachment, Stephen retrieved a cup of coffee from a large percolator outside the kitchen. He then led Cliff into the side room where they would soon have their first meeting.

"You mean you haven't heard?" Cliff said, taken aback.

"Heard what? Is there some reason Jim might not come?" Stephen began distributing handouts onto the thirty chairs that encircled the perimeter of the room. On a small central table were a Bible and a self-standing cross. He knew there might be justification for Jim's absence, but he could scarcely believe it. At last year's retreat, the group had digressed into an awkward and heated "debate" over the issue of divorce and remarriage, and he and Jim had ended up on opposite sides. Sadly, they had left without resolution. Stephen's anger had fully subsided on the drive home, but his preoccupation with his then private struggle with his ministry and his move from Respite to Witzel's Notch made it too easy to put off mending the breach in their twenty-five-year friendship. He wondered now how his longtime friend would take his impending announcement.

"Well, you need to sit down for this, because of all people you may find this hard to believe." Cliff helped Stephen finish, and then after topping off their coffees, he led Stephen back to some overstuffed leather chairs by the fire.

"You remember," Cliff began, "that Jim had accepted a part-time position at Southwestern Seminary, teaching courses in practical pastoral theology?"

"Yes, while he pastored a local Presbyterian church." Stephen rose to nudge a half-burned log closer into the fire's core.

"That's right. I heard he was one of Southwestern's most-liked teachers. His classes were always full, while his church kept growing. Everything was going great. Then on the first Sunday of October he resigned from his church...."

"What?" Stephen said, returning his attention sharply to Cliff.

"That's right. I was told that he stopped right in the middle of worship when he was about to lead the congregation in the Lord's

Supper. He asked the elders to meet with him immediately in the parlor. After twenty minutes, the head elder returned to inform the congregation that their pastor had submitted his resignation and would not be returning. Within two weeks, Jim and his large family had vacated the parsonage."

Stephen sat slowly back into his chair, staring at Cliff with the look of a doubting Thomas, stunned that he had heard nothing of this, from Jim or anyone. If it was true, it would be much too coincidental.

"But why? This can't be true."

"I don't know any more details, and I haven't spoken with Jim since the last time I was here," Cliff said. "I heard all this from Scott Turner at a meeting in January."

"But how could Jim abandon his charge right in the middle of worship?" Stephen demanded. "Cliff, this is absurd. To resign is one thing, but to stop in the middle of worship—in the middle of the Lord's Supper—leaving the congregation sitting, wondering, confused? Jim's commitment both to Christ and his calling are too strong for this to happen."

Stephen rose for a coffee refill. "But Scott and Jim will be here soon, so then we can lift the skirts on this mystery. Can you do me a favor? How about taking the role of greeter this morning, welcoming the guys as they arrive? I need to call Sara."

"Sure, no problem."

Stephen headed into the kitchen where Mrs. Cousineau was putting another tray of cinnamon rolls into the oven. "Good morning, Mrs. Cousineau."

Suzette Cousineau was always a pleasant, nostalgic sight for Stephen. She and her husband, Tom, were as active and energetic as any sexagenarians could be. Tom had been a fisherman on the St. Lawrence River before retiring to help his wife run this retreat house. The land-locked life had done him well. Besides tending their nearly year-round garden, Tom hunted and fished the woods and streams surrounding their wilderness getaway. Suzette dedicated most of her efforts to her favorite pastimes, cooking and eating, evidenced by her robust figure.

"Stephen, welcome back," Mrs. Cousineau said in her French Canadian twang as she came from behind her kitchen island to give this familiar boarder a hug. "Is everything all right? Are you finding what you need?"

"It's good to see you, Mrs. Cousineau," Stephen said, returning the embrace. "Yes, everything's great as always."

"Good. Are you ready for some French Canadian cooking?"

"Looking forward to it," Stephen said, stretching it a bit. Mrs. Cousineau's cooking was indeed delicious, but as French Canadian cooking went, it was on the heavy side. Everyone's growing indigestion became the running joke during the retreats, but they carefully kept this from her. She was much too generous to chance hurting her feelings. "Is Mr. Cousineau home?"

"Tom should be back tomorrow. He's on pilgrimage to St. Joseph's Oratory in Montreal, and he'll be very repentant at that for leaving me here alone to do everything for you boys. But don't you worry. I won't burn your eggs."

"Please, may I use the phone to call Sara?"

"Sure, go ahead."

After keying in his number, Stephen only had to wait one ring before Sara picked up. "Hello!" She yelled into the receiver.

"Geez, Sara, what's with you? You nearly burst my eardrum."

"Oh, I'm sorry," Sara said in a much reduced tone. "Danny and I are having a brouhaha over his getting up late and missing the bus. William doesn't need to drive in until ten, so I'll have to drive Danny myself. I was standing next to the telephone when you rang, and it startled me. I didn't mean to direct my anger at you, but then again, you know how it is. How was your trip?"

"Just fine, nothing out of the ordinary." Stephen saw no reason to go through his unexpected encounter with Walter Horscht. "Cliff Wilson is here."

"Cliff? Great. How is he doing? Are they back together?"

"No. Cecilia moved out, remarried, and took the kids with her. Cliff's been helping me get ready. No one else has arrived yet, except of course for Mrs. Cousineau, who's here in the kitchen making another pan of her famous cinnamon rolls."

"And you tell her," Mrs. Cousineau spoke up, "that I'll make some for her if you husbands ever bring your wives along."

"Maybe next year, Mrs. Cousineau," Stephen said. "Sara, I do need to go finish setting up, but I just heard an outlandish rumor about Jim Sarver."

"What's that, honey? *Danny, please, get your shoes on!*" Sara yelled, driving Stephen away from the receiver. "Oh, sorry, Stephen."

"Oh, that's OK. I didn't need that ear anyway."

"Well, just remember that being home alone with these boys for three days is not my idea of a *retreat,*" Sara said with rising emotion.

"I understand, dear," Stephen said carefully, hesitant to arouse the demons, "and I do appreciate your letting me come."

"Just don't enjoy yourself too much," she said with controlled humor. "Now what was that rumor you wanted to tell me?"

"Oh, nothing. Nothing that can't wait."

"Mom!" Stephen heard in the background.

"Listen, honey," Sara said, "I've got to go. Please, have a good time with your friends, and say hello to everyone that I know. And don't eat too many of those cinnamon rolls."

"Oh, you know I will. Love you."

"Love you, too."

Hanging up, Stephen stood motionless, questioning whether he was ready to face any new arrivals. He turned to see Mrs. Cousineau once again absorbed in kneading dough.

"Thanks for the use of the phone," he said. "I guess I better go and greet the newcomers. By the sound of it, a few of the more rowdy ones have arrived."

"Yes, Stephen, you get out there and keep 'em in line! And what you can't catch, I'll reel in with my cinnamon rolls at nine-thirty sharp."

"Great, see you then." Stephen left the kitchen and found himself in the welcome arms of a dozen old friends. As they exchanged the usual pleasantries, others arrived at a steady pace. As usual, most had been intent on getting there in time for Mrs. Cousineau's famous rolls.

At nine-thirty, the kitchen serving windows opened and a fine spread of rolls, English muffins, juice, and coffee awaited the hungry crowd of thirty-three guests. Most of the regulars as well as a few new faces had arrived, except for Jim Sarver. Recalling his usual promptness, Stephen wondered if maybe this year Jim wasn't coming.

"Hey, guys," Stephen yelled through the growing commotion. "Before we feed our faces, let's take a moment to thank God for safe journeys and for giving Mrs. Cousineau the heavenly gifts that produced these delicacies. Scott, would you lead us in prayer?"

"Yeah, thanks Stephen," Scott Turner said, with feigned indignance. "Just because I'm the bulkiest person here, you think this will keep me from getting first in line. OK, that's fine, but I warn you: don't keep your eyes closed too tightly."

All laughed, but as they prayed, more than a few kept at least one eye open. Once the prayer was complete, the kitchen window was rushed, and Stephen, hanging back until last, prayed that this retreat would be as inspiring and rejuvenating as those in the past. He also prayed again that this swarm of friends caught in a mock feeding frenzy might help him return home with solid answers and much clearer direction.

3

STEPHEN SAT IMPATIENTLY in the makeshift chapel-meeting room. It was thirteen minutes past the scheduled start of their second group discussion, and being a stickler for schedules, Stephen was getting annoyed.

The rest of the men were nursing their post-lunch coffees, clustered around the hearth. Through the open door, Stephen could see several talking and laughing. One was Larry Wycliffe, who had led the discussions last winter. Larry was one of the more popular regular attendees—a strong, handsome ex-Marine who had found Jesus in a prisoner-of-war camp in Korea. A piece of blazing shrapnel had given his left cheek a distinctive wound.

Larry of all people should know better than to ignore the schedule, Stephen grumbled. *Once we get off track, it's hell trying to get back.*

Stephen glanced again at the wall clock to which they seemed oblivious.

Are they taunting me on purpose? Would they belittle me if I tried to herd them in? Would they press me to let them stay out there? But I put so much effort into this!

The inner voices were taking advantage of his inherent insecurities to discourage and deflect him from his spiritual goals. As well-liked as Stephen was, he still struggled with self-doubt, questioning the sincerity of any friend's affection. Often he caught himself absorbed in mental scenarios in which he was defending himself against supposed combatants or disgruntled church members.

As he continued to stare through the open door, torn between getting up to call them in or waiting for them to come on their own, he happened to catch Larry's eye. Larry was talking with Scott Turner, whose back was to Stephen. Larry glanced at his watch and exclaimed, "Hey!" His booming voice stopped all conversation. "Come on, guys. Stephen is waiting. Let's go, into the chapel." Larry and Cliff began corralling the group in, and no one hesitated, offering apologies all around.

"Sorry, Stephen," Scott said as he took the chair next to him. "Lots of catching up to do."

"That's all right. Hey, before we get started, I need to ask..."

At that moment, as the men crowded into the small room, the voice of Birch Herbert blurted out over the din of rustling chairs, "Don't give me that!" He was feigning an argument with Cliff Wilson. "UConn doesn't have a prayer. I'll bet you ten-to-one the Blue Devils go all the way." Birch was fulfilling his usual role of keeping their non-discussion times focused on anything but the spiritual, which usually meant sports. Cliff was an avid Connecticut basketball fan and a patsy for Birch's blustery brags.

"If I wasn't so much holier than you, I'd take that wager," Cliff said.

"Well, excuuuuuse me!" They laughed as they took their seats, assuring all around of their levity.

The buzz of the crowd was subsiding, and attentions began focusing toward Stephen.

"What was it you wanted to ask?" Scott responded.

"I guess we'll have to talk later," Stephen said. "It was about a rumor I heard—about Jim Sarver."

Scott shook his head slightly. "Yeah, can you believe it? I was half hoping he'd show up, but I guess I didn't expect him to."

"But is it true?"

"I'm afraid so," Scott said.

"Then we need to take a walk after the discussion."

"Sure."

Their morning devotions and first discussion had gone well. To a man, the group seemed ready for this retreat, each expressing a hope for some spiritual, personal, or vocational breakthrough.

As they gathered for their second meeting, they were to have re-read St. Paul's First Letter to Timothy. Stephen was about to drop a bombshell, and he wanted this to fall on well-prepared minds.

Reaching over to touch the knee of a man sitting across from him, Stephen asked, "Hank, will you open us with prayer?"

"Sure, Stephen. Guys...let us pray."

Hank Fabrey, dressed in a white shirt and blue paisley tie with his white hair meticulously combed, stood up, which brought a similar response from the rest of the men. "Father God..." Hank began in his usual manner.

Stephen found it comical that each of the pastors had their own peculiar yet predictable prayer ritual. Hank always began in a deep pastoral tone with "Father God," and Stephen knew why. Hank was of the old school and fought endless battles with modern feminists who berated him to use gender-neutral language. But Hank refused to budge, and spitefully stepped up his emphasis on the Fatherhood of God. Taylor Cummins, on the other hand, standing ironically on the opposite side of the room, de-emphasized the fatherhood of God. He rarely referred to God in any other way except as "God"— seldom as "He" and never as "Father." Others present addressed their prayers either to Jesus, or the Holy Spirit, or, under the impulse of being free and independent, a different person of the Trinity every time.

The more Stephen considered these differences in verbal piety, the more it reinforced what he was about to present. But he also realized that he had missed most of Hank's prayer. As Hank drew to a close, the inner voices of doubt again picked up their attack. With the communal "Amen," Stephen struggled against the urge to abandon his plans and lead them in a less threatening discussion.

The men retook their seats, while Stephen stepped to a wooden lectern in the rear of the room, facing the door.

"Thank you, Hank. Now before I begin, does anyone need a *Rolaid*?" Laughs rose all around, accompanied by affirmative facial gesticulations. "Tom, did you bring the annual supply?"

"Sure did." Tom Sylvan, by far the largest in girth of the attendees, held up an extra-large bottle of multi-flavored antacids. Over the years, this had become Tom's unofficial responsibility—partially out of his own need for relief—as well as a regular source of light-hearted jesting.

Allowing the noise to subside while the bottle made its journey around the room, Stephen began the discussion that he had been both anxiously anticipating and dreading for weeks.

"As most of you know, I've been an ordained minister now for about nineteen years. I've pastored three churches and am now five months into my fourth. I've come from being an assistant at a medium-sized church, to the solo pastor of a tiny country church with no staff, to the pastor of a slightly larger semi-rural church, again with no staff, to my current position as the senior pastor of a large congregation with a staff of six, a seven-figure budget, and an evangelical reputation. I do believe that the church I now pastor is probably the largest in membership represented here. I suppose you could say I've arrived—at least that I am now pastoring the size of congregation with the kind of opportunities I only dreamed that one day I would have. And I suppose that at least one of you is a bit envious of my present situation." He smiled at Kyle Reuther.

"Boy, you can say that again!" Kyle blurted out to everyone's knowing laughs. Kyle's pastorate was everything that "difficult" meant. The search committee that convinced the congregation to hire this extraordinarily gifted, confident, yet gentle man two years before had blatantly lied, both to him and to the liberal-minded congregation. After nearly everything he did—from sermons to committee meetings to weddings and funerals—he received nasty complaints. More often than not, some member threatened to have him fired; and more often than not he considered quitting. Being a uniquely devout man of prayer, however, he was certain that he was to stay "come hell or high water"—unless he heard differently from God, and he had come to this retreat hoping to hear.

"I suppose that in knowing your situation, Kyle, every one of us should count our blessings," Stephen responded, hoping that what he was about to say would not sound like sour grapes. "But even in saying this, and recognizing the real problems you have faced where God has planted you," he said, pointing affectionately at Kyle, "I want to explain to all of you why I have decided to resign."

"What?" Cliff blurted out, as similar comments came from around the circle.

Stephen held up his hands and waited patiently as the reaction of his audience subsided. "For a few of you, this should come as no surprise," he said, glancing at Cliff, Kyle, and Scott. "In the past I've told you my concerns, but when you appointed me as this year's discussion leader, I couldn't shake the conviction that God wanted me to tell the rest of you.

"I also need to stress that no one in my congregation or family—especially my wife, Sara—knows that this is coming. Over the years,

I've given Sara all the data, but I don't think she as yet has connected the dots. If she had, I wouldn't be here this morning!" This brought some confirming yet subdued laughs.

Pausing to study their familiar faces, he continued. "I've coveted this moment with the hope that you, with your own ministry experiences, can help me find a different solution. But before any of you speculate too far afield about what terrible thing I must have done to necessitate my resignation, let me assure you: I no longer beat my wife, I've returned all the money I've embezzled from my last three churches, and I have more than enough incriminating information on my mistresses to guarantee their silence."

"I don't know, Steve," Tom Sylvan added, "I think news has leaked about our escapade last year with the coeds up on Mount Lafayette." Everyone laughed freely, for Tom's size and far from winsome appearance were ample proof of their jocularity.

"No, I'm not quitting because of some gross moral or ethical failure, though God knows I've plenty of faults." A fleeting picture of the woman at the convenience mart crossed Stephen's mind. "I'm leaving the pulpit because I question whether I have any right to preach from it any more. I'm simply no longer confident that I can stand before my people and tell them that I *know* what is *true*. Not that I doubt Jesus," he said as he glanced at a foreign-looking portrait of Jesus hanging on the back wall. In it, Jesus was pointing to a large red three-dimensional heart painted on his chest. "I love Him as much as ever, maybe even more." His emotions were rising, causing his voice to crack and his eyes to tear.

"What I doubt is whether as an ordained pastor I can speak authoritatively on anything else—whether anything I believe is more than just *my* opinion. If this is so, then how can I be certain that what I am teaching my people has any eternal significance–whether what I claim to be the gospel has any resemblance to what Jesus taught His Apostles two thousand years ago?"

Stephen caught himself starting to preach, so he backed off. He paused, listening and looking for some sign that his audience was with him. Cliff, Scott, Larry, Birch, Kyle, Hank, and the men in between all sat, silently dazed and seemingly willing to hear him out.

"If you will bear with me, I want to draw your attention to a few things in Paul's first letter to his son in the faith, Timothy, which I believe clearly illustrate my dilemma. My intent is not to focus solely on my personal crisis, but to challenge you to examine your own authority as ordained ministers.

"I'm assuming that you've all read through the entire First Epistle as I asked," Stephen posed rhetorically, receiving a few nods, "so if you would, allow me to walk you through a few significant sections. I ask only that you save your comments until I'm done. There'll be plenty of time for discussion." Stephen knew that if they got embroiled in a debate, they would never hear his point.

"That's fine, Stephen," Cliff interjected, standing up, arms raised, "but I'm immediately distracted by what you've just dropped on us. Resigning is a drastic move," he said, using a quisical glance to reference their earlier discussion. "Are you serious or just exaggerating to make a point?"

For a second that seemed like hours, Stephen weighed the myriad times this question had consumed his thoughts. Was he *truly* serious about resigning or just being dramatic? *Or am I just floating this for shock value to get them to take me seriously?* No, he knew that he could no longer face his congregation with a clear conscience.

"Cliff, I'm serious about this. I wish it was only for shock value, but for now, if you can, put that thought on hold."

Cliff sat down, but Stephen knew he had shaken his friend.

"As we consider this epistle, it helps to envision Timothy sitting in his first-century robes, at a rough-hewn wooden table, inside a small plaster and thatch house, somewhere in the primitive village of Ephesus in Asia Minor. A messenger arrives delivering a papyrus scroll sealed with the Apostle Paul's imprint. Timothy, who serves as the pastor or overseer for this region of the mission field, anxiously breaks the wax seal and unrolls the scroll. He sees the familiar handwriting and begins to read:

> Paul, an apostle of Christ Jesus by command of God our
> Savior and of Christ Jesus our hope...

Stephen began his running commentary, as one loving shepherd to another.

*   *   *

THE DIGITAL ALARM EXPLODED with its annoying electronic bleats. Walter awoke from his daytime nap with a jump and slammed down hard on the off button. Instantly he feared he had broken the darn thing. Walter sat up, pulling his bare legs out from under the sheets and onto the floor, brushed back his thinning hair with his hands, hooked his wire glasses behind each ear, and looked around at his new surroundings.

Their new home was in much worse condition than the one they had left behind. At first glance, Helen had been convinced that this two-story, field-stone, antebellum house had great potential. The wallpaper in their bedroom, however, was soiled and peeling from a roof leak. The entire house bore a musty smell, probably from the damp basement. Walter wondered, shaking his head, *wouldn't it be better to just tear it down and build a new one?* But, like Helen, he was excited about restoring this hidden treasure.

"Helen?" he called out affectionately. Afternoons were their best windows for marital intimacy. There was no answer, even after a second try, so Walter assumed with disappointment that Helen must be out either shopping or getting acquainted with the neighbors. *In that case, I might as well make that call.*

Donning his robe, he retrieved a cup of overcooked coffee and sat at their antique oak dinette in the breakfast nook. Through a tall window that showed the imperfections of its age, he studied the infinite chores facing him in the backyard. Thankfully, six inches of snow made procrastination easy. The trimming of the overgrown hedges and the reseeding of the pock-marked lawn, where the last owners had kept their "beloved" beagle imprisoned at the end of a chain, could wait until spring.

From his shirt pocket, he removed a tattered address book. Locating the number, he dialed. The telephone at the other end rang, which was rare. Normally the line was busy, either with other calls or because they were connected to the Internet.

After two rings, the familiar female voice answered.

"Good afternoon, FC2C. Can I help you?"

"Yes, hello, Virginia, this is Walter Horscht." He always enjoyed calling the offices of FC2C, partially because Virginia was such a pleasant gatekeeper.

"Oh, hello," she said politely. "Did you get settled into your new job and home?"

"Yes, we did, thank you. I think the family will be happy here." Walter thought about adding "for the time we have left" but held back, not knowing Virginia's take on the apocalyptic. "Is the Reverend available?"

"I think so. Just wait a second and I'll see."

"YES, VIRGINIA," Reverend Harmond said in the intercom.

"Walter Horscht is on the line for you."

"Virginia, I asked you to shield me from him whenever he calls."

"I know, but he just sent in a large donation. I figured the least you could do..."

"You're right," Harmond said, "but you owe me one. Put him through." After a few seconds of a classical guitar rendition of "Amazing Grace," he heard the click of the connected line.

"Walter, great to hear from you. Long time no hear."

To the Reverend Gary Harmond, Walter was an enigma, at times showing an elusive Dr. Jekyll-Mr. Hyde personality. Generally, Walter came across like an average-Joe evangelical who could chat freely about his faith in Jesus or the chances for the Patriots in the Super bowl. But mention Catholicism, and he seemed to grow hair and scowl like a caged beast. Walter's convictions about the growing Catholic conspiracy and the imminent Rapture exceeded even Harmond's.

Now in his mid-fifties, Harmond was quite comfortable to be out of the pulpit and no longer fighting denominational superintendents, church boards, or ladies' guilds. As the director of this para-church ministry, accountable only to his hand-picked board of advisors, Harmond enjoyed his freedom—especially since his ex-nun wife had left him—to travel the country speaking in churches about the horrors of the Catholic Church and the Pope's supposed role in the coming tribulations.

The early afternoon was generally the slowest time of his day, and he usually struggled to keep awake after his traditionally ample lunch. He cradled the receiver within his double chin, and clutching his afternoon coffee in one hand, he sketched random images on a blank page of his daily planner with the other.

"Just fine, Reverend Harmond," Walter said. "The Lord has been good to us as usual. The new position's much better than the last, more pay and better benefits, although this time it's the graveyard shift."

"That's a shame. When you gonna get a respectable job like mine?"

"Right, kicking back and relaxing off my donations. How many golf memberships have I financed so far?"

"Only the one at Palm Beach, which I only use four or five times a year." Both knew this was fiction, for Harmond was hardly an athlete, let alone a golfer. "What's on your mind?"

"Oh, just calling to re-establish connections."

"Come on, my friend, I can tell by your voice that something's wrong. What's eating you?"

"Well, do you remember, oh, about a year ago when we talked about my previous pastor? The one you confirmed sounded like he might be an infiltrator?"

"Sure...ah...I'd never heard of a more certain candidate." Harmond quit sketching triangles and set his mind at recall. He was certain about the growing threat of the Catholic Church and was always glad to hear from a convinced follower. "Have you come across more incriminating evidence?"

"Well, the Lord certainly has a strange sense of humor. When Helen, Stacy, and I attended our new Congregational Church here in Witzel's Notch, guess who we discovered was our new pastor?"

Harmond laid his pencil down. "You're kidding. He's your new pastor?"

"That's right. My glasses nearly fell off when I recognized him."

"That would have made quite a racket."

"Very funny."

"Sorry. Remind me, what was it that first convinced you he might be a Catholic priest posing as a Protestant?" All Harmond could remember was that it indeed had sounded intriguing.

"Well, I can't repeat word for word what he had said—it's been several years. But one night in a Bible study, he stated that he believed contraception was a sin. He said it prevented a married couple from being fully open to God's gift of children. He said it reduced intercourse to merely an act of pleasure, and eliminated the need for responsible stewardship of one's sexuality."

"That's right," Harmond remembered, "contraception. Responsible stewardship of one's sexuality?"

"Yes. By using contraception, men and women can enjoy promiscuity without procreation."

Harmond pondered this while he sketched a couple embracing. He could not recall if this was exactly the Catholic party line, but he was positive that no Protestant minister he knew ever took this stand. Most ministers felt a responsibility *under God* to tell engaged couples about the good stewardship of using contraception to delay or limit the size of their families.

"What did you say his name was?" Harmond asked.

"Reverend Stephen LaPointe."

"That's right," Harmond said, though he had hardly remembered, "and what church?"

"First Congregational Church of Witzel's Notch."

Harmond made a note. Since this was so close, he would probably make the call himself. He loved a good debate—especially if it could mean uncovering a papal infiltrator in front of his own congregation. So far he had struck out, but he knew that one day he would confirm his hunches.

"Reverend Harmond," Walter proceeded cautiously, "you know we've discussed how I understand my calling before God—to be His obedient centurion, no matter where or when He calls, no matter what the cost. I'm beginning to think that all the chips are falling into place in His bringing me to this spot."

Normally this kind of thinking put Harmond off, remembering with guilt and melancholy the days when he viewed his own calling with the same enthusiasm. But having had to eat his own apocalyptic predictions so many times had jaded this fervor. Yet respecting Walter's sincere and almost childlike faith, Harmond chose to affirm him like a brother.

"Well, Walter, you just hold tight to that. I do think you are on to something. Why don't you let me follow up on this, and then let's talk. Together we can figure out what God might be calling you to do. By the way, now that you live closer, have you called the local FC2C fellowship group?"

"No, not yet. We've only been here a few days."

"Well, Virginia will give you Raeph's phone number."

"Raeph?" Walter said with pleasant surprise. "Raeph Timmons?"

"That's right."

"He and I are old friends. I forgot that he lived so close."

"Then he'll be glad to hear from you," Harmond said, sipping his coffee, "and if you're planning to face the evil one head-on and wondering what God wants you to do, you'll need the support and discernment of Christian brothers."

"Of course, Reverend Harmond. Thanks for your encouragement."

"Don't mention it. It's always good to hear from you. I'll call you as soon as I've spoken with Reverend LaPointe. And don't worry, I won't mention your name. I'll just see what tidbits I can uncover."

"Thanks."

"No problem. Talk to you soon, and God bless." Harmond switched Walter off and pressed the intercom.

"Yes, Reverend Harmond?"

"Please, Virginia, lookup the number for the First Congregational Church of Witzel's Notch and see if you can get me an appointment with the Reverend Stephen LaPointe."

*   *   *

WALTER REFILLED HIS CUP and retired to the living room. The newly purchased navy blue curtains on their picture window matched nothing else in the house, but they were the starting point for Helen's redecorating, her greatest interest and talent. She had outdone herself in their last home, which had made it doubly hard for them to leave, stretching every spare dollar to turn their Depression-era Cape Cod into a veritable castle. Generally he just stayed out of her way, because he knew that whatever she did would be worth bragging about.

He pushed the curtains aside and watched the snow fall, adding to the drifts that covered his lawn and driveway. Silently, he thanked God for Reverend Harmond and the FC2C. Both had been a continuing source of encouragement over the years. He prayed for guidance, and then returned to his bedroom to dress against the winter onslaught.

4

"I T CROSSES MY MIND as I read Paul's words," Stephen continued, anxious to finally be candid with his friends, "by whose authority am I a pastor? Twenty-some years ago I sensed a call, a desire to serve Jesus full-time. A local minister and some friends confirmed that call. I went to seminary and got good grades, and then a group of lay leaders and ministers laid their hands on me." Stephen extended his hands, palms down in the posture of a blessing, but then morphed them into claws. The men confirmed his parody with boisterous guffaws.

"They declared me ordained to the pastoral ministry, in the name of the Father and the Son and the Holy Spirit, and called down the Holy Spirit to empower me for ministry. Each one of you went through the same rite of passage, and I assume experienced the same empowerment."

Stephen returned his hands to the lectern. "Since then, by God's grace, I've done an adequate job. Nevertheless, when I envision Timothy being ordained at the hands of the Apostle Paul, I wonder: did any of the people who laid their hands on me have this same authority? The Apostles, whom Jesus chose and ordained, confirmed Paul's calling and self-confidence: Jesus to the Twelve to Paul to Timothy.

"By what line of authority did those men who ordained me gain the right to declare that I was specifically chosen or sent by God as His representative—set apart—to declare His truth? You might say they were acting merely as channels of God's grace, but think about it. Can anyone claim he has the authority to ordain, especially given the grossly divergent opinions about what ordination means? About what ordination requires, or who can be ordained, or even what it *does* to us? Why is our ordination of any more certainty than, let's say, the self-declared, uneducated, mail-order-confirmed minister who lead thousands of independent store-front churches all across America?"

"Now Stephen, come on…" Taylor Cummins began to comment.

"Please, Taylor. Let me get through this in one piece or it'll take all day."

Stephen returned to the text. "Verse three:

> As I urged you when I was going to Macedonia, remain at
> Ephesus that you may charge certain persons not to teach
> any different doctrine, nor to occupy themselves with myths
> and endless genealogies which promote speculations rather
> than the divine training that is in faith.

"Already during that first generation of Christians there were leaders—ordained or not—teaching doctrines contrary to what the Apostles had delivered. From Paul's description, it sounds as though they were mixing Jewish and pagan ideas with different aspects of the Christian gospel. This is similar to the warning Paul gave to the Galatians when he wrote, 'I am astonished that you are so quickly deserting him who called you in the grace of Christ, and turning to a different gospel.'

"A different gospel." As Stephen looked around at his friends, he could also see in his mind's eye the myriad faces that stared back expectantly every Sunday morning.

"Let's consider these unnamed false teachers. They presumably had won the hearing of some Ephesian Christians, drawing them away into other gatherings. Is it not possible that these teachers *believed* that they had received an authentic call from God and that their interpretation, application, and proclamation of the Christian gospel was true, even if it contradicted what Paul was teaching? Put yourselves into this situation. Given how differently we each teach from one another as well as from a vast majority of Christians, how can we be certain that we are teaching 'the divine training that is in faith' rather than wandering off into different doctrines and myths?"

Seeing several poised to respond, Stephen said quickly what he presumed was on their lips: "We might claim that the measure is the Bible. In other words, are you or I following the clear teaching of Scripture? But bear with me, and listen carefully to what Paul writes. Verse five:

> [W]hereas the aim of our charge is love that issues from a
> pure heart and a good conscience and sincere faith. Certain
> persons by swerving from these have wandered away

into vain discussion, desiring to be teachers of the law,
without understanding either what they are saying or
the things about which they make assertions.

"I pray that the aim of our ministries aligns with these three
crucial compass headings—love that issues from a pure heart, a
good conscience, and sincere faith—but how can we be certain?
How can we be sure, for example, that our consciences are *good*? As
American Congregationalists we shout from the rooftops our
inalienable right to freedom of conscience, but is it not possible that
our consciences have become so *free* that they are no longer *good*,
and therefore no longer trustworthy?"

Stephen worried that he was being too abstruse, and losing any
who might be struggling under the deadening aftereffects of lunch.
Yet the eyes of every man—including Birch, who was being only
slightly fidgety—were bright and their expressions keenly focused.

"The important question to ponder here is not 'What did Paul
say?' but 'What did Paul *mean*?' How can we know whether our
consciences are *good* and leading us correctly when we teach our
people whether having an abortion is right or wrong? Or whether
baptism is a mere symbol or an indispensable means of grace? Or
whether Jesus was merely a wise and gifted human being chosen by
God as His sacrificial lamb, or one of the three persons of the
Trinitarian Godhead?

"It's too irresponsibly easy to bark, 'Believe the Scriptures!' or
'Listen to the leading of the Holy Spirit,' when neither the Bible nor
the Holy Spirit are that indisputably clear on these and hundreds of
other important issues. How many of you have clergy friends from
other denominations who believe that the Bible answers every
question, yet argue with you about some biblical issue that you are
certain you have interpreted correctly? How do you determine which
of you is correctly following Paul's three crucial compass headings?"

Stephen glanced nonchalantly at his watch. *Two-thirty! Good Lord.*
He had only a half-hour left and way too much material. He forged
on.

"Jumping over to verse eighteen:

This charge I commit to you, Timothy, my son, in accordance
with the prophetic utterances which pointed to you, that

inspired by them you may wage the good warfare, holding faith and a good conscience. By rejecting conscience, certain persons have made shipwreck of their faith, among them Hymenaeus and Alexander, whom I have delivered to Satan that they may learn not to blaspheme.

"There is nothing more important to me, and I'm sure to you, than to 'fight the good fight,' to hold true to the faith, and to do so with a good conscience. But how can you or I know for certain that we are more correct than Hymenaeus and Alexander, Christian leaders who apparently fell away and blasphemed? Imagine being immortalized for all time in the Bible as a false teacher."

"But Stephen," Taylor insisted, "Paul states clearly that the *reason* they fell away was that they rejected conscience. This is a direct affirmation of our emphasis on conscience as a trustworthy guide."

"Not if understood in the context of this letter. Let me ask you this, Taylor. What does your conscience teach about whether abortion is murder?" Stephen had not planned to pinpoint Taylor, but Taylor had asked for it.

Taylor flushed slightly. "That is an issue of conscience."

"But do you mean it is up to our consciences to define whether abortion is murder, or to determine whether abortion is an act contrary to sound doctrine?"

"There are many factors in a woman's life that one's conscience must take into account," Taylor replied. "This is not a black-or-white issue."

"Who says that abortion is not a black-or-white issue? The Bible? No, it makes no mention of abortion. Then whose conscience, yours or mine, is to determine which factors should or should not be tallied to determine morality? And if, as relativists insist, truth is determined only by an individual's conscience, then, contrary to what Jesus said, there is no truth that can set us free."

"But Stephen, there are truths which our collective consciences confirm..."

"Taylor, stop. We've been there and you know we've done this before." Stephen had anticipated that Taylor would be the first person to divert his presentation off on a tangent. "But actually our perennial disagreement on this issue illustrates my point perfectly. We both accept the Bible as authoritative and infallible, yet we cannot agree on such an important issue."

Stephen backed away from the lectern, directing his comments now toward Cliff. "This struck home hard last week as I was preparing my sermon. Remember how we were taught in seminary to prepare a sermon?"

"Well, I can tell you one thing," Cliff said, hoping to diminish the heat, "I've never come close to the 'one-hour-per-minute-of-delivery' that old Newlan hammered into us!"

"Ain't that the truth!" Birch added, knowing he was lucky to get in one minute of study per one minute of delivery.

"Wait a second," Scott asked with feigned horror. "You mean that was one hour per *minute* of delivery? I thought he said one hour per *second!*"

The laughter this brought was a relief to everyone, especially Stephen.

"You and I are all in full stride in our ministries, two weeks behind in everything at best, including our commitments to our families. We do the best we can in preparing a meaningful and truthful Sunday message. We were taught to resist the temptation of resorting too quickly to commentaries. We first are to study the text thoroughly on our own, so that we come first to our own conclusions. Then before we drop our conclusions on our congregations, we were taught to check our findings with biblical commentaries written by well-respected scholars and theologians." Stephen got a few confirming nods, and took the non-nods as signs of token agreement.

"I have tried to stick to this order for the last nineteen years. I have never dedicated thirty hours before any thirty-minute sermon, but I rarely crack a commentary before Friday morning.

"But this week, when Friday rolled around, I was still struggling with all the implications of my text. I began to reach for one of my favorite commentaries, and something disconcerting occurred to me. Like you, I have an extensive library, but also one that, because of space, must be intentionally compact. There are few books in my study that I fail to open at least once per year. The rest I weed out to make room for new additions.

"As I reached for this highly favored commentary, I realized that my shelves only hold those commentaries that reflect my personal evangelical convictions. Rarely do these scholars and I disagree enough to change my conclusions. Do you get my drift?"

Most were waiting, but Taylor was fuming.

"You see, from week to week, I actually only check myself against *myself*. The conclusions I eventually deliver to my people, therefore, are never actually challenged for their truthfulness. I wonder how many times my carefully chosen commentators and I have been blindly wrong on some important point of Scripture?"

A suitably illustrative subject flashed through his mind. "Some of us here baptize only believing adults while others baptize infants—this variety being the gift of our Congregationalist freedoms. I baptize infants, because I see this as a visible symbol of our salvation by grace. I don't, however, believe in baptismal regeneration. Most of my commentators confirm me in this. The Episcopal pastor down the road, however, teaches infant baptism as well as baptismal regeneration. We read the same Bible. Which of our carefully chosen commentators are correct?"

"Stephen," Scott countered hesitantly, "Episcopalians believe this because they are blinded by a raft of other presumptions."

"But Scott, isn't that basically what we say about everyone who disagrees with us? They are blinded by their presuppositions. Well, if we only listen to those who agree with us, how can we be sure that we aren't the blind ones? I wonder if old Hymenaeus and Alexander only compared notes with one another? As a congregation of two, did they confirm each other's gut instincts that what Paul and Timothy were teaching was contrary to the 'gospel?' Yet, they are immortalized for their misled consciences. How can we be certain that we here, united in our evangelicalism, are not eternally wrong in some important aspect of the faith?"

Several of the men wanted to comment, hands raised like children in a schoolroom, but a quick look at his watch forced Stephen to charge on.

"Because of time, I better jump ahead to,"—Stephen skimmed the ensuing verses to determine how he could rein in his grossly overplanned exposition—"chapter two, verse eight, where you'll find an interesting illustration of what we've been discussing:

> I desire then that in every place the men should pray,
> lifting holy hands without anger or quarreling; also that
> women should adorn themselves modestly and sensibly
> in seemly apparel, not with braided hair or gold or pearls

> or costly attire but by good deeds, as befits women who
> profess religion. Let a woman learn in silence with all
> submissiveness. I permit no woman to teach or to have
> authority over men; she is to keep silent.

"OK, gang, how many of you obediently follow these scriptural instructions? Come on, not all at once."

"Right, Stephen," Birch answered with humor covering a history of pain. "In my church, you'd think that Paul had ordered the men to shut up." This brought an interesting number of confirming nods.

"But Paul was writing to a first-century culture with first-century rules and hang-ups," Taylor responded without humor. "Our job as interpreters is to reinterpret the text for our modern context and culture."

"Excuse me, Taylor," Stephen said, glad that Taylor had swallowed the bait, "by what authority do you decide which scriptural mandates apply only to the first century and which are timeless? As far as I know, there is nothing in Scripture," holding up his Bible, "that mitigates these commands or any others by Paul, John, James, Peter, or Jesus as merely temporary. Yet, we in this room are unanimous in our opinion and practice that Paul's constrictions on women apply only to the early church. OK, but there are also Christian groups today that follow these instructions to the 'T.' We use terms of derision to describe them: 'Fundamentalists' or 'legalists;' churches where women are required to dress plainly without jewelry, to wear head coverings, and to keep quiet. Now which of us are more faithful to the Word of God? They, or us? Or has most of modern Christianity merely buckled under the pressure of feminist politics or the threat of raised rolling pins?" This brought a few grins.

"You guys know I'm not calling us to go home and implement these instructions," Stephen continued. "If I did, you'd never see me again!" This brought guffaws from most, except Hank, who was visibly exasperated.

"What I am trying to point out is this: on the one hand, we hold up the Bible as the sole source of our authority and of the truth we proclaim. Yet, on the other hand, we raise ourselves up above it when we pick and choose those things we wish to defend, or to ignore. And chapter three, verse one is a good example of this: 'If any one aspires to the office of bishop, he desires a noble task.'

"OK, friends, where is the office of bishop in the Congregational Church? How can we be so certain that we have interpreted these passages correctly, when we are surrounded by other Christian churches with bishops, deacons, and even priests? The Reformers and our Congregationalist forefathers interpreted the word 'bishop' to mean 'elder' or 'overseer,' and instituted church structures which we know from history were at best the minority view for the first fifteen hundred years of Christianity. Does it truly make no eternal difference how a church is structured, or is it possible that our tradition has merely opted out for institutionalized individualism, rejecting a more ancient and scriptural hierarchical system?"

"Now, wait a second." Hank could no longer contain himself. He jumped up, slamming his chair against the wall. "Our Congregational structure is no mere invention of man, but the most ancient and authentic. We all know this from our studies of the early Church and from Scripture." He looked around for confirmation. "It was the Catholic Church, enamored with the power of the Roman emperors like Constantine, that imposed an authoritarian hierarchy on the once free churches, and persecuted those who would not bow to papal dictatorship. Scripture teaches that, 'Wherever two or more are gathered in My name, there am I in the midst of them.' This means that Christians have the freedom to gather in His name, to worship Him, to love Him, and to proclaim His truth, without the imposition of popes, bishops or other tyrants."

Though Stephen could tell that not everyone agreed point-by-point with Hank's recitation of the old party line, none were jumping up to contest him either. Instead, what Stephen saw was a room of faces waiting to see how he would answer this beloved, elderly pastor.

"Hank, please, for now I don't want to debate you on that. Please sit down, just for a moment more." Hank remained stolidly in place, while Stephen continued cautiously. "What you have just said I, too, have believed all my life, but this only reinforces my point. This is what we Congregationalists have believed with a vengeance, especially here on this continent. Yet, millions of other Christians—Lutherans, Episcopalians, Methodists, Baptists, Presbyterians—believe differently. Are you willing to say that only we Congregationalists are teaching what is true?"

"No, but I'm not ready to proclaim that what we

Congregationalists have been teaching for five hundred years is wrong, either," Hank replied.

"I understand, Hank. I'm uncomfortable doing that, too, but it's this confusion that's got my goat. Please, Hank, sit down for just a moment longer." Hank sat, though obviously not conceding Stephen's point.

Turning to the entire group, Stephen asked: "Do you remember the words of the Salem Covenant of 1629, the agreement signed by all the settlers of the Salem church? I memorized it in seminary:

> We covenant with the Lord and one with another, and
> do bind ourselves in the presence of God, to walk together
> in all His ways, according as He is pleased to reveal Himself
> unto us in His blessed word of truth."

Stephen choked up as he delivered the words of this concise creed. It pained him that by his statements he was stepping on the graves of these sincere Pilgrim forebears.

"This covenant of Christian love sounds great, and it has been a constant inspiration as I've tried to instill spiritual unity to churches infested with bickering and pride," he said. "There is a problem with it, though. Not in what it says, but in what it leaves out.

"Hank, you expressed the beliefs of a sizeable portion of Christendom. But there are millions of Christians who believe otherwise. How can we be sure that how we are walking, in contrast to all these others, is, as the Salem Covenant states, 'according to how He—God—has pleased to reveal Himself unto us?'"

Stephen noticed by the inverted hands on Cliff's watch that he was losing time. "But please, Hank, I need to push on. Verse fourteen reads:

> I hope to come to you soon, but I am writing these
> instructions to you so that, if I am delayed, you may
> know how one ought to behave in the household of
> God, which is the church of the living God, the pillar
> and bulwark of the truth.

"There are several things in this passage that I cannot answer, especially when compared with other New Testament passages,"

Stephen said. "First, Paul admits that he is writing this letter because he cannot be there in person. In other words, his preferred means of instructing was by word of mouth, not by letter. Does this not imply that Paul could have communicated other important instructions to his assistant by word of mouth that never made it into this letter? In fact, most of what we find in the New Testament letters are solutions to specific problems at local churches. Is it not possible, even probable, that there were many teachings and practices that were known at the local level and needed no correction by Paul, and therefore were not mentioned in Scripture?

"Is it not possible, for example," Stephen said, focusing away from Hank, "that the local churches were organized into a hierarchical structure with bishops, pastors, and deacons, as intimated earlier, and since the structure was working fine, Paul didn't waste valuable papyrus writing about it? And what about the content of early worship? The New Testament gives few details about what they did, said, or sang when they worshipped. Does this mean that there was no commonly accepted order or liturgy, or that there were as yet no liturgical controversies that required Paul's written attention, except for those at the church of Corinth?"

Stephen saw at least one nod of agreement from Taylor Cummins, and this troubled him. Taylor was drawn to the more liberal, "higher critical" views of the Bible, which insinuated that much of the New Testament was not historical but a later concoction of the Church. This was not the position Stephen wished to promote.

"Certainly, this may all be written off as an argument from silence, but on the other hand, why should we assume that only what is found in these letters is the sum total of what is true and gospel?" he said. "In Second Thessalonians 2:15, Paul wrote: 'Stand fast and hold to the traditions which you were taught by us, *either* by word of mouth or by letter.' Doesn't this imply that there were other things not recorded in Scripture that Paul assumed they should believe and pass along?"

Several of the men began paging through their Bibles to check whether this was what was written.

"But more significantly, let's go back to this verse from First Timothy. Paul refers to the church as the bulwark and foundation of truth. The church? Which church?" As he said this, more heads dropped to their Bibles.

"Several years ago, at a board meeting of my second solo pastorate, one of my board members cornered me with this verse. Actually, what he did was first ask, in front of the rest of the board, whether it was true that we evangelicals consider the Bible to be the primary source of Christian truth. I responded, 'Yes, of course,' as I presume all of you would do. Then he asked, 'Where in the Bible is this taught?' I then drew the board's attention to the verses that all of us use to prove the sufficiency of Scripture. Seemingly satisfied, he then asked whether this meant that we believe that the Bible is the bulwark and foundation of truth, and I said 'Yes.' He responded, 'Well then, why does the Bible teach something different?' and he asked me to read this passage to the board.

"Now, like you, I've read this epistle many times, but for some reason, the implication of this text never struck me until that moment. As I read it, first to myself and then to the board, it was as if I had never seen this verse before. For several seconds I stood speechless. I then gave the board the usual explanation about the 'invisible church,' blah, blah, blah, and changed the subject as soon as I could, but I knew in my heart that I had no adequate response."

Looking at Cliff, Stephen asked, pleading, "What does Paul mean by 'the church of the living God?' Did he mean what the sixteenth-century Reformers defined as the 'invisible church'—the loosely connected family of believers all around the world and throughout time, regardless of whether inside or outside any organized church? Or did he mean the churches united around the bishops, pastors, and deacons he wrote about earlier in this very letter? And to which church or churches today can we point to as this 'pillar and bulwark' of truth?"

Some of the men still stared into their Bibles, hesitant to lift their gaze and meet Stephen's inquiring eyes. Even Hank had sunk back into his chair.

"But I need to go on or we'll miss our break time. Chapter four, verse one:

> Now the Spirit expressly says that in later times some will
> depart from the faith by giving heed to deceitful spirits
> and doctrines of demons, through the pretensions of
> liars whose consciences are seared, who forbid marriage
> and enjoin abstinence from foods which God created to

be received with thanksgiving by those who believe and
know the truth.

"On the surface, many Christians see in this the Roman Catholic
Church. Yet, you and I also know many other groups that fit this
description—Christian sects as well as certain New Age cults—
which delve into the occult, forbid marriage, and call for abstinence
from certain foods. How are we to identify which groups Paul is
warning us to avoid? Have we been wrong in maligning Catholics in
this way?"

"Just as I thought," Hank shouted. "You've also turned papist."

An awkward stillness filled the room. All stared at Stephen,
wondering, against their better judgment, whether Hank had stumbled
upon the truth of Stephen's crisis. Stephen, on the other hand, glared
blankly back at Hank.

"What are you talking about?" Stephen said flabbergasted. "I
have never even for a moment considered the Catholic Church a
viable option for my life."

Hank sat down reluctantly, unconvinced.

"My point is," Stephen said, addressing himself directly to Hank,
"that we mindlessly presume that the Catholic Church is the
fulfillment of Paul's apocalyptic warning, but we might be wrong,
and if so, we falsely condemn millions of innocent people."

Turning from Hank's piercing glare, Stephen continued. "Jumping
ahead to chapter 4, verse 12:

> Let no one despise your youth, but set the believers an
> example in speech and conduct, in love, in faith, in purity.
> Until I come, attend to the public reading of Scripture,
> to preaching, to teaching.

"I suppose few of us here need to worry any longer about being
despised because of our youth," Stephen said, hoping to add some
levity, but he had no takers. "But what does Paul mean here by the
word 'Scripture?' We all know that the only Scripture that Timothy
could have had or that Paul could have referred to as 'Scripture' was
what we call the Old Testament. At what point and why did Christians
start including other books under the highly selective category of
Scripture? Who authorized this?

"From our seminary studies, we also know that there were many other letters and books floating around—such as the Didache, the Epistle of Clement, or the Shepherd of Hermas—that some considered equally as inspired as those that eventually were included in the New Testament. We also know that these same Christian leaders judged some New Testament books, such as Hebrews, Revelation, and Second Peter, as inauthentic. Why are we certain that this Bible, which we base so much of our lives and ministries on, qualifies for what Paul here refers to as Scripture?"

One might think, as Stephen himself suspected, that this group of middle-aged men, corralled together in a stuffy room in the middle of the afternoon after a heavy lunch in a warm cabin in the outback of the New Hampshire mountains, would by now be overly anxious for this long presentation to be over. They might be fighting boredom, nodding off, or anxious to shovel snow from the basketball court for some serious one-on-one.

The opposite, however, was true. They respected Stephen and presumed that he had gained the position of senior pastor because he was no slouch. Consequently, they listened as he explained his dilemma. What they were beginning to wonder, however, was what were they to *do* with all of this. What Stephen was interpreting as impatience was actually their wrestling with this internal quandary. He kept going, however, convinced that he probably had alienated most of these men whom he had once called friends.

"Given what I've said so far, consider Paul's statement in chapter six, beginning with verse three:

> If any one teaches otherwise and does not agree with the
> sound words of our Lord Jesus Christ and the teaching
> which accords with godliness, he is puffed up with
> conceit, he knows nothing; he has a morbid craving for
> controversy and for disputes about words, which produce
> envy, dissension, slander, base suspicions, and wrangling
> among men who are depraved in mind and bereft of the
> truth, imagining that godliness is a means of gain.

"My friends, I can tell you without hesitation that each one of us teaches contrary to some of the specific things Paul commanded Timothy to teach," Stephen said. "Are we therefore puffed up? Were the founders of the Congregational movement puffed up? Were the sixteenth-century Reformers who disagreed with one another on many important details of theology all puffed up? How can you and I make certain that we are not 'men depraved in mind and bereft of the truth, imagining that godliness is a means of gain'?

"But Paul continued:

> There is great gain in godliness with contentment; for we brought nothing into the world, and we cannot take anything out of the world; but if we have food and clothing, with these we shall be content. But those who desire to be rich fall into temptation, into a snare, into many senseless and hurtful desires that plunge men into ruin and destruction. For the love of money is the root of all evil; it is through this craving that some have wandered away from the faith and pierced their hearts with many pangs."

Stephen hesitated as he considered his commentary on this section. "I suppose I could have skipped this portion, since this may seem unrelated to the issues I'm presenting. Yet, I wonder whether this section doesn't hit right at the heart of the matter."

This said, he looked at Taylor, his present polite nemesis, and continued.

"It is easy for you and me to preach these verses from the pulpit, exhorting our people to avoid materialism, feeling fairly self-righteous about our own commitments. We smugly believe that as ministers of the gospel, we have shunned more financially rewarding careers. But let's be honest. Every one of us here receives a salary higher than our average parishioner. We might argue that, because of our training, experience, and responsibilities, we deserve it. But couldn't Paul have said the same to Timothy? Paul was a highly trained Pharisee before he converted to the Christian sect. He had far more training and experience, and shouldered more responsibilities than any in his congregations. Yet he chose to remain poor for the sake of preaching the gospel, supporting himself by making tents." A few raised eyebrows told Stephen he was stepping on toes.

"So here is the point: to what extent have money, prestige, power, and position blinded us from taking Scripture seriously? To what extent are we unwilling to challenge our people in controversial areas because it might cost us our job, our reputation, our friends, or our colleagues?"

Stephen looked around for signs of confirmation. He thought he got one from Cliff, and maybe from Larry, but in general the men had glazed, stern eyes, staring with minds seemingly elsewhere. His wristwatch had passed three, so he skipped to the end.

"Paul closed his letter with this:

> O Timothy, guard what has been entrusted to you. Avoid the godless chatter and contradictions of what is falsely called knowledge, for by professing it some have missed the mark as regards the faith.

"Friends, I can only speak for myself, but as I've tried to explain, I am no longer confident that I am faithfully guarding the truth Paul entrusted to Timothy," Stephen said. "How much of what we have accepted and now believe, teach, and preach is nothing more than the 'godless chatter and contradictions of what is falsely called knowledge?' Let's face it, with so much diversity among Christians around the world, there must be some Christian preachers and teachers who fit into this category. How can you or I be certain that we are right and they are wrong; that you or I aren't the ones who have 'missed the mark as regards the faith'?"

Stephen closed his Bible, and after a momentary hesitation, moved it from the top of the lectern into a compartment beneath.

"My brothers in ministry, it is for these reasons that I have decided to resign. I place these thoughts before you, confidentially, as a friend, as a fellow minister of nineteen years, as someone who loves Jesus Christ, and as someone who takes my responsibility as a shepherd seriously. What will I do next? Probably go back to school for a Ph.D. so that I can teach, but how ironic," he said with a grin. "I resign from my pastorate because I'm insecure about what is true so that I can teach. How will I support my family? I haven't a clue, but I do know that God will provide.

"But let me close by sharing what proved to be the final straw that sealed my decision to resign." Stephen placed his hands in his pockets and stared down at what he could see of the worn Bible that had been his good friend for so many years.

"During these first five months of my new pastorate, our congregation has experienced an unusually large number of deaths. Soon after I arrived, an elderly member of the congregation had a stroke and fell into a coma. I visited him every afternoon, praying beside his bed, wondering as we all do whether people in this condition can hear anything we say.

"Then last Thursday, after I had finished reading a psalm to him and opened my eyes from a prayer, I realized that his wife, Ruth, had slipped in behind me and was sitting quietly by the door. I went over and sat next to her, taking her hands into mine. She sat motionless, staring at her husband of more than fifty-three years. I said hello, but she remained silent. I waited patiently, content to sit silently next to her if this was all she wanted.

"And then she spoke. Her stare never faltered, but as a tear formed and flowed down her cheek, she asked, 'Pastor, is Frank going to heaven?'

"I wasn't expecting that question, but now that it was out, I squeezed her hand and prepared to give my standard evangelical answer: since he had put his faith in Christ and believed that he would one day stand face-to-face before God, covered with the righteousness of Christ, we could be quite confident that he would enter into God's loving presence.

"But I hesitated. You see, it crossed my mind that if instead of being an evangelical Congregationalist I were a Methodist minister, I would be giving a completely different answer. Or if I were a Baptist, or a Lutheran, or a Presbyterian, or Assembly of God, or a Disciples of Christ, or a Pentecostal minister, or you name it—I would be giving a different answer based on different criteria. In that split second it even crossed my mind that my usual evangelical answer differed greatly from what a staunch Calvinist would say—about predestination, about the elect, and the chosen.

"Instead of giving my pat answer, however, I put my arm around her, gazed with her at her husband, and said, 'Ruth, we need to trust in God's mercy and His love, and pray without ceasing.' I led her in a tearful recitation of the Lord's Prayer, for I didn't want to tarnish the moment with any improvisational pastoral rhetoric. I left the hospital knowing that I had no right to remain a pastor. My prayer is that through God's love in Jesus Christ, you and I may be full recipients of what Paul requests for Timothy at the close of his letter: 'Grace be with you.'"

With that, Stephen sat down to await whatever might fall.

The room remained silent for more than a minute. No one ventured a retort to Stephen's long soliloquy, until Scott, sitting next to him, reached out and gently patted Stephen's knee as a sign of brotherly affection.

"Stephen," he said. "Thank you for the intense effort you put into that, and for your candor. You said many things that make sense. I admit that I have never taken the time to think through all of those verses or even all of those issues. I've never even second-guessed my calling or what I believe or teach. I'm unsure, though, what to do with all you've said. Maybe I'm afraid to ask those questions, but regardless, I do think you've made some strong points that I promise I won't forget easily."

Larry Wycliffe responded next, with less sympathy. "Stephen, I'm hesitant to throw my hat into this ring, but I must say that I come up with different conclusions. I believe that the Bible is sufficient, as Paul wrote in Second Timothy 3:16, to teach us everything that is necessary for our salvation in Christ. Sure, there is great diversity on many things in the Christian world, but these conflicting opinions are about nonessential things. Remember what Augustine said: 'In essentials unity, in nonessentials diversity, in all things charity.' The problem as I see it is *not* that we disagree about so many things, but that we are so uncharitable in our disagreements."

Stephen was prepared and willing to reply, but Cliff beat him to it. "Yes, Larry, that is true. Nevertheless, what I think Stephen has correctly pointed out is that Christians disagree over which things are essential. We here on this retreat may think we are united about what we consider essential or nonessential, but if we took the time to examine the bigger picture as Stephen has, we would realize that there is more than a lack of charity that separates the thousands of branches of Christianity. Christianity is disunited in almost everything."

Hank was ready to take them all on in defense of classic Congregationalism. "Our forefathers, who put their lives and families in peril to escape political and religious tyranny, sailed to this land..."

A door slammed somewhere in The Widow's Mite, and Hank paused as they listened to someone scurrying across the stone floor of the lobby, dragging a piece of luggage with squeaky wheels. Then a face and body burst through the rear door of the room.

"Hey, guys, sorry I'm late!"

Everyone turned at the sound of a familiar voice, one that no one expected to hear at this year's retreat. There, with bags in hand, his winter clothes and boots wet with snow, and a ready smile to greet his old friends, stood Jim Sarver.

"I'm sorry. The snow and ice were worse than I expected. For a while I almost decided to turn back, but I really wanted to see you guys. Have I missed much?"

For what seemed an eternity, they all sat like statues. All that Stephen could see were the backs of their heads and the face of Jim beaming above them. Then as if on cue the heads turned and glared at Stephen. Together they sat in silence, wondering who would make the next move.

5

In all of her classes, Stacy Horscht sought out isolated chairs in the back rows where she could watch the rest of the class as if detached from a distance. Being a new student—and a stunningly beautiful one—she created a distraction wherever she went, and though she was the talk of the school, she wanted none of it. Her only quest was to return to Red Creek, to her friends and everything that meant anything to her. After three days at this upper-middle-class high school, she was still so seething with resentment toward her father for dragging her away from her home and friends that she refused to speak to anyone.

It, of course, was his uncontrollable temper that had caused all of this. Whether at home or at work, once his rage reached a certain level, there was no stopping it. But it was his paranoia about the end of the world and the Catholic Church that had cost him his job and their friends.

What bothered her most was his hypocrisy. He insisted that they put on the air of a faithful and contented Christian family, but all she ever experienced was his anger—especially since she had flowered into a young woman. It was as if he assumed that every boy she talked to had ulterior motives. Eventually, he always drove them away—except for those special, secret friends....

The sound of final bell broke Stacy from her enraged introspection. She heard the teacher announce: "...our discussion on Gettysburg. Your assignment is to read on through Appomattox."

Stacy collected her unopened books and with her face hidden behind the protection of her shoulder-length blond hair, she made a quick exit.

"Excuse me."

Stacy gave no sign that she had heard this greeting.

"Please, Stacy, can we talk."

A gentle hand touched her elbow as a voice somehow reminiscent of her past cut through her resistance. She stopped, but didn't turn. A tall boy walked around in front of her and smiled a kind greeting. It was the same curly-haired young man she had noticed in church on Sunday. Her heart began to beat faster.

"Hi, I'm William. I'm new too. We moved here five months ago, and, well…" William wasn't sure whether he was getting through, because Stacy was facing the wall. "I heard the teacher call you Stacy, and you looked so familiar. I was just wondering whether..."

Stacy looked up at him through her blond veil. Yes, it did look like him. It hadn't crossed her mind on Sunday, but, of course, that was what her father had said. Their new pastor was Reverend LaPointe.

"William," she said with an emerging smile, "is it really you?"

"Yes," he replied anxiously. He wanted to reach out and lift this beauty from his past up off her feet—he couldn't believe she was so awesome-looking—but he held back. She took the first move and extended her hands, and he responded with his. He stood mesmerized.

"William, it's been so long. How are you? You say that you're new here, too?"

"Yeah. My father took the job at First Church, so we pulled up stakes and moved here from Respite."

This was the first student to whom he had freely spoken about his father, the minister. His parents didn't know that William was tired of being known as a "PK," especially now as a senior in high school. He felt like he had circles all over him from people keeping him away with ten-foot poles. He was sure that all the so-called cool kids in school had avoided him on purpose. They didn't invite him to their parties, and they seemed to get quiet whenever he came around. For these reasons, he was determined to make a fresh start here, and do whatever was necessary to break the mold.

"What brings you here, Stacy?" he asked as they began walking together down the hall, to the dropped jaws of every boy in sight.

"Pretty much the same. My father got a new job."

"Hey, do you have time for a Coke or something before you go home?" he asked. "There's a convenience store across the road. I'll buy."

"I'd love to, but…" She quickly glanced out the corridor window toward the parking lot, and she saw it—their embarrassing gray-whale wagon. Through the windshield she saw the glint of the sun off her father's glasses.

"William, I've got to go," she said as she ran from him.

"But Stacy, wait," he said, trying to keep up.

"My father is out front waiting."

"How about meeting me in the senior lounge tomorrow morning before first bell?"

But without an answer, she was gone. William stood gawking, amazed at his good fortune. He turned and stumbled over Steve Turner and Brad Corvey, two of his new friends.

"Wow, Willy boy, how'd you ever break through? She hasn't said word one to anyone."

"Let's just say that some's got it and some's don't. Come on, I'll buy Cokes across the street."

The three grabbed their coats and ran off, spinning fanciful stories about their successes in the dating world.

IN THE CIRCULAR DRIVEWAY in front of the high school sat the gray Caprice wagon, dark exhaust spewing from its tailpipe. It looked like a contagious disease among the newer horde of minivans and SUVs. The driver, though, gave it no mind. Occasionally, Helen had suggested that they trade it in on a newer, roomier vehicle, but sticker shock always sent Walter home. It was better stewardship to keep the Caprice—especially given what he knew might happen in the coming months. Within weeks the faithful might be gone, raptured mercifully into the presence of God, leaving the rest of the world behind to fight the great final battle. Walter looked out into the growing crowd of students, trying to identify his daughter, and wondered what kind of world was ahead for them.

He removed his glasses for cleaning, more a mindless habit than a necessity. Out of his car's speakers droned the voice of a popular preacher and writer narrating his most recent best-selling apocalyptic novel. Every word confirmed Walter's suspicions—as the Bible foretold, somewhere in this world, even as he sat wasting time in his idling station wagon, the Antichrist was winning converts and rising in political power. And as Walter presumed, the Pope was at least the Antichrist's right-hand man, the servant of Satan, claiming to be the image of Christ in this age. There were no seams to his convictions: the Roman Catholic Church was truly the Whore of Babylon, a scourge on the name of Jesus Christ.

As he listened to this fictional portrayal of the End Times, Walter knew that his own time to act must be near. He still was uncertain exactly what this act would be, but he knew that it would be so final that his life and that of his family would never be the same. It might even mean his own martyrdom, but he was willing.

He looked impatiently through the crowd, worried whether some boy with out-of-control hormones had cornered his Stacy. The crowd was thinning out, yet no sign of her. No, wait, there she was, running toward him with her books in one hand and her coat in the other.

"Sorry, daddy. My sixth-period teacher wanted to know how much of what we were studying I had already completed."

As she entered, he replaced his glasses, turned off the cassette, and then greeted her with a kiss on the cheek. For a minute, the kiss she gave in return was a token of genuine affection. He was here for her. Her father. The work-hardened hands, the care-worn face, the coat and tie, all reminded Stacy that he was the pillar of the family. She depended on him, and he provided for her. Lord knows, he reminded her of it often, the sacrifices he made for her. Even this move was supposedly for "her" own betterment.

But before the minute was gone, all the warmth and feeling of the kiss had ebbed away. She had caught the words of the tape he had hastily shut off. *That crazy Rapture story.* Her dad was crazy. *"Meet any boys?"* he was going to ask in a minute.

"So, Stacy," he asked with his fatherly smile, "meet anyone new today?"

Yup, right on cue, but should I tell him? she wondered. The memory of how her father acted on Sunday, however, screamed *"No!"*

"Oh, Daddy, don't worry. I've hardly spoken to anyone."

She lied. On the surface, she tried to portray the sweet and loyal daughter, but underneath her life was crumbling away like sand behind a receding tide.

"Why is that?" her father pressed. "Are these rich kids too stuck up to talk to the likes of us?"

"No, Daddy. They're talking to me, I..." She hesitated. "I just haven't been talking back. I still miss my old friends." She turned her face to the window, hoping he would stop interrogating her.

He backed the station wagon out and then drove around the circle out onto the main thoroughfare, heading for home. For several blocks they rode without words, until Stacy, now ill at ease with the silence she had created, decided to alter their focus.

"How's work going, Daddy?"

He shot her a glare, but then softened. "Oh, just fine, sweet pea. Between you and me, let's hope that this time I can keep my temper." He reached over and grasped her hand. "I'm sorry we had to move and leave all of our friends. You know I didn't mean to hurt you and Mother." But his facial expression turned to a familiar gray seriousness. "It's just that I know some things about our future, about this world, that none of these people around us, in their big fancy cars and country-club memberships, can see. They are blinded by their materialism and political correctness."

Stacy's stomach turned whenever her father talked this way. Sometimes when challenged, especially if someone called him *crazy*, he would lose control. Apparently, this was what happened at his last job. Ever since, he had spent most of his free time locked away in his bedroom or in a utility room in the basement. She didn't know what he did down there, but she did know that it was there that he kept a large collection of Vietnam War memorabilia.

"Daddy, you know I love you," Stacy said nervously, squeezing one of his large rough hands.

"And I love you, too, Stacy." He squeezed her hand back, and for the rest of the trip home they talked about a wide assortment of mundane things, leaving the end of the world for another time.

6

"WHAT DID I WALK INTO?" Jim Sarver asked with suspicion as he gathered with Stephen and Scott in the warmth of the hearth.

Most of the retreatants had already made round trips to their rooms for athletic clothes for the annual "Greater New England Evangelical Congregationalist Pastors Basketball World Championships." The older men, who shared a mortal fear of the pace set by the younger, either holed up in their rooms for a long winter's nap or headed out for a meditative stroll in the woods.

After Jim had so abruptly added his presence to the already uncomfortable atmosphere of the meeting, Ron Stang had risen. The tension in *his* annual retreat was causing him to panic. Praying that hot heads would be tempered by charitable hearts, he had interjected, "Hey, it's pushing four o'clock, and if we expect to get the first round of the annual b-ball championships completed before dinner, we better get out there."

"That's right," Cliff said, now more than willing to abandon his unspoken convictions and surrender to sports—anything to escape the impending debate. "I've been waiting four years to teach Birch a few new moves."

"What do you mean! You've forgotten more moves than I'll ever know...I mean..."

The crowd of men laughed at Birch's twist of words, as did Birch once he realized his own *faux pas*.

"Oh well," he quipped, "when you reach my weight and girth, you always have more moves than anyone else, no matter what you're doing."

Again, the men laughed as they rose for closing prayer. Hardly had the "Amen" left Ron's lips when the group bolted for the exit, exchanging basketball talk for the previous conundrum. Only Stephen, Scott, and Jim remained.

"You were an unexpected, unsuspecting exclamation point at the end of a well-put argument—one that few of these men were ready to hear," Scott answered as they retrieved cups of coffee and gathered in front of the fire. "And Stephen, I agree with most of what you said, though not your decision to resign."

"Stephen, what did you say?" Jim demanded.

"Jim, I didn't expect to see you this year," Scott said with friendly hesitation.

Jim lowered his head and said, "Well, this group represents the best friends I have in the world. I've always come to get recharged. I knew there'd be lots of rumors and questions, and I owed it to everyone to pay the piper and face you in person. I don't regret my decision, even for a moment, but I am sorry for any hurt I may have caused. Was this what you were discussing when I came in?"

"No, it wasn't," Scott responded, "but it's possible that the sight of you may have convinced some that you were the cause for Stephen's confusion."

"What confusion, Stephen? What is happening?" Jim asked. "What's this about *your* resignation?"

"First, tell us about yours. I only heard about it this morning from Cliff," Stephen said as he threw two more logs on the fire, a visual statement that they were ready to hear it all.

Scott pulled a leather chair up close to the right side of the fireplace, while Stephen did the same on the left, leaving Jim to a chair in the middle, front stage. They sat back with their feet crossed comfortably on the hearth, cradling their coffee cups and staring into the fire. What they each witnessed was quite different.

In the yellow and white tips of the flames, Scott saw two close friends in great turmoil. He understood their questions, basically, but didn't share their conclusions.

Stephen felt a weight on his heart, for he feared that he might have alienated his dearest friends. As he peered into the red flames, he saw irresolvable confusion and wished he could just run away. He had prayed that in these friends he would find receptive, empathetic hearts. Instead, he found men who were unable to express support because to do so would demand that they follow suit. It might mean putting their own careers in jeopardy, which they were not prepared to do. In the flames, he saw himself, a fool, and he really didn't want to hear about Jim's decision, distracted as he was by his own debacle.

Jim, on the other hand, admired the blue and green highlights of the fire with a growing sense of peace and energy. He had hoped for just such an opportunity to talk to these two old friends, but had not expected it so quickly. He was certain they would listen with charity, but where to begin? *Maybe what I will say will be of help to Stephen*, he thought. As he watched the flames flicker off the faces of his friends, Jim prayed for wisdom and a clear tongue.

"I don't know what you guys have heard, but it is true that I've left my position at Clymersville Presbyterian. I'll also admit to you two friends that Cindi is far from happy about my decision, but I had no other choice."

"Why did you have no choice?" Scott asked.

"Actually, it started last year at this retreat," Jim began. "As you remember, we had that big brouhaha over divorce and remarriage. For as long as I can remember, I have supported the basic Evangelical slant on these issues—that divorce is wrong in the eyes of God, except when the marriage is broken by adultery. If someone approaches us wanting to be remarried after they have been divorced, we do our best to determine how 'necessary' the divorce was. We listen to their explanation of the circumstances and how hard they have tried to reconcile differences.

"In the end, two things always force our hand. First, we recognize that divorce isn't the 'unforgivable sin,' and second, if God can forgive them, than so should we. As a result, I've performed seventy-five plus remarriages, some for people who had been divorced several times."

"I guess you can throw my hat into that ring, too," Scott said. "Just last weekend I performed a ceremony in which the best man, the attendants, the maids of honor, even the ringbearers, were children or grandchildren from the couple's previous marriages. From the beginning of our premarital meetings, I had wanted to scream 'No,' but, well, what can I say—they and their families are powerful people in the church as well as the community. Besides, by the time the third session had rolled around, they had sent out the invitations and bought everything. All I could do was leave them to God's mercy."

"Count me in, too," Stephen added. He returned his stare to

the fire. There were far too many questions about marriage, divorce, remarriage, ceremonies, music, customs, sacraments, symbols, and the like that had helped drive him into his present despair.

Recently before performing a marriage ceremony for a divorced member and her non-believing fiancé, Stephen had spent hours struggling over these issues. He had pastor friends who taught that marriage was a pseudo-sacrament, or that intercourse was marriage's consummating sacrament. He believed that marriage established an unbreakable covenant, and that the marriage ceremony symbolized this. But as he led the couple in their vows, he wondered whether what he was doing had any more meaning than if they had been hitched by the justice of the peace.

"But Jim," Scott said, "we've all wrestled with the contradictions, in, through, and after seminary, and now we just trust in God's mercy, and I guess His forgiveness, knowing that we are but ignorant children, who know only in part. What more can we do but the best that we can, given the circumstances?" As he said this, he realized that he had unintentionally critiqued Stephen's entire presentation.

"OK, I agree," Jim said, "and for nearly fifteen years I used that same self-rationalization to excuse me from all kinds of things I knew weren't exactly right."

"Jim, that's a bit strong," Stephen said, drawing back into the conversation.

"Is it? Now, guys, we're old friends here, so no offense, but I need to talk about this as openly as I can."

"Yes, but it's in there between the truth of what Scott said and where I'm sure you are headed that right now I'm lost," Stephen said. "Yes, we are but ignorant children, seeing dimly as in a glass and all that rot. But this is no excuse for the embarrassing confusion and rampant compromise that plagues Christianity. With one foot on each side of this morass, where does one lean his weight?"

"Stephen, I remember thinking like that on the way home from last year's retreat," Jim replied. "As you remember, I was the loudest and strongest advocate for the accepted Evangelical position. And the louder I got, the more polarized everyone became. Most argued other positions just to argue, just to make a point. Some pushed the far end of the liberal envelope, questioning whether we have any right to deny anyone's request for divorce and remarriage. Others argued the other extreme, posing that marriage was for life and eternity, and therefore no one had the authority to break this bond. Even you, Stephen, if you remember, argued for this interpretation."

"Well, as usual, the heat of the moment caused some of us to take sides stronger than we might normally take, especially before our congregations," Stephen said. "I apologize if our year of silence had anything to do with our strong words. I often thought about calling, but just kept putting it off."

"I'm sorry, too, but my silence was more from the craziness of my year. Last year you argued for what is certainly the minority view among Protestants. Did you know you were arguing like a Catholic?"

To Stephen this sounded too much like the charges being leveled by "Thevoiceoftruth."

"Only slightly," he said, "and of course with no intent. I really don't know or care what the Catholic Church teaches about divorce and remarriage. We were just fighting sides, a safe, idealistic, pugilistic debate without gloves. If I believed and taught what I was arguing, I'd be out of a job."

There was silence as Jim and Scott stared back at Stephen until he returned his eyes to the fire.

"Touché, Stephen. Why *are* you quitting your job?" Jim asked.

Stephen started to answer, but instead retorted, "No, I want to hear your story first."

Jim looked at Scott and then continued. "Last year, we ended that argument with jests all around and then as usual went out to play basketball, but I couldn't shake a strange, sick feeling in my gut. I had so forcefully argued for divorce and remarriage that I woke myself up to what I was truly saying and believing. I had been defending things that Jesus could never have intended His followers to teach.

"Later, on the long drive home, I wrestled with how often we compromise in our preaching. We exhort our people to turn from sins that they, essentially, give us permission to scold them for—laziness, selfishness, stealing, lying, fornication, adultery, you know the list. But Jesus taught just as strongly against divorce and remarriage, as the Apostle Paul also taught strongly against allowing people to receive the Lord's Supper unworthily. But try teaching what Jesus and Paul clearly taught, and you and I would be in deep doo-doo."

Stephen listened intently. Jim hadn't been there for his earlier soliloquy, but he was arguing from the same page.

Jim continued: "It was these two scriptural mandates by Jesus and Paul that got me into trouble. After I arrived home, I read everything I could find on what Jesus taught about divorce and remarriage. I examined the writings of theologians from every major Christian denomination, including the Catholic Church. I read stuff by the Reformers as well as Christian writers from the second and third centuries. In the end, it was clear that the majority view among Christians of all traditions from the beginning of the Church through most of history—right up until the early years of this century—was the more literal, conservative view: against divorce for any reason and against remarriage.

"In the stillness of my office, I therefore discovered that what I believed to be true put me at odds with both my congregation and my denomination, and, fear of all fears, on the same page as the Roman Catholic Church. At this point this only meant chalk one up for the Catholics where Protestants had compromised—had thrown out the marital baby with the bathwater."

Jim emptied his cup and made a round trip to the coffee urn as he spoke. "I didn't know what to do with this new information, except that I could no longer justify remarrying divorced people. So, as you both know, I was on the road to trouble."

"Where does your Presbyterian denomination stand on this issue?" Scott asked.

"Actually, they are fairly conservative on this. They support divorce only in cases of adultery or gross sexual misconduct, and remarriage only in those cases. In practice, however, most ministers bow to congregational pressure."

Stephen rose. With a poker he rearranged the new logs which had failed to ignite, and felt like he was enacting a symbolic representation of what life was often like in the pastorate— particularly with issues like divorce and remarriage. He might have strong views about whether a couple should or should not get married, but too often he was like a log in the midst of a devouring fire, prodded and pushed around by the powerful influences of public opinion or pillar families. The logs burst into flame.

Jim gazed into the comfort of his steaming coffee cup and continued: "My conclusions were solidified one morning when I was confronted with the status of my own marriage. I've talked to you about this in the past, so there are no secrets. You both know that Cindi and I have had problems ever since we were married during my first year at seminary, especially whenever her monthly hormones kick into high gear. For over fifteen years we've had about one good week a month. The other three weeks can be a progressive, screaming chaos until the last week can become an earthly hell. I don't know whether your marriages are this way, but during those difficult weeks I feel like a complete hypocrite: on the one hand preaching love, peace, and forgiveness to my congregation, while on the other hand, struggling at home to survive a screaming free-for-all. Many times I have been on the brink of leaving."

Stephen's focus shifted from the fire to Jim directly. "I suppose if we were to compare notes, Jim, we'd find that our marriages aren't all that different. In many ways, becoming a *successful* pastor has required becoming equally skillful at hiding marital strife. Only our children truly know how difficult things can get, and I worry about this."

"To some extent this is also true for us," Scott chimed in, "but not to the same degree. Dianne and I have been graced from the beginning with an amazing ability to talk it out before tempers escalate. I can't remember our last knock-down, drag-out fight."

"You're indeed blessed," Jim said, smiling. "But one Sunday morning about six months ago, I barely put a foot out of bed to leave for the early service, when Cindi started in on me. Everything that was wrong with the family and the world was my fault. I strained to resist responding in anger, but I lost it. Here I am getting ready to preach on the joy of being a Christian, and we're at each other's throats.

"I left in a huff for my office, trying to settle down so I could stand before my people with some semblance of the joy I was about to exhort them to have, and it was clear that I had reached the end of my rope. I was ready to leave. In fact, I had decided that as soon as I finished the last service at twelve noon I would pack up and leave, without any plans for the future. But then…well, have you ever preached a sermon only to discover that the message was mainly for you?"

"I suppose," Scott responded, "but I probably never listened."

"Well, this time it was too obvious. My text was from Ephesians 5 on the love between husbands and wives."

"Yipes!" Scott said.

"You're a lot smarter than me," Jim responded, "because it took a crisis for me to *hear* what I had spent an entire week preparing to *teach* my congregation. As I read verse 22, I became more angry... 'Wives, be subject to your husbands, as to the Lord'? I wanted to scream this at Cindi. I wanted her to hear this and to live it. To quit treating me with such disrespect, especially in front of our children. To quit ridiculing me in front of our friends and family.

"But then I read verse 25... 'Husbands, love your wives, as Christ loved the church and gave Himself up for her, that he might sanctify her, having cleansed her by the washing of water with the word, that He might present the church to Himself in splendor, without spot or wrinkle or any such thing, that she might be holy and without blemish.'"

"Boy, you've got that verse down pat," Scott said.

"I've been reciting it every morning since," Jim said. "I considered how faithfully Jesus has remained with us, His church, His body. No matter how rebellious, or difficult, or disrespectful we have been, He has never broken His promise to never 'leave us or forsake us.' I immediately knew in my heart, as if by a powerful, painful, spiritual implantation, that there was, therefore, no reason I could ever use to justify leaving my wife."

"But what about adultery? What about that passage in Matthew?" Stephen shot back. Though he was decidedly against divorce, seeing it as the scourge of America, yet there had been times he had confirmed a spouse's desire to leave a husband or wife once adultery had been discovered, based on this scriptural warrant.

"Even adultery, for there are many examples in Scripture as well as in history when God's people ran after other gods, playing the harlot, yet God never turned His back on them," Jim said. "When Jesus made His reference to the writ of divorce, He said that it was a concession made by Moses for the people's hardness of heart. But this is not what God had intended. And besides, the out-clause for unchastity is only in Matthew and not the parallel passage in Mark. There Jesus says clearly: 'Whoever divorces his wife and marries another, commits adultery against her; and if she divorces her husband and marries another, she commits adultery.' Jesus was calling His followers to a higher level of faithfulness, and for this He gave us new hearts. He also called us to forgive one another as He has forgiven us, and in the same passage from Mark, 'What therefore God has joined together, let no man put asunder.'

"Most of this came into my mind while I was reading my sermon text from the pulpit, and I knew standing there that I had been a false prophet. I had sanctioned the breakup of many marriages that I had no authority to break. I had performed the remarriages of many divorced people, many who weren't even members of my church. I knew in my heart that what I had done was wrong in the eyes of God. I had misled God's people.

"I finished the sermon almost in a trance. But it was communion Sunday, and as I began reading the communion liturgy from the Presbyterian Book of Common Worship, I stopped dead in my tracks. I had just finished reading the words of consecration from 1 Corinthians 11, verses 23 through 26, and was beginning to read the warning in verses 27 through 30. Scott, please pass me your Bible."

Scott reached for it and handed it over. "Here. I think I know where you're headed, but I don't think you needed to come to such a hard conclusion on yourself."

"Why not? Isn't what Paul writes infallible Scripture? Doesn't it apply today?"

"Yes, but..."

"Please, listen. The Apostle Paul wrote:

> Whoever, therefore, eats the bread or drinks the cup of the Lord in an unworthy manner will be guilty of profaning the body and blood of the Lord. Let a man examine himself, and so eat of the bread and drink of the cup. For any one who eats and drinks without discerning the body eats and drinks judgment upon himself. That is why many of you are weak and ill, and some have died.

"As I read this before the congregation, I saw out of the corner of my eye my wife and children watching, listening, and two things struck me quickly and hard. First, though all are guilty of taking the Lord's Supper unworthily—we're all sinners saved by grace—I was more guilty and unworthy because through my leadership I had led my people to practice things that were wrong. I had enabled them to be complacent about things that Jesus and the New Testament writers had clearly said were sin. I had no right to be in that pulpit."

Stephen was sitting up straight. He placed his empty coffee mug down on the mantle to listen more intently to Jim's description of his nearly identical experience.

"But then something else became clear. The thing that Paul warned should not be done in an unworthy manner was the eating and drinking of the *body and blood of the Lord*. He said that to do so was *profaning the body and blood*—not the bread and wine that are mere symbols helping us remember Jesus' sacrifice, but the *body and blood*. He even said clearly that *any one who eats and drinks without discerning the body, eats and drinks judgment upon himself.* Excuse me, but if our celebration of the Lord's Supper is but a mere symbolic, memorial feast, then how can our taking of it unworthily bring judgment upon us? Especially when Paul's emphasis is not upon receiving communion with unforgiven sins, or with anger in our hearts, or with heretical beliefs in our heads, but specifically because we do not discern *the body*. What did Paul mean by this?"

Scott started to answer, but Jim held up his hand. "As I stood there reading, lifting up in one hand a silver plate with a broken loaf of home-cooked bread and in the other a silver cup of unfermented grape juice, watching the elders standing before me ready to pass out silver platters of dissected cubes of white bread followed by plastic shot-glasses of juice, I knew we were miles away from understanding, let alone obeying what Paul had written. Discerning the body? What body? And there I was, preparing to lead my congregation in this farce. What kind of judgment was I about to bring down upon us?"

"But Jim," Scott interrupted, trying his best to respond. "I wasn't there in front of your people feeling what you were feeling, so it's too easy for me to critique now, but I've always understood that the key to this passage is what happens by faith in our hearts. During the Lord's Supper, Jesus Christ is present in a unique and mysterious way through our faith. If our hearts aren't with it, if we don't believe, if we're more distracted by sin than grace, then, therefore, we bring judgment down on ourselves."

Stephen looked on anxiously for Jim's response because he was nervous about where this was headed. He, too, had struggled with the meaning of the sacraments because, like so many other things, the opinions among Christians about what the sacraments mean and accomplish are highly diverse and contradictory.

"That was my internal response," Jim said. "But as I gazed out over my congregation, seeing people who had divorced and remarried under my blessing, who came to church week after week with brightly cleansed exteriors but whose interiors I knew from my heavy counseling load were far from *discerning the body of Christ*, I just couldn't do it any longer."

Scott was about to respond, but again Jim stopped him. "For you see, there is more to this than you know: the regular order of worship for Holy Communion as presented in the Presbyterian Book of Common Worship omits this warning. It quotes First Corinthians only through the words of institution and then abruptly stops. Years ago I had reinserted these words, but their significance had not hit me until that moment. In that brief moment, which seemed like eternity, I asked myself: why had these important verses been removed? Was it because those who framed the Presbyterian Order of Worship years ago had recognized that there was something at least awkward, if not downright contradictory, between the way we Presbyterians believe and the literal meaning of Paul's warning?

"Listen, I'm not saying that you should do what I did," Jim concluded. "I only know that I had to stop immediately, put the symbolic elements of communion down, call the elders together under closed doors, and resign."

"What did you tell them?" Stephen asked. He had contemplated the many ways he might one day resign, but never anything so dramatic.

"I simply left the sanctuary and went to my office," Jim replied. "I sat quietly as each elder entered and shuffled for a chair. Eleven of the twelve sat before me in a semicircle. I told them I was sorry and sad about this, but as of that moment I was no longer their pastor. I didn't give a detailed explanation then, but promised that I would at the next session meeting. I told them that I would take no more salary as of that day, but only asked that my family be allowed to remain in the manse for at least two weeks to give us time to find another place to live.

"The president of the session tried to dissuade me, but I told them firmly that I believed that this was the right thing for my family, for me, and for the congregation. After a few more words of apology and appreciation for their work, I got out of that place as fast as I could, leaving them to inform the congregation. I also asked the head elder to pull Cindi and the children outside and ask them to come home, and I went home to wait for them."

"Jim, I can't imagine what happened next," Stephen said. "I've known you and Cindi for a long time. She must have exploded."

"Stephen, it wasn't pretty. She came into the house running, afraid that I was sick or something. When I told her I had resigned, she screamed 'What?' so loud, I swear they heard it over at the church. I tried to give her at least a summary of why, but she couldn't hear anything over her fears of my being unemployed and unemployable. She was aware of my concerns over divorce and remarriage, but she never took them seriously. There's a lot of deep stuff here, but suffice it to say, Cindi has always been more nominal about her faith in private than she is in public. She couldn't understand how I could let my convictions put our family in peril. And I really don't blame her.

"The next few weeks were rough. I did everything without her support. I found us a new house, and though a few elders and friends helped, I moved almost everything myself. Thankfully we had some inheritance money put away, so I could devote some time to discerning what God wants me to do next."

Stephen and Scott sat silently waiting for Jim to continue, but when nothing came, Stephen asked anxiously, "OK, what are you doing? Are you still teaching, or have you found another job?"

Jim rose and stood before the fire, warming his hands. "A lot has happened in the last few months—God has been very merciful and generous—but I suppose the most significant thing to tell you is that this coming Easter I'll be entering the Catholic Church."

"What?" Stephen asked incredulously, spilling the remainder of his coffee on his shoes. It was as if he were hearing a ghostly echo from his past confrontation with the McBrides.

Jim looked at his longtime friend, knowing this was beyond Stephen's comprehension. "Stephen, you know me as well as anyone. We go back a long way. You know that I have always viewed the Catholic Church in the same light as you; in fact, I probably helped convince you in the early days of your conversion to hate Catholicism. When I resigned, I had no intention of considering the Catholic Church. I only knew that I could no longer be a Presbyterian pastor."

Stephen stared silently at Jim, shaking his head from side to side.

Jim continued. "I first searched through the Encyclopedia of Christian Denominations, looking for some denomination where I could hang my hat. But as I read through the descriptions of over two hundred different Christian groups, three things struck me. First, though most of these groups accept the Bible as the sole authority for their faith, there was a disturbingly broad range of interpretations and applications. One group, for example, takes the closing verses in the Gospel of Mark literally and teaches that true believers should handle snakes to prove their salvation. This sounds crazy to us *sophisticated* believers, but yet that is what the Gospel of Mark says, so who has the authority to say that their interpretation is wrong?

"Second, I realized, as I closed the book having found no denominations that fit my criteria, that I was searching for a denomination, not that was right, but that was right for *me*. I had elevated myself as the judge and jury for every Christian denomination in the world and found them wanting.

"And third, as I reflected on what I had read, it became clear that for the last five hundred years, each denomination had essentially played follow-the-leader. They had each left a previous denomination with the hope of establishing a more perfect, biblical, loving, and true church. Then in time, another leader from within their midst would get discouraged or disgruntled and leave to make yet another try at perfection.

"Later I discovered in a larger *Encyclopedia of Christianity* that there are over twenty thousand different Christian groups in the world, with a new group starting every five days. I knew there had to be something wrong with this picture, but I couldn't put my finger on it."

The yells from the basketball court drew their attention toward the exterior door just as a crowd of exhausted players burst in. Four were struggling to carry Birch to a couch.

"What happened?" Stephen asked, rising.

"Oh, nothing," Birch complained in obvious pain. "Just this bum ankle, but I'll be fine."

"I think there's a crutch in the closet if you want to finish the game," Cliff said with a smirk.

"Just because you're ahead," and the old rivalry went on.

"Listen, my good friends," Jim said to Stephen and Scott. "I guess I'll need to finish this later."

"Yeah," Stephen said. "Besides, I need to prepare our next discussion, but Jim, I do want to hear it all, even if we have to drive into town to be alone."

"I'm with you on that," Scott said. "We're glad you're here, Jim, no matter what crazy-headed thing you're planning to do. Our friendship is bigger than that."

Accepting their hands of friendship, Jim said, "Thanks, guys. I appreciate it, more than you know. The last six months have been a mind boggling mixture of joy and despair. And the battle is far from over."

The noise became overpowering as the rest of the aged basketball stars entered the lodge. Jim and Scott joined the ranks, but Stephen held back, watching. Jim seemed happy enough as he greeted his long-lost friends, but his story was having a paralyzing affect. It had not only confirmed his concerns, but made them more complicated. Up until hearing Jim, he had yet to consider the long-term implications of his looming resignation. The question was: did he have the courage to see it through? To accept being jobless? To abandon his respected, high-profile position of religious authority for whatever job he might find to pay the bills? But the issue of greatest terror, which drew his eyes toward the mesmerizing glow of the fire, was: did he have the courage to face the certain and justified wrath of his wife?

*   *   *

"Hey, stephen. Can we talk a moment?"

"Sure, Ron."

The basketball players were ascending the stairs to their rooms to shower. Fortunately, other than Birch's twisted ankle, none of the other middle-aged men had sustained any life-threatening injuries, other than deflated egos. Cliff Wilson's three-man team had won the day and was still gloating with high-fives all around.

Ron Stang beckoned Stephen to join him outside. The two walked silently away from the din of the others to a small grove of junipers beside the partially frozen pond. For a moment, they watched a beaver working near the entrance of a small gurgling creek.

Stephen began, "Actually, I'm glad you asked. I'm afraid I dropped too heavy a bomb on the group. This wasn't my intent, but now I'm afraid my selfish goals have distracted these men from the reasons they came: to pray, fellowship, and get recharged."

"Don't short-change yourself so quickly," Ron replied. "I believe you presented exactly what the Lord intended. When I initiated these retreats, I didn't want them to be safe, soft havens away from reality. Let's face it, as conservative evangelical pastors in an increasingly liberal association of independent churches, it's a battle out there. These men need to be confident about who they are, what they believe, and why. What you gave was a challenging check-up on our convictions."

Stephen was surprised to hear this, especially from Ron, who had remained mostly silent during his presentation.

"As far as what conclusions should be drawn," Ron continued, "each man must answer this in his own heart. Each came with different baggage, and returns to different situations, different crises." With this said, Ron hesitated, straining for the right words.

"For this reason, Stephen, I was wondering whether it might be better for someone else to lead the rest of the retreat. You are obviously subsumed in your discernment process, which I do not belittle. I hate to see you resign and hope we can discuss this in private later, but I'm concerned that with you in the leadership role, the discussions might remain too affected by your personal issues rather than on the needs of the group. Not that I believe you intended this; it's just that I question whether they can break from this distraction."

Stephen watched the beaver push a branch three times its size through the water toward his dam. "I suppose to put a positive spin on things, I used my personal crisis to awaken the men to the difficult but real issues raised by the Apostle Paul. Now someone else like yourself should step in who can re-focus the men away from me and back onto their pastorates."

"You don't mind if I step in?"

"No, not at all."

"Thanks, Stephen. Could you start the meeting with prayer and then give some explanation to help ease the transition?"

"Sure, no problem."

"Good," Ron said, turning back to the pond. "Well, it looks like that old beaver is a lot like us. Always something to do, whether at the church or at home."

"Yeah, funny. Watching him made me remember some remodeling I promised Sara I would do on her new kitchen, but I don't see a clear time window for months. Yet here I am, lounging by this mountain pond, jawing, and watching a bunch of old men trying to feel like teenagers."

"I wonder if beavers ever have heart attacks or nervous breakdowns?"

"I was wondering if Mr. Beaver finally got around to pushing that branch because Mrs. Beaver was on his case all day?"

They both laughed the kind of laugh that needed no explanation—not a critique of complaining wives, but an affirmation of their own need to be prodded. The two turned to go in for dinner, Ron placing his arm over Stephen's shoulder to communicate that all was well.

7

DURING DINNER, Scott polled Jim and Stephen whether Burson's Tavern was a good choice to continue their earlier discussion. All had agreed.

The dinner and group meeting came off without any controversies. The only person still steaming from Stephen's earlier presentation was Hank, but once Stephen turned the meeting over to Ron, the focus flowed easily into a discussion of how as Congregational ministers they could help their people hear, understand, and accept biblical truth.

At first, from the back of the room, Stephen listened with great interest. But as the discussion gravitated into tangential issues and illustrations, Stephen became frustrated. He wondered by their comments whether anyone had heard a thing he said. It reminded him of the many times Jesus had struggled to convey something to His hand-picked Apostles, but the meaning would pass right over their heads. He recalled one such story when Jesus told the parable of the sower. The seeds fell on four different kinds of soil, but only one produced fruit. The disciples didn't get it. Later, when they asked for an explanation, Jesus, frustrated by their obtuseness, had to explain the parable's meaning, emphasizing that the reason the fourth group of people produced spiritual fruit was because they heard and *understood!*

Stephen berated himself for comparing himself to Jesus. Obviously, in his own case, it wasn't that he was smart and these men obtuse; rather, he must have been confusing. He probably was too self-centered, too self-occupied.

Gazing around at his friends, he felt a deep sense of embarrassment. *Have I now so alienated these men that they may never take me seriously? Admittedly, I'm only in the discernment stage, but what if I come back next year still the pastor of First Church? Will they merely conclude that this year's "heart-on-my-sleeve" presentation was nothing more than insincere grandstanding?*

He had hoped they would help him through this, but what he had done was focus the whole retreat on solving his own problems. *What about their problems, their needs, their ministries?* Stephen felt ashamed. He slipped out of the room for a cup of coffee and stood by the fire. There were those flames. The reds, blues, greens, yellows, and whites. *Jesus, forgive me,* he prayed silently as he felt his heart calmed by the fire.

"Stephen, you all right?" Cliff had quietly followed him out.

Stephen was startled by his friend's voice, but glad to see him.

"Well, I'm a bit embarrassed by the mess I made of this afternoon, and sorry for it."

"Sorry? Stephen, your presentation was right on. It's just that few of us want to think that hard about what we are doing. We each have so many situations and problems to focus on that most don't want to stand back and uncover more and deeper ones. For them to reconsider whether anything they are doing is out of line and false is too threatening.

"As for me," Cliff continued, turning his attention toward the fire and pausing to button his thick cable-knit sweater to his neck, "I need time to let what you said sink in. With all that's happened in my own marriage and ministry, I think you've touched on some foundational issues that may explain the frustrations I've been feeling, but couldn't put a finger on."

"Thanks, Cliff. I was wondering whether these guys thought I had anything left upstairs."

"Oh, I'm sure some saw you bring in your suitcases, so..."

Stephen looked at his friend to see if he was serious.

Cliff laughed softly. "Oh, I know. Stephen, I can't speak for them. Yeah, a few at dinner were rationalizing away everything you said, but I could tell that more than a few were sitting silently, reflecting. And hey, since when did you give a rip what the peanut gallery thought?"

"I'm a whole lot more insecure than you might think. Listen, after the meeting, Scott, Jim, and I are sneaking out for a late-night snack. Want to join us?"

Looking back toward the meeting room and discerning his loyalties, Cliff said, "Thanks, I appreciate that. I'm sure that the answers you and Jim are running after are much closer to what I need than the answers those men are running away from."

*   *   *

"EGAD, why won't that guy turn off his brights!"

"Probably more intent on looking for deer than your comfort."

Stephen squinted, looking slightly to the right until the oncoming car passed. It took a moment for his eyes to readjust.

"You were saying?" Jim prodded Stephen to continue.

As soon as they had made their getaway from The Widow's Mite, into the car and out onto the road toward Burson's, Jim had asked Stephen to summarize what he had said that afternoon. Stephen had almost finished when he was temporarily interrupted by the oncoming traffic.

"Yes, well, the end result is that I apparently have come to the same conclusion you did—I have no right to remain in my pulpit," Stephen concluded. "If I'm so doubtful about whether what I am teaching, preaching, and doing as a pastor is true, then I shouldn't pass myself off as a spiritual leader. I'm a hypocrite or, as Jesus called the Pharisees, a blind guide."

"Stephen, I still think you're being much too hard on yourself," Cliff said. "We all have questions about certain aspects of what we teach, preach, and do. We all know that there is great confusion, even great contradiction, among the different Christian denominations. But as the Apostle Paul said, 'For now we see in a mirror dimly, but then face to face. Now I know in part; then I shall understand fully....' Now we walk by faith, even in the midst of confusion. We must trust that the Holy Spirit is guiding us, as we seek to understand and proclaim His truth."

"Cliff, that sounds all well and good. But listen," and as he spoke he pointed to the dark silhouette of a country Methodist church they happened to be passing. "The good, faithful man that pastors that small country church: doesn't he believe those same things?"

"Of course, but..."

"But nothing. He believes all those things, trusting that the Holy Spirit is guiding him, but what he believes his congregation needs to hear for their salvation is different than we do. Don't you think this is a problem?"

"But, Stephen," Scott chimed in, "if we went where your logic is leading, no Christian pastor should be preaching in his pulpit."

Stephen didn't answer, because this was the same conclusion to which he had no counterargument. *If so many Christian pastors believe that the Scriptures are sufficient, yet disagree with one another, then who can be certain that they are accurate enough to "stand with confidence and not shrink away from Him in shame at His coming?"* Stephen knew that he could not do this, and he wasn't sure what he could do to regain this confidence. *If Scripture isn't a reliable enough authority, then what is?*

"Guys, I remember an incident many years ago when I was still in college," Stephen reflected, "not long after my adult conversion." He turned to Jim and smiled. "Two Mormon missionaries came to my off-campus apartment while six of us were having a Bible study. Jim, you were away for some reason, and I was struggling to explain some Gospel parable to five new recruits. I did my best to counter the claims of these missionaries, but as they left, they gave us a copy of the Book of Mormon. I tried to refuse, but they insisted, saying that if we prayed before we read it, asking for the Holy Spirit's guidance, then He would help us discover the truth that was in their book of scriptures.

"It immediately struck me as funny that the same words they used to encourage me to read the Book of Mormon, I had just used to encourage these new recruits to read the Bible. Now one might say, 'OK, let's put the Holy Spirit to the test. Which book is true?' But there are a significant number of Mormons in the world—in fact, many more Mormons than Congregationalists or Evangelicals— who have taken this test and been convinced that the Holy Spirit had confirmed the truth of the Book of Mormon. Now if the Mormons, Jehovah's Witnesses, Seventh-Day Adventists, Unitarians, Pentecostals, Tennessee snake handlers, you, and I all use the same criteria and yet come to completely different but certain conclusions, then how can we determine which of us is right?"

They had reached the parking lot of Burson's and were turning into a vacant space near the door.

"But, Stephen, some of those groups aren't even Christian," Scott responded. "We can use other criteria to eliminate their claims before one gets to the test of the Holy Spirit."

Stephen turned the engine off, and all left the car.

"Scott, I've considered that same question," Stephen said, "and when I enumerate the criteria one might use to make these initial distinctions—to narrow the list to only those churches one might consider most trustworthy—you know what I found?" They were now walking two by two across the parking lot.

"What?"

"I found that every distinction was based on an interpretation of Scripture, not on a clear *statement* of Scripture." Stephen stopped them for a second on the snowy front step. "For instance, what separates us from the Unitarians? The doctrine of the Trinity. But the word 'Trinity' is not in Scripture. It's a term coined sometime in the early centuries of the Church to make sense out of the many verses that describe God the Father, Jesus the Son, and the Holy Spirit in sometimes conflicting ways. Nowhere in Scripture is the doctrine of the Trinity clearly stated as we understand it—one God in three persons. The Trinity is only alluded to. So where do we get the criteria to determine which of us is right, the Unitarians or us Trinitarians? Not from Scripture, but from early Church tradition. But what is the authority of this? Which early Church traditions do I consider reliable and authoritative, and which do I ignore? We might shout, 'Show it to me in Scripture!' but then we're back to where we started, because as I tried to demonstrate this afternoon, the Bible nowhere states that one must prove truth by reference to itself. This idea is a tradition—a non-biblical criterion."

"Hey, guys, I'm getting cold!" Cliff cried, holding his coat almost over his head.

"Yeah, come on inside," Scott said, kicking the snow from his shoes, socks, and pants. "Hope the coffee's hot and fresh."

"I'm hoping for something a bit stronger," Jim said with a laugh.

They entered the uniquely warm and welcoming atmosphere of Burson's Tavern, a renovated and expanded old log cabin converted into a comfortable local hunters' and fishermen's hangout. The lights were dim. The wood-paneled walls were strewn with the local taxidermist's handiwork: an assortment of fish, furry critters, and deer and moose heads. Mixed in were photographs of successful hunters and fishermen. The bar stools around the long, highly polished wooden bar were occupied by boisterous locals, either bragging about recent exploits in the woods or on the river, or arguing about who would win this year's Stanley Cup playoff. The booths around the outside of the room were about half full with similar clusters of men and an occasional mixed couple.

When the four strangers entered, the local patrons paused in their conversations to study these obvious outsiders with their studious, clean-cut appearance, and the one a black man. For a split second, eyes met, and the strangers pondered whether this had been a good idea. But then just as quickly the conversations resumed, covering the intrusion.

"Hey, here's a booth," Scott pointed to a table in a corner to the right, under a suspended 40-watt bulb shaded by a brittle, smoke-stained buckskin. The four passed an interesting assortment of locals, once again receiving their momentary scrutiny, until they crowded safely into the booth. Jim and Scott sat with their backs to the rear wall, and Stephen and Cliff faced them, away from the noisy room. A waiter with a scruffy black beard, a torn brown knit hat, a white t-shirt rolled up over his biceps, and a soiled apron, came to their table, wiping his hands on a dishtowel.

"What can I get you boys?"

"Coffee for me," Stephen said.

"Me, too," said Cliff. Scott nodded the same.

"If you guys don't mind," Jim said, "I'd like something a bit stronger. What's your local beer?"

"Got a couple of locals, but most drink Moosehead on tap."

"That'll be fine."

Stephen, freed up by Jim's bold order in the face of these evangelical ministers, looked around and said, "Well, actually, now that you mention it, if you guys don't mind, I'll have a glass of red wine."

"You others want to change your orders, too?" the waiter asked Scott and Cliff with a smirk.

"No, coffee's fine for me," Scott responded, avoiding the eyes of the waiter and of his friends. Cliff nodded.

The waiter turned and yelled as he walked to the kitchen, "A moose, a red wine, and two blacks."

"Sorry to cause problems, but I'm really in the mood for a beer," Jim said sheepishly.

"Oh, that's all right," Cliff said. "I've had a taste or two at special occasions myself."

"What gets me though, Jim," Stephen said, "is that you used to be the only person at fraternity parties who refused to touch a drop. Even at seminary, when a few of us used to leave campus for a nightcap or at the annual off-campus clam-bake, you were always a strict teetotaler."

"Yeah, I know, and now I look back embarrassed, even ashamed at my hypocrisy. Don't get me wrong, I'm against getting drunk, or for telling those with drinking problems to throw their worries to the wind. I just discovered that I was greatly mistaken when I claimed that it was wrong for Christians to drink."

"I guess you are becoming a Catholic," Scott said. "Most of the Catholics I knew in college seemed more committed to their freedoms than to their Catholic faith."

"Actually, I discovered this several years before the thought of becoming Catholic entered my mind, but for similar reasons. It also has a lot to do with what you were talking about earlier, Stephen."

"Hey, don't use me as an excuse for your drinking. I've just never lost my taste for wine from my pre-Christian drinking days. I'm a sinner, depraved and all that," he said with a nervous laugh, still feeling awkward for choosing wine in front of his abstaining friends.

"Well, let me ask you this," Jim said. "Where does it teach in Scripture that it is un-Christian to drink alcohol?"

Scott, an avid proponent of abstinence, chimed in quickly, "In Ephesians 5:18, 'Do not get drunk with wine, for that is debauchery; but be filled with the Spirit.'"

"But, Scott, what does that verse truly say?" Jim pressed. "I am against getting drunk, but where does it say 'don't drink', especially when the same author, Paul, encourages Timothy in his first letter,

'No longer drink only water, but use a little wine for the sake of your stomach and your frequent ailments'? Actually there are many verses in Scripture where, although drunkenness is strongly discouraged, drinking is not. And remember that when they ran out of wine, Jesus didn't say, 'Good, you shouldn't be drinking anyway,' but instead changed more than a hundred gallons of water into the best wine."

"But we don't know whether that was fermented wine."

"Scott, be serious. If what Jesus made was grape juice, it would make a farce of the story. What impressed the steward of the feast was that the best wine—which unbeknownst to him Jesus had made miraculously—had been saved until last. He would have been insulted by unfermented grape juice."

"But you don't know that," Scott insisted.

"But, Scott," Stephen interrupted the debate, "let's not get sidetracked on the issue of whether Christians can drink. The point Jim is making, which is precisely what I tried to say this afternoon, is that Scripture isn't dead clear about the issue of drinking. As a result, there is a great breadth of opinions among Christians. Some think one cannot be a Christian and drink, just as some think one cannot be a true Christian unless he speaks in tongues. But there are equally sincere Christians using the Bible as their source to promote the opposite opinions. You, Scott, preach that drinking can keep someone from Heaven; I do not. Which of us is correct, and how can we be certain? Or does it not matter? What does matter?!" he said sarcastically.

"I hope these do," said a young buxom waitress, dressed in a colorful, flower-print dress covered by a white apron identical to the previous waiter's, but clean. Stephen received his red wine, took a generous gulp, and then sat looking into the dark goblet.

"Stephen, I'm sorry," Scott said. "I didn't mean to get us off on that. Jim, please, tell us why you want to become a Catholic."

"Well, on the one hand, there's really too much to go through now. It involved a tremendous amount of reading, arguing, prayer, and soul-searching as I examined the doctrinal and traditional issues. But on the other hand, I suppose it all comes down to the same issue we've been discussing all evening: the issue of authority, and how one determines what is true."

A large, roughly dressed, unshaven hunter seated behind Stephen turned and glared over the bench seat. With what he had been overhearing for and against drinking, and now about authority and truth, he just had to get a glimpse at the nature of the beasts sitting behind him.

After he turned back around, Jim said, smiling, "And I suppose I better keep this down or we may be shown the door—or I should at least include a few stories about the big ones that got away." They all laughed, but when the hunter took one more glance over the seat, they stifled their laughs and resumed drinking their beverages with a tip to his health.

"You know from our discussion this afternoon what led me to resign my pastorate," Jim continued in a subdued tone. All four sat hunched forward over the table as if conspirators. "Cliff, rather than go through it all again, let me just say that I became so convinced that my Presbyterian viewpoint and practice concerning divorce, remarriage, and the sacraments were wrong, that I knew I could not with a clear conscience continue leading my people. I felt I was at least partially responsible for helping them break the warning Paul gives in 1 Corinthians 11. I was contributing to the delinquency of their souls," he said with a tip of his draft, drawing laughs from all. "And given the constraints of our Presbyterian creeds and system of elders, I couldn't easily do otherwise.

"At first I thought I would just move to another denomination, but after examining every major Protestant denomination, I decided that there wasn't one in which I could serve comfortably. The Catholic Church was never an option, for lots of reasons, but especially because I am married with a family, so the Catholic priesthood was out.

"But then what started me toward the Catholic Church was a study of the Gospel of John. As I said, I had been confronted by the seriousness with which Paul speaks of the Lord's Supper in 1 Corinthians 11. So I began examining other scriptural references to the body and blood of Christ and was startled by what I found in John chapter six. Mind you, I have preached and taught through this Gospel many times, but I never saw what was truly there. I've always taught that John 6 was an episode dealing with the importance of believing in Jesus. But I missed how radically Jesus expected His followers to trust and believe in His words."

Given his previous experience with this text, Stephen listened with keen interest.

"We didn't bring our Bibles and I haven't memorized all the key verses, but essentially I discovered that Jesus states without hesitancy over six times in the course of ten verses that to be His follower— to have life, to abide in Him, to experience eternal life—one must, and I emphasize *must,* eat the flesh of the Son of Man and drink His blood. I studied these verses every which way. I looked at the Greek. I looked at how all the terms were used in other biblical passages as well as in classical Greek references, and in the end, I could not get around the fact that Jesus was speaking literally. And this was exactly how His Jewish audience took him: the Jewish scribes and Pharisees were horrified by Jesus' offering His flesh to eat, and as a result, many disciples abandoned Him.

"Now, everyone of us teaches that Communion is symbolic, right?"

They all agreed with differing signs of affirmation.

"Well, if Jesus had meant His words to be taken symbolically, He easily could have recalled His disciples. He could have said, 'Hey, wait, wait, I didn't mean this literally. Don't be so serious! I meant that you must eat of My teachings, and drink of the living water that comes to your heart through the Spirit,' or something like that. But He didn't do this. Later, when He was alone with His remaining twelve Apostles, He still didn't straighten this out. Instead, He asked them, 'Do you also wish to go away?'

"But what was particularly striking was what the Gospel writer recorded several verses earlier. Those disciples who left Jesus complained that what Jesus demanded 'was a hard saying; who can listen to it?' This confirms that they understood Jesus to be speaking literally.

"From there, I said to myself, 'OK, if Jesus was speaking literally, both here in chapter six and later in His institution of the Last Supper, does this make sense of the rest of Scripture?' So with the assumption that Jesus literally meant to eat His body and drink His blood, I began rereading the many Scriptures that refer to the Lord's Supper as well as Old Testament references to the Passover. Eventually, I became convinced that this assumption made the most sense of everything I had read, especially Paul's warning in 1 Corinthians 11."

"But doesn't the Catholic Church demand," Scott said, "that when the priest repeats the words of consecration the bread and the wine literally change into the body and blood of Jesus, even though they still look and taste like bread and wine? This is nonsense."

Cliff and Stephen nodded in agreement and awaited Jim's answer.

"That's exactly what I believed. I was repulsed by the craziness of this Catholic dogma, but the more I struggled with it and prayed about it, a couple of things became clear. First of all, the doctrines of the Incarnation, the Virgin Birth, the Trinity, as well as the inerrancy of Scripture, are *equally absurd* as far as human logic goes. Imagine standing beside Jesus when He roamed the back roads of Galilee in the first century. To look on Him, to touch Him, to smell Him, He would have appeared in every way to be a normal Palestinian peasant. It would have been impossible to discern with your senses that He was the creator of the universe! Millions have rejected Christ's divine nature, explaining Him in more palatable terms, all leading to strange heresies. How many today still believe that Jesus was no more than a mere man and at best a good teacher chosen by God? But if this is true, then, as C. S. Lewis said, Jesus was in fact a liar or a lunatic.

"Or how can a woman who has never had intercourse give birth, not only to a human being but to the very God of the universe? And you know how hard it is to explain the Trinity in logical terms— evidence so many Unitarians within Congregationalism."

"But, Jim," Stephen asked, "what bothers me about this literal interpretation of the Lord's Supper is that it shows up no where in the book of Acts. If it was so essential, than why don't we hear Peter and Paul emphasizing it as they made converts and planted new churches?"

"And can't the same be said about the doctrine of the Trinity?" Jim replied. "There are many verses that imply this doctrine, but just as many that lead to other conclusions. Like Simon Peter's first Christian sermon, where he called Jesus a man attested to by God through whom God did mighty works, and whom God raised up. Many heresies have arisen from these texts."

Stephen sat silently, because he realized that any rebuttal he gave only played into his own confusion.

"But let me return to points about the Eucharist," Jim said. "Since the miracles of Jesus clearly emphasize that all things are possible with God, why is it so hard for us to believe that what may look and taste like bread and wine, may also be, beyond our limited and tainted understanding, the real presence of Jesus? When Peter walked on water, must we presume that Jesus had first turned it into a lake of ice? No, this would have been a different kind of miracle. The Gospel writers clearly implied that the water Peter and Jesus walked on had all the qualities of liquid water. How could this be?

The power of God. Five loaves and two fishes fed over five thousand. How could this be? A miracle of sharing? Hardly. But a miraculous, inexplainable work of God. And so is the Eucharist."

The audience of three considered challenging his argument, but to do so would force them to present some criteria for distinguishing between miracles. And none could quickly think of any.

After an ample swig of Moosehead, Jim continued. "And third, still struggling with all this, I examined what the Catholic Church meant by the term 'transubstantiation,' and realized that what was wrong was not the Church's teaching but my information. I've come to the conclusion that there are basically three reasons so many people reject the Catholic Church: ignorance, prejudice, and bad Catholics. Ignorance, because most non-Catholics haven't a clue what the Catholic Church truly teaches; prejudice, because many non-Catholics *think* the Catholic Church teaches things it doesn't; and bad Catholics, either because the Catholics we know are poor models of their faith or we don't understand what Catholics are doing. We see a woman with a lacy head covering praying with beads before a statue and conclude that she is a superstitious idolater. The true problem, again, is our ignorance."

Scott and Cliff were ready to break in, but Jim was on a roll. "With the doctrine of transubstantiation, the Church is merely doing the best she can to describe in philosophical terms a mystery that has been believed since the beginning of the Church.

"But the fourth thing that convinced me was that the literal interpretation as well as this somewhat difficult philosophical explanation offered by the Church made the best sense of what I found in the early Church Fathers. Do you guys remember reading anything from the early Church Fathers when you were in seminary?"

"I remember a book that summarized their teachings," Cliff responded, "but little of what they wrote connected with what I believe or teach."

"That's exactly what I thought in seminary," Jim said. "I probably read the same collection in the same class and underlined maybe a half-dozen statements. But when I recently reread them, I was so overwhelmed by what I found, that now there might be only a dozen or so statements that aren't underlined. You see, I used to judge them by how I always believed and taught. But, Stephen," he said, turning his focus to his longtime friend, "I guarantee that if you read them you'll find challenging answers to the questions you're struggling with.

"I wish I had a copy with me right now, but there is one significant statement from Irenaeus I have memorized. Irenaeus was a second-century Christian bishop who learned the faith from Polycarp, also a bishop, who had learned the faith directly from the Apostle John. These connections are clearly documented. In his treatise 'Against Heresies', Irenaeus wrote:

> If the body be not saved, then, in fact, neither did the
> Lord redeem us with His blood; and neither is the cup of
> the Eucharist the partaking of His blood nor is the Bread
> which we break the partaking of His body.

"I'm not quoting this as a proof text, but to demonstrate that the literal meaning makes the best sense out of how the early Christians understood the Eucharist as they learned it from the Apostles."

Jim paused for comments. The noise of the room was increasing as more locals were entering and congregating around the bar. The nature of the clientele was slowly being transformed as the older "Field and Stream" crowd was being joined by college-aged young adults.

"OK, let's accept the literal meaning for a moment," Stephen said, "but why not become an Episcopalian or a Lutheran?"

"Well, yes and no," Jim answered. "I wrestled a lot with clarifying the differences, but just when I was getting close, I was confronted by the real, more essential issue: once I can explain clearly each position, how will I determine which one is true? Should I pick the one *I* think best explained Scripture? But isn't this merely returning me to the beginning, duplicating what so many others have done throughout history: *me* claiming that, with the help of the Holy Spirit, I can most accurately discern what is true, and then go off and start a new, more true, more biblical church?

"With this question, I turned to Scripture as well as the writings of the early Church Fathers and became convinced that the authority for determining what is truth was left by Jesus not in the Scriptures alone, or in individual Christians, but in the Church, founded in His Apostles centered around the Apostle Peter."

Seeing that his audience of three was becoming increasingly distracted by the escalating noise as well as the mushrooming population of scantily clad co-eds, Jim knew it was best to summarize. "Suffice it to say that I took Jesus at His word. He appointed Peter the rock upon which He would build His Church, and I accepted this as literally true. He said He would send the Holy Spirit to guide His Apostles into all truth, and to be with them always, and I took this to be literally true. He also said that His Church would consist of both wheat and weeds, good and bad, and I accepted this as the best description for what has happened throughout history in the Catholic Church, sometimes leading even to schism. So I accepted this to be true. And I can only say that the more I read, the more I am convinced that the Catholic Church, for all her peppered history, is still the Church that Jesus established in His Apostles."

At that moment, a roar arose from the bar, fists flew, and a smelly, drunken man landed on their table. "Hey, that's enough of that!" came a voice from the kitchen, and out stepped their original waiter. The drunken man's friends collected him, and with looks of derision toward the younger patrons now controlling the bar, they left in protest. Burson's Tavern then returned to its previous level of increasing chaos.

"Maybe it's time we made our escape," Cliff said.

"Yeah, let's go. I'm getting tired anyway," Scott added.

They paid their bills and made their retreat to the safe haven of The Widow's Mite.

8

A FAINT RAY OF SUN broke the next morning's silver-gray horizon and crept over the mountainous forest of evergreens and the leafless skeletons of oak, maple, and birch trees. The ray leaped the lower peaks of the mountains surrounding Mount Washington and the immortal stone face that watched the slopes of Mount Lafayette. It found a second-floor window of the isolated Widow's Mite, slipped in between the embroidered seams of a white lace curtain, and fell on the yet unopened eyelids of a man who had only just succeeded in falling asleep. Try as it might it could not awaken him, until it was rudely assisted by the man's digital alarm.

Stephen jerked straight up in response to both the light and the alarm, and winced from the strain on his lower back. Carefully he eased himself back down, grateful for no spasms from his chronic disc problem. Age and vocational stress had certainly taken its toll. Starting again, he rolled to his side and swung his knees over, causing him to sit up without pain—following the instructions of his surgeon. A few minutes of stretching every morning as well as such cautionary routines were a small price to pay to avoid the table and the knife.

The digital clock blinked 7:15.

"Good," he muttered. Stephen wanted to get packed and gone before anyone else arose. Yesterday had gone every way but how he had hoped and expected.

After a quick trip to the bathroom, he threw on a clean plaid lumberjack shirt and his khaki pants from the day before, and threw everything else into his suitcase. With a final glance around to ensure that nothing had been overlooked, Stephen cautiously opened the door and slipped down the central staircase to the living room. No one else appeared to be awake. The fire, however, had been rekindled, probably by Mrs. Cousineau, and was already blazing. To avoid being trapped into a long explanation of why he was leaving so early, Stephen crept clear of the kitchen window.

Making his exit like a boy guilty of raiding the cookie jar, he was stopped by a faint, beckoning whisper. He turned to see Jim in a blue robe and a pair of moose-skin slippers, waving him down.

"Stephen, I'm glad I caught you. I wanted to give you this." Jim extended a book. "Last night when we came in, I noticed this on the Cousineaus' bookshelf. I'm sure they won't mind my giving it to you once I tell them why. This book was a great help to me in working through my questions and presumptions."

Stephen looked down at a well-read copy of a book entitled *Catholicism and Fundamentalism.* He hesitated between taking it or shoving it back. He took it to avoid any delay in his departure—but taking it didn't mean he had to read it.

"Thanks, Jim. Let's talk soon, but right now I've got a mess of things to work through."

"I understand, but you know my number if you need me. If I don't hear from you in a few weeks, I'll call you."

They heard other footsteps descending the staircase.

"Gotta go. Please pray for me," Stephen said, turning.

"I will, Stephen. God bless!"

Stephen trudged through nine inches of fresh and leftover snow and then into his car, still clear of snow from their late-night excursion. The engine started right up, but Stephen didn't relax until he was on the two-lane paved mountain road leading toward the Interstate. He figured he'd drive about halfway home before holing up in a motel. Sara and the church staff didn't expect him home for two more days, so why give up the needed window of solitude?

As he drove, the events of the night before came at him in one anxious image after another. The sun, now half visible over the eastern mountains, forced him to shift the visor over. It only partially blocked the glare. He leaned over to the right onto his elbow, steering with his left hand, until he found a position where his eyes were shaded. Staring down the road, he resumed his recollection, and remembered—last night he had performed the same maneuver to avoid a similar irritating flash from an oncoming motorist.

"Lord God," he pleaded, "what are You trying to tell me through all of this?" Stephen was quite certain that God had brought him on this retreat, but now what? Was he running away from or toward the answers he needed?

Down the highway he sped, hunched to one side, a lone car in the misty morning, emancipated from anyone's oversight or judgment, except, of course, from God's.

*   *   *

THE SETTING ASIDE OF A ROOM at Witzel's Notch High School as a lounge for seniors had been the brainchild of the Student Council of the Class of 1976. The faculty and staff had voiced their reservations, but the argument that this would provide a quiet space for the more mature, last-year students to discuss their plans for the future had won the day. And to some extent this had proven true. Over the years many seniors could be found talking about which colleges they were considering, which degrees, which careers, which parts of the country, and, for some, which branch of the armed services.

But as most had suspected, the senior lounge was more often a place of rendezvous—a semi-private escape, away from the suspicious eyes and ears of parents and teachers, where a boy and a girl could strategize, discuss intimacies, or just get to know each other better. Yes, there were adult advisors who took their turn at the chaperone's desk, and generally there were other students present, so it would be difficult to get away with anything untoward—though rumor had it that over the years certain students of famed prowess had accomplished *great* things beneath the gaze of faculty supervision.

Because of these rumors, the room was kept brightly lit, and the many stuffed couches and chairs were arranged well in view of the chaperone's desk. The green-and-white striped walls (the school colors) were strewn with a collage of pictures, drawings, and other mementos from several decades of senior classes. Various concession machines were available, dispensing sodas, snacks, and instant cappuccino for those with more sophisticated tastes.

At 8:45 a.m., William entered this private hangout for the first time. His new friends had invited him, but up until yesterday, he had had no reason to use this place of rendezvous.

Sure enough, as he entered, Miss Duryea was there at the chaperone's desk, as he had been warned. She had a pretty enough face and for a teacher a pleasant personality, but her beauty was buried beneath mounds of excess flesh. In general, the students liked her, but the less sensitive, more immature students used a nickname for her that involved an alternate phrasing of her last name. William had been told that she rarely interfered in their private discussions, except when they became too raucous or crude.

William decided to take the direct approach. "Good morning, Miss Duryea," he said as he walked up to her desk, extending his hand. The image of Eddie Haskell from *Leave It to Beaver* passed through his mind, but he carried through with his greeting anyway.

"Good morning," she responded. "You must be one of our new students?"

"Yes. My name's William LaPointe. We recently moved here from Respite. My father's the new pastor at First Congregational."

"Well, how do you like our school?"

Before William could answer, the door opened again and it was Stacy.

"Oh, excuse me," William said as he turned physically, mentally, and emotionally to greet her. Miss Duryea no longer existed.

"Stacy, you came," William said with hard-to-contain excitement.

"Hi." She lowered her eyes and followed William to a pair of facing loveseats. Her shyness moved him. Her modest dress and demure expression told him that she was pure and untainted, though girls a lot younger and less attractive than she were already on the pill or in trouble.

Must...not...do anything...to spoil it, he thought, though her encouraging smile made him wish for the hundredth time that he didn't have such a sterling reputation to uphold.

"Sure, why not?" Stacy continued, "My father thinks I had an early class."

"I just didn't...when is your first class?"

"Actually, it's first bell, English IV, with Miss Duryea over there." Her directed glance was one of derision, which William noticed changed again to a smile when she returned her attention to him. "What about you?"

"Trig with Mr. Abkie," William said, then dropped off into awkward silence.

"Do you remember when..." they both said simultaneously, and then laughed as the familiarity of their childhood returned. For the next forty minutes, they recounted their childhood adventures playing knights and maidens at Rogers Park or skipping stones in Wadkin's Brook; they recalled how William would defend her from Brad, the local bully, or how he had helped her home after she had cut her knee riding down "Dead Man's Hill." The memories surged through both of them and brought to each a joy they hadn't felt in years.

In time, the approach of first bell turned their small talk to making plans. They would meet again tomorrow morning, same time, same place.

William held the door for Stacy as they left for class. "Have a nice day, Miss Duryea," William called over his shoulder, playing the image that had always won him adult respect.

"You, too, William, and, Stacy, is it?" Miss Duryea asked.

"That's right," she answered with a semi-polite patronizing glance, then exited the room.

Awkwardly, William smiled, and with a farewell nod, left to catch up with Stacy.

9

Around ten-fifteen, Stephen awoke for the second time that morning. He hadn't set an alarm. He figured he'd let his body determine how much additional sleep it needed.

Fighting against nodding off at the wheel, Stephen had given in to the inviting glow of a motel sign. He had stayed here once before, years ago, when he was stranded in a snowstorm. Familiar ground would be good.

After checking in, he had headed right to bed. Usually he and naps didn't get along well. Short naps seemed to help more than long ones, which often left him disoriented and groggy. Now as he eased his legs over the side of the bed, bringing his body up to a slouched but erect position, he remembered one particular nap he had taken years before in seminary. Upon awakening, he had noticed through dreary eyes that the time was after 6:30, so he quickly showered, dressed, and rushed downstairs to the dining room to catch breakfast, only to find out that he had just missed dinner.

He rechecked the electronic alarm radio next to his bed to make sure what time of day it was and confirmed it with a glance through the curtains. After a quick shower and a clean set of casual clothes, he sat at the desk, conveniently provided to entice business travelers, for his morning devotions.

Stephen intended to begin with a meditative read through the fourth chapter of Philippians and a prayer for guidance, and then devote the rest of the day in reflection on all that had recently happened.

But as he began his reflection, his mind was still too overwhelmed by what he had discovered: *Jim, of all people, had also been blindsided by the same unavoidable concerns.*

Stephen decided, therefore, to get some R&R before returning to the heavy discernment of what he would do with the rest of his life. An hour in the pool and whirlpool and a chapter or two of a Clancy novel would do the trick.

But as he reached into his briefcase for his half-read copy of *Debt of Honor*, he found the book Jim had forced upon him. He glanced at the back cover. A summary stated that the author "defends Catholicism from fundamentalist attacks."

What the heck, Stephen thought. For Jim's sake, he would read at least a little.

Changed into his swim trunks and robe, he left for the indoor pool, carrying also *Debt of Honor*, in case the Catholic book was too boring or strange.

$$* \qquad * \qquad *$$

THE ALARM JARRED WALTER from his daytime sleep. He grabbed for it, missing several times, knocking his glasses to the floor, before finally turning off the incessant clatter. He groped in the artificial darkness of his curtain-shrouded bedroom for his glasses. Failing to locate them immediately, he became irritated. Without them he was clinically blind. For years he had admonished himself to buy an extra pair, but had always put it off. Would this be the day he regretted this?

Under the nightstand, then under the bed he searched. "Where are they?" he complained. Carefully he crawled around on all fours. He was heading away from the bed toward the bathroom when his right hand bumped against them. "Thank God," he said as he pulled them to his face, his hands shaking slightly as he wrapped the flexible stems around each ear. He rose and made his way drowsily to the bathroom.

After a quick shower and a change into clean clothes, Walter felt refreshed. On the kitchen table he found a note from Helen. She was out shopping. *As usual,* he thought. *Spending my money before I've even received my first paycheck.* The note said he would find leftovers in the refrigerator.

"Great," he muttered. Helen had many qualities Walter was proud of, but cooking wasn't one of them. He poured himself a can of soda over ice, and began working through some cold chicken and baked beans.

After finishing what was edible, he still had fifteen minutes before he had to leave to get Stacy, so he returned to the dark solitude of the bedroom and switched on his computer. Since arriving in Witzel's Notch, he had found little time to try out his Internet dialup.

Thankfully the new provider had allowed him to use his old login. When prompted, he typed it in: "thevoiceoftruth." For his password, he also used his old one, though everyone advised him to change it periodically: "onlyhiswill."

He hit "Enter." As his modem dialogued with another somewhere out there in cyberspace, he listened to the familiar honks and bleeps. Once connected, his monitor burst with color as he linked to his Web page of choice: *Former Catholics To Catholics*. He did not qualify as a "former Catholic," but this was unimportant. All that mattered was that FC2C spoke more to his heart and convictions than any other Christian Website.

Across the top of the page flowed FC2C's signature banner in bright red letters:

DO YOU KNOW A CATHOLIC WHO NEEDS TO KNOW JESUS?

Beneath this was a menu of choices: conversion stories, resources to purchase, on-line apologetic instruction, a message from the founder, and a high-powered search engine. Walter chose the latter.

The familiar rectangular input-box appeared. FC2C claimed that its search page combined ten other Internet search engines, providing a uniquely extensive and thorough exploration of the entire Web.

He typed in what only recently had crossed his mind as the most obvious thing for him to search: "Stephen LaPointe," and pressed enter. As the familiar hour glass appeared indicating that his hard drive and FC2C's search engines were racking their collective brains, Walter sipped his soda in nervous anticipation. *Will I possibly find some indisputable evidence that will prove my suspicions?*

After thirty seconds, the results were posted: twelve hits. The first was to an article LaPointe had written in 1998 for the New England Journal of Pastoral Ministry: "What is the Punctuation of Your Faith?"

A quick read told Walter that this was nothing more than a rehash of a sermon he had heard LaPointe preach at Red Creek. Nothing incriminating.

Links two through eleven were all newspaper announcements

about LaPointe's involvements in funerals, weddings, and an ecumenical Thanksgiving service.

His ecumenical sympathies certainly betray his interest in a one-world religion, but I need more.

Link No. 12 was to the head office of the American Association of Congregational Churches. It was LaPointe's pastoral biography. Walter followed the link and received a paragraph summary of his life:

> LaPointe, Stephen William. Born June 3, 1954, in Frenchtown, MI. Parents: Robert and Willamette LaPointe. Siblings: Francis (born 1956) and Clare (1960). Graduated summa cum laude from State College with B.A. in Business (1976). Received M.Div. from New England Evangelical Seminary (1981). Ordained to pastoral ministry at First Congregational Church, Boston (1981) where he served as minister to young adults. Has since served as assistant pastor at Sleepy Meadow, VT (1982-84), pastor at Red Creek, VT (1984-92), and Respite, NH (1992-1999). He is currently senior minister of First Church, Witzel's Notch, NH. Married to <u>Sara (Bondforth)</u> with two children: William (1982) and Daniel (1986).

Walter studied the posting carefully: though there was nothing overt, was there anything between the lines? *Frenchtown. The French were generally Catholics. Maybe that's the clue. "Francis" and "Clare." Catholic names, for sure—St. Francis and St. Clare!*

But nothing else. He glanced at his watch. *Two-fifty. Gotta go.*

But he noticed that Sara LaPointe's name was a hyperlink.

"Why not?" he said as he entered the link. This connected him to a shorter bio in the same association's database:

> LaPointe, Sara (Bondforth). Wife of Rev. Stephen W. LaPointe, senior minister of

First Church, Witzel's Notch, NH. Born
Norwich, CT (1955). Graduated magna
cum laude with B.A. in American History
from Campion College, S. Boston (1977);
received masters in history from same
(1982). Two children...

Walter stopped, pulling his face away from the monitor's glare. "Campion College," he said in breathless excitement. "But it must be!"

Once in a book about the history of the Reformation, he had read about a man named Campion. *Edmund Campion. He had been a Catholic priest during the reign of Queen Elizabeth. He had tried to bring the Catholic religion back into England. Eventually, though, he was caught, tried, and justly drawn and quartered.*

"It must be a Catholic college...named after this heretic Catholics glorify as a 'martyr.'" After a moment's reflection, he exclaimed, "That means that his wife must also be a Catholic! They're both in on this.

"Yes!" he shouted as if having struck gold. Ignoring the usual protocol, he switched his computer directly off and burst from his room down the hall to the garage. His only disappointment was that at that moment he had no one to tell.

*   *   *

AFTER A QUICK DIP in the indoor pool, Stephen progressed quickly to the whirlpool. Lounging like a contented sea lion in the soothing, frothing water, he presumed, being the sole occupant, that he could remain as long as he wanted. With one dry hand, he picked up *Catholicism and Fundamentalism* by Karl Keating.

With the first word of the preface, Stephen's interest was piqued. Keating's style was engaging yet pleasant and though obviously a Catholic writing to a Catholic audience, Keating didn't appear to be writing with a vendetta against anti-Catholics.

The book began with a detailed description of the origins of American Fundamentalism, which to Stephen was quite fascinating. Though he was technically an Evangelical, he knew there were many points of crossover, but had never explored how fundamentalism arose from the seemingly dying embers of nineteenth century Protestantism. After a discussion of the basic "fundamentals" that all fundamentalists hold dear, the following statement arrested Stephen from his relaxation:

> The key problem with fundamentalists' understanding of the Bible is that they have no rational grounds for what they believe. That sounds harsh, but it is true, and fundamentalists admit it. As E. J. Young says, "If the Bible is not a trustworthy witness of its own character, we have no assurance that our Christian faith is founded upon truth."…We believe the Bible to be true, say fundamentalists, because to adopt any other position is to deny the truths in which we otherwise believe.

With all that had been consuming his thinking for so many months, even years, this statement struck directly at Stephen's core. He reread it several times, but its circular reasoning disquieted him.

In the solitude of the whirlpool he formulated his thoughts out loud: "Bible-believing Christians are convinced that what we believe is based upon the Bible as the sole authority of truth. But as I have embarrassingly discovered, the Bible nowhere makes this claim about itself. This conviction has been imposed upon the Bible by believers…" he paused before he completed this thought, "…to ensure the foundation of truths we already hold."

Never before had he admitted this so clearly. Fidgeting now in the swirling warm waters, he allowed his body to sink deeper into the froth, wondering: *If what I have believed and taught all these years is nothing more than the Evangelical-Calvinist spin on Scripture, then in essence I have elevated my tradition—my opinions—above the Bible and have in turn used the Bible to defend my opinions. And if the Bible doesn't claim itself to be the sole infallible authority of Christian truth, then what? Am I left only with the circular reasoning of this fundamentalist writer—believe the Bible to be true because to adopt any other position is to deny the truths which I otherwise believe?*

Stephen set the book aside and slid completely beneath the warm water. He allowed the pulsating jets to ease the tension in his muscles and concluded: *I can't accept this, but neither can I jettison the authority and inerrancy of the Bible.* He knew from experience the truth, the depth, the power, and the beauty of the Scriptures. Beyond any doubt they were inspired by the Holy Spirit.

Returning to the surface with a gasp for breath, he knew that he was unprepared to answer this dilemma. Drying his hands, he returned to his reading. The second chapter was about "The Anti-Catholic 's Sourcebook," a classic book called *Roman Catholicism* by a Presbyterian clergyman named Boettner. Stephen knew this book well. A friend gave him a copy years ago, and ever since he had placed a copy in the libraries of every church he had pastored. He always presumed that it contained irrefutable evidence of the flaws of the Catholic Church.

Keating began, however, by pointing out the numerous flaws of this book, which Keating attributed to Boettner's failure to do his homework. Keating claimed that Boettner merely passed along unfounded and unsubstantiated myths. Stephen found most of this interesting, but not necessarily convincing. *How can I be sure Keating himself isn't just passing along unfounded counter claims?*

But then one paragraph caused Stephen to sit straight up in the steaming water. Once from the pulpit at Sleepy Meadow Church, he had ridiculed Catholics for their idolatrous practice of praying to statues, relics, and icons. To back his critique, he had quoted from Boettner's exposition of Catholic idolatry. But here Keating identified Boettner's ignorance:

> Do Catholics give slivers of wood, carvings of marble, and pieces of bone the kind of adoration they give God? That is what Boettner seems to say. What if a Catholic were to say to him, "I saw you kneeling with your Bible in your hands. Why do you worship a book?" He would rightly answer that he does not worship a book. He uses the Bible as an aid to prayer. Likewise, Catholics do not worship the Cross or images or relics. They use these physical objects to remind themselves of Christ and his special friends, the saints in heaven. The man who keeps a picture of his family in his wallet does not worship his wife and children, but he honors them....No one really thinks the pictures are themselves the objects of worship.

Up until that moment, Stephen had never doubted his presumption that Catholics were idolaters. But Keating's argument seemed logical. Could Keating be trusted?

Stephen closed the book, exchanged it for his towel, and returned to his room to dress for a late lunch. Through a cheeseburger, fries, and Coke, Stephen was haunted by Keating's words.

Back in the privacy of his room, he returned to where he had left off reading and was immediately confronted by a statement made by a famous Catholic bishop, Fulton Sheen:

> …few people in America hate the Catholic religion, but many people hate what they mistakenly believe is the Catholic religion—and…if what is hated really were the Catholic religion, Catholics would hate it, too.

A passing shadow drew his attention from his book to the window. Most of the outside light was blocked by the gold, motel-grade curtains, except for what entered through the thin vertical space between them. A family was walking by. First, a small boy appeared and vanished. Then a slightly older boy and a girl. Then their mother carrying a baby, followed by the father, fumbling with a large key ring. Then they were gone.

This parade of strangers became a parable in his mind. On the other side of his window was a whole world of reality. But *his* world was limited to the shelter of this room, confined, constricted, *prejudiced* by his curtained windows, through which he perceived only a partial glimpse of the outside. And the meaning of what he saw outside was shaped by his truncated perspective.

This reminded him of a section in the book he had just read. Leafing back, he found it:

> This is a good example of a common failing among fundamentalists, and not just those who are actively anti-Catholic. They memorize their lessons well, but they memorize selectively because they are taught only certain things. Although they read the entire Bible, with, naturally enough, special emphasis on the New Testament, verses that do not mesh with what their pastors have told them are either skipped or just not perceived as being trouble

> spots. On any one topic, they learn verses that,
> concatenated, seem to prove conclusively their position,
> and it is on these that they concentrate their apologetics.
> Few of them seriously ponder the meaning of those large
> chunks of the Bible that are pushed into the background.

This is exactly what I tried to tell them yesterday, Stephen thought with frustration. He didn't necessarily agree with Keating's last quip, yet what he said was true. He and others *did* skip over Scripture passages that didn't align with their theological presumptions to focus instead on those that did.

Returning his gaze to the book, Stephen read with a sense that the curtains were being thrown back on the windows of his mind.

Over the next few hours, a great number of his presumptions about the Catholic Church were disturbingly challenged. Most of these were low-level issues, like why Catholics cross themselves, why the Catholic Bible includes the Apocrypha, or why the Bible was at times forbidden to laity. The more he read, the more he felt curiosity mixed with shame for the many things he had passed along to his congregations without adequate examination.

In time his stomach told him it was time for dinner. With Keating in hand, Stephen went down to the restaurant, where he figured he would enjoy more of these new insights over a medium-rare T-bone, a glass of red wine, and an open mind.

*   *   *

IT WAS 3:10 A.M., and only the desk lamp lit the room. Stephen inserted a piece of tissue paper in the beginning of chapter seventeen called "Peter and the Papacy," where he planned to begin in the morning. Throughout the evening he had bounced back and forth between Keating and Clancy. Whenever Keating became obnoxiously Catholic, Stephen got disgusted and returned to *Debt of Honor*. But his curiosity could not be ignored. So many of his presuppositions were being challenged in chapters on the inspiration of the Bible, the reliability of Sacred Tradition, the development of doctrine, fanciful histories, salvation, the baptism of infants, the forgiveness of sins, and purgatory, that he now just sat in exhausted awe, his face buried in his hands.

But it wasn't Keating's Catholic arguments that had won the day, for Stephen's heart was far from ready to take the Catholic turn that Jim's had. Rather, the implications of his own convictions were being driven home simply because the Catholic Church could be considered at all. His problem now loomed even larger, for even more potentially valid opinions clouded the theological horizon.

Though it was late, he turned back once more to the chapter on Tradition. There Keating had quoted the famous Anglican convert, John Henry Cardinal Newman. This writer directly refuted the answer Stephen had once so confidently recited to Larry Howe at that Respite board meeting.

> It is quite evident that 2 Timothy 3:17 furnishes no argument whatever that the Sacred Scriptures, without Tradition, is the sole rule of faith; for, although Sacred Scripture is profitable for these four ends, still it is not said to be sufficient. The Apostle requires the aid of Tradition (2 Thess. 2:15).

Stephen grabbed for his Bible a bit nervously. At this late hour he was pulling a blank on what 2 Thessalonians 2:15 stated, and he certainly wasn't aware of any Scripture that implied that tradition was required. He found the verse, there among others he had underlined, and read: "So then, brethren, stand firm and hold to the traditions which you were taught, whether by word of mouth or by letter from us."

But of course. Stephen knew this verse. Only recently he had been startled by its emphasis on both the oral and written transmission of the gospel. For some reason, however, he hadn't noted the significant emphasis on "traditions." He sat, staring. Once again a verse he had read before jumped out at him as if for the first time. *Stand firm and hold to the traditions.* It clearly implied that for the Apostle Paul and the leaders he was teaching, the oral traditions were as authoritative and *sufficient* as Paul's written epistles—which eventually would be considered *Scripture.*

Stephen set the Bible aside and leaned back in the lounge chair, raising the leg rest. With his eyes closed, he begged the Lord for guidance, for clarity, for direction, and for mercy. He began reciting and claiming, possibly for the thousandth time, the promise of Proverbs 3:5 and 6, "Trust in the Lord with all your heart; and lean not unto your own understanding. In all your ways acknowledge Him, and He will direct your paths," and fell asleep.

*   *   *

THE BRIGHTLY LIT, yet otherwise dingy work area was deafeningly loud with the mechanical drone of four injection-molding machines spitting out plastic cups, plates, and butter tubs. Eight operators hovered around the equipment, ensuring that the bulk resins and additives didn't run out, the temperature and other critical settings didn't budge, and the finished product was within spec. If all went well, their work was fairly routine. Basically they could watch while drinking coffee, but if one factor went amiss, they had to scramble. A five-degree drop in extruder temperature for one minute could alter the molten plastic temperature and resultant texture so drastically that hundreds of finished product would end up in the scrap bin. This would cost the company money, and if this occurred too often, it would cost them their jobs.

The operators kept a vigilant eye on their equipment, but this night they also were conscious of their new foreman's eyes on them. There, twenty feet above the production floor, in a glass-front cubicle, well-insulated from the constant pounding of the injection molding machines, Mr. Horscht watched over them. The men barely knew their new foreman, so they were on best behavior. His thick glasses and stern features, along with his German name, made them think of the commandant in a classic television sit-com about prisoners in a Nazi prison camp. So far they had found him exceedingly fair in his expectations, though a bit more pensive than their last foreman.

As on his first few nights, Mr. Horscht was there in his cubicle, staring out, over, and around them, rarely moving. But to the minds of those operators who stole a glance, he looked more stern than usual. He sat dead still, peering down. They wondered if they were doing anything wrong or at least differently. They couldn't know that Walter's thoughts were elsewhere.

At that moment Walter cared little about injection-molded cups or butter tubs. His thoughts were consumed with reviewing over and over again what he had discovered that afternoon. The rest of the world, including his family, was asleep, but he was lost in a world of conspiracy theories and apocalyptic scenarios.

He began to conclude that what he was to do—what he *must* do—was crucial for the salvation of hundreds of souls. For the first time he was beginning to apprehend the full impact of the radical task to which he was being called. And how greatly he would be misunderstood, even hated, even by his own family. But the words of the prophet Isaiah speaking of Jesus entered his recall: *"He was despised and rejected by men; a man of sorrows, and acquainted with grief; and as one from whom men hide their faces he was despised, and we esteemed him not."*

Surely, Walter concluded, *I too must be willing to sacrifice all for the defense of my Lord Jesus and his truth—even if it means sacrificing my life.*

Walter sat brooding, staring blankly out over the production room, his chin resting in the palm of his left hand, his right hand tapping the window before him with the point of a pencil, and his thick glasses making what was directly in front of him crystal-clear but everything to the sides distorted and out of focus. To Walter, his glasses were a symbol for what his task must surely be: he must forge straight ahead with his commission and not be dissuaded by any interior or exterior voices that misunderstand the truth as he alone had come to realize it.

The men below worked more carefully than usual under the intense stare of their foreman. They listened to his constant tapping on the control-room glass, trying to discern what it meant. They even chose to forgo their coffee to avoid any impression that they were doing anything but focusing on their work. And the night went on, the machines and the operators churning out cups, plates, and butter tubs, all within tolerance, while their foreman pondered his destiny.

Part VI

Thou Preparest a Table Before Me

1

"GOOD MORNING...it is seven...o'clock...a.m...time to get up," the digitally processed voice declared to Stephen after he had clumsily retrieved the phone from its cradle. He responded with a habitual "thank you" and hung up, and then felt stupid for thanking a recording. He threw back the covers and carefully repeated his usual routine for getting out of bed. After only four hours of sleep, he wasn't ready to get up, but he had much to do. He went to the curtained picture window to discover what the weather was like. Though it was still dark, he could see that about three inches of new snow had fallen. Enormous flakes were still wafting down. He would need to start home this morning, or he might possibly be snowed in.

After a quick trip to the bathroom, Stephen started a pot of coffee and dressed in the clothes he had worn the day before. It crossed his mind with a stab of guilt that he ought to let Sara know where he was. *As far as she knows, I'm sleeping soundly and happy as a clam at The Widow's Mite. But if I told her that I was hanging out, she'd probably guilt me into coming home and I'm not ready yet.*

He was anxious to return to Keating's book, for after a few hours' sleep, he was wondering whether he had been reading and listening clearly. *Had there been flaws in Keating's arguments that I missed in my enthusiasm?* He would find out in a moment.

The coffee was done, and as he added the non-dairy whitener to his first cup of the day, he remembered that it was Wednesday morning and he had not glanced at his sermon for Sunday. He had planned to work on it little by little during the retreat, but with all that had happened and then becoming absorbed in Keating's book, he had forgotten all about it. In fact, for the moment he couldn't remember which text he had scheduled and had Marge print in the bulletin.

He threw Keating aside and dug into his briefcase for the sermon folder. The folder tab read "Matthew 16:13-20."

"Good Lord, you've got to be kidding!" he exclaimed out loud.

Inside were his notes from the sermon he had preached nearly four years before at Respite, entitled "Who Do <u>YOU</u> Say I Am?"

"I can't believe that I scheduled this text again—especially with all the junk I'm going through."

Coffee in one hand and his sermon notes in the other, Stephen retired to the lounge chair by the window. He anticipated no problems in making this already-revised sermon work for Witzel's Notch. *If my memory serves me correctly, I think I already mellowed down the controversial parts.*

As was his usual routine, he began by rereading the familiar text, until he reached the verse of Protestant-Catholic contention:

> And I tell you, you are Peter, and on this rock I will build my church, and the powers of death shall not prevail against it.

Stephen remembered how, sitting in the stale air of his substandard Respite office, under the oversight of the black velvet Jesus, a commentary by a Jesuit scholar had effectively countered his anti-Catholic disclaimers for this text. He remembered how this had become one of the crucial signposts along his road to confusion: *The Jesuit's explanation was at least as plausible as any other. So which, if any, is true?*

"But wait," Stephen said aloud in the stillness. Setting his sermon notes aside, he grabbed Keating's book. "Isn't this what the next chapter is about?" Sure enough, the next chapter was entitled "Peter and the Papacy." Skimming, he saw that Keating dealt directly with this text from Matthew.

"How providential," he said wryly. He glanced at the digital clock. "I'll read this at breakfast."

Locking the door behind him, he passed down the empty motel hallway to the restaurant, where over some eggs and ham he hoped to find a flaw in Keating's argument—a speck of incredibility that might allow him to rest once more in the comfortable assumptions of his past.

*　　　*　　　*

"Good morning," William said with guarded passion as he watched Stacy enter the senior lounge. She had made a more conscious effort to look her best, and she did, in a black sweater and closely tailored, calf-length camel skirt that shouted her maturing figure in a way that made William feel faint.

"Hi." Stacy took the cushioned seat across from him.

Miss Duryea was seated in her usual spot, watching them over her morning coffee. "You two want any coffee?" she asked. "Help yourselves."

"No thank you, Miss Duryea," William said, his concentration shattered by her interruption. "But thanks for offering." He turned back to Stacy. "How are you this morning? You…you look great!"

"Oh, come on, William," she said demurely, "this is just some old stuff that I got out because of the snowstorm. It looks like it might get pretty bad."

"I've heard they might send us home early if it doesn't let up. If that happens, would you need a ride home? I've got a car."

Her head dropped slightly. "No, my father will be here."

They sat in silence until William continued with his agenda. "Stacy," he began hesitantly, too insecure to look Stacy in the eye for long. "I was wondering, with you also being new and all, well, has anyone asked you to the Winter Formal?"

Again Stacy's head dropped shyly, but after a few seconds, she said, "No. No one has asked."

"Well, I was wondering…you see, I originally hadn't planned to go. I hadn't met anyone I wanted to go with, and, well, I also wasn't that interested in making much of an effort, what with leaving all my friends last fall." Unable to see her eyes, William felt even more awkward. "But then I saw you, and well, I didn't know if maybe…"

"Yes."

"What?"

Looking full into William's eyes, she said, "If you're asking, I'd love to go."

"You would?" His exclamation got Miss Duryea to peer up from her grading and over her reading glasses. "I mean," he said more softly, "you would?"

"Yes, I was hoping you would ask," she said with a smile that made William melt, "but I figured you had already asked someone." Again dropping her glance, "But there's a problem. A major problem."

"What's that?" He leaned forward.

"My Dad. He's...paranoid that every boy in the school, every man in the world, is after me, and he's determined to protect me. In the past he's let me go to dances, but every date has had to pass muster like being interviewed for the FBI."

"What do I need to do?"

"I don't know. I'm afraid to introduce you to him too quickly. I'm even afraid to leave the school too close to you or any boy."

"What do you mean, afraid?" He asked with a heightened edge of concern.

Stacy looked into William's face. "Oh, not what you might think. My father would never be violent with me or anything. I'm his prized pearl," she said with an edge of sarcasm. "The man I bring home will have to be more perfect than Jesus Christ to meet my father's expectations."

Troubled by the strange distance in her eyes, he said, "Well, won't he think differently once he learns that I'm your pastor's son? You didn't know this, but I saw you in church Sunday. I didn't recognize you then, but I saw you."

"I saw you, too, William, but I didn't know it was you. You were up front, right?"

"Yeah, in the front row, with my mother and brother. You know—we need to give that good, godly impression of the minister's family all together there right up front," he said with feigned cynicism.

"I don't think I noticed. My father is what you might call an *enthusiastic* Christian. He drags us to all kinds of Christian events. We never miss Sunday morning worship, and rarely a Sunday or Wednesday night meeting. Don't get me wrong," she continued, looking a shade to the side, "I'm a Christian and all that—my father made sure of that by sending me to Sunday School and to more Bible camps than I can remember—but, well, I wish church and Sunday School weren't such stone-cold obligations."

Stacey's openness drew William in. "I couldn't agree more. Sometimes I wish I could go because I wanted to, and not because it was my duty as the pastor's son."

Noting the time, he returned their attention to the topic at hand. "But do you think this will soften your father enough to let me take you to the dance?"

"I'm sure it will. If he's in a good mood, I'll ask him today when he picks me up. I'll let you know tomorrow. If he's the least bit open, he'll want to meet you right away so he can make up his mind."

"Great."

First bell rang. They had five minutes.

"Can I walk you to class? Here, let me carry your books."

They walked out together, leaving Miss Duryea to her grading and her third cup of coffee.

*   *   *

"ANOTHER CUP, sir?" the waitress asked as she cleared away Stephen's soiled but empty breakfast dishes.

"Yes," he said without looking up from the pages of Keating. He was halfway through the chapter on "Peter and the Papacy," right to where Keating was beginning his explanation of Matthew 16.

So far, Keating had reviewed the more commonly held assumptions about Peter, espoused by most evangelical preachers, including Stephen himself: that Christ never appointed Peter as the earthly head of the Church; that the papacy was merely a man-made institution that arose out of fourth-century Roman politics, with no connection to the New Testament; and that Peter had never been in Rome. Keating countered these with evidence from early Christian writers. These quotes were particularly intriguing. Other than a few scant references to the Apostolic Fathers in seminary, Stephen had ignored them. Occasionally during the past few years, however—especially with his curiosity piqued by Ginny McBride and now Jim—he had wondered how the first-century writers dealt with the proliferation of novel interpretations of the Bible. He made a note to buy himself a collection of their writings.

Keating then repeated the arguments that Stephen had previously read in the Jesuit Bible commentary, but then progressed to a portion of the Matthew text that Stephen had always skirted over:

> I will give you the keys of the kingdom of heaven; and
> whatever you shall bind on earth shall have been bound
> in heaven, and whatever you shall loose on earth shall
> have been loosed in heaven.

Since Jesus had said this also to His other apostles, Stephen
had given little thought to whether this implied anything unique for
Simon Peter. Stephen presumed that every pastor, every single
Christian, under the indwelling guidance of the Holy Spirit, had
this power to "bind and loose," for hadn't Jesus promised that
whatever anyone asked in His name He would grant?

Nevertheless, Stephen read Keating's explanation:

> Here Peter was singled out for the authority that provides
> for the forgiveness of sins and the making of disciplinary
> rules. Later the apostles as a whole would be given similar
> power, but here Peter received it in a special sense; the
> later grant to them did not diminish the uniqueness of
> what was granted Peter. Indeed, Peter alone was promised
> something else.

"He was?" Stephen said aloud.

"Excuse me, did you need something?" said a passing waitress.

"Huh? Oh, nothing, sorry," he said with a smile, and then
returned to his reading.

> "I will give to thee [singular] the keys to the kingdom of
> heaven." In ancient times keys were the hallmark of
> authority. A walled city might have one great gate and
> that gate one great lock worked by one great key. To be
> given the key to the city (an honor that exists even today,
> although its import is largely lost) meant to be given free
> access to and authority over the city. The city to which
> Peter was given the keys was the heavenly city itself. This
> symbolism for authority is used elsewhere in the Bible (Is
> 22:22; Rev 1:18).

Stephen paused, closed the book slowly, then picked up his

coffee with both hands. Once again he had encountered a verse that previously he had always conveniently passed over. For a second, that inane Irish jingle about a four-leaf clover once overlooked ran through his mind, in a whining vaudevillian tenor. He smirked and wondered whether this verse he was now "looking over" would prove to be a lucky or unlucky omen.

How have I explained the meaning of the keys? He couldn't remember having said anything about this in a sermon or a Bible study, or could he recall any discussion about this in seminary. Surely one of his professors had proposed an explanation, but he couldn't remember.

And Isaiah 22…what does this have to do with it?

He left a healthy tip, paid his bill, and returned quickly to his room. Once inside, he grabbed for his Bible. *Isaiah 22, verse 22.* Finding this verse, he read slowly, silently:

> And I will place on his shoulder the key of the house of
> David; he shall open, and none shall shut; and he shall
> shut, and none shall open.

"This, of course, points forward to Jesus, the Messiah," he said aloud. *But who in the context of the verse was to receive the key "on his shoulder?"*

He sought the answer to this in the preceding verse:

> In that day I will call My servant Eliakim the son of
> Hilkiah, and I will clothe him with your robe, and will
> bind your girdle on him, and will commit your authority
> to his hand; and he shall be a father to the inhabitants of
> Jerusalem and to the house of Judah.

But who was Eliakim, and what was his significance? A cross-reference on the side of the page pointed him to 2 Kings 18:18.

> And when they called for the king, there came out to
> them Eliakim the son of Hilkiah, who was over the
> household…

Stephen closed his Bible and leaned back in the lounger. After a moment's reflection, he could see all the interconnections of the Catholic—of Keating's—argument: Isaiah prophesied that the keys of the kingdom of Judah would pass from the king, David's descendant, to Eliakim, the overseer of his household; then, in Matthew's Gospel, Jesus the King, the son of David, gives the keys to Simon Peter, designating him as overseer of His household, the Church.

The implications were clear, and for Keating—as apparently for Stephen's life-long friend Jim—this was enough to prove papal authority. But not yet for Stephen, for to his dismay this merely reconfirmed that the Bible *alone* is insufficient, since it can so easily be interpreted or misinterpreted.

OK, so what am I going to preach from this text this time, from this pulpit to these people?

He looked out the window. The snow was falling harder and faster, and as the digital clock by the bed turned ten, Stephen decided he'd better start home. He would call Sara, then mull and pray over all he had discovered as he drove back. Certainly somewhere between this motel and Witzel's Notch, the Lord would give him a hand up from the quagmire of his confusion.

2

SARA HURRIEDLY transferred the wet clothing from the washer to the dryer, slammed the lid shut, and spun the control knob. With a tap on the start button, the dryer began humming. She then poured a roughly measured cup of detergent into the washer, followed by an armload of unsorted dirty clothes. Assuming all the settings were within range, she pulled the knob to start, flicked off the lights, and hurried upstairs.

Unaware that her husband was reading a book challenging his assumptions, Sara was more than halfway through one that was fortifying hers—a book she hoped to finish before Stephen got home.

Earlier in the week, Molly Torquist, the Christian education director at First Church, had called in a panic. She desperately needed to find a replacement teacher for an adult Sunday school class. Sara was hesitant to assume leadership so late in the semester, but when Molly told her the title of the book they had been reading together, Sara quickly relented. It was a collection of conversion stories: twenty Catholic nuns who had left the Catholic Church to become Protestant. Given her previous encounters with Ginny and Adrian, and that abhorrent book by the Cardinal, she considered this an immensely comical twist of fate. After Molly had brought the book over last night, Sara could not put it down, reading it into the wee hours of the morning. Now she was squeezing it in between her chores.

Back in the living room, Sara returned to her chair by the fire. She picked up the book she had left spread open and inverted on the couch. The book's cover portrayed a joyful woman, in normal dress, holding a Bible. Sara turned the book over and began reading about an ex-nun named Donna.

Donna had been raised in a large Catholic family that had also produced two priests. She went through all the usual Catholic institutions and, to the joy of her parents, had entered the convent immediately upon graduation. She wrote that, though she was taught all the doctrines of the Catholic Church, she had never owned or read a Bible until after she had been in the convent for ten years. This she had received from her ex-Catholic, charismatic younger brother, who had found Christ through the witness of a nondenominational campus ministry. Though her brother was relentless in arguing from Scripture that she must flee the Catholic Church to find new life in Christ, she resisted—yet she yearned to have his bold assurance of salvation.

For five more years, Donna followed along with other nuns who were experimenting with a wide assortment of New Age spiritual techniques that had become in vogue within her religious order. Nothing brought her joy and peace. Finally, after fifteen years of "emptiness," she left the convent with another nun. The two proceeded from bad to worse as they supported each other in their decision to abandon all forms of religion.

In despair, she eventually cried out to God and experienced a powerful change of heart and mind. Immediately the Scriptures came alive to her, and she considered this moment her true conversion to Jesus.

Donna ended her testimony by exhorting any who were trying to earn their salvation through the rigors of religious life as a Catholic nun or priest to trust fully in the free gift of salvation through grace by faith in Jesus Christ alone.

Everything this ex-nun said confirmed Sara's belief that Catholics seek salvation through rituals and works and are forbidden to read the Bible for fear they might discover the falsity of their church.

Sara was on to the next conversion story when the phone rang.

"Hello? …Oh, hi, hon. How's the retreat going?"

Sara listened as Stephen described in vague terms how, though the retreat had not gone as planned, the overall experience had been a good one.

"Well, good. Are you ready to come home? The weather's getting pretty dicey."

"I'm starting home now," Stephen said. "After a brief stop at the church, I'll be home around five. I was wondering if we could go out for dinner tonight? I'd like to tell you about some of the things I discovered this week."

"Oh, honey," she blurted out, "I can't wait to tell you about…" but she stopped, deciding instead to tell him later.

"What was that?" Stephen asked. "I didn't get the last part. Must be bad reception."

"Oh, nothing. Nothing, dear. I'll tell you tonight over dinner."

After hanging up, reassured by the distant hum that the washer and dryer were still running, Sara returned with a joyful vengeance to her book.

*   *   *

THE GRAY CAPRICE WAGON was parked as usual in the circular driveway of the school. Walter sat peering carefully around, studying every exit and as far inside as he could see through the shaded glass of each entrance. He was determined to spot any interaction between boys and his Stacy. He saw other students laughing and walking arm in arm. He just knew that these girls, unbeknownst to their trusting, naive parents, were sluts who had surrendered under the constant pressure of sex-crazed adolescent boys. He knew this because he remembered what he had been like, before his adult conversion to Jesus. He knew what these boys did and said because he had done and said it all, and this shameful memory strengthened his resolve to ensure that this would never happen to his daughter. Stacy might not understand, but one day she would thank him for helping her preserve herself until her wedding night.

"There she is." He spied her exiting the main entrance, by herself as usual. And, as usual, a contrary voice hounded him: *But why is such a beautiful girl as Stacy always alone? Do these rich kids think they're too good for us?*

But he was more relieved to see her free of male influence. As she approached the car, he noted that she was running with a joy he had not seen in months. Her face was beaming. *What could it be?*

"Stacy, my precious. What is it? You seem so happy." His voice had a suspicious edge.

"Oh, Dad, I had a great, great day."

"Well, that's good, Stacy. But why? Please tell me. What happened?"

"Will you promise to hear me out? I've got something exciting to tell you."

"Sure, OK. What is it?"

"Dad, a nice young man talked to me today."

With that, Walter shot her an angry glance.

"Now, Dad, you promised. Please hear me out and trust me. I share your views about dating, remember?"

Walter softened and, with a slight smile, returned his attention to the road ahead. "I'm sorry. You know me, Mr. Four-Eyes Protection Agency."

They both laughed.

"His name is William. He's an honors student and a first-string forward on the basketball team. But best of all..."—Stacy hesitated for effect, then proceeded—"...he's the son of our new minister."

Walter's upper torso went tense and straight. His foot hit the brake, forcing the car to an abrupt halt in the middle of a busy intersection. Car horns honked as Walter exclaimed with increasing intensity, "What did you SAY?"

"Daddy, what's wrong? Why are you reacting like this? They're honking at us!"

Walter broke from his angry trance and pulled the car to the side of the road onto someone's front yard. Throwing the shift lever into park, Walter turned to face Stacy directly and demanded: "Once again, what did you say?"

Stacy was overcome with tears. Cringing back against her door, she answered cautiously, "I said that he is the son of our new minister. His name is William LaPointe."

Hunched over, glaring at the jewel of his heart, Walter said, almost breathless, "You must not see this boy, ever again."

"But why, Daddy? Of all the boys I could be interested in, why are you so angry that I talked with our minister's son? Don't you remember him? I grew up with him."

"That doesn't matter, you don't know his father."

"What do you mean? He's our minister."

"Stacy, you don't understand. There are things I know about our minister that force me to demand that you stay away from his son." With this, Walter looked into the rear-view mirror and turned the Caprice wagon back onto the road, heading for home.

He set his face to communicate that the subject was closed, but Stacy was not ready to give up. More controlled, she continued. "Please, Daddy, please. Talk to me. What have I done wrong? I stay away from the other boys as you wish, but William is different. He's a committed Christian and a minister's son. What is there about Reverend LaPointe that demands that I stay away from William? I heard his sermon on Sunday, and it was good. What's wrong?"

Walter knew that his daughter and Helen were tired of his conspiracy theories; he also knew that he had lost some of their respect. Consequently, he had kept his suspicions about LaPointe to himself. *One day, however, they will know that I have been right all along. But maybe,* he reconsidered, *Stacy needs to know a little about this so she could more fully appreciate my strong warning.*

Stopping at a light, he turned toward her with intense seriousness. "Stacy, all I can say is that I have proof that Reverend LaPointe is not what he claims to be. I have known LaPointe for years, and though I know this sounds bizarre," he turned back to the road ahead and said cautiously, "I am convinced that he is secretly a Roman Catholic priest posing as a Protestant minister."

Stacy stared at him in confused bewilderment. "Daddy, what are you talking about?" She wanted to ask more, but surrendered to tears.

"Stacy, please, I know this sounds crazy, but you must trust me. I only want what's best for you and our family, and I only want to defend our Lord Jesus."

"But, Daddy..." Stacy pleaded. Walter stopped her short with a glare, and she cowered back against the door.

Walter drove the rest of the way home as if in a trance. On the one hand, he felt enraged, even violated. The battle had now escalated—his own family was being infiltrated. On the other hand, however, this attack had energized him. It was as if his quest for clearer directions had now been given marching orders. He must act, soon.

After pulling into the garage, Walter stormed from the car and slammed the door, leaving his daughter. His mind was elsewhere. He charged through the kitchen.

"Hello, honey. Everything all..." Helen said from the sink, dish towel in hand. Walter ignored her. He descended into the basement, locking the door behind him.

"Walter," Helen said from the kitchen side of the door. "Is everything all right?"

"Yes, yes, just fine," Walter yelled up as he unlocked a private closet under the stairs. He reached up to the back of an upper shelf for a green metal box.

Helen rattled the knob. "Walter, what's wrong?" she cried in panic. "Why is this door locked?"

"Please, Helen. Nothing is wrong. Just leave me alone."

He fumbled with the combination lock several times before the tumblers finally meshed. He opened the lid and there it was, still wrapped in a bloodstained bandana. He picked the bundle up, studied it with nostalgia, and then slowly, carefully unwrapped it. For nearly thirty years he hadn't looked upon it—since he had wrenched it from the rigid hand of a dead North Vietnamese officer. It looked to be in perfect condition–*but would it still fire?*

"Please, Walter, open this door! You're scaring me!"

He stood statuelike, eyes closed, holding the bundle forward, slightly elevated, as if he were offering it as a sacrifice to God.

3

"WILLIAM, you're in charge, so after you and Daniel finish cleaning up your dinner..." Sara directed.

"Yeah, thanks a lot. We get hot dogs and leftover beans, while you and Dad eat steak."

"What do you mean? We'll probably order meatloaf or liver and onions."

"Yeah, right," Daniel said, looking grudgingly at his plate.

"When you're done, put everything in the dishwasher, then finish your homework. If you're done by 8:30, you can watch the game on television."

"Yes! The Celtics are playing the Bulls at home. Can we make popcorn?"

"If you don't make a mess."

"All right!" The boys slapped high fives.

"But you've got to get your work done first," Sara added.

"We'll do it. Come on, Daniel, let's get honking so we can see the game." The two dug into their leftovers. "You two have fun."

"All right. We'll be at the Wayside Inn if you need us."

"Meatloaf or liver and onions, my foot," Daniel said, submitting one last vote of protest.

Sara just smiled as she closed the door and walked to the car. The engine was running and the inside was getting toasty as Stephen shoveled a few spots the boys had missed.

"The boys did a fine job keeping ahead of the storm," he said as he got behind the wheel, rubbing and blowing into his chilled hands. Though the snow had stopped during the afternoon, the temperature was still falling, now into the lower twenties.

"The weather report said it might get down into single digits tonight," Sara replied.

"I guess we'll find out whether the pipes in this new house can stand the freeze."

The Wayside Inn was about thirty minutes away when the roads were clear, so Stephen figured it might take close to an hour given the icy conditions. But they both knew the drive was worth it, because the food and atmosphere were great, and also because the distance from the church conveniently insured that they would have a peaceful, uninterrupted evening alone, beyond the watchful eyes of parishioners.

The Wagoneer turned off their lane onto a larger suburban neighborhood thoroughfare, and then finally onto old Route 30, the primary route across lower New Hampshire for more than 200 years.

"Were the boys cooperative during my time away?"

"Yes, just fine. What with basketball practice and Daniel's extra orchestra rehearsals for the upcoming Easter concert, they didn't have time for mischief. I think William might have a new flame, though."

"Oh, really. What's her name?"

"I don't know. I'm actually just guessing," she said. "He came home from school on cloud nine, a smile pushing his ears together at the back of his head. Daniel was teasing him, but William wouldn't let out a clue."

"Well, that's good, I hope. It might help him get his mind off his old friends, and especially his old flame, Susan. In some sense, I half-justified our move just to nip that relationship in the bud."

"On that we both agree," Sara replied with an emphatic sigh of relief. "Now let's pray that any new girl he falls head over heels for will be more in line with our moral expectations."

For a Wednesday evening, and a cold one at that, the road was unusually congested. Stephen could have chosen the four-lane highway to avoid the occasional bottlenecks of this old two-lane road, but he and Sara preferred this more scenic route. The disappearing sun peeked from behind the trees to the southwest of the road, and the glare of oncoming cars sporadically illuminated them. An occasional comment or question about the scenery broke their silence, as each waited for the right moment to launch into their respective agendas. Then, as Stephen cautiously passed a farm tractor hauling a load of alfalfa, Sara broke their stalemate.

"Well, tell me, what is it you discovered this week on your retreat?"

"Oh, yes, well, let's wait until we get to the Inn. There's a lot to tell."

After a few more minutes of awkward silence, he said, pointing off to the right, "Looks like we're here." He glided his four-wheel-drive into the parking lot.

The Wayside Inn was a 150-year-old timber-frame restaurant and pub. Its once visible, hand-hewn beams, lattice-work, and white plaster filler were now covered over with the graying cedar shakes common across New England. Inside, the ceilings were low, reminiscent of a time when the average height of Americans was several inches shorter. The round, Shaker-design tables were candle-lit, and the waitresses wore long cotton dresses with white aprons and bonnets.

After being led to a table reserved directly in front of the expansive stone fireplace, Sara and Stephen both ordered the special, a lamb dish with turnips and new potatoes. They were toasting with their first glass of Beaujolais when Sara solicited more details of Stephen's getaway. Looking into his glass of dark red wine, unaware of Sara's own discoveries, he told her that Jim Sarver had resigned from his Presbyterian congregation and was becoming a Roman Catholic.

A spray of wine spewed from Sara. Customers around them ceased their drinking, eating, and discussions in mid-sentence, while Stephen kicked back his chair and stood up, shaking wine from his shirt and suit coat.

"Sara?!"

"Oh, Stephen, I'm so sorry," she said as she rose to help with the cleanup. "I didn't mean to…" she said both for his and the onlookers' benefit.

"It's OK, it's OK," he said, motioning her back to her seat. He waited until a waitress had changed the table linen and the onlookers had resumed their meals before he continued.

"Now what was that all about?" he demanded.

Sara sat, stunned. Given the confluence of her concerns, this was the worst possible news she could imagine. It was Jim who had led Stephen back to faith, and throughout the years he had always had a strong influence on Stephen's thinking. The implications of this frightened her.

Calmly, she spoke. "Is this really true about Jim? Why would he do such a foolish thing?"

"Yes, unfortunately it is true. He gave us the gory details, which

I can go through later if you want, but let me tell you more about the retreat."

A waiter came with their salads and a basket of fresh rolls.

"All went well up until my second presentation. Remember, I told you I had planned to share my concerns about the pastorate with this small gathering of like-minded friends. Well," he paused to chew a large bite of salad, contemplating the impact of his next statement, "the bomb dropped when I prefaced my talk with the news that I was considering resigning from First Church."

"What?" she exclaimed, choking on a bite of roll. Stephen rose to help her as she began coughing loudly. Drinking, eating, and discussions again ceased momentarily around them. As she wiped her mouth with her napkin, she repeated softly, "What did you say?"

Stephen was taken aback by her strong reaction. "Sara, this is really nothing new between you and me. You know that this has been a running concern for me for years, and that coming to this larger church has only made things worse."

"What do you mean? Sure, I've known you've been struggling with the great range of opinions among Christian churches and ministers, but what has this got to do with resigning from First Church? We just got here."

By the edge in her tone, Stephen knew he needed to be careful, so he hedged. "Sara, I didn't say that I was going to resign, but that I was considering it. I told this to the group more for effect than for certain. But Sara, I can't deny that I've been wondering whether this is what I should do, to clear my conscience."

He began buttering a roll, trying to convey to all eyes an air of composure. He was glad none of the retreatants had been here to overhear his cowardly deception. "Please, Sara hear me out on this. You know that in many ways I have lost confidence in my ability to discern what is true. This might seem like a mere academic or philosophical problem, but it is much more than that. When I stand in the pulpit, I accept a great responsibility—to speak the truth to those who trust me. I am responsible to Jesus for how I lead, teach, and preach. But when I recognize how contradictory my conclusions from Scripture are from those of other faithful ministers, I question whether I should ever step into a Christian pulpit again."

Stephen studied his wife, but saw only a cold, glazed expression. "This is basically what I presented to the group. I walked them through a brief study of First Timothy, illustrating how differently we contemporary Christians think and teach compared to how Paul taught Timothy. Later, Jim, Scott, Cliff, and even Larry admitted to the same concerns, but the rest of the group weren't ready to hear these concerns or where they might lead. So," he took a bite of roll, then continued, "at Larry's request, I relinquished leadership of the retreat."

Sara couldn't hear anything past Stephen's threat of resignation. "But Stephen, what will we do if you resign? We just moved here! How will you support us?"

His intuition was to downplay his thoughts about resignation, but instead he chose to face it squarely. "Sara, I haven't thought it all through yet, because I wasn't planning to resign immediately, so please don't panic."

She shot him a look that said, "Don't you tell me not to panic when you're leading us into destitution!"

"Please, Sara, I promise I won't do anything drastic until our future is well mapped out. But, honey," and he extended his hand across the table for hers, "the concerns I'm grappling with are important, and I don't know how long I can continue preaching from that pulpit when I'm not sure whether what I'm preaching is true."

Sara accepted his gesture and tried to calm down. "But, Stephen, you've been doing this for years. Can't you merely avoid the more controversial issues? Just preach the basics?"

"But there's great controversy even with the basics—about salvation, about the meaning of the Church, about sacraments like Baptism and the Lord's Supper, about how a church should be structured, about the authority of my ordination."

The waiter arrived to remove their salad dishes and distribute the main course. Sumptuous plates of lamb, turnips, new potatoes, cranberry sauce, and a local blend of succotash were placed before them. Another waiter refilled their wine glasses and asked, "Is there anything else we can do?"

"No, thank you. It looks great," Stephen said.

They ate in silence. After what seemed like an eternity, he

resumed. "Anyway, after Ron agreed to lead the rest of the retreat, I decided to escape. Early yesterday morning, I left and holed up in a motel to pray and attempt to make some sense of all this."

"You weren't at the retreat these last few days?" Sara asked, her eyes raised from her braised lamb.

"Well, I guess you might say 'yes and no.' I wasn't at The Widow's Mite, but I was still on retreat." He could see that Sara's ire was again on the rise, but all he could do was keep on going. "The night before I left, however, Scott, Cliff, and I went out with Jim for a nightcap to hear about his resignation and decision to become Catholic. Then Jim gave me a book that had helped him more clearly understand the Catholic Church. I spent most of yesterday and this morning reading it, and in the end, it only further confirmed that I have no place in a Protestant pulpit."

Panic rose in Sara like a dormant volcano as the memories of her Catholic encounters—Campion chapel, Ginny and Adrian, the Cardinal's book, the Pope's message to Cuba, and the ex-nuns' testimonies—converged in her mind.

"Stephen, stop." She sat poised before him, her hands resting on the table, one clenching a fork and the other a knife. "I don't understand all you are going through or the reasons you have lost your grip on reality, but the Catholic Church is not the answer."

"The Catholic Church? I didn't say anything about my becoming a Catholic."

"But your questioning of Protestant assumptions and the sufficiency of the Bible is setting you up to become vulnerable to the arguments given by Jim or the books you are reading," she declared. "You must stop."

"Sara, the book I read didn't convince me to become Catholic," Stephen protested. "But it did demonstrate that Catholic beliefs are at least another viable interpretation of Scripture, which therefore adds one more contradictory voice to my confusion."

The set of Sara's eyes told all. She was ready to explode.

"Sara, please understand, I can't be afraid to pursue truth, for Jesus promised that the Holy Spirit would lead and protect my mind."

"But isn't this what all Protestants believe?" she pressed him. "If this is true—if the Holy Spirit leads into all truth—then why are there so many different conclusions? Is the Holy Spirit all mixed up?

Or not listening? Or not even there!" This declaration of doubt rose deep from within, surprising them both.

"What do you mean by that?"

After a cautious pause, Sara admitted, "Stephen, most of what I believe, I have learned from you. I accepted it at your word, because I am not about to read all your deep theology books. I believe in God, in His Son Jesus, in the basic Christian truths, particularly as you have preached and taught them. But as I have watched and listened to your growing struggles with 'conscience,' I, too, have wondered whether what I have come to believe is really true."

"Sara, the basics of what we believe—the Trinity, the divinity of Christ, the truths expressed in the Apostles' Creed, salvation by grace through faith—none of these basics are up for grabs. I haven't questioned for a second any of these essential Christian truths."

"But why not?" she demanded. "Haven't I heard you admit that doctrines like the Trinity and the divinity of Christ are mysteriously hidden in Scripture? And don't we have pastoral friends, like Bob and Connie Lundy, who disagree with these 'basics'? They're Unitarian Universalists who believe that everyone is saved and that the goal of evangelism is to tell those who don't know it."

He had no quick response.

After a sip of wine, Sara continued with increased intensity. "What I'm saying is this, Stephen. If you resign because you are uncertain of Christian truth, then I just might decide to resign from Christianity altogether."

"Sara…"

"If the Bible is insufficient to teach what we need to believe, then as far as I am concerned, everything we've believed is up for grabs. And I'm not about to let some old man in Rome, who thinks he's Jesus Christ come to earth, tell me how to believe or live, either."

The energy of this declaration was drawn from the painful guilt of the secret she still vowed her husband would never know—a sorrowful, irreversible act that she feared might be unforgiveable, both in the eyes of those she perceived to be Catholic bigots as well as through the eyes of her own pro-life husband.

Stephen sat paralyzed, caught in his own trap. He had been blind to how his struggles were affecting Sara's faith, but how could he merely set his concerns aside? They were too real.

He wanted to assure her that his questioning did not necessarily lead to Sara's conclusions, but he knew that at this moment she could not hear him.

They finished their meals, then sat quietly sipping coffees.

"Anything else?" A waiter asked.

"No, thank you," Sara said tersely. "We're done. May we have our bill?"

With that, she stood up, threw her napkin on the table, donned her coat, and left for the car. Stephen sheepishly extended his credit card to the waiter and waited. While he strained to ignore the cloud of witnesses eyeing him, he nevertheless abused himself with the words of the psalmist, *He who digs a hole, falls into it himself.*

4

Pᴜʟʟɪɴɢ ɪɴᴛᴏ ᴛʜᴇ ᴘᴀʀᴋɪɴɢ ʟᴏᴛ punctually at eight a.m., Marge noticed Reverend LaPointe's office light already on.

"Good," she muttered. "He'll never get through his mail and e-mail in a month of Sundays."

"Good morning, Marge," Stephen yelled from his office sanctum as he heard her opening the front door, beating her to the punch.

"Morning, Pastor. Have a good retreat?"

"Just grand. Everything fine here?"

"Nothing out of the ordinary. A few people want all of your time, and your e-mail and mail inboxes are overflowing." She began the morning coffee.

"That's why I came in early." He lied a little. "It truly is amazing how enslaving e-mail can be. When I started in ministry, there was no e-mail, no Internet, no computers. Now I can't imagine working without 'em, even if they do eat up most of my time. It's beyond me how the Apostles accomplished anything!"

Marge almost responded that they didn't have computers back then, but caught herself. She wasn't always quick on the uptake when it came to jokes.

She brought Stephen his mug of coffee and cream and then a

ponderous pile of letters and files. "I've already weeded out the junk mail, so have fun."

"Thanks, Marge," he said with feigned offense. "Couldn't you have answered a few of these? Especially these letters from the National Headquarters."

"Not my job, boss."

"Ain't you lucky." They exchanged signs of sympathy and resignation as she left, closing the door behind her.

Stephen's e-mail was open before him, but his mind was elsewhere. Sara wasn't speaking to him. During their ride home the previous night, she had sulked in silence. He had tried several times to break through, but she refused to speak. Before he had turned off the engine, she had stormed from the car, charged through the mudroom and into the kitchen, slamming the door. As he entered, he was hit in the chest with a book—a collection of conversion stories of ex-nuns.

"Here, read the truth about the Roman Church you feel so attracted to," she had exclaimed. "Until you read this, I will hear nothing more about your resigning." She then stomped upstairs and locked the bedroom door.

Stephen had retreated nonplussed to the living room, where he made a fire and considered whether to read Sara's book. He skimmed the front and back covers and then turned randomly to a short conversion story in the middle, but after completing one, he found he really wasn't in the mood.

Stephen was feeling as if his life was without moorings, as if he were adrift in a rough billowing sea beyond sight of land or landmarks. He had glanced over at his favorite seascape above the couch, its beauty now forever scarred by the crease for which Sara had never given him an adequate explanation. She had rehung the newly framed painting, but had remained evasive about the "accident."

Staring at it, his ire had risen as he tried to ignore its flaw. He had considered marching upstairs and demanding an explanation, but then his reason logged in: *Every good general chooses his battles.*

But what had so lit Sara's flame last night? Stephen thought now as he gazed blankly into his computer monitor. *How could she have been that oblivious to the implications of my concerns? But I suppose my stating it so matter-of-factly was a bit much.*

"Ain't that an understatement!" he said castigating himself.

But why had she become so distracted by Catholic issues and accused me of wanting to become a Catholic? Me?! My views about the Catholic Church may have softened, but that doesn't mean I want to become one! Jim might make such a rash move, but I certainly won't.

He turned toward the wall of books beside him, the intellectual tools of this trade he so loved, and thought: *I might have to resign from being a pastor, and maybe leave Congregationalism, but that is no mandate to become Roman Catholic. But where will I go? Which Christian denomination most clearly stands where I do on truth?*

He decided to do what Jim had done, and opened before him an encyclopedia of denominations. Occasionally sipping his coffee, he skimmed it from beginning to end, and then threw it back on the shelf. *Just as Jim had said. I can find something to like and dislike about every one. And besides, this is a distraction; I've work to do.*

But for one more moment, he stared at the encyclopedia resting precariously on its shelf while the question that had crossed Jim's mind crossed his own: *Who am I to stand in judgment of all those churches?*

Up until then, Stephen had been questioning how he might determine which of the many conflicting interpretations of countless Christian beliefs was the most true. But now he was passing his "omniscient, omnipresent, and omnipotent" judgment on entire denominations—each one believing that its interpretation of the Bible or of tradition or of conscience was true. He dropped his face into his hands, bewildered by the complexity and hypocrisy of his situation: *I sit in this office, in this church, because I am their leader. But how can I have the audacity to lead if I haven't a clue where I am going?*

*   *   *

WILLIAM FOUND A CROWD OF STUDENTS in the senior lounge.

"You've discovered our secret hideaway! Welcome," Brad Corvey declared from a cluster of male and female students where three or four conversations strained for attention. "Step up and have a cappuccino on me."

"Actually, I've been here the last few mornings," William said, searching through the crowd for Stacy, "and none of you were here. I figured this was a forgotten spot."

"Hardly. We're here most mornings, but the last few days we've been meeting with the prom committee," Brad said.

William recognized a few other faces, but no Stacy. He joined Brad at the cappuccino maker, pushed the button for café latte, and turned to see Stacy enter.

The din of voices subsided as male and female faces studied the newcomer, and the initial emotional responses ranged from indifference to jealousy to lust.

Brad, the group's self-appointed spokesman, said, "Hello! Come on in and join us."

Spotting William, Stacy said pleasantly but detached, "No, thank you," and passed around the crowd to William. She lowered her voice. "We need to talk."

"Sure." Retrieving a café latte for Stacy, he motioned her to a pair of stuffed chairs separated from the crowd near Miss Duryea's desk, ignoring the stares and comments from the gang. "Let's go there."

As they sat down, Stacy said, "Well, I've got good news and bad news." She paused for a sip from her steaming cup. "The good news is that I'm still alive. The bad news is that I can never see you again."

"What? You're not serious." He was puzzled by this emotionless revelation from his new heartthrob. "What do you mean, *alive?*"

"Oh, I'm just joking about that," she said, though William wasn't convinced. "My father hit the fan, not me, when I told him about talking with you yesterday. But he was even more angry when I told him who you were. He went crazy." Stacy was beyond crying. For years she had dealt with her father's wrath, but this last fit of craziness was far beyond her last straw.

"I don't understand. You thought it might make him more open to me."

"My extremely suspicious and conspiracy-crazed father thinks that your father is secretly a Catholic priest."

"A *what?*"

"A Roman Catholic priest posing as a Protestant minister to 'infiltrate and subvert our Protestant faith.'"

William was lost. "But that's absurd. Wacko! My father has never been a Catholic. He never even mentions the Catholic Church at home. Whenever he talks about the Catholic Church in sermons or Bible studies, he always points out its heretical beliefs. Where'd your father get such a ridiculous idea?"

"I don't know. He didn't say, but he's totally convinced and insists that I stay away from you—'for the good of my soul.' And given what he has done before, I'm sure that he will be even more vigilant in watching my every move." Tears glistened in her eyes.

William looked up and noticed that the crowd was watching. "Come on, Stacy, let's go. I'll walk you to class." They dropped their cups in the waste container and walked past the other students, who returned to their conversations. As they passed, William noticed a wink from Brad. He responded with a friendly smile as he led Stacy out.

"Now what, though?" William asked. "I want to keep seeing you, even if I can't take you to the Formal."

Stacy stared ahead as they walked down the main school hallway. "I don't know, but this time I'm not giving in to my father's craziness." She stopped and turned toward him. "I'll tell you what. Let's meet again on Monday, same place, same time. By then, things may have subsided. I doubt it, but regardless, I think by then we'll know what we need to do. See you then." Stacy stood on her tiptoes and gave him an unexpected kiss on the cheek. William dropped his books as he watched her walk away.

"But what about tomorrow morning?" he called after her, but she was gone.

"I saw that! I saw that!" Brad said from behind a cluster of freshman girls.

"Spying on us!" William said with feigned indignation.

"Not spying. Just keeping track of my friend's conquests."

William slammed him with a biology book as they jolted toward class at the ringing of first bell.

*   *   *

"Please hold my calls, Marge," Stephen said as he walked from his study. "I'm going into the sanctuary."

"Fine." Marge was accustomed to Stephen's solitary escapes for prayer. She herself couldn't fathom praying alone for more than five minutes and had often considered spying on him to see what he actually did.

He left the newer office annex, constructed in the mid-'70s, and followed the freshly shoveled sidewalk to the church. Like so many other New England churches, First Congregational of Witzel's Notch was a large, white wooden structure with a single central steeple. The main entrance was on the south side facing the parking lot. Because the sanctuary temperature was kept around 60 degrees during the week, he left his coat on. To the left of the entrance was a bank of light switches. He turned on only the sconce light above the communion table positioned directly in front of the central pulpit. The rest of the sanctuary was softly hued from natural light passing through the slightly swirled, imperfect surfaces of the 130-year-old clear glass windows.

Up the center aisle he paced and felt the familiar strangeness he always felt when the church was empty. *This was made to be full of souls worshipping their Savior.* When he reached the front, he stepped up into the pulpit. He turned and looked out at the empty pews, envisioning the faces that normally gazed upward, and felt the weight of his pulpit responsibility being challenged by his growing hopelessness.

The text on which he was to preach in two days came to mind. Without reservation, he knew that he could boldly proclaim from the housetops, let alone this pulpit, the same answer Simon Peter had given to Jesus' question—that Jesus was and is the Son of God, our Savior, our Redeemer, our Lord and King. *But beyond that eternal truth,* he wondered, *what more can I proclaim so boldly?*

The empty pews reminded him of the thousands of people who over the years had occupied them expecting to hear the Christian faith preached "in the manner to which they have become accustomed."

For some reason, that haunting text from Second Thessalonians flashed through his mind: *Stand fast and hold to the traditions which you were taught by us, either by word of mouth or by letter.*

Stephen knew that this was how God sometimes tried to get his attention, to redirect his thinking or confront his convictions.

Looking out intently from his pulpit as if he were preaching, he wrestled mentally with the confluence of this verse and the many other things with which he had been struggling.

Assuming that the traditions Paul taught orally were precisely what Jesus had taught His Apostles, who then, under the guidance of the Holy Spirit, had passed them on faithfully to their disciples and to new converts and so forth, wouldn't this make these "traditions" equivalent to Jesus' words? But isn't this what constitutes the New Testament?

Not necessarily, Stephen realized, again with discomfort. A previous revelation surged through his mind: *These traditions had been delivered by word of mouth as well as by letter, and it is obvious that many of the things Paul taught his churches were never recorded in any New Testament document. How then am I to "stand fast and hold" to unrecorded teachings of Jesus?*

He recalled that many of the denominations listed in the encyclopedia claimed that "they" had preserved these early traditions, and therefore believed that they were more faithful to the early Christian witness. *Yet each one came up with different conclusions and models. Which, if any, of these self-proclaimed authorities is reliable?*

"Preach it, brother!" A voice rang out from the shadows under the rear balcony. In the dim light, Stephen couldn't tell who it was, but the voice was familiar.

"Who goes there? Come forth and reveal thyself," Stephen responded in Shakespearean prose.

"'Tis I, your lost, infidel friend." Jim Sarver stepped into the light.

"Jim, what are you doing here?" Stephen bounded from the pulpit, elated to see his good friend.

Clasping hands, Jim said, "After the retreat was over, I hung around by myself for a while, and then decided to check up on you on my drive back to Connecticut."

"How long can you stay?"

"Actually, only a few minutes, because I need to get home. Things there aren't on an even keel yet. I still need to find a job."

"Other than my sermon prep, I'm basically free until a three o'clock appointment," Stephen said. "Come, let's go across the street where we can talk."

They left the church together, walked through the snow and across the country lane, and into the homey warmth of the Pewter

Duck, a village inn with roots that went back almost as far as First Church across the street. They drank coffee and ate freshly baked muffins as Stephen recapped all that had transpired since he left the retreat, including his unsettled disagreement with Sara. He then shared the big question which had plagued him in the pulpit.

"Stephen, that is the same thing that drove me from my pulpit, but as I told you, that is also why I am becoming a Catholic."

"But why?" Stephen said with curtailed intensity because everyone in the restaurant was either a member of his congregation or knew who he was.

"Stephen, did anything that I said on Monday make sense? And by the way, did you get a chance to look at the book I gave you?"

"Yes, I've read much of Keating, but most of what you and he have said only add mortar and bricks to my dilemma. If the Catholic Church is not the 'whore of Babylon,'" he said with sarcasm, "but can be considered at least as valid as any other Christian denomination, then this is just one more contentious opinion to throw into my pot of confusion."

"Stephen, I want to speak straight with you, and then I need to go. I am becoming a Catholic because of this very issue—because I believe, through the witness of Scripture and history, that the Catholic Church is the only church that has a valid claim to the authority needed to solve this dilemma. A famous Anglican minister who converted to the Catholic Church named John Henry Newman once wrote, 'To be deep in history is to cease to be a Protestant.' Stephen, this is exactly what I have found to be true. The more I examine Scripture and history, the more I am convinced that only the Catholic Church can claim to be the continuing church that Jesus Christ established in His Apostles—and every other Christian denomination or tradition is essentially in schism. Why? Because the flip side of what Newman said is also true: to *cease* to be deep in history is to become Protestant.

"Tell me, Stephen, how many Christians can you name between the Apostles and Martin Luther?"

"Augustine and Francis of Assisi and..." Stephen was already pulling a blank, "...and of course Tyndale, Wycliffe, and John Huss."

"And that's all?"

"Well, of course there were thousands more."

"Yes, but name some of them."

Stephen was embarrassingly frustrated. "But that's the problem. The Church was hijacked in the fourth century by the pagan Roman emperor Constantine and lost its moorings. Sure, there were always believers in Christ, but they were the ones persecuted by the Catholic Church."

"Stephen, the names you mentioned are revealing for they fit nicely with the revisionist, pro-Reformation slant on history we were taught in seminary. The Reformers proof-texted from Augustine to buttress their rebellion; Tyndale, Wycliffe and Huss were rebels who set the stage for the Reformation; and, of course, everyone loves St. Francis. But what few Protestants recognize is that Augustine and Francis were unswerving, tireless defenders of the Catholic Church against her attackers. Do you know what Augustine said about schism?"

"No," Stephen answered matter-of-factly.

"In a letter to a Luther-type reformer of his own day, he wrote that no matter how bad leaders might get in the Church, there was never any justification for schism, primarily because schism implies putting private judgment above the authority of the Church, which is heresy according to Scripture. Therefore, bad popes, bishops, or priests never negate the Church's authenticity any more than do the liberal, self-justifying leaders of your Congregationalist or my Presbyterian denominations. Not one of the churches—Roman Catholic, Congregational, Presbyterian, Methodist, Episcopal, Eastern Orthodox, Assembly of God, Church of Christ, etc., etc., etc., have any claim to perfection. All Christian churches are hospitals for sinners. The question is, *which* of these thousands of churches is *true*? I think what you are missing is *not* more faith, or a more thorough knowledge of Scripture, but a more accurate knowledge of history."

Jim thanked with a nod the waitress who had topped their coffees, then continued.

"Too many Christians think that all they need is the Bible, as if it somehow dropped out of Heaven in King James English with the words of Jesus in red, detached from any historical context. But we still believe in Jesus in the year 2000 specifically because the Christian faith and the Church have been around for 2,000 years since His birth, death, and resurrection. There is a continuous history of millions of faithful men and women who lived and died for Christ and His Church. If you want to know how to discern which of the hundreds of contradictory opinions is true, you need to look back through history to discover which church has always, continually, and sacrificially spoken for Christ."

"But how can one do this?" Stephen said. "There are so many contradictory presentations of history."

"You start with the Early Church Fathers, the writers who learned their faith directly from an Apostle or a disciple of an Apostle."

"I guess this is what I keep hearing from you and Keating, but why haven't I heard this before?"

"Isn't that obvious? Because the Church of the Early Fathers is the Catholic Church of today. This is what converted Newman. One hundred fifty years ago, he had achieved a great reputation as an Anglican preacher and writer. He undertook an exhaustive study of the Early Fathers to prove that the Anglican Church was the true Church, the true middle way between Catholicism and Protestantism. But in the end, his studies convinced him that the early Church was Catholic, and that he had no choice but to resign and become Catholic in the midst of a dangerously anti-Catholic England."

"But Jim, last night Sara shoved a book in my face that contains conversion stories of nuns who left the Catholic Church to become Protestant. Twenty ex-nuns!" Stephen exclaimed. "How do I answer this? If what you say is true, then how is it that Catholic nuns don't discover the Bible or Jesus until after they leave the Catholic Church?"

"Stephen, I've read that book and a similar collection of one hundred conversion stories of Catholic priests who became Protestant. I read them both from cover to cover because their claims stood as a stark contradiction to my journey. But in the process I discovered something significant about these stories. Tell me, in your new-members classes, from which Protestant denominations have you received transfers?"

"I suppose, over the years, from every mainline denomination—Lutheran, Episcopal, Methodist, Baptist, Presbyterian. We've even received a few ex-Eastern Orthodox and an ex-Mormon."

"And in the process of their 'conversions' to Congregationalism, did any of them claim to have discovered Jesus for the first time, even though they had received continuous religious training in the churches of their birth?"

"Not all, of course," Stephen admitted. "Some married into the Congregational Church, but yes, many profess powerful conversions to Christ and have little if anything good to say about their previous churches."

"Exactly," Jim answered. "What those priests and nuns experienced is far too commonplace. Thousands of people from every denomination have had similar testimonies: they passed through the religious 'conveyor belts' of their denominations, into seminary, and on into the pastorate without encountering Christ. What they were taught hardly entered their minds, let alone their hearts. Don't you know Protestant ministers who seem to have little faith in Jesus?"

Stephen considered Jim's explanation. Sure, he knew ministers who seemed far from being "Christian" and some who had found Jesus long after seminary. He also remembered with frustration a young man in his first congregation named Derrick, who left in a huff to join an independent, fundamentalist church because Stephen was not teaching the gospel as they were in his new church.

"But Jim, the explanation for these nuns' conversions can't be this simple."

"Remember Jesus' parable of the Sower? The same seed fell on four different types of soil, but only one out of four produced fruit. Remember that great book by the English Puritan Richard Baxter, *The Reformed Pastor*? Back in 1650 he was desperately trying to inspire renewal among Anglican ministers, and he complained that it was a sin when a man became an ordained minister before becoming a Christian. This is not a new phenomenon, or a uniquely Catholic one."

"But Jim, priests and nuns!"

"Stephen, it is sad that priests and nuns can spend so many years dedicating their lives to a Savior they have not come to know. But in the end their conversions to Protestantism say nothing about the validity of the Catholic Church, let alone any church."

"Yes, but in the one story I read, the ex-nun claimed that during her fifty years as a Catholic and more than thirty as a nun, she had never owned a Bible. When she finally received one from a Protestant friend and read it, she discovered the gospel for the first time and left the nunnery for evangelicalism."

"Stephen, I want to believe the sincerity and honesty of this sister in Christ, so I won't presume otherwise," Jim replied. "I suppose it is possible that she never owned a personal copy of the Bible, just as it is possible for Protestants. But to never hear or read Scripture is literally impossible for any Catholic—priest, nun, or lay. Every Mass of every day of the week has two or three major readings from Scripture. And every priest, religious sister, or brother is required to pray the Daily Office of the Church, which consists of readings from the Psalms and other Scriptures. Between the Mass and the Daily Office, they would easily read through the entire Bible every two or three years. The only way a Catholic nun or priest could go thirty years without hearing the Bible is by not listening. Sadly, this obviously happens and the devil laughs. Catholics as well as Protestants own Bibles and catechisms that serve more to hold down coffee tables than to inspire their faith."

Jim waved to the waitress for the bill.

"Tell you what, Stephen. I need to go, but I know a spiritual director not far from you who can help. He's a priest out at St. Francis de Sales parish in Jamesfield, about two hours northeast of here. His name is Father William Bourque."

"I don't know, Jim. I'm not ready..."

"No, Stephen, not for that. Father Bourque is a holy, Christian man. I know from experience that he can help you work through this. He helped me a lot. I spent a week at St. Francis under his direction discerning what I should do. What makes him particularly sensitive to what you are going through is that he is a clergy convert."

"A clergy convert?"

"He was a Lutheran minister before he converted to the Catholic Church and became a priest. He's an author of several books on the spiritual life."

Jim rose from the table. "Stephen, this is just a thought, but I really do need to get back on the road. Please, call if you have any questions. I want to help you through this in any way I can."

"Thanks, Jim." Stephen hugged this great old friend. "You were there twenty-five years ago when I needed your witness. I'm sure you'll hear from me."

Jim left for his car while Stephen returned to his office to give attention to his flood of e-mails and other correspondence and to finalize his sermon. As he cut through the church toward the office annex, he glanced hesitantly toward the pulpit, and confronted himself: *What will I have the courage to preach in that pulpit in which I am so unworthy to stand?*

5

"Hello, is this Raeph?"

"Yeah, who wants to know?"

"Hi, Raeph, this is Walter. Walter Horscht."

"Walter, hey, great to hear from you. How are things up there in the North Country?"

"Actually, we don't live up north anymore. We moved down to Witzel's Notch, New Hampshire."

"That's still too far north for my blood, but now you're closer. Great," Raeph said. "How are things going?"

Walter felt reassured as he heard the voice of this familiar brother in Christ—who fully understood and shared his convictions about the impending apocalyptic crisis. "Everything's fine, but I've got a quick question for you. I only have a few minutes, but I need your advice."

"Go ahead, shoot."

Walter was startled by Raeph's choice of words. "Remember when we used to talk about the urgency of things? How the timetable of God's judgment was more imminent than ever, and that we might be called upon to make drastic choices, even dangerous ones if necessary?"

"Of course, and you should have been at our last meeting. Reverend Harmond's last novel about the Rapture has become a best-seller, on the front shelves of every bookstore in America. People have been calling the FC2C office from all over the country."

"Raeph, do you truly believe that Catholic priests have infiltrated our churches?"

"Believe it? Walter, how can you doubt it? Whenever I see liberalism destroying another church or another believer—whenever I hear someone claim that it doesn't matter what religion you believe— I know that behind it is the watering-down influence of Catholic propaganda. In the past, the Catholic Church claimed that it was the only true church, but do you know what the Pope recently did? He led a worship service that included Buddhists, Hindus, Muslims, and even Jews! And wherever you encounter this relativism, you encounter the influence of a Catholic."

On the surface this seemed to confirm Walter's hunches; yet did it justify the drastic measures to which God was calling him?

"Raeph, do you recall how during the English Reformation, Catholic priests and laity who were secretly infiltrating England to restore the Catholic faith were captured, imprisoned, and then executed? Do you think this was justified?"

"Justified? Walter, if the faithful had not done what they did, England would probably be a Catholic nation today! All over the world, Catholic infiltrators needed to be squelched, even here in New England, but don't forget what they did to us—the millions of faithful people who were innocently murdered during the Inquisition and the reign of Bloody Mary. And don't for a second listen to Catholic apologists who claim that these actions ran contrary to official Catholic teaching. I read just last night that none other than their most prized theologian, Thomas Aquinas, defended the burning of people they considered heretics for the same reason that counterfeiters were executed. Whenever we Protestants have resorted to force, it has been in retaliation to their brutality and in the defense of the innocent."

Walter responded hesitantly, "But would these kinds of actions be justified today?"

"That's a hard question, but in drastic times, sometimes the faithful need to take drastic measures. Why are you asking all this?"

Walter wanted to tell it all, but a voice from within stopped him. This was to be an act that he alone was to carry out—like the secret missions of his military past. It was to be between him and the Lord.

"Oh, nothing particular," he said. "I guess I've felt out of touch up here where no one, including my family, shares our convictions."

"It's a scary time to live, but also a glorious one. Imagine: we ourselves might soon experience the great and powerful hand of God!"

"Yeah, that's exciting," Walter said with mixed emotions. "Raeph, I need to go. Maybe I'll see you at the next FC2C meeting."

"Great, Walter. You take care, and remember, don't let the papists bite!"

"See you, Raeph."

Walter hung up and for a moment stared at the phone. He then hurriedly retrieved his coat and rushed to the car to pick up Stacy...*before that papist's son steals her heart!*

*   *   *

"Reverend lapointe, a call on line one," Stephen heard Marge call over their archaic intercom. *That stubborn board,* Stephen complained to himself. *Convincing them to install a newer, digital version was like telling the inventor of shoestrings that Velcro works better for kids.*

"Is it urgent, Marge? I've got to get this sermon done, and my three o'clock appointment will be here any minute."

"The call is from a Reverend Gary Harmond, who also called yesterday. He wasn't clear about why he was calling." Marge held back on the rest of what she knew; she preferred to remain neutral on all controversies.

"Reverend Gary Harmond?" Stephen wracked his brain. "Marge, I know that name, but I can't place it. Is he a local minister?"

"He says he's the president of a ministry called FC2C: Former Catholics To Catholics."

"Oh, *that* Gary Harmond."

"There's more than one?"

"Yeah, well, his literature and anti-Catholic tracts are quite well known," Stephen said. "But why is he calling me?"

"Like I said, he wasn't clear," she lied. "Do you want me to take his name and tell him you're unavailable?"

"Oh, no, I'll take the call, thanks." Stephen thought it strange that he was receiving a phone call from the nation's foremost anti-Catholic writer and speaker when for the first time in his life he was considering the Catholic side of things. *Providential, or what!*

"Good afternoon, Reverend Harmond," Stephen said as he answered the phone. "What a pleasant surprise."

"Then you know who I am, Reverend LaPointe?"

"Why, of course, and please call me Stephen. I've been familiar with your writings for years, and I suppose much of what I've told my congregations about the dangers of the Catholic Church has been lifted from them, if you don't object?"

"Of course not, and please call me Gary, though enemies have an assortment of other nicknames."

"Gary, I have a counseling appointment in five minutes that I can't postpone, so it's your nickel. What can I do for you?"

"Well, if you know who I am, and you're familiar with the FC2C's tracts, then you should know the motivation behind my work. And since you indicated that you've actually used, if not plagiarized, our materials..."

"Incessantly."

"Good," Harmond said. "Then it makes it easier to pose my question without beating around the bush. One of your parishioners called me, very concerned. He said he once heard you teach—when you've been defending your pro-life positions, which I strongly commend you for—that using contraception is a sin."

"I don't remember stating it quite that strongly, but yes, I do believe that contraception is wrong. But why has this aroused your attention?"

"If you don't mind, Stephen, may I ask how you arrived at this position?"

Sensing the need to be cautious, Stephen, nevertheless, decided to answer straight away. "It's connected to my convictions against abortion and my awareness of how easily our culture has blindly accepted this form of murder. At one time I was basically pro-choice. I thought it was the more loving, sensitive position. Then in seminary and during my first years in the pastorate, I became convinced that abortion was the least loving thing to do for the mother, the fetus, and the father, and in magnitude abortion is the modern holocaust, worse in numbers than even Stalin's or Hitler's programs of mass extermination. What shocked me was recognizing how our culture had grown to accept what only a hundred years ago all Christians agreed was murder.

"Did you know, Gary, that up until 1930, all Christians were equally against abortion and contraception, seeing them both as grave sins? But after the Episcopalians boldly accepted contraception that year at their annual conference, the majority of Christian denominations eventually folded under the pressure of the pro-contraception lobby. Now most Christians not only accept contraception, but also support a woman's right to abort her baby. It occurred to me that these two issues were interconnected. Eventually, I became convinced that contraception is just as lethal a tool for preventing life as abortion, especially since most contraceptive devices are abortifacients. It is clear that the contraceptive mentality of our culture has altered how we view sex, marriage, and the family, and the results are all around us—the traditional family has been replaced by every conceivable alternative. As bad as abortion is, I believe that the across-the-board acceptance of contraception has been the more heinous tool used by the devil to lull our society into its present immoral culture of death."

"But as you said," Harmond responded, "this isn't an across-the-board acceptance. You do know that the Catholic Church still teaches what in essence you believe."

"Yes, that is true. Actually, I discovered that later and was quite surprised."

"Why was that?"

"Well, Gary," Stephen played the devil's advocate, "given all that your tracts reveal, I was surprised to discover how firmly they stood against so much opposition for a position so contrary to the devil's agenda. As the whore of Babylon, led by the Antichrist, it seemed odd that they would take such an unpopular, Christlike stand."

"It's all a smokescreen, of course. You know as well as I do that the average Catholic in the pew doesn't follow Roman Catholic teaching. You see, the Catholic Church projects this calculated position precisely because it appears so Christlike, thereby attracting people who want to be faithful to Jesus Christ. But then in time, after their sensibilities have been numbed by rituals and other convoluted teachings, the innocent are allowed to drift into immorality, under the guise that whatever they do, of course, can be forgiven with one visit to the confessional."

"But, Gary, that is absurd. Are you admitting then that the use of contraceptives is un-Christlike?"

"I'm only confirming that whatever appears Christlike in Catholic teaching is but a sham."

Stephen didn't like where this was leading. It might be fun to debate Gary, especially now that his eyes had been opened to how fanciful and uninformed Gary's accusations were, but this was the wrong time. Plus, he was still curious as to why he called.

"Listen, Gary, why don't we continue this discussion another time—as I said, my counseling appointment is probably waiting for me even as we speak. But back to where we started, why does my stand on this issue warrant your call?"

"It seems that your parishioner was so upset by your apparent Catholic position on this and other things, that he has become convinced—now hold onto your seat—that you are a Catholic priest in disguise, infiltrating the Protestant Church to destroy it from within."

"*What?*" Stephen said, dumbfounded. Laughing, he repeated, "What? Where in God's name did he ever get this idea? Who is this man?" He was at a loss, but then remembered: *Thevoiceoftruth.*

"I'm not at liberty to divulge this, you understand," Harmond said.

"But this is ridiculous. I just told you how much I've read and used your own tracts throughout my pastorate to teach against the Catholic Church."

"Stephen, hey, I only called because I promised him I would check things out. I didn't say I believed him."

"But I presume you're a busy man, so your call tells me that you consider his accusation at least plausible."

"He begged me to call and, well, to get him off my back, I promised him. Are there Roman Catholics infiltrating Protestant pulpits? You've read my stuff, so you know I believe this could be possible. But to be honest, I find your views on contraception quite extraordinary."

"Pastor LaPointe?" Marge's voice echoed over the intercom. "Your counseling appointment is waiting."

"Thank you. Please tell him it will only be a moment."

Stephen returned to his phone call. He felt the urge to push the envelope with this ex-Catholic, anti-Catholic apologist, whom Keating had specifically demonstrated was blindly misinformed by his inadequate Catholic formation.

"Gary, I'm far from being your Catholic infiltrator, but I have come to see that much of what you teach about the Catholic Church is untrue. Your tracts are laced with half-truths that build on innuendo, claiming that Catholics believe and practice things that the Catholic Church does not teach and has always taught are heresy and forbidden for Catholics."

"*Excuse* me?" Gary responded with rising anger.

"I was just saying…"

"I know what you said!" Gary answered in such a way that Stephen knew this anti-Catholic apologist was standing, yelling into the phone. "How dare you challenge my integrity. In case you don't remember, I was brought up Catholic. I know from experience what the Catholic Church teaches."

Remembering his conversation with Jim, Stephen countered, "I realize that, but I also know lots of ex-Lutherans, ex-Episcopalians, and ex-Presbyterians who claim they know their childhood faith, but in reality never…"

"That makes no difference. What I've printed I know to be true, and anyone who claims differently is the devil's mouthpiece!"

Stephen had stuck his hand into a hornet's nest. "Gary, sorry. I didn't mean to offend you. Listen, I do need to go. Perhaps we can pick this up another time?"

"Gladly, in any arena. You name the time and the place."

Stephen recalled with regret that Reverend Harmond was notorious for taking on all comers in debates across the country, and Stephen had no interest in going there. "Please leave your phone number with my secretary, and maybe sometime next week we can continue this conversation over the phone."

"That's fine, but…"

"Please, I do need to go. Here's Marge, she'll take your number." He punched the hold button and breathed a sigh of relief. *That was crazy!* But thinking twice, he recognized how providential this call was. *This is certainly how God works. But why?* It struck him that Keating's description of this sometimes volatile apologist was right on. *But why such pent-up anger?* He wondered how much of the rest of what Keating had said was equally true.

Marge knocked first, then opened his door. "Pastor, I hope you don't mind, but I fibbed about your appointment. He had to cancel, but by what I could overhear of your conversation with Reverend Harmond, I figured you might want a way out."

"You were right on that score," Stephen said gratefully. "Did you get Reverend Harmond's phone number?"

"That and a lot more." Her eyes rolled with feigned bewilderment.

"We'll talk about that later. Thanks."

After Marge had left, Stephen sat in the privacy of his office, taking in all that he had experienced over the last few days. He considered taking a few moments to review his sermon notes, but then realized that in two hours he would need to go home and face an extremely upset and confused Sara. He picked up the book that she had insisted he read, but conceded that Jim's analogy more than explained what little of the stories he had read. He decided instead to spend his remaining time in prayer.

He also thought a dozen roses might help.

6

THE DIM, DANCING LIGHT of a scented candle illumined the pages of an open Bible and a green, cloth-bound journal. Stephen sat motionless, his hands flat together and his head bowed in the privacy of his basement study. This was actually just the corner of the basement in their new home, but Stephen had designed the space to be quite cozy. An old door laid on top of a pair of two-drawer filing cabinets for a desk, self-standing bookshelves all around, and a curtain from ceiling to floor to his left to block out extraneous noise. It was to this private, holy space that Stephen had retreated this Saturday morning, like every morning, around six a.m. for devotions, prayer, and journal-writing.

Sometime during his seminary years, he had begun lighting a small candle as a part of this morning ritual. Through his readings, he had learned about the ancient tradition of lighting a candle as a symbol of one's prayer being elevated to the Father. This was scriptural and traditionally liturgical, and even though as a confirmed

Congregationalist he wasn't keen on traditions, he liked the aura of God's presence that seemed to arrive whenever his small candle was lit and the thin wisp of its black smoke rose to the heavens. Stephen considered this spot more holy than the cold, barren, public atmosphere of First Church's sanctuary.

To anyone observing him, Stephen would have appeared the holiest of saints, lost in prayer, communing with the Father. But inside, he was in utter turmoil. Never in his life could he remember feeling more perplexed, as if lost in an endless woods without a compass. No matter how much he tried, he had been unable to console Sara. She would not have it. It was as if a demon of anger and bitterness had been hiding deep in her heart for years, waiting for just the right moment to emerge, and had done so with a vengeance. Nothing Stephen said or did could regain the affection of her heart. It was as if someone had convinced her that he could no longer be trusted; that his words of assurance were nothing more than sugar-coated deception. For the third night in a row he had been relegated to the couch, their bedroom door locked from the inside.

This had all been instigated, of course, by telling her of his growing conviction that he *must* resign from his pulpit. *"Must" is a powerful word.* He certainly understood how unsettling this was for Sara, for his only option if he resigned was to return to school, and how would he support his family?

He also sensed that her wall of anger had been particularly exacerbated by his admission that he had read a Catholic book. *But why would this turn the tide so drastically?* Sure, the witness of Jim, both in words and in action, along with the winsome logic of Keating's book, had made the Catholic Church appear less threatening for the first time in his life. *But become a Catholic? Why would she accuse me of this?*

It was the first time this possibility truly crossed his mind. As he gazed at a picture of his family, distorted by the rising heat of the candle, he sensed a new panic rising within. *Is Jim's conclusion—is Ginny's, or Keating's—the only answer to my dilemma? Is it inevitable?* Stephen's longstanding and deep-seated prejudice still spoke louder than anything these otherwise trustworthy voices might claim.

He dropped his hands. Before him was a pile of notes for

tomorrow's sermon, Sara's book on the ex-Catholic nuns, and a book of quotes from early Church writers he had found in a box of lesser-used books from seminary. The urgency of reviewing these three screamed for his attention. His sermon was getting more awkward every time he looked at it, because he felt uneasy about ignoring the Catholic implications of Simon Peter's confession and Jesus' response. On the other hand, Sara's book of ex-Catholic testimonies stood as a constant objection to any positive Catholic consideration. And in between these two contradictions was a book on the Early Church Fathers.

As he scrutinized its red cover, his attention was arrested by the simple white drawing of the *Ichthus*, Greek for "fish", just below the title. This ancient symbol of Christ from the times of the catacombs and early martyrs flashed at him with a light much brighter than the flickering glow of his now dwindling candle. Focusing on the *Ichthus* symbol he sensed that in this book he would be connecting over the expanse of nearly two thousand years with voices he might be able to trust—who had learned directly from the Apostles or from their disciples exactly what Jesus had taught and meant.

Stephen opened the book randomly to the *First Apology* written by St. Justin the Martyr, a Christian philosopher who lived from approximately 100 to 165 A.D. Stephen began reading until he came across a section in which Justin described how a new believer was brought into their Christian community:

> Whoever is convinced and believes that what they are taught and told by us is the truth, and professes to be able to live accordingly, is instructed to pray and to beseech God in fasting for the remission of their former sins, while we pray and fast with them. Then they are led by us to a place where there is water; and there they are reborn in the same kind of rebirth in which we ourselves were reborn: in the name of God, the Lord and Father of all, and of our Savior, Jesus Christ, and of the Holy Spirit, they receive the washing with water. For Christ said, "Unless you be reborn, you shall not enter into the kingdom of heaven" … The reason for doing this, we have learned from the Apostles.

As Stephen read this alternative explanation to how he had always explained being "born again," he felt as if this ancient witness was somehow selecting and then connecting the dots from amongst the wide range of opinions that had been plaguing and destroying his confidence. Justin emphasized that conversion involved becoming convinced, then believing, professing, being instructed, and being *born again* through Baptism.

Stephen felt weak and yet exhilarated at the same time. *How different this view of Baptism is compared to anything I've ever taught.* But he also realized that it wasn't obscure, for he knew that this was basically what Episcopalians, Catholics, Eastern Orthodox, and other traditionalist Christians taught. *Who am I to say they are wrong?*

He then came across Justin's description of early Christian worship:

> After we have thus washed the one who has believed and has assented, we lead him where those who are called brethren are gathered, offering prayers in common and heartily for ourselves and for the one who has been illuminated, and for all others everywhere, so that we may be accounted worthy, now that we have learned the truth, to be found keepers of the commandments, so that we may be saved with an eternal salvation.

According to Justin, therefore, salvation for those who have been baptized and thereby illumined to the truth will depend on whether they are "accounted worthy…found keepers of the commandments." So far Stephen had found no mention of the sole necessity of Scripture as the primary criterion of faith, let alone "faith alone." He continued reading:

> Having concluded the prayers, we greet one another with a kiss. Then there is brought to the president of the brethren bread and a cup of water and of watered wine; and taking them, he gives praise and glory to the Father of all, through the name of the Son and of the Holy Spirit; and he himself gives thanks at some length in order that these things may be deemed worthy. When

> the prayers and the thanksgiving are completed, all the
> people present call out their assent, saying, "Amen!"
> "Amen" in the Hebrew language signifies "so be it". After
> the president has given thanks, and all the people have
> shouted their assent, those whom we call deacons give to
> each one present to partake of the Eucharistic bread and
> wine and water; and to those who are absent they carry
> away a portion.

Stephen recognized nothing unique about this early description of the celebration of the Lord's Supper, except possibly the implication that it might be a frequent celebration, whereas First Church and most other Protestant denominations celebrate Communion only once per month, if at all.

> We call this food Eucharist; and no one else is permitted
> to partake of it, except one who believes our teaching to
> be true and who has been washed in the washing which
> is for the remission of sins and for regeneration, and is
> thereby living as Christ has enjoined.

This was different, though. Few Protestants use the sacramental, Catholic term of "Eucharist," and even fewer bar anyone from communion. But what Stephen read next convinced him that what he taught and how he celebrated the Lord's Supper was at least contrary to what Justin reported:

> For not as common bread nor common drink do we
> receive these; but since Jesus Christ our Savior was made
> incarnate by the word of God and had both flesh and
> blood for our salvation, so too, as we have been taught,
> the food which has been made into the Eucharist by the
> Eucharistic prayer set down by Him, and by the change
> of which our blood and flesh is nourished, is both the
> flesh and the blood of that incarnated Jesus. The Apostles,
> in the Memoirs which they produced, which are called
> Gospels, have thus passed on that which was enjoined
> upon them: that Jesus took bread and, having given

thanks, said, "Do this in remembrance of Me; this is My Body." And in like manner, taking the cup, and having given thanks, He said, "This is My Blood."

Another dot in the wide range of doctrinal options was connected in Stephen's mind, and again, disturbingly, it was more Catholic than Protestant. And with this reference to the real presence of Christ in the Eucharist, he knew he was truly walking on Catholic turf.

In the margin of the page, he saw a reference to another writer. He turned to some quotes from St. Ignatius, the third bishop of Antioch, who died a martyr in the arena in 110 A.D.:

> I have no taste for corruptible food nor for the pleasures of this life. I desire the Bread of God, which is the Flesh of Jesus Christ, who was of the seed of David; and for drink I desire His Blood, which is love incorruptible…Take care, then, to use one Eucharist, so that whatever you do, you do according to God; for there is one Flesh of our Lord Jesus Christ, and one cup in the union of His Blood; one altar, as there is one bishop with the presbytery and my fellow servants, the deacons…the Eucharist is the Flesh of our Savior Jesus Christ, Flesh which suffered for our sins and which the Father, in His goodness, raised up again.

Another marginal reference led him to St. Irenaeus, the second bishop of Lyons, who lived from 140 to 202 A.D.:

> If the body be not saved, then, in fact, neither did the Lord redeem us with His blood; and neither is the cup of the Eucharist the partaking of His Blood nor is the Bread which we break the partaking of His Body…He has declared the cup, a part of creation, to be His own Blood, from which He causes our blood to flow; and the bread, a part of creation, He has established as His own Body, from which He gives increase to our bodies.

Further references led Stephen to other early theologians and bishops. He encountered St. Cyril, a bishop of Jerusalem who lived from 315 to 386 A.D. This place and time were significant in Stephen's mind: *Though this bishop lived during the period when Emperor Constantine made Christianity the official religion of Rome, he nonetheless lived hundreds of miles away in Jerusalem—the home of Jesus and the Apostles. Maybe he was unaffected by any "Romanization" of the faith?*

Stephen read:

> Let us, then, with full confidence, partake of the Body and Blood of Christ. For in the figure of bread His Body is given to you, and in the figure of wine His Blood is given to you, so that by partaking of the Body and Blood of Christ, you might become united in body and blood with Him. For thus do we become Christ-bearers, His Body and Blood being distributed through our members. And thus it is that we become, according to the blessed Peter, sharers of the divine nature...Do not, therefore, regard the Bread and the Wine as simply that: for they are, according to the Master's declaration, the Body and Blood of Christ. Even though the senses suggest to you the other, let faith make you firm. Do not judge in this matter by taste, but be fully assured by the faith, not doubting that you have been deemed worthy of the Body and Blood of Christ.

He was stunned at how clearly these early witnesses confirmed the *Catholic* teaching of the Lord's Supper. He supposed that he could twist the interpretations of the quotes to support other views, but their most direct understanding, individually and together, was the more literal view that somehow by God's mysterious grace, the bread and wine become truly the body and blood of Christ. This ran against more than his senses; it was offensive; it was downright cannibalistic, *as had been the charge leveled against these early Christians by their pagan persecutors,* he remembered, *"flesh-eaters."*

The smoke rose from his devotional candle. *I wonder how many fewer martyrs there would have been if they had insisted that the Lord's Supper was merely symbolic?* But as this last quote from Cyril emphasized, he was not to base his beliefs on his senses, but on faith.

As he further considered this, it also occurred to him that these were the same reasons people throughout the ages have struggled with the doctrines of the Trinity and the Divinity of Christ. *As Jim said, would the first-century Palestinian Jews who saw, touched, and heard Jesus have been able to tell by their senses that He was also the very God and Creator of the Universe? No! Then why base our understanding of the Lord's Supper on our senses and logic, when the literal understanding makes the most sense of the Scriptures and the reports from these early Christian writers?*

Stephen glanced past the book over to his sermon notes and panicked as he realized how much more complicated these voices from the ancient past were making his presentation.

He heard steps coming cautiously down the stairs. He turned to face the curtains, hoping this might be Sara coming to apologize. But a hand reached around the curtain that he knew wasn't hers.

"Dad?" William said softly as head followed hand.

"Yes, William, good morning. Come in." Stephen closed the book and set it aside, out of sight.

"Morning. Hey, sorry to interrupt you, but can we talk for a moment?"

"Sure, what is it?" He directed his oldest son to a slowly disintegrating stuffed chair next to his desk. "Have a seat in Grampa's favorite chair. But don't get lost in it."

William sat and squirmed until he found a position where the loose springs weren't jabbing him.

"Dad, I've got a strange question to ask." William hesitated. He and his father rarely had problems talking, but he was about to cross uncharted territory. "I've met a new student at school from our past. Do you remember the Horschts? From Red Creek?"

Stephen had not expected to hear this name so early on Saturday morning. "Yes, and that's right," he said, looking with new light at his son, "they did have a daughter named Stacy that used to play with you."

"That's right, and they also moved here a couple of weeks ago. She's pretty sharp. We've been talking nearly every day this week, and I'd like to take her to the Winter Formal."

Stephen and Sara had different views about the pace with which the boys should progress into dating, he being more conservative than she. He didn't want his boys making the same mistakes he did.

"Well, that's good, William. You remember, of course, the guidelines we've laid down?"

"Sure, Dad. Everything's under control. Nothing passionate going on." William, of course, wasn't going to share all that was exploding in his heart. "The problem is, though, well, her father is set against her seeing me."

"I can understand why."

"What?"

"Oh, nothing. He's pretty strict, eh?"

"To say the least, but there's more to it," William said. "We thought he'd be more receptive to Stacy going with me to the dance once he found out who I was, but when she told her father, he went berserk. He demanded that she never see me or talk to me again. He told her that he is convinced that you are, well, a Catholic priest in disguise sent to infiltrate the Protestant church."

"He's the one!" Stephen said, reviewing mentally and now understanding the misguided animosity of his anonymous e-mailer. "He actually told her that?"

"Yes, Dad, but what's this all about?"

"William, I really don't know. Apparently, Mr. Horscht is suspicious because he doesn't like some of the things I teach. More likely he has been influenced by the teachings of fanatical anti-Catholics. But nevertheless, I can assure you that his accusations are, of course, absurd."

"I knew that, but what should I do?"

Normally, Stephen would have used humor to prove the foolishness of such accusations. But given his present circumstances, he didn't feel like laughing.

"William, I am certainly no Roman Catholic in hiding, but I am less 'anti-Catholic' than Mr. Horscht. I don't know how to allay his suspicions, though, since many of my views are, at least to him, clearly Catholic. And if he's here this Sunday, he might be even more convinced," he said, thinking out loud.

"What's that, Dad?"

"Oh, nothing. Look, son, I don't know what else to say right now except that his allegations aren't true. But let me think on it. If there is anything I can do, you know I will. Now, let me ask you: are you planning to see her anyway?"

William looked at his father, reading his eyes. "Well, yes, I think so. We meet every morning in the senior lounge to talk…which you know is chaperoned and always crowded with other seniors."

"Just be careful that you don't make things more difficult for her."

"We won't. Thanks, Dad."

"It's OK. Have you seen your mother yet this morning?"

"Yeah, and it doesn't appear that her mood has improved any. She made coffee and then went back to her room. What happened, anyway?"

"Oh, the usual. We misunderstood one another and now we're paying for it. My hope is that we can straighten it out sooner than later."

"I think I'll just stay out of the way," William said as he awkwardly extracted himself from the chair.

"I don't blame you. See you later, son."

"Sure, Dad." William left through the curtain and returned upstairs.

Stephen stared as the curtain settled to stillness. *This is weird,* he thought. *Just when I am recognizing, for the first time in my life, that the Catholic Church is a whole lot closer to the truth than I ever imagined, some fundamentalist whacko wants to burn me at the stake for being a subversive! And if I give even one hint that I'm softening my anti-Catholic views, I'll be confirming his suspicions, destroying my son's love life, and mortifying my wife, possibly driving her away from the faith entirely.*

He turned back toward his desk: a book of ex-Catholic nuns now joyfully in love with Jesus; a selection of quotes from the Early Church Fathers sounding awfully Catholic; and a half-finished sermon getting less and less finished.

"Aw, to hell with it," Stephen said as he pushed away from his desk. "I'd rather shovel snow!"

*   *   *

"Helen, where's stacy?" Walter asked in as calm and controlled a voice as he could muster. The morning's rest had done him well, but all night at work he had wrestled with his daughter's cavorting with that papist's son. He decided, by the grace of God, that the only way to protect her was to love her.

"She's in her room, why? You left in such a huff last night, I doubt if she wants to speak with you."

"I don't blame her," he replied. "She's got every reason to be mad at me. I just want to apologize."

Helen had long since given up trying to change her husband's mind about anything. That only made matters worse.

Walter walked upstairs and then down the hall to Stacy's new room in their home of two weeks.

"Stacy?" He tapped lightly on the door. "Can I talk with you?"

At first he heard nothing, then a soft rustling, then the slow turning of the lock, and finally the door opened slightly. Walter cautiously pushed the door open farther and, walking in, saw Stacy standing by her window gazing blankly out into their new back yard. She was still in her robe and slippers.

"Stacy, honey." He walked toward her. "I'm sorry about yesterday. I didn't mean to get angry. I promised that I wouldn't lose my temper any more, but well, you know me. I can never seem to follow through on anything."

Stacy stood silently, staring out at an empty, disheveled doghouse left by the previous owners and, next to the garage, the pile of trash they had removed from the house when they moved in.

"I just want what's best for you," he continued. "I'm afraid of the same things happening to you that happened to girls I grew up with and, frankly, what I did to girls before I came to know Jesus."

"But Dad, this Catholic stuff about William's father. This is absurd. William told me that he has never seen anything that gives even a hint to what you claim. He said that the Catholic Church is never even mentioned at home."

Walter was getting angry again. *How dare she challenge what I know to be true! Of course his father—or his mother—wouldn't talk about it, even at home. I bet their son doesn't even know.* This thought calmed him down.

"Stacy, I'm sorry that I said this to you. I hadn't planned to say anything to you or your mother, but it slipped out. You know me and my conspiracy theories." He knew that he was a fool in their eyes, but someday he would show them all.

"Listen, honey, let me think on it for a while," he said. "For the time being, I only ask that you be careful. Don't be alone with him, or any boy for that matter. Stay safely in groups, and you won't be tempted to do something you'll regret for the rest of your life."

Stacy turned from the window, surprised to hear her father speaking so sensitively. "Dad, if I promise to stay with a group, may I go with William to the Winter Formal next Friday night?"

Walter studied his daughter and saw the love of his life. There was no one more beautiful in his eyes. Any young man would love to have this maturing young woman. He only wanted to protect her.

"Stacy, I'll think about it. I promise," he said with a smile, knowing that by next Friday, this might be a moot point.

"Thank you, Daddy." She turned and hugged him, while he hugged her back.

But from past experiences, she knew that this kind of promise essentially meant "no."

Looking at herself, over her father's shoulder in the mirror above the dresser, she made herself a promise—a promise she would not break, come what may.

*   *   *

STANDING IN HER BATHROBE and slippers, Sara watched from her second-floor bedroom window as her husband shoveled an inch of overnight snow from their driveway. She studied his motions, his familiar gait, his favorite green-knit ski cap, his tan insulated coveralls, and his calf-length, insulated boots. She watched this man to whom she had been married for nineteen years, with whom she had shared her bed and conceived two wonderful sons. She looked with an aching yearning, for there was the man she had known and loved for so long; yet, she wondered whether she really knew him at all.

During their first years of dating and marriage, he had been so enthusiastically focused in his ministry. This had been so contagious that she caught it herself, basking in the limelight of being a pastor's wife. Her husband's faith had also been irresistible, and in time, most of the remnants of her agnostic, liberal, feminist rebellion had melted away. Almost overnight, she had become a card-carrying evangelical conservative. She had become fluent in the jargon and had even accepted leadership roles in various church women's fellowships.

But as she studied her husband—this man who now apparently doubted his *call* and even some of his basic Protestant convictions—she wondered how she had ever been drawn along so far and for so long at his word. *Who was that man, and who am I?*

She turned from the window and returned to her reading chair. Pulling the comforter back over her legs, she considered whether to return to the mystery novel she had been reading since 6 a.m. It was an effective escape, but was that what she needed?

Instead, she reached for her white leather Bible, praying silently that she might find some scripture to give her hope. She turned to Philippians, her favorite book, and then to chapter four, where she found a familiar text underlined:

> Have no anxiety about anything, but in everything by prayer and supplication with thanksgiving let your requests be made known to God. And the peace of God, which passes all understanding, will keep your hearts and your minds in Christ Jesus.

"Lord Jesus," she prayed softly as she closed her eyes and bowed her head. "I do thank You for all the blessings You've given me, and my family, and ever so much for Stephen. Please forgive me for my doubts and my anger, but right now I feel so confused. I don't understand all that he is struggling with, and I'm afraid of where he seems to be headed. If he resigns, what will we do? And if he decides to follow Jim or Ginny, what should I do?"

Without warning, the sharp, guilt-ridden images of her trip to the clinic so many years before flashed before her eyes.

"Lord, there is no way that this is what You would want! Please *guard our hearts and minds*; help us to *understand* Your will. And please silence the doubt in my heart."

Another verse came to mind, so she turned to the book of Romans, chapter eight, verse twenty-eight:

> And we know that in all things God works for the good

of those who love him, who have been called according
to his purpose.

Considering this for a moment, she admitted, *Stephen
certainly loves God with his whole heart, mind, and strength. He's
not perfect, but he does love God, and I believe that he has been
called according to God's purpose. Lord Jesus, please help me trust
that You will work out everything for the good if Stephen...if we
decide to make some radical changes.*

Then, as if from the voice of an angel, another verse cut her to
the heart. She turned to Ephesians four and read with contrition:

> Be angry but do not sin; do not let the sun go down on
> your anger, and give no opportunity to the devil.

Sara knew that her anger had crossed into sin, that she had let
the sun go down three days in a row on her anger, and that the devil
had played havoc with her emotions.

"Lord Jesus," she prayed with renewed conviction. "Please
forgive my sins—*all* of them—and give me the courage and willpower
to tell Stephen I'm sorry."

She returned to the window. *Yes, Stephen was still shoveling.*

Quickly, she began changing into her winter work clothes. She
wanted to get out there in time to help, and maybe even (she chuckled
at the thought) push him into a drift!

7

DRIVING CAUTIOUSLY on this crisp early Sunday morning, Stephen
felt as if he were passing through a mystical dreamland. A warm
front had passed through during the night, bringing unseasonably
warm temperatures and a soft rain. When Stymie their cat woke
him at 3 a.m. wanting desperately out, he presumed the warm rain
would make the world a slushy mess by morning. But after the warm
front passed, the freezing temperatures returned. Now everything

from sidewalks and roads to tree branches and twigs was glazed with a beautiful, yet treacherous layer of thin ice.

It was in moments like this that Stephen thanked God for his trendy four-wheel-drive SUV, but even so, he needed to creep along to keep from torquing sideways at every stop or curve. Finally, with white-knuckled caution, he pulled into the church parking lot without incident. Ned, the custodian, had already scattered a de-icing compound, so once on the cleared blacktop, Stephen felt like a tightrope walker having reached the distant platform.

The lot was already half full, and worshippers were making their way toward the narthex door. *So,* Stephen thought with satisfaction, *the freezing couldn't deter this congregation from coming to pay homage to their Lord.*

"Morning, Ned. Some weather we're having!"

"Eh-yup. Caught the tip uh that storm outta the Carolinas."

"Well, thanks for cleaning 'er up for us."

"No problem, Pastor."

Stephen trudged up the steps and into the annex, stamping his feet vigorously on the metal-grate porch. Upon entering, he took off his old timers' rubbers, hung up his overcoat and wool English walking hat, and went straight to the coffee pot.

"Ned is truly a righteous man," he said, finding the coffee ready and waiting. This had been one of the many unexpected perks of this new pastorate. At his previous churches, it had fallen to him to start the Sunday morning coffee because he was generally the first to arrive. But every Sabbath since he began in September, Ned had beaten him to church and started the coffee percolating. "Well done, good and faithful servant," Stephen said with gratitude, for he knew Ned did little things like this out of service to God.

Though too humble to admit it, Ned was like the artisans of old who dedicated their lives to crafting intricate statuary high up on the roofs of cathedrals where no human being would ever see. Ned believed his work as a janitor was as important and holy as anything Stephen did as pastor. But Stephen knew that he was wrong: Ned's unselfish, behind-the-scenes efforts were more holy, more righteous. *Oh, that I could know that what I will do this morning from the prestigious height of my pulpit was as pleasing in the sight of God.*

Feeling unworthy, he took his coffee and glanced at the clock. *Twenty minutes before the service. Just enough time to pray and think one last time through the sermon, such as it is.* The first half and the ending were fairly clear in his mind, but the middle was a muddle of reservations. Still torn about how to address the controversial passages, he presumed the Spirit would guide him when he arrived at them.

He closed his office door against the world outside and upon his own world of nervousness and confused convictions.

"COME ON, DANIEL, we'll be late!" Sara yelled as she and the boys rushed to get out the door on time.

"I can't find one of my shoes."

"Well, whose fault is that? We'll be waiting in the car."

William was already out in the garage, warming up the van. Sara joined him as Daniel followed, hopping on one shoed foot, carrying the other shoe.

"I swear there's someone else living with us who always hides my shoes."

"Yeah, right," Sara said. "Don't swear, just get in. We're late."

As William backed the car out onto the slick driveway, she yelled, "Jeez, be careful."

"Don't worry, Mom. Dad sprinkled salt, and I'm sure the roads will be fine."

Sara watched with apprehension as they rode to church on the still icy roads. She regretted deeply that once again they headed for worship in a tense mood. No matter how hard she tried, they were always rushing on Sunday mornings, and invariably she lost her temper. She wondered if they ever entered worship with hearts ready with joy.

With a significantly more controlled and calm voice she said, "William, you're doing just fine. Thanks for driving. And Daniel, I'm sorry. I think I'm the culprit. I found your one shoe and threw it in your closet, assuming the other one was there." After a pause, "Tell you what, let's talk your dad into taking us out for lunch. He was gone for a few days this week, he owes us."

"Yeah, great! How about pizza?" Daniel exclaimed.

"Pizza?" William said. "No way, we can do better than that. Seafood, shrimp, clam chowder."

"Sounds good to me," Sara said, smiling.

By the time they entered the parking lot, it was nearly full. William had to park in the row furthest from the door.

"Good turnout this morning, regardless of the weather." Sara was pleasantly surprised.

"They must have been captivated by Pop's sermon title posted on the billboard," William said cynically.

"More likely the bad weather discouraged them from going anywhere else," Daniel shot back.

Rushing across the freshly cleared lot and in through the narthex doors, they took their usual seats as the organist played the introduction to the first hymn. Careful about drawing attention, William looked stealthily for Stacy until he found her sitting several rows back. Their eyes met and they exchanged smiles. But a quick glance from her father forced William to turn back around.

The congregation rose and shyly sang the first verse:

"Come, Thou Fount of every blessing,
Tune my heart to sing Thy grace;
Streams of mercy, never ceasing,
Call for songs of loudest praise."

Sara watched her husband pass, proceeding down the center aisle and then up to his chair behind the pulpit. As usual, he was wearing his black academic robe with a green seasonal stole hanging down to the floor. Only his white shirt collar and the knot of his red and blue striped tie were visible above his robe's V-neck. Hanging around his neck and positioned centrally on his chest was the silver Celtic cross. He always wore this when he preached, even if he wasn't wearing a robe, almost as if it were a good-luck charm. But knowing that Stephen didn't believe in luck, Sara knew he wore it as a symbol of Him Whom he served.

With mixed convictions, the congregation sang the final verse.

"Prone to wander, Lord, I feel it,
Prone to leave the God I love;
Here's my heart, O take and seal it,
Seal it for Thy courts above."

And sealed it with a surprisingly harmonic, "Amen."

"Let us pray," Stephen said from the pulpit, pausing as the congregation bowed their heads in one of their few accepted forms of religious ritual.

Sara listened to her husband pray. Her head was bowed and eyes closed, but her mind concentrated on the tone of his voice, not his words. *He sounds as confident as ever, but how can he stand up there, leading with such self-assurance, if his concerns are as serious as he says?*

"Amen. Now, before you take your seats," Stephen said with a smile, "please take a moment to greet those around you in the name of the Lord."

The stillness of the sanctuary was broken by the din of more than three hundred souls greeting one another. There were "Hellos," "Good mornings," and "How you beens" all around. Some left their seats to greet friends across the aisle. Sara donned an air of congeniality and dutifully greeted those behind her, but she always considered this hand-shaking ritual out of place. To her, it broke the reverence of the service just when they were ready to hear the Scriptures. She knew the arguments, she had heard them many times from Stephen—"This is an enactment of Jesus' command to be reconciled with one another before we approach the altar"—but she always argued that this was a phony, artificial reconciliation at best, and besides, *there is no altar.* He always countered, "You know what I mean." *But isn't that the point? Was Jesus being merely symbolic, or didn't He literally mean "reconcile before you come to worship?"* But she never won the day.

Stephen sat down, signaling everyone else to do the same, while Molly Torquist came forward. The children began emptying the pews to gather around her for the children's sermon.

"In the Gospel message for today," Molly spoke in a tone for small children, "Jesus asks His disciples, 'Who do people say I am?'"

STEPHEN HAD MIXED FEELINGS about children's sermons. He was glad that he himself was beyond this—he had plenty of humorous horror stories of children saying embarrassing things or wetting their pants. He also recognized that this simple preview of the day's Gospel sometimes helped many adults in the congregation grasp the concepts he would present later. And of course parents and grandparents were always pleased to see young ones up front, acting angelically cute.

Nevertheless, Stephen often felt this gathering of screaming meemies made a circus out of this holy time. He was also convinced that when the kids were up front on stage, under the gaze of an audience of smiling faces, they heard little of Molly's message. *After the self-imposed one-year moratorium on major changes,* he promised himself, *I'm going to have Molly lead the children out of the sanctuary and down to Fellowship Hall where they can be taught in a more conducive environment.*

Then he checked himself: *If I'm still here, that is.*

He glanced out at the surprisingly full congregation. The regulars were there, plus the many others he had yet to meet—and might never. The sea of faces were all fixed on Molly and the children. Then he tensed as he saw Walter Horscht, his wife, and William's new heartthrob, Stacy.

In contrast to most of the congregation, Walter and his wife were hardly the picture of contentment. Their faces were stiff and stern, but Stacy's seemed to radiate with expectant joy. He could see why his son was drawn to her—she was more than pretty, and compared with how he vaguely remembered her from last Sunday, much more interested in being here. She had obviously done herself up right this morning.

Stephen returned his gaze to Walter, and they locked eyes. Walter sat up stiffly and averted his gaze. Stephen likewise turned toward Molly, who was dismissing the children.

Forgive me, Lord, he prayed silently, *but I wish this ... strange man wasn't here.*

A gentleman whom Stephen didn't recognize came forward to read a lesson from the Old Testament. Stephen greeted the stranger with a nod as he took the pulpit. While the man read, Stephen prayed for guidance and peace of heart.

WALTER WAITED NERVOUSLY, but eventually glanced back at LaPointe. Seeing that he was no longer being scrutinized, Walter relaxed. Now that he had broken his silence with his daughter, he presumed that she had told William, who would have squealed to his father. Consequently, LaPointe knew that he knew.

What should I do? I wonder if he's guessed that I am "Thevoiceoftruth"? Walter didn't know how aggressive an undercover Catholic might be, but he knew that whatever came, he would not take it sitting down. He was ready to act. *When I have completed my assignment, the truth will come out, and I will be vindicated. If not, then whatever punishment comes will be for the cause of Christ.*

The reader drew to a close, and Walter asked the Lord for a sign. *Let me hear from the lips of this traitor some clear proof that what I believe is true. Please, don't let me make a mistake.*

THE CHOIR STOOD to deliver the choral call to prayer. For over a hundred years there had been a formal adult choir at First Church, and as Stephen watched them rise proudly in their white satin robes, he was certain that several were charter members. In general, they harmonized well, but a few had long since lost their ability to stay on pitch. The high warble of one particular white-haired matriarch was mimicked regularly by many of the children. If Stephen stayed long enough, he planned to add at least two more choirs, one for teens and another for contemporary music, to alternate in the loft.

Allowing a few seconds for silent prayer and for the congregation to recover from the choir's number, he rose to lead Morning Prayer. Though he generally preached without notes, he often would pen a short outline of thoughts for these petitions—events and people to remember, sins to be avoided or forgiven, virtues to pursue, etc. This morning, as he prayed through his notes, he inserted a few impromptu concerns he had never previously considered: "Lord Jesus, help us to be more understanding of Christian brothers and sisters in other denominations and traditions. May we love one another over and above our differences, and put aside any feelings of prejudice and bigotry. If we are guilty of the things that divide us, have mercy on us, and help us work towards reconciliation. Amen.

"And now, let us return to the Lord a portion of all he has graciously provided for our needs."

Stephen returned to his seat as the ushers began their rounds. The choir stood and transgressed all bounds of musical decency to sing a maudlin "We Give Thee But Thine Own." Stephen questioned whether their harmonization was good stewardship of the congregation's eardrums.

Finally, the organist struck the signal chord, and the congregation stood to sing the Doxology as the ushers brought forward the morning's collection: "Praise God, from whom all blessings flow..."

After the Preparation Hymn, "Fairest Lord Jesus," the congregation sat down. Stephen rose and approached the pulpit. He opened the large King James pulpit Bible to Matthew. He didn't always read from this, but he knew it pleased the older members of the church when he did.

"Please turn with me to the Gospel of Matthew, chapter sixteen, verses thirteen through twenty." He waited for the rustling of pages from pew and personal Bibles to cease. "Before I begin, let us pause in prayer: Heavenly Father, in the words of this morning's Gospel, your Son, Jesus our Lord, poses an important question. May your Holy Spirit, who dwells within our hearts, open our ears and minds to hear Him plainly, so that in the clamor of so many modern voices, we can make the same profession of faith that Simon Peter made. And may our focus be not so much on the speaker, but upon Your Son, Jesus Christ our Lord, for it is He whom we have come to see. Amen.

"Hear now the words of the evangelist and Apostle, Matthew:

> When Jesus came into the coasts of Caesarea Philippi, He asked His disciples, saying, "Whom do men say that I the Son of Man am?"
>
> And they said, "Some say that Thou art John the Baptist; some, Elias; and others, Jeremias, or one of the prophets."
>
> He saith unto them, "But whom say ye that I am?"
>
> And Simon Peter answered and said, "Thou art the Christ, the Son of the Living God."

Stephen wished that he could end his reading here and focus their attention only on the text up to this point. But he knew that he couldn't get away with it—the entire passage had been printed in the bulletin, and surely some would read too much into his omission.

And Jesus answered and said unto him, "Blessed art thou,

> Simon Bar-jona: for flesh and blood hath not revealed it
> unto thee, but My Father which is in heaven. And I say
> also unto thee, That thou art Peter, and upon this rock I
> will build My Church; and the gates of hell shall not
> prevail against it. And I will give unto thee the keys of
> the kingdom of heaven: and whatsoever thou shalt bind
> on earth shall be bound in heaven: and whatsoever thou
> shalt loose on earth shall be loosed in heaven.
>
> Then charged He His disciples that they should tell
> no man that He was Jesus the Christ.

He turned his attention from the printed page and began preaching.

"Who do you say that Jesus is? There is an interesting twist in the wording of this question, for I believe that Jesus is directly challenging us here this morning in at least two specific ways.

"Do you remember the setting of this story? Jesus had just fed four thousand men with seven loaves and a few small fish, so the disciples had personally witnessed his miraculous powers. Then the Pharisees and scribes demanded a sign from Heaven. The miraculous feeding of the four thousand had not impressed them. Or had their prejudice blinded them to the truth right before their eyes?" He knew that this particular morning, much of his preaching would be to himself. "As a result, Jesus warned His disciples to 'Beware of the leaven of the Pharisees.'

"Now, I remember once hearing a Southern radio preacher expounding on the leaven of the Pharisees. This radio preacher proclaimed with great conviction, 'You know why Jesus told His disciples to have no mind of the leaven of the Pharisees? Because there were twelve of them!'"

This brought the expected chuckles, followed by a second ripple of guffaws from those slower on the uptake.

"Jesus was warning them to beware of the teaching of the Pharisees, but what was wrong with the Pharisees' teaching? Later in Matthew, Jesus will tell His disciples that the Pharisees didn't practice what they preached. They laid heavy burdens on people which they themselves wouldn't carry. They'd dress in showy clothing and take the more prominent seats at banquets. In essence, their religion was an external religion of show for the sake of prestige and power. And as Jesus said earlier in Matthew chapter six, the Pharisees were already receiving their reward—horizontal praise and respect from man—but losing the one reward that counted—vertically from God. The disciples were to be careful who they listened to, who they imitated, and who they followed, because there would be many, many voices trying to lure them away from Him, their Savior and Lord.

"You see, it was easy for the Apostles to report what others believed. This required no personal convictions. But when Jesus asked in those beautiful, reverent words of the King James, 'But whom say ye that I am?,' the crowd of disciples became speechless.

"There are several ways to envision what happened next, since the Gospel writer recorded only the basic facts without the colorful details. It's possible that Simon, in his usual bold, 'Betty, don't bar the doors' brashness, yelled right out, 'You are the Christ, the Son of the living God!'

"On the other hand, knowing how far he would soon fall when he denies Jesus three times, I envision something quite different. Do you remember that old Laurel and Hardy movie when they're in the French Foreign Legion? The commander asks for a volunteer and the line of soldiers steps back, leaving Laurel and Hardy standing alone. I wonder whether this is a little of what happened here. Did the other Apostles take a big step back, leaving the brash fisherman to fend for himself? At this point in his spiritual journey, Simon might not have had the courage to step boldly forward, but he at least didn't step backwards. But however this happened, he was standing alone, and as Jesus waited for his answer, Simon didn't back down. He professed his faith in Jesus as their Messiah."

WALTER'S HEARTBEAT BEGAN TO RISE. He sat up erect, listening intently, for he recognized this passage. It was the passage papists use to defend the primacy of the pope. He couldn't believe that LaPointe was actually preaching on this text.

What will LaPointe say? Will he give the usual Protestant disclaimer for this text, or present what Catholics claim it says?

And then he realized an even greater significance in this text. *What LaPointe says in the next few moments may be God's "yes" or "no" to my marching orders—and I hope it's a "yes!"*

"In jesus' answer to Simon's brave profession," Stephen continued, "I can't help but envision the same sentiments Jesus once felt toward another man who boldly expressed faith in Him. This other Gospel story is important for its parallels with today's text. If you remember, a rich young man, of higher standing and class than the peasants surrounding Jesus, came and knelt before Him—humbling himself before this crowd. He asked Jesus, 'Good teacher, what must I do to inherit eternal life?' Now Jesus answered first, 'Why do you call Me good? No one is good but God alone.'

"It is important to recognize that Jesus was pointing out that this man's bold profession was somewhat akin to what Simon Peter would later profess. The young man had cast aside all of his cultural privileges to abase himself before Jesus—like Simon standing out from the rest of the disciples. Jesus attempted to help him see the true significance of what he had said: 'You have recognized that I am a good teacher, but only God is good. Can you see, therefore, that I am God?'

"But Jesus went on with His answer. He said, 'You know the commandments.' And the rich young man responded, 'Teacher, all these I have observed from my youth.' And Scripture states that 'Jesus, looking upon him, loved him.'

"Now if things had turned out differently, this bold young man might have ended up an apostle. But as far as we know, his response to Jesus was otherwise, and Jesus said, out of love for this sincere man, 'You lack one thing: go, sell what you have, and give to the poor, and you will have treasure in heaven; and come, follow Me.' Scripture then says sadly that 'At that saying his countenance fell, and he went away sorrowful; for he had great possessions.'

"As I envision today's text, I see Jesus looking upon Simon and also loving him. But Jesus, through His omniscience, sees exactly who Simon is with all of his shortcomings, how he will respond, and what he will do for the glory of Christ—even eventually unto death by crucifixion, upside down on Vatican Hill in Rome."

At this mention of Peter's presence and martyrdom in Rome, Walter's head jerked up, dislodging his glasses. He scrambled for them, causing enough of a commotion to capture Stephen's attention, who then paused for a second. Oblivious to what had startled Walter, Stephen went on.

"Jesus responded gently to Simon. I envision Jesus reaching out to him, placing His hands on Simon's shoulders and saying, 'Blessed are you, Simon son of Jonah, for flesh and blood did not reveal this to you, but My Father who art in heaven.' Simon's insight and profession had been a gift of grace from the Father."

Stephen was feeling unusually tense. Sweat was beading up on his forehead and dripping onto the open Bible before him.

Where should I go from here? he asked himself. He had planned to ignore the next section—the controversial section—and cut to the conclusion, the charge. *But what is true?* He had pledged when he was ordained to always proclaim the truth of Christ to his people. *Am I like Simon Peter, or the rich young man?* He chose, for the moment, another dodge.

"Again I'm reminded of Jesus' parable of the sower. The seed fell on four soils, but the only soil that produced fruit was the good soil, or as Jesus would later explain, the person who heard and understood. Understanding was the difference, and Jesus pointed out to Simon that his understanding of who He was as the Son of Man was a supernatural gift of God. And because of this, Jesus proclaimed that this supernatural insight set Simon apart for a unique purpose."

OK, Stephen thought, *where to now?* He stood silently in the pulpit, awkwardly. He looked down at Sara and then over to several of his board members and others he had come to know well, and then back behind them toward Walter.

WALTER AND SARA BOTH noticed Stephen's delay, his awkward scanning of the congregation. It wasn't like him. He looked nervous, unsure of himself. They watched him look back down at the pulpit Bible and then up again.

Sara grew uneasy. *What's wrong with him?* she thought. *What is he thinking of doing?* She watched him struggling, standing speechless, and recalling what his friend Jim had done, she suddenly felt the urge to stand up and shout, "No! Don't you dare!"

SARA'S LOOK OF PANIC was not lost on Stephen, who glanced one more time at the text. *"Thou art Peter, and upon this rock I will build My Church."* He began to speak cautiously.

"Friends, we've reached a very controversial point in today's text, as some of you know. Over the past twenty years of my ministry, whenever I've preached or taught on this passage, I've proclaimed with great emphasis and assurance the one interpretation that is most widely accepted amongst Protestants—an opinion which is decisively and intentionally anti-Catholic. This opinion downplays the more obvious literal implications of the text, explaining it away, to mean that Jesus was referring only to Simon Peter's faith, and not to him personally.

"But over the past few years, I have come to discover something that troubles me—it troubles me a lot."

He glanced over at Bill Walker, who had advocated hiring him, and wondered how this good man would respond to what he was about to say.

"You know that I take my responsibility as your pastor and teacher very seriously. I believe that I will be accountable to God one day for all that I have taught you, and I would rather die a thousand deaths than mislead you.

"You also know how deeply I believe that this book," Stephen raised the heavy pulpit Bible high above his head, "is the inerrant Word of God. You know that I have taught consistently that everything we need to believe for our salvation is to be found here."

He noticed many heads nodding in agreement.

"Yet, is it not true," he said as he lowered the Bible back to its place on the pulpit, "that you and I know other Christians who accept the Bible as the infallible Word of God yet believe differently than we do? Who believe things that completely contradict what we believe?

"Now you might say, 'Well, then of course they are wrong, but don't be too hasty. They love and have faith in Jesus, just as we do; they believe that the Holy Spirit is guiding them in their interpretation of Scripture, just as we do; and yet, they have concluded that we are the ones who are wrong—that we have misheard the Holy Spirit, just as we claim of them."

He waited for this to register and then confessed with great relief, "The significant question which has driven me to my knees and continues to haunt me is, how can we determine with eternal certainty which of us is right?"

Sara grabbed for william's arm. He was paying closer attention than usual to his father's sermon. William looked at her and saw that she was white as chalk.

"Mother, are you all right?"

She said nothing in reply, only stared up at her husband preaching out over her to the congregation.

"The quandary with this particular text," Stephen continued carefully, "is that there is a wide range of heated opinions as to how it should be interpreted. People have persecuted and murdered over how this text should be applied. Do you remember the movie *A Man For All Seasons,* about the life, arrest, and execution of Thomas More? Most of us consider him a great man of conviction who would rather have his head cut off than go against his conscience. But what was the specific issue of conscience on which he was unwilling to bend? It was the literal interpretation of this text: that Jesus promised to build His Church on the leadership of Simon Peter."

This was the sign, Walter thought. All that he had presumed was true. LaPointe was being theatrical about it, but this was just what Walter might suppose. *This papist is attempting to win our sympathetic ear by twisting our reason through our emotions.* He knew now that he must act, and soon.

"What struck me most as I reconsidered this text," Stephen said in a softer tone, "was the next thing that Jesus promises—that 'the gates of hell shall not prevail against' this church established on the faith and the person of Simon Peter. Well, my friends, what does Jesus mean here by 'church'? Does He only mean the nebulous, invisible Church that we Congregationalists and other Protestant Christians believe in? The worldwide, invisible fellowship of those who are truly born again, regardless of institution, tradition, or creed? This is what I've always believed and taught: that what Jesus meant here is that the world will never be without the witness of a born-again believer, even if there is only one left.

"But I also recognize," he raised his voice in emphasis, "that there are millions of Christians of drastically different traditions and beliefs who are convinced that their particular church or denomination is more than a mere manmade institution; that it is in fact the truest expression of the Church established by Jesus. Many claim with great conviction that Jesus intended from the beginning to establish a visible church, with bishops, pastors, and deacons with authority to preserve, protect, and proclaim the truth down through the ages, unspoiled by the opinions of each age, under the continual guidance of the Holy Spirit."

SARA SAT IN SHOCK, wondering if in a few minutes the elders would carry her husband out on a rail.

HE WAS ON A ROLL, poised to let it all out, and let the chips fall where they must. "But do you realize that there are over twenty thousand different, separate Christian groups in the world? A handbook on my desk outlines two hundred of these denominations in the United States alone, and none of them agrees on what the Church is, let alone what every Christian must believe to be saved. When I think about what Jesus said to this humble apostle who had taken a bold stance in the face of all other opinions, I doubt that this confusion is what Jesus intended when He said He would establish His Church.

"Later in the Gospel, on the night when Jesus was betrayed, when He and His Apostles were gathered in the upper room, He led them in prayer. We find the words to Christ's high-priestly prayer in John chapter seventeen." Stephen turned the pages of the pulpit Bible back to this prayer, as did many in the congregation who were anxious to discover where their pastor was leading.

"In verse eleven, Jesus prays, 'Holy Father, keep through Thine own Name those whom Thou hast given Me, that they may be one, as We are.' Then in verse twenty, 'Neither pray I for these alone, but for them also which shall believe on Me through their word, that they all may be one...'

"My friends, what kind of unity do today's more than twenty thousand separate, sometimes conflicting, Christian groups represent? What is wrong here? Has the Holy Spirit failed to guide us properly? Is the Holy Spirit's guidance hopelessly confusing? Or have we failed, in our ignorance, in our prejudice, in our pride, to listen, understand, and obey?

"And given this shameful, contradicting disunity, have the gates of Hell, therefore, prevailed against the Church?" Stephen proclaimed with great force, focusing on the man who had called him to be their pastor. "I think not. Scripture tells us that 'The prayer of a righteous man has great power in its effects.' Well, there is no more righteous man than Jesus Christ, the sinless Son of God, so whatever He asked in prayer must be true. Therefore, His Church must have been established in Simon Peter, it must be unified, and it must still be standing strong against the onslaught of the gates of hell."

FEELING FAINT, Sara rose from her pew, steadying herself on William's shoulder. Daniel followed them out. The sound of nearly three hundred people taking a sudden inhale added a dramatic hush to their exit.

STEPHEN WATCHED SILENTLY, realizing fully what his words had done. As Sara left the sanctuary, the congregation returned their attention to the front, and confronted him with a sea of concerned faces, some angry, some blank in a state of unknowing, and a few smiling anxiously.

He continued cautiously. "The bottom line in all of this is the same question Jesus posed to His disciples: 'Who do *you* say that I am?' But He is not merely asking for our mental affirmation that He is the Son of God, our Savior and Lord; He is asking that if we truly believe this, do we therefore take Him at His word and act accordingly? Do we trust Him enough to follow Him no matter where He leads, as He demanded of the rich young man—to go, sell all that we have, to give it away if necessary, so that we can follow Him without encumbrances? Are you willing to take a stand for who Jesus truly is and what He expects of you, regardless of what people around you might say—regardless of what the consequences might be?"

Stephen turned his attention to the few in the congregation he could call close friends, hoping for support. "All my adult Christian life, I have been committed to these convictions. Now I want nothing to stand in my way of proclaiming and following Jesus faithfully, without wavering, wherever He might lead. And I also pray this for you. Will you be like Simon Peter, or will you turn away like the rich young man? Please, let's keep one another in prayer so that regardless of the many contradictory opinions and pressures that may surround us, we can together follow our Savior faithfully. Let us pray."

"MOTHER, WHAT CAN I DO? Can I get you something?" William said as he helped his mother to a bench in the church narthex.

"Here's some water," Ned the custodian said as he handed her a cup.

"Thank you." Sara gulped the water down. "Thank you, that helps."

"Mother, what happened?" Daniel asked.

"Nothing, Dear. Look, I feel dizzy. I must be coming down with something. William, can you take me home?"

"Sure, I'll bring the car up to the front entrance."

She sat waiting, silently, fighting back tears, holding Daniel's hand tightly.

AS THE ORGANIST PLAYED the introductory measures of the closing hymn, "Turn Your Eyes Upon Jesus," Walter forcefully directed Helen and Stacy to follow him out of the pew. Stacy resisted, but with a glare from her father that said, "Don't you dare disobey me in front of all of these people," she quickly fell in line and followed him down the aisle and out of the church.

"What are we doing, dear?" Helen demanded cautiously.

"I just want to beat the rush. Please let's go."

As Stacy opened the back door of the Caprice, suppressing her disappointment in missing William, Helen sat obliviously in the front. Walter prayed privately, taking his place behind the wheel: *Thank You, Lord, for Your confirmation. I will follow You no matter where You lead, no matter what the consequence.*

*   *   *

"WHAT WERE YOU *THINKING*?" Sara screamed as soon as Stephen entered from the garage.

"What do you mean?" he said with diminishing resolve. He had assumed that Sara would explode the moment he walked in. Watching her bolt from the sanctuary, he guessed that she was expecting him to announce his resignation—as Jim had—without warning to his congregation or family. All the way home, he prayed that he would respond to her justified concerns with love and compassion. He was determined not to return anger for anger. But the moment he encountered her rage, he failed, as he had done so many times before.

"What do I mean?" she continued. "You promised me you wouldn't do anything rash. That you were just *thinking* of resigning. How dare you do this without telling me! How dare you embarrass me in front of that entire congregation!"

"So that's all you really care about—how embarrassed you might be." His resolve was gone. "You have no concept of how important this issue is for me, for my career, and for our family." He threw his hat and coat in the direction of the hall closet, where they fell on the floor.

"No concept? You're going to put us out in the cold without a job!"

From the entrance to the living room, William and Daniel watched and listened, as they had done many times before. Slowly, as their parents' voices and tones escalated, they backed into the living room toward the fireplace, letting the swinging door close between them and their arguing parents. They sat on either side of the wood stove, avoiding each other's eyes.

On the verge of tears, Daniel stared down at the floor, while William looked blankly into the stove where the embers from the morning's fire were almost cold. He was far less affected by this conflict than his younger brother, for he had had more years to grow accustomed to his parents' battles. He and his father had talked many times about these fights, so he understood intellectually: whenever two people come together in marriage, though they truly become one by the grace of God, they are yet sinners with different backgrounds, upbringing, experiences, personalities, and emotions—like two strong rivers coming together into a massive rapids to form one stronger river. His father wished they would never fight, but he also knew that this side of Heaven, their sinfulness would always lead them to fail. He was sorry, and William knew it; but William also watched with growing cynicism as week after week his father spoke of love, forgiveness, and patience from his elevated pulpit.

Watching one last ember cool from bright to dim red, and hearing the intensity of the voices from the kitchen continue to rise, William wished his father wasn't a minister. And he wished he wasn't a minister's son.

The kitchen door burst open, slamming against the living-room wall.

"I've had it!" Stephen yelled as he crossed the living room for the stairs. "For nineteen years I've sacrificed for you and this family, and all I ever get are complaints." He paused in his stride as he saw the bewildered faces of his sons, and then with a look of shame resumed his flight up the stairs.

"That's right. Go ahead and leave," she shouted from the kitchen. "See if I care! Resign from the church, and resign from the family!"

William returned his gaze to the fireplace. He had watched this scenario before. His mother's anger would continue to escalate, and his father would retreat, bewildered, impotent to do anything.

For a few moments the house was silent. The boys sat dead still waiting for the next volley of words. And then their father came down the stairs with a suitcase. There was less energy in his steps than when he had ascended. He paused as he passed his sons.

"Boys, I'm truly sorry for this. Please forgive me...forgive us. I'm going away for a while, to figure this all out. Please take care of your mother...I do love her, you know that, and I love you."

Without waiting for a response, he left the house by the front door, walking outside and around the kitchen to the garage. He threw his bag into the Wagoneer, backed out, and was gone.

"Damn you!" Sara screamed from the kitchen.

William watched as the last glimmer of red heat faded into gray-white ashes and Daniel's tears began to flow freely.

Part VII

In the Presence of Mine Enemies

1

"Helen, thank you for lunch," Walter said as he pushed back from the table. "Good as always."

"Right! Since when did you start liking my tuna casserole?"

"Now, honey, like I said, it was as good as always. I can't help it if tuna casserole ain't my favorite dish. But, honestly, thanks for your effort." He kissed his wife on the cheek, and started toward the garage.

Helen noticed that he had been acting strangely ever since they left church, kind of nervous. Convinced that his pleasant tones were no more than self-serving placations, she demanded, "Where you going?"

"Oh, just out for a short drive. I won't be gone long. Ever since we moved here, I haven't had a chance to look around, to map out the necessary stores and services. I'll be back in an hour or so."

"But, Walter..."

He was already out the door. Lifting the garage door as noiselessly as possible, he glanced up and down the street. "Why am I being so cautious?" he mumbled, belittling himself.

He walked back and got into his Caprice wagon. Before starting the engine, he reached under the seat to confirm that the blood-stained bundle was still there. It was, and the touch of it brought a surge of conflicting voices, some shouting, *Yes! Yes! Do it! For the sake of God and the gospel,* while others countered, *No! Stop! For God's sake, don't!*

He started the already warm engine and, seeing a hole in the traffic, backed out.

For nearly fifteen minutes he drove from the south side of the city suburbs around to the northwest, out into the country, where newer homes were being built on larger, more spacious lots. He turned down a lane, then onto another, until finally he pulled his car to a stop by the curb. He sat watching, waiting. Down the street, slightly around a curve, at the end of the lane, about five hundred yards away, was a nicely landscaped, white two-story home. He could make out nothing through the dark windows, so he couldn't tell if anyone was home. The two-car garage door was open, with one stall empty and a red minivan in the other. A blue Jeep Wrangler was parked out in the street. He knew that LaPointe drove a green Wagoneer, so it appeared that he had not arrived home from worship.

Walter decided to wait anyway, rolling up his collar against the rising cold. *What else can I do? This is my destiny.*

*   *   *

WHILE STEPHEN HAD BEEN EATING, a frigid winter wind with sleet had added a thin layer of ice to his car. After scraping the windshield and restarting the engine, He once again headed aimlessly north.

I should have followed my instincts, he mused with regret. *I guess everybody seeing everybody else parked outside assumed that everybody else was at that restaurant because it was great food. We were all wrong. Greasy, overcooked. I'll need a full roll of antacids just to survive.*

The restaurant, a truck stop badly in need of paint, had been the only one open along the snow-blown, nearly deserted Interstate.

On the seat beside him lay his red-striped tie and the Celtic cross he had worn that morning in the pulpit. When he left the car for lunch, he had removed them both with a violent jerk, as if leaving these behind was a symbol of his flight.

Through the fogged up windshield and wipers slapping against the oncoming sleet, he tried to read a road sign. FORBESGATE 30 MILES; JAMESFIELD 63 MILES. Then he remembered. *Jamesfield. Jim had recommended seeing a priest in Jamesfield.*

He immediately rejected the idea and passed on to other thoughts. He was overwhelmed by an aching, bitter sorrow over the events that put him on this road to nowhere. Nothing in his life had gone as he had planned—his ministry and maybe his marriage were in shambles.

In time, he passed a second sign and a third, and reconsidered.

But how can this priest, an ex-Protestant minister, help me without bias? As the exit to Jamesfield approached, he locked his eyes to the center of the road, but the broken center line passing rhythmically, looking too much like a turn signal, taunted him. Within 30 feet of the exit, he still intended to pass by, but at the last second the Wagoneer swerved to the right, off toward Jamesfield.

At the light at the bottom of the ramp, he remembered. "Jamesfield. I've been here. Irene and Elsie and...*the exorcism!*" he had come to call it. *But what else could it have been?*

And then he remembered the inexplainable pursuit by those men in the car.

He turned onto First Street, forcing the feeling of dread behind him. Five blocks to the east, he could see the Church. Its square, stone bell tower with four pointed corner spires overshadowed the smaller buildings all around. Between the spires stood a tall stone cross. In the distance, where First Street intersected the downtown congestion, were taller, newer office buildings, but none as artistically attractive as this stone building of worship.

On this cold Sunday afternoon, First Street was deserted, so Stephen had no problem finding a parking space directly in front of the church. An unlit sign declared, *St. Francis de Sales Parish.*

Before he opened the car door, he sat for a moment, staring. In many ways, this Catholic church looked like so many other older Episcopalian, Methodist, or Lutheran churches. He was no student of architecture, so he couldn't identify the style. All he knew was that it shouted of permanence.

The entire front façade consisted of three elevated arched doorways—one in the base of the central bell tower, the other two on either side slightly recessed. Concrete steps led up to each. Above each door was an arched stained-glass window. In the midday light, however, it was difficult to identify what each window portrayed. From his car he could see that the left side of the building consisted of five more enormous windows. Nothing so far looked particularly "Catholic," except possibly a symbol on the bell-tower entrance. From where he sat, it looked like a skull and crossbones. Stephen presumed this wasn't the case, but he couldn't tell otherwise. So, he got out.

Only once before had he entered a Catholic Church. In '98, the

Thanksgiving ecumenical service had been held at St. Anne's Parish in Respite, but that parish had been so modern that inside and out it was indistinguishable from most modern Protestant churches. St. Francis de Sales Parish, however, looked like the kind of Catholic Church he had always been warned to avoid like the plague. Compared to First Church, Witzel's Notch, it appeared ominous. Approaching the massive wooden doors, he felt as if he was under the menacing shadow of a medieval fortress.

Upon ascending the central stone steps to the bell-tower entrance, the details of the symbol became clearer, revealing not the sign of pirates and buccaneers but a large crest. It contained a domelike crown above two crossed keys. The symbol was unfamiliar and at first he didn't get it, but then it struck him: *The keys of the Kingdom, of course; the authority of Peter, the Rock.*

He hesitated, then tried the door. It was bolted tight. *To be expected,* he muttered. *It was Sunday afternoon, and worship was over.* He was content to take this as permission to move on, but decided instead to try the other doors, *just in case.* Down the steps and up those on the right, but that door was also locked. So again down the steps and over to the remaining stairs on the left. A voice from within said to pass up this third door, for surely it too must be closed, but his curiosity was too strong: *How different is an old Catholic church like this from your average Joe Congregational church?* He ascended to door three, presuming it would be immobile, but when he pulled, it opened easily.

He glanced in from side to side, and seeing no one, he entered the small outer hall. To the left, a cork bulletin board announced an upcoming Lenten Series on *True Repentance.* The presenter, Father William Bourque. The flier included a picture of a smiling, jovial priest in his sixties with receding black hair. His eyes were friendly and unthreatening, but Stephen wasn't convinced.

To the right was a large rack of magazines, books, and pamphlets, with a padlocked box for donations. He glanced over the selection and from the unfamiliar titles and authors he knew he had entered a different world: *Enthronement of the Sacred Heart, The Eucharist and Christian Perfection, The Three Ways of the Spiritual Life, True Devotion to the Blessed Virgin, Hell, The Furrow, The Soul of the Apostolate.* Stephen backed away toward the swinging doors that led into the sanctuary.

Through the red pane of a stained-glass portal he got his first glimpse of a traditional Catholic church. The only light inside, besides what came in through the enormous, now brilliantly lit picture windows, was a large red candle suspended to the left of a center altar.

He pushed the door open, entered, and was immediately taken aback. Before him was the opposite of the stark empty sanctuary of First Church. This enormous room, with high vaulted ceilings supported by black, spiral columns, was overflowing with pictures, statues, candles, and symbols. Seen from the inside, the picture windows appeared on fire, each presenting a scene from the Gospels: the visit of the angel to Mary, the birth of Jesus in a manger, Jesus praying in the garden, His ascension. Below the windows and around the room, just above eye level, were a dozen or more carved reliefs of scenes from Christ's crucifixion. As he walked down the center aisle, other images caught his eye, some quite unusual and eerie: statues of a brown robed monk holding a skull, a small child dressed in flowing robes, and a painting of two bright red hearts, one with a crown of thorns, and the other pierced with many swords.

Up front over dozens of rows of wooden pews, he saw three altars: one to the left with a statue of Mary, another to the right with the statue of a man holding a hammer and square, and in the middle a massive, white altar, consisting of spires and arches, with three shelves holding flowers and candles. In its center, about shoulder height, was a finely detailed golden door about a foot square. Above the altar the ceiling was covered with a mural of angels surrounding what he assumed was an artist's rendition of the Trinity: an old, bearded man on a throne, pointing down to His Son Jesus on the cross, from which flew a white dove representing the Holy Spirit.

Stephen slipped cautiously into the front pew, resting his eyes from their visual feast. It was all beautiful, like the beauty in a museum, yet so strange and foreign. He searched for something familiar, but only found more strangeness: a tiered table holding hundreds of candles, some lit; a life-sized mural of a woman in blue standing on a serpent; and the statue of a priest holding a book. He felt his head spin. *What am I doing here? What does all this stuff mean?*

He rose from the pew and started to leave.

"Hello," a deep muted voice echoed from a side door. "May I help you?"

Stephen stopped, startled. He turned toward the voice and saw against the afternoon light the silhouette of a robed man with one arm raised.

"Reverend Bourque?" Stephen asked nervously, relinquishing his hope for escape.

"That's right," the priest said, extending his right hand in friendship. "Have we met?"

Once the man stepped from the back light, Stephen recognized him as the priest in the flier, the same welcoming smile and joyful, warm eyes. He was dressed in a black monk's robe tied with a white cincture. Hanging at his side was a large silver chain of black beads, which Stephen presumed was a rosary. The priest wore a clerical collar, and around his neck hung a silver crucifix three times larger than Stephen's preaching cross. His grip was firm, warm, and dry, but his hands were surprisingly rough and callused. He spoke with a slight accent, which matched his French or French-Canadian surname.

"No, but we have a mutual friend, Jim Sarver," Stephen answered him."

"Why yes, and how is Jim doing?"

"Well…" Stephen wasn't sure what to say. *Does this priest know?* "Fine, if you can call resigning your ministry, putting your marriage in jeopardy, and being without a job, 'fine.'"

"Yes, he does need our prayers, but tell me, what is your name and your relationship to Jim?"

"My name is Stephen LaPointe, and I'm the pastor of the First Congregational Church of Witzel's Notch."

Every time he announced his church in this fashion, Stephen felt he was giving it an exaggerated sense of importance. "Jim and I went to college and seminary together."

The priest motioned toward the front pew. "And what brings you to St. Francis de Sales?"

Stephen was siting directly before a life-size statue of Mary clad in blue and white robes and holding the baby Jesus. She was extending an arm, offering a string of beads, and her beckoning smile gave Stephen the willies.

"Jim suggested that I come," he answered. "I suppose you might say I'm suffering the same malady that drove him from the pulpit, but I haven't accepted the same cure. He said you might be able to help me sift through my options."

"I'm no magician, Stephen, but I'll gladly do what I can. Jim is a good and faithful brother in Christ, and any friend of his is a friend of mine. You are more than welcome here. Are you just passing through, or like Jim, away until you can return with answers?"

Stephen looked into the priest's brown eyes for a hidden meaning, but saw nothing. "Well, I..."

"You can stay in the rectory guest room if it will help, the same room that Jim uses whenever he comes."

"Thanks, but what will be the charge?"

"Oh heavens, nothing. That's what the room's for. And since tomorrow's my day off, we'll have plenty of time to talk."

Stephen felt himself being studied. Then the priest asked, "Is this your first time in a Catholic church?"

"No, but the only other time was in a more modern church. This is quite different," he said, gesturing around him.

"I remember my first visit to a Catholic church," the ex-Protestant-minister-now-priest said. "Any questions about what you see?"

"Oh, not now, thanks. Maybe later. I'm a bit overwhelmed, as you can imagine. This is all quite contrary to my Congregationalist sensibilities."

"Yes, yes, I quite understand, but here, before we retire to the rectory—dinner is almost ready—let me point out one very important and uniquely Catholic item."

He beckoned Stephen to follow him up onto the raised platform of the sanctuary.

"Many Protestant churches are adding these, but I dare say few know why. Lots of things in this church are uniquely Catholic—the pictures, statues and icons. But this points to what makes this sanctuary truly significant and unique. See that red candle suspended from the ceiling?"

"Yes, I noticed that when I came in."

"Then it served its purpose perfectly. When lit, that candle tells us that Jesus is truly present in the Tabernacle." He pointed to the gold door in the center of the altar. "I realize that as a Congregationalist this is foreign to you; it was even to me as a

Lutheran. I believed, as a Lutheran, that Jesus was uniquely present in the bread and wine of the Lord's Supper, but not in this way. As a Congregationalist, I presume you believe that the celebration of the Lord's Supper is at least a symbol, pointing to Jesus and his sacrifice for our sins. I dare say that Lutherans and Congregationalists as well as other Protestants settled for lesser views of the meaning of the Eucharist because their minds would not accept what their senses could not see, taste, or feel. But, using the words of John chapter six, we Catholics 'believe and have come to know'—truly, spiritually *know*—that our Lord Jesus Christ, the Son of God, the Creator and Savior of the World, is truly present, body, blood, soul and divinity, there in that ornate box."

Stephen wanted to shoot back, "So, in St. Francis de Sales Parish you have God in a box." Instead he asked, "But how can God be any more present there on your altar than in all the world at large?"

"Yes, our omnipresent God is truly everywhere, especially in the heart of every believer. But we believe Him at His word that he is uniquely present there in the tabernacle under the accidents of bread."

"Accidents? What do you mean?" The immensity and intensity of the unknowns that surrounded Stephen were beginning to play havoc with his nerves.

"A philosophical term. It describes the physical appearance of something apart from its substance, what something truly is," the priest replied. "Assuming your background is similar to mine, you probably never studied philosophy, did you?"

"No," Stephen said. "Philosophy is man's dead-end attempt to explain all of life and reach God on his own intellect and reason." Being able to explain at least something of familiarity helped calm him, but Stephen noticed his hands shaking.

"Yes, that is true. Some philosophies are dead ends, because they are built on false assumptions. Just as some traditions are good and trustworthy, while others are faulty. But beginning with the right assumptions, it is amazing how close to God man can reach through his reason."

Nothing bucked so hard against Stephen's beliefs than this statement about reason. Since his days in seminary, he had been thoroughly convinced that apart from God's special revelation, man cannot find God on his own, and the confusion of the world was proof of this. Then Stephen had discovered that even among those who had God's revealed written Word in their hands, who studied it and prayed over it constantly, there was endless confusion and contradiction. And now this Catholic priest had the audacity to stand before him and, on the one hand, claim that—contrary to anyone's senses and logic—Jesus was bodily present in that golden box in the form of wafers, while, on the other hand, state that, given the right assumptions, any man using his logic can come close to God!

In less than fifteen minutes in this Catholic enclave, Stephen felt further away from discerning what was true than he had in years. Swiftly that red candle which this priest considered so beautiful and meaningful had become to him a beacon of utter chaos and deception. Add to this the peculiar statues and paintings, and he suddenly felt claustrophobic, trapped.

He turned from the altar and, stumbling toward the rear of the church, said, "Please, I need to leave."

"Stephen, what is it?"

Without an answer, Stephen hurried down the center aisle toward the front door.

"Stephen, wait!" the priest called after him, but Stephen wasn't listening. He burst through the front door and immediately felt release. The cool, crisp winter air was fresh and free. He nearly flew down the steps to his car, started the engine, threw it into gear, and sped away.

Within minutes he was on a two-lane country road leading west out of town. Where it led was of no concern; he was merely driving. The late afternoon sky in front of him was washed in the reds and oranges of the setting sun. It was that time of day when one isn't quite sure whether headlights are necessary; some of the cars coming at him had theirs on, others didn't, and the glow from one made the next hard to see.

His entire world was spinning, and every solution he considered seemed fleeting and groundless. He couldn't return to the life and ministry he had left behind—for myriad reasons that had accumulated over the years—yet he couldn't go forward.

Lost in his thoughts, he didn't notice how fast he was driving, now well over the speed limit, fifty-five, sixty miles per hour. He swerved in and out of the left oncoming lane, passing cars as if they were parked. He tried to pray, but felt detached from God. Every word of supplication seemed to echo back: *No one is listening, no one up there cares!*

His speed reached sixty-five, and as he approached a curve, a never before considered thought entered his mind: *What do I now have to live for? My life is a mess, as a result of my own stupidity. Why keep going on?*

The road ahead curved to the right and under a railroad trestle. His Wagoneer leaned dangerously to the left as he took the curve at sixty-five, but he didn't care. Coming out the other side, he saw headlights coming directly at him, drawing him in, entrancing him. As the road continued its arch to the right, Stephen no longer responded. Following the tangent of the curve, he headed straight for the oncoming headlights. Within five feet of Stephen's car, the oncoming vehicle, horn blaring, swerved dangerously to its left, just missing Stephen's car on the right. As the other car swerved back into its own lane, Stephen's tires left the pavement.

He awoke immediately as if from a trance. He retook control of the steering wheel, still traveling nearly sixty miles per hour the wrong way down the gravel- and snow-covered berm on the wrong side of the road. The Wagoneer bounced along against four-foot-high snowdrifts as Stephen gently tapped the brakes to avoid a skid. Another car passed on the pavement to his right. He heard its horn blaring in the distance, its tone dropping in pitch and fading away.

His speed had eased down to thirty. After letting another car pass to his right and seeing both lanes clear, he veered back onto the pavement and across to the correct side of the road. He continued slowing down, pulled over to the side, and stopped. He shoved his car into park, turned off his ignition, and dropped his head into his hands, crying.

"Oh, Lord, dear Lord. I'm sorry. So sorry," and as he considered how miraculously fortunate he was, his prayer changed: "Thank you, Lord. Thank you, precious Jesus. Thank you for saving me."

Stephen remained parked for quite a while, weeping tears of both sorrow and joy, but still without any idea as to what he should do.

2

Father bourque knelt in the small private chapel in the rectory. Ever since Stephen had left in such a panic, he felt ashamed for coming on so strong. *I should have known better.*

He had led evening Mass hoping Stephen would return, but saw no sign of him. During Mass, however, he sensed deep within that someone was passing through some great spiritual trial, maybe someone out in the congregation or at home. He didn't know whom, but from past experience he trusted the veracity of this inner voice: someone was dangerously under spiritual attack. Silently, he offered the Mass for whomever this might be. Afterward, when he greeted people out front, no one mentioned anything significant, so he relinquished it to the infinite mercy of God.

On through dinner, he prayed and waited patiently for Stephen's return, but nothing.

Now alone in the chapel, praying the Evening Office and, as the English say, telling his beads, he begged God to help Stephen work through his vocational despair, wherever he was.

The priest crossed himself and rose to leave. Opening the chapel door, he heard a distant knocking. Passing down the central hall, the knocking grew louder. He reached the front door, and looking through the peephole, he saw that God had heard his prayers.

"Stephen, come in, please," Father Bourque exclaimed, opening the door. Stephen was huddled against the evening cold.

"Thank you, Reverend Bourque." He entered quickly.

"Where did you go? I mean…I'm sorry if I offended you."

"No, it was all me," Stephen said, kicking snow from his shoes. "Everything just came rushing in, and I panicked."

"Well, I'm glad you came back. Here, let me take your coat. Would you like coffee? There's a fresh pot in the kitchen."

"Sounds great. I guess I should ask, is the offer still open for the night?"

"But, of course. Your room is down the hall to the left next to mine, and everything's ready for you."

"Thank you. I truly appreciate it."

Father Bourque handed him a large mug of coffee and led him to the study. "Come, sit down, and let us start over. I've a warm fire burning, so how about a bit of your history?"

"Thanks, but how about yours first?" Stephen said as he sat in a large bentwood rocker to the right of the fire facing Father Bourque, who sat in a similar rocker to the left. "Jim told me that you were a pastor."

"Still am," the priest said with a grin.

"I mean..."

"I know. Yes, I was a cradle Lutheran, you might say, born in central Canada. From as early as I can remember, I knew God was calling me into the ministry. I've always loved Jesus, almost from baptism on, which I admit is quite rare. And my life was basically on one track: from confirmation to Lutheran high school to Lutheran seminary and then, finally, ordination to the Lutheran ministry. During seminary, I married a beautiful, holy woman named Lucy." He gestured toward a small black and white photo on the table beside him.

"We discovered with regret that we could never have children, but with hindsight, I'm certain it was God's perfect though mysterious will. During my second pastorate, Lucy contracted leukemia, and her life for the next sixteen years was one growing hell. And this was the beginning of my search, for my wife's suffering turned me—turned us—into Catholics."

"Is there anything else I can get you? You seem cold?" The priest rose to provide whatever aid was needed.

"No, thank you, please, I'm feeling much better. The fire and the coffee are working wonders," Stephen said. "But please, tell me more about your journey. How did suffering make you into a Catholic?"

Father Bourque sat back down with some reluctance. "Stephen, how do you as a Congregationalist understand suffering? How do you explain to people why God lets them or their closest family and friends suffer and die from terrible diseases, like cancer or leukemia, or allows an innocent child to be killed in an auto accident?"

Stephen looked from the priest into the blazing fire, considering this mystery. Suffering was certainly one of the more difficult issues for which he had encountered many conflicting explanations, all based on some combination of biblical texts. He had placed this mystery safely on the back burner.

"Reverend Bourque, I don't know," he finally said. "For every explanation, I can find an alternative. I guess it's an elusive combination of God's mysterious yet perfect will, our own sin and rebellion, and the workings of the devil."

"Yes, there is a great mystery to suffering. But what bothered me most about it, what led me almost to despair, was its meaninglessness," the priest replied. "I could encourage my parishioners to trust in God's wisdom and mercy, or to remember that 'all things work together for good for those who love God,' but none of this worked for me. I watched Lucy suffer in excruciating, continuous pain, and I could discern no good reason behind it, especially with all I believed about the powerful work of Christ's redemption. In His earthly life, Jesus had healed so many, and you and I know that He still heals to this day. But He would not heal Lucy." He rested his hand gently against the photo.

"One night, about two years before Lucy died, she was enduring an extraordinary amount of pain. We sedated her, and as she fell peacefully to sleep, I went into my study and broke down, crying as I had never cried before. And two things happened that changed my heart and my life. First, in the midst of my tears I realized that I was suffering as much as Lucy, but in a different way. Oh, sure, I had gone through hours of 'Why me, Lord?' but this was different. I realized that my suffering in concern for Lucy—not for myself, but for her—was somehow just as real and just as significant as hers. And in that, I sensed that somehow our suffering together, for one another—for then I realized that she too was suffering inside for what this was doing to me—was not a mere mysterious question mark, but a purposeful part of God's plan for us. I still didn't know what this might be, but I knew that there was purpose here, true meaning."

He rose to get more warmth from the fire. "Then a second thing happened. I turned to Scripture, imploring God for guidance, for some reason to hope, and almost miraculously—not almost, it truly was God's providence—I turned to some verses I had read many times before, but had never heard quite so clearly. Romans chapter eight, verses sixteen and seventeen. Do you know these verses?"

"I've certainly studied and read Romans many times," Stephen said, "and know by memory several verses around that section, like verse twenty-eight, which you just quoted. But I can't recall those."

"I've since memorized them, because they truly changed my life—it changed our lives. Paul wrote to the Romans: 'When we cry, "Abba! Father!" it is the Spirit himself bearing witness with our spirit that we are children of God, and if children, then heirs, heirs of God and fellow heirs with Christ, provided,'—and this is the important point—'provided we *suffer* with Him in order that we may also be glorified with Him.'

"That night, as I prayed and prayed over these verses, I literally became Catholic in my thinking, even though I was oblivious to it. What does this simple and clear verse say? It first reminds us of what our salvation is truly all about. Protestants too often think of salvation only in terms of a legal court in which God declares our sins forgiven because of what His Son did for us. But here Paul emphasizes that our salvation truly means a new relationship with God the Father—Abba—and with Jesus Christ, our Brother. And if we are therefore truly children of our loving heavenly Father, as the First Epistle of John also emphasizes, then why aren't we responsible for our actions, just as children are?"

Now warmed, the priest sat back down and leaned toward Stephen as he spoke. "The more I reflected on this, it seemed as if this was something I had always believed but couldn't put into words, given my Lutheran categories. Children are not called to 'sin boldly,' as Luther had boasted, or to ignore their wicked behavior, presuming upon a father's forgiveness won by an elder brother's sacrifice made on their behalf. And even if an elder brother did sacrifice everything on our behalf, we would be spitting in his face if we didn't recognize that how we live our lives is as important as our willing acceptance of his sacrificial act!

"Anyway, I'm drifting, sorry," the priest said, taking a sip of coffee. "The most significant thing this verse helped me to discover was that suffering is not only an important part of being children—in terms of formative discipline—but it's also an eternally essential part of our salvation. Remember what that verse said: 'provided we suffer with Him.' This was a curious construction, so I looked it up in the Greek—which, of course, tends to be the highest authority for Protestant exegetes, is it not?" he said with a smirk.

"What do you mean?" Stephen replied.

"When you as a Protestant pastor question the accuracy of a particular translation of the Bible, is not your first recourse to check the Greek for yourself? To see what Greek word is truly in the text, to parse it, and then, if you don't know the word, look it up in a Greek-English dictionary?"

Stephen considered all angles to this before replying: "Yes, generally that's true, Hebrew or Greek, depending upon the Testament."

"OK, now consider this," Father Bourque asked, rocking slowly. "Let's say you question a word that the committee chose when they produced the Revised Standard Version of the Bible. You go through your exegetical process, and eventually decide on a different word that you feel better translates the original Greek. Have you ever done this?"

"Many times," Stephen responded with the enthusiasm of one wanting to disclose a discovery. "Recently I was preparing to preach on Psalm 121, which in most Bible translations opens with the phrase: 'I lift up my eyes to the hills. From whence does my help come?' After doing my exegesis, I concluded that another possible, and I believe more probable rendering was, 'I *lifted* up my eyes to the hills. But from whence *came* my help?' You see, most people interpret this passage as if looking to the hills was a good thing, when in fact looking to the hills was a form of apostasy. The psalmist had been essentially running away from God, cavorting with idol priests and worshippers in the 'high places.' So, this psalm was the confession of his conversion back to the God of Israel who had come to his aid."

"Interesting translation," the priest said, with a mischievous smile, "but think about this for a second: did you then preach on this? Did you share your translation with your congregation instead of the one given in their pew Bibles?"

"Yes, I did," and as he said this, Stephen realized how arrogant this sounded.

"If you don't mind my asking, in the end, where did the authority rest in your translation: with the Greek New Testament, the RSV Committee, the Greek-English Dictionary, or you?"

Stephen sat looking at his inquisitor, his mind racing. He took a long sip of coffee and then, with a soft tone of self-resignation, he said, "Me...but I proceeded on the assumption that the Holy Spirit was guiding me."

"That's right, but in reality, the final authority for most Protestant preachers is themselves: they preach what they decide a verse means."

"Reverend Bourque, you're hitting at the core of my problem. I've always believed that the Bible was the sole foundation for my faith, but, as you say, in the end what I've believed and preached has been based too often on my own opinions or those of some interpreter, scholar, or religious leader I trust."

"And as a Lutheran pastor," the priest said, "what I preached was a combination of what Luther and Melanchthon believed 'brought up to date' by some biblical scholar, but still, when I stood before my people, I preached what *I* concluded was true—never the Bible *alone*."

Stephen stared into the fire, his anxiety rising again. This conversation was only recapitulating his own crumbling life.

"But you were saying about suffering?" he prodded.

"Sorry, Stephen. I'm afraid you'll have to bear with my tangential mind. Old age is taking its toll. Tell you what, I'll give the quick conclusion to my story, and then back to what we were discussing, because I believe that in it you will discover the answer to your dilemma.

"I turned to the Greek New Testament to check the translation of that verse from Romans, because to my Lutheran sensibilities, the phrase 'provided we suffer with Him' seemed too strong. It demanded too much of us. How can our salvation *depend* upon whether we have suffered with Jesus? I looked it up and found that this was exactly what the Greek words meant; there was no getting around it or softening it. Jesus called us to suffer *with* Him, and as I watched Lucy suffer, knowing her faith, I realized that her suffering somehow involved a meaningful sharing of Christ's suffering on the Cross.

"Then in my daily devotions, a Scripture passage confronted me that I had always avoided because, frankly, I couldn't explain it.

In Colossians 1:24, the Apostle Paul wrote:

> Now I rejoice in my sufferings for your sake, and in my flesh I complete what is lacking in Christ's afflictions for the sake of His body, that is, the church.

"Stephen, how can anyone, let alone the Apostle Paul, given his horrendous persecutions while in prison, rejoice in their sufferings? To me, this seemed both crazy and yet exhilarating. The Scriptures teach that Christ's suffering and sacrifice were complete and sufficient for all sinners, so what could be *lacking?* I didn't know, and in a real sense still don't, because this is a mystery. Yet, I came to realize that our sufferings are a participation in Christ's redemptive suffering for others *if* we accept them as such, with joy and without complaining.

"Stephen, this changed my life, but even more miraculously, it changed Lucy's."

Father Bourque dropped his head into his hands. When he raised back up, the glow of the fire reflected in his moist eyes.

"I was hesitant to share this with her—how could I, in perfect health, tell Lucy, in constant agony, to *rejoice in her sufferings?* But I gently and lovingly told her what I had discovered, and Stephen, she already knew it. She didn't understand the underlying theology, but in the midst of her pain the Spirit had told her—that her suffering was for others."

Stephen wanted to understand, but this was contrary to everything he believed about faith and redemption, suffering and sin.

The priest left the room briefly and then returned with a plate of oatmeal cookies. "The handwork of Sister Agatha."

Returning to his rocker, he continued. "One evening, Lucy, in her soft, pain-ridden voice, read me a passage from Romans 12:

> I appeal to you therefore, brethren, by the mercies of God, to present your bodies as a living sacrifice, holy and acceptable to God, which is your spiritual worship. Do not be conformed to this world, but be transformed by the renewal of your mind, that you may prove what is the will of God, what is good and acceptable and perfect.

"She then closed the Bible, letting it slide down out of her weak hands onto the bed, and said, 'Honey, I pray that somehow my suffering is for the good of Christ and the salvation of souls.'"

Father Bourque turned to the fire to hide his tears. "She was right, you know. Her mind had been transformed. She was no longer conforming to the values of this world. She was presenting her body, with all its pain and suffering, as a living sacrifice to God, completing in some mysterious way the afflictions of Christ and his Church."

The priest turned back to Stephen with an air of composure, "To make a long story short, I knew that this was not Lutheran theology, or Protestant for that matter, but I didn't know that it was Catholic until someone gave me a small book entitled *The Christian Meaning of Suffering,* written by Pope John Paul II. This changed my life. I had never read anything by a Catholic, let alone a pope, so I cynically expected a long collection of doctrinal mumbo-jumbo built on earning one's salvation through works and suffering. Instead, what I found was the clearest, most profound *Bible study* of the gospel message I had ever read. The first paragraph began with the verses I had been studying, and by the time I reached the end, I was a Catholic. Here, let me show you."

He rose and crossed to a bookshelf that covered the entire wall behind Stephen. From a collection of thin paperback books, he removed one that was worn from use.

"Here, listen." The priest returned to his chair, thumbing through pages which Stephen could see were underlined and annotated. "It's hard to find one simple quote that expresses succinctly all that John Paul teaches about suffering—you'd need to read it from cover to cover. But bear with me on this long quote from paragraph twenty-seven:

> St. Paul speaks of true joy in the letter to the Colossians: "I rejoice in my sufferings for your sake." A source of joy is found in the overcoming of the sense of the uselessness of suffering, a feeling that is sometimes very strongly rooted in human suffering. This feeling not only consumes the person interiorly, but seems to make him a burden to others. The person feels condemned to receive help and assistance from others, and at the same time

seems useless to himself. The discovery of the salvific meaning of suffering in union with Christ transforms this depressing feeling.

"This is what happened for Lucy and me. When we discovered the meaning of our suffering together, we were filled with an inexpressible, supernatural joy. Let me continue:

> Faith in sharing in the suffering of Christ brings with it the interior certainty that the suffering person "completes what is lacking in Christ's afflictions"; the certainty that in the spiritual dimension of the work of Redemption he is serving, like Christ, the salvation of his brothers and sisters. Therefore, he is carrying out an irreplaceable service. In the Body of Christ, which is ceaselessly born of the cross of the Redeemer, it is precisely suffering permeated by the spirit of Christ's sacrifice that is the irreplaceable mediator and author of the good things which are indispensable for the world's salvation. It is suffering, more than anything else, which clears the way for the grace which transforms human souls. Suffering, more than anything else, makes present in the history of humanity the powers of the Redemption. In that "cosmic" struggle between the spiritual powers of good and evil, spoken of in the letter to the Ephesians, human sufferings, united to the redemptive suffering of Christ, constitute a special support for the powers of good, and open the way to the victory of these salvific powers."

Father Bourque set the book aside. "But as I said, the entire book is one continuous Bible study on the meaning of suffering, and in the end it led us to become Catholics. Not overnight, mind you. I first had to face up to my own ignorance. Most of what I thought the Catholic Church taught was inaccurate; I had accepted blindly what non-Catholics or even anti-Catholics had written."

This was all so familiar to Stephen, as he remembered that evening with Ginny and Adrian.

"Lucy and I began studying the Catholic faith together, and

everything we learned rang true. In time, I had no other choice. I resigned from my pastorate, and on Easter Vigil 1985, we were received into the Church.

"Six months later, Lucy died. I thought my life was over. But now it was my turn to accept the redemptive meaning of suffering, or, as Catholics say, 'Offer it up!' And God blessed unbelievably. The bishop called me in, and everything from then on flew by like a whirlwind. After three years in seminary, I was ordained to the priesthood. And here I am, unworthy as I am."

Moved by this priest's candid testimony, Stephen nevertheless said, "I'm taken aback by hearing about you and Jim, Protestant ministers resigning to become Catholic. Other than you two, I've never heard of such a thing. I've heard of Catholic priests, nuns, and laity becoming Protestant, but the only Protestants I've known who became Catholic did so through marriage."

"It is a well-kept secret, isn't it? Actually the number of converts to the Catholic Church, both lay and clergy, is quite large and constant, and has been ever since the Reformation. Many books tell the stories of clergymen, high Church leaders, scholars, doctors, lawyers, writers, and other professionals who have converted during the last several hundred years. But since Protestants rarely read Catholic books, they don't know this. There are so many clergy converts today, in fact, that there's an international network of converts from more than sixty different denominations. Jim and I are only the tip of a growing iceberg."

Stephen was incredulous. "This is hard to believe. Why are these men—and women, I presume—converting?"

"For a variety of reasons and circumstances, but usually it boils down to the issue of authority—the authority to determine what is true. Isn't this what you're struggling with?"

Stephen stared at the priest, certain that he had not revealed this. "As a matter of fact it is, and as a result, my life is a disaster."

"Well, maybe that's why God brought you here. Listen, it's late, and I apologize for rambling on so long."

"Oh, no, Reverend Bourque. It was very pertinent to where I am."

"I'm anxious to pick up our earlier discussion about interpreting Scripture, but we can do that in the morning," Father Bourque said, rising. "Morning Mass is at seven o'clock, if you'd like to come, and then breakfast at eight. After that we can come back here. Sound all right?"

"Yes, fine," Stephen said as he also rose.

"Do you need to call your family?"

"No, they know I'm away on retreat to sort this all out," Stephen said, curious as to how much this priest might have guessed. "I'll call them tomorrow." He turned toward the hall.

"Fine, but before we head off to bed, let's end our time in prayer."

Stephen halted, bowed his head, and closed his eyes.

"Heavenly Father," the priest spoke softly, "thank You for bringing Stephen here. In Your infinite wisdom and knowledge, You know his needs and struggles even more than he does. Help him through Your indwelling presence to hear Your voice and follow Your guidance, wherever You desire to lead him. This we ask in the name of the Father and of the Son and of the Holy Spirit. Amen."

"Thank you," Stephen said, extending a hand. "I am glad to be here."

"You're welcome, my friend. Here, let me show you to your room."

He led Stephen down the hall to a small bedroom that contained a single bed, a padded chair, a desk and lamp, a sink, and a mirror.

"Thank you, Father Bourque. Good night," Stephen said, for the first time addressing the priest as "father." He had avoided this all day, given the scriptural mandate against calling any man "father," yet with Father Bourque it somehow seemed right. He would ask him about this in the morning.

"Good night, Stephen. Pleasant dreams." With a slight wave, the priest passed down the hall.

Stephen closed the door, undressed, and retired quickly to bed. In the darkness, he lay amazed at all that had transpired during the day—from his sermon to his fight to his flight to his near-death on the road and now his evening with this sincere clergy convert, Catholic priest. He pondered God's hand in it all, but before he had any answers, he was asleep.

*   *   *

THE ACTIVITY ON THE PRODUCTION-ROOM FLOOR appeared to be progressing normally. The familiar faces were in their assigned stations, and the evening's end product—marble-textured ABS plastic lunch trays—were being retrieved from the injection molding machine, trimmed, and stacked for cooling.

All was well, so Walter returned his attention to the open Bible before him. He still felt chilled to the bone after sitting nearly five hours that afternoon in his car. He pulled the electric space heater closer so the radiant heat could flow more directly onto his legs and then up his body.

Since the beginning of the year, he had been following a *Read-the-Bible-in-a-Year Guide* that Raeph had sent him for Christmas. Though Walter had studied most of the Bible, he had never read it consecutively from cover to cover, but this was one of his resolutions for this first year of the new millennium.

Today's reading: Deuteronomy 13.

Moving his desk lamp closer, he began reading:

> If a prophet arises among you, or a dreamer of dreams,
> and gives you a sign or a wonder, and the sign or wonder
> which he tells you comes to pass, and if he says, "Let us
> go after other gods," which you have not known, "and
> let us serve them"…

"Now if that don't sound like those wild Pentecostals down the street, nothing does," he said, shaking his head. "And the God they worship sure doesn't sound like the one I do."

He continued:

> You shall not listen to the words of that prophet or to
> that dreamer of dreams; for the Lord your God is testing
> you, to know whether you love the Lord your God with
> all your heart and with all your soul. You shall walk after
> the Lord your God and fear Him, and keep His
> commandments and obey His voice, and you shall serve
> Him and cleave to Him.

"Testing me." Walter knew that much in life was intended as a test of his loyalty. *To what extent, though, am I willing and able to walk, fear, keep, obey, serve, and cleave unto Jesus?* He read on:

> But that prophet or that dreamer of dreams shall be put to death, because he has taught rebellion against the Lord your God, who brought you out of the land of Egypt and redeemed you out of the house of bondage, to make you leave the way in which the Lord your God commanded you to walk. So you shall purge the evil from the midst of you.

He didn't remember reading this before. It was strong, awfully strong, but it was real. And it was from the very Word of God.

> If your brother, the son of your mother, or your son, or your daughter, or the wife of your bosom, or your friend who is as your own soul, entices you secretly, saying, "Let us go and serve other gods," which neither you nor your fathers have known, some of the gods of the peoples that are round about you, whether near you or far off from you, from the one end of the earth to the other, you shall not yield to him or listen to him, nor shall your eye pity him, nor shall you spare him, nor shall you conceal him; *but you shall kill him; your hand shall be first against him to put him to death, and afterwards the hand of all the people.*

His sat back hard in his swivel chair. From years of use by heavier foremen, the chair ball-joint squeaked and leaned him slightly to the right. He stared out through the production office window, out over the whirring machinery and the computers and the men working nervously under his supervision, and he wondered how peaceably his nemesis was sleeping that night.

"What more do I need to know?"

3

Sᴛᴇᴘʜᴇɴ's ᴇʏᴇs ᴏᴘᴇɴᴇᴅ into the darkness of pre-dawn, and for a moment he didn't know where he was. The room was darker than his bedroom at home, which even in the middle of the night was partially lit by the glow of a distant street lamp.

Then he remembered. He had spent the night in the rectory of a Catholic church, miles away from Sara and the boys. His heart ached, mostly from guilt, but also sadness. *Lord Jesus, what am I doing to my family?*

He threw off the sparse covers, white institutional bed linen and a thin wool blanket. Kicking his legs over the side and sitting up, he ran his fingers through his hair and then sat in the darkness, head in hands. He begged God for forgiveness and "the peace that passes all understanding."

His mind was a whir of voices, all talking at once—some encouraging, others accusing, rationalizing, or pleading. Yet in the midst of this, as if from deeper in his heart, a calming, soft, *still* voice whispered: *Be patient and trust. Be not afraid. Be not afraid.* As the other voices raged for his undivided attention, his heart kept repeating these last three words of faith.

A soft tapping interrupted him. Then again, gently.

"Stephen?" came the soft voice of Father Bourque. "Stephen, are you awake?"

"Yes, Father Bourque," Stephen said, rising from his bed, groping toward the voice and the door. He glanced at the phosphorescent dial of his watch: 6:39 a.m.

"I hope I didn't wake you," came the voice through the door.

"No, no, I was awake."

"Good. I just thought I'd remind you about morning Mass— just in case you changed your mind."

"Just a moment." Stephen felt around for the light switch. After being momentarily blinded, he quickly dressed. Now presentable, he opened the door. The priest was dressed in the same black robe cinctured by a rope.

"Thank you for asking, but I don't think so, not yet," Stephen declined.

"That's OK, I understand. Just make yourself at home. Feel free to pay a visit to the chapel down the hall or browse through my library. I'll be back around 7:45 for breakfast. Sister Agatha will be our cook this morning." He hurried off, grabbing his overcoat from a rack by the front door.

Stephen watched briefly and then closed himself back into his room. Fully reawakened to his self-imposed exile in this strange land, he decided that adhering closely to his normal routine was the best solution. A quick shower, a clean change of clothes, and Stephen was ready for his morning quiet time.

At the small desk, he opened his Bible to where he had left off Saturday morning—he generally skipped Sundays, figuring that morning worship and other church activities more than sufficed for the day's devotions. He began to read, but remembered the chapel down the hall.

"Why not?" He collected his Bible and journal and exited for the chapel.

The door was ajar and light flickered from the other side. He slowly pushed the door open. Inside the dimly lit, tiny room were several chairs and kneelers that faced a small front altar covered with candles, vases of flowers, religious pictures, and a central silver box like that in the church sanctuary, only smaller. A candle in a red glass fixture hung from the ceiling and hovered just to the left of the altar. The sight brought back yesterday's panic, but this time that still, small voice calmed his heart: *Be not afraid.*

He eased into a chair. The flickering light of a dozen candles gave an eerie feel to the religious pictures. The eyes on one particular portrait of Mary seemed to stare right at him, beckoning him. She wore a full-length blue dress with a white mantle, and her arms were outstretched, her palms opening toward him. She was smiling, inviting him to come to her.

Until reading Keating, Stephen had always assumed that Catholics worshiped images like this. But Keating had argued that Catholics no more worship a picture or a statue than does a child standing before a picture of his mother or a statue of a great war hero. Pictures of saints, he had said, help people remember and then emulate their faithfulness or spiritual heroism.

But Catholics do go a step further, Stephen mused, *for they actually pray to the saints whom these images represent.* This was probably the most difficult Catholic practice for him to stomach—the closest to idolatry. But Keating had claimed that this was no different than asking any friend or family member to pray for us—the saints are just closer to the source, as witnessed in the book of Revelation.

Stephen wasn't convinced. He forced his attention down to his Bible and began reading.

After a few paragraphs, though, his eyes drifted up to the ornate crucifix above the altar. He had just read a verse that had always been a puzzlement. In Paul's letter to the Galatians, the Apostle was writing to Christians who had never seen or heard Jesus in person, but had learned the faith through Paul's preaching.

So what does Paul mean by this strange statement, he wondered:

> O foolish Galatians! Who has bewitched you, before
> whose eyes Jesus Christ was publicly portrayed as
> crucified?

"Publicly portrayed as crucified." What was Paul referring to? he asked himself, or was he asking God? Studying the sinews of the emaciated, bleeding plaster corpse that hung limply from a cross with a drooping crossbeam, he thought: *Is it at all possible that Paul was referring to just such a crudely crafted crucifix?*

Another item on the altar caught his eye, a round gold fixture that looked like a picture frame with golden spikes all around it. He got up to examine it more closely. In the center of the circular glass compartment was a small white six-pointed star surrounded by silver rays, and glued in the center of this was a tiny brown chip of something. Underneath the star was a white nameplate that contained the words: *S. Franc. Sal. ECD.*

He had never seen one, but he knew what this was—*a relic! And that brown chip must be a piece of bone from some saint!*

Stephen understood none of this. Retreating to his seat, he tried to redirect his mind back to his Bible, but the immensity of everything in this small private chapel was too intense. He rose and backed out and into the comfortable familiarity of his temporary bedroom. *Lord Jesus, what am I DOING here?*

And yet, the still quiet voice from deep within whispered: *Be not afraid.*

*   *   *

BENEATH THE MORNING SHADOW of a grove of Norwegian spruce, William parked his pristine sky-blue Jeep Wrangler, his pride and joy. Since it first graced their driveway seven months ago, he had learned a lot about taking care of the engine. In many ways, this 10-year-old Jeep was in better shape than when it sat in the used-car lot in Respite. Other boys souped their cars up with overhead cams and hood scoops, lowered the suspensions with those new wide, thin-walled tires, and installed extreme music systems with bass that could be heard and felt four cars over. William, however, just kept his Jeep to its original specs, spotlessly clean and purring like a kitten. He had added an in-dash CD player, which was yet to be invented when this puppy rolled off the assembly line, but it was a conservative model— for the listening pleasure of the occupants, not for everyone else in the great outdoors.

He liked to park out here, the most remote section of the high school lot, partly because he liked the scent of the small spruce grove, but also because he could retreat to this friend and sit uninterrupted. He did this often when he had a long, empty period between classes. Though he had made the basketball team and found new friends, he still felt like an outsider at this predominantly upper-middle-class school. He missed his old friends, both male and female, and though things were looking up now that Stacy had dropped back into his life, it wasn't the same.

This dreary winter morning, however, William had another reason for lingering in the privacy of his personal space on wheels, for now he knew what it felt like when one parent leaves home. He had friends whose parents were divorced, or even unmarried. And though his parents had their regular episodes of fighting and yelling, he never dreamed that they would separate. *My dad's a minister, for heaven's sake! He would never let their marriage fall apart. God wouldn't let this happen!*

But maybe it was happening.

He also knew that ministers were just like anyone else—equally tempted to sin. And maybe even more so. His father had often explained that people in positions of great potential for the kingdom of God were a greater threat to the devil and his schemes. When a minister falls into sin—when his marriage crumbles—the faith and confidence of his congregation weakens, and the devil wins a battle.

Well, Dad, I guess you blew it!

Yesterday had been horrible. His mother had vented her frustration on Daniel and him, making them clean practically everything in the house. Off and on all night, he heard her crying in her room, as well as Daniel in his. He thought about going in to soothe her, but she was so unpredictable—sometimes she would respond in kindness, other times with bitterness. So instead he just lay in his bed, without tears, hoping his dad was all right, certain that he would be back in the morning when he awoke.

But he wasn't. No calls, no Wagoneer in the garage. So before his mother and Daniel awoke, William had dressed and driven to school. Now he sat alone, waiting for class, wondering whether, in the hearts of other kids whose parents had blown it, this ache ever went away.

He looked at his watch. In five minutes the doors would open. *Would Stacy be there waiting?* He had caught her eye in church yesterday morning, but hadn't been able to talk with her. *I wonder if her father has softened any?*

The influx of cars was increasing, so William decided to go in and beat the rush.

"Good morning, William," Miss Duryea said as he came through the senior lounge doors. "You're here bright and early. Anxious to start a new week of classes?"

"Now, Miss Duryea, you know full well why I came here so early," he said as he dispensed himself an instant cappuccino.

She smiled. "Discussions about New Hampshire history? Yes, she's very pretty."

William had guessed that Miss Duryea was more "with it" than the other students' cynical putdowns implied.

"Yes, she is. You probably know from personal experience that senior lounges are not for getting a jump on homework."

Again she smiled, but with a hidden sadness—for her, student lounges had always been for homework.

"William, let's just say I'm not oblivious to why you students come here." She took a sip from her own coffee. "And that's all right with me, as long as you don't do something foolish to mess up your lives."

"Not under your ever-watchful eye," he said, smiling and winking.

"Well, let's just not take advantage of my occasional turned back." She winked back.

The door opened, and it was Stacy.

"Excuse me," William said. He turned his focus to the beautiful girl walking toward him.

"Hello, Stacy," he said, fighting the same emotional butterflies he had felt at their first reunion. He wanted to tell her how great she looked, but nothing came out.

"William," she responded with a dark tone. "We need to talk."

"OK. Would you like something to drink?"

"No, thank you." She led him to a stuffed love seat off the beaten path of the room.

"William, I need your help desperately," she said, wiping her eyes with a handkerchief, glancing momentarily up into his eyes and then down toward the floor.

"What has happened?" William said with a panic, ready to fight whatever threatened her.

"Nothing has happened, yet, but I'm terrified that something will. Father is acting strangely, like he did once before when—well, I just don't want to go through that again. I can't."

She buried her face in her hands, muffling sobs with her kerchief. Cautiously he put a soothing arm around her shoulders, and to his surprise she welcomed it. He glanced at Miss Duryea, who cast them a concerned glance.

"What can I do?" he asked.

Stacy suddenly scooted slightly away from William. She lifted her head and the tears were mysteriously gone. With renewed enthusiasm and inner strength, she whispered, "William, I need you to help me escape. I'm running away."

"Stacy, is it really that bad?"

"My father is unpredictable. He can be so protective, but at the same time so violent. He calls me his prized pearl, his sweet pea.

William, I'm afraid." As she said this, she grabbed his hands and looked into his eyes.

"What do you want me to do?" Any reservations he might have had melted away.

She dropped his hands and spoke softly, deliberately.

"Tomorrow afternoon, immediately after class, I need you to drive me away from this school to a place about fifteen miles north of town. Some of my old friends will be there waiting to take me to where I'll be safe."

"But Stacy, what if your father..."

"I know where you park your car. I can get out to it without him seeing me. I'll stuff my backpack with clothing rather than books, and then tomorrow after last bell, you just come out to your car. I'll be there hiding in the back seat." She took his hands. "William, I'll be greatly indebted to you if you help me."

He looked into her blue eyes, which crowned her soft, winsome smile, and he was hers.

"OK, I'll help you. But I'm nervous about this."

"Don't worry. It will work just fine."

She turned and rose. "And after I'm safely away, I'll keep in touch with you by e-mail. Listen. Let's meet again here tomorrow morning, just to make sure everything is going as planned. Then I'll be waiting for you after school in your Jeep. OK?"

"OK, Stacy, but..."

Several other students whom neither of them knew came into the lounge.

"Thanks, William." She gave him a light kiss on the cheek and left.

He stood there watching as the door closed behind her. The other students were oblivious to this, but he did sense two watchful eyes from behind him. He turned to see Miss Duryea's concerned gaze.

"Anything wrong, William?"

"No, nothing," he said, unable to hold back his exploding smile.

"So, what'd we learn today about New Hampshire history?" She quipped as he crossed toward the cappuccino machine.

"Nothing, but I think we might be making some."

4

"Stephen, how 'bout throwing a few logs on the fire. I'll be with you in a few minutes with fresh coffee. Cream or sugar?"

"Cream, please." Stephen left his napkin on the breakfast table next to his dishes and retired to the study. Sister Agatha's breakfast had been delicious—Western omelets, sausage, fried potatoes, English muffins, juice, and Earl Grey tea. He was stuffed. *No wonder Father Bourque is far from wasting away.*

More than Sister Agatha's hospitality and cooking had captured Stephen's attention, though. He was mesmerized by the Sister herself. Given her name, he had expected an older, grandmotherly woman. But Sister Agatha was less than 30, beautiful, and to his unyielding curiosity, dressed in a traditional nun's habit—a black, full-length, loose-fitting robe that disguised her feminine form. Only visible were her hands, red and chapped from kitchen duty, and her face, beaming from beneath a white-lined black cape that trailed down her back to her waist. Stephen struggled to keep from staring at her, but every time she brought something in from the kitchen, she focused only on her task and never on him.

In time, Father Bourque had noticed his staring. Once after she had left the room, he asked, "Quite pretty, isn't she?"

Stephen had felt embarrassed, certain that he wasn't to look upon a nun with such admiration. "Yes, she is. I didn't expect..."

"You didn't expect a woman named Agatha who has committed herself to lifelong celibacy to be that young and beautiful."

"Right."

"Maybe we can talk more about this later, but suffice it to say there is no sorrowful malady that has forced this beautiful young woman to escape from the world, robbed of sexual and marital fulfillment. On the contrary, she is so in love with Jesus her Lord and so certain of God's calling in her life that she is more than willing to dedicate her entire life and all her energies to serving Him and His Church. She doesn't feel robbed; instead she feels highly and richly blessed."

Now in the study, Stephen noticed that the fire was down to red coals. He placed three quarter-split logs into the wood stove and closed the front glass-and-cast-iron door. Within seconds the fire was rekindled, blazing from the well-engineered draft.

While he waited, he looked through Father Bourque's extensive book collection. Except for the wood stove, windows, and door, every wall was covered with shelves and books. Scanning titles, he noticed sections on theology, philosophy, Church history, Scripture, biography, and finally the collection of paperbacks from which Father Bourque had retrieved the booklet on suffering. Alongside it were other books by the same author.

"Our present pope is quite a writer," Father Bourque said as he entered the room carrying two coffees in large pottery mugs. "He's not only an author of books on theology, Scripture, and philosophy, but also a playwright. But being a convert, what impressed me most about this man was how biblically sound his writings are. Every book is essentially a Bible study. You really ought to read something by him."

"I might do that," Stephen said doubtfully as he looked at the pope's book *Mother of the Redeemer*. He winced at the glorified picture of Mary and child on the cover and quickly returned it to the shelf.

"Father Bourque, before we pick up where we left off last night, may I ask a few questions?"

"Of course." He motioned Stephen to the rocker nearest the fire.

"Here's my dilemma. As I hole up here in your rectory, I'm essentially playing hooky from my life and responsibilities—from my family and my job as a minister. And all of this because, essentially, I can no longer be certain that my interpretation of the Bible is trustworthy. Now, for most people in the world, this is a non-issue. They believe that truth is basically relative—each person can decide his or her own truth. If they heard of my dilemma, they would just say, 'Get a life! You're taking yourself too seriously.'"

"But you and I both know that this proposition is illogical," the priest said.

"That's the point. Truth isn't relative; it's very real, eternally real. And you and I, as ministers of the gospel, will one day stand before Jesus responsible for how we proclaimed His truth. But I've become mentally paralyzed by the seeming contradiction of millions of sincere, Bible-believing Christians divided into thousands of denominations who disagree over what this truth is. Many try to justify this by claiming that God ordained these divergent groups, each with its own unique gift for the kingdom, to meet the diverse needs and temperaments of people. Yet, scratch any group of Christians, and in the end they bleed that only their denomination has a corner on the truth."

Stephen paused to sip his coffee, staring into the fire. For a second, he felt like he was back staring into the hearth at the pastors' retreat, sharing the same frustration with his friends.

Father Bourque waited quietly for him to continue.

"I lost my anchor when I realized that *sola Scriptura* cannot be trusted as the definitive foundation for truth. I was always aware of problems in interpretation, but just went on blindly believing that 'all we need is the Bible' to know what is true. Then it was brought to my attention that the Bible itself nowhere makes this claim. In essence, I was stymied by the same illogical circular argument that destroys relativism. Then a parishioner pointed out where the Bible claims that the Church, not the Bible itself, is 'the pillar and bulwark of the truth.' All this has left me confused and stressed out—it affects everything I do, everything that I am. I've got a family to support and a wife to please, but the only thing I know how to do, I can't do any longer.

"And discovering that the Catholic interpretation of Scripture is at least plausible," he continued, "only complicates things—one more opinion, held by millions of people, adding countless new permutations to my dilemma. I would love to challenge you with dozens of questions about why Catholics pray to saints or meditate on relics or wear ancient robes or require celibacy of priests or call priests 'Father,' but in the end it's all just one more sliver of the pie claiming to be the only true sliver.

"And to top all this off, the only people I know who also see the problem have either become or are becoming Catholics...like you. Maybe what Catholics believe is a whole lot different and less repulsive than I thought, but to become Catholic? This runs cross-grain to everything I've ever believed—everything that I am. And as our friend Jim has shown us, it means sacrificing everything—maybe even my marriage."

Stephen wondered what Sara might be doing at that moment. *Is she crying? Is she bitterly angry? Is she glad I'm gone?*

"So, Reverend Bourque, right now I can't see any way out of this dilemma except to ignore it—to come down off the mountain to the proverbial molehill—and spend the rest of my days wearing Congregationalist blinders, oblivious to the contradictory opinions of thousands of other sincere, well-informed Christians."

The priest broke in. "Stephen, my friend, let me assure you that I do understand most of what you are going through—for I went through it myself. Trust me, there is a clear answer to this dilemma. Granted, you might not like the answer, but the whole situation is quite easily explained. In reality, I suppose the complete explanation is a bit more complicated and convoluted, but let me give it a try.

"It all boils down to the issue of authority: who has the God-given authority to determine which of the millions of opinions out there is true? Which of the millions of authors, scholars, ordained ministers, self-proclaimed prophets, denominations, sects, or even cults has the rightful authority to stand up and claim they have found the truth?

"Remember several years ago that bumper sticker that said simply 'I Found It'? Now, we Christians knew what this meant, but the more I thought about it, the more this bumper sticker became a symbol of Protestant arrogance and confusion. You see, Stephen, I was asking some of the same questions you are from beneath my Lutheran clerical collar. In the phrase 'I Found It,' where should the emphasis be placed? On 'It,' or 'Found,' or 'I'? This is hardly an expression of grace or humility. Shouldn't it have been more accurately phrased, 'It Found Me'? And who was to define what 'It' was? The presumption was that one should follow the driver to find out—but which church parking lot would he drive into? Whose opinion of 'It' had the 'I Found'? Maybe it should have been 'He Found Me,' but then again, depending upon which lot you were led into, you'd end up with a different description of who 'He' is, or was, or is to come. You might even end up with 'She Found Me'!"

They both laughed.

"A similar criticism might be made of the present craze around the statement 'What Would Jesus Do?'," Father Bourque added.

"My secretary uses it as her screen saver," Stephen said. "She intends it as a periodic check to frustration or impatience, but I think it's become more a Pavlov's signal to reach into her lower desk drawer for another snack."

"I don't remember Jesus downing a Twinkie whenever he felt frustrated," the priest answered with levity. "Seriously, though, on the surface this sentiment sounds wholesome. But, criminy, that's been the problem for the past two thousand years: it's not always clear *what* Jesus might do in certain situations. This statement essentially reinforces the idea that it's every Christian for himself to determine what is true—unless there *is* an authoritative voice out there that can say without hesitation exactly how we are to imitate Jesus.

"Stephen, consider this: at the conclusion of the Gospel of Matthew, when Jesus gave his disciples their final marching orders, did he say, 'Now go and tell people to do what they think I would do'?"

"Of course not," Stephen answered. "His instructions were to make disciples of all nations, to baptize them, and to teach these new disciples what He had taught them."

"Correct, though your summary is telling. Assuming you left out the Trinitarian formula for brevity, there are three things, though, that must not be overlooked. One, Jesus began His Great Commission with the statement, 'All authority in heaven and on earth has been given to Me.' Two, He concluded with the promise, 'Lo, I am with you always, even to the close of the age.' And three, in the middle was the word 'all.' They were to teach 'all' that He had commanded them, not merely what they were comfortable with or what made sense to their limited reason. In these instructions, we find the passing of the baton of visible authority from Christ to His hand-chosen Apostles. They were to go forth to teach, not on their own authority, but on the authority of He who would always be with them, teaching *all* He had taught them, making and baptizing new disciples who would then carry on this work. Do you remember what Jesus promised them on the night He was betrayed?"

"Well, lots of things." Stephen knew where the priest was headed, but wasn't convinced he wanted to go along.

"Most significantly, Jesus promised that after He was gone He would send the Holy Spirit who would bring to their remembrance all that He had taught them, and then guide them into all the truth. So the short of it is that immediately after Jesus had ascended, how did the Apostles and their first disciples know what was true?"

"Well, they had the Sacred Writings—what we call the Old Testament—and what the Apostles said Jesus taught them."

"Exactly, and there are lots of Scripture verses to reinforce this. What about one or two generations later, to those believers who had not seen or heard Jesus in person, but learned about Him through the testimony of the original Apostles and disciples? How would they know what was true, especially if they were being persecuted for their Christian beliefs?"

Stephen waited to give his answer. He wanted to be accurate, not merely a purveyor of opinions he had accumulated along the way. "I presume they knew that something was trustworthy because it was written in the letter of an Apostle?"

"But why trust the word of someone like Paul who himself had not seen or heard the living Jesus?"

"His authority as an Apostle was based on his powerful conversion experience on the road to Damascus where he heard and saw the risen Christ."

"His self-proclaimed conversion," Father Bourque observed. "Lots of people claim conversions to Jesus, even drastic ones like Paul's, but that doesn't prove they can be trusted. Why did the Christians, who once knew Paul as their enemy, eventually accept his authority to teach truth or to write epistles like Galatians that expected their obedience?"

Stephen had always assumed that it was the witness of the Holy Spirit in people's hearts that had confirmed which first-century epistles were to be considered authentic or phony. But before he could answer, the priest continued.

"Here, Stephen, it's actually quite clear. In Galatians 1:18, Paul reminds his readers of the reason his gospel is to be trusted as opposed to those preaching 'a different gospel':

> Then after three years I went up to Jerusalem to visit Cephas, and remained with him fifteen days. But I saw none of the other apostles except James the Lord's brother.

"It's important to note the emphasis on Peter, here identified in Aramaic, Cephas. Later Paul writes:

> Then after fourteen years I went up again to Jerusalem with Barnabas…I went up by revelation, and I laid before them…the gospel which I preach among the Gentiles, lest somehow I should be running or had run in vain…and when they perceived the grace that was given to me, James and Cephas and John…gave to me and Barnabas the right hand of fellowship…

"Do you see the significance of what is happening?"

"Yes, but doesn't Paul eventually make a big thing about how he belittled Peter's authority and leadership, accusing him to his face of hypocrisy?"

"Stephen, that's the smokescreen Protestants always use to avoid facing the *reason* Paul mentions any of this in the first place. In reality, all that Paul's railing of Peter proves is that Peter is a sinner, susceptible to failing, and that Paul had the authority to criticize him. But what is most important about this section—the reason Paul includes it—is to establish that his gospel is to be accepted because his authority had been confirmed and established by the original Apostles. And this chain of authority went on. In Paul's Second Letter to Timothy, chapter two verse two, we read:

> What you have heard from me before many witnesses entrust to faithful men who will be able to teach others also.

"Jesus passed His authority on to the Apostles, who passed it on to men like Matthias and Paul, who passed it on to men like Timothy, who then ordained others, who in turn could ordain others. This is what the Church has always called 'apostolic succession.' A man could not just *decide* Jesus was calling him to preach and go off and start his own church. He had to be authorized and sent by the Apostles or one of their representatives.

"This is what Paul meant in Romans 10 when he exclaimed rhetorically:

> But how are men to call upon Him in whom they have
> not believed? And how are they to believe in Him of
> whom they have never heard? And how are they to hear
> without a preacher? And how can men preach unless
> they are *sent?*

"Do you see the significance? Belief was based on what was *heard*, not read—people heard the gospel proclaimed by preachers, but not just any preacher: preachers who were *sent*. Why? Because a man is not authorized to preach unless he has been sent with the apostolic authority of the Church."

"Yes, I think so." Stephen's mind was spinning with new information, but he was taking it in. "This is all a bit askew from how I was taught and what I teach, but it's making more sense. I've always presumed that the authority of the Apostles and their oral teaching was transferred to the written Gospels and pastoral epistles that became the New Testament?"

"Yes, in a sense, but never in the sense of *sola Scriptura*, because the Scriptures were never used this way, either in Old Testament times or during these early years of the Church. In Acts 15, we read about the Jerusalem Counsel where the Church decided whether Gentile converts had to be circumcised. What was the problem? A group of Jewish Christians was insisting that ritual laws of the Scriptures be obeyed—they were essentially the first 'Bible only' Christians. But in the end, the Church, under the authority of her apostolic leaders, overrode the authority of the written word and declared that Gentile converts did not have to be circumcised. The Church put this into a letter to be circulated among the churches, but nevertheless, the book of Acts says that with this letter, Paul and Barnabas continued *'teaching and preaching the word of the Lord.'* The written letter did not supplant the spreading of the apostolic deposit of faith through oral tradition. Here, let's turn to Second Thessalonians 2:15."

"Let's not," Stephen said jokingly. "Up until the last few years, I didn't know that verse was even in the Bible. Now I'm running into it almost every day."

"I know what you mean. That began happening to me with a vengeance when I went through all this myself. Allow me then to point out another interesting tidbit. First Corinthians 11. Here Paul confronts the Corinthian Christians on how unworthily they were receiving the body and blood of Christ in the Eucharist, or Lord's Supper. In verse two, he begins: 'I commend you because you…maintain the traditions even as I have delivered them to you.' Now given what Paul stated in his letter to the Thessalonians, how did he deliver these traditions to them?"

"I guess by preaching and teaching, by word of mouth or by letter."

"Stephen, it is obvious to anyone with an open mind that the gospel message and apostolic traditions were spread *primarily* through the spoken word and only secondarily through the written word," Father Bourque declared.

As Stephen pondered this, he noticed that the fire was burning down and needed rekindling. He got up to retrieve three more logs, and as he did the imagery of the fire impressed him. *Lord Jesus, am I like this fire being restoked?*

"Stephen," the priest said as Stephen took his seat, "let me show you two more things before we take a break. I hope I haven't piled it on too deep. You told me you have lost track of how to authoritatively determine what is true now, essentially two thousand years since Jesus delivered His gospel to His Apostles. And when one looks at the thousands of separate and contradictory Christian traditions, it's obvious that there are millions who have equally lost touch with apostolic truth, even though they don't know it."

"I suppose in some sense it is consoling to know that I'm not the only one lost in a sea of voices," Stephen said, "but it's disconcerting when we remember Christ's prayer that His followers be united as one. How could Christ's righteous prayer have gone so unanswered?"

"Yes, it is disconcerting, but let me promise you that His Church is still one, united by the power and guidance of the Holy Spirit. Consider this: after the first years of the Church, after the Apostles and their immediate disciples were dead, after their letters had been written and copied and passed around from church to church, how did Christians dispersed throughout the Mediterranean, Europe, and Asia determine what was true? Remember, the New Testament was not finally compiled until late in the fourth century. Have you read much of the Early Church Fathers?"

"Not until recently." Stephen wondered if all these Catholics read from the same script.

Father Bourque reached behind his rocker to a bookshelf and removed a well-worn leather book.

"Then listen to what one important Early Church Father said about this issue. St. Irenaeus was the second bishop of Lyons in what is now France. He lived from approximately 140 to 202 A.D. As a youth he was converted by St. Polycarp, who had been a disciple of the Apostle John. So in Irenaeus we have a direct transmission of the apostolic tradition."

"Father Bourque, pardon my skepticism, but how do we know this?" he challenged. "Jim told me the same thing, but what proof do we have that Irenaeus knew Polycarp or that Polycarp knew John, or that any of these guys even lived?" He uttered that last comment with deep frustration.

"Stephen, I know how you feel. 'Is this just some sort of Catholic fiction designed to fortress its own myths?' But what I am claiming and showing you is equally accepted by all biblical scholars and historians, Protestant or Catholic. We still have copies of ancient records, both Christian and secular, which back this." He paused to ensure that Stephen was still with him, and seeing him nod, Father Bourque continued. "In Irenaeus' well-documented book *Against Heresies,* we read the following:

> For the Church, although dispersed throughout the whole world even to the ends of the earth, has received from the Apostles and from their disciples the faith in one God.

"After a summary of what we recite in the Apostles' Creed, Irenaeus then makes a long speech about the authority of the tradition:

> As I said before, the Church, having received this preaching and this faith, although she is disseminated throughout the whole world, yet guarded it, as if she occupied but one house. She likewise believes these things just as if she had but one soul and one and the same heart; and harmoniously she proclaims them and

teaches them and hands them down, as if she possessed but one mouth. For, while the languages of the world are diverse, nevertheless, the authority of the tradition is one and the same.

Neither do the Churches among the Germans believe otherwise or have another tradition, nor do those among the Iberians, nor among the Celts, nor away in the East, nor in Egypt, nor in Libya, nor those which have been established in the central regions of the world. But just as the sun, that creature of God, is one and the same throughout the whole world, so also the preaching of the truth shines everywhere and enlightens all men who desire to a knowledge of truth.

Nor will any of the rulers in the Churches, whatever his power of eloquence, teach otherwise, for no one is above the teacher; nor will he who is weak in speaking detract from the tradition. For the faith is one and the same, and cannot be amplified by one who is able to say much about it, nor can it be diminished by one who can say but little.

"We certainly live in a different world today, don't we?" Father Bourque said. "There is little unity among the many Christian traditions in any of these places. Yet, the Catholic Church is still there, teaching one and the same thing."

"The exact same thing without changes?" Stephen asked skeptically.

"I'll talk later about the development of doctrine, how the Church matures and doctrines are fine-tuned to meet the growing needs and circumstances of the Church. In essence, though, there is nothing we believe today in matters of faith and morals that contradicts anything the Church has taught from the beginning. This cannot be said, however, of the thousands of national and independent churches around the world today."

Stephen sat silently listening.

"Lastly, let's turn to an Early Church Father who lived nearly 250 years later. All we know is that Vincent of Lerins died around 450 A.D. and lived in the same region as St. Irenaeus. He wrote a book entitled *Commonitorium* in which he gave many arguments and examples on how the Christian faith was to be preserved and protected against the onslaught of heresies. In a chapter on "Progress in Church Doctrine," he commented on Paul's command to Timothy to 'guard what has been entrusted to you. Avoid the godless chatter and contradictions of what is falsely called knowledge.' As I read, consider how this compares to what you were taught in seminary and what you preach from your pulpit. Vincent of Lerins wrote:

> Keep that which is committed. What is committed? It is that which has been entrusted to you, not that which you have invented; what you have received, not what you have devised; not a matter of ingenuity, but of doctrine; not of private acquisition, but of public tradition; a matter brought to you, not created by you; a matter you are not the author of, but the keeper of; not the teacher, but the learner; not the leader, but the follower.
>
> This deposit guard. Preserve the talent of the Catholic Church unviolated and unimpaired. What has been entrusted to you may remain with you and may be handed down by you. You received gold; hand it down as gold.

"Does this accurately describe your training and ministry?"

"Yes, to some extent I think it does," Stephen answered hesitantly, "for we were supposedly taught universal doctrines which have been believed and accepted by Christians of all ages as they applied Scripture to their lives. But," he reconsidered, "as I've been discovering, what I learned in seminary does not represent a single line of truth over the two thousand years of Christianity. Much of what we were taught merely traces back to the doctrines of the sixteenth-century Reformers, and even in that, few modern-day Calvinists preserve all that Calvin taught. I have to admit that much of what we Protestant pastors proclaim must be chalked up as *invented or devised*."

The priest let this go by without comment, and said, "Listen now carefully to this longer section:

The question may be asked: If this is right, then is no progress of religion possible within the Church of Christ? To be sure, there has to be progress, even exceedingly great progress…But it must be progress in the proper sense of the word, and not a change in faith. Progress means that each thing grows within itself, whereas change implies that one thing is transformed into another…

The growth of religion in the soul should be like the growth of the body, which in the course of years develops and unfolds, yet remains the same as it was…The course of the years always completes in adults the parts and forms with which the wisdom of the Creator had previously imbued infants…

In the same way, the dogma of the Christian religion ought to follow these laws of progress, so that it may be consolidated in the course of years, developed in the sequence of time, and sublimated by age—yet remain incorrupt and unimpaired, complete and perfect in all the properties of its parts and in all its essentials…so that it does not allow of any change, or any loss of its specific character, or any variation of its inherent form.

From a drawer in the small stand next to his rocker, Father Bourque removed a glossy photograph and placed it in his leather book as a bookmark. He then turned his attention to the blazing fire.

"Stephen, my friend, there is so much I'd like to read to you from these great and wise saints, but I fear it might be lost on both of us. Vincent of Lerins makes some very prophetic statements about how truth should be preserved as well as how it can become corrupted. I believe what he warned has become true both in Protestantism as well in some aspects of Catholicism."

Stephen studied his face and saw for the first time in those warm eyes a troubled soul. His continual and contagious smile had flattened into sadness.

"Father, what is it?"

The priest studied the dancing fire for a moment before he answered. "I fear on the one hand that I am not doing justice to the beauty and eternal trustworthiness of Christ's spouse, the Church. That my ramblings are but clouding her salvific clarity. On the other hand, I am also well aware that this grand Church, the *true* Church if I might add, the one that has sought against all odds to follow the guidelines of saints like Vincent of Lerins, is yet far from perfect. Whenever I speak with sincere men like you who are seeking truth with your whole heart, part of me wants to grab you, shake you, wake you up and scream, 'Cast aside the prejudice, the false myths, the bigotry, the confusion, every barrier that stands in your way, and come home to the beauty, the depth, and the joy of this wonderful Church.' But part of me also knows from experience that if you look with open and receptive eyes, what you'll see might not be so appealing."

"What do you mean?"

"One might look at the Reformation as the greatest wrenching apart that Christianity has ever suffered—that is, next to the fourth-century Arian heresy or the eleventh-century schism of the Eastern Orthodox Churches. But in some sense, the revolt happening within the Church today is far worse than any of these previous crises."

There was a knock at the study door.

"Yes?" the priest called out.

The door opened slightly and Stephen caught a glimpse of the black and white of Sister Agatha's habit.

"I'm sorry to bother you, Father, but you have an important call."

"Excuse me for a moment, Stephen." He left the room, closing the door behind him.

Beyond the stillness of the room, Stephen could hear but not make out the soft muffle of voices. Then they were gone.

The room was brighter now with midmorning light entering through the lone window. There was much for Stephen to mull over, but expecting Father Bourque's imminent return, he postponed starting. Instead, he watched the room dust rising and falling through the light beams.

"It looks like I may be out for a while after all," Father Bourque said as he re-entered and reclaimed his rocker. "An elderly parishioner is being taken to the hospital."

"Well, please don't worry about me. I've got more than enough to think about."

"I don't need to be there for about an hour, so that leaves me just enough time to explain where I left off, if you don't mind?"

"No, of course not."

The priest held up before him his rough left hand, fingers drawn into a fist. "For fifteen hundred years, up until the Reformation, the average Christian layman as well as village priest learned what was true from five sources, in essentially this order.

"First," he extended his thumb, slightly curved by the ravages of arthritis, "they trusted the Church to preach what was true—the bishops in union with the Bishop of Rome, the pope. Christians trusted that the Holy Spirit guided the Church as Christ had promised, to preserve, protect, and propagate the faith as delivered by Christ to His Apostles. They also trusted the Church to apply the truth to changing times and situations so that, as Vincent of Lerins taught, the truth would not be changed or altered but mature, develop, as an acorn into an oak.

"Second," extending his first finger, "they learned the truth through Sacred Tradition, the same deposit of Faith the Church was protecting and preserving. Third," extending his next finger, "and closely connected to Sacred Tradition, was Sacred Scripture, which is essentially a part of Sacred Tradition. I put them in this order because, remember, up until the invention of movable type and the printing press around 1450 A.D., few Christians even had a Bible to look at, let alone read. In both cases, Tradition and Scripture were known basically by memory or through the medium of art or music—the great stained-glass windows or Stations of the Cross, or the chants, and so on."

Extending his next finger, "Fourth, they learned truth by the working and confirmation of the Holy Spirit in their hearts, helping them discern truth from near-truth; from that which the Church, Sacred Tradition, and Scripture actually taught from what some innovator tried to sell them. And finally," extending his last finger, "they had themselves. This was last, in submission to the teaching authority of the Church, Tradition, and Scripture through the leading of the Holy Spirit. And as individual Christians tried to live their lives faithfully, they knew *what Jesus would do* because their hearts had been nurtured and trained by the Church, Tradition, Scripture, and the Holy Spirit," extending each finger again respectively.

Stephen found this all strangely fascinating and listened with great expectation—in the midst of this finger exercise, might he find the answer to his dilemma?

"But this of course didn't guarantee that all these Christians were saints. Far from it," Father Bourque continued. "Since everyone is free to act however they choose—to resist even the most perfectly changed heart—than obviously not everyone hears or listens to the teachings of the Church, Tradition, Scripture, or the Holy Spirit.

"It's safe to say that by the time of the Reformation, a large part of Christendom had lost the 'joy of their salvation.' Religion for the common man had become mostly external, focused on pilgrimages, relics, rituals, buying indulgences, doing whatever they thought might put them right with God and, as David had prayed in Psalm 51, restore the joy of their salvation. Many within the Church were calling for and working for reform and spiritual renewal, some in ways faithful to the sources of truth, others in ways contrary.

"In my view, this is what happened—and I'll point my finger at Martin Luther for convenience," the priest said with a smirk, recognizing the childishness of his finger exercises. "When you read his life, it is obvious that he was a Catholic priest for whom joy was elusive, a troubled man for whom his Christian faith brought no peace. In the end, though, he claimed to find peace by essentially redefining the sources of truth." With this he held up his hand with all fingers extended like the plumage of a peacock.

"The first source that Luther attacked and eliminated was the Church, the bishops in union with the pope." With this, he closed his thumb. "Luther declared that the pope was the Antichrist, the cardinals and bishops his demons, and the Catholic Church the Whore of Babylon. He declared that the Church could not be trusted to protect and preserve truth, because it had become corrupt.

"Second," closing his next finger, "Luther claimed that Sacred Tradition could not be trusted, since it too had been corrupted over the years by the Whore of Babylon. The only thing that could be trusted as the 'pillar and bulwark of the truth' was the written Word—Scripture alone. This was an essentially new idea—none of the Church Fathers or even Scripture itself defended this—but the charisma and convictions of Luther, backed by the growing support he received from other Reformers, influential political leaders, and frustrated laity, carried the day. What he left as sources of truth, which should sound familiar to your Protestant ears, were Scripture as the primary source, the inspiration of the Holy Spirit, and, third, ourselves."

This did ring true to Stephen, for essentially this was what he had always taught his people, though from a different, more positive angle—as if Luther had done a great service for Christianity, freeing it from the clutches of the Catholic Church and its empty traditions. So far, what this priest explained fit the data, as well as the outcome.

"But things didn't remain this way," Father Bourque continued, "for without the authoritative guidance and constraint provided by the Church and Sacred Tradition, Protestant theologians began developing almost limitless interpretations of Scripture, all claiming the leading of the Holy Spirit. Within twenty years, there were at least a dozen different divided Protestant sects, all basing their truth on Scripture alone. But in time Scripture also fell."

With this he closed his middle finger, leaving only two.

"The German theologians and higher critics began 'proving' through their exegetical theories that Scripture could not be trusted. They claimed Moses didn't write the Pentateuch but that it was written by different redacting 'committees' writing over a thousand years. And the New Testament was basically a creation of the growing Church, sometimes putting words into the mouth of Jesus to buttress the growing power of bishops. In fact, some higher critics charged that little of what the Gospels claimed Jesus did or said could be trusted as authentic—they were all myths. So what was left as sources of truth were the Holy Spirit and Christians themselves. And denominations died and others sprouted up, some with far-out ideas, until intellectual doubt and skepticism even eliminated the Holy Spirit..."—he closed the second-to-last finger—"...leaving only ourselves as the source of truth. Is this not descriptive of our world today?"

"Yes, it is," Stephen said quickly, "but among evangelical Christians there has been great faith and trust in the Bible as well as the certainty of the Holy Spirit. Evangelicals particularly have fought against the stupefying effects of the higher critics, emphasizing the inerrancy of Scripture and the traditional views of the Trinity."

"Yes, that is true," the priest acknowledged. "God is not dead, as many liberals claimed in the '60s, and He has not let His witness die out. During this century particularly, there has been a constant resurgence of spiritual renewal within Protestantism. But in almost every case—and I challenge you to examine this—as time goes on, every Protestant group eventually loses its original fervor and branches off: new renewal-minded factions break away from the older-line groups which have grown staid and sometimes liberal in their theologies. Isn't this true in your own Congregational denominations?"

"Yes, but…" Stephen thought for a second, then reconsidered, "Yes, it is. And this is the problem I've seen and which has led to the dilemma I'm in. As an evangelically-minded Congregationalist pastor, I just represent one of a bazillion of these splitting factions."

Returning to his explanation, Father Bourque raised his hand again, but flip-flopped. "Because of this resurgence of spiritual renewal among what Catholics call our 'separated brethren,' a whole new phenomenon has arisen, a reordering of the sources of truth. And this is true for what we call modern-day 'cafeteria Catholics' as well as Protestants, for the first source of truth for so many millions is in fact themselves.

"In Protestantism, this shows itself in the "me and Jesus" heresy of indifferentism. The final arbiter of all truth becomes the individual, and these Christians pick and choose which church or Bible translation or doctrine best fits their lifestyle. In Catholicism, this essentially means that each person becomes his own pope. Oh, these modern Catholics give lip service to the authority of the Church, Sacred Tradition, Scripture, and the inspiration of the Holy Spirit, but these are all subjugated under self, or as some moderns prefer to say it, *conscience*. 'One must never act against one's conscience,' they say, but what they're actually doing is raising themselves up above and in judgment of all other sources of truth. In many ways this has played itself out in ways similar to what happened in the Reformation, but, as I said earlier, in worse ways.

"I would say that in the 1940s and '50s, the spiritual lives of many Catholics were much like those of the fifteenth century: externally focused," the priest added. "They did everything right, but too often failed to experience the *joy of their salvation*. As a result, when the renewal measures of the Second Vatican Council began to emerge, the disgruntled and the discouraged became overzealous. They overapplied and overstated what they termed the 'spirit of Vatican II,' instituting reforms never intended by the Council. As a result, many of the treasured sacramentals of the faith—rituals, relics, artwork, liturgies—were rejected as empty distractions and replaced by newer forms and community-centered liturgies.

"In many ways, Stephen, I believe a Protestant spirit has been unleashed in the Catholic Church. The authority of the Church and Sacred Tradition as well as the reliability of Sacred Scripture have all been challenged by many Catholic scholars, educators, and religious leaders, often with the essentially Protestant motive of *returning the Church to the unspoiled norms of the early Church*. So often when something old is replaced by something new, the rationale is generally, 'But this is the way they did it in the early Church!' Have you not heard this before, within Protestantism?"

"Of course," Stephen replied. "That's the motive behind the start of every new church: a return to the pristine simplicity of the early, more biblical church."

"An abandoning of the mature adult for a return to the underdeveloped infant; rejecting the majesty of the oak for a return to the acorn. This has left millions of Catholics with a great inner sadness."

Father Bourque folded his hands before him and turned his gaze back toward the fire.

"Stephen, I tell you all this, because I want you to know that as a Catholic I have nothing to hide. I wish all Catholics lived the truth faithfully and walked in holiness and love, but Jesus didn't say His Church would be this way. He said it would consist of both wheat and chaff until the end, good and bad fish. Many anti-Catholics bewail the litany of bad popes, cardinals, bishops, priests, religious, and laity, and all I say is 'Amen,' for 'there but for the grace of God go I.'

"But even with all of the Church's problems, and especially with the discouragement of the Church today, I have no regrets whatsoever about becoming a Catholic. This is the Church Jesus Christ founded in His Apostles, and she, in her Magisterium centered around the Seat of Peter, is still as trustworthy as ever. She preserves, under the protection of the Holy Spirit, the integrity of Sacred Tradition and Scripture, so that you and I, even in the midst of a thousand contrary voices, can know without a doubt what is true."

Again a knock at the door, this time a bit more frantic.

Father Bourque reached over, grasped Stephen's shoulder and said, "Stephen, I will pray for you in your search. Please forgive me if I seem to push, pull, or prod you towards the Catholic Church. I just want to stand beside you and offer whatever help I can. Excuse me."

He went out into the hall and then returned quickly. "I guess I need to go now. Will you be here when I get back, for dinner?"

"Yes, if that is all right?"

"Of course, Sister Agatha will provide lunch, and then just relax here and enjoy the warmth and resources of my study until I return."

"Thank you, Father Bourque," Stephen said, extending his hand, "for all you've said. You've given me much to think about."

"You're welcome, my friend." The priest cradled Stephen's hand in both of his warmly, and then left the room, leaving Stephen alone.

Before him on the table beside Father Bourque's rocker was the old tattered copy of the Early Church Fathers. Sticking out was a glossy photograph. With unrestrained curiosity, he removed it and saw that it was an oval picture of a young nun with the name *St. Therese of Lisieux* scrolled across the bottom. He turned the picture over and found her name printed again, with the additional words *'Her prayer to know God's Will.'* Stephen began to read:

> Lord, grant that I may always allow myself to be guided by You, always follow Your plans, and perfectly accomplish Your holy will. Grant that in all things, great and small, today and all the days of life, I may do whatever You may require of me. Help me to respond to the slightest prompting of Your grace, so that I may be Your trustworthy instrument. May Your will be done in time and eternity, by me, in me, and through me. Amen.

Stephen closed his eyes and prayed softly to himself: *Jesus, may this, too, be my prayer.*

5

"Good afternoon, First Congregational Church," Marge said as she turned the volume of her CD player down to a whisper. On Mondays, when both her boss and Molly took the day off, she kept herself company with her favorite Elvis, Slim Whitman, and Willie Nelson albums.

Her legs were comfortably crossed and elevated on an adjacent chair, and cradled in her hands was a half-read Barbara Cartland romance she had purchased at the supermarket on her way in. Her lunch of ham and cheese on rye, potato salad, yogurt, and coffee was spread out across the desk, hardly touched.

"Hello, Marge. How's everything at the shop?"

Her feet hit the floor, the book flew under the desk, and the CD was switched off, all in one motion.

"Reverend LaPointe, now there you go calling me again on your day off," she said with mock scolding. "How long is it going to take to convince you that I can handle things just fine without your constant meddling for at least one day a week?"

"I know, I know," Stephen said. "I just need to hear your sweet voice. Any urgent calls or e-mail I need to follow up on?"

"Well, to tell you the truth, I've answered more calls this morning than on any previous Monday. You've received e-mail from members of the congregation I didn't even know were computer-literate. What did you say yesterday?"

"Weren't you there, Marge?" he said in a mock scolding.

"Sorry, boss. It was my mother's seventy-fifth birthday. I spent the weekend in Braintree." To Marge, this sounded convincing enough. It was partially true, of course, for it was her mother's birthday, but she didn't need so plausible an excuse to avoid one of Stephen's gospel-in-your-face sermons. Often she just stayed home—keeping the Sabbath in her own way. Or she might visit the Unitarian Church in Weymouth, where the pastor, the Reverend Thomas J. Potsherd, preached love and ecological responsibility with nary a mention of sin.

"But what did you say?" she continued. "Most of the callers wouldn't tell me what they wanted, but I could tell by their urgent anxiety that they were either gravely concerned or angry."

"I merely told them that the text had more than one equally plausible explanation. What's a few rustled feathers?"

"A few? The whole henhouse is cackling for answers." She absent-mindedly took a bite of her sandwich, and then said through stuffed cheeks, "Wha do ah tall tham?"

"Whatever you say, please finish your lunch first. I'm sure you'll think of something. Guess you should'da been there. Now, are there any calls I can't put off until I return?"

"You received a call first thing from a Reverend Billings of Lincoln, Nebraska. He said he wants to talk with you as soon as possible."

"Jack Billings? Are you positive?"

"That's what he said. An old friend? He talked as if you were old buddies."

"We go back a long ways, but I'm intrigued by his timing." He considered Jack a kindred spirit within the wide theological spectrum of Congregationist ministers, but they hadn't spoken for several years. "Did he leave a number?"

"He gave me both his office and cell phones. He did sound urgent."

"OK, I'll give him a call. Did my wife call?"

"No, haven't heard from her. Are you away today?" As soon as she said this, Marge wished she hadn't. It sounded too much like she was gathering grist for the gossip mill.

There was a pause before he answered. "Yes, I'm unexpectedly out of town for at least two days. I'll let you know if my plans change, so just keep on keeping on, and Katie-bar-the-doors if necessary. I'll put out any fires when I return."

"OK, boss. You know me, ever vigilant."

"Well, just make sure your Slim Whitman CD is off if a trustee stops by," Stephen said and then hung up.

"What?"

For a second Marge wondered whether she should dispense with her music, since Reverend LaPointe was obviously privy to her Monday goings-on.

"What the heck," she said, as she restarted her Willie Nelon CD. To the tune of "Moonlight In Vermont" she finished both her lunch and another chapter of Cartland, with her phone off the hook and her computer scrolling *WWJD?*

*   *   *

STEPHEN SAT IN FATHER BOURQUE'S ROCKER next to the phone, deliberating whether to call Jack now or wait. *What could be so urgent?*

He scanned Father Bourque's diverse assortment of books, wondering what issue, doctrine, or strange Catholic teaching he should bone up on for their next marathon discussion. As he rose to examine a small book entitled *The Roots of the Reformation*, he reconsidered, being drawn back into the rocker by an inner voice screaming, *Call Jack! Don't procrastinate! Get it over with. It will do you good.*

He dialed Jack's office phone. After a few rings, an unfamiliar woman's voice answered, "Third Congregational. May I help you?"

"Yes, hello. Is Reverend Billings in?"

"May I ask who is calling?" the voice requested, officially detached.

"Reverend Stephen LaPointe."

"Just a moment. I'll see if he is available."

Stephen felt like yelling, "I'm returning his call, you dumb…" but resisted the temptation. He hated when church secretaries acted like they were corporate executive assistants rather than the church's first ambassadors of Christ. As he stewed, he also realized that this secretary was doing exactly what he had instructed Marge to do: screen all calls.

"Stephen! How're you doing?" Jack Billings answered. "Thanks for calling back so quickly."

"I'm keeping my head above water. How about you? What has it been, a year since you took the senior position at Third?"

"Almost. A year ago Easter, and all I can say is that I've certainly landed with both feet running. The last minister had initiated so many lay-run educational and outreach programs during his last few years of ministry that I'm just now getting a handle on how to rein in the leadership. His ideas were great—the only problem with them is that I hadn't thought of them myself! This is a great church."

437

"Are they comfortable with your evangelical and pro-life views?" Stephen knew there had to be some fly in this ointment.

"Actually, they are quite receptive and, as a whole, quite orthodox. The main divisions, surprisingly, are between the staunch Evangelicals and the flaming Charismatics—most of the liberals have long since left Third for Memorial downtown. How about your new congregation?"

"Basically fine. Nothing that can't be worked out over time."

"Stephen, I have a luncheon meeting in about ten minutes, so let me get to the point. Yesterday I spoke with Ron Stang. He said a few things about you that troubled me, and I just thought I'd make sure you were all right."

"Well, Jack, I appreciate that, but what did he say?" Stephen had wondered when the backlash from his retreat speech would come around to bite him.

"He essentially said that you were so fed up with the mass confusion of Protestant opinions that you were planning to resign. Is that true?"

"Jack, I said that partially for effect and partially because for years I've been seriously considering it."

"But Stephen, come on. I agree that the disagreements between Christians are a sad scene, but we've known this from the beginning. You and I knew when we started in ministry that we would be in the minority, and if necessary we would tough it out, even if we were the last faithful voices of authentic Christianity in a sea of deception."

Do I really want to go through all this again? Stephen thought with dread. *And, besides, he's only got ten minutes.*

"Listen, Jack, I know. The problem is I've lost confidence in my ability to discern whether you and I are truly of the remaining faithful."

"Are you going the same route as Jim Sarver?"

He was startled by the question itself as well as Jack's pressing boldness. "No, of course not."

"Are you sure? From what Ron told me, it sounds like you two old peas-in-a-pod might be making the same mistake."

This tapped a nerve. "Who are you to judge that I am making a mistake?"

"Listen, Stephen, I know the Catholic Church. You probably

didn't know this, but I was born, baptized, and catechized a Catholic. My parents are still Catholics and have yet to reconcile to my Protestantism. But by the grace of God, I was saved from that hellhole while a teenager. Stephen, a lot of things may sound great on the surface about the Catholic Church, especially in the face of the seeming confusion of Protestantism. But believe me, you don't want to go there. I know plenty of Catholics who would gladly leave if they could. If I'd have known what Jim was contemplating, I would have stopped him, too."

"Jack, I didn't say I was becoming a Catholic—just considering leaving the pastorate." He paused wondering whether he truly wanted to tamper with the apparent rage that lay bridled behind this vehement ex-Catholic. "Yet, I must admit that for the first time in my life, I'm looking open-mindedly at the teachings of the Catholic Church."

On a roll, Stephen spoke quickly and forcefully to avoid interruption. "I've come to the conclusion that I was grossly mistaken about much of what I thought the Catholic Church taught. I think I've also come to the conclusion that the reason there is so much confusion within Protestantism is that its primary pillar—*sola Scriptura*—doesn't work and isn't even scriptural."

"Whoa, Stephen, back up a bit. I can see you've been had by some Catholic propagandists. Every claim made by a Catholic is easily countered by Scripture. Are you familiar with *Former Catholics to Catholics?*"

"As a matter of fact, I recently spoke with the founder, Gary Harmond."

"Really? Well, are you familiar with their new book *True Roman Catholicism?* It contrasts the teachings of the new Roman Catholic Catechism with the Bible, revealing how unscriptural the Catholic Church truly is."

"No, I haven't seen this," Stephen said, his curiosity piqued. After discovering how untrustworthy his other anti-Catholic books were, he wasn't in the mood for another polemical collection of myths and accusations. But then again, maybe this was exactly what he did need. *Could there be something in this up-to-date book that might cut through all the propaganda to the truth?*

"Stephen, are you on the Internet?"

"Of course."

"Then go to FC2C's Web site. You can read or download this new book. They want everyone to have this irrefutable information."

Stephen heard a soft beep over the phone line.

"Just a second, Stephen, hold on." The phone line clicked, and Stephen was left with some unfamiliar contemporary Christian female vocalist rising to a grand crescendo about how only in Jesus Christ all things work out for the good. The tune wasn't bad and the scriptural sentiment was timely, but he hadn't called to be serenaded.

"Sorry about that. My luncheon appointment is here, so I've gotta run. Please read this book. I guarantee it will counter any leanings you might have toward the Catholic Church."

"Thanks, Jack. I'll do that."

"And please, call me before you make any rash decisions. Gotta go. God bless."

"You, too."

Stephen heard the dial tone and then hung up. He sat rocking, his elbows on the rocker arms and his hands together before his face, fingertips to fingertips. The implications of Jack's comments reverberated through his mind, bouncing off a host of other opinions, and for a long moment he rocked in a mental haze. In time, his eyes focused on the thin book on the Reformation he had earlier considered. He walked over and removed it from its place among dozens of other books on the Reformation, but as he turned it over to examine the recommendations on the back cover, he instead put it back. *I've got to look at that Web site.*

After a quick trip to his room, he returned with his laptop. Attached to the rectory phone line, he connected through the Internet to the world's most active anti-Catholic Web site.

He browsed the index of online resources and articles, a Catalog of books and tapes, several e-mail discussion groups, and links to other anti-Catholic sites. In the online resources, he found links to many tracts he had already read or seen laying around for unsuspecting Catholics to find and "be saved." Near the end was the link to *True Roman Catholicism.* He clicked the appropriate icon and was taken directly to a fully downloadable book.

Unlike most of the tracts, this book was not written by Gary Harmond, but by someone Stephen had never heard of, a John

Richards. A bio indicated that Richards and his wife had been born, raised, and catechized Catholics. Then they *saw the light*, accepted Jesus as their Lord and Savior, and converted to Protestant Christianity. Now they were dedicating their lives to helping other Catholics learn the truth.

In this, Richards' first book, he proposed to contrast the teachings of the new Catholic Catechism with Scripture, proving that the Catholic Church was unbiblical to the core.

Even before examining the detailed evidence, the cumulative effect of the chapter headings was making an impact on Stephen, for they sounded unchristian, unbiblical, even idolatrous. The ones that particularly jumped out included "The Catholic Church presumes the power to forgive sin," "Salvation by works *alone*," "Salvation through the Sacraments," and "Mary our Coredemptrix and Advocate."

Assuming that the author was honest and sincere, Stephen was appalled that the Catholic Church could possibly make these claims.

He turned to the first chapter on "The Catholic Church presumes the power to forgives sin" and began reading.

> Roman Catholicism proclaims that it has the authority and power to forgive sin. This claim is clearly made in the Catechism. "There is no offense, however serious, that the Church cannot forgive" (#982). "By Christ's will, the Church possesses the power to forgive the sins of the baptized" (#986). "The Church, who through the bishop and his priests forgives sins in the name of Jesus Christ" (#1448).

This was followed by a long collection of Scripture texts which emphasized that only God has the authority to forgive sins, such as Mark 2:7—"Why doth this man thus speak blasphemies? Who can forgive sins but God only?" and Ephesians 4:43—"And be ye kind one to another, tenderhearted, forgiving one another, even as God for Christ's sake hath forgiven you."

Stephen felt sick to the stomach. He skimmed the next chapter and then the next, and his queasiness grew into a warm, familiar conviction. In every instance, whenever he had to choose between the quotes from the Catechism or from Scripture, the answer was always obvious: the inerrant Scriptures—the divine, authoritative Word of God—must be preferred, believed, and followed.

The chapter examining the Catholic Church's beliefs about Mary as our Coredeemer sounded absolutely repulsive. He was amazed that any intelligent person could believe these things. *But I thought Catholic priests were highly trained. How could they accept this tripe?*

By now, the panic that had driven him out of the Catholic sanctuary and almost to suicide was rising again in his heart. He looked at his watch—4:50 p.m. Reverend Bourque would probably return any moment. He contemplated collecting his bags and leaving, but fought the impulse.

What better place to face once and for all these accusations of the Catholic Church? I will lay them before Reverend Bourque when he returns and examine his reaction as well as his response.

Stephen sat, waiting nervously. He hated confrontation, especially heated debates. He had seen the kind, understanding, winsome side of this convert priest. *But how will Bourque respond to these documented proofs that the Catholic Church is at best unscriptural and at worst directed by a conniving servant of Satan?*

He waited, anticipating that in the next few minutes his dilemma might at least be simplified as this oldest of Christian denominations was once again proven false.

6

"WALTER, WHERE ARE YOU GOING NOW?" Helen's voice pleaded from the kitchen. After a moment of silence, she repeated louder but cautiously, "Walter!"

"What!" he called from the hallway leading to the garage.

This time, she repeated more gently, "Where are you going? You left yesterday afternoon and didn't come back until after dark."

He was not in the mood to justify his actions: she would not understand and would be shocked if she even knew. *Besides, I don't need her permission to leave the house.*

"I'm just going out again," he called. "And don't hold dinner for me, because again I might not be back until late."

"But Walter...?"

The garage door slammed, leaving Helen alone in the kitchen. She wanted to scream; to storm out into the garage demanding an explanation, but she was much too afraid. Instead, she sat down on a dining room chair, shaking from pent-up anger as well as her years of marital despair. Stacy was in her room upstairs. Helen hoped she hadn't heard and prayed that Stacy would remain safe and unaffected by her husband's unpredictable fury.

Walter entered his Caprice wagon and checked: it was there. He pulled out of the driveway and then north toward town. It wasn't quite dinnertime, so he presumed LaPointe would still be in his office. After a fifteen-minute cruise through the back streets of several large neighborhoods, he drove into First Church's parking lot, but the green Wagoneer wasn't there. A light was on, however, in the church office.

"The secretary must be in," he mumbled. *But should I stop by? I don't want anyone to get suspicious. Maybe he went home early? Or maybe he's away somewhere—why waste time in front of his house if he's gone?*

His mind was a battle of voices.

He pulled the Caprice up next to the only other car in the lot, a blue, undistinguished sedan. For nearly a minute he sat wrestling over whether to go in or leave, and then decided. He left his Caprice and proceeded up the freshly shoveled sidewalk into the office annex. Out of the sides of his eyes he saw no one watching, no movements other than a few birds pecking in the snow beneath an empty feeder.

Through the window by the door, he saw a woman sitting before a computer. She was chewing, and the glow of the monitor gave a surrealistic tint to her pudgy face. Over the sound of passing cars, he could faintly hear a familiar Willie Nelson tune. He entered.

Marge reached to turn the music off and asked, "Good afternoon, can I help you?"

"You don't have to turn Willie down on my account," he said. "It's great to find someone with my taste in music."

She smiled. "He helps me get through the long afternoons. Is there something I can do for you?"

He had already decided that hiding his identity was unnecessary. They needed to enroll anyway, and besides, if he was successful, it might be good for people to see that he wasn't prowling around like a common crook.

"Yes, my name is Walter Horscht, and my family and I have recently moved into town. We'd like to enroll."

For ten minutes, they volleyed questions and answers until Marge had completed the necessary forms.

"You see, we've known Reverend LaPointe for several years," he said. "He was our pastor in Red Creek, and it was actually he who encouraged me to come back to Christ."

"That's nice," Marge said, hiding her indifference.

"In fact, he was with my wife, Helen, when Stacy was born. He's been a real blessing to our family." This said, a dagger of guilt pierced his heart. *Yes, he has been good to us. What has he ever done to deserve what I am planning? But you had been duped. You and hundreds of others! A fox in sheep's clothing.*

"By any chance is the pastor in?" he said matter-of-factly.

"No, this is his day off."

"Oh, I didn't know. So he'll be in tomorrow?"

"Well," she hesitated, "I'm not sure. Best call first if you plan to stop by."

"I'll do that, and thanks for your help." He turned toward the door, but stopped and said with a smile, "I'll think we'll like this church."

"I think you will, too, Mr. Horscht."

"Good day," he said, and left.

Once beyond the office window, he sprinted to his car.

"He's home!"

Walter left the lot and headed north, following a different route than the one he took yesterday. Once there he again pulled to the curb on the last curve before their home. The garage door was open.

"Damn!" Walter exclaimed. "His car isn't here."

He turned off the headlights and engine, and waited, watching. Gray, billowy snow clouds completely shrouded the afternoon sun, and the temperature seemed to drop a degree a minute. He wrapped himself in a threadbare army blanket and reviewed what he would do once his task had been accomplished. *Should I make no effort to avoid the authorities, or publicly proclaim my motives for all to hear and understand? Surely they will recognize the mandate I followed,* he mused. *But then again, you just don't know any more. These people have infiltrated everything and everywhere. Maybe I should leave town and avoid any suspicion—for the safety of my family? Lord, what should I do?*

For two hours he waited and watched. Only once was there movement from the house. A young man came out—Walter presumed it was the boy that Stacy liked—and drove away in his blue Jeep. Walter scooched down below the window to avoid being seen.

Cold, angry, and frustrated, he eventually gave up again and returned home. *But I'll be back tomorrow and the next day, whatever it takes.*

THROUGH THE CURTAINS in the kitchen window, Sara saw car lights come on out in the street and then drive away. *Now who could that be?* she asked herself as she held the curtains aside, but she didn't recognize the car.

For a fleeting second, the thought crossed her mind that it was Stephen keeping an eye on her, but she easily discounted this. Stephen wasn't like that. *He's probably relaxing in some hotel, sipping a glass of red wine, lost in a Clancy novel, without a thought about me or the boys.* But she knew that Stephen wasn't like that, either.

Looking out into the blue-gray stillness of the winter night, one circle of their road lit by a lone streetlight, she asked softly, "Where are you, Stephen?"

William was at the library and Daniel was upstairs fighting some intergalactic war on his computer, and here she sat nursing one more cup of tea, her eyes swollen from crying. But she wasn't crying any longer. Probably the boys had heard her sobs all night long and presumed she was mourning their father's departure. But she had been crying for herself—for what her decision years ago to marry this religious fanatic had now gotten her into. Yes, she loved him, and she was thankful for the joy he had brought into her life over the years—especially for their two sons.

Yet, given all this, could she go on with the masquerade? For nearly twenty years she had struggled, almost daily, with trying to be the good minister's wife that he and their congregations expected. Thousands of times she had put up with the petty complaints and hypocritical expectations of well-meaning church women. But there were so many things she had hoped to experience and achieve that instead had been left behind and put out of her mind—especially her desire to get a Ph.D. in history so she could teach at the college level. This had been her dream since high school—her "calling," to steal Stephen's thunder—but had it been right to set her calling aside for his? And now after all this, he was thinking of throwing his calling away. *After all I've sacrificed!*

She felt guilty about keeping all of this walled up inside of her for so long. *But isn't this what he has done? Sure, I knew he was frustrated about lots of things in the church and about being a pastor, but how was I to know that he was thinking about resigning? And to what extent has he thought out all the ramifications of resignation? What about the needs of the boys? What about my needs?*

Another thought crossed her mind that made her want to throw the cup across the room. *And is it possible that he is seriously thinking of doing what Jim is doing?* All she had to do was remember Campion Chapel, or the book by that arrogant cardinal, or those escaped nuns, or especially that mistake from her past to know that she could never become a Catholic.

But shouldn't I wait to find out his decision? She had asked several friends what exactly he had said on Sunday and learned that, thankfully, he had not resigned. *But regardless, his trajectory is certainly in that direction.*

She rose and went to the living room. She sat in Stephen's recliner. *So when he does call, as I know he will, what will his plans be? His explanation? His options? His demands? And what will be my answer?*

Glancing up she saw his favorite painting—the one with the flaw she had caused. And it reminded her of herself: *Was I not also his favorite? Did he not say that he would always love me, no matter what happened? No matter how hard things got?* And then the flaw: *But don't I also have a flaw, a hidden imperfection about which I can never tell him? Imagine sitting in the darkness of a confessional, telling some bored priest that I murdered my first born! There is no way that I can do this.*

She stood to leave the room but noticed the unopened mail

resting on the table beside her. Sitting back down, she mindlessly shuffled through the short stack: mostly bills, a few advertisements, a few ministry-related promotionals. And in the middle, there it was. Another letter from Rockport.

Since their unexpected reunion, Frank had written several times. Initially, she refused to answer—she didn't want to encourage a friendship that could not and should not be rekindled. But then about a year ago, after a previous disagreement with Stephen—not all that different in tone and effect from the present one—she had responded. Since then they had corresponded surreptitiously, writing merely as if but old friends. Sara liked this, for Frank had truly changed. His conversion seemed real, and his words were tinged with a gentleness he had lacked when he had been her husband. Over the years, only once had he hinted at getting together, but this she quickly rebuffed.

Now as she stared at the envelope with its familiar return address, she was taken aback by its timing. Before opening it, however, she went for one last cup of tea, and returned with a knife.

Carefully she unfolded the cream-colored stationery, imprinted at the top with his name and address, and read silently with a mixture of guilt and intrigue.

> Dear Sara,
>
> The weather out here on the tip of the North Shore has been brutal. That nor'easter that struck last week buried us two feet deep in new snow, so schools were canceled and I'm holed up here, thinking of you.
>
> I'm sorry for continuing to bother you. I know I shouldn't, but, hey, what can I say? After all these years, and after all the mistakes I've made, I still miss you.
>
> As I sit looking out over the rocky ledge to the north sea, I mourn for having treated you so unforgivably. Thousands of times I've wished I had it

to do all over again. You were my wife—
in my hands was the greatest opportunity
in my life, to be a loving and faithful
husband, to make you happy, even to be a
father. But I was too blind, too self-
centered, too lost in sin. (And Sara, I
am so sorry, so, so sorry for what <u>I made</u>
<u>you do</u>. Always remember that it was my
fault, my selfishness; never blame
yourself.)

    Sara, I'm not saying this in an attempt
to win you back—I'm certainly not trying
to break up your marriage. Every day I
pray for you and Stephen and the boys. I
want you to be eternally happy together.
I guess I'm just hoping that somehow
through sharing this with you I can grow
to forgive myself.

    Always remember that I am here for
you if there is ever anything you need.
Please know that I will always love you,
and that you are always in my prayers.

Your friend always,
Frank

Tears stained the page before she crumpled it between her hands. "Dear God, why are you doing this to me?"

She went to the bathroom for a Kleenex and to wipe her face with a wet cloth. After drying off, she stood staring into the mirror. At 45, her auburn hair still greatly outnumbered the infiltrating gray, and the smoothness of her complexion was winning the war against crow's feet. She gazed into her own eyes, as if prospecting for hidden answers, while combative voices fought within her psyche. After a prolonged meditative gaze, a slight smile came to her otherwise forlorn composure.

"So he wants to resign. So he questions everything that he has believed and taught."

She continued staring, looking through the woman she had become to rediscover the woman she could have been.

"I'm certainly not too old to reclaim my dreams."

7

Dinner was long since over, but still no Father Bourque. Sister Agatha had long since removed the dinner dishes, and Stephen was in his room anxious, impatient, and struggling with guilt. He knew he needed to call home. He needed to go home and get on with life, but he wanted to hear what this priest had to say to Richards' arguments. He wanted to get this Catholic thing settled once and for all.

Pacing, he rehearsed his impending confrontation. He envisioned Bourque becoming offended and evasive or even speechless under the weight of Richards' claims. He pictured himself becoming angry at this priest who had purposely concealed these things and then stomping out, heading home vindicated.

For the hundreth time, he glanced at his watch and then out the window to the parking lot. He sat down at the small desk and opened his Bible randomly, but then got back up. *Lord Jesus, I'm sorry for all this mess. Please help me to know Your truth.*

A distant door slammed. He heard feet stamping and then walking briskly down the hall toward him. The steps paused briefly and then resumed until they stopped outside his door.

"Stephen," came the priest's unsuspecting voice. "Are you still here?"

"Yes, Reverend Bourque," Stephen said in a tone much friendlier than he had heard earlier inside his head. He opened the door and was startled by the priest's appearance. He was visibly fatigued, leaning against the door jamb.

"Are you all right?" Stephen asked.

"Oh, I guess my long day is showing. Yes, I'm fine."

"Is there anything I can do?"

"Tell you what. How about making us a fresh pot of coffee, and then I'll meet you in the study in about ten minutes. I need to change my clothes, make a short visit to the chapel, and then we can talk. OK?"

"Yes, fine."

The priest smiled, nodded slightly, and walked slowly to his room. When the door had closed behind him, Stephen turned off his own room light and went to the kitchen. As he measured the coffee, he wondered what possibly could have happened, considering the demands and duties of his own pastoral work. *An accident or an untimely death? A confrontation with a church official or a disgruntled parishioner? Or had he spent the afternoon fending off some local fundamentalists?*

With the coffee brewed and poured into two large mugs, he proceeded to the study. It was empty, so he placed Father Bourque's mug by his rocker and then sat in the other. After waiting a few minutes, he decided to start the fire, which had long since grown cold. It wasn't until the fire was fully ablaze, though, and he had finished half of his coffee that the priest finally entered. He had changed into a clean black robe.

"Thanks, Stephen," he said as he sat and took his mug, "and thank you for making the fire. I have a chill that won't go away." The priest sat rocking quietly, sipping his coffee, staring into the fire.

Eventually Stephen could no longer take the suspense. "What happened, if you don't mind my impatience?"

"A man in my parish died today. Jeremiah Eames. He wasn't an active member; in fact, as far as I know, he hadn't entered the doors of this or any other church in over 40 years, since his mother's funeral. He was baptized here shortly after World War I and received the Sacrament of Confirmation during the first year of the Depression. I knew little else about him, except that he never married and lived his entire life in the house where he was born, about four blocks from here. After his parents died in the '60s, he outlived his three siblings, spending the last nine years alone and bitter to the core. I know of no one who liked him. Over the years, the priests of this parish have tried to pay their annual visits, but we were never welcome. Through the locked front door he would just call us 'blind bastards' and 'viper's brood!'"

The priest took a sip of coffee and then smiled. "He was a likable old cuss. Run across any of these in your ministry?"

"I suppose," Stephen said, but he was too anxious to get on with his own agenda. Once at Red Creek he had tried persistently, with the gospel of love, to break through the cynical and vicious heart of one such unchurched neighbor, but had only walked away humiliated. "Kicking the dust off his shoes," he had concluded that he had more than enough willing people who needed his pastoral attention. And then, of course, there was crotchety old Mr. Bernstein at Sleepy Meadow.

"This morning Jeremiah was rushed to St. Luke's Hospital, dying," Father Bourque resumed. "Apparently the delivery boy from the local market who brought Jeremiah his weekly order found him lying motionless on the living-room floor. The squad took him to emergency and put him on life support."

"Were they the ones who called you in?"

"Actually, no. The owner of the market is a parishioner. He made the first call, but Jeremiah himself made the second."

"You're kidding."

"No, after about a half hour, Jeremiah regained consciousness, and, true to his character, cursed everyone in sight for bringing him there. They said he tried to escape but was too weak, so he gave up. They restrained him and basically left him alone. It was then that somehow he called me."

"What did he say?" Stephen asked, now slightly more interested.

"Simply, 'Father, we need to talk,' in a surprisingly humane voice, and then hung up. When I got to his room, he was lying still, like a corpse glaring out into the unknown, tubes running everywhere, his eyes locked on the ceiling. He appeared much more emaciated than the last time I saw him, about a year ago. I walked forward, touched his arm, and said hello, and without altering his gaze, he said weakly, 'Father Bourque, I'm sorry, I'm sorry for so much.' Then, after a pause, Jeremiah turned his face and beckoned, 'Father, can you hear my confession?' Stephen, it's an understatement to say that this was the last thing I expected to hear from this Scrooge of a man. In fact, that's exactly what went through my mind: I envisioned the converted Scrooge and wondered whether old Jeremiah had seen a few ghosts. For nearly two hours I sat beside Jeremiah and heard his life's story. At times he wept, but toward the end a smile had finally won the battle for his face."

"But what did he say?" Stephen asked, now quite intrigued.

"Well, now we're caught in the privacy of the confessional, since most of our conversation was enclosed by the bookends of his request for confession and my bequest of absolution. What I can say, though, is that Jeremiah's life was a perfect example of what happens when a person allows the seed of bitterness to sprout in his heart, to establish roots, and then grow unchecked for years. As a boy, he had wanted to become a priest because he loved the Lord and His Church dearly, but the Depression had so impoverished his large family that his priest told him to stay home and help them survive. Years later he reconsidered the priesthood, but the U.S. had entered World War II and he was drafted. He came back depressed and angry, mostly because his hands had been used to kill so many when his dream had been to heal with love.

"In the '50s he closed himself in against the world, and his heart soured as in self-pity he turned the world in on himself. He became mad at everyone, especially the Church for rejecting him when it could have prevented him from a 'life of murder' as he called it. At the end of his confession, though, I can only say that his heart was clean and free, and, as King David had petitioned in Psalm 51, restored with the joy of his salvation."

"But if he had been this bitter for so long," Stephen asked, "what changed his heart to want to talk with you?"

"Apparently, I wasn't all that far from the truth. Jeremiah claimed he had seen some kind of vision, an image of his dead father, who told him he was about to die and to get himself ready. This vision involved quite a lengthy conversation, which in the end caused Jeremiah to faint. He hit his head on something and fell to the floor out cold until the delivery boy found him. When Jeremiah was done cleansing his heart from the guilt of years of sin, I asked him to make an act of contrition, and he recited from memory the traditional prayer with more meaning than I have ever before heard."

"The traditional prayer?" Stephen said, puzzled, for of course, as a Congregational minister, no one had ever asked him to hear their confession. *Why would they? They only need to go directly to Jesus!*

"With eyes closed and his hands poised in the posture of the altar boy he was 80 years ago, Jeremiah prayed, 'O my God, I am heartily sorry for having offended Thee, and I detest all my sins, because I dread the loss of heaven, and the pains of hell; but most of all because they offend Thee, my God, who are all good and deserving of all my love. I firmly resolve, with the help of Thy grace, to confess my sins, to do penance, and to amend my life. Amen.' I stayed beside him for a few more hours while he drifted in and out of consciousness. A doctor and a few nurses began making a fuss over him, but there was nothing they could do. Around six, he died, at peace with the Lord."

The memory of the exorcism and similar death of Elsie Drewer—in an apartment not all that far away—rushed Stephen's mind. *What's with this town?* he thought. She, too, had exuded the same joy, once she had been freed from her torment. And then he thought of the myriad times he had sat beside dying members, sending them off to meet their Maker, and wondered: *Did I do all that I could to prepare them?*

"So, Reverend Bourque, did Jeremiah Eames, after a life of bitterness and sin cleansed at the last minute, go straight to heaven?"

"What's wrong, Stephen?" the priest said, surprised at the bitterness in Stephen's voice.

"Oh, it's this very issue, this setting of the minister and the dying man, that has caused me the most concern over the years. Every Protestant tradition has a different set of criteria for entrance into heaven, and now I'm reminded that you Catholic priests believe that you have the God-given authority to forgive a person's sins: you perform last rites and, hocus-pocus, a person is saved."

"Come on, Stephen, out with it. What do we need to discuss?"

Stephen hesitated, but the priest was inviting him. "This afternoon I spoke with an old friend—an ex-Catholic who is now a Congregational minister. He was shocked by what he *thought* I was considering. He challenged me to read a book that is posted on the Internet. I spent the afternoon reading it, and, well, I must admit I found its arguments convincing. The author compares the Catholic Catechism with Scripture, and demonstrates over and over again that the Catholic Church is unscriptural."

"And what book is that if I may ask?"

"True Roman Catholicism."

He expected Father Bourque to be offended, or at least skeptically curious, but instead the priest just sat quietly, rocking slowing, smiling.

"Stephen, come here."

The priest rose, directing him to follow. Together they walked across the study to the front right corner where Father Bourque pointed to a shelf about six feet off the floor.

"See these books?" the priest asked. "Examine, if you would, their titles."

Stephen cocked his head to read the titles, and saw before him dozens of anti-Catholic books. In the midst were several he had in his own library, including Boettner's *Roman Catholicism*. Father Bourque reached to the far right end of the stack and pulled out a colorful paperback. The cover picture depicted a medieval portrayal of the devil holding in his hands St. Peter's Basilica in Rome. Above the picture was the title: *True Roman Catholicism.*

"You've got the book," Stephen exclaimed, his voice trailling off with embarrassment.

"I may have the most thorough library of anti-Catholic books in the world, at least for a Catholic priest. You see, I have lots of Protestant friends who fear that I lost my soul when I became Catholic. They constantly send me everything they come across, hoping a book or cassette tape might be the ticket to my salvation. In every case, I've read their books or listened to their tapes, and then sent back my critiques, hoping instead to open their hearts. None has responded, of course, but it has kept me abreast of anti-Catholics' ignorance of history, philosophy, Scripture, and particularly what the Catholic Church truly teaches. Come, let's sit and examine this particular book."

He directed Stephen back to their seats.

"Stephen, I guarantee that we can easily answer all of this author's arguments—not because I'm so smart or he's so obtuse, but because his arguments are built upon the blindness of his convictions. He starts with anti-Catholic assumptions and then backs these up with isolated quotes from the Catechism and Scripture."

Handing Stephen the book, he said, "Actually, I couldn't ask for a better way to help you see why Protestant methods of discerning truth are flawed—which you have discovered on your own—and why one needs to trust the Church as the Spirit-led guarantor of truth."

Though Stephen felt a warm closeness to this understanding priest, he yet steeled his heart to listen with care.

"Setting aside the Catholic issue for a moment," the priest began, "have you read any books written by one Protestant tradition defending its beliefs and practices against another?"

"Certainly," Stephen replied. "Over the years, I've read several Protestant textbooks trashing my Calvinistic views on baptism, salvation, justification, etc., which also contradicted each other. As a matter of fact, I remember years ago when I was preparing a sermon on God's predestination of the elect. After four days of Scripture study, I checked my Calvinist interpretation against several Methodist, Lutheran, and Baptist commentaries in a local seminary library. In the end I had four separate, irreconcilable interpretations about how God's will and our wills control our destinies.

"When I asked other pastors about this, I got basically two responses: either they were so convinced their respective interpretations were right that they couldn't see the problem, or they confessed the contradictions but wrote them off as the natural result of our human depravity. But Jesus promised that 'if we continue in His Word, we will know the truth.' That Sunday in the pulpit was the first time I knew there was a big problem, and so my search began."

"Stephen, I've also read similar Protestant books that attacked my Lutheran background. Now, consider this: didn't each of these Protestant authors anathematize their Protestant opponents by quoting Scripture?"

"Yes, I suppose." This reminded Stephen of the times when he and Malone battled it out. It was always a test of who could quote the most verses and less an open-minded search for truth. He added: "And sometimes they present an opponent's position inadequately to make it easier to destroy."

"For example?" the priest queried, taking a sip of coffee.

"Well, take baptism, for example. Baptists, who teach 'believer's baptism,' claim that infant baptism is a contradiction of salvation by faith alone. They quote verses that emphasize the necessity of personal faith in Christ and then point out the obvious: infants are incapable of personal faith. They also show that the Bible nowhere promotes infant baptism, claiming that this was a pagan practice added later by the Catholic Church."

"Do you baptize infants?"

"Yes, I do

"OK, what's your rationale?"

"I emphasize that salvation is a gift of God's undeserved grace, and the baptism of an infant is the ultimate sign of this. To make reception of baptism dependent upon a person's act of faith is akin to making salvation dependent upon his *work*." As he spoke, Stephen couldn't escape the implications for his own practice of proof-texting. "I then fortify my position with lots of verses that emphasize grace as a free gift, that whole families were baptized in the book of Acts, and that baptism was the New Covenant's replacement for infant circumcision."

"Now, asking this as an ex-Lutheran: do either of you—you or your opponent—believe that baptism saves you?" Father Bourque asked.

"No, of course not. We both believe that baptism is a visible sign of one's saving faith, a sign of God's grace working in the heart of either an innocent, helpless infant or an adult believer."

"Then how do the two of you understand the statement in First Peter 3:21, 'Baptism...now saves you...through the resurrection of Jesus Christ?'"

Stephen laughed. "Well, there's another one of those verses we conveniently read around. I have no adequate explanation for that verse, which both sides generally avoid in their arguments."

"Precisely. Now, Stephen, back to this anti-Catholic book. As far as how Richards has framed his argument, he is correct. But his method is so flawed that I end up feeling sorry for him in his misled sincerity.

"His first underlying false assumption, which we have already discussed, is that the Bible alone is sufficient to define truth. Your battle over what is more biblical—believer's or infant baptism—is a good illustration. Would you not agree that this assumption is flawed?"

"Yes, I now admit that," he said with cautious resignation. "To do so is scary, but I know that I can no longer rest my faith on this assumption."

"Richards' second underlying false assumption is that for something to be true, it must be found somewhere in the Bible. 'Show it to me in the Bible!' is their constant mantra, with the implication that if the Catholic Church—or another Protestant group for that matter—believes something that isn't mentioned specifically in the Bible, it therefore by definition must be false. Is this not true?"

"I suppose."

"But what do you think now, Stephen? Tell me, where in the Bible does it say that I have to show it to you in the Bible?"

Stephen turned to the fire, distracted by the popping of an ember. *Had these not been Ginny McBride's exact words?*

Finally he answered: "I admit, from what I have read and observed, that the Bible nowhere makes this claim. This disclaimer could have been initiated by the Reformers themselves to justify using the Bible alone to denounce whatever Catholic practices they didn't like."

"By George," Father Bourque said with theatrical surprise, "I think he's got it! With just those two disclaimers you can pretty well discount all of Richards' arguments."

"But, yet," Stephen insisted, "the things he claims that the Catholic Church teaches are backed up by direct quotes from the Catholic Catechism?"

"Yes, on the surface these quotes do seem incriminating, so let's examine another flaw in his method: he misrepresents Catholic teachings by extracting one doctrine from others that explain it. By doing this, he can make something sound boldly heretical which otherwise makes complete sense. He then defends his caricature by pulling isolated quotes from the Catechism, ignoring the supportive context. Finally, he selects Scripture references that make his caricature sound obviously heretical.

"For example, let's look specifically at his chapter on 'The Catholic Church presumes the power to forgive sin.'"

Father Bourque directed Stephen to the chapter and then held the book so that together they could read by the combined light of the lamps and the fire.

"The author begins by caricaturing the Church's position and then backs this with a quote from the Catechism. For instance, from paragraph 982 he pulls out this quote: 'There is no offense, however serious, that the Church cannot forgive.' On the surface, this sounds pretty arrogant, doesn't it?"

"To say the least."

"But let's look at what else the Catechism says." The priest reached to the books under his nightstand and pulled out a well-worn copy of the Catechism. He located the quote and held the book up. "Stephen, do you notice anything significant about where this quote is located in the Catechism?"

Stephen turned the book toward him to study the page where the quote was located.

"No, I mean look at the spine. Don't you see that this quote is located at least one-third of the way into the Catechism?"

"Yes, but..."

"The point is that this Catechism is arranged and organized systematically. In this case, Richards is quoting from a long section in the Catechism on the Nicene Creed, and specifically from an explanation of the line, "I believe in the forgiveness of sins,' which as you know is near the end of the creed."

Stephen nodded.

"Two hundred and fifty-six pages of explanation proceed this quote. By extracting this quote and ignoring its preceding context, Richards grossly misrepresents the Church's understanding of its responsibility as a channel of God's forgiveness and love."

Through another cup of coffee and two new logs on the fire, Father Bourque proceeded to lead Stephen through a thorough and sometimes tedious examination of the Catechism, section by section, until they reached the paragraph immediately preceding the section quoted by Richards.

"The Catholic Church's understanding of her authority to forgive sins is built, first, on the authority Jesus gave Simon as the Rock and the bearer of the keys of the kingdom, second, upon the authority to loose and bind that Jesus gave all the Apostles, and finally on the authority to forgive sins Jesus gave His Apostles in the upper room. It is only logical, therefore, that since Jesus intended the Church to last far beyond their specific lives—until the whole world was reached with the Gospel—this authority would pass from them to their successors, the bishops of the Church. Listen to how this is fleshed out in paragraph 981:

> After His Resurrection, Christ sent His apostles "so that
> repentance and forgiveness of sins should be preached in

His name to all nations." The apostles and their successors carry out this "ministry of reconciliation," not only by announcing to men God's forgiveness merited for us by Christ, and calling them to conversion and faith; but also by communicating to them the forgiveness of sins in Baptism, and reconciling them with God and with the Church through the power of the keys, received from Christ.

"The Catechism then reinforces this with a quote from St. Augustine:

> [The Church] has received the keys of the Kingdom of heaven so that, in her, sins may be forgiven through Christ's blood and the Holy Spirit's action. In this Church, the soul dead through sin comes back to life in order to live with Christ, whose grace has saved us.

"Finally we have reached the paragraph from which Richards quoted, but note the entire paragraph:

> There is no offense, however serious, that the Church cannot forgive. "There is no one, however wicked and guilty, who may not confidently hope for forgiveness, provided his repentance is honest." Christ who died for all men desires that in His Church the gates of forgiveness should always be open to anyone who turns away from sin.

"Then in the next paragraph the Catechism backs this with quotes from three universally respected Early Church Fathers:

> St. Ambrose: The Lord wills that His disciples possess a tremendous power: that His lowly servants accomplish in His name all that He did when He was on earth.
> St. John Chrysostom: Priests have received from God a power that He has given neither to angels nor to archangels....God above confirms what priests do here below.

St. Augustine: Were there no forgiveness of sins in the
Church, there would be no hope of life to come or
eternal liberation. Let us thank God who has given
His Church such a gift."

Setting the Catechism aside, Father Bourque picked up *True Roman Catholicism.*

"Now, Stephen, can you at least affirm, given a wider examination of the Catechism, that what this author argues against is a misrepresentation of what the Church actually teaches?"

Stephen picked up the Catechism, feeling its weight, and compared it mentally to the plethora of creedal statements that shape, define, and constrict what Protestants believe.

"Yes, but what troubles me deeply," he said, "is how flippantly I've viewed and taught forgiveness. Like so many Protestants, I made forgiveness a 'me and Jesus' thing, without any need for the Church or baptism or any apostolic authority. I've portrayed the Catholic Church as an arrogant, power-hungry institution, set on controlling its members' lives and preventing them from following Christ freely. But I fear I've been greatly misled."

"Stephen, I'll not deny that there have been individuals in the Church—popes, cardinals, bishops, priests, religious, and laity— who were arrogant and sinful. I'll also admit that I fall far short of being the kind of priest I should be. But this in no way hinders the Church from being exactly what Christ established her to be: His very Body in the midst of this world of sin."

Father Bourque put the anti-Catholic book back up on the shelf with the others. "I fear that my long-winded explanation has not answered all your questions, but I'm feeling quite spent. Is there anything else we need to discuss tonight?"

Stephen had a long list of questions, but sensitive to Father Bourque's demanding day, he replied, "No, not tonight, but maybe in the morning if you have time. I'll probably start home tomorrow afternoon."

"So you've called your wife?"

Stephen looked into the priest's eyes. "No, I haven't," but the priest's otherwise stolid poker face was broken by his fatigue, "how did you know?"

"I guessed last night when you came back. Given my experience counseling other clergy converts, it was obvious that this was having a devastating effect on more than your job."

Before this man of God, Stephen felt ashamed.

"Listen, my friend," Father Bourque said, "there's one thing of which I'm certain: nothing happens in our lives apart from God's will and good pleasure. Your marriage is a significant part of His plan, as is your vocational struggle and your visit here. If you don't mind my meddling, I think you need to call her. Let her know you're all right, and that you'll be home tomorrow."

"You're right, and that's exactly what I will do."

The priest rose from his rocker and crossed to the bookshelf on the opposite side of the room. "Before you go, though, I noticed that a particular book was sticking out of my shelf." He removed it and read the title. "Yes, just as I hoped. A very helpful book."

"I started to look at it this afternoon."

"You couldn't find a more balanced examination of the causes behind the Reformation than this small book by Professor Karl Adam. Tell you what, if I may, let me give you an assignment for this last evening here. After you've squared things with…?"

"Sara."

"…Sara, spend the rest of the evening reading *Roots of the Reformation.* It's less than one hundred pages. I'm positive it will answer a host of lingering questions. Then tomorrow morning after breakfast, my time is yours for whatever conundrums you might ask. Sound fair?"

"OK," Stephen said, accepting the small book.

"Please, feel free to stay in here and use my phone. Just call direct, and I'll see you in the morning."

"Thanks, Father Bourque."

"Good night, and God love you."

With that, the priest left Stephen alone with the phone and his growing anxiety about calling home. *What has Sara been thinking? How will she respond after my day and a half of silence?*

He stared at the phone, considering a host of reasons to procrastinate. But in the end, he couldn't argue against reason, for he heard that familiar inner voice: *Be not afraid!*

He dialed and waited. It was now almost 9:30 p.m. The boys

would be in their rooms finishing their homework. Sara might be in the living room watching television, or alone in her room.

The phone rang twice, three times, and then she answered, "Hello?"

Her voice was surprisingly calm.

"Sara, hi. It's me."

"Oh, hello."

The phone was silent. Stephen was unsure how to proceed. It was clear that she wasn't ready to apologize. But having been the one who ran away, he knew that the ball was in his own court.

"Sara, honey, I'm sorry for everything. I'm sorry for the confusion I've caused in our lives, and for putting you and the boys through all this stress. Can you forgive me?"

"Of course, darling. I miss you."

He was relieved to detect at least a crack in her resistance.

"Where are you," she said, "and when are you coming home?"

Stephen, however, wasn't about to hedge his bets and sacrifice one step forward for three back. "I've got a room near Jamesfield, and, if you don't mind, I'd like to come home tomorrow afternoon."

"Are you planning to resign?"

Carefully, he responded, "Honey, I promise I won't do anything drastic unless you are in complete agreement. The last thing I will ever do is put you and the family in jeopardy. Please, trust me."

The line remained quiet for an uncomfortable moment, but then she said, "All right. So I'll see you tomorrow night?"

"You know, honey, I'm also sorry for our last dinner at the Wayside. How about letting the boys take care of themselves tomorrow evening, and meet me there again for dinner at, say, five o'clock? We need to redeem our favorite place."

"That sounds fine. There are a few things I also want to discuss."

This made him pause, but he was certain that this time, whatever it was, he would handle things differently.

"How are the boys taking this?" he asked.

"Well, Daniel has cried most of the last two nights, and William, well, he's been quiet. I guess he's become acclimated to our battles."

"When I get home, I'll have a long talk with both...no, we'll have a long talk with both of them. We need to apologize and make certain they know how much we love them and each other."

Stephen ached to be with her. "They need to know how much I love you."

"And I love you."

"Thanks, dear. I worried that I had lost you through my craziness. We'll make it all up tomorrow night. Get a good night's sleep."

"You, too," she said.

"Good night, darling."

"Goodbye."

They hung up. The tone of her farewell was a mite strange, but he must have been mistaken. Checking the clock, he picked up *The Roots of the Reformation* and went to his room.

Before opening his door, though, he saw the door to the chapel ajar. Led by the prompting of that still small voice, he decided to spend some time first on his knees. He had so much for which to thank God—much more than he had ever dreamed when he stumbled into this place yesterday afternoon.

8

Except for the flickering light of the suspended red altar light and a single votive candle, the chapel was dark. Father Bourque entered and checked the status of the votive candle, which he had lit the night before as a private prayer offering for Stephen. He had hoped to find Stephen waiting to join him for Morning Prayer, but as of yet there was no sign of him.

He considered knocking on Stephen's door. *But would this be pushing him too hard?* For a few seconds, he lingered outside Stephen's room, listening, but heard no movements. He tapped lightly, but no response. Again a little louder and called out softly, "Stephen, are you awake?" But still no answer.

Then it crossed his mind: *He must have left during the night! Heavenly Father, I pressed too hard, forgive me.* He tapped again, this time hard enough that no one could sleep through, but still no response. He tried the door, but it was locked. He checked his pockets, but didn't have the master key.

Dejected, he returned to the chapel. *He seemed fine when we parted, genuinely interested and open.* Then another thought occurred to him: *Maybe problems at home required him to leave in a hurry? But if that were the case, he would have left a note.*

In the chapel, he genuflected before the Tabernacle and knelt on the central prie dieu. In lieu of yesterday's profusion of blessings, he now felt empty and a failure. He opened his Breviary and began the Office of Readings, offering them for Stephen and his family, for Stephen's search for truth, and for Jeremiah Eames. *May God pour out his mercy abundantly on them all.*

He gently pierced the stillness of this inner sanctum with the pleading recital of the Psalter, a reading from the Old Testament, and then turned his attention to the second reading—a selection from the *Discourses Against the Arians* by St. Athanasius, bishop of Alexandria. Athanasius was one of the champions of the divinity of Christ at the important Council of Nicaea in the fourth century A.D.

As he meditated on this important work of antiquity, one particular sentence caught his attention in the light of his discussions with Stephen:

> But because the world was not wise enough to recognize God in His wisdom, as we have explained it, God determined to save those who believe by means of the "foolish" message that we preach.

When Athanasius penned this around 358 A.D., the canons of the Old and New Testaments would not be finalized for another fifty years. The New Testament documents had been copied over and over by hand, translated into many languages, and distributed all over Europe and Asia. But there also had been hundreds of other writings—Christian, pseudo-Christian, and pagan—which were held in varying levels of esteem by the Christian community. Out of this uncertainty arose many heretical groups, like the Arians. But as Athanasius emphasized, it was the *preaching* of the Apostolic Tradition that spread the truth of the gospel to the tens of thousands of Christians and pagans who could not have read a New Testament Epistle if they had had one in their hands. It was the apostolic preaching, preserved, protected, and passed down through the ages that ensured the correct interpretation of Scripture, not the other way around.

This reminded Father Bourque of a verse from the First Letter of Peter, where the Apostle reminded the early Christians of "the things which have now been announced to you by those who preached the good news to you through the Holy Spirit sent from heaven..."—the blessings of the Apostolic Tradition, preserved, protected, and proclaimed by the Church.

He finished the Office of Readings and Morning Prayer, crossed himself, and rose to leave. Passing the votive candle, he prayed that God would allow him one more opportunity with Stephen.

Donning his black overcoat and gray tweed cap, he walked from the rectory to the church. The winter morning air was crisp. There wasn't a cloud in the sky except for the vapor of his breathing. He tried the side door to the sanctuary and as usual found it open. Fred O'Reilly, the retired Army colonel who volunteered as the church janitor, couldn't be more faithful if he were paid a salary.

Like the small rectory chapel, the church was dimly illuminated by the sanctuary lamp, the few votive candles that still had flames, and the morning light filtering through the large picture windows. He crossed between the pews on his right and the Marian altar on his left and, genuflecting, passed before the tabernacle. He switched on the sanctuary spotlight and the ceiling lamps over the front third of the church. Besides the usual dozen or so regulars, he noticed a figure kneeling in the back pew. The priest squinted, but unable to identify the man, he proceeded into the sacristy to prepare the elements for Mass.

He robed while reciting the private liturgical prayers that accompanied this ritual. From the sanctuary he heard the voice of Mrs. Defidi leading those who had gathered for the morning rosary. Listening to their familiar voices, he asked God to bless their efforts and to have mercy on those who through ignorance or bigotry did not understand the benefits of the rosary. With embarrassment, he recalled what he had thought as a Lutheran—that the rosary was exactly what Jesus had warned against when he taught not to "heap up empty phrases as the Gentiles do." But the rosary was hardly "empty phrases," since the prayers and stories recited were predominantly from Scripture. And as for the repetitiveness, he had found it was a wonderful way of resting in the Lord—trusting that God knows more about what we truly need than we can ever express with our limited language and intellect.

When the church carillon began pealing seven bells, Father Bourque entered the sanctuary, signaling the congregation to rise. He kissed the altar and then blessed the congregation. Reciting the Trinitarian formula, he again noticed the figure in the back of the church, now standing, and by the colored lights of the brightening stained-glass windows, he could see that it was Stephen.

Thank you, Lord! he thought with great excitement.

He progressed through the rubrics of the Mass, distracted, for he was anxious to discover how Stephen was doing on his journey of faith.

Lord Jesus, he prayed as the lector rose to read the first lesson, *may this day truly be a day of mercy and insight for my friend and Your servant, Stephen.*

*   *   *

"WILLIAM!" a voice whispered from around a corner in the main high school hallway.

He stopped abruptly and turned to see Stacy motioning to him.

"Good morning," he said as she pulled him further back, out of view. "Is everything all right?"

"Yes, just fine. Neither of my parents suspects a thing."

"Stacy, are you sure you want to do this? Have you thought through…?"

She turned on him with a look that could raise the hair on a cat. "Don't you turn on me, too." Her expression softened, and she touched his sleeve. "William, I really have no choice. I've got to get out now before he goes crazy again. You're still going to help me, aren't you?"

"Yeah, I guess." He knew this didn't sound convincing, but he wasn't excited about how his parents would react if they ever found out.

"Great!" She turned and pointed to two dark bundles in the corner. "My things are in those two backpacks."

"How'd you get those past your parents?"

"I told my mother when she drove me in this morning that the senior class was hosting an Easter clothes drive for some needy students. She asked no more questions and didn't even check what I was stashing. Could you be a dear and put them in your car? Like I said, we'll meet there immediately after last bell. You walk to your car and just drive away. I'll be crouched down in the back seat."

Any resistance melted into excitement as he looked into the winsome blue eyes of this young woman who so trusted him, needed him, and even wanted him. He remembered those mysterious eyes from his childhood when, they were only five or so, she had thanked him for protecting her from the neighborhood bully. They had locked eyes and then, even though she had already turned back to the swings as if nothing had happened, he had felt what he now knew were the first tinges of love.

"Stacy, I'll do whatever you think is best. Should I meet you in the lounge?" he said as he picked up the bulging backpacks.

"I can't this morning. I need to make one final call to ensure that my friends will be there to meet us. Thanks again, William." With this, she moved up close, looked up into his eyes, and kissed him affectionately on the lips. He kissed her back, wondering, in his inexperience, what to do with his hands. Before he could decide, she had pulled away, smiled, and scurried down the hall.

He watched her disappear around a corner, debating whether he could manage the backflip his heart wanted him to attempt. Instead, he grabbed the backpacks and practically flew out to his car, knocking down two freshman girls in the process.

*   *   *

"The mass is ended; go in peace to love and serve the Lord."

"Thanks be to God," the fifty-plus parishioners responded in sync. Some knelt to continue in prayer; some sat to read or meditate; some stepped out, genuflected, and hurried off to the business of the day; while others just left, lax in their practice of Catholic tradition.

Father Bourque transported the Eucharistic vessels to the sacristy and began the ceremonial removal of his outer liturgical garments.

"Good morning, Father."

The priest turned toward the now-familiar voice. "Good morning, Stephen! It's great to see you. I was worried about you."

"Worried?"

"Yes, I stopped by your room to see if you would join me for Morning Prayer and you weren't there. I thought maybe I had driven you away again."

Stephen beamed. "No, not this time, though I was tempted to sneak out after talking with Sara. That single bed felt awfully empty last night. But no, everything's just fine. In fact," he glanced back through the sacristy door toward the Tabernacle and said with a smile, "I'd have to say that my life has been *altered* dramatically."

"Well then, Stephen, you'll just have to tell me about it. Come, let's have breakfast."

As he prepared for the brief trip through the cold, Father Bourque asked hesitantly, "What did you think of Mass?"

"Awesome, to use my sons' word. I'll elaborate later, but it was truly a blessed experience."

Bundled against the winter cold, they hustled without words from the church through the brisk and bright near-freezing air to the rectory. "Ever read Lewis' *Chronicles...of...Narnia?*" the priest asked as he removed his galoshes. "*The Lion, the Witch and...the...Wardrobe?*"

"Many times, to my boys. Why?"

"Well, it just occurred to me that this winter cold might be a symbolic penance specifically for you. Remember our talk about the true meaning of suffering? Well, maybe our heavenly Father is making you endure this winter chill as a sign of the spiritual springtime that awaits you around the corner."

"If that's the case, then at about two a.m. I felt that the *winter of my discontent* was over, and then about twenty minutes ago I was absolutely convinced."

They gathered at the breakfast table where Sister Agatha met them with the morning coffee.

"Good morning, Father, Reverend LaPointe."

"Good morning, Sister," the two beggars said. The breakfast entrees of pancakes, mixed fruit compote, fried eggs, sausage, bacon, and English muffins were already in place.

"Sister Agatha, once again you've done us up well," Father Bourque declared. "But I thought Tuesday was Sister Christina's shift?"

"She was a bit under the weather," Sister Agatha said with a bright, cheerful voice, "and besides, she didn't grow up with brothers. I knew you two needed a good, hearty breakfast." She nodded slightly and exited into the kitchen.

"Sister Agatha's a great blessing," Father Bourque said. "She keeps us in the right attitude."

They filled their plates and began eating.

"OK, Stephen, tell me. What was it that has ended your winter of discontent?"

After finishing a mouthful of pancakes and fruit compote, Stephen responded: "It was that book you lent me. After speaking with Sara, I went to my room to read. I was worried I might doze off, so I grabbed another cup of coffee. But the book was so engrossing, I couldn't have fallen asleep if I tried."

"What specifically impressed you?"

"First, could I ask a big favor? Can I buy that book from you? I want to reread it more carefully."

"My friend, the book is yours. Just promise to repay the favor by encouraging another friend to read it."

"That's exactly what I want to do with several pastor friends. There are many important things the author said that I had never heard or considered—that I was never told in seminary—about the true issues of the Reformation. But the one thing that most impressed me, and in the end convinced me that I can no longer remain a Protestant..."—he paused to let this sink in, both in Father Bourque's mind as well as his own—"...was his contention that the revolt initiated by Luther and the other Reformers was flawed in its core motive.

"Luther fought against the idea that we are saved through works," Stephen summarized. "He couldn't live up to the faith as he had learned it from his Renaissance professors, or the rigorous expectations of his monastic environment, or the demands of his own scrupulosity. So, in his desperate search to ease his conscience and restore joy to his life, he *discovered* a new and novel interpretation of the gospel: salvation through faith *alone* without works. He believed he was returning a misguided, corrupt Church back to its roots.

"In reality, however, he was fighting against a misrepresentation of the true Catholic faith, a cancer specific to his own time and place. He caricatured the Catholic Church as teaching that salvation can be earned through works or bought through indulgences, and to this day millions of people take Luther at his word and believe this. In the end, Luther essentially invented a new religion, and then the other Reformers—Melanchthon, Calvin, Zwingli, Bucer, Knox, Cramner—each took Luther's revolt further in more radical directions, until there were not only dozens of different faiths but, as we have today, thousands.

"But as I have only recently discovered," he said, smiling at his new priest friend, "the Catholic Church has never taught salvation through works. In fact, it has consistently declared that this idea is a heresy. If we want to know how the Catholic Church teaches we get to heaven, we only need to read Ephesians: 'For by grace you have been saved through faith, and this is not from you; it is the gift of God; it is not from works, so no one may boast.' Faith, as used here, means more than mere mental assent to truth; it includes the active application of truth in our lives. Faith requires that we live in obedience, or as it states in Romans, 'the obedience of faith.'"

"But, Stephen, where does this put you as a Congregational minister?"

"In many ways, the founders of Congregationalism were worse than Luther and the other major Reformers. At least the Reformers were trying to reform the authentic Church. The independent Congregationalist founders rejected all aspects of institutionalism. They traced their spiritual heritage back through all the schismatic groups that have ever fought against hierarchical control. The only way to accept Congregationalism is to believe that the original Apostles misheard Jesus about how the Church was to be structured and then from the beginning misdirected their followers. If this was true, however, then Jesus had broken his promise to his Apostles to be with them forever, the Holy Spirit had failed to lead them into all truth, and the gates of hell have prevailed."

The two sat silently, chewing their breakfast, mulling over what needed to be said next.

"But, Stephen, you said that something else sealed your journey?"

He looked up at Father Bourque with a smile: "It was something I did not expect."

Again he paused, feeling the power of the emotions that had turned his heart so decisively. "After little sleep, I woke up early, around five. I stopped to reconsider what I had decided before I went to bed—that I could no longer remain a Protestant, let alone a

Protestant minister—but I knew this was the only correct choice. I then sensed an inner calling, leading me to go over to the church to pray. It had so repulsed me on Sunday that I wanted to revisit it, to look at it with new eyes. Thankfully the doors were open, so I walked in and, still a bit intimidated, I sat in the back. I began pouring everything out to God, asking for forgiveness for my bull-headedness and my sins. I thanked Him for opening my eyes to the truth, and I pleaded with Him for some kind of confirmation; some clear, indisputable sign that I was not being misled by *the prince of liars*.

"I prayed like this for at least an hour, studying every statue and picture in the church, asking for insight and understanding, until people began coming in. I presumed they were coming for morning Mass, but then, for the first time in my life, I heard the rosary. Being ignorant of this kind of prayer, I yet forced myself to listen with an open heart and immediately recognized one of its benefits: it enabled the entire group to unite their hearts, minds, and voices together in concerted prayer for nearly twenty minutes. It was amazingly peaceful and reverent."

"Well, sadly, Stephen," Father Bourque said, pushing his breakfast dishes aside and bringing his coffee mug center stage, "too many Catholics pray the rosary as if they're in a footrace, just as some priests think completing the Mass in record time earns them special points. But not so with those who gather here early at St. Francis de Sales. These are sincere believers who rightly believe their prayers make a significant difference in the working out of God's will."

Stephen again envisioned the thirty or so men and women, kneeling in the pews, fingering their beads, staring at the ornate gold Tabernacle on the altar or at the agony-ridden crucifix on the wall above it, reciting in unison the biblical prayers of the rosary. He was impressed that these men and women came of their own volition, daily, while still in the morning twilight, to humble themselves in prayer before God.

He then compared this to the weekly prayer meeting he led at First Church, the only other time during the week his members made any effort to gather for worship or prayer. There were eight to ten regulars, and sometimes the numbers swelled to fifteen. Other than an occasional spontaneous reading or recitation of Scripture, the prayers were impromptu, extemporaneous, and presumed by their emotive content to come from the heart. After 19 years, however, of leading various renditions of these, Stephen had come to the conclusion that the prayers of these otherwise sincere people—mostly women—were hardly extemporaneous. The same terms and phrases were constantly repeated, and though the prayers were directed upwards, it was obvious that sometimes the intended audience was those seated around the room.

"Are you all right, Stephen?" Father Bourque broke the silence.

"Oh, yes, Father," Stephen said as his attention returned. "When you finally began the Mass, I was more than nervous. I had resolved that I could no longer be a Protestant minister, but I certainly wasn't ready for the alternative. I watched and listened, admittedly not as a participant but as an outside observer—as a *critical* outside observer. And, Father, my simple conclusion is that I witnessed the kind of reverent Scripture and prayer-centered worship I have sought to instill ever since I was ordained, but unsuccessfully. Many things you did were similar to our monthly Communion services, except for the sacrificial language. But there were three powerful moments that cut to my heart and sealed my journey, or I suppose you might say, my fate," he said with a nervous chuckle.

"The first was the Words of Institution. I use the same words from First Corinthians when I lead Communion. But when you recited Christ's words—'This is My body'—slowly and with great awe, and held high the large flat disk of wheat…"

"The consecrated host," Father Bourque added as a gentle correction.

"…the consecrated host, pausing in obvious worship, I somehow knew that this was real—that the host was truly the body of Christ my Savior. I don't know how—as I don't know how to adequately explain the Trinity or how God created everything *ex nihilo*. All I know is that scales of stubbornness, pride, and ignorance fell from the eyes of my heart, and I believed Jesus at His word. He isn't just here in our hearts or in our midst by the dwelling of the Holy Spirit; He is miraculously and uniquely present in what appears to be only a flat piece of bread."

"Stephen, your acceptance of this is quite a miracle in itself. It took me a long time to truly accept it, given my near-Catholic Lutheran views of the Eucharist compared to your merely symbolic Calvinist views."

"I know. I myself was startled by this realization, but it wasn't over. After we said the Lord's Prayer and greeted each other, you brought our focus back to the altar. The congregation sang some phrases in Latin and then knelt together. Once again you held up the host, this time broken in two pieces, and you said something that I as a Protestant minister could never comfortably say. You drew our attention directly to the elevated host and, quoting the words of John the Baptist, you proclaimed, 'The Lamb of God, who takes away the sins of the world. Happy are those who are called to his supper.' The implication was obvious. You were professing that the consecrated host in your elevated hands was Jesus, the Creator and Savior of the world. My rational brain said 'No! It's only bread,' but my heart—not my emotions but my soul—knew that it was true." His eyes became misty.

"But, Father, the real miracle happened next."

"Next?" Father Bourque looked on, listening, puzzled.

"It was as if everyone around me knew exactly how I felt. It was, in fact, a great sign of the spiritual wisdom of the Church, for I heard the congregation recite in unity and with great sincerity the words of the centurion in the Gospel—the very words that described how I was feeling: 'Lord, I am not worthy to receive you, but only say the word and I shall be healed.'

"Up until that moment, I had not taken part in the Mass. I had remained seated in my pew, never kneeling, feeling too self-conscious to do any of the, quote, *Catholic* things. But when I heard the congregation humbly confess this, I was driven to my knees, and wondered if I would ever be able to get up—if I ever should get up—for all that I have done in my life; for how I have sadly misled so many people. And I watched as the men and women went forward to receive Jesus, wishing that I could be so worthy."

Stephen's head dropped in shame, and Father Bourque reached over to comfort him.

"Stephen, this is one case where I can say I know how you feel, for I too was devastated when I realized that the sacraments I had led for so many years were invalid. But, Stephen, take heart. What you have done has always been out of sincerity and out of ignorance. Given your Protestant formation, you really had no way of knowing. And for this, God forgives you. He knows your heart, your motives, and your desire to lead faithfully. As a result, I'm positive he pours forth his grace into the hearts of your congregation and you.

"But, Stephen," he continued, "now you know differently." He paused for a sip of coffee, and then asked, "What are you going to do now, my friend?"

Stephen stared at his hands. He then wiped his eyes and, with a smile, looked into the priest's and said, "Oh, I guess I'll just hang around here with you for the rest of my life."

They both laughed.

"Yes, that would be fun," Father Bourque replied. "In time, we could solve all the world's problems, but your wife and family might start to miss you."

"I suppose," Stephen said, turning serious. "As I said, I now know that I can no longer serve as a Protestant minister—I can no longer promote the Protestant agenda. It is as if I've been transported back to the Reformation, and though the Church desperately needed renewal, I now know that the Reformers' methods were wrong: Church renewal does not come through divorcing oneself from the Church and starting a new one. This is the sin of schism, which has only led to thousands of other schisms. No, Church renewal begins in the heart, and that means it begins right here."

With this, he tapped his chest with a closed fist, the way he had seen several parishioners do that morning in Mass.

"But as for becoming a Catholic," he held up his hands and shook his head, "I'm not ready for that. As you yourself must understand, there are still a lot of things that are strangly foreign to my Protestant eyes and ears."

Father Bourque laughed, "Ain't that the truth! I remember especially how uncomfortable I felt the first time I prayed before a statue of Mary. I knew in my mind that as a Catholic I wasn't worshipping her—the statue was only to draw my attention to her, and Jesus is pleased whenever we honor His mother—but still it felt awkward, even idolatrous. Even to this day, I often have to pray like the man who wanted Jesus to heal his son: 'I believe; help my unbelief!'"

"That's exactly what I prayed this morning!" Stephen exclaimed. "While the congregation confirmed my unworthiness, I prayed, 'Lord Jesus, I believe, I believe! Now please, please, help my unbelief.'"

Sister Agatha entered with a fresh pot of coffee.

"Thank you, Sister." Waiting for her to exit, Father Bourque continued. "What now, then? Are you ready to go home, or is there something else we need to discuss?"

"Oh, there are far too many things I don't understand, but maybe after I've straightened things out at home and at my church, I can break away for another visit."

"Come back any time, but call me if there is anything I can do in the mean time, and remember: it is not my desire to push, pull, or prod you into the Catholic Church. I only want you to have the fullness of what Christ wants for you."

"Thank you, Father," Stephen said. "I don't feel pressured, only loved." He rose from the table. "I think I'll take the rest of the day to drive home. I'm meeting Sara for dinner, where tactfully I'll try to tell her most of this, and a long, casual, roundabout drive through the snowy countryside will help me think this through."

"Sounds good, Stephen. Just keep it within the speed limit."

"Right, Father! Well within the limits."

"Come, though. Let me pray with you first, and give you God's blessing."

They went together down the hall to the chapel. As they entered, Father Bourque knelt on the prie dieu before the Tabernacle, and Stephen for the first time joined him. He bowed his head slightly, praying silently: *I believe, help my unbelief!*

The priest reached over and, placing his hand on Stephen's shoulder, prayed, "Heavenly Father, thank You for Your infinite mercies, for Your abounding love, and Your freely given grace. Help Stephen, Your servant, to continue to grow to know Your word and Your will. Soften any hardness in his heart that he might follow You with abandon wherever You desire to lead him. And may You shower Your blessings on his family, especially on his marriage as he considers how to tell Sara the ways in which You have opened his heart. We recall how Abraham's own wife Sarah laughed when she heard she was to have a child in her old age. May we believe deeply in our hearts the answer You gave her: 'Is anything too hard for the Lord?'"

Standing and positioning his hands on Stephen's head, he continued, "The Lord bless you and keep you; the Lord make His face to shine upon you, and be gracious to you; the Lord lift up His countenance upon you, and give you peace."

Then, tracing the sign of the cross, he said, "In the name of the Father, and of the Son, and of the Holy Spirit, Amen."

Feeling self-conscious, Stephen traced the sign of the cross on himself for the first time in his life.

"Thank you, Father," he said as he rose. He reached to shake the priest's hand, but instead Father Bourque enveloped his friend in a brotherly embrace. Stephen gratefully reciprocated and, as he did so, he felt as if he was re-enacting the biblical image of the prodigal son being received back into the fold by his loving, forgiving father.

"Wait a second, Stephen," Father Bourque said as Stephen turned to leave. "I have something to give you."

He left the chapel and then returned quickly. "I realize that this is a bit outside of your theological comfort zone, but since your name is Stephen, it's appropriate that you become more aware of the saint after whom you were named." He handed Stephen an oblong silver medal about an inch and a half long with a bas-relief image of St. Stephen, the first Christian martyr. "This isn't some kind of magic charm or talisman. When you carry or wear it, you are to reflect on Stephen's bravery for the faith and pray for his intercession. We choose particular saints because their lives of faith are an inspiration. I'll also ask that St. Stephen pray for your guidance and protection."

"Thank you, Father Bourque," Stephen said. Unsure what to do with this token of Catholic piety, he deposited it in his left shirt pocket. With a final glance of farewell, he retrieved his luggage and overcoat and headed toward the entrance.

"One more thing, Stephen."

As Stephen turned, the priest stuffed a paperback book into the inside pocket of his overcoat.

"And have a copy of the Catechism on me," the priest said with a confirming tap. "It'll answer any of your reservations about this Church too many call the 'whore of Babylon.'"

"That's kind of you, Father, but I can't..."

"Please, I guarantee you'll find some life-changing truths in that book."

"Then thanks again. I'll let you know what I've found."

With a final shake of hands they parted, Stephen to his car and Father Bourque to the rest of his duties.

Driving away, Stephen looked again at the insignia on the front door of the church and prayed silently: *Lord, I believe; please help my unbelief.* And a soft voice from within his heart responded: *Be not afraid!*

*   *   *

"So, DEAR, what have you discovered on your afternoon jaunts around town?" Helen asked as pleasantly as possible, setting before her husband a plate of leftover meatloaf and potatoes. Walter had slept longer than on most recent mornings, allowing only twenty minutes for lunch before he needed to pick up Stacy.

"Oh, the usual stuff. There is a huge bookstore by the strip mall that sells coffees and snacks, with a large Christian section. I've been spending some of my time there." He turned his undivided attention to his plate.

"That's nice," she said, "I'd like to go with you some time." She worked her hands through a sink of dirty dishes, not fooled a lick by his feigned interest in her day-old meatloaf.

He just ate.

After a few minutes of silence, she said, "By the way, I put another bag of clothes in your car to give to Stacy."

"Bag of clothes? What are you talking about?"

"Stacy said the seniors are having some kind of Easter clothing drive. She took two backpacks full this morning, but I found some more sweaters and things in the basement that she will never wear. They're in a sack in your back seat."

"Stacy never mentioned any clothing drive to me," Walter said, forcing down another bite of well-ketchuped meatloaf.

"Probably because it's more a 'mom' thing that she didn't want to bother you with."

"Um," he grunted as he finished up and placed his napkin on the table. "Thanks for lunch. Gotta get ready." He kissed her on the cheek and left the kitchen for their bedroom upstairs.

The extra sleep had done him good, but it was never enough. Maybe after a few months, he might get used to midnights. As he passed Stacy's room, he thought: *But why even worry about it?* The door was slightly ajar, so he paused to look in. He smiled as he looked around at her things. There was nothing he wouldn't do for her happiness, even though for now she couldn't understand his fatherly caution.

The room was in its usual state of partial disarray, books strewn across her desk, the bed unmade, the dresser drawers only partially closed. He started to leave, but stopped. Something about the usual clutter bothered him. He looked again, and this time noticed that her vanity, normally a mélange of makeup bottles and other paraphernalia, was stripped clean, empty.

Strange, he thought. He continued looking. The top dresser drawer was open. He started walking toward it, and as its contents came gradually into view, he saw that it too was empty. He yanked open the second drawer, empty, and the third. And he knew.

He threw back the bedroom door with a loud slam against the century-old plaster wall and rushed recklessly down the stairs.

"What is it, dear?" Helen asked as Walter ran past.

He said nothing.

Part VIII

Goodness and Mercy

1

THE FINAL BELL RANG, and William was first out the door. Advanced algebra was his favorite class, but hardly a word of his instructor's lecture on limits theory had entered his brain. In fact, he hardly heard a word all day. All he could think about was helping Stacy escape—well actually, all he could think about was Stacy, her kiss, and her promise of gratitude. He was uncertain where this would lead, but for now he was in love, and apparently she was, too.

He forced himself to walk calmly to avoid undue attention.

"Hey, Willie boy." The voice of Brad Corvey caught him from behind. "Slow down, my man. How 'bout some hoops over at my place? A dozen or so guys are coming."

"Love to, but can't. Got a commitment. Catch you tomorrow."

He waved Brad off and kept going. But Brad pursued closely behind.

"Willie, what's up? You've been somewhere else all day. Has that Stacy chick stolen your heart?"

If William hadn't liked Brad, he might have knocked him one, but instead he said with a wink, "Actually, you're not too far off. Listen, I've got to go, but I'll tell you later. Sink a few for me."

He and Brad shared a contemporary handshake of friendship—grasping fingers more than hands—then continued toward the parking lot. Brad, honored by his friend's candor, let him go on alone.

William left the school by the rearmost door and walked along the back fence to his Jeep. The doors were still open, as he had left them, and without checking the back seat, he slid in behind the wheel. He started the engine and asked, "Stacy, are you there?"

"Yes, just drive," came an abrupt, nervous voice from behind. "Is my father's gray wagon anywhere?"

Maneuvering the Jeep through the crowded, haphazardly filled lot, he looked.

"I don't think so. Where does he usually park?"

"In the front circle, directly out from the front entrance."

William chose an alternative exit—a gravel drive that circled the football practice field. Stopping at the main road, he glanced toward the front of the school and saw the car. "Your father's there, waiting. I can't see inside, but it's your station wagon all right."

"Can he see us?"

"I don't think so. He's a long way off, and his car is facing the other direction."

"Good, just step on it," she ordered with angry impatience.

"Relax, Stacy, and stay down. We'll be away in a moment."

He turned from the school down Main toward the Interstate. Once they were up the ramp and cruising safely along with the Interstate traffic, Stacy sat up. She shot a quick glance back. Seeing the coast clear, she swung her head around, her blond hair flowing around her face, and yelled, "Yes! I'm free! Come on, William, let's go!" She caressed his shoulders with her hands and smiled at him in the rear-view mirror.

Elated by her affection but unsure how to respond, he just kept his focus on the road and his pedal to the metal. He drove north on the Interstate according to her instructions. He yearned to ask her something more intimate, to fish for signs of affection, but he could not jump-start his courage.

Finally, he blurted out, "Stacy, where will you be staying? How will I get in contact with you?"

"I'll be with friends, and I'll contact you by e-mail." She said nothing more.

They continued north, past city limits, into open country. The scenery became less and less civilized as subdivisions, convenience stores, and service stations evolved into trees, boulders, and distant mountains.

"Do you have enough money?" he asked, trying to spark conversation.

"Yes, plenty, and besides, my friends will take care of me."

Again she retreated into silence, while William kept driving, staring awkwardly down the highway.

Thirty-five miles into freedom, Stacy yelled, pointing, "Here it is! Take this exit!"

William responded with a jerk, taking the off-ramp. Other than the usual New Hampshire winter wonderland, the only landmark was an abandoned two-pump gas station at the crossroads to the right.

"Pull in down there," she commanded, pointing.

As he drove the remaining hundred yards and on into the snow-swept station, William looked for signs of life, but saw none. The windows were boarded up, the front door askew on its hinges. Haphazardly strewn around the lot were several partially stripped and rusting cars—and two motorcycles.

"Are you positive this is the right place?" he asked.

"Yes, I'm positive."

"They must be late then."

"No, they're here," she said with excitement.

William glanced quickly behind and saw Stacy looking right past him. He slowed, turned in, and parked beside one of the abandoned pumps. He turned to speak to Stacy, and was startled by what he saw. Coming toward the car from the gaping door of the station was a tall figure in a mirror-faced helmet, black leather jacket, jeans, and knee-length, black leather boots. Two more riders in similar but different-colored helmets, outfits, and boots followed. William could tell by the cut of the jeans and the shape of the coat that the third rider was a girl.

"Stacy…," he started to yell, but she ignored him and burst from the back seat into the arms of the tall rider. He swung her off her feet, and William knew that this stranger was more than a mere friend.

"My bags are in the back," he heard her shout as the mirrored rider placed her back on the ground.

Without a word, the rider motioned, and the second male rider opened the door and retrieved her bags.

"Hey, wait," William said, but the helmeted figure only slammed the door shut. He attached one bag to the second cycle, and then the girl rider joined him. With one kick, the still-warm engine started, and they shot off down the road, heading east. While the tall rider attached the other bag to his cycle, Stacy walked quickly toward William's window.

He rolled it down and demanded, "But Stacy, I don't understand…?"

"William, thanks a lot. You don't know how much I appreciate this." She turned away.

"But Stacy, who are these people?"

She stopped and glared back at him with a demeaning face he would never forget.

"Look, you're a good kid. I'm sorry that I used you, but forget about me. And if my father ever asks, just tell him to go to hell!"

She mounted behind the tall rider whose face William never saw and was gone from his life. The cycle spewed stones at his Jeep as it sped off after the others.

William sat dazed in a wrenching state of confusion, anger, and rejection. He watched until both cycles were mere dots that disappeared over the horizon of a snowy hilltop. Hands shaking, he shifted his car into drive and cautiously pulled back onto the road, heading west.

He was at a loss what to think, but as he turned from the crossroad onto the highway, he was already starting to heal. He began considering all the negative things that *must* be true if Stacy would do something like this and with this coldness. Accelerating up to highway speed and melding into the southbound afternoon traffic, he was already feeling less jilted and more downright lucky. He then remembered that he hadn't told his mother anything about his plans for the afternoon, but surely she would accept his explanation if he told her he had been playing basketball at Brad's and lost track of time.

In the congestion of the late afternoon traffic, he became trapped behind a slow 14-wheeler. He waited impatiently as other cars passed before trying to pull out.

Then he saw him: his father, speeding by in his green Wagoneer.

But did he see me? No. His father was focused foward, seemingly in his own fight through the traffic.

William thought about honking and waving to get his attention, but caught himself. *How will I explain what I am doing this far north at this time of day?* Instead, he held back, allowing several dozen cars to pass before he edged out.

"The best thing to do," he said aloud, "is just go to Brad's and explain later." *But this must mean that Dad is coming home!"*

With a joy close to tears, he sped on toward Brad's, ready to "forget what lies behind and press onward," as his Dad would so often quote.

And as his car disappeared over an overpass, he gave one last glance in the rear-view mirror.

"God, be with her," he mumbled, far from truly over her. "And God help me…"

*　　　*　　　*

"WHAT DO YOU MEAN, you know nothing about what happened to my daughter? I am here every day at the same time to meet her, and she comes out the same door, every day, at the same time. Where is she?"

The school principal, Mrs. Elaine Scornsby, could offer nothing to calm this out-of-control father. Though she towered over him with her unusual height, she knew her slender frame would bend like a weed if push came to shove. She beckoned to every teacher and staff member within hailing distance to come to her aid.

"Please, Mr. Horscht, I said I will do all I can to find out where she is. Are you sure she didn't get a ride home with a friend?"

"Stacy has no friends here!" he screamed, his glasses steaming with rage. "We just moved here, and she told me that no one at this snobby school has even tried to speak with her."

Mrs. Scornsby turned to her aides, who had formed a protective cluster around her. Peering out over them, she asked if anyone had any information, but they all shook their heads, glancing curiously at this distraught, frenzied father.

"I'm sure, Mr. Horscht, that there is a logical explanation. Could she have walked home?"

"Stacy would not have done that!" he screamed, pushing the principal and her human fortress back with the mere force of his anger. "She knows that I come to pick her up, and she knows better than to do anything other than wait for me. Where is she?" He slammed his fist down next to Mrs. Scornsby on the office windowsill.

With this, a woman broke through the crowd. "Here, wait. Excuse me."

Everyone turned as a heavy-set woman pushed to the front.

"Miss Duryea," Mrs. Scornsby cried out nervously. "Do you know anything about this?"

"Well, I was passing by and heard you mention the name Stacy," she said, motioning toward Walter. "Did you say your daughter's name was Stacy?"

"Yes," he turned on her, ready to pounce. "Where is she!"

"I don't know, but if it is the same Stacy I know, she has been meeting with another student every morning in the senior lounge."

"A boy?!"

Miss Duryea saw the fire in his eyes, but she had some fire of her own. Unlike most of the staff, she had a personality that felt little fear in the face of adversity. She didn't know where Stacy and William were, but she could understand why Stacy might need to seek friendship behind this raging father's back. Being Walter's height, she stared straight into his eyes as she moved toward him.

"May I ask your name, please?"

"Mr. Walter Horscht."

"Well, Mr. Walter Horscht, I'm not at liberty, or under any obligation, to tell you the name of the student with whom she has been meeting." She spoke with a firmness that made him back pedal. "And I have no idea whether she is even with this student, and neither do these innocent teachers. We don't know where she is, and it is not our responsibility to know. Therefore, I would suggest that you turn around and go home peaceably. It's likely that when you get there, she'll be waiting. This was probably all just some miscommunication."

"Miscommunication? There was no miscommu..."

Miss Duryea took another step closer, staring at Walter nose-to-nose. Calmly yet firmly, she said, "I again suggest that you turn around and go home, and then call us if she hasn't arrived, say, by dinner. Otherwise, I will have security forcibly carry you out and deposit you in your car!"

Walter was fuming, but under the pressure of this fearless woman and her great cloud of witnesses, he had no choice but to leave. He wanted to scream some invective, but stomped out without a word.

Walking to his vehicle, he looked around through the huddled groups of gauking students, but saw no sign of her. *Where can she be? Who has she been meeting...?*

He froze. *William LaPointe! The papist's son! They have won her over, against my will!*

Driven with rage, he jumped into his car, started the engine, and screeched the tires as he sped from the school, heading first for home. He prayed that she would be there and his worst fears proved for naught. *Maybe another friend did bring her home. Maybe we just missed connections. Maybe she didn't see my car for some reason. No, she had to see it! It was in the same place as always!*

He banked his car around every corner, running every stop sign and light, until he pulled into his driveway. Kicking the car door open and letting it rebound against its hinges, he ran to the front door of his home. It was locked. He pounded several times but no answer. He fumbled for the key, and then the door opened. It was Helen.

"Walter, what is it?"

He pushed her aside, releasing some of the residual frustration from his abortive confrontation at school. She fell back against the wall and into the living-room couch.

Pressing toward the kitchen he yelled, "Where is she!"

"Stacy? Isn't she with you? Wasn't she there to meet you?"

He stopped short and turned to face her. "You mean she isn't here?"

Helen had seen that look before. She cringed deeper into the couch. *Fifteen years ago, or was it more recently?* He had thought she was seeing another man, and nothing she could say could convince him otherwise. He had pushed her, twisting her arm badly. To protect him—to protect them—from the gossip of the community, she had told everyone that she had fallen. Most had believed. But she never wanted to experience that rage again. So now she said nothing and only shook her head frantically, waiting for the repercussions.

Walter ran back out the front door, set on finding and correcting his daughter—and making certain that that son of a papist never spoke to her again. He jumped back into his car, backed out of the driveway without any concern for traffic, and jammed his car into drive. *First to the LaPointes', and if she's there, there'll be hell to pay!*

2

"D<small>ANIEL</small>, where is William?"

"Don't know; haven't seen him." Daniel stared into his computer monitor, where he had successfully achieved a level in his three-dimensional aerial attack game that even his older brother had not reached.

"But I need to leave to meet your father." She checked her watch. "And I need to leave now..." *if I am to be there waiting when he arrives.* Sara wanted to establish claim to home territory.

"Listen, Daniel. I'm sure William will be home soon, but I need to go. Just stay put, don't let anyone in. In case of an emergency, go next door to the Franklins' or call *911*."

Daniel glared intently at the computer.

"Daniel, did you hear me?"

"Yeah, Mom. No problem," he said, absorbed in his high-speed dogfight. "Don't worry. I'll be fine."

Sara watched her son conquering the cyberworld for the side of good against the dark lords of evil, and knew that her son would be fine.

"William should be home soon. Your father and I will be back, oh, around eight. We're meeting for dinner at the Wayside Inn if you need us for any reason. Love you."

No response.

She figured Daniel didn't even notice that she had left. After checking all the doors, she went out to the garage and backed out the van. Once in the street, she started forward, and then remembered, *Oh, the garage doors,* and pushed the switch again, closing both doors for the security of her boy home alone.

She pulled out around the first corner and passed a car racing in the other direction. It looked vaguely familiar.

Probably somebody needing to turn around. She kept driving, concentrating on only one thing: putting everything straight once and for all with Stephen.

A<small>S SHE PASSED</small>, Walter ducked down but still caught a glimpse of her face. *Yes, that was his wife.* He recognized her from when she had left early on Sunday morning and from their days at Red Creek.

Intent on having this one out, he drove directly into the driveway and up to the garage door. He peered in the garage-door window. *No cars at all?*

He knocked on the front door, and then again, but no answer. He looked in through the window and saw no movement.

Then it crossed his mind: *Maybe Mrs. LaPointe was driving to meet them somewhere. Of course! They knew that I would come after them as soon as I found out!*

He ran to his car. Surging back out, he tore off down the street at twice the speed limit, intent on catching up with the LaPointe van. At the main intersection, he looked in both directions, but saw nothing. He had a hunch, though: *away from town.* He turned right and sped out toward the country.

A mile down the road, he passed a Shell station on the left. He saw the van parked next to a pump. *She must have needed gas. Thank You, Jesus!* In the rear-view mirror, he watched her turn back onto the road in his direction about a quarter of a mile behind him. Up ahead on the right was a Ma-&-Pa grocery, so he pulled in and waited. When she passed, he eased back in about a hundred yards behind her. Together they drove west out away from the city.

Walter had no idea where, but he knew one thing for certain: *She is either driving to meet up with Stacy and her son, or she is going to rendezvous with LaPointe.*

He reached down below his seat. *Still there!*

THE MOUNTAIN DRIVE had been beautifully relaxing, and just as Father Bourque had predicted, the winter weather, taking a turn for the better, was a symbol of Stephen's spiritual change of heart. The sky had become clear, the sun warmer, and his soul had basked in mile after mile of breathtaking New Hampshire scenery.

Eventually, he worked his way over to the Interstate. All afternoon he had wrestled with how much to reveal to Sara. He was unable to tell her state of mind from the tone of her voice, and even so, she was so unpredictable. *If she had a bad day today, who knows how she might be now. But then again, she sounded more remorseful last night than ever before. What had changed? Lord, what should I do?*

He listened for that clear, still voice, but nothing came.

As he reflected and prayed while he drove, the scenery outside merged with all that he had obtained inwardly in his short time with Father Bourque. He also ran through various scenarios of how he would tell his friends about his decision. There were a few who might understand, but only one or two who might agree, and Jim, of course, was one. He thought about calling Jim, but didn't have the time.

He left the Interstate at Route 30 and headed west. *Sara might be driving on this very road,* he thought with a smile. But a careful look ahead and into his rear-view mirror revealed no van like hers.

The Wayside Inn was about three miles away, so with the time left, he decided to pray. After petitions for guidance and patience and particularly for tact, he remembered Father Bourque's example and the explanation Keating had given about the protective intercession of the communion of saints. This was as far out in left field as a Congregationalist got, but Stephen needed all the help he could muster. So he began asking for help from every saint whose name he could recall: St. Joseph, St. Francis of Assisi, St. Thomas More, St. Augustine, St. Christopher, St. Francis de Sales, and, still constrained by caution, the Blessed Virgin Mary. As he asked for her prayers, he thought: *Didn't she herself admit in the Gospel of Luke, "Henceforth all generations will call me blessed?"*

"Oh, and of course, St. Stephen, please pray for me," he said as he tapped the silver medal in his shirt pocket.

Ahead in the dimming twilight, he saw the lights of the Wayside Inn. He pulled into the parking lot, looking for Sara's van. *There it is. I'll park next to it.* But as he drove toward it, he saw a station wagon that looked disconcertingly familiar. *That looks like...Walter Horscht's car, but it can't be. We never see parishioners out this far. But wouldn't it be funny if it was? Wouldn't he have a cow if he knew where I've been!*

Chuckling to himself, he pulled in. Turning off the lights and buttoning his knee-length overcoat against the decreasing evening temperature, he stepped out and made his way toward a rendezvous he hoped would be a turning point in their marriage.

Sara watched as he left his vehicle. The spring in his step told her that he was in a great mood. She pulled back a bit, not wanting to appear too anxious, and they caught each other's glance. When their eyes met, Sara was reborn. If there had been any doubt in her mind—even with plans that might not now include him—she knew that she still loved him deeply. *Please, Lord, help me to listen, to understand, and to love him no matter what...*

STEPHEN SAW HER there through the front picture window, at a table with two candles, giving him the familiar welcoming smile that had won his heart so many years before. He now knew that everything would be fine.

His gaze shifted to the front door. As he approached, about five feet away, a figure stepped out from the dark side of the building. At first, Stephen couldn't tell who it was, for the man's head was covered by the hood of a sweatshirt and the rest of his body by a full-length wool coat. But then the light from a street lamp illuminated his face.

"Walter, hello. What a strange coincidence meeting you here."

Then the coat fell open, and the barrel of a revolver was pointed directly at him.

"Walter, what is this? What are you..."

The revolver fired, and the impact drove Stephen back. He screamed in pain, "Lord Jesus!"

"You'll not corrupt my daughter or my family!" Walter cried.

The revolver discharged again as Stephen tripped and fell, trying to get out of range.

"Lord Jes..." he cried out as his face hit the pavement.

Walter leaned forward, placing the revolver to the back of Stephen's head. He was beginning to press the trigger when he heard Stephen utter faintly, "Jesus, please...forgive...him..."

SARA NOTICED HER BELOVED STOP to talk with someone standing out of her line of vision. *Must be someone he knows, because he is smiling.*

Then she saw his face change from friendly recognition to shock to fright. He mouthed several words, and then she heard a loud explosion and he was thrown backwards. Then another. She watched with horror as Stephen hit the icy pavement headfirst.

"No!" she screamed as she kicked her chair back into the people behind her and raced to the door. Others began running with her. Someone beat her to the door, and once outside they found Stephen lying motionless, steaming blood forming a red slush in the snow.

"Oh, my God…" Sara wailed as she threw herself down beside him, clinging to him with all her might, certain that he was gone.

"Did you see anyone?" someone yelled to others coming out. "Quick, help me look around. Someone help this man. Someone call 911!" Men began circling the restaurant.

"Here, look out," came a voice from the crowd, "I'm a doctor." He reached quickly for the carotid artery in his neck to take Stephen's pulse. "He's still alive, but failing fast. Someone get some towels and blankets and something for his head."

But Sara refused to let go, desperately trying to awaken her husband.

"Stephen! Stephen! Please wake up! Please, God, don't let him die!"

Some of the men returned from circling the building. "We didn't see anyone."

"Quick, search the parking lot. He's got to be nearby, but be careful. The gunman might still be trigger-happy."

The men crouched down between cars, peering carefully into each, fanning out toward the highway. Then they heard the screeching burn of tires.

"There he goes!" someone yelled.

A gray Caprice wagon spun its wheels on a patch of ice between the lot and the road. But once clear, it shot forward, swerving as the driver struggled for control and sped off toward the west.

"Someone call the sheriff!"

Then off in the distance, they heard the faint whine of sirens. Knowing help was on its way, the crowd stood vigil, waiting, wondering, watching as a grieving wife held her beloved and the assassin escaped from their grasp.

*　　　*　　　*

"Raeph, raeph, is that you?" Walter whispered into the mouthpiece of a payphone stretched from the booth into his driver's-side window.

"Yeah, sure. Who is this?"

"It's Walter. Horscht."

"Well, hey, Walter. How goes it? And why are you whispering?"

"I did it."

"You did what?"

"I...I eliminated the papist."

"What are you talking about?" Raeph demanded.

"The minister at our church, whom I told you about...the one I was positive was a Catholic infiltrator...he was trying to steal my daughter...I shot him."

"You what? You can't be serious."

"But the other day...you said..." Walter stammered.

"Walter, don't you dare say I said," Raeph said, incredulous. "We were only talking hypothetically...what we *might* do if..."

No longer whispering, Walter protested, "But my situation wasn't hypothetical, and neither is what I just did! I need your help."

"Help? Walter, I can't believe you actually did this! And now you want to bring *me* into it?"

Walter's face jerked from the receiver as he heard sirens. "But you *are* in this. You and Harmond and the rest. I asked you about this, and you agreed."

"But I never expected...how did you know this for sure?"

Walter started to answer—but then remembered with shock for the hundredth time Stephen's last words. "But I thought that Catholics didn't believe...yet in the end...he called on Jesus...and he forgave..."

Sirens were now approaching from both directions, and the pulsating glow of the red and blue lights were starting to reflect on everything around.

He threw the receiver from the window. "Damn you!" he screamed.

With headlights off, he slowly pulled his car around to face the road. A patrol car whirred past from the east, its siren shifting octaves. Then two cars approached and passed from the west, but immediately slammed on their brakes. Walter panicked and shot out onto the road toward the west. In his rear-view mirror, he saw the second two patrol cars turn around and come after him at full speed. In front of him, the brake lights of the first patrol car came on and the headlights swerved around into his direction.

"But why am I running?" he cried aloud. "Won't they understand?"

No, you fool! a voice screamed from within. *You're dead meat.*

As the red and blue lights gained on him, boxing him in, he

noticed a farm road off to the left. He took the icy turn onto the snow-covered road at sixty. Then his right rear tire slid into a stump the local farmer had always planned to remove. The Caprice went airborne, spinning over and over, until it landed upside down against the barn.

The patrol cars arrived within seconds, but not before the leaking fuel exploded, engulfing the gray Caprice wagon in 15-foot-high flames.

3

THE YELLOW-WHITE FLAME of a shallow candle fluttered violently as the last of the wick and wax evaporated. This particular candle had burned for many hours, as had the dozen others before it, visible symbols of the many prayers being offered.

But before it could melt away into a cold stillness, a loving hand replaced it with a new candle, carefully transferring the flame from the nearly spent wick to the fresh one. Fed by fresh wax, the rejuvenated flame stretched to full height and bathed the altar of the hospital chapel with joyful brightness. This bright joy, however, could not assuage the aching sorrow reflected in the illumined face, for the hand that replenished it extended from an anxious wife whose husband's life hovered between this world and the next.

As she looked down upon the dancing flame, her tears nearly thwarted her effort. With the edge of a handkerchief, she wiped tears from her swollen eyes and gazed upwards at the brass cross above the altar. *Please, dear Sweet Jesus, spare my husband. He's a good husband, he tries to be a good father. Please let him live so that somehow we can start our lives over.*

With that, she turned her attention to a second candle whose flame burned brightly. *And Lord Jesus, please watch over Stacy, wherever she might be. Guard and protect her, and please, please, turn her heart toward home.*

Helen bowed her head and returned to the front wooden pew, where she sat alone in the empty chapel.

The door suddenly opened slightly, letting in a band of new light. A nurse spoke softly.

"Mrs. Horscht?"

"Yes?"

"He's awake and wants to see you."

"Thank God!" she exclaimed, leaving with the nurse.

Once out in the hallway, her world changed dramatically. People scurried everywhere: doctors in blue-green gowns, frantically checking their charts; orderlies pushing patients on gurneys or wheelchairs; recuperating patients walking precariously along the halls pulling IV apparatus; visitors searching for the rooms of loved ones.

Down the hall and to the left. Helen knew her way now without thinking. For three days she had been waiting anxiously for Walter's condition to take a turn for the better. Thank God, the patrolman had reached him and smothered the spreading fire with foam. Twenty minutes later, using the Jaws of Life, the emergency squad had freed him and brought him here. Nevertheless, eighty percent of Walter's body had been scorched and, coupled with multiple fractures, contusions, and a severed spine, his prognosis was grave. And since being admitted, he had not regained consciousness.

From a distance, Helen could see that the door to Walter's private room was open, and a uniformed policeman was seated in the usual spot. Every four hours a different officer would take a shift, watching over a prisoner who most likely would not stand trial.

When Helen and the nurse approached, the policeman rose and spoke in a sympathetic voice. "He's barely awake, and you can see him." He held up a hand to slow her down. "But I must remind you: he is under arrest, and I must be with you as he speaks. If he's coherent, I need to read him his rights just in case he gives us a clue as to why he did it."

Helen tried to push past him. "May I please see my husband?"

"Yes, of course." He let her pass, then followed her in quietly.

Walter was propped up slightly on pillows. Bandages covered most of his body, except for scant openings for his eyes, nose, and mouth. An oxygen apparatus assisted his breathing, and intravenous tubes provided medication and nutrients, food and water. Attached to his right wrist, concealed mostly by his blanket, was a set of handcuffs locking him to the rail of his bed.

"Helen...my darling..." Walter said breathlessly as she walked into his view. She leaned to hold him carefully, working around the tubes, cuffs, and gadgets.

"...my glasses..."

She looked among the bottles and other paraphernalia that cluttered his bedside table until she found them. "Here, honey," she said, positioning them precariously on his nose.

He smiled faintly as the face of his loving wife came into focus, but then his expression changed. His eyes widened and his smile vanished. He inched his arm toward her. Seeing this, she reached down to him, but he grabbed her hand tightly.

"Walter, what is it?"

"Is he...is he alive? Did I get him?"

"Excuse me," the officer said leaning forward, "I'm sorry, but Mr. Horscht, I must warn you that you are under arrest, and anything you say can be used against you in a court of law."

"...Helen..." Walter said with as much force as he could muster.

"Yes, Walter."

"Yes, what?"

"Yes, Reverend LaPointe is going to be fine. By God's mercy. He bled a lot, but apparently he was never in any danger."

Walter's hand fell away as he released his grip. With eyes closed, he said, "No...I...failed."

"But Walter, why did you do it?" she pleaded. "Why did you do such a thing?"

"For you...for Stacy...for God..."

"But, Walter..."

"I had to do it...don't you understand..."

His eyes began to close, then reopened with a look of confusion. "But...he called on Jesus...and forgave..." His voice trailed off as he fell back into unconsciousness.

"Oh, Walter," she said, collapsing on the bed beside him, weeping uncontrollably. The policeman and nurse pulled her up.

"Please, Mrs. Horscht. He needs his rest," the nurse said as they led her out into the hall, closing the door behind them. "Would you like to go back to the chapel?"

"Yes, please."

The nurse assisted her down the hall, through the mesh of other lives touched by pain, sickness, tragedy, and the unknown.

Once inside the solitude of the chapel, Helen checked first on her candles. Seeing them both burning steadily, she sat, turning her gaze to the figure of a man who had been nailed innocently to a cross, for the sins of His executioners. And she remembered His words. Looking upon him, she repeated them for her husband: "Father, forgive him, for he knew not what he was doing."

WHEN SARA LEARNED that it had been Walter Horscht who so savagely had tried to assassinate her husband, and that he was actually recovering downstairs in the same hospital, she had to fight the temptation to go downstairs and disconnect his IVs. By the second day, however, when she came to realize that Stephen would recover completely, her hatred slowly subsided into pity. Nevertheless, she knew she could never forgive him the way Stephen apparently had.

Then something Stephen said on the second night of his recovery helped make sense out of everything. After dinner and while he was resting, she had asked him through tears, "Why would God let this happen, just as we were getting back together?"

Quoting a verse she hadn't recalled hearing before, he answered: "'Now I rejoice in my sufferings for your sake, and in my flesh I complete what is lacking in Christ's afflictions for the sake of His body, that is, the Church.' Sara, I don't know exactly why Walter did it, but I have a hunch. All I know for certain is that God is calling me to accept my sufferings with joy, maybe in reparation for the many acts of ignorance and prejudice that Christians do to one another, even sometimes in the name of Christ."

"I don't understand."

"With God's help I will rejoice in my sufferings, and I want you to rejoice also. God has always been more than generous and merciful to us. This suffering is but a small price to pay for the suffering He endured for us on the cross. Through all of this, He has not left us alone. We must forgive Walter, pray for his recovery, and especially be merciful to his family."

Sara had leaned over and kissed him on the forehead, then said affectionately: "You're a better man than I am, Gunga Din."

Now on this third evening of Stephen's recovery, as she and the boys hurried down the hallway from the elevators, she noticed a half dozen or so visitors waiting in the lounge across the hall. Some she recognized, others she didn't, including an elderly dark-haired Catholic priest. When they saw her and the boys approaching, the visitors rose.

"Hello, Sara," Adrian McBride said as he and Ginny greeted her.

"Adrian and Ginny," she replied, taking their hands affectionately. "I can't believe you came this far. Thank you."

"We were so shocked when we heard, yet so relieved that he will be fine."

"God is good."

Ginny hesitantly offered an embrace. Sara took it gladly. Holding each other, Ginny whispered softly, "And thank you so much for your kindness. You and Reverend LaPointe were so much help."

"But…" Sara responded, puzzled, "is everything fine with you two?"

"Yes, just fine. God is truly good."

The priest came forward cautiously, extending his hand. "Good evening, Mrs. LaPointe. My name is Father William Bourque."

To everyone's surprise, Sara walked past his hand and encircled him with her arms. "Oh, Reverend Bourque, thank you for all you've done." Her eyes began to tear up. "He has told me so much about you. I know that it was the encouragement he received from his time with you that got him through this. God bless you."

"Well, God bless you, Sara. It was God's mercy and Stephen's faith that got him through."

As Sara stepped back, wiping her eyes, she noticed another gentleman standing back away from the group but obviously waiting to see her. She extended her hand and introduced herself. "Hello, I'm Sara LaPointe. Are you here to see Stephen?"

He replied nervously, "Yes, I am. Can we see him tonight? I came yesterday, but I missed visiting hours. Is he fine? Will he be fine?"

"Yes, it looks like he will recover completely."

"Thank God," he said, closing his eyes and raising his palms as if in prayer.

"I'm sorry, I didn't get your name."

"Oh, I'm Reverend Harmond. Gary Harmond."

"Well, here, let me take you in to see Stephen. I presume he knows you?"

"Yes, we've talked on the phone. In fact, just a few days before the...incident." He looked away.

"Fine. Let's see how he's doing." Turning toward the room, she continued, "The boys and I spent a lot of time with him this morning, so he's probably anxious for new faces."

As they entered his room, Stephen was sitting on the edge of his bed in his hospital skivvies.

"Oh, just a moment," he said as he carefully eased himself back into bed and covered up with a blanket. "Come on in."

Sara walked up to the bed and embraced her husband briefly. "How you doing?"

"Ready to break out of this joint," he said with a laugh that made him cringe with pain, "as soon as these ribs heal up a bit more."

"Well, you've got a waiting room full of visitors. Are you ready for some new faces?"

"Sure, bring 'em on."

She turned, expecting to see Reverend Harmond, but he hadn't followed her in. She walked back to the door.

"Reverend Harmond," she whispered around the corner. He was cautiously waiting outside. "Please come in. He'll see you now."

Gary Harmond followed her in and hesitantly extended his hand. "Hello, Reverend LaPointe. It's extremely good news to hear that you're going to be fine."

"Thank you. I didn't quite hear your name. Have we met?" Stephen thought this white-haired, well-groomed man in a finely tailored, three-piece suit looked familiar, but he couldn't place him. He vaguely remembered seeing him somewhere on a poster.

"I'm Reverend Gary Harmond."

"Reverend Harmond! Well, what a surprise. This is quite a long way to come. Were you in the neighborhood giving a talk or something?" Stephen didn't know how to read this well-known anti-Catholic's visit, but he felt somehow honored.

"No, actually I flew in from Boston the moment I heard the details of your, ah, incident." He glanced back toward Sara, then said softly to Stephen. "Do you think we could talk in private?"

"Sara, could you excuse us for a moment? How about making sure the boys haven't broken another video game?"

"I'll be down the hall if you need me."

After she had gone, Harmond reached for a chair and asked, "Do you mind, Reverend LaPointe?"

"No, go ahead, and please, call me Stephen."

"Yes, well," Harmond stammered, hesitant to begin. "I came as soon as I could, as soon as I learned the details of what happened. In fact," he said, raising his hands toward Stephen in despair and remorse, "I know a whole lot more about this probably than anyone. Reverend LaPointe…Stephen…I'm so sorry for what has happened. Walter Horscht called me just last week, as you know from our conversation on Friday, but I had no idea he would ever go to such measures. Then I was told by one of our members that Walter called him immediately after he shot you. I've always thought he was a bit wacko, but I never dreamed…please understand, we may be against the Catholic Church, but we would never advocate violence against anyone. If I had had any inkling that he might do this, I would have warned you and had him arrested. Surely you understand how fanatics and conspiracy freaks like Walter can sometimes go to extremes."

Stephen remained still, listening, studying the pleading of this famous anti-Catholic. Then using the electronic control, he raised the mattress so that he sat upright.

"Gary, could you close the door for a second."

"Yes, yes," he said. He pushed the door closed, then turned back to Stephen.

"Listen, I'm grateful for your visit. I know that you and your organization do not advocate violence. And I've forgiven Walter for his overzealousness. I believe he acted out of ignorance as well as a deep desire to obey God faithfully. His problem was that the people he trusted to know and teach what was true misled him. He was wrong, because they are desperately wrong. And for this, I do hold you responsible."

"But, Stephen…"

"Listen, Gary, I'm not up for a debate right now," he said, readjusting his position.

"Yes, I know. I'm sorry," Harmond said, raising his hands, imploring forgiveness.

"Maybe another time, and don't misunderstand me—I appreciate your visit. Like I said, I know that you did not intend for this to happen, but the false information and accusations you publish in your literature fed the flames of this man's righteous indignation. I can tell you without any doubt that most of what you have written about the Catholic Church is false." Stephen gasped in pain.

Harmond rose to do what he could to help.

"I'm fine, just fine," Stephen said, holding his breath until the pain subsided.

Harmond sat back down, waiting, and then responded. "Stephen, when you are well, I would like us to talk, as friends." He looked down with obvious shame. "Over the years, I admit that I haven't taken the time I should have to check the accuracy of what I sometimes pass along in my preaching, my books, and tracts. I also know through the witness of good Catholics in my own family that a lot of what I rail against is insignificant, mindless hype. I'm ashamed to admit this, but half the reason I don't 'fess up to this is because my whole life and reputation is built upon my anti-Catholicism."

He paused, looking at Stephen with his upper torso and shoulder wrapped in bandages.

"But I promise that this incident has awakened me to my own blind fanaticism. I'm not saying that all of a sudden I'm pro-Catholic, because I still have lots of unanswered concerns. But I am going to take the time to check the veracity of what I believe and teach."

"Then I tell you what," Stephen answered, extending his right hand. "After a few months of examination, give me a call. I'd like to hear what you've discovered."

"It's a deal," Harmond said, shaking on it. "But I guess I've got another visit to make while I'm here."

"Yes, I heard that he came out of his coma, briefly."

Harmond responded with a sigh, "Yes, but I don't think he's supposed to make it. I only hope I get the opportunity to apologize to him, too. Take care, Stephen."

"You, too. And thanks again for stopping by."

After Harmond left, two familiar faces from the past poked around the corner.

"Hello, preacher!" Adrian exclaimed. "Up for a pastoral call?"

"What a pleasant surprise. Please, come in."

"It's so wonderful to hear that you will be fine, but what a shock," Ginny said.

"I guess with some people, God has to use extremely drastic measures to get their attention," Stephen joked.

They all laughed nervously.

"We wanted to thank you for your kind counsel," Ginny said. "It really helped."

Stephen nodded his acceptance with a smile.

"And," Adrian asked, "I've been meaning to talk to you about your last sermon."

"What do you mean, my *last* sermon?"

"I don't mean that. I mean the last sermon you preached. I mean…"

Again they all laughed nervously.

"I was told by one of your parishioners at First Church that you said some things that, well, sounded like you were questioning your commitment to Protestantism. Then add to this finding Father William Bourque outside waiting to see you…"

"Father Bourque is here?" Stephen said, leaning forward. "Ah!" he screeched, out of breath, in a spasm of pain. He eased back into the sheets.

"Now, you mustn't excite him," a nurse said from the hallway. "He's got a lot of healing to do."

"Oh, they're fine," Stephen replied carefully. "My fault, or," turning to Adrian and Ginny, "as Father Bourque taught me, *mea culpa!*"

They laughed, carefully.

"Father Bourque is a good and holy man," Stephen continued. "But in answer to your earlier question, your allusion was more right than you know, for my next sermon probably will be one of my last sermons. I've decided that I can no longer remain a Protestant minister."

"But are you then…" Adrian started to say, but Stephen silenced him with his hand.

"At this point, I've only decided to leave Protestantism. I recognize now, especially through the loving counsel of Father Bourque, the validity of the Catholic Church as the one, holy, catholic, and apostolic church."

"Well, if it looks like a duck and quacks like a duck…" Ginny began.

"Just hold on," Stephen interrupted with a smile. "There are a lot of ramifications if I were to consider converting. What will I do for a living? What about my call to the ministry? My ordination? And besides," he added with hidden concern, "I'm positive that Sara is far from ready to consider this. We've barely had time to talk about my decision to resign."

"Is there anything we can do?" Ginny asked.

"Just pray for us as we work through both my recovery and our discernment of the future." He fell quiet for a moment, then continued.

"Friends, I am drawn to the Catholic Church, for lots of reasons, but maybe the most significant reason is because of Catholics like Father Bourque. Getting to know him has convinced me that sincere Catholics are deeply committed to Jesus Christ, and that the things I thought unchristian about Catholicism are not so unchristian once you understand them. Through him I discovered that being a Catholic means becoming exactly what Jesus called us to be: holy as He is holy."

He held his hands out and grasped theirs in a ring of friendship. "When I'm out of here, and I've worked through all the hubbub of my resignation, let's get together. It's good to have friends in this, because few of my family or other friends will understand."

Adrian smiled as he grasped Stephen's hand firmly: "You can count on both of us for this, Reverend LaPointe, for we, too, know how our families are going to react to our decision. We'll be entering the Church this coming Easter Vigil."

With a smile that revealed a hint of sadness, Stephen said, "Adrian and Ginny, please just call me Stephen. The ramification of what I have come to understand about my ordination to the Protestant ministry at least implies that those who ordained me had no true, God-given authority to do so. They were well-meaning souls, but for now, I need to accept that I am only a well-trained and experienced layman. Please pray for me as I work through all of this. Right now I feel very inadequate and disoriented."

"We'll do that, Rev...Stephen," Adrian answered.

"Now, please ask Father Bourque to come in for a minute."

"Sure. We'll stop by again soon," they said as they left the door. A moment later, a familiar face appeared.

"Father Bourque, please come in."

He came in and grasped Stephen's hands, standing silently as they shared tears of joy.

"I didn't expect to see you again this soon, Stephen."

"And I didn't expect to get such a prompt, hands-on lesson in suffering," he said with a sly smile. "But seriously, everything you taught me about suffering was timely and made all the difference in the world."

"Our God has mysterious ways of doing things."

"You can say that again." Stephen pointed to two objects resting on his bedside table. "Remember these?"

"Blessed Jesus!" the priest exclaimed. Among an assortment of snack wrappers and hospital paraphernalia were the paper Catechism and the silver St. Stephen's medal. The priest picked them up with emotion. The medal was no longer flat but concave, as if someone had tried to pierce it with a nail, and through the side of the Catechism was a hole, blocked at one end by a flattened bullet.

"I guess I'm alive today because of good ol' St. Stephen and the teachings of the Catholic Church," Stephen said with a tearful smile. "Walter's first shot was aimed square at my heart, but that book and medal stopped it. My ribs and lungs are badly bruised, but I'm alive. His second shot grazed my neck, which released a lot of blood, but not seriously. He apparently was planning a third but for some reason he stopped."

"Most people would see this as just coincidental or superstitious," the priest said, "but this is how God works."

"I know. He has done merciful things like this all my life. Speaking of 'coincidence,' open the Catechism to where the bullet lodged."

When the priest did, the book fell open near the front. The first thirty pages were bound together by a round gray stud.

"Please read the sentence directly beside the bullet," Stephen said, pulling his body up straighter against the headboard.

Father Bourque read:

> But I would not believe in the gospel, had not the authority of the Catholic Church already moved me.

"Our God is so good," Stephen said. "All my adult life, I have been searching for a firm foundation for my faith. I thought I had it in the Bible alone, but like the author of this quote—St. Augustine—I now know that the foundation of my faith in Jesus is the faithful witness of the Church."

"Yes, Stephen, God is very good," the priest said, placing Stephen's life-saving treasures back beside his bed. "I don't mean to push, but are you any clearer on what steps you want to take?"

Stephen lowered the back of his bed, and then turned carefully over onto his side. He motioned the priest to the chair by the bed.

"In all honesty, Father, I feel like I'm in no-man's land. I'm convinced that the Protestant experiment—regardless of how sincere the Reformers might have been—was the wrong answer to Church renewal. Therefore, I cannot remain a Protestant, nor can I just go out and start my own new church as so many independent pastors have done. This is just Protestantism to the most arrogant, self-centered degree.

"But neither am I ready to become a Roman Catholic. There are just too many customs, statues, paintings, rituals, and beliefs that seem strange or foreign. I may understand them intellectually, and recognize the scriptural foundations for the authority of the Church and the pope, but a battle stills rages in my heart. The inner voices of my anti-Catholic past won't leave me alone. Just when my mind starts to accept the Catholic explanation of some strange dogma or practice, a voice tells me I'm being duped by the devil himself."

"Stephen," the priest laughed, "every single person I've known, clergy or lay, who has gone through the conversion process from a background like yours has struggled with the same things. Old prejudices die hard. But what's crucial right now is that you never abandon, even for a moment, your faith in Jesus and His abiding love."

"Actually, Father, my faith in Jesus is deeper now than it has ever been, primarily because of what I have learned through my study of Catholicism. If only the Lord will help me get through stuff like the Infant of Prague and scapulars. Please pray for me that my stubborn heart will accept the fullness of Catholic truth."

"Stephen, you are in my prayers daily. A candle burns brightly in my chapel for you twenty-four hours a day as a symbol of not only my prayers, but the prayers of my entire parish. For now, though, your job is to rest and recover.

"As far as what you'll do once you finally tender your resignation, don't worry. Remember Jesus' command: 'Have no anxiety about tomorrow; the day's worries are sufficient for the day.' And besides, Jim and I are already working on this. We won't let you starve."

"Thanks, Sara and the boys will appreciate that."

They both laughed, which caused Stephen to cringe in pain.

"Now, Stephen, no laughing. We don't want any setbacks. You better quit reading that book of 'Far Side' comics I see someone has left you," he said with false severity, "and keep to more solemn and substantial reading like Augustine's *Confessions* or Thomas Aquinas' *Summa Theologica*. Here, you better let me take that," he said with a grin as he reached for the collection of Gary Larson drawings.

"Don't you dare! They're what keeps me sane in here!"

They both laughed again, which again sent Stephen back in pain.

"Sorry, Stephen."

"I'll just offer this pain up," he said forcing his tensed chest muscles to relax, "for all those stick-in-the-muds who can't appreciate the deep theological insights of Larson."

"That's the spirit! How about a word of prayer before I go?"

"Please do Father."

Father Bourque reached into his pocket for a rosary made of green, hand-knotted cord. "Here's a gift. I know you're still uncomfortable about this, but for now, just pray an *Our Father,* a *Hail Mary,* or a *Glory Be* with each knot, offering each up in thanksgiving to God for some friend, family member, or church member. For tonight, let's meditate on the mystery of Christ's resurrection. Let's thank God for His mercy in giving you back your life. We begin with the Apostles' Creed."

"He has certainly done that, many times. And thank you, Father," Stephen said as he accepted his first rosary. He followed the priest's lead in crossing himself, and together they began praying, "I believe in God, the Father Almighty…"

*   *   *

THE WAITING ROOM WAS EMPTY, except for Sara, William, and Daniel.

The boys were watching a rerun of an old *Andy Griffith* program, while Sara was only half-focused on a mystery novel.

"Mrs. LaPointe?" a nurse called from Stephen's room.

"Yes?" Sara said, turning.

"The Reverend needs rest from all these visits. Why don't you pay him a quick one and then call it a night."

"Fine, thank you."

Letting the boys finish their fill of Andy, Barney, Gomer, and the rest, she went alone to Stephen's room. As she slowly pushed the door open, she heard, "In the name of the Father and of the Son and of the Holy Spirit, Amen." Over the priest's right shoulder, she saw Stephen bless himself with the sign of the cross and then halt abruptly when he noticed she was watching.

"I'll be in to see you again in two days, so hang in there, my friend," the priest said as he turned to leave. Seeing Sara, he said, "Come Sara, he needs you more than this old fuddy-duddy."

"Thanks, Reverend Bourque, thank you for everything."

"Oh, don't mention it. Now you just pamper him with love."

"I don't want to spoil him too much," she said with a smile, giving the priest a farewell kiss on the cheek. After he left, she turned to Stephen's bedside and grasped his hands.

"Long evening," he said. "What you just saw wasn't what you might think…"

"Stephen, there's a lot we both need to talk about, but it can wait until you get out. For now, just know that I believe, as you do, that just as God has brought you miraculously through this experience, He will take care of us come what may."

"Thank you, my darling. God truly blessed me when He gave me you."

She leaned over to kiss him just as Daniel interrupted.

"Come on, Mom! You'll crush him."

Sara straightened up, laughing. William and Daniel entered, grasped their father's hands, and kissed him on the cheek.

"How are you boys doing? Ready for me to come home and spoil all your fun?"

"We miss you, Dad," William said. "There's a few things we need to talk about, and besides, I'm not shooting so well without you in the stands."

"Well, I should be home in a few days and in the stands cheering for you."

"Come on, boys, we need to give your father some rest." Shooing the boys out, she gave her husband a farewell squeeze of the hand and left for the night.

*   *   *

STEPHEN LAY ALONE in his room, relieved that the night's visits were over. He had much to think over; so many new thoughts and impressions from his visits—with Gary Harmond, with Adrian and Ginny, with Father Bourque, and again with his family.

He lay under the institutional sheets, with the warmth of only a thin blanket, not moving a muscle, still, peaceful, moving only his tearful eyes, looking around the room for some sign of the guardian angels, the interceding saints, for even the Lord Himself—for surely they had all been there, guiding and blessing this evening. He felt so mercifully blessed, for all he had been through, to even be alive, but mostly to have been graced by the Holy Spirit with an open mind and heart to hear and receive the truth.

In one hand he fingered the strange string of knots, while in the other he rubbed the life-saving dent in the silver medal to St. Stephen. He prayed: "Lord Jesus, thank You for reminding me constantly not to be afraid, for with You as my Savior, my Lord, and my guide, there is nothing whatsoever to fear."

4

Several months later...

"LOW IN THE GRAVE HE LAY, Jesus, my Savior!
Waiting the coming day, Jesus, my Lord!"

The choir and standing-room-only congregation of First Congregational Church, Witzel's Notch, sang with cautious exuberance. It was a day of great celebration: Easter. *Christ has risen! Christ has risen indeed!*

"Up from the grave He arose, He arose,
With a mighty triumph o'er His foes; He arose;
He arose a victor from the dark domain,
And He lives forever with His saints to reign;
He arose! He arose!
Hallelujah! Christ arose!"

But it was also a day of pensive sadness, for their pastor of only eight months was leaving.

Family and friends who rarely crossed the threshold of First Church, except for weddings, funerals, and Christmas, were present for their annual Easter observance. The front of the sanctuary surrounding the elevated pulpit, as well as the steps on both sides, were overflowing with lilies and more candles than usual to signify the light of the risen Christ. The choir in the loft behind and above the congregation was at unusually full strength, dressed in white robes with red sashes. The congregation, clad in bright flamboyant spring colors, looked like the color chart at the local paint store. And up front, Stephen's senses feasted on this triumphant Easter celebration. Breathless from a mixture of joy and sorrow, he could barely emit a sound, so he mouthed the words.

Glancing around, Stephen studied the multitude of familiar faces intermixed with the faces of strangers. Most were singing with eyes glued to the lyrics in their hymnals, but many were looking up at him. Some smiled, eyes streaming with tearful, yet joyful support of his decision. Others stared with blank expressions, which he took for signs of confusion over why he would resign so soon after being hired. But a few glared with unreserved hostility, and it was these few that cut to his heart. *Will they ever understand? Will they, in their ignorance, prejudice, and pride, even hear what I have to say?*

Yet, as the third refrain ended, Stephen wasn't certain himself what he would say in this, his last sermon at First Church—possibly his last sermon, period.

During his week in the hospital and then several more at home, Stephen had vacillated over what Scripture and topic should be his swan song. The congregation knew that he was leaving and why, from his detailed explanation in the newsletter, but to what extent should he reveal the other discoveries that had forced his hand?

Repeatedly he had rewritten and revised his sermon, until in the end, he had thrown the whole thing out. *I'm nothing more than a lame-duck pastor, with nothing that this congregation now cares to hear.* He concluded that his best bet was to thank them, praise them, apologize, give them hope, and in the end, turn their focus to Jesus and away from himself.

When the choir and congregation had concluded the hymn with the obligatory "A-men," they sat and waited for their pastor to rise and enter their pulpit for the last time. But he lingered in his chair longer than usual, thinking, praying, and a bit nervous. He glanced to the right of the ornate wooden pulpit and saw the space in the front pew where Sara and the boys normally sat. This morning it was empty, for they were gone.

Yes, Jesus had said that any who would follow Him might lose their families for His sake and the sake of the gospel; Stephen just never expected this to happen to him.

His heart ached with sorrow when he remembered the glare of her eyes and the set of her lips as she left. Nothing he could say could break her resolve. Repeatedly she said she still loved him, but there was always a disclaimer. In the end, they were both contrained by their convictions. Her last words were, "I married a Protestant minister, and for 19 years I gave up all my dreams to fit into your world. Now you've decided you were wrong—that we were wrong. Well, it's time for me to reclaim my dreams while I still can."

He would leave the pastorate, and she would return to graduate school. He tried to convince her that their choices were not at varience—he would gladly support her in this if she wanted—but somehow his openness to Catholicism had made him a stranger in her eyes.

Or was there something else, something just below the surface of her past or present that was standing as an insurmountable barrier to their future?

She began pulling away from him both in public and in private, and then several weeks after he was released from the hospital, she took the boys to live temporarily with, of all people, her mother—until she could get settled somewhere near a school on the north shore of Boston.

With great effort, Stephen brought himself back to the present. Following Jesus would be a lonely and sorrowful road. *Where is the joy, Jesus? Where is the joy?*

Though his body was on the mend, he was grateful for the added amplification of his lapel mike, for it still hurt to project his voice in his usual manner. Before uttering his first words, he took one last preparatory glance around, absorbing all the courage he could muster from the many supporting faces, and said: "Please, before I read today's text and deliver my final sermon from this illustrious pulpit, join with me in prayer."

Even he was surprised by how weak his voice sounded. He waited as the usual rustling subsided, until every head was bowed and every pair of hands was folded peaceably.

"Heavenly Father, on this Easter morn in which we celebrate Your great and loving act of sacrificial mercy and victory, fill our hearts with joy, for Your Son, our Savior and Lord, is risen! May we live each day in the full realization of His resurrection. Lord Jesus, please bring healing and hope to this congregation. Bring them a new pastor who will faithfully lead them into all truth, a leader after Your own heart."

His prayer came to an end, but not an inner voice that berated him for failing these people, for putting his hand to the plow and looking back, for abandoning his post in the midst of a storm.

Where are you, Lord? he pleaded. *Why must I feel so alone?*

He opened his mouth and began, trusting that the Holy Spirit would lead.

"The text for this Easter morning is the account of the empty tomb and the Resurrection as told by the Apostle John. But before I read, I must take this opportunity to thank you for showering my family and me with so many expressions of love and support, even after I announced my decision to resign."

And even though he was surrounded by a sea of smiles, it was again those blank or angry glares in their midst that drew his attention. Sara and he had agreed to keep their separation a private matter, so he was certain that their rage was limited to his decision to abandon them, not her.

"I realize that the situation of my leaving might be too distracting for a regular sermon, but the importance of this day of Christ's Resurrection, the day that changed the entire course of human history, greatly overshadows the mere insignificance of one pastor's resignation. So let us focus on the message of the gospel, and then with the Holy Spirit's help, I will give some brief thoughts for reflection. Hear now as I read the Gospel of the Resurrection from John chapter twenty."

And there was none present more angry with him than his secretary, Marge. Ever since his announcement, she had treated him as if he had betrayed her personally. She refused to look him in the eye, and limited her communication to a modicum of terse words, but only when necessary. The one time she failed to contrain her temper she castigated him for doing this all behind her back, for leaving her in the dark, and making her out to be a fool.

And there she sat, in the furthest left corner of the back pew, too distant for Stephen to make out the details of her scowl, but he knew that it was there.

It would have helped if Jim had made it as he promised, but the aftershock of his own crisis had continued unabated. He now was fighting to avoid the same marital separation that had befallen Stephen.

Stephen opened the pulpit Bible and prepared to read, but the significance of the moment still left him speechless. He loved to preach, to expound on Scripture, to proclaim with great energy and conviction the message of God's love and mercy in Christ Jesus his Son. He also loved to move and motivate people to evangelical action, and he believed in his heart that this was why God had created him. This was his *raison d'etre.*

But this might be his last time—not by force or coercion, but by choice. Again he heard that haunting voice of self-doubt, second-guessing his decision: *You fool! What have you done? What are you doing? You don't have to do this. No leader in the Congregational Church—or the Catholic Church for that matter—is making you do this. How can you be so deluded to think that this is God's will for you? Maybe He's disgusted that you acted so rashly. You were at the front lines of His service, and now you're nothing more than a retreating coward.*

The voice was getting the better of him. He fought the impulse to raise his hands and yell, "Wait! Wait one damn minute! I have changed my mind! I was wrong. I will NOT resign!"

But then the familiar, comforting, soft voice of his Savior cut through what he knew was just the usual spiritual attack: *Stephen, Stephen. Be not afraid. Trust me.*

With a nervously soft voice, Stephen began. "Please follow along prayerfully as I read:

> Now on the first day of the week Mary Magdalene came to the tomb early, while it was still dark, and saw that the stone had been taken away from the tomb. So she ran, and went to Simon Peter and the other disciple, the one whom Jesus loved, and said to them, "They have taken the Lord out of the tomb, and we do not know where they have laid Him."
>
> Peter then came out with the other disciple, and they went toward the tomb. They both ran, but the other disciple outran Peter and reached the tomb first; and stooping to look in, he saw the linen cloths lying there, but he did not go in.
>
> Then Simon Peter came, following him, and went into the tomb; he saw the linen cloths lying, and the napkin, which had been on his head, not lying with the linen cloths but rolled up in a place by itself.
>
> Then the other disciple, who reached the tomb first, also went in, and he saw and believed; for as yet they did not know the Scripture, that He must rise from the dead.

Turning his attention now to his audience, Stephen began to preach.

"The most obvious point of this story is that the tomb was empty. To the elated surprise of Mary Magdalene, Simon Peter, and 'the other disciple,' whom we presume to be John, Jesus was no longer there. As the Gospel describes in intimate detail, the linen burial cloths were lying empty on the stone slab, and the napkin, which had been on His head, was not lying with the linen cloths but was strangely rolled up in a place by itself. The good news is that He was risen just as He said, which He soon would prove to them when He appeared before them in the upper room."

SITTING CLOSE TO THE FRONT, hand in hand, were Adrian and Ginny McBride. This likely would also be their last time in a Congregational church, for last night at the Easter Vigil Mass at St. Anne's Parish in

Respite, they were received into the Catholic Church. Many had warned them not to expect too much—emotions do not necessarily accompany the reception of God's grace in the sacraments. But for them it had. They were overcome by joy, and for the rest of their lives they would witness to how the Holy Spirit had come powerfully into their hearts, purging them of sin.

Tears streamed down Ginny's face as she listened to this pastor who had been so sensitive and open to their plight. As suspected, she and Adrian had reaped the rejection of their families, in whose eyes their conversion to the Catholic Church was a direct, spiteful denial of their ancestral tree. She had anticipated this reaction with regret, but hadn't been swayed by it. Instead, she prayed that her conversion would be the first step in returning her family to the fullness of the faith.

As she listened to the good news of the Resurrection, she prayed silently that God would open her parent's and sibling's hearts, and also that He would open the floodgates of His grace so that Reverend LaPointe would not only find work quickly, but that he and his family might find their way home to the one, holy, catholic, and apostolic Church.

"APART FROM THE OBVIOUS significance of this text," Stephen continued, "there are a few less obvious points I want us to consider.

"Remember that John most likely wrote his Gospel many years after the other Gospels had been writen, when he was an old man, maybe even the last remaining Apostle alive. Tradition tells us that all the other Apostles died as martyrs for the faith; only John died of natural causes.

"With all that he could have said about this important event, the few details he chose to mention are therefore of unique significance. Notice, for example, who John mentions as the first person to witness the empty tomb. Was it not Mary Magdalene, the harlot whose multitude of sins had been forgiven, who anointed Jesus' feet with oil even when ridiculed by some of the Apostles? Are not those who are forgiven the most sometimes the most grateful?"

IN THE BACK PEW, out of sight from the rest of the congregation, sat Helen and Stacy Horscht. Together, they shared a panoramic view of the nearly full sanctuary. Mostly they saw the backs of people's heads, but occasionally a face would turn and study them—the widow and daughter of the man who had tried to murder their pastor. Helen considered attending a different church, but it didn't matter. Witzel's Notch was too small. Everyone in every church knew who she was. Her choices were either to move away, or quit church altogether, or to be brave and return to where by rights she should expect to receive the love of Christ through His people.

At first, the reception had been mixed. Besides words of rejection and disgust, one woman even spit in her face. But under Stephen's example, the congregation eventually let her and Stacy attend worship without provocation. A few even extended hands of forgiveness, support, and prayer.

Helen's life, though, would never be the same. This side of heaven, she would never know exactly why he did it. But, at least Stacy had come home.

Several days after her father regained consciousness, she returned on her own accord, repentant and remorseful. She had been determined never to see her father again, but then there he was, his face an item on the evening news. Her friends laughed, thinking this vindicated her escape from his craziness, but it drove her to despair. Through all her father's unpredictable and sometimes hysterical fanaticism, she still loved him, and now she was ridden with grief that her running away might have pushed him over the brink.

When she finally reached the hospital and entered the room, she was shocked by his appearance. He looked like a mummified corpse. He was awake but weak and feeble, and unable to move his face to greet her. For an hour, she held him tenderly and wept, pouring out remorseful sorrow. It was then that Reverend LaPointe had come in. He had tried several times previously to see her father, but had always found him asleep. Now when her father saw the enemy he had tried to destroy, he asked her softly to leave them alone.

She would never know what they said to one another. After a few minutes, she went outside for a smoke—a habit her father had never discovered and now never would. When she returned, the pastor was gone. In the stillness of her father's room, she found him weeping. She enveloped him with her arms and whispered, "Daddy, what is it?" He whispered back, "Stacy, I'm sorry, so sorry. Please...forgive me." And with all the strength he could muster, he raised his one free arm and drew her to him. "Please, take care...of your mother," and he was gone.

Many more attended his funeral than had been expected.

"It is also significant that, with all the excitement of the moment, John did not enter the tomb right away," Stephen said. "The text reads: 'They both ran, but the other disciple'—John's way of describing himself—'outran Peter and reached the tomb first; and stooping to look in, he saw the linen cloths lying there, but he did not go in.'

"Why was this detail so significant for John to mention? Biblical scholars give various explanations, but was it not simply because the young Apostle deferred to the head of the Apostles, Simon Peter? Throughout Scripture, in nearly every instance where groups of Apostles are mentioned, Peter is listed first or serves as the Apostles' spokesman."

In the back row of the balcony sat a well-groomed, white-haired man in a three-piece suit. He listened carefully to Stephen's final sermon, anxious to talk with him later in private.

"But there is one final, seemingly insignificant detail, that I believe, speaks volumes. The text reads: 'Then the other disciple, who reached the tomb first, also went in, and he saw and believed.'

"Did you notice the difference between how Peter and John responded? Scripture says nothing about what Peter *thought* about what he had found in the empty tomb, but it states clearly that John saw and believed. Even though the Gospel writer emphasized that the Apostles did not as yet know the Scriptures that specified that Jesus must rise from the dead, John yet saw and believed. He saw and believed."

Stephen closed the pulpit Bible, and leaned forward on his elbows, studying his congregation for the last time.

"Friends, I've often wondered what a privilege it would have been to be one of those first disciples, to have walked with our Lord, hearing Him, watching Him heal and perform miracles, and then to have been there when He appeared, risen and alive, in His resurrected body. How easy it would have been to believe, to know fully, and to trust completely."

Becoming more animated, he stepped away from the pulpit, speaking now almost in his usual, booming voice.

"To have heard firsthand all the teachings of Jesus—not just the ones that ended up condensed and recorded in the Gospels or passed on indirectly in the New Testament Epistles, but to have listened as Jesus instructed His Apostles precisely how to organize, lead, and then propagate the new Church—how easy it would then be to know exactly what must be believed, not merely to be saved, but to be faithful to God's expectations of you and me as His adopted children."

Stephen returned to the pulpit and once again rested his weight on his elbows.

"But we didn't live then. We live now, two thousand years later, and the number of interpretations of what Jesus taught or intended or required of us is almost limitless. Just think for a moment of the many different opinions held by your own neighbors, friends, or family about who Jesus is. Which of these opinions is right? How can you be certain you are right? Upon what will you base your decision? This book?" he said, raising high the pulpit Bible.

"But how many of those holding opinions contrary to yours also believe that they are merely giving the most accurate and obvious interpretation of this book?" He set the Bible back down and returned to studying his people.

"The Apostle John *saw and believed.* I think the problem today is not necessarily one of belief, for people today believe all kinds of things. We are truly people of faith, for we Americans live our lives as if there is no end to the prosperity of our technological age. We believe in progress. We trust in the new, the innovative, the immediate. We trust that just as the sun comes up every morning, defining clockwork, so our lives will continue to get better and better and better.

"And we Congregationalists particularly believe that all we need to do is listen to our consciences to know what is true. And yet even we in this one small congregation disagree on so many significant things, such as when we should consider the child in a mother's womb a viable human being.

"No, our problem is not in *believing*, but in *seeing*. We are blinded by our progress, our prosperity, our prejudice, our ignorance, and by our carefully crafted reconstruction of history, reconstructed specifically to justify what we as Protestant Americans cling to as true. But through it all we do not *see*, and therefore we end up blindly believing many things that are not true."

Stephen stepped away from the pulpit and removed his red stole from off his shoulders. He folded it carefully and draped it over the pulpit. He then unzipped his black preacher's robe, uncovering a dark gray suit, white shirt, and red-striped tie. He folded and laid the robe upon the pulpit. His Celtic preaching cross he carefully removed, and fighting back tears, kissed it, and stuffed it into an inner pocket of his coat.

"Friends and fellow laymen, by God's grace—and only by God's merciful grace—I have come to *see* how lost I was in my own blindness. I have come to *see* that Jesus and the New Testament writers made it very clear that today's confusion was not what Jesus intended for His Church. In His final great priestly prayer Jesus proclaimed:

> Now I am no more in the world, but they are in the world, and I am coming to Thee. Holy Father, keep them in Thy name, which Thou hast given me, that they may be one, even as we are one.

"Then Jesus prayed specifically for you and me, and the millions of other believers throughout history who have believed because of the preaching and writings of these original Apostles:

> I do not pray for these only, but also for those who believe in Me through their word, that they may all be one; even as Thou, Father, art in Me, and I in Thee, that they also may be in us.

"Unity. This is what Jesus desired for His Church," Stephen declared. "Oneness like that experienced between the three Persons of the Trinity. A oneness built on love and unity of heart and mind."

He looked out upon these people whom in only eight months

he had so come to love—these people whom God had sent him to lead. And he knew that he could no longer hold back the truth he had come to see, come what may.

"My friends, I have come to *see and believe* that this unity, this oneness with Christ, this true abiding can only be fully experienced in the one Church Jesus built on the testimony and faith of His Apostles. The one Church built, protected, and preserved for nearly two thousand years on the Rock, the leader of His Apostles, Simon Peter, and his successors. The one Church that has always accepted her responsibility under the guidance of the Holy Spirit to protect and preserve the deposit of faith as delivered by Christ to His Apostles. And this one Church, I have come to *see and believe*, is none other than the Roman Catholic Church."

Stephen saw immediately that more than a few were startled that he actually had the audacity to say this from this Congregationalist pulpit. The noise level rose as comments passed between couples, friends, and families. He raised his arms, requesting silence, and the congregation obeyed, but for this pastor, the last time.

"I stand now before you a layman, but not a mere layman, for the term 'mere' should never be used to describe what you and I are in Christ. No, I prefer to see myself as one of those described by Simon Peter in his first Epistle, and in closing, may this be the challenge I leave with you, my dear friends:

> Like newborn babes, long for the pure spiritual milk,
> that by it you may grow up to salvation; for you have
> tasted the kindness of the Lord.

Stepping out from behind the pulpit, Stephen concluded, "I realize that many, maybe most of you, do not understand or agree with what I have come to *see* or *believe*. All I ask is that we keep one another in prayer, and as one final request, please stand and join me in the hymn that most clearly describes how willing we should be to follow Jesus, wherever He might lead: 'Be Thou My Vision.'"

He descended the pulpit steps and stood alone in the space normally reserved for his family. He would have liked to receive Sara's reaffirming kiss—confirming that she was with him and proud of him. He wished he could look over at the loving smiles of William and Daniel, his pride and joy. Instead, he listened alone as the organist played the introduction to the last hymn he would sing in his last church as a Protestant minister.

ON CUE, the congregation rose. The white-haired, well-groomed man in the balcony also stood. Tears were flowing freely for the first time in years. For so long his heart had been too hardened by bitterness and anger to *hear,* or to *see.*

Lord Jesus Christ, have mercy on me, a sinner. And please, if it be Thy will, let me also come home.

HAVING FINISHED HER INTRODUCTION, the organist raised the volume and led the congregation into the hymn that Stephen always considered the clearest expression of his faith. The congregation began singing, but without the unreserved exuberance he believed this song deserved.

But what could he expect? *Lord Jesus, please bless these people!*

> Be Thou my Vision, O Lord of my heart;
> Naught be all else to me, save that Thou art;
> Thou my best thought, by day or by night,
> Waking or sleeping, Thy presence my light.

He felt a tap on his shoulders and turned to see Adrian and Ginny anxious to greet him. They hugged and crowded around him, holding his hands as a sign of support and unity.

> Be Thou my Wisdom, and Thou my true Word;
> I ever with Thee and Thou with me, Lord;
> Thou my great Father, and I Thy true son,
> Thou in me dwelling, and I with Thee one.

More friends began coming forward, offering hands of support and tears of love. Some were people Stephen hardly knew, while others were faithful members and friends whom he feared would never speak to him again. Their smiles told him differently.

> Riches I heed not, nor man's empty praise,
> Thou mine inheritance, now and always;

Thou and thou only, first in my heart,
High King of heaven, my treasure Thou art.

Through this crowd of supporters pushed a man in a three-piece suit. When he reached Stephen, he held out his right hand cautiously.

"Gary!" Stephen said, embracing the Reverend Gary Harmond as if they were old friends.

"Thank you, Stephen, for your courage. Right now, all I can say is that God has used you—and Walter, Lord forgive him—to reach me, to help me *see and believe* again. Thank you."

"God bless you, my friend,' Stephen said. "Who knows, maybe we can go home together."

Others who had overheard this man's testimony also began greeting him.

And then Stephen felt another tap on his shoulder. He turned, and for an eternal moment the congregation, the music, the church were no longer there. Only him and his sweetheart.

"Sara!"

They grasped each other and held tightly, oblivious to the rest of the world.

"Oh, darling," she whispered, "I'm sorry for leaving. Please understand, I'm not where you are in your thinking, but I couldn't leave you. I can never leave you."

"And I will never leave you," he said as William and Daniel crowded in beside them.

Stephen turned to Adrian and Ginny, to Gary Harmond, and to Sara and his two sons, and proclaimed, "God is so good. So good!"

High King of heaven, my victory won,
May I reach heaven's joys, O bright heaven's Sun!
Heart of my own heart, whatever befall,
Still be my Vision, O Ruler of all.

AUTHOR'S AFTERWORD

Those who are familiar with my family's spiritual journey may wonder to what extent this novel is autobiographical. Let me begin by stating that all of the story's main characters, names, places, and incidents are fictitious. This is a novel, not a biographical conversion story.

However, the story is based loosely around a composite of the actual journeys of many living people whose love for Jesus Christ and His Church took them on similar journeys. Yes, in some ways, the experiences of Stephen most resemble my own spiritual journey as a Protestant minister, but still very loosely. In this work I have tried to express the actual reasoning and emotions that many ministers like myself have experienced, yet in a fictional format. It is particularly important to note, however, that the experiences of Sara LaPointe do <u>not</u> parallel those of my wife, Marilyn.

Most of the books and authors mentioned are real and still in print (see the accompanying bibliography).

There are many friends I need to acknowledge who made this work of fiction possible. First, to those whose witness brought me to a love for Jesus and His Church: Rev. Elmer J. Melchert, Rev. Quentin Battiste, Rev. Tom Witzel, Rev. Dr. Gary Stratman, Dr. David Wells, Dr. Scott Hahn, Rev. Tom Cebula, Rev. Ray Ryland, Rev. Benedict Groeschel, Rev. Mitch Pacwa, Rev. Ray Bourque, Mother Angelica, and of course many others. Also, to those dear friends whose journeys most directly inspired this book: Dr. Kenneth Howell, Dr. Scott and Kimberly Hahn, Stephen Wood, Bruce Sullivan, and the many other converts who are members of the *Coming Home Network* or who have been my guests on the *Journey Home* television program.

I also owe an overwhelming gratitude to the many friends who have read and helped edit this book: Bud Macfarlane Jr., John O'Brian, Dr. Tom Howard and his daughter Gallaudet, Carol Kean, Barbara Brown, Noah Lett, Todd and Joan van Kampen, Joseph Pearce, Fr. Ray Ryland, Karen McClelland, and the staff and many members of the *Coming Home Network*.

There is none, though, to whom I owe more thanks than to my loving and patient wife, Marilyn. In the end, it was only through her encouragement that this book was able to reach fruition.

Please feel free to pass along any comments or questions, and may the Lord bless you as you seek to follow Him faithfully.

Marcus Grodi
Feast of St. Mark the Evangelist

ENDNOTES

(by page number)

5. Mk. 9:42
6. Prv. 3:5-6.
26-27. Mt. 24:9-14
27. Mt. 24:40-42.
34. 2 Tm. 3:1-5; 1 Tm. 4:1-3.
36. Loraine Boettner, *Roman Catholicism* (Philadelphia, PA: The Presbyterian and Reformed Publishing Company, 1962), p. 450.
38. Ps. 51:10-12.
42. 1 Cor. 7:32-34a.
63. 2 Tm. 3:16-17.
65. Mt. 24:36, 42; 24:6-12; 24:40-41.
66. 1 Tm. 4:1-3.
67. Mt. 24:13; Mk. 13:13, Rom. 8:28-30.
79. 2 Tm. 3:16.
90. Phil. 2:14-15, 3:13-14, 4:5, 11, 19.
92. Heb. 6:4-6.
103. Mk. 10:21.
113-14. Mt. 16:13-20.
117. Paraphrased from Karl Keating, *Catholicism and Fundamentalism* (San Francisco, CA: Ignatius Press, 1988), pp. 210-11.
121. Mt. 5:11-12, 10:23.
124. Harry Chapin, *Cat's in the Cradle*, 1974.
130. Heb. 4:12; 2 Tm. 3:16-17.
137. 1 Tm. 3:14-15.
138. 2 Thes. 2:15.
139. 1 Cor. 11:2, 4:17; 2 Tm. 2:2.

140. 2 Tm. 3:14-15; 1 Tm. 3:15.

145-46. St. Francis de Sales, *Introduction to the Devout Life* (New York, NY: Image Books, 1989), pp. 54-55.

148. James Gibbons, *The Faith of Our Fathers* (Rockford, IL: TAN Books, 1980), p. 68, 71.

156. Eph. 6:12.

163. Gibbons, 58.

166. St. Augustine, c. 418 A.D., *Discourse to Church at Caesarea*, 6.

169. Pope Paul VI to the editor in chief of the New American Bible, September 18, 1970.

178. 2 Thes. 3:10, Mt. 25:21.

180. Jn. 6:53-55.

188. Jn. 6:53.

188-89. F. F. Bruce, *The Gospel of John* (Grand Rapids, MI: Wm. B. Eerdmans Publishing, 1980), p. 159.

189-90. Barnabas Lindars, *The New Century Bible Commentary* (Grand Rapids, MI: Wm. B. Eerdmans Publishing, 1972), pp. 266-68.

190. Rodney A. Whitacre, *Johannine Polemic: The Role of Tradition and Theology*, Society of Biblical Literature Dissertation Series, no. 67 (Chico, CA: Scholars Press, 1982), p. 129.

190-91. Raymond E. Brown, S.S., *The Gospel According to John, i-xii, The Anchor Bible,* vol. 29 (Garden City, NY: Doubleday & C., 1978), pp. 284-85.

192. Mt. 6:33; 1 Thes. 5:3; Mt. 18:6.

195-96. Pr. 3:5-6.

201. Mt. 5:48.

204. Jn. 8:31-32.

209. Jn. 8:28, 30.

210-11. Jn. 8:32-33.

212. Jn. 8:34-36, 59.

212. Rom. 3:23.

213. cf. Rev. 2:7, 11, 17, 25, 26; 3:5, 12, 21; 1 Cor. 5:17-18.

214-15. 1 Cor. 5:17-18; Eph. 2:4-9.

215. Jn. 15:7, 11.

236. 1 Tm. 1:1.

243. 1 Tm. 1:3-4.

243-44. 1 Tm. 1:5-7.

244-45. 1 Tm. 1:18-20.

247-48. 1 Tm. 2:8-12.

248. 1 Tm. 3:1.

250. Williston Walker, *The Creeds and Platforms of Congregationalism* (Philadelphia, PA: Pilgrim Press, 1969), p. 116; 1 Tm. 3:14-15.

251. 2 Thes. 2:15.

252-53. 1 Tm. 4:1-3.

253. 1 Tm. 4:12-13.

254. 1 Tm. 6:3-5.

255. 1 Tm. 6:6-10.

256. 1 Tm. 6:20-21.

258. 1 Tm. 6:21b.

268. Mk. 10:11-12; 1 Cor. 11:27-29.

271. Eph. 5:22, 25-27; Heb. 3:5; Mt. 19:9.

272. Mk. 10:11-12; 1 Cor. 11:27-30.

281. 1 Cor. 13:12.

285. Eph. 5:18.

286. 1 Tm. 5:23.

291. St. Irenaeus, c. A.D. 180, *Against Heresies*, 5, 2, 2.

302. Karl Keating, *Catholicism and Fundamentalism* (San Francisco, CA: Ignatius Press, 1988), p. 20.

303. Ibid., p. 40.

304. Ibid., p. 49.

304-5. Ibid., pp.101-2.

306. Ibid., pp. 135-36.

307. Pr. 3:5-6.

308. Isa. 53:3.

312. Mt. 16:18.

316. Mt. 16:19; Keating, p. 207.

317. Isa. 22:20-22; 2 Kgs. 18:18.

336. 2 Thes. 2:15.

338. John Henry Cardinal Newman, *An essay on the Development of Christian Doctrine* (Notre Dame, IN: University of Notre Dame Press, 1989), p. 8.

352. St. Justin Martyr, c. A.D. 155, *The First Apology*, 61.

353-55. Ibid., 65-66.

355. St. Ignatius of Antioch, c. A.D. 107, *Letter to the Romans*, 3:3, *Letter to the Philadelphians*, 4:1, *Letter to the Smyrneans*, 7:1; St. Irenaeus, c. A.D. 180, *Against Heresies*, 5, 2, 2.

356. St. Cyril of Jerusalem, c. A.D. 350 , *Catechetical Lectures* 22 (*Mystagogic* 4), 3.

362. Phil. 4:6-7; Rom. 8:28.

363. Eph. 4:26-27.

370-71. Mt. 16:12-20.

373. Mk. 10:17-22.

374. Mk. 4:3-20.

377. Jn. 17:11,20.

378. Jas 5:16b.

392. Jn. 6:69.

397. Rom. 8:28.

398. Rom. 8:16-17.

399. Ps. 121:1-2.

401. Col. 1:24; Rom. 12:1-2.

402-3. Pope John Paul II, *On the Christian Meaning of Human Suffering: Salvifici Doloris.* (Boston, MA: Pauline Books & Media, 1984), pp. 46-47.

406-7. Dt. 13:1-9.

410. Gal. 3:1.

419. Mt. 28:18-20.

420. Gal. 1:18.

421. Gal. 2:1-9; 2 Tm. 2:2.

422. Rom. 10:14-15; Acts 15.

423. 1 Cor. 11:2.

424-25. St. Irenaeus, c. A.D. 180, *Against Heresies*, 1, 10, 1-2.

426-27. 1 Tm. 6:20; St. Vincent of Lerins, c. A.D. 445, *A Commentary: For the Antiquity and Universality of the Catholic Faith against the Profane Novalties of All Heresies*, chap. 22.

430. Ps. 51:12.

439. This and any subsequent quote of the fictitious book *True Roman Catholicism* is based on material in the web site *The Roman Catholic Church Do They Teach God's Word?*, www.geocities.com/CapitolHill/Parliament/3491/rc_directory.html.

455. Jn. 8:31-32.

456. 1 Ptr. 3:21.

464. St. Athanasius, c. A.D. 358, *Discourse against the Arians*, Oratio 2, 81, 4.

465. 1 Ptr. 1:12.

470. Eph. 2:8-9; Rom. 1:5.

473. Jn. 1:29; Mt. 8:8.

474. Mk. 9:24.

475. Lk. 1:37; Num. 6:24-26.

490. Lk. 1:48.

504. St. Augustine, *Contra epistulam Manichaei, 5,6:* PL 42, 176.

506. Mt. 6:34.

513. Jn. 20:1-9.

518. Jn. 17:11, 20-21.

519. 1 Pt. 2:2-3.

BIBLIOGRAPHY

The following books were either quoted or referenced in the text, and are highly recommended for your spiritual edification:

The Holy Bible, Revised Standard Edition Catholic Edition. San Francisco: Ignatius Press, 1966.

Pope John Paul II. *On the Christian Meaning of Human Suffering: Salvifici Doloris.* Boston, MA: Pauline Books & Media, 1984.

Keating, Karl. *Catholicism and Fundamentalism.* San Francisco: Ignatius Press, 1988.

Catechism of the Catholic Church. Rome: Libreria Editrice Vatican, 1994.

Gibbons, James (Cardinal). *The Faith of Our Fathers.* Rockford: Tan Books & Publishers, 1980.

Newman, John Henry Cardinal. *An Essay on the Development of Doctrine.* Notre Dame: Univerity of Notre Dame Press, 1986.

Adam, Karl. *Roots of the Reformation.* Translated by Cecily Hastins. Steubenville: Coming Home Resources, 2000.

Jurgens, William. *The Faith of the Early Fathers.* 3 vols. Collegeville: The Liturgical Press, 1970.

de Sales, St. Francis. *Introduction to the Devout Life.* Translated by John K. Ryan. New York: Image Books, Doubleday, 1989.

FURTHER READING

If you enjoyed this novel, you might also enjoy these **true** stories of conversion:

Journeys Home by Marcus C. Grodi; Queenship Publishing

Rome Sweet Home by Scott & Kimberly Hahn; Ignatius Press

Suprised by Truth 1 by Patrick Madrid; Basilica Press

Surprised by Truth 2 by Patrick Madrid; Sophia Press

Crossing the Tiber by Stephen K. Ray; Ignatius Press

The Path to Rome by Dwight Longnecker; Gracewing

There We Stood, Here We Stand by Timothy Drake; 1st Books Library

My Life on the Rock by Jeff Cavins; Ascension Press

One Shepherd, One Flock by Oliver Barres; Catholic Answers

Literary Converts by Joseph Pearce; Ignatius Press

Continued...

Home at Last edited by Rosalind Moss; Catholic Answers

The Ingrafting edited by Rhonda Chervin; Remnant of Israel

Newman to Converts by Stanley Jaki; Real View Books

Born Fundamentalist Born Again Catholic by David B. Currie;
Ignatius Press

Classic Converts by Fr. Charles P. Connor; Ignatius Press

And a great new book on the Apostolic Fathers:

Four Witnesses: The Early Church in Her Own Words
by Rod Bennett; Ignatius Press

Marcus Grodi received a B.S. in Polymer Science and Engineering from Case Institute of Technology. After working four years as a Plastics Engineer, he attended Gordon-Conwell Theological Seminary where he received a masters in divinity degree. After ordination he served first as a Congregationalist and then eight years as a Presbyterian pastor. He is now the President / Executive Director of *The Coming Home Network International* and hosts a live television program called *The Journey Home* on *EWTN*. His wife Marilyn and he live with their three sons—Jon Marc, Peter, and Richard—and a cadre of animals on their small farm near Zanesville, Ohio.

For more information
about the author and
The Coming Home Network International,
please write, phone, or visit their website:

The Coming Home Network
PO Box 8290
Zanesville, OH 43702-8290

1-800-664-5110

http://www.chnetwork.org
or
http://www.hfaf.com